65
Great
Spine
Chillers

Merry Christmas Kyle
Lots Of Love From
Auntie Carol
X X

65
Great
Spine
Chillers

Edited by
Mary Danby

This edition first published in Great Britain in 1982 by
Octopus Books Limited
59 Grosvenor Street
London W1
in collaboration with
William Heinemann Limited
10 Upper Grosvenor Street
London W1
and
Martin Secker & Warburg Limited
54 Poland Street
London W1

ISBN: 0 86273 045 7

Printed in the
United States of America

Contents

6   Contents

Contents

Lodgers

Joan Aiken

'Are you *sure*, doctor?' said Rose Burdock. 'You really mean that *he*'s got mumps and *she*'s got measles? You couldn't be mistaken?'

'No mistake,' said Doctor Cobb briskly. 'Seen too many cases this week – half the town's got one or the other. Bob's got the stiff neck – Titch has the spots. Nothing you can do but keep 'em warm, give 'em aspirin and lots to drink. Wrap up their necks and ears and keep 'em isolated, because what's sure to happen is that in a couple of weeks they'll swap bugs; it's then you'll *really* have to worry, because they'll be a bit pulled down by the first bug so they may take the next one harder.'

'How long will it last?' she said faintly.

He was scribbling prescriptions. 'Umn? Oh, you'll probably have 'em both at home for about a month from first to last. Here, this is for Titch, every four hours round the clock, and these are for Bob, same, till their temperatures are back to normal. Call me if the fever goes on for more than two days or if there is any delirium.'

'Delirium!'

'Not likely unless mumps-meningitis sets in. Watch out for bronchitis or pneumonia, though, of course. Have *you* had mumps and measles, by the way?'

'Oh yes.'

'Well, you can get mumps again, so look out,' he said with callous cheer, running down the front steps. Rose dully watched him go. There was a small disused graveyard beside her house. A heavy rain followed by a sharp January frost had left all the gravestones neatly cased in ice. They looked like playing-cards laid out for patience. Patience ... How peaceful, she thought, to be lying stretched out in one's bones under there, with an ice-pack overhead; and went back into the house where Titch, hot and miserable, wanted a drink and to be rubbed with eau-de-cologne; Bob, feverish, and with acutely painful glands, wanted a hot poultice round his neck to take away the pain; both asked to be read aloud to and both wished to be made instantly better.

Rose presently dragged herself wearily downstairs for the next disagreeable duty.

'*Woman's Scene* – can I speak to Mrs Joubert, please? – Mrs Joubert –
this is Rose Burdock. Mrs Joubert – I am most *terribly* sorry, but it looks
as if I shan't be able to get to the office on Monday. Both my children
are sick: one with mumps, one with measles, and my lodger left two days
ago – I've got no one at home to look after them. – Yes, of *course* I will.
But – yes, I know. Yes, I do realize that. Yes I *know* Wednesday is Press
Day. I'll certainly see what I can do. I just thought I had better warn
you in case – Yes, yes, I will. Yes, of course.'

'You do remember, Mrs Burdock,' came the editor's clear voice over
the wire, 'that when we gave you this job it was on the strict understanding that there were to be no extra days off, no emergencies or crises, that
if you came to us you promised *never* to leave us in the lurch on press days?'

Rose remembered the conversation extremely well. Mrs Joubert, who
had a face like an isosceles triangle on its apex with a crest of blue hair
and two zero signs for eyes had terrified her so much that she had made
the promise unhesitatingly with every intention of keeping it. Besides,
with a well-disposed lodger who was always home at teatime before the
children had finished school, the future had seemed secure. Who could
have foretold that the lodger would be summoned to Scotland to nurse
a dying mother, or that the children would succumb to mumps and
measles simultaneously?

'I'll do my very best, Mrs Joubert,' she said in despair.

'Please do, dear. Because this sort of thing really mustn't happen, you
know. We've been *very* good to you – made special arrangements for you
to work a four-day week——'

'Yes – I know——'

'Very well then.'

After the formidable click with which Mrs Joubert rang off came the
immediate peal of the front door bell. Oh god, now what? Rose thought,
and dragged herself to the door. If that's the meter man it means another
electricity bill.

It was not the meter man, but a frail-looking woman with badly-waved
hair dangling on either side of her face like a cocker-spaniel's ears. Her
face was somehow ineffectual – pale and long, with anxious grey eyes and
a mouth that made efforts to be firm but kept dropping back into a weakly
placating curve. Her skin was dry and chalky and her clothes hung on
her like dead leaves after the first rains of winter.

'Mrs Burdock?' Her voice was placating too, refined yet shallow, as if
she never took in quite enough breath. 'You won't know me but I've
heard of you through your professional associates – well, through Mrs
Joubert actually——'

'If it's life-insurance I'm afraid I'm not interested,' said Rose swiftly.

'And – you must excuse me, but I've two sick children in the house – I have to get back to them——'

'No, *no*, you misunder*stand* me – I'm giving Mrs Joubert as a *ref*erence – actually she's a friend of my husband's father's, Admiral Colegate at South Dean.'

'Oh, I see.' In fact Rose saw nothing; it was true that Mrs Joubert had a weekend cottage at the village of South Dean five miles away, and no doubt she knew dozens of admirals there, but why should that bring this dithering woman to stand on her threshold?

'The fact is, we're a bit desperate, my husband and I,' Mrs Colegate went on rapidly with what she seemed to hope was a winning smile, 'and we happened to hear – through the local grapevine you know – that you might have some rooms to let in your house – we wondered if there might be a chance for us to rent them?'

'You want to rent *rooms*?' Suddenly the sunlight on the graveyard's frosted grass seemed to have acquired the heat of midsummer; Mrs Colegate's chalky face was haloed in a golden fuzz of hair. 'Oh, now I do see! Please come in and look at them, won't you? I'm afraid they're nothing very grand – just two rooms, a bathroom and kitchenette – won't you come upstairs?'

'We don't *want* anything grand,' pattered Mrs Colegate in her soft, conciliating voice, following up the stairs. She had to duck her skimpy length to get in at the spare bedroom door, for the house was Tudor, with lintels to match, and she quite tall; nonetheless she instantly exclaimed, '*Oh*, how delightful! Why, this would suit us down to the *ground*! It's really an answer to prayer, you see, as my husband has been disqualified from driving for six months – just on a technicality, you know, so silly – and he has to catch the eight-fifteen twice a week to town and there's no bus to South Dean and I'm a wretched driver in a fog and you *know* how many fogs we've been having, these mornings – We have been living at South Dean with the Admiral, you see, my husband's father, ever since we had to come back from Iran so suddenly – Desmond had an *excellent* job in Tehran, it was so sad when things got difficult there——'

All this flowed out in a gentle unaccented stream as she, rather inattentively, it seemed to Rose, inspected the bathroom, kitchenette and two bedsitting-rooms. 'Quite perfect! And is there a shed or something where we can garage the car?'

That, Rose was obliged to confess, there was not. Her own Mini lived across the lane where there was a slot just big enough for one car – 'But I'm afraid they won't allow any more. You can park overnight in the main square, though, that's only three minutes' walk.'

Mrs Colegate declared that that would be absolutely super, and that the whole thing was just what they had been looking for. 'Only three minutes to the bus, too – couldn't be more convenient. May we move in this afternoon?'

'Don't you want your husband to come and look first?' said Rose, a little startled.

'No need; no need at all. He'll love it just as much as I do.'

'There's just one thing——' Rose hesitated, feeling that, heaven-sent though this chance seemed, it behoved her to be honest. 'I have two children aged six and eight——'

'Oh, the *pets*! We *love* children!' cried Mrs Colegate. 'I've had children of my own, you see – grown now, alas! – We shall be so *happy* to live in a house with children once more.'

'Oh – that's – I'm very – But the thing is,' went on Rose desperately, 'that one of my children has mumps at present, and the other has measles, and in about ten days' time or even sooner they are due to reverse the pattern. Are you sure you want to face that? Have you had mumps and measles, Mrs Colegate?'

'Bless you, yes, my dear, long ago, and so has my husband. Mumps and measles are *nothing* to us! We shall be happy to nurse your children for you. It will make us feel needed; I gather you go up to town every day? I feel quite certain that we are going to fit into your house *very well*. That's all settled, then, and we'll move in this afternoon between three and four – if that is a good time?'

'Yes of course,' Rose said. 'I'll give you some keys.'

Mrs Colegate's smile had been so continuous and persevering that it was rather a shock for Rose to observe the violent shaking of her hands as she received the keys. Poor thing, perhaps she had arthritis – or Parkinson's Disease, was it, that made the hands shake? Or somebody's palsy?

'Who was that at the door?' called the children's voices from their separate bedrooms. (It was no use putting them in together; first they argued, then they quarrelled; finally they fought.) Rose went to tell them that two new lodgers were due to arrive who would be happy to read aloud, fetch drinks, and do shopping errands. Bob took the news indifferently; he had a temperature of 102°; Titch's face fell.

'I thought *you'd* stay at home to look after us,' she said dolefully.

'Honey, you know I'd like to but I can't; I have to go to my office. But I'm sure Mr and Mrs Colegate will be very nice . . .'

At two-thirty the bell rang again, and it was a short, very fat man with a green eye-shade over his face, who held an immense untidy bundle wrapped in a red baize cloth.

'Mrs Burdock? I'm Desmond Colegate. Delighted to meet you. Can't shake hands, ha, ha. May I carry this little lot upstairs?'

His voice was startlingly high and shrill; the only thing higher, Rose thought, would be a bat's squeak. What she could see of his face, below the green shade, was almost as startlingly white and moist; like the underside of a plaice. Taking her silence for assent, he nipped past her and, locating the stairs by instinct, it seemed, went quickly up with his load. Finding her wits, Rose followed and directed him into the lodgers' rooms.

'Delightful; delightful,' he said, dumping the cloth-wrapped bundle on the bed and crossing to the window.

'I'm sorry it looks out on the graveyard,' Rose said after clearing her throat. 'My son's room does too. I do hope you don't mind.'

'*Mind?* Why should I mind? Oh!' he said chuckling, 'you mean worry about the spirits of the departed, that sort of thing? But, my dear young lady, that little graveyard is *old*; why, I daresay no one has been buried in it for a hundred years. Nothing spooky is going to come out of there. Dear me, no. A very pleasant prospect. Aha! I believe I hear my wife down below——'

'You mean – only recent graves produce ghosts?' Rose asked trying for a light note, as she followed him downstairs again.

'Spirits, my dear – spirits! Of course! They wear *out* in the end – burn out, if you like – just like a candle flame. Spirits are not immortal, any more than bodies – they simply have more energy and a longer life-span. Thank you, Laura,' he added, receiving a plastic garment-bag, evidently stuffed with clothes, from his wife, who stood nervously by the open front door. 'And of course,' he added to Rose, nonplussed in the hall, 'it is when they have just left their bodies that spirits are most agitated; not yet knowing, you see, quite where they *stand*, ha, ha!' His chuckly was like ice cubes falling into a glass. He retired up the stairs again with the dress-bag and Mrs Colegate went back to their car, which was parked on the pavement outside with a policeman eyeing it thoughtfully.

'I hope you don't mind our coming a little earlier than we said?' Mrs Colegate fluttered up the front steps again with a bundle of golf-clubs and fishing-rods and the tube of a vacuum cleaner. 'The Admiral thought it would be more practical to leave during the *daylight*; it gets dark so early these days, and then it's so hard to find things.'

She handed the clubs and rods to her husband, who, still in pursuit of his previous theme, said airily, waving a butterfly net, 'Yes, yes, spirits, when they have just left their bodies, buzz round in quite a panic – like wasps, you know – positively distilling energy!'

He bustled off up the stairs again – he could move amazingly nimbly for one so fat – calling back what sounded like:

'That's the time to catch them!'

Rose went away into her own kitchen to be by herself. She supposed she had better make the Colegates a cup of tea; that was the proper way to welcome people. She wished that she had not taken such an instantaneous aversion to Desmond Colegate. Probably he was quite ordinary and pleasant when one got to know him; he couldn't help that unnerving voice and fishlike complexion.

During the weekend the Colegates seemed to settle in very completely, in their own way. They had brought no furniture – indeed, they had no need to, for the rooms were furnished – but they had an incredible quantity of paraphernalia, bundles, boxes, rolls, frames, cages, baskets. As they carried these up, Rose could not conceive where they would stow all the stuff in her two moderate-sized rooms; and indeed, when she tapped and entered with the ceremonial cups of tea, the floor was completely covered with objects dumped higgledy-piggledy, and the owners were making no attempt to organize the chaos. They were seated, he on the chaise-longue and she on the divan, each with a half-empty glass in hand. A Johnny Walker bottle stood on a box midway between them.

'You see us exhausted, my dear Rose,' chirped Mr Colegate. 'I may call you Rose, may I not? Such a charming name – recruiting our strength before embarking on the next stage of our labours. Ah, tea! What a considerate thought! How delicious!' But Rose noticed when she carried the cups down again that he had hardly touched his, taken no more than a courtesy sip. Was the silence interrupted by her entry a sullen silence? An acrimonious silence? A conspiratorial silence? There had been a positive quality to it, of that Rose felt certain. And, on the Sunday, as she went about her weekend tasks, and tended the children, she could not avoid the irrational notion that the Colegates, mousy-quiet themselves (they seemed to be late risers) were, as she swept, or clinked pots in the kitchen, or merely ran up and downstairs, sitting motionless, as she had first discovered them – *listening* to her.

On Sunday evening Dr Cobb dropped in, unannounced.

'Passing by, thought I might as well. Temperatures down yet? Never mind, it has to take its course. Keep 'em in bed, though; no getting up to watch telly. That measle-bug is a bad one; young Pete Finn, the vet's son, know who I mean? Round-faced boy.' She nodded. 'Took pneumonia – died this morning. Couldn't get the temperature down.'

'*Pete?* Pete Finn?' She was transfixed by a pang of pity and terror. 'But he's such a big strong boy; we know him well. He's – was – a friend of Bob's.'

Cobb shook his head. 'Didn't make it. Don't tell you this to scare you – just to warn. Well – keep on with the pills. All you can do.' He made for the door fast, turned to say with a touch of inquisitiveness and something else – malice? – under his good-nature – 'Hear you've got new lodgers.' He jerked his thumb upwards. 'They didn't stay in his father's house too long!'

'You know the admiral then?'

He nodded; he knew everybody. 'Patient. Haven't met the younger generation though; been in foreign parts, haven't they? Good thing they left the old boy; rubbing him up the wrong way. He said they were hastening his end. Behaving themselves here, are they?'

'They seem fine – why?' She was instantly alarmed.

'Oh, nothing; nothing. Glad you found somebody. Only I did hear——' He gestured, tipping up an invisible glass.

Oh, thought Rose, that would explain the shaking hands and trouble about driving. '*Both?*' she mouthed unhappily. He shrugged.

'Only in moderation, I daresay. Could be worse. Could be heroin! Take care, now – call me at the least worry.'

With a carefree slam he was into his car and away.

On Monday, a prey to hideous qualms and misgivings, Rose drove to the office of *Woman's Scene*. She had left prepared food of every kind ready to be fed to her children; a paper tacked to the wall with her phone number, the doctor's number, the plumber, electrician, hospital; typed instructions stuck on all the household appliances. For Mrs Colegate had asked if she might use the washing machine, the iron, sewing-machine, vacuum. 'My father-in-law was always terrible difficult about letting us use his things,' she confided.

Press week on the magazine was always a scramble of last-minute work; Rose found it impossible to leave the office before six-thirty. She arrived home late and in trepidation, though Mrs Colegate, that morning, had been wholly friendly and reassuring. (Mr Colegate had not been visible.) 'Don't you worry about a *thing*, my dear; it will really be a pleasure to look after your nice children, dear little things.'

She had seemed decidedly calmer than on the day they arrived; her hands shook less.

When Rose opened the door, her house was totally silent; and downstairs, all in darkness. She flipped a switch; no light. In a panic, she ran up the stairs. Here there was darkness too, though dim lights came from the children's rooms. When she went in to see Titch, Rose discovered the source of this subdued light; Mr Colegate was there, reading *Kim* aloud to her daughter by the flicker of two candles. His high, monotonous bird-like voice – which had seemed, as she entered, mysteriously to come from somewhere up in the ceiling – ceased when he saw Rose.

Despite the dim light, he was still wearing his eye-shade.

'Ah, there you are at last, my dear,' he said graciously to Rose. 'Then I will retire.'

'Has – has everything been all right?' Rose hoped that the nervousness and dislike in her voice were not as audible to him as they seemed to her.

'Just as right as it could be!' Mr Colegate declared with greater gaiety. He added judiciously, 'But I believe your daughter is not very used to *men*——'

husband died when she was only three——'

'Ah, I see – That explains it. So long ago.' He sighed. 'Might I ask – Did your husband live here, when he was alive? In this house?'

'No, we moved here after his death.'

'Ah, too bad.' He seemed disappointed. 'I was asking the children about him——'

He took a step, and a strong sweetish scent, of whisky and hair-oil, was released.

Rose longed for him to be gone. She could see, what seemed to have escaped Mr Colegate's notice, under the eye-shade and the dim light, that Titch was in a silent agony of terrified tears that might any minute reach screaming-pitch.

'Well, goodnight, Mr Colegate – thank you so much –' and, as he mercifully left the room, and she heard his own door shut behind him:

'My *lamb*! What's the matter?'

Titch flung herself, quivering into her mother's arms. 'He's *horrible*! I couldn't understand a *single* word he *said*! Not a word! His voice is so strange! It seemed to come from the roof. And he smells *awful*. Please don't let him come in here any more.'

'No, of course I won't.' With sinking heart Rose wondered how this was to be achieved without mortally offending Mr Colegate; she suspected that he might be a very touchy man.

As soon as she could detach herself from the panic-stricken Titch, Rose went to visit Bob. Here the scene seemed calmer. Bob was sitting up in bed, flushed, but impassive, wrapped in a quilt, playing cards on a pastry-board with Mrs Colegate. Two more flickering candles lit the room.

'Your son has a natural aptitude for cards,' Mrs Colegate said, smiling, ducking out from under the sloping roof. 'I've taught him Spider; and before that he learned Napoleon, Streets and Alleys, Klondyke and The Beleaguered Castle. He learns like lightning.'

'Bless him.' Rose stroked the tousled fair head. 'It's so kind of you . . .'

With relief she saw that Bob, though not in the best of spirits, had not been reduced to Titch's state of despair. She felt his forehead. It was very hot. He twitched away nervously from her street-cold hand.

'Why all the candles?' Rose asked. 'Did the main fuse blow?'

'I can't say.' Mrs Colegate looked vague. 'Something went wrong. But, anyway, my husband and I really prefer candlelight.'

Rose did not. In a Tudor house, largely constructed of timber and lath, candles were too great a fire-hazard; and she groped her way down to the cellar and mended the three separate fuses that seemed to have blown. However, even when the rest of the rooms were blazing with light, she noticed (when outside fetching her briefcase from the car) that only a dim flicker still emanated from the Colegates' windows. I hope to God they've tidied up all that clutter, she thought apprehensively; she could hardly forbid the Colegates to use candles if such was their preference, but it did seem risky with all those obstacles on the floor to trip them. Perhaps they were straight by now, though.

Later on in the evening she was obliged to visit their room. The phone rang: it was a male voice asking for Mr Desmond Colegate.

'What name shall I say?' inquired Rose.

'Hugh Morgan-Sleigh – Admiral Colegate's solicitor. I have been trying this number all day!' said the voice irritably.

'I'll see if they are in; but I rather believe I heard them go out half an hour ago,' said Rose.

As she gulped down her late, hasty supper she had heard footsteps and mutterings on the stairs.

Pondering, she tapped on the Colegate's door. Twice during the day she had tried to phone home in order to ask after the children, but had got no reply on either occasion.

Were the Colegates telephone-shy?

The tapping produced no response, and she cautiously opened the door, automatically switching on the light. Something scurried hastily in a corner; she caught a glimpse of a smallish, whitish creature which vanished under a corner of blanket hanging from the divan.

The Colegates were nowhere to be seen. And the rooms were still just as untidy as they had been four days ago. A guttering candle leaned precariously over the edge of a saucer. Rose extinguished it and went back to the phone.

'They must be out, I'm afraid. Shall I leave them a message to call you?'

'*That* won't be any use,' he said sourly. 'I suppose I shall have to come and see them to explain the Admiral's intentions.' He sounded as if he found the prospect intensely disagreeable.

'You might catch them at friends – if you had any idea where to phone?' Rose suggested.

'More likely in a pub,' he muttered, to himself, not Rose, and rang off.

She had intended to wait up in order to tell them about the call, and also ask about the creature – *what* could it have been? a ferret! a lizard! a coypu? – but they returned home so extremely late that by the time they came in she had given up and, exhausted, retired to bed. She slept lightly, though, and heard their shuffling feet on the stairs, after the church clock struck one. Not a pub then; Mr Morgan-Sleigh must have been wrong about that.

In the morning there was no sound from the Colegate area. Not daring to leave the children – both running fevers – without being certain that somebody was alert enough to attend to their needs, Rose waited as long as possible, then tapped at the door. A very long silence ensued. Rose tapped again. A drowsy voice called, 'Who is it?'

'It's me – Rose. I'm sorry to disturb you——'

After another long pause Mrs Colegate came flapping to the door in a faded silk wrapper that must once have been memorably ornate. Her face was chalk-pale, her hands shook wildly.

Rose passed on the lawyer's message – which Mrs Colegate received without expression – and then added, 'I'm sorry to bother you——' why did she keep saying that, it wasn't true – 'but I've just phoned the doctor, and he says, if the children's temperatures aren't down by noon, get in touch with him and he'll come round. Just phone him and he'll come,' she repeated, as Mrs Colegate continued to look unreceptive.

'Phone the doctor … ? Oh, I won't do that, I'll run round to the surgery,' Mrs Colegate said after a pause. 'I've seen it, it's in the square, isn't it?'

'Yes,' said Rose, rather astonished. 'But you'd much better phone. He won't be there, he'll be on his rounds – they'll have to find him.'

'I'll go,' repeated Mrs Colegate. 'I like the fresh air.'

'You won't forget, will you?' There was something so odd about the woman that Rose was deeply troubled at having to leave the children in her charge. She went on, 'I don't like to seem like a silly fussing parent, but since the news about poor little Peter Finn's death——'

'Peter Finn's death?' Mrs Colegate looked a little more intelligent. 'The vet's boy at South Dean? Such a sweet boy – he used to wash our car and my husband taught him to play cribbage——'

Mention of the vet reminded Rose of something. 'By the way – do you have a pet? When I looked in last night I thought I saw – The thing is, I hadn't really reckoned – The house isn't very big——'

For several moments Mrs Colegate remained quite silent, her face non-committal. Then, as if after reflection, she said, 'A pet?'

'I thought, when I went up about the phone call I saw something like a ferret——'

'Oh, you mean my sister's Chinese rabbit?' Mrs Colegate said, as if suddenly enlightened. 'Don't worry, I'll take it back to her today.' And she added, '*We* don't like pets at all. Don't worry,' she finished absently.

Rose nodded, left the house, and ran to her car. She was very late. And it was beginning to snow.

On both the following evenings the lights were all fused when Rose arrived home. Some activity of the Colegates apparently put an excessive strain on the wiring. Mending the fuses, Rose resolved to ask them about it when she had a little more time – but there were so many things on her mind as well. The children's still soaring temperatures, the unsorted mess in the Colegates' rooms, visible whenever they briefly left the door open – ought Rose to help them tidy it? – the intermittent snow, which made driving a terror to Rose, never confident in a car at the best of times – the hectic going-to-press nonstop action at the magazine.

Then, on Wednesday evening, there came a call from the police.

'Mrs Burdock? Sar'n't Grimbold here, I believe you have a Mr Cole-gate staying with you who owns a white Cortina, registration DDR 01 439 J? Would you mind telling him he's parked it illegally in Mary Lane and unless it's removed within half an hour it will be towed away at his expense?'

'Oh yes – I'll tell him – very kind of you to tip him off,' Rose said to Sergeant Grimbold, who was an old friend, and he said:

'Confidentially, they keep leaving their car in all sorts of crazy places. You'd better warn them or they're in for trouble.'

'Oh, good *heavens*!' said Mr Colegate irritably when Rose relayed this message to him, somewhat watered down. 'I must say, it is a *great* pity we are not permitted to put our car in the graveyard next door. There would be *plenty* of room among the graves. This town is so awkward and confusing at night, as the streets are so poorly lit.' Ironic that he, with his preference for candlelight, should complain of that, Rose thought. He went on, 'Quite often, in the morning, other people have parked so inconsiderately that it is almost impossible for us to locate our car. My poor wife had to spend *several hours* today searching for it.'

This explained Bob's complaint. 'We didn't get our lunch today till four, Mum. Need these Colegates stay? I don't really like them.'

'Oh, dear, love. Nor do I, much. But they *are* keeping an eye on you. And they've paid a month's rent in advance. What don't you like about them?'

'Everything! And his puppets are the absolute *end*!'

'Puppets?'

'He makes them out of china or something. They clink. He showed me a couple this afternoon when we were playing cards. One moved by itself – horrible! We played canasta and he said if I won I could have one of the smaller puppets. But I wouldn't want one; they give me the creeps. Anyway I didn't win.'

On Thursday morning, early, Mrs Joubert sent for Rose. The maga-zine had been safely put to bed; there was time to draw breath. Rose hurried to the editor's office wondering what fault or omission of hers had come under scrutiny; she could think of several possibilities in the last few desperate days.

But this summons was of a personal nature. Mrs Joubert came to the point directly.

'I've just been talking to my housekeeper at South Dean – she tells me she heard the young Colegates had rented rooms in your house.'

Young Colegates? Rose would hardly have classified them as that, but she supposed that, compared with the Admiral in his late eighties, they rated as young.

'Yes, that's right.'

'Well, *get them out at once*! You *can't* let them stay in your house.'

'But – but——' Rose stammered, utterly taken aback, 'they gave *you* as a reference! That – that was why I let them come——'

'Like their impudence. They'd no right to,' Mrs Joubert said incisively. 'My dear, they nearly drove that wretched old man mad! He said they were hurrying him towards his end. They are an appalling couple!'

'What's the matter with them?'

'Well, they drink like fishes for a start. But there are much worse things – they have all kinds of murky habits – you have *got* to get rid of them!'

'But they've paid a month's rent!'

'Pay it back. Get them out.'

'How can I possibly do that?'

'Invent something. Say you've got your mother-in-law coming to live with you. I'm serious.'

'But – they are looking after my children who have mumps and measles.'

Rose felt herself close to fainting with sheer despair.

'You'll just have to take some time off,' Mrs Joubert said impatiently. 'Lucky we've just gone to press ...'

In a small, detached, ironic corner of her mind, Rose wondered if the time off would have been granted otherwise.

'Don't come in till next Monday. Tell them some story – fix *something*. Okay? And you'd better leave early today.'

Nonetheless there was much clearing-up to do after the scrambled press-day. The January afternoon was darkening by the time Rose parked the Mini opposite her front door. The sight of Dr Cobb's car arrogantly straddling the double yellow lines across the road turned her cold with apprehension.

'I'm afraid the lad's coming down with measles too,' the doctor told her, outside Bob's door. 'This is going to be the really tricky time ... I've left a new lot of medicine for him to take. Try an ice-pack. And lots of fluids. I'll be back later this evening.'

'You don't think he should go into hospital?' Rose tried to keep her voice level.

'My dear they're packed to the gills. Still – don't worry. See you later.'

Don't worry, Rose thought, pressing both hands against her aching temples.

Ten minutes afterwards, as she ran up the stairs with a jug of barley-water, she found her way impeded by Mr Colegate, fatly occupying most of the narrow landing.

'I'm taking these in to amuse him,' he chirped gaily.

She was too exhausted to pretend.

'No, he doesn't want anything like that, Mr Colegate. He's far too sick.'

Yet there was something rather repulsively fascinating about Mr Colegate's puppets, which he held dangling from either hand. China, Bob had said, and she had thought he must be mistaken, but in fact the puppets were made of ceramic – a series of bell-shaped pottery pieces, a large one for the body, with painted face, and smaller ones for the arms and legs, each slotting into the one above, threaded on leather thongs. They clinked slightly as they moved. The faces, though depicted by no more than half a dozen strokes of black and white paint, wore such expressions of malign hostility that it was easy to see why they had upset Bob. Thank heaven Titch had not seen them.

'He's too sick,' Rose repeated firmly.

'Poor boy,' Mr Colegate sighed. 'It's hard – when one is young – to be so very ill. You're sure I couldn't show him just *one* puppet? I have a big one – bigger than these – which moves all by itself; I've trained it to do that. He liked that one.'

'No thanks, Mr Colegate.'

Mrs Colegate opened their door and put her face round. She looked fatigued and frightened. For a moment Rose thought she could hear a faint, high-pitched crying coming from the room behind her. Then she stepped out and closed the door.

'Ventriloquism,' said her husband. 'Did you know I could throw my voice, my dear Rose?'

He twitched his face, and a squeaky voice came from among the rafters up above them.

'*Let me out, let me out!*'

'*Don't* do that, Desmond,' said his wife hastily. 'Tell me, where did you put the collecting-bottle? I need it for——'

'I am trying to divert our dear Rose, Laura.'

'Well she isn't amused. Where did you leave the bottle?'

'I daresay it is in the car,' he replied pettishly.

'Where's the car?'

'God knows if *you* don't!' he snapped, and went into their room, slamming the door. For the instant that it was open, Rose thought she heard the crying again. Then there was a thump, and silence. Am I going mad? she wondered, carrying the barley-water in to Bob. He was slightly delirious, and pushed her away crying, 'Don't you let them near me or I'll smash them!'

Titch, too, was worse that evening, and complained of pains all around her neck. But she would still take fruit juice, which Bob refused. Rose, squeezing oranges in her kitchen, was interrupted by Mr Colegate, who seemed aggrieved.

'I am very *fond* of your children,' he announced aggressively.

'That's kind of you, Mr Colegate ... I'm sure you are.'

'Then why does your daughter scream like a maniac when I go into her room?'

'She's very sick. She's only eight. She's not used to men.'

'She's used to the doctor.'

'That's different. She's known him for years.'

'I would like to teach her how to play clock patience. *Any* child her age can learn that.'

'Mr Colegate, I would rather you didn't go into her room, just at present.'

He looked at Rose loweringly; but at this moment his wife came in, flustered, brushing snowflakes off her shabby headscarf.

'Desmond, I can't *find* the car. Can't you remember where we left it last?'

'*You* were driving.'

'No I wasn't——' she began, but he dragged her sharply out into the passage.

Rose heard them squabbling.

'You *must* remember.' 'Well I don't.' 'You *were* driving.' 'Shut up! Try to think where you put it.' 'I didn't put it *any*where.' 'I've looked all over the town. If we don't find the bottle soon it'll be – they're getting fractious.' '*I* don't hear anything.' 'That's because you're deaf, Desmond.'

He *was* a bit deaf, Rose had noticed; often she had to repeat things she said to him.

'Did you try in the alley next to the library – where it says "Librarian Only"?'

'No, I didn't.'

'I think it might be there; go and see.'

'You go and quiet them down, then; put them in the birdcage.'

When the Colegates had departed, Rose took Titch her orange juice. She thought she could hear a kind of scuffle taking place in the Colegate's room, mixed with subdued curses.

Just as she was carrying the empty beaker downstairs again, Mrs Colegate came in through the front door. Evidently her quest this time had been successful; she bore a heavy-looking gallon-sized flagon made of black glass. It was encased in a sort of basketwork which was covered all over with beads – black, green, blue, red and white. The beading formed letters, which ran criss-cross, up, down and sideways, like a crossword puzzle; in her brief glimpse Rose saw no words she recognized, but noticed the letters O, A, T, N, E and S. It was an extremely foreign-looking article; perhaps the Colegates had brought it back with them from Tehran. What could they keep in it that was required with such urgency? Although the black glass looked massively thick, the frail Mrs Colegate appeared to be able to carry it without too much difficulty, as if the contents were light. It could be oxygen, thought Rose. Or crushed laurel leaves for killing moths – why did they call it a collecting-bottle?

She went upstairs again to read aloud to Titch, who complained that she ached all over.

The crying from the Colegate's room had ceased. Rose decided that she had imagined it.

Dr Cobb came back at eleven and said that Bob was holding his own.

'You get a bit of sleep now, and have a look at him around two. Call me if you're at all bothered,' he said. 'Try to sleep a little now.'

'Okay. You're very good,' Rose muttered.

The Colegates, according to evening custom, had gone out. Rose suppressed an urge to bolt the front door so that they could not get back in. She could not resist the temptation to peep into their room. The floor was still covered with things. The plastic garment-bag hung from a rafter, swaying slightly. Near the door stood the large birdcage, covered by a square of red baize. Gingerly, Rose twitched the baize up – and let it drop again with a shudder of disgust. On the floor of the cage were three smallish, whitish wrinkled things, huddled together motionless; what could they have been? They resembled embryos with horrible little tapering attenuated limbs. They reminded her vaguely of William Blake's paintings. They couldn't have been alive, they couldn't have been real, she told herself. It was just a pile of chamois-leather, or something like that. Bits of crumpled plastic perhaps.

Tomorrow she would give the Colegates notice to go. The first thing in the morning. As soon as she saw them.

Trembling, she shut the door again, went to her own room, set the alarm for two a.m., and fell on the bed fully clothed. She had thought she would never go to sleep, but she went off instantly, as if she had swallowed a knockout dose, and immediately began to dream.

She dreamed that she was watching Desmond Colegate and her son play cards. The cards were laid out like gravestones all over a flat board, and the room was lit by two candles, one black, one white. Mr Colegate pointed to the candles, and said, 'You remember what the Egyptians believed. We are split into ten parts, of which this is the kha, or double, and that the khu, or spirit. Are you paying attention, boy?'

'Yes,' Bob said sleepily – he was lolling back on the pillow, hardly able to keep his eyes open.

'Very well; we shall play Devil's Bed-Posts,' Colegate said, and he began moving the cards into a square formation. 'The winner takes both candles – right?'

'*Don't play with him, Bob!*' Rose wanted to scream, but her voice remained trapped inside, her lips would not open.

The players began moving the cards about, murmuring incomprehensible terms. 'I buy the devil.' 'I cross the equator.' 'Cold hand takes the tiger.' 'Go now!' 'Queen of the night takes ten.'

Suddenly Colegate slapped all his cards down on the board, shouting:
'*Dead Hand!* I win!'

And, picking up a black conical candle-extinguisher, he snuffed out
both flames and put the candles in his pocket.

Rose thought she had woken herself by shrieking, but found that it was
the shrilling of the alarm in her ear that had roused her. She stumbled
out of bed and quietly opened her bedroom door.

On the landing she was dismayed to see Desmond Colegate, also fully
clothed. He seemed to be coming from Bob's room, and was carrying a
flashlight which cast a small round pool of light before him on the floor.
He did not observe Rose; he opened his own door and exclaimed in a
harsh whisper:

'Laura. *Laura!* The little brute got away. Where did you leave the
bottle?'

Her sleepy voice answered, '... It's back in the car.'

'*Where's the bloody car?*'

'Don't you remember? You left it in the graveyard.'

He spun round and Rose heard the thump of his feet down the stairs,
and the soft slam of the front door. Aghast, she stepped to the landing
window, which also looked out on to the graveyard, thrust back the
curtain, and saw, in bright moonlight, against the snow, the Colegate's
car drawn up askew just inside the gate. She was in time to see Colegate:
he held the wicker-wrapped flask in one hand, what looked like a white
towel in the other; he was dashing about among the gravestones,
apparently in pursuit of some elusive and darting quarry. He made
frantic flaps and lunges with the cloth; blundered into the stone slabs,
tripped, picked himself up again, and stumbled on.

But presently, dropping the bottle, he pressed both hands violently
against his breastbone, as if coughing or choking – stood in this position,
anchored, for several moments – then fell, heavily, on to the snow, and
lay still.

Rose heard a shallow breathing behind her, and turned to see Laura
Colegate looking past her shoulder.

'What is it, what *is* it?' she muttered apprehensively, pushing aside her
dangling hair with tremulous hands.

'Your husband is out in the graveyard, Mrs Colegate,' said Rose
bleakly. 'I think you had better go to him; he seems to have been taken
ill.'

Whimpering in distress, the other woman shuffled down the stairs.
'Desmond, Desmond, why couldn't you wait for me?' she called plaintively, and the door slammed behind her. Rose waited a moment; saw
her approach her husband's body, stoop and recoil with upflung hands,
glancing suspiciously round her as if expecting crowds of onlookers.

Rose turned and ran to her son's room. His window stood wide open.

A scatter of cards lay over the quilt. Bob was sprawled in the bed motionless, with his face to the wall. Rose, trying to keep her fingers steady on his wrist, could find no pulse. She ran down the stairs to the telephone.

'Mum? I'm thirsty!' came in a feeble croak from Titch's room.

'Just a minute, love; shan't be long.'

Rose began dialling the doctor's number; as she did so she heard the front door close, and Mrs Colegate's dragging steps cross the front hall.

The Playfellow

Lady Cynthia Asquith

Laura Halyard wondered whether she would ever grow more accustomed to the loveliness of her new home. Each time she looked at the beautiful Tudor house she still wanted to rub her eyes.

After the din and glare of New York, the mellow beauty and green silence of Lichen Hall and its perfect surroundings lay like a spell on its new mistress. It was just six months since her husband Claud Halyard had succeeded to the property at the death of his elder brother, who had died childless. Since his marriage to Laura business had kept Claud in America, so he had never met her unfortunate brother-in-law. Yet she often thought of him, so strongly had his sad story impressed her imagination; the early loss of his adored wife, the accident which left him a hopeless cripple, and the ghastly tragedy of his only child, a girl of ten, who had perished in the fire which twelve years ago had destroyed a small wing of Lichen Hall.

The building had been so skilfully restored that it was difficult to believe in that fatal fire. Laura felt herself lapped in an atmosphere of peace, and found it impossible to associate anything so hideous as the death of that poor child with this place. Could such a thing have happened here, and only twelve years ago? In these serene surroundings it seemed so unimaginable.

Laura Halyard had the extraordinary adaptability of her race, and as she sat in the great hall one December evening, her slim, delicate beauty glowing in the flicker of the firelight, she looked wonderfully in tone with her setting. She was giving tea to the old parson, whose faded eyes blinked appreciatively at the grace and beauty of his hostess. He wished he didn't feel it was time to end his visit.

'If I may be permitted to say so,' he said, reluctantly dragging his stiff limbs from the depths of the easy-chair, 'If I may say so, Lady Halyard, it is very pleasant to have a châtelaine here again. Lichen Hall has been a sad place these last twelve years.'

'Yes,' responded Laura sympathetically. 'I don't suppose my poor brother-in-law ever recovered from the terrible tragedy of that poor, poor child.'

'A broken man is a phrase one often hears,' said the parson, 'but I am thankful to say that in the course of a long life it has only been my lot to know one man to whom I felt the phrase could be justly applied. That man was your brother-in-law. He did his duty by this place. No one could have done it better. But after Daphne's death, duty was all the world ever held for him. Nothing else remained. To see such grey ashes and have no power to kindle one spark has been a great pain to me. Such loneliness! Scarcely anyone ever came here during these last years. Just a few old friends, but I always felt he only suffered them out of consideration for *their* feelings.

'I often wondered why your husband never came. In spite of the twenty years between them, they had always appeared to be such devoted brothers. It seems strange he should never once have returned to his own home until he succeeded to it.'

'I know,' said Laura. 'Of course he was very tied by business, but still he could have managed it in his summer holiday. I often urged it, but he always said he thought next year would be better. I don't know why it was. Of course, Mr Cloud, he's very sensitive. He shrinks from things. Perhaps – I sometimes think – he felt he simply couldn't face his brother's misery.'

'Possibly,' said the parson. 'But I wish he had come. It might have made a big difference.'

Laura detected a hint of reproach in the kind old voice.

'It isn't that he doesn't love this place,' she eagerly assured him. 'I can't tell you how much it means to him.'

'I know, Lady Halyard, I know. You see, I remember him as a boy. Why, his love for his home was quite a household joke. Once he gave a visiting schoolfellow a black eye because he dared to say his home was more beautiful than this! Bright days those were, when he and all his sisters were young.' The parson's pale eyes widened as he stared wistfully back into the past. 'I always think this garden clamours for children. It's wasted when there's none about. I assure you, it's a real joy to see your little girl tearing up and down the grass slopes.'

'I can't tell you how happy Hyacinth is here,' exclaimed Laura. 'Her day is one long rapture.'

'Bless her!' said the parson. 'How lovely she is and how extraordinarily like——'

'Like? Like whom?'

'Like her poor cousin – like poor little Daphne. Why, surely the resemblance must have struck your husband?'

'No. At least he hasn't said anything, but then perhaps he wouldn't. Even after all these years he can't bear to speak of his niece. He never mentions Daphne's name.'

'I know it was a great shock to him,' agreed the parson. 'He was so fond of her. I remember he was always playing with her. But then we all loved her. Yes, there was a real fascination about little Daphne.'

'And was she really like our Hyacinth?'

'Like?' exclaimed the parson. 'Why, it's the most astounding resemblance! I assure you it gave me quite a start the first time I saw your girl peering at me through the bushes. Yes, it took me back twelve years. She's ten, isn't she – your Hyacinth?'

Laura nodded.

'Well, you see, poor Daphne was just the same age the last time I saw her – the day before. Yes, yes, I can see her now. Just the same mop of red-gold hair framing the pale, pointed face – the wide eyes and the same eager look – something so extraordinary *vivid*.'

'Really,' said Laura. Her voice trembled and the hall swam in a blur of tears.

'Yes, a most extraordinary resemblance,' continued the old man. 'Voices a good deal alike, too. And your Hyacinth seems to have a similar passion for play. I never saw any being like Daphne for filling the day. She always seemed to want to cram as much fun into each hour as it could possibly hold. It was almost as though she knew she had no time to lose. Do you remember that passage in Maeterlinck about those he calls "Les Avertis"?'

'Yes, I do.' Laura's voice was heavy.

'Well, well, I must be going now,' said the old man. 'Thanks, dear lady, for a very pleasant afternoon. Give my love to Daph – Hyacinth. She must come to tea with me.'

'Good night, Mr Cloud. Come again soon,' said Laura rather mechanically. Turning to the fire she kicked one of the large logs with her foot, and then stirred amongst the embers with a poker until they blazed into flames. She felt cold and tired. She started when the clergyman re-entered the room. He apologized for having forgotten his gloves.

'Oh, what colour are they?' asked Laura absently, as though a variegated assortment of gloves were likely to be lying about the hall.

'Grey. Here they are. I'm so sorry to have troubled you.'

'Stop one moment, Mr Cloud. There was something I meant to ask you. How do you think my husband is looking?'

'I think he looks well, Lady Halyard, quite well. He always was a magnificent fellow. Yes, I think he looks quite well. But, since you ask me, the only thing I notice about him is a sort of strained expression on his face – in his eyes, and on his forehead. It's as though he were making some kind of mental effort – as if he were trying to remember something.'

'Trying to remember something?'

'Yes, he looks as I feel I must look when I'm struggling with my daily crossword. No doubt it's the result of all his work in that office. I'm so glad to see him out of it. Somehow I can't picture any Halyard in an office. Oh yes, Claud was always made for country life. Good night, Lady Halyard, good night.'

Left to herself, Laura crouched over the blazing fire. 'Claud made for country life?' Yes, so she had always thought. In America he had seemed an exile pining for his native land. And yet, now that they were at his beloved home, and it had proved more beautiful than even his rhapsodies had led her to expect, what was the matter? To her growing disappointment she could not help admitting that her husband's spirits – never steady – were on the whole much lower than they used to be. A sultry gloom seemed settling on him. Then that look of strain the parson had noticed. Others had commented on this. What could cause it, now that the present and the future seemed so fair? Business worries? Laura wondered almost hopefully. No, what business worries could he have? He told her everything. Told her everything, did he? Laura almost laughed aloud. That very afternoon she had re-encountered that threadbare phrase. The heroine of the bad novel she had been reading, a woman in total darkness concerning her husband, had confidently asserted, 'He tells me everything!' How could any human being ever tell anyone *every*thing?

No doubt Claud had got something on his mind. Since their homecoming, she had been conscious of a barrier between them. In old days, if challenged, he would often admit to a fit of depression. Now he seemed rather to resent any inquiry as to his health or spirits. If she said, 'Is anything the matter?' he would answer almost irritably, 'The matter? No, nothing's the matter. Don't suggest things.'

Laura was not left to her reflections for long. Her husband, a tall, handsome man, came into the room with their daughter Hyacinth riding on his shoulders, her mop of red-gold hair shining above his dark head.

The three of them settled round the fire. Hyacinth, with her knees drawn up to her pointed chin, and her wide eyes staring into the flames, made but a poor pretence of listening to her father reading *Ivanhoe* for her benefit. The moment the chapter was finished she sprang on to the tips of her toes and stood quivering, like a flame released.

'May I go now?' her whole eager being seemed to express.

Struck afresh by the gleaming quality of her beauty, her father gazed at her lovingly. So breathlessly full of life! Ought she perhaps to have playfellows of her own age?

'Are you lonely, Sprite?' he asked her tenderly.

'Lonely! Oh no! I'm never, never lonely here!' There was a note of exultation in the child's happy laugh.

'I must go now!' she said excitedly, and, slipping out of her father's arms, she darted up the dark oak stairs and, with a wave of her hand, disappeared from her parents' gaze. Long after she had turned the corner that took her out of sight, they heard her running footsteps and her voice trilling out 'Come, Lasses and Lads, Take Leave of your Dads'.

'Hyacinth's voice matches her face so marvellously, doesn't it, Claud?' said Laura. "Not many people's do. Hers has that piercing quality of crystal youth. It's like cold, cold water or biting into an apple.'

Claud rose to throw another log on to the blazing fire.

'Laura, what does Hyacinth mean by saying she's never lonely *here*?'

'I don't know, Claud. But, now you ask, haven't you noticed how different she is since we came here? Do you remember how listless she sometimes used to seem? I often got quite worried, and thought that perhaps I ought to borrow some bright child to keep her company. But now she's always as happy as the day is long. In fact – to tell the honest truth – I can't help rather missing her moods – or at least her dependence on me. You see, she used so to want me. Don't you remember how she was always imploring me to read to her or tell her stories?'

'Doesn't she now?' asked Claud.

'No; nowadays I can scarcely ever persuade her to stay with me. She's always rushing away, as though she had something better to do. It's little I see of her beyond her heels and the back of her head! She's so strangely self-sufficient. Between you and me, Claud, I think she's almost disquietingly happy.'

'Disquietingly happy? What do you mean, Laura?'

'Well – I mean – it's almost uncanny. Really, I don't know how to put it into words, but it's – it's as though she had some resource we don't know about. She seems so *occupied*. Yes, that's it – occupied. It sounds too silly, but it's as though being by herself were not being alone. She's grown a queer new sort of smile lately, too, a stealthy, sidelong smile, and the comings and goings of that smile don't have any connection with what any of us say or do. Haven't you noticed it? Claud, do you remember what that spooky friend of mine said about Hyacinth?'

'No, I don't,' Claud answered shortly. 'Some absurdity, I'm sure, from what I remember of her.'

'She said, "Now there's a child that should *see* things. Her 'muddy vesture of decay' is too transparent to 'close her in'." She said she had what she called "listening eyes", and the thinnest lids she had ever seen. Nonsense I thought it at the time, but now, Claud, I sometimes wonder ... This old place——'

'Oh, Lord! For Heaven's sake don't start any of that psychical rot here.'

Surprised at the annoyance in her husband's voice, Laura laughed.

"I know, dear, you think no American can come near a stately home of England without peopling it with ghosts, but I assure you I haven't – to relapse into my native tongue – "sensed" anything unpleasant here. I've had neither sight nor sound of abbots carrying their heads, nor of ladies in blood-speckled shrouds. No, indeed! On the contrary, I am conscious of a something that's happy – gay – blithe I don't know what to call it, but there seems a sort of *liveliness* about the atmosphere of this house – especially upstairs, and most especially in that room Hyacinth insisted on having as her playroom, the old day-nursery.'

'I didn't want her to use that room,' said Claud gruffly.

'I know, dear, I know,' his wife responded sympathetically. 'But she *insisted*.'

Poor fellow, she thought, how sensitive he is! Of course it had been his little niece Daphne's playroom. Probably she had romped in it just before her life ended so tragically. Laura reproached herself. She should never have allowed Hyacinth to appropriate that particular room. For Claud, its associations with Daphne were too strong. She should have remembered how he winced at any reminder of that poor dead child. Laura shuddered at the thought of the horror of her death. Ten years old! Just the same age as Hyacinth!

'I promise you there's nothing unpleasant in that room,' Laura went on. 'But – please don't think me silly – I do feel an atmosphere in it – a happy, youthful one. When I sit in that room, as I often do, memories of my own childhood break out of the past and come thronging round me. I feel the years simply slipping off me.' She laughed. 'Why, I get funny impulses to play, to dance, to jump about. My toes begin to twiddle. It's as though there were some *invitation* in the room. You'll think me too absurd, but once I actually found myself hiding in the cupboard, just as though I expected someone to come and search for me. And yet all the time I knew Hyacinth must be in bed and asleep. Sometimes I long to mount the old rocking-horse and have a gallop. I would, too, only I'm so afraid of being caught by one of those terribly grown-up housemaids.

'Once I thought I heard light, scuffling steps and a sort of soft tittering. Imagination, of course! . . . And yet, I suppose generations and generations of children have played in that room?'

'Yes,' said Claud. His voice was very gruff, and as he spoke he raised *The Times* and held it, like a wall, between him and any further confidences. Conscious of having annoyed him, Laura went away to tell Hyacinth it was bedtime. It was half an hour before she found her in the hayloft, and then she had great difficulty in coaxing her indoors. At last she handed her over to her maid, Bessy. The moment she returned to the hall her husband rose, saying he would go and say good night to Hyacinth.

'You won't find that little flibberty-gibbet in bed. I had such a tussle to get her in. It's the same thing every night. However late I leave her, she always says, "I haven't had nearly time enough to play!" '

'Not nearly time enough to play?' echoed Claud. '*She* doesn't say that; not Hyacinth?'

'Yes, why shouldn't she?' exclaimed Laura, puzzled by the violence of his manner.

But, giving no answer, Claud hastened from the room. That night at dinner, when Laura asked him why he had been so struck by those very ordinary words of Hyacinth's that she had repeated, he said he had no idea to what she was alluding, couldn't remember her quoting Hyacinth, and that it must be one of her 'silly fancies'.

Puzzled and hurt, Laura dropped the subject. Claud did not look well, and tonight that expression of strain was very noticeable. How had the old person described it? 'As though he were trying to remember something'? No, she didn't think that was what the expression in Claud's cavernous grey eyes suggested. But when she tried to define it to herself, she felt completely baffled.

A few days later, the Halyards were walking in the garden. A strong wind blew, the trees were bare, and crisp leaves, the colour of Hyacinth's hair, rustled around their feet. As usual their thoughts turned on their adored child.

'I thought Hyacinth looked very pale at luncheon,' said Claud.

'Yes,' answered his wife. 'Naughty child, she went out of doors last night!'

'Out of doors?'

'Yes. Bessy found her shoes and stockings drenched this morning, and when I asked, the little wretch owned she had gone out long after we were in bed. Just think how cold it must have been! She wouldn't tell me why she had done it, and when I said she must promise not to do it again, she burst into tears.'

'Little sprite!' laughed Claud. 'She still thinks of sleep as waste of time! I hope it may be – heavens! Just look at her now! What is she doing? I never saw a child run so fast, all alone.'

Hyacinth, her face wildly tense, flashed past them on long, spindly legs. Her speed, surprising for her age, never slackened until, with arms outstretched to touch it, she reached an acacia tree, at the foot of which, panting and laughing, she flung herself to the ground.

Her parents approached.

'Well done, Hyacinth! You *were* going fast!'

'I nearly won that time!' exclaimed the excited child, her green eyes blazing. 'Oh, so, so nearly!'

'You nearly *won*? What do you mean, by you "nearly won"? Were you racing one leg against the other?'

Hyacinth flushed, smiled nervously, sprang to her feet and in an instant had run out of sight behind the great yew hedge.

'Funny child!' said her mother, with an uneasy laugh. 'She's always running off, just as though she had an appointment elsewhere. She never seems to need me now. Do you remember how she used to think it such a treat to sleep with me? Now she never wants to. You know, Claud, it sounds ridiculous, but nowadays, when I go into that child's room, I feel as if I were – interrupting.' As she spoke, Laura gave a slight shiver. Her own words seemed to crystallize vague misgivings of which she had scarcely been aware.

'Interrupting?' echoed Claud. 'Interrupting what?'

'I don't know,' she answered hopelessly, and turned towards the house. Claud whistled for his dogs and set of for a long walk.

That evening Laura went to see Hyacinth in bed.

'Darling,' she said wheedlingly, 'wouldn't you like to come and sleep with Mummie tonight? We'll have early morning tea together and play ludo on my big pillow.'

An anxious look flitted across the child's sweet but rather set face.

'Thank you, Mummie darling,' she answered shyly but decidedly, 'only I'm so happy in my own lovely room. I love it, and I don't think it would like to be left.'

Intense relief shone in her bright eyes when, in silent aquiescence, her mother kissed her good night.

'Good Mummie,' she cooed, and, with a little ecstatic wriggle, she turned her radiant face towards the window.

That night it was very late before Laura rejoined her husband after dinner. The great bow window in the hall was uncurtained and the moonlight streamed in, its slanting green shafts mingling with the flickering red from the blazing fire by which Claud sat, an unopened book on his knee.

'Where have you been all this time, Laura?' he asked, glancing up at her face. 'What have you been doing? I hope Hyacinth hasn't been up to any more of her pranks.'

'No,' Laura answered quickly. 'But I have.'

'What do you mean?'

'I mean, I've been what you'd call silly. You remember what I told you about those funny feelings I get in the play-room? Well, directly after I left you over your coffee, I felt I wanted to go to the playroom. Don't frown, Claud, I couldn't help it. I simply *had* to go. My feet just took me there. Well, as I went along the passage, I heard a faint noise – a queer sort of a rushing noise. I opened the door. What do you think I saw? Claud, the rocking-horse was plunging to and fro – going furiously – *without a rider!*'

'Well,' said Claud, 'no doubt Hyacinth heard you coming, and, knowing she should be in bed, jumped off and ran out of the other door.'

'So I thought – so I hoped! But I rushed straight to her room, and found her fast asleep.'

'Well, then it must have been one of the maids.'

'No, there was no one about. They were all down at their supper. When I got back to the playroom, the rocking-horse was gradually subsiding. I watched it; and soon it was quite motionless.'

'No! You *do* surprise me!' jeered Claud.

'The queer thing,' said Laura solemnly, 'was that even while the rocking horse was galloping so fast, the stirrups were not swaying as they naturally would. No, they were quite taut – stretched out forwards – just as if——'

'Look here!' exclaimed Claud angrily. 'What are you driving at? What have you been reading? What have you been eating? Rocking-horse, indeed! It sounds more like a nightmare! I never knew Hyacinth had a rocking-horse. Who gave it to her?'

'No one. We found it here. It was Daphne's. You must have seen it. Vermilion nostrils and minus a tail. But, do you mean to say – haven't you ever been in the playroom since you came home?'

'No.'

'How extraordinary!'

'Why should I?' Claud's voice was fierce and he glared at his wife.

'Quite, quite!' said Laura nervously. She was surprised and shocked at the tone of his voice and the expression on his face. Why, for a second he had looked at her as though he hated her. Was it possible? Claud, her gently, courteous husband, whose devotion to her was almost a joke to their friends. 'Oh, I've forgotten my spectacles,' she said confusedly, 'I'll run up and fetch them. I shan't be two minutes.'

With this excuse she ran upstairs, leaving her husband moodily staring at her spectacles, which lay, conspicuous, on the table where she had just placed them.

Five minutes later she returned. Glancing at her, Claud knew that if she had not been flushed she would have been very pale.

'What is it now?'

With her back to him, Laura stood facing the fire. She spoke quickly, in a very low voice, as though she feared to hear her own words.

'As I got near the playroom, I heard the gramophone playing. I thought I heard dancing feet, but when I opened the door there was no one in the room. You won't believe me, Claud, but there was no one in the room. No one! And yet a *record had just been set going*. It was "Boys and Girls come out to Play". Before I found the electric switch, I thought I felt something very light brush past me. Almost before I was aware of it, it had gone. Oh, so quickly – just like a puff of wind! To make sure, I went to all the maids' bedrooms. One of them might have started the gramophone, but they were all in bed. Then I went to Hyacinth's room. I crept in, so as not to wake her, if she was asleep, and she was – yes, sound asleep. But as I looked at her, I heard a tap-tap at the window. It *might* have been a branch. Anyhow, it woke her. She sprang up in a second, wide, wide awake, with such a joyful welcoming expression on her excited little face ... Then she saw me, and she looked sort of scared and sorry – yes, *very* sorry to see me. Oh, Claud! I couldn't bear the look on her face when she saw me!'

Laura's last words came from her like a cry, and she turned to Claud with outstretched arms, as though appealing against she knew not what.

'Damnation!' he cried, springing to his feet. 'I can't stand any more of this! Look here, Laura darling, we'll all go away tomorrow. It's obvious you need a change. We've been here too long. After all, you aren't used to staying like a tree in one place. Besides, it will be great fun to take Hyacinth to London, won't it? Laura, my sweet, darling Laura, say you like this plan!'

'Of course I should love it,' murmured Laura, clasped in his arms.

It was such joy to feel herself carried on this wave of tenderness back into the haven of love, in which, until recently, she had felt so secure, that any proposal would have seemed welcome.

If only he would go on looking at her now, with love in his eyes, what matter where they went? And yet, even in the intensity of her relief, Laura was conscious of the irony of his wishing to leave the home he had always described as the Earthly Paradise. It was decided that they should leave the very next day, but, alas, when tomorrow came, their plan could not be carried out. Hyacinth had sprained her ankle very badly and was unable to put her foot to the ground. When told the news, Laura hurried to her daughter's room. She found her sitting up in bed. Her face was flushed and she looked shy.

'Poor darling! This is sad. However did it happen?'

'I'm so sorry, Mummie.' Hyacinth spoke hurriedly and nervously. 'But I'm afraid I've been naughty again. Don't be very angry with me, but I went out again last night and——'

'You went out? Oh, Hyacinth darling, you promised you wouldn't!'

'I'm so sorry, Mummie, but it was such a lovely night – such bright, bright moonlight. It made me forget I mustn't, and I simply *couldn't* say no.'

'The sooner you learn to say no to yourself the better. I shan't be able to trust you any more. You've hurt yourself, so I won't scold you, but you must never, never do such a thing again. Anyhow, what happened? How did you hurt your silly self?'

'I had a fall.'

'What, running?'

'No,' answered Hyacinth reluctantly. 'I was climbing a tree.'

'Climbing a tree? Good heavens! You might have broken your leg and lain out all night. Which tree?'

'The big elm. The one Daddie made a house in when he was little. A branch broke——'

'Well, you've had what Nannie used to call a "natural punishment". So I won't say any more. Lie still now, until the doctor comes.'

After the doctor had bound up Hyacinth's ankle, her mother went to look at the elm tree. She was appalled at the height of the broken branch. It seemed almost a miracle that the child was not more seriously hurt.

She returned to question her.

'You don't mean to tell me you fell from where a branch is broken off right up near the top of the tree?'

'Yes, but you see, there were so many branches that I paused on all the way down. I only really fell just the last bit.'

'But I had no idea you could climb so high. Surely you can't have got all that way up without any help?'

'Oh yes, I did!' cried Hyacinth triumphantly. 'And she climbed even higher, but then, of course, her legs are a little longer.'

'She? Who is She?'

Hyacinth flushed scarlet, and in confusion flung her arms round her mother's neck. Glancing quickly all round the room, she put her finger in front of her mouth.

'Don't tell Daddie. Oh, Mummie, *please, please* don't tell!' she said in a scared, panting voice. Not one word more would she say. After that one unguarded moment, her whole being was clenched in silence. At first her mother tried to coax her into an explanation, but, alarmed by her flushed excited face, she took her temperature. Finding her a little feverish, she did not like to press her any further. She seemed so troubled.

Laura did not tell her husband of Hyacinth's strange slip.

'*She* climbed even higher'? How could she tell him of that? She dreaded to hear him speak in that new, sharp way, so utterly unlike his old self.

After all, Hyacinth's fall must have been a considerable shock. Perhaps she had not known what she was saying. The next day the child seemed better, and Laura made another attempt to cross-question her about her accident, but, at the first word of inquiry, the child's flower-like mouth set in a thin, hard line, and an expression came into her eyes that was like a shutter between her and her mother.

During the following days she was affectionate but somehow guarded, and Laura felt strangely out of touch with her. On everyone's account she longed for a change and chafed at the enforced postponement of their plans. Claud, though now uniformly gentle in his manner, seemed increasingly depressed. Laura was determined to leave the first possible day, but unfortunately Hyacinth's injury proved more serious than had been supposed, and her ankle took a long time to recover. No bedridden child had ever been so little trouble. In fact she seemed almost unnaturally contented. Whenever her mother read aloud to her, she was politely aquiescent, but her manner was that of one who makes a necessary concession and waits with as good a grace as can be commanded.

Her gladness when the book closed was evident, and when her mother turned to leave the room she would wave her hand over-gratefully, and raise herself a little on her pillows, with a look of relief and a hovering smile of happy expectancy. Though Laura tried to shut her mind to the impression made by Hyacinth's manner, she could not succeed. Stung out of her usual self-control, she once cried out, 'What is it, Hyacinth? Why are you always waiting now – waiting for me to go?'

A look of fear quivered across the child's sensitive face.

'Waiting? What do you mean, Mummie? Why do you think I want you to go?' And with unskilled evasiveness she began to talk of irrelevancies – the cat's kittens, the new gardener, the pony that had kicked the groom – anything that came into her head.

With a heavy heart and a sense of absurdity, Laura aquiesced in making conversation with the child whose confidence she had once so completely possessed.

Though Hyacinth was full of strange whims, the one her mother thought the queerest was her insistence on having the rocking-horse brought into her bedroom.

'But, darling, it will take up so much room. And whatever is the use of having a rocking-horse you can't ride?'

But Hyacinth's pale, peaked face set in obstinacy.

'I want it. I need it,' was all she would say.

So the shabby old rocking-horse was dragged along the passage and stood in arrested prance at the foot of the child's bed.

That evening, as Laura came into the room, Hyacinth gave an obvious start, and, turning to her mother in flushed uneasiness, said querulously:

'Aren't I old enough yet, Mother, for people to knock at my door before they come into my room? You always tell me I must knock at your door.'

Amazed and hurt, Laura looked at the usually so gentle child, whose worried gaze she noticed was now fixed on the rocking-horse. Glancing at it herself, her glance became a stare. Was it her fancy, or was it slightly, almost imperceptibly moving?

'Have you been out of bed, Hyacinth?' she asked suspiciously.

'Oh no, Mummie, why?'

'Only I thought perhaps you had been very naughty and got on the rocking-horse. When I came in I thought it was just moving, as if it had been in motion and wasn't yet quite still. But of course it must have been my fancy.'

With unwonted eagerness, Hyacinth said:

'Will you read to me now, Mummie?'

Laura readily consented.

'Before I begin, though,' she said, 'I must tell you some good news. The doctor says you may get up in a week, and the very day after you get up we are going to take you to London.'

'You're going to take me to London?' Hyacinth's voice was sharp with dismay.

'Yes, darling. Won't it be fun?'

To her distress, Hyacinth burst into tears.

'Oh no, Mummie! No, no, no! Please don't take me away from here. I can't go! I won't go! It wouldn't be fair!'

'What do you mean, you absurd child? You'll have a lovely time in London. We'll take you to the Zoo and Madame Tussaud's and have pink ices at Gunther's. We'll do all the treats I used to tell you about in New York.'

Hyacinth's eyes welled with tears.

'Oh, please, Mummie,' she implored, 'don't take me away from lovely here.'

'But my darling, I love you to love this place, but you can't always be here. It will be all the more fun to come back to it.' She tried to laugh the child out of her distress. 'After all, you goose, it won't run away because we leave it. Everything will be exactly the same when we return.'

'I don't know, Mother,' sobbed Hyacinth. 'You can't tell. I'm afraid to go – besides, it wouldn't be fair.'

'Not fair, what do you mean?' questioned Laura, now completely bewildered.

'Oh! I don't know, Mummie! But I'm so happy here. Mayn't I stay? *Please*, please, *please*!'

Seeing Hyacinth so hysterically excited, Laura said firmly: 'We won't talk about it any more now,' and began to read aloud to unlistening ears.

The next day Hyacinth seemed much more sensible. Laura told her their departure was quite settled, and she made an obvious effort to accept the inevitable with as good a grace as possible, but she looked pale and strained and her manner was even more usually preoccupied.

'She looks as though she were trying to propitiate herself,' Laura explained to her husband.

'Trying to propitiate herself? What an absurd phrase!' he laughed. 'The ideas you have about that child!'

'I haven't any ideas about her.' Laura was astonished at the vehemence of her own voice.

Laura spent most of Christmas Eve decorating a small tree for Hyacinth. When she brought it upstairs, gay with glittering tinsel, gilded walnuts and shiny ornaments, the child clapped her hands with delight. Saying she would return in about an hour to light the candles, Laura placed the tree on a table in front of the fire.

When she came back she was surprised to find the room illuminated by the glimmer of little wax candles. Hyacinth seemed asleep, but sat up as the door opened. Assuming the child had prevailed on Bessy the maid to light the candles, Laura merely said:

'Well, I must say, after all my trouble, I do think you might have waited for me. Never mind. Now let's pull the crackers together.'

Shamefacedly Hyacinth pointed to the coloured tatters of two dozen exploded crackers. Her bed was strewn with paper caps, mottoes, and little tin musical instruments.

'Sorry, Mummie, I just couldn't wait,' she mumbled. 'I *love* candles. Flames are such fun, aren't they? May I have some toy fireworks? Please, Mummie!'

'I don't know. I think they're rather dangerous.'

'Oh no, Mummie. They aren't! Please say I may have some. I know! I'll ask Daddie to give me some. He told me to tell him what I wanted.'

Laura went to find Bessy.

'You should have asked me before lighting the candles on the Christmas tree,' she said severely. 'It wasn't at all safe to leave Miss Hyacinth alone in the room with all those candles alight. They often set fire to a bit of the tree. There should always be someone at hand with a wet sponge. I'm surprised at you, Bessy.'

'I didn't never light no tree, my lady,' said the astonished maid. 'I haven't been into Miss Hyacinth's room, not for two hours.'

Laura hurried back to Hyacinth.

'I don't want to scold you on Christmas Eve, but it was very naughty of you to get out of bed to light the candles, when you know perfectly well you're still forbidden to put your foot to the ground. And isn't it rather selfish to pull the crackers by yourself?'

Hyacinth blushed, but the expression on her face was unmistakably one of relief.

'Sorry, Mummie,' she said, 'so sorry,' and impetuously she flung her arms around her mother's neck and kissed her quickly – lovingly – just as she used to in the days when she was lonely.

At last Hyacinth's ankle was sufficiently recovered to allow the Halyards to make all their plans for leaving the next day. That evening Claud was to dine out with an old school-fellow who lived about four miles away. Before starting he went up to say good night to Hyacinth. Her half-packed trunk was open, and she was practising getting about the room.

'Don't ruin my tie!' he cried, as, hopping towards him, she flung her thin arms around his neck.

'Bother your tie!' she laughed. 'Oh, Daddie, darling Daddie. Thank you for the lovely, lovely box of fireworks. They came by the afternoon post. Aren't they gorgeous? Look at the lovely pictures on the lid. Whizz-bangs, catherine wheels and all!'

'Oh, they've come, have they? Well, mind, you aren't on any account to touch them. I'll let them off for you the first evening we come home. I'll carry them away now and lock them up somewhere safe.'

'Oh, mayn't they stay here, Daddie? I like looking at the pictures.'

'Certainly not. I can't trust you not to touch them.'

Hyacinth stood flushed and pouting. Suddenly she turned towards the window.

'Oh, look, Daddie,' she cried, pointing. 'Look at that great white owl. Oh, what a lovely Mrs Fly-by-Night!'

'Where, Hyacinth? I can't see it.'

'No, Daddie. You aren't looking where I'm pointing can't you see? She's just flown over the church tower.'

But look where he might, Claud could see no owl. He was still trying to be guided by Hyacinth's erratically pointed finger, when the butler came in and announced his car.

'Well, then, I must give the owl up,' he said. 'My friend's a great stickler for punctuality,' and kissing Hyacinth, who made no effort to detain him, he left the room, quite forgetting the box of fireworks he had left lying on the table.

As he was about to step into his car, he overheard a mocking 'To-whit-a-whoo!' Remembering an accomplishment of Hyacinth's — she could imitate an owl by whistling through her hands — he looked up towards her window. There she was, leaning far out, her red head gleaming, her pale face strangely elfin in the moonlight. Claud was startled by her beauty.

'Go to bed, Sprite,' he called.

Hyacinth waved her thin white arms.

'Good night, Daddie. See you in the morning!'

Though bitterly cold, the still, starlight night was so beautiful that Claud decided to walk home, and dismissed his car. He and his friend found much to say to one another, and it was past midnight before he started home. As he strode across the frozen fields, he began to regret his dismissal of the car. The cold, clear silence was only broken by his own footsteps, the occasional hoot of an owl, and the far, far away bark of a lonely dog. He felt too much alone in a white, unshared world.

The present — in which Claud always strove to enwrap himself — receded and faded. Quite powerless to protect him from the past, it became a mere dissolving mist.

A man maimed by one memory, he depended on contact with immediate external things to preoccupy him, to claim his attention so urgently that his senses might not be reassailed by certain ineffaceable impressions.

Just now he felt abandoned to the past, unprotected by the passage of time. What were time and space but modes of thought? There could be no putting distance between yourself and any experience. What had all the intervening years availed to release him? Nothing.

Claud Halyard had paid dearly for his inheritance. That strained expression friends noticed on his face was due not to the effort to re-member, but to the effort to forget – to expunge from his consciousness a haunting memory from which there was no release.

> And if I seek oblivion of an hour,
> So shorten I the stature of my soul.

In Claud's life there is one hour of which he ceaselessly and desperately seeks oblivion. Struggle as he may, he is now caught back in that hour, forced to relive each agonizing instant. It is superimposed on his present, and all the impressions of twelve intervening years are powerless to soften any of its intensity.

Twelve years ago; it is a moonlight night and, as now, he is walking towards Lichen Hall, the beautiful home of his childhood, the home which so obsesses his imagination that to him it seems the core of the entire world. Such love, he feels, should surely establish ownership, but Lichen Hall is not entailed on the male line, and, at the death of its present owner, his widowed and crippled brother, it will pass to that brother's only child, Daphne, who in time will marry and transfer all that wonderful beauty to strangers. He reaches the edge of the park. What is it that so startles him? What strange, terrifying sounds? God! the alarm bell in the great tower is clanging furiously. 'Fire! Fire!' he hears the word shouted.

Sick with dread, he rushes towards the house from which his horror-struck eyes see wreaths of smoke curling. Terrible crackling sounds are coming from one wing, and from the little turret tower in that wing long ribands of flame flutter towards the white moon.

Breathless, he reaches the lawn. The distracted servants have just carried someone out of the house. It is his crippled brother. Claud rushes to him. Struggling to raise his paralyzed body, the agonized man clutches at Claud and, pointing towards the house, shrieks, 'Daphne! Daphne!'

Claud realizes the situation. The fire brigade has not yet arrived, and Daphne, who sleeps in the turret tower of the burning wing, has not been got out. The alarm has only just been given, as it is merely a few minutes since the servants were aroused, the fire having gained a strong hold before any of them awoke. So far they have only just had time to carry down their helpless master. The child, they hoped, would have woken and escaped. They expected to find her outside but, to their dismay, she is nowhere to be seen

With a reassuring shout, Claud dashes into the house. The staircase leading up to the burning wing is already dense with smoke. Claud smashes a window and, choking, fights his way up and into the suffocating room where he sees Daphne on the floor – lying close to the window. The smoke has been too much for her. She is unconscious – quite unconscious, but breathing. He is in time! Quite easy to fling that light burden over his shoulder, to dash down the stairs and carry her safely out into the blessed air. Vividly Claud sees himself doing this – sees the joy blaze in his brother's eyes.

Simultaneously, an alternative picture presents itself. The child left lying as she is – unconscious – quite unconscious, not suffering, not dreading, not knowing, just *not reawakening*. Unaware. His own future? Lichen Hall?

His body seems to act without any conscious volition. Something takes command of his limbs. 'I never told myself to do it! I never told myself to do it!' How often thereafter was he to mutter these words!

Stooping, he lifts the light body. The burnished red hair brushes against his cheek. In a moment he has shoved her safely out of sight. Now for the stairs. They have become almost impassable. He emerges, choking. 'I can't find her!' he gasps to the horrified crowd. 'She's not in her room. She must have got out.' A frantic scream from his brother. Two minutes later the fire brigade dashes up. Claud takes control, directs the firemen to search for Daphne in every room except her own.

Now he sees the glowing, writhing roof of the little turret tower fall in. Soon the flames are extinguished. All the pictures are saved. The body of a child is found.

'Unfortunately the poor girl had taken refuge beneath her bed, and therefore her gallant uncle was unable to find her.' The coroner's verdict!

Daphne's father. Oh, God, his eyes!

Claud has lived through each moment just as intensely as twelve years ago. Shaking, dripping with perspiration, he drops back into the present.

He still sees his brother's eyes.

Had he loved his Daphne as I love my Hyacinth? At the thought Claud's heart contracts agonizingly. Suppose he had. Why not? Was she not as lovely, as piercingly sweet and young? Her eagerness! Had he not loved her himself – his dear little niece. The 'perfect playfellow' he used to call her. That last evening he had gone to say good night to her in her little Carpaccio bed.

'Time to go to sleep,' he had said.

'Oh, bother sleep!' she had exclaimed, imploring him to remain. 'I haven't had nearly time enough to play!'

Once more he feels the light burden in his arms, the unconscious little body that would so easily have revived to entertain its eager spirit – to welcome it back to the life it loved.

'Not nearly time enough to play?' Claud's mind struggled from the past to the present, to the past again and back to the present. Not nearly time enough to play!

The galloping, riderless rocking-horse? Hyacinth running races alone? His wife's strange impulses? Hide and seek? Who is it that seeks? These and other things flit through his strained mind.

He is nearly home now – home to Laura and Hyacinth – and tomorrow night they will all three be far from here. Yes, but in the meantime he is still so much in the grip of that fatal hour twelve years ago that he seems actually to hear that awful clanging and the cries of 'Fire! Fire!'

Heavens, how *real*, how outside himself these hideous sounds seem! But this is past bearing. Are his senses hopelessly haunted? This way lies madness. He must go away – let the house – return to America.

The sounds are insistent – grow louder. The illusion is complete.

God, can it really be *now*?

Turning the corner which brings the distant house into view, Claud stares. Yes, it is true! The present and the past have fused. The bell, the shouts are actual – immediate! It is twelve years later, but Lichen Hall is again on fire, and burning – burning furiously. How can a fire have taken so strong a hold? Every modern device for extinguishing an outbreak had been installed. Claud tears up the hill and reaches the lawn. This time it is the other wing that has caught fire that in which he, Laura and Hyacinth sleep. Its top story is already blazing. A crowd stares upward – pale faces red in the reflected glow. That shrieking woman, struggling to escape from arms that hold her back, can that be Laura? Disjointedly, from various voices, Claud learns the situation. The water supply is frozen – all the pipes useless. The telephone wires are broken down, but the car has gone for the fire brigade. Any moment now they should be here. In the meantime the child – the child – is upstairs, and the wooden staircase is impassable, was already so before anyone got up to bed, and, as only the family sleep in that wing, no one was there. The child is alone up there, trapped in that red horror, and the longest ladder cannot reach to the window of her room. A second ladder? Yes, they are tying two together with ropes, and several men have offered to climb up.

Claud shouts that he will go himself. Thank God the ladders are now securely fastened together! There is still time, but none to lose. The roof must soon fall in.

The ladder has been placed against the wall under Hyacinth's room. Claud's foot is already on its second rung, when something catches his eye. At a window there to the right of the one to which he is climbing he sees a child appear. The window is open. Her long, thin arms are outstretched, her red head gleams in the flaring light.

'Move the ladder, quick, quick!' Claud yells distractedly. 'She isn't in her bedroom. She's gone into the other room – the playroom. There! There! Can't you see her? There, hanging out of that window!'

No one sees anything, but blindly they obey. There is a rush and eager arms carry out his orders. The ladder is dragged away to the other window, at which Claud is pointing. It's ready now. Cheers ring out. Claud climbs up, up, up. Near the top he raises his head and finds himself staring into the smiling face of the girl who had perished in the flames twelve years ago. As Claud stares transfixed, the lovely, smiling face blurs and fades away. No one is there.

With a cry no one below could ever forget, Claud hurls himself down the ladder.

'The other window,' he gasps. 'Back to the other window!'

Wonderfully quickly the ladder is moved and replaced, but not quickly enough. The delay has been fatal. Just as the fire engines roar up the drive, the roof falls in.

Again every picture is saved, and a little body is recovered.

The Amorous Ghost

Enid Bagnold

It was five o'clock on a summer morning. The birds, who had woken at three, had long scattered about their duties. The white, plain house, blinkered and green shuttered, stood four-square to its soaking lawns, and up and down on the grass, his snow-boots planting dark blots on the grey dew, walked the owner. His hair was uncombed, he wore his pyjamas and an overcoat, and at every turn at the end of the lawn he looked up at a certain window, that of his own and his wife's bedroom, where, as on every other window on the long front, the green shutters lay neatly back against the wall and the cream curtains hung down in heavy folds.

The owner of the house, strangely and uncomfortably on his lawns instead of in his bed, rubbed his chilly hands and continued his tramp. He had to watch on his wrist, but when the stable clock struck six he entered the house and passing through the still hall he went up to his bathroom. The water was luke-warm in the taps from the night before, and he took a bath. As he left the bathroom for his dressing-room he heard the stirring of the first housemaid in the living-room below, and at seven o'clock he rang for his butler to lay out his clothes.

As the same thing had happened the day before, the butler was half prepared for the bell; yawning and incensed but ready dressed.

'Good morning,' said Mr Templeton rather suddenly. It was a greeting which he never gave, but he wished to try the quality of his voice. Finding it steady he went on, and gave an order for a melon from the greenhouse.

For breakfast he had very little appetite, and when he had finished the melon he unfolded the newspaper. The door of the dining-room opened, and the parlourmaid and housemaid came in and gave him their notice. 'A month from today, sir,' repeated the parlourmaid to bridge the silence that followed.

'It's nothing to do with me,' he said in a low voice. 'Your mistress is coming home tonight. You must tell her of these things.'

They left the room.

'What's the matter with those girls?' said Mr Templeton to the butler who came in.

'They haven't spoken to me, sir,' said the butler untruly; 'but I gather there has been an upset.'

'Because I chose to get up early on a summer morning?' asked Mr Templeton with an effort.

'Yes, sir. And there were other reasons.'

'Which were?'

'The housemaid,' said the butler with detachment, as though he were speaking of the movements of a fly, 'has found your bedroom, sir, strewn with clothes.'

'With my clothes?' said Mr Templeton.

'No, sir.'

Mr Templeton sat down. 'A nightgown?' he said weakly, as though appealing for human understanding.

'Yes, sir.'

'More than one?'

'Two, sir.'

'Good God!' said Mr Templeton, and walked to the window whistling shakily.

The butler cleared the table quietly and left the room.

'There's no question about it,' said Mr Templeton under his breath. 'She was undressing ... behind the chair.'

After breakfast he walked down his two fields and through a wood with the idea of talking to Mr George Casson. But George had gone to London for the day, and Mr Templeton, faced with the polish on the front door, the polish on the parlourmaid, and the sober look of the *Morning Post* folded on the hall table, felt that it was just as well that he had not after all to confide his incredible story. He walked back again, steadied by the air and exercise.

'I'll telephone to Hettie,' he decided, 'and make sure that she is coming tonight.' He rang up his wife, told her that he was well, that all was well, and heard with satisfaction that she was coming down that night after her dinner-party, catching the eleven-thirty, arriving at twelve-fifteen at the station.

'There is no train before at all,' she said. 'I sent round to the station to see, and owing to the strike they run none between seven-fifteen and eleven-thirty.'

'Then I'll send the car to the station and you'll be here at half-past twelve. I may be in bed, as I'm tired.'

'You're not ill?'

'No. I've had a bad night.'

It was not until the afternoon, after a good luncheon and a whisky-and-soda, that Mr Templeton went up to his bedroom to have a look at it. The cream curtains hung lightly blowing in the window. By the fireplace stood a high, wing, grandfather chair upholstered in patterned rep. Opposite the chair and the fire-place was the double bed, in one side of which Mr Templeton had lain working at his papers the night before. He walked up to his chair, put his hands in his pockets, and stood looking down at it. Then he crossed to the chest of drawers and drew out a drawer. On the right-hand side were Hettie's vests and chemises, neatly pressed and folded. On the left was a pile, folded but not pressed, of Hettie's nightgowns. Mr Templeton noted the crumples and creases on the silk.

'Evidence, evidence,' he said, walking to the window, 'that something happened in this room after I left it this morning. The maids believe they found a strange woman's nightgowns crumpled on the floor. As a matter of fact they are Hettie's nightgowns. I suppose a doctor would say I'd done it myself in a trance.'

'Two nights ago?' he thought, looking again at the bed. It seemed a week. The night before last as he lay working, propped up on pillows and cushions and his papers spread over the bed, he had glanced up, absorbed, at two o'clock in the morning and traced the pattern on the grandfather chair as it stood facing the empty gate with its back towards him, just as he had left it, when he had got into bed. It was then that he had seen the two hands hanging idly over the back of the chair as though an unseen owner was kneeling in the seat. His eyes stared, and a cold fear wandered down his spine. He sat without moving and watched the hands.

Ten minutes passed, and the hands were withdrawn quickly as though the occupant of the chair had silently changed its position.

Still he watched, propped, stiffening, on his pillows, and as time went on he fought the impression down. 'Tired,' he said. 'One's read of it. The brain reflecting something.' His heart quietened, and cautiously he settled himself a little lower and tried to sleep. He did not dare straighten the litter of papers around him, but with the light on he lay there till the dawn lit the yellow paint on the wall. At five he got up, sleepless, his eyes on the back of the grandfather chair, and without his dressing-gown or slippers he left the room. In the hall he found an overcoat and his warm snow-boots behind a chest and unbolting the front door he tramped the lawn in the dew.

On the second night (*last* night) he had worked as before. So completely had he convinced himself after a day of fresh air that his previous night's experience had been the result of his own imagination, his eyesight and his mind hallucinated by his work, that he had not even remembered (as he had meant to do) to turn the grandfather chair with its seat towards him. Now, as he worked in bed, he glanced from time to time at its patterned and concealing back, and wished vaguely that he had thought to turn it round.

He had not worked more than two hours before he knew that there was something going on in the chair.

'Who's there?' he called. The slight movement he had heard ceased for a moment, then began again. For a second he thought he saw a hand shoot out at the side, and once he could have sworn he saw the tip of a mound of hair showing over the top. There was a sound of scuffling in the chair, and some object flew out and landed with a bump on the floor below the field of his vision. Five minutes went by, and after a fresh scuffle a hand shot up and laid a bundle, white and stiff, with what seemed a small arm hanging, on the back of the chair.

Mr Templeton had had two bad nights and a great many hours of emotion. When he grasped that the object was a pair of stays with a suspender swinging from them, something bumped unevenly in his heart, a million black motes like a cloud of flies swam in his eyeballs; he fainted.

He woke up, and the room was dark, the light off, and he felt a little sick. Turning in bed to find comfort for his body, he remembered that he had been in the middle of a crisis of fear. He looked about him in the dark, and saw again the dawn on the curtains. Then he heard a chink by the washstand, several feet nearer to his bed than the grandfather chair. He was not alone; the thing was still in the room.

By the faint light from the curtains he could just see that his visitor was by the washstand. There was a gentle clinking of china and a sound of water, and dimly he could see a woman standing.

'Undressing,' he said to himself, 'washing.'

His gorge rose at the thought that came to him. Was it possible that the woman was coming to bed? It was that thought that had driven him with a wild rush from the room, and sent him marching for a second time up and down his grey and dewy lawns.

'And now,' thought Mr Templeton as he stood in the neat bedroom in the afternoon light and looked around him, 'Hettie's got to believe in the unfaithful or the supernatural.'

He crossed to the grandfather chair, and taking it in his two hands was about to push it on to the landing. But he paused. 'I'll leave it where it is tonight,' he thought, 'and go to bed as usual. For both our sakes I must find out something more about all this.'

Spending the rest of the afternoon out of doors, he played golf after tea, and eating a very light dinner he went to bed. His head ached badly from lack of sleep, but he was pleased to notice that his heart beat steadily. He took a couple of aspirin tablets to ease his head, and with a light novel settled himself down in bed to read and watch. Hettie would arrive at half-past twelve, and the butler was waiting up to let her in. Sandwiches, nicely covered from the air, were placed ready for her on a tray in a corner of the bedroom.

It was now eleven. He had an hour and a half to wait. 'She may come at any time,' he said (thinking of his visitor). He had turned the grand-father chair towards him, so that he could see the seat.

Quarter of an hour went by, and his head throbbed so violently that he put the book on his knees and altered the lights, turned out the brilliant reading lamp, switched on the light which illuminated the large face of the clock over the mantelpiece so that he sat in shadow. Five minutes later he was asleep.

He lay with his face buried in the pillow, the pain still drumming in his head, aware of his headache even at the bottom of his sleep. Dimly he heard his wife arrive, and murmured a hope to himself that she would not wake him. A slight movement rustled around him as she entered the room and undressed, but his pain was so bad that he could not bring himself to give a sign of life, and soon, while he clung to his half-sleep, he felt the bedclothes gently lifted and heard her slip in beside him.

Feeling chilly he drew his blanket closer round him. It was as though a draught was blowing about him in the bed, dispelling the mists of sleep and bringing him to himself. He felt a touch of remorse at his lack of welcome, and putting out his hand he sought his wife's beneath the sheet. Finding her wrist his fingers closed round it. She too was cold, strange, icy, and from her stillness and silence she appeared to be asleep.

'A cold drive from the station,' he thought, and held her wrist to warm it as he dozed again. 'She is positively chilling the bed,' he murmured to himself.

He was awakened by a roar beneath the window and the sweep of a light across the wall of the room. With amazement he heard the bolts shoot back across the front door. On the illuminated face of the clock over the fire-place he saw the hands standing at twenty-seven minutes past twelve. Then Mr Templeton, still gripping the wrist beside him, heard his wife's clear voice in the hall below.

The Face in the Mirror

Denys Val Baker

I saw him watching me in the wide mirror of the barber's saloon. He was a wiry, little man of about forty, with a round bullet-like head, going bald. He was drabbly dressed in baggy flannels and a faded brown jacket, with a mackintosh over one arm and slouching trilby hat balanced on his knees. He seemed a subdued and insignificant figure, yet there was something disturbingly familiar about him. His face, which was rather ugly, with protruding front teeth and deep, unsightly eye-sockets, was not a stranger's face. Something about it provoked in me an odd feeling of impending surprise, of startled recognition to come. I felt I ought to have known his face immediately, but somehow it remained shadowy and indefinable – slightly, and worryingly, outside the focus of my understanding.

It was about four o'clock and I had dropped in for a shave on my way home from work. I was leaning back with my eyes half-closed, pretending to be immersed in an animated conversation with the barber, and I don't think the little man realized I had observed his interest. I remembered that he had come into the barber's shop just behind me. I had taken the proffered shaving chair, while he had taken off his hat and mackintosh and sat down on the bench for waiting customers. As far as I knew, he had picked up one of the newspapers on the bench and started reading it. It was only by chance, while the barber was filling the hot-water mug from a can in the corner, that I happened to look in the mirror and see the little man staring across the room with bright, burning eyes. With sudden uneasiness I realized his gaze was aimed specifically in my direction. It was not a casual, not a mildly curious gaze, but rather the fierce, almost wolfish gaze of a man who had suddenly set eyes on a prey for which he had long been seeking. The eyes seemed to burn into the mirror with a sort of consuming hatred. I felt a chill creep into my reclining body. Of course, I was being quite ridiculous, I told myself, fighting hard against a tremendous desire to turn my head away and pretend it was all a dream. I was imagining things. In a moment or so I would see the man's eyes drift away and return in bored unconcern to their newspaper. But, unfortunately, they did not. They remained, instead, fixed unwaveringly upon me, two pin-points of steely menace that bored into my very existence. They seemed to be alight with an evil flame, and they were growing brighter and brighter.

I stuck it for a while, wriggling uncomfortably in my seat and trying unsuccessfully to let the monotone of the barber's voice lull me into a sense of security. Then I felt the little man's gaze becoming fiercer, more impelling, and I began to get really perturbed.

'For God's sake, hurry up and finish!' I muttered to the barber out of the corner of my mouth, so that the little man wouldn't notice. I drummed my fingers nervously on the side of the chair while the barber, disgruntled, gave a hasty wipe of a towel over my face, then roughly whisked off the cover sheet.

As I rose from the chair I looked casually into the mirror. The eyes of the little man rose upwards with me, following my movements steadily. I couldn't be quite sure (his face was still blurred), but it seemed that a quick look of cunning flitted across his face, as if he were making some rapid decision to cope with the new problem created by my imminent departure. For a moment I hesitated, wondering if he would rise and dutifully take the seat which the barber was now politely offering to him. Indeed, he *was* beginning to rise – but some flash of intuition warned me that he had no intention of taking the seat. I hastily thrust a coin into the barber's hand. 'Keep the change!' I said hurriedly. Then I grabbed up my mackintosh and hat and ran out of the shop, swinging the door back behind me viciously.

I didn't dare to look back, but I felt sure that the little man had come after me. I began walking down the street as fast as I could without actually running, intent on finding some sort of hiding place. When I came to a Woolworth's on the corner, I darted through the entrance. Inside, there was a thick crowd of shoppers: I threaded my way among them, burrowing deeper and deeper into the mass of sticky humanity. When I reached the stationery counter at the far end of the shop, I felt safer. Looking back I could see a jumble of housewives, old men and children, but no sign of the little man. I breathed easier and began walking slowly up and down the counter. I felt a tempting sensation of relief stealing over me. It would be all right now. Probably the little man's view had been temporarily blocked at the particular moment I stepped into Woolworth's. He would have gone hurrying by ... I would give him a few minutes, then come out of the shop and get a bus home.

I began wandering from counter to counter, looking at the goods with idle curiosity. I passed from stationery to kitchenware, then to hardware, then back to stationery. Passing the hardware counter for the third time, I felt the assistant eyeing me, and hastily picked up a coloured mixing bowl. 'I'll take this,' I said, smiling brightly at her. She took my silver and moved away to get change. I found myself smiling into a long, rather dirty mirror which lined the wall behind the counter. I went on smiling rather mechanically, then felt the grin slowly freeze across my face. Standing at the counter behind me I could see the little man, his slouch hat pulled down over his eyes, his mackintosh thrown untidily over his shoulder. He was pretending to examine a writing pad, but all the time his eyes were darting round the shop. Feeling like a hypnotized rabbit, I stood there without moving and watched his gaze travel round until it alighted, abruptly, on me. For a moment we remained like two statues; then the little man started to move. I had an extraordinary feeling that he was going to vault over the counter towards me. Crying out in sudden terror, I dropped the bowl on the edge of the counter, cracking it into a dozen pieces, and started running down the corridor leading to the nearest exit. Behind me I heard the startled cry of the assistant; shoppers and other assistants turned a sea of surprised faces in my direction; but before they could make any move to stop me, I had plunged through an exit swing-door. As I did so I fancied I caught a glimpse of the little man irritably pushing his way through a converging crowd of people.

Outside in the street again I felt bare and defenceless, like an animal caught in the open. Seeing another big store on the other side of the road, I made a dash for it, skipping neatly across the path of a tram and passing smoothly through a revolving door. As I went in I looked across the road and saw the Woolworth's door bursting open, and I knew that he was after me.

This was one of the higher-class stores, mostly clothing and drapery. The tall counters and drooping fabrics offered some excellent cover. I hurriedly skirted round the shop, keeping an occasional eye on the entrance to see if the little man would come in. Unfortunately, while doing this I backed into a precarious tower of carpet rolls and brought the whole lot tumbling down, spread-eagling me on to the floor. Terrified by a sudden fear that the little man would come leaping down on me, I scrambled to my feet and started running away without waiting to repair the damage – taking with me a blurred vision of a shopwalker's stout, reddening face, convulsed with indignation. I went on, turning two or three corners, passing through the ladies' underwear and brassiere sections. Then I began to wonder whether, during my accident, the little man had entered the shop and was even now waiting for me behind some tall display stand. It would certainly be safer to transfer myself to some other floor. Looking around I saw a convenient sign pointing: LIFTS. I hurried along and, in luck's way, I found the lift waiting, the uniformed girl about to close the gates.

'Hey, wait!' I cried, running up. The girl smiled demurely and stepped aside. I went in and flopped on to a welcome bench. The girl called out:

'Going Up!' Some other passengers crowded in after me. Then she clanged the gate and the lift started rising.

Something made me take uneasy stock of my surroundings. My nearest neighbours were two faded old ladies, out for an afternoon's shopping. Next to them were a mother and her small girl. Beyond her ... beyond her I caught a glimpse of the side of a man's face. There was something about it. One of the old ladies turned, sweeping her wide-brimmed hat out of my line of vision. Then indeed, I nearly died. The little man was standing exactly opposite with only one or two women between us.

At the sight of me a ferocious grin split his face into an evil mask. His drawn-back lips seemed about to mouth fearful epithets. For the first time I realized how incomparably sinister a figure he was, how threatening was the whole of his hard, shrivelled-up menacing presence. Now, indeed, there was no longer any room for doubt, no chance of pretending otherwise than that it was a chase for life or death.

My tongue parched in my mouth. I tried to utter words.

'Help!' I said. 'Help!'

I thought I was crying out, but the words must have stuck in my throat.

'What floor did you say?' said the lift-girl, looking at me.

I didn't reply. I just stared fascinatedly at the little man, and he stared back at me. I noticed he had a small unkempt moustache and a stubble of beard, and a sharp pointed nose. (I suddenly thought of a miniature Mephistopheles.) At any moment he would brush aside the old ladies with a wave of his hand.

'Third floor,' said the lift-girl unemotionally.

'Here, let me get out!' I cried wildly. With a terrific surge of strength I seized one of the old ladies around her waist and half-lifted, half-threw her into the path of the little man. Then I dived out of the lift, knocking the surprised lift-girl against the side. Seeing some stairs running beside the lift-shaft, I darted to them and began bounding down them two at a time. I heard someone call out after me: 'He must be mad! Stop him!' It was probably the old lady. Or, more likely, the little fellow. He would be after me down the stairs, like a terrier.

I beat him to the exit, however. I flew out of that store even faster than I had left Woolworth's. This time I gave up all pretence and began running hell-for-leather down the street. I saw people staring at me, and a policeman raised his eyebrows, but I didn't care how much attention I aroused. I only wanted to get a long way away. I ran the whole length of the main shopping street and then took a turning at random into a smaller, secondary street. I was puffing: it was some years since I had done any running. The trouble was my lunch was still a weight on me. It had been a good and heavy one ... And I bitterly regretted my two mild and bitters. I could hear them swishing about inside me.

Looking back I couldn't see any sign of the little man; so I slackened

my run to a panting walk. I wasn't fool enough to think I had given him
the slip, but at least I had time to think and manoeuvre. Although I could
hear my heart beating with heavy thuds, I felt much cooler in the head.
I remembered reading in detective stories that danger sharpened the
brain. Well, something like that was happening to me. It was high time
I forgot all about how, three-quarters of an hour ago, I had been walking
home from work, like I had done for nineteen years, and how I'd thought
it might be a good idea to have a shave. (I like now and then to have
the thing done professionally.) It was high time I forgot all about that
and concentrated on the job in hand. Here I was, walking down a dusty
side street which I didn't rightly recognize, going in the opposite direction to my home in the suburbs . . . and not far behind a little man with
a bullet head was after me, peeping in and out of the shop fronts. (I gave
him credit for that: he looked a thorough sort.) I would have to fox him,
and fox him properly. It couldn't be done lightly: it had to be thought
out carefully.

I seemed to be moving into the business quarters. I passed big blocks
of offices, inhabited by hundreds of formal, unknown 'Messrs.' I wondered whether to slip into one of the buildings and hide for a while, but
decided the risk of arousing suspicion, possibly of being captured by a
truculent commissionaire, was too great. I went on, walking about twice
as fast as would ordinarily be the case. It was tiring, but it helped to keep
up my morale. I kept crossing from one side of the road to another, and
taking right turnings and then left turnings. In this way I reckoned to
mix the little man up a good deal. Also, in the process, I got myself
completely lost. Indeed, I was gradually overcome by a fantastic feeling
that I was now in a completely strange town, without any knowledge of
locality or direction. It was possible that, in fact, many of the streets were
normally familiar to me. But as I turned down one street and up another,
I began to feel that I was in some gigantic maze, whose towering walls
were nebulous and unreal. Twice I became so lost that I found myself
back at a street corner which I had passed a few moments previously. On
the third occasion that this happened I found myself walking back on my
tracks and saw, some way ahead of me, a disturbance at a street-crossing.
I didn't know how he had done it but I guessed that the little fellow was
on my trail again, pushing his way through a crowd. I turned round and
began running again.

It was exciting in a way. There was always the persistent thrill of
danger, arising out of the knowledge that I was being chased. There was,
too, always the possibility of my coming round a corner and walking
straight into the little man. I wondered which of us would have the
presence of mind to act first. I rather prided myself that we would at least
be about even. I had worked out a very neat plan for lowering my head,
butting him hard in the stomach and then dashing away – when coming

round a corner I bumped straight into a tall, heavy policeman, knocking him sideways and staggering backwards myself.

'I'm terribly sorry, officer,' I said.

Then I didn't wait for any more because I recognized his face and knew that I had already walked past him four times, in four different streets. I had a dim idea that he shouted something after me, but by that time I had disappeared down an alley-way. It was a very long alley, and towering buildings shut out most of the light. I walked along it feeling more and more alone and frightened. When I eventually emerged from it into a rather dingy shopping street, I was so exhausted – after three imaginary encounters in the shadows with the little man, and one terrifying episode in which I saw the policeman starting towards me out of a lamp-post – that there was sweat dripping off my forehead and a weak feeling in my legs.

That's the trouble with being chased. It doesn't matter really who's chasing you: if it goes on long enough, it gets to the stage where you feel like everyone's chasing you. For instance, it wasn't long before I was going round not only with the little man and the big policeman on my track, but also with the knowledge that if I passed their way again at least three other people (a vegetable stall man, a newspaper seller and a squat Jewish woman shopkeeper) would decide I was either a criminal or a madman, and start chasing me themselves. For that reason I made a concentrated effort to move steadily away from the district where I had been wandering for an hour or so. When I came out into the shopping street, one of the suburban type, I knew that I was succeeding to some extent. The street was less crowded – there was more space between the buildings – and the trams had that emptying look, as if they were penetrating further and further out of the town.

All this time, it was true, I hadn't seen the little man. But I knew that he was after me. There was something so very sure about him that I felt he wouldn't be thrown off easily. Indeed, I remembered once seeing a film about something like that, where a fellow was chased all over the place by a gunman. No matter what this man did, the gunman kept tracking him down. In the end he cornered him in his own sitting-room, with his wife in a faint on the floor, and shot him three times through the head. It turned out, of course, that the fellow being chased had played a dirty trick on the gunman in the past; so it was all made to seem quite reasonable. My trouble was that I felt quite sure that the little man would keep finding me, but I couldn't for the life of me think of any reason for his interest. It was possible he hadn't got a gun (I shivered – his eyes were bad enough). But it was possible he had. I was glad that I hadn't gone home, following my first impulse; at least I wouldn't drag my wife into it. I hadn't forgotten my wife. I knew that already she would be somewhat worried. Most evenings I got home by five o'clock and we always

had supper at six; now it was well after six, and getting to be dusk. Several
times I thought, 'Well, I'll 'phone her, anyway,' and crossed over to a
telephone box. But each time I went inside and heard the door bang on
me, a terrifying feeling came over me. There I was, all nicely cooped up
in an oblong box. The next moment I would see the little man glaring
in through the glass panes. The moment I had that thought I pushed back
the door and dashed out of the box. What's more, I was always pretty
sure that if I hadn't done so, he would have been round the corner and
on top of me.

I felt happier on the move. The trouble was that I had suddenly
become conscious of my physical body. It was tired, dead tired. Not for
ten years had I walked and run so much. My head urged me to wander
on until I had shaken off the little man. My legs and the rest of my body
just ached and ached. Aching like that can wear down anything, even
the most rigid of purposes. It just goes on and on, gets heavier and
wearier, until you feel you'll drop down dead about three steps forward.
I didn't see much point in that. I began looking around for some shelter.
Besides it was getting dark, and there might be some real chance of giving
him the slip.

I picked in the end on a small cinema, tucked away among a block
of shops. It suddenly struck me as a brilliant idea. I fished two bob out
of my pocket and darted in, thrusting the money at the box-office girl,
grabbing the ticket and plunging into the welcome darkness. It was all
smoky and hazy inside, but it was shelter. I found a seat at the end of
a row. It was soft and cushioned . . . I sank into it with a sensuous feeling
of comfort. I stretched my legs out luxuriously, leaned with heavy
pleasure on the arm rests. I turned my attention to the screen and tried
to forget about the little man.

It was about two minutes from the end of the big picture – something
about a matador in Spain, the scene a bullfight finale – when I heard
the little man coming into the cinema. There's no way of explaining how
or why: I just knew it was him. There was a faint light from the door;
then I saw a shadow – a small shadow – floating down the aisle. There
wasn't any girl or anyone else, just him. He was pretending to be a
stranger, looking round casually for a seat. But I was watching him like
a hawk and I saw him stop at the end of my row and slide himself into
the first seat. A moment later he was sitting in the fifth seat; then he'd
dropped into the seventh seat. There were four seats between him and
me, and the bull in the film was just making its death charge, when I
leaped out of my seat and fled towards the cinema exit. It was a familiar
feeling; only this time I did it quicker than ever before. I fancy even the
little man was surprised.

It was dark when I got outside. It gave me a feeling of security, just
like the cinema. I began loitering past the shops, trying to catch the sound

of the little man's footsteps. The next thing that happened was someone shone a torch full on me, dazzling me, bathing me in relentless light. There wasn't time for any thinking. I just lowered my head and made a wild rush at the light. I think my head went about straight into the centre of a stomach. The light went out and I heard a strangled 'Ouch!' of pain. I must admit it gave me a thrill of sadistic pleasure, that moment. The action was so completely and devastatingly successful. It put me temporarily in supreme control of the situation. I felt a shadow sprawling on the pavement and started running away into the darkness. The wind was on my face as I vanished into the darkness ... Indeed, it was almost exhilarating.

I guessed that had made him mad. I heard some shouting and saw the torch come on again, whirling savagely. I also heard the surprising sound of a shrill whistle. A few minutes later there was an answering whistle somewhere ahead of me. These things, happening one after the other, got me rather confused, but I had enough presence of mind to take a turning and sprint down it deep into the night.

I had to stop running pretty soon. I had to lean against a lamp-post and take great heaving breaths. Otherwise I felt I should have collapsed. I stood there for several tense moments, getting my breath back and at the same time listening for the sound of chasing footsteps. But by some miracle the quiet remained unbroken. My ears had to be content with the dull rustle of wind in the tree-tops that lined the road and with far-off occasional hoots of cars. It was very eerie – very eerie indeed. For, I suddenly realized, because there were no footsteps it did not mean I was not being followed. I would be a fool not to concede more than average intelligence to the little man. He was the sort, I decided, visualizing his small, crafty face, alive with hidden cunning, who would possibly wrap cloth over his boots – or even take them off. In a flash all sense of temporary relief vanished. Standing there I became aware, with a blinding horror, that every shadow, however vague, every rustle, however muffled, might not be what it seemed. Even the solid shapes of the trees might not be real ... I think it was when I got to that state of mind that I gave up all efforts to preserve my morality, my sense of ethics, my character of an ordinary citizen who some hours previously had been sitting in his respectable office, doing his respectable job. There, swimming in the menacing shadows of a suburban residential street, I gave it all up and became the hunted fugitive, the animal who must use his cunning – not only to outwit his chaser, but to dispose of him.

I can remember how clear and simple it all became. It was as if a tremendous load had fallen away. I felt a wave of confidence pouring into me. At the same time I felt myself in powerful control of my senses, became aware of newly-acquired strength. I waited not in fear, but in expectancy, for what I knew would eventually come. I didn't mind how long the wait now that I knew exactly what course of action to follow, exactly what events were going to take place. And it *was* a long wait. I felt the cold night air creeping into my clothes, enveloping my feet, my fingers, my ears, sinking into my limbs. I didn't dare stamp or flap my arms for fear of giving my position away. For now, the whole essence of success was surprise. I had moved close into the shadow of a tree, merging myself into its frame. I could not possibly be seen against that dark outline. There I waited, breathing as quietly as possible, hardly daring to move a muscle. In fact, I felt it would be dangerous even to think – I might weaken in my new resolve – so I deliberately devoted my mind to counting numbers.

I had reached one hundred and forty-five, I think, when I heard him coming. Probably to anyone else it would have sounded just like a rustle of wind in the trees, or a leaf blowing about – but, of course, that was just what he would have wanted me to think. I envisaged now his triumphant smile, his sense of achievement, and smiled to myself. There was hardly any sound, just that faint, occasional, apparently casual rustle. I can't imitate the sound in writing, but it was rather like some-body turning over the pages of a newspaper. And that, of course, re-minded me of how I had first seen him, sitting there in the barber's shop, so insignificant, so innocent. A huge burning indignation swept over me at the thought of all the trouble he had given me. What had I ever done to him? Who was he to hound me down like a criminal? What right had he to bring terror into my life? It would take me weeks to recover from that one evening. And my wife – God knows what she would be thinking.

I has just reached the apex of these thoughts when I saw him. He was only a few feet away from me – the vaguest of shadows – but a sixth sense told me that it was him. He was sliding along, like some dirty, little sneak thief. I counted as he came nearer, giving him a certain number of steps to come level. One – two – three – four – five – six. 'Seven,' I said out loud, or I might even have shouted it, to startle him. Then I leapt forward and clutched him, and we went rolling on to the ground.

I had taken him completely by surprise. I was able to get my hands round his neck just where I wanted to. I knew exactly what to do: I had read it all in considerable detail in a crime novel. I held my fingers firmly into the flesh of his neck, pressing my body hard down on him, and with my two thumbs I felt for the narrow stem of his windpipe. I had got him – I knew I had got him. I could feel him suddenly struggling convulsively, like a drowning man. I maintained my grip, pressing tighter and tighter. I could feel my nails cutting into the flesh of his neck. I could hear the breath ebbing out of him. My strangle-hold sank deeper and deeper ... Then, suddenly, like an immense nightmare, the darkness seemed to swoop down on me, pouring over me in a gigantic wave of pain. Conscious of a helpless, detached sensation of bewilderment, I felt myself falling away ... falling, falling, falling ... down into a deep, black oblivion.

When I opened my eyes again it was no longer dark, but bright daylight. I was no longer fighting for my life in a quiet back street, but lying in bed in a hospital ward, with sunshine pouring through a window and falling in great streaks across the white coverlet.

There was a white-coated nurse sitting at a table in one corner. When she saw me open my eyes, she got up and came over. She was smiling – somehow it warmed me through and through to see her smile. I felt I just wanted to lie back there and drowse away, with everything big and white and peaceful, with the sunshine pouring in, and the nurse smiling. But there was something stopping me, something small and hard-pressing far away at the back of my mind. I didn't quite know what it was, and I couldn't quite express myself.

I looked up beseechingly at the nurse. She smiled and bent down, putting a cool hand on my head.

'It's all right, you just relax,' she said. 'You've had a nasty experience, a terrible shock, but you're going to be all right now. You just lie back and go to sleep again.'

But I couldn't go to sleep, I couldn't. She must have known that, I thought irritably. I tried to tell her what I wanted with my eyes. I looked at her pleadingly, passionately, begging her to answer my unformed question. For a few moments she stood looking down at me, a puzzled line creasing her forehead. Then she seemed to understand.

She gave a wide, reassuring smile.

'Now, don't you worry. You've had a nasty shock. Some madman tried to strangle you. Your neck's been cut about a bit ... But there's nothing permanently damaged. A week or two here and we'll be able to pack you off home.'

I looked at her dumbly. I felt as if I were about to tumble over the edge of a terrifying precipice, which I had climbed painfully and laboriously. I motioned her nearer, struggling to speak. The words came out at last, each one hurting the dry swollen lining of my throat.

'Please,' I said. 'Please, bring me a mirror.'

The nurse hesitated, then nodded. She went over to the corner of the room and came back holding a large oval hand-mirror.

'There you are,' she said soothingly. 'Only some bandages around your neck. Nothing very frightening, is it?'

But I didn't answer her. I looked in the mirror and the face I saw was a familiar one. It was small and ugly, with protruding teeth and sunken eyes, and the head was bald and round, like a bullet.

Caterpillars

E. F. Benson

I saw a month ago in an Italian paper that the Villa Cascana, in which I once stayed, had been pulled down, and that a manufactory of some sort was in process of erection on its site. There is therefore no longer any reason for refraining from writing of those things which I myself saw (or imagined I saw) in a certain room and on a certain landing of the villa in question, nor from mentioning the circumstances which followed, which may or may not (according to the opinion of the reader) throw some light on, or be somehow connected with, this experience.

The Villa Cascana was in all ways but one a perfectly delightful house, yet, if it were standing now, nothing in the world – I use the phrase in its literal sense – would induce me to set foot in it again, for I believe it to have been haunted in a very terrible and practical manner. Most ghosts, when all is said and done, do not do much harm; they may perhaps terrify, but the person whom they visit usually gets over their visitation. They may, on the other hand, be entirely friendly and beneficent. But the appearances in the Villa Cascana were not beneficent, and had they made their 'visit' in a very slightly different manner, I do not suppose I should have got over it any more than Arthur Inglis did.

The house stood on an ilex-clad hill not far from Sestri di Levante on the Italian Riviera, looking out over the iridescent blues of that enchanted sea, while behind it rose the pale green chestnut woods that climb up the hillsides till they give place to the pines that, black in contrast with them, crown the slopes. All round it the garden in the luxuriance of mid-spring bloomed and was fragrant, and the scent of magnolia and rose, borne on the salt freshness of the winds from the sea, flowered like a stream through the cool, vaulted rooms.

On the ground floor a broad pillared *loggia* ran around three sides of the house, the top of which formed a balcony for certain rooms on the first floor. The main staircase, broad and of grey marble steps, led up from the hall to the landing outside these rooms, which were three in number, namely, two big sitting-rooms and a bedroom arranged *en suite*. The latter was unoccupied, the sitting-rooms were in use. From here the main staircase continued up to the second floor, where were situated certain bedrooms, one of which I occupied, while on the other side of the first-floor landing some half-dozen steps led to another suite of rooms, where, at the time I am speaking of, Arthur Inglis, the artist, had his bedroom and studio. Thus the landing outside my bedroom, at the top of the house, commanded both the landing of the first floor, and also the steps that led to Inglis' rooms. Jim Stanley and his wife, finally (whose guest I was), occupied rooms in another wing of the house, where also were the servants' quarters.

I arrived just in time for lunch on a brilliant noon of mid-May. The garden was shouting with colour and fragrance, and not less delightful after my broiling walk up from the *marina*, should have been the coming from the reverberating heat and blaze of the day into the marble coolness of the villa. Only (the reader has my bare word for this, and nothing more), the moment I set foot in the house I felt that something was wrong. This feeling, I may say, was quite vague, though very strong, and I remember that when I saw letters waiting for me on the table in the hall I felt certain that the explanation was here: I was convinced that there was bad news of some sort for me. Yet when I opened them I found no such explanation of my premonition: my correspondents all reeked of prosperity. Yet this clear miscarriage of a presentiment did not dissipate my uneasiness. In that cool fragrant house there was something wrong.

I am at pains to mention this because it may explain why it was that, though I am as a rule so excellent a sleeper that the extinction of a light on getting into bed is apparently contemporaneous with being called on the following morning, I slept very badly on my first night in the Villa Cascana. It may also explain the fact that when I did sleep (if it was indeed in sleep that I saw what I thought I saw) I dreamed in a very vivid and original manner, original, that is to say, in the sense that something which, as far as I knew, had never previously entered into my consciousness, usurped it then. But since, in addition to this evil premonition, certain words and events occurring during the rest of the day, might have suggested something of what I thought happened that night, it will be well to relate them.

After lunch, then, I went round the house with Mrs Stanley, and during our tour she referred, it is true, to the unoccupied bedroom on the first floor, which opened out of the room where we had lunched.

'We left that unoccupied,' she said, 'because Jim and I have a charming bedroom and dressing-room, as you saw, in the wing, and if we used it ourselves we should have to turn the dining-room into a dressing-room and have our meals downstairs. As it is, however, we have our little flat there, Arthur Inglis has his little flat in the other passage; and I remembered (aren't I extraordinary?) that you once said that the higher up you were in a house the better you were pleased. So I put you at the top of the house, instead of giving you that room.'

It is true that a doubt, vague as my uneasy premonition, crossed my mind at this. I did not see why Mrs Stanley should have explained all this, if there had not been more to explain. I allow, therefore, that the thought that there was something to explain about the unoccupied bedroom was momentarily present to my mind.

The second thing that may have borne on my dream was this.

At dinner the conversation turned for a moment on ghosts. Inglis, with the certainty of conviction, expressed his belief that anybody who could possibly believe in the existence of supernatural phenomena was unworthy of the name of an ass. The subject instantly dropped. As far as I can recollect, nothing else occurred or was said that could bear on what follows.

We all went to bed rather early, and personally I yawned my way upstairs, feeling hideously sleepy. My room was rather hot, and I threw all the windows wide, and from without poured in the white light of the moon, and the love song of many nightingales. I undressed quickly, and got into bed, but though I had felt so sleepy before, I now felt extremely wide-awake. But I was quite content to be awake: I did not toss or turn, I felt perfectly happy listening to the song and seeing the light. Then, it is possible, I may have gone to sleep, and what follows may have been a dream. I thought anyhow that after a time the nightingales ceased singing and the moon sank. I thought also that if, for some unexplained reason, I was going to lie awake all night, I might as well read, and I remembered that I had left a book in which I was interested in the dining-room on the first floor. So I got out of bed, lit a candle, and went downstairs. I entered the room, saw on a side-table the book I had come to look for, and then, simultaneously, saw that the door into the un-occupied bedroom was open. A curious grey light, not of dawn nor of moonshine, came out of it, and I looked in. The bed stood just opposite the door, a big four-poster, hung with tapestry at the head. Then I saw that the greyish light of the bedroom came from the bed, or rather from what was on the bed. For it was covered with great caterpillars, a foot or more in length, which crawled over it. They were faintly luminous, and it was the light from them that showed me the room. Instead of the sucker-feet of ordinary caterpillars they had rows of pincers like crabs, and they moved by grasping what they lay on with their pincers, and then sliding their bodies forward. In colour these dreadful insects were yellowish grey, and they were covered with irregular lumps and swellings. There must have been hundreds of them, for they formed a sort of writhing, crawling pyramid on the bed. Occasionally one fell off on to the floor, with a soft fleshy thud, and though the floor was of hard concrete, it yielded to the pincer-feet as if it had been putty, and crawling back, the caterpillar would mount on to the bed again, to rejoin its fearful companions. They appeared to have no faces, so to speak, but at one end of them there was a mouth that opened sideways in respiration.

Then, as I looked, it seemed to me as if they all suddenly became conscious of my presence. All the mouths at any rate were turned in my direction, and the next moment they began dropping off the bed with those soft fleshy thuds on to the floor, and wriggling towards me. For one second the paralysis of nightmare was on me, but the next I was running upstairs again to my room, and I remember feeling the cold of the marble steps on my bare feet. I rushed into my bedroom, and slammed the door behind me, and then – I was certainly wide awake now – I found myself standing by my bed with the sweat of terror pouring from me. The noise of the banged door still rang in my ears. But, as would have been more usual, if this had been mere nightmare, the terror that had been mine when I saw these foul beasts crawling about the bed or dropping softly on to the floor did not cease then. Awake now, if dreaming before, I did not at all recover from the horror of dream: it did not seem to me that I had dreamed. And until dawn, I sat or stood, not daring to lie down, thinking that every rustle or movement that I heard was the approach of the caterpillars. To them and the claws that bit into the cement the wood of the door was child's play: steel would not keep them out.

But with the sweet and noble return of day the horror vanished: the whisper of wind became benignant again: the nameless fear, whatever it was, was smoothed out and terrified me no longer. Dawn broke, hueless at first; then it grew dove-coloured, then the flaming pageant of light spread over the sky.

The admirable rule of the house was that everybody had breakfast where and when he pleased, and in consequence it was not till lunch-time that I met any of the other members of our party, since I had breakfast on my balcony, and wrote letters and other things till lunch. In fact, I got down to that meal rather late, after the other three had begun. Between my knife and fork there was a small pillbox of cardboard, and as I sat down Inglis spoke.

'Do look at that,' he said, 'since you are interested in natural history. I found it crawling on my counterpane last night, and I don't know what it is.'

I think that before I opened the pillbox I expected something of the sort which I found in it. Inside it, anyhow, was a small caterpillar, greyish-yellow in colour, with curious bumps and excrescences on its rings. It was extremely active, and hurried round the box, this way and that. Its feet were unlike the feet of any caterpillar I ever saw: they were like the pincers of a crab. I looked, and shut the lid down again.

'No, I don't know it,' I said, 'but it looks rather unwholesome. What are you going to do with it?'

'Oh, I shall keep it,' said Inglis. 'It has begun to spin: I want to see what sort of a moth it turns into.'

I opened the box again, and saw that these hurrying movements were indeed the beginning of the spinning of the web of its cocoon. Then Inglis spoke again.

'It has got funny feet, too,' he said. 'They are like crabs' pincers. What's the Latin for crab? Oh, yes, Cancer. So in case it is unique, let's christen it: "Cancer Inglisenis".'

Then something happened in my brain, some momentary piecing together of all that I had seen or dreamed. Something in his words seemed to me to throw light on it all, and my own intense horror at the experience of the night before linked itself on to what he had just said. In effect, I took the box and threw it, caterpillar and all, out of the window. There was a gravel path just outside, and beyond it a fountain playing into a basin. The box fell on to the middle of this.

Inglis laughed.

'So the students of the occult don't like solid facts,' he said. 'My poor caterpillar!'

The talk went off again at once on to other subjects, and I have only given in detail, as they happened, these trivialities in order to be sure myself that I have recorded everything that could have borne on occult subjects or on the subject of caterpillars. But at the moment when I threw the pillbox into the fountain, I lost my head: my only excuse is that, as is probably plain, the tenant of it was, in miniature, exactly what I had seen crowded on to the bed in the unoccupied room. And though this translation of those phantoms into flesh and blood – or whatever it is that caterpillars are made of – ought perhaps to have relieved the horror of the night, as a matter of fact it did nothing of the kind. It only made the crawling pyramid that covered the bed in the unoccupied room more hideously real.

After lunch we spent a lazy hour or two strolling about the garden or sitting in the *loggia*, and it must have been about four o'clock when Stanley and I started off to bathe, down the path that led by the fountain into which I had thrown the pillbox. The water was shallow and clear, and at the bottom of it I saw its white remains. The soaking had disintegrated the cardboard, and it had become no more than a few strips and shreds of sodden paper. The centre of the fountain was a marble Italian Cupid which squirted the water out of a wineskin held under its arm. And crawling up its leg was the caterpillar. Strange and scarcely credible as it seemed, it must have survived the falling to bits of its prison, and made its way to shore, and there it was, out of arm's reach, weaving and waving this way and that as it evolved its cocoon.

Then, as I looked at it, it seemed to me again that, like the caterpillars I had seen last night, it saw me, and breaking out of the threads that surrounded it, it crawled down the marble leg of the Cupid and began swimming like a snake across the water of the fountain towards me. It came with extraordinary speed (the fact of a caterpillar being able to swim was new to me), and in another moment was crawling up the marble lip of the basin. Just then Inglis joined us.

'Why, if it isn't old "Cancer Inglisensis" again,' he said, catching sight of the beast. 'What a tearing hurry it is in.'

We were standing side by side on the path, and when the caterpillar had advanced to within about a yard of us, it stopped, and began waving again, as if in doubt as to the direction in which it should go. Then it appeared to make up its mind, and crawled on to Inglis' shoe.

'It likes me best,' he said, 'but I don't really know that I like it. And as it won't drown I think perhaps ——'

He shook it off his shoe on to the gravel path and trod on it.

All the afternoon the air got heavier and heavier with the Sirocco that was without doubt coming up from the south, and that night again I went up to bed feeling very sleepy, but below my drowsiness, so to speak, there was the consciousness, stronger than before, that there was something wrong in the house, that something dangerous was close at hand. But I fell asleep at once, and – how long after I do not know – either woke or dreamed I awoke, feeling that I must get up at once, *or I should be too late*. Then (dreaming or awake) I lay and fought this fear, telling myself that I was but the prey of my own nerves disordered by Sirocco or what not, and at the same time quite clearly knowing in another part of my mind, so to speak, that every moment's delay added to the danger. At last this second feeling became irresistible, and I put on coat and trousers and went out of my room on to the landing. And then I saw that I had already delayed too long, and that I was now too late.

The whole of the landing of the first floor below was invisible under the swarm of caterpillars that crawled there. The folding-doors into the sitting-room from which opened the bedroom where I had seen them last night, were shut, but they were squeezing through the cracks of it, and dropping one by one through the keyhole, elongating themselves into mere string as they passed, and growing fat and lumpy again on emerging. Some, as if exploring, were nosing about the steps into the passage at the end of which were Inglis' rooms, others were crawling on the lowest steps of the staircase that led up to where I stood. The landing, however, was completely covered with them: I was cut off. And of the frozen horror that seized me when I saw that, I can give no idea in words.

Then at last a general movement began to take place, and they grew thicker on the steps that led to Inglis' room. Gradually, like some hideous tide of flesh, they advanced along the passage, and I saw the foremost, visible by the pale grey luminousness that came from them, reach his door. Again and again I tried to shout and warn him, in terror all the time that they should turn at the sound of my voice and mount my stair instead, but for all my efforts I felt that no sound came from my throat. They crawled along the hinge-crack of his door, passing through as they had done before, and still I stood there making impotent efforts to shout to him, to bid him escape while there was time.

At last the passage was completely empty: they had all gone, and at that moment I was conscious for the first time of the cold of the marble landing on which I stood barefooted. The dawn was just beginning to break in the Eastern sky.

Six months later I met Mrs Stanley in a country house in England. We talked on many subjects, and at last she said:

'I don't think I have seen you since I got that dreadful news about Arthur Inglis a month ago.'

'I haven't heard,' said I.

'No? He has got cancer. They don't even advise an operation, for there is no hope of a cure: he is riddled with it, the doctors say.'

Now during all these six months I do not think a day had passed on which I had not had in my mind the dreams (or whatever you like to call them) which I had seen in the Villa Cascana.

'It is awful, is it not?' she continued, 'and I feel, I can't help feeling, that he may have ——'

'Caught it at the villa?' I asked.

She looked at me in blank surprise.

'Why did you say that?' she asked. 'How did you know?'

Then she told me. In the unoccupied bedroom a year before there had been a fatal case of cancer. She had, of course, taken the best advice and had been told that the utmost dictates of prudence would be obeyed so long as she did not put anybody to sleep in the room, which had also been thoroughly disinfected and newly white-washed and painted. But ——

The Damned Thing

Ambrose Bierce

1: One Does Not Always Eat What is on the Table

By the light of a tallow candle which had been placed on one end of a rough table a man was reading something written in a book. It was an old account-book, greatly worn; and the writing was not, apparently, very legible, for the man sometimes held the page close to the flame of the candle to get a stronger light on it. The shadow of the book would then throw into obscurity a half of the room, darkening a number of faces and figures; for besides the reader, eight other men were present. Seven of them sat against the rough log walls, silent, motionless, and the room being small, not very far from the table. By extending an arm any one of them could have touched the eighth man, who lay on the table, face upward, partly covered by a sheet, his arms at his sides. He was dead.

The man with the book was not reading aloud, and no one spoke; all seemed to be waiting for something to occur; the dead man only was without expectation. From the blank darkness outside came in, through the aperture that served for a window, all the ever unfamiliar noises of night in the wilderness – the long nameless note of a distant coyote; the stilly pulsing thrill of tireless insects in trees; strange cries of night birds, so different from those of the birds of day; the drone of great blundering beetles, and all that mysterious chorus of small sounds that seem always to have been but half heard when they have suddenly ceased, as if conscious of an indiscretion. But nothing of all this was noted in that company; its members were not overmuch addicted to idle interest in matters of no practical importance; that was obvious in every line of their rugged faces – obvious even in the dim light of the single candle. They were evidently men of the vicinity – farmers and woodsmen.

The person reading was a trifle different; one would have said of him that he was of the world, worldly, albeit there was that in his attire which attested a certain fellowship with the organisms of his environment. His coat would hardly have passed muster in San Francisco; his foot-gear was not of urban origin, and the hat that lay by him on the floor (he was the

only one uncovered) was such that if one had considered it as an article
of mere personal adornment one would have missed its meaning. In
countenance the man was rather prepossessing, with just a hint of stern-
ness; though that he may have assumed or cultivated, as appropriate to
one in authority. For he was a coroner. It was by virtue of his office that
he had possession of the book in which he was reading; it had been found
among the dead man's effects – in his cabin, where the inquest was now
taking place.

When the coroner had finished reading he put the book into his
breast-pocket. At that moment the door was pushed open and a young
man entered. He, clearly, was not of mountain birth, and breeding:
he was clad as those who dwell in cities. His clothing was dusty, however, as from travel. He had, in fact, been riding hard to attend the
inquest.

The coroner nodded; no one else greeted him.

'We have waited for you,' said the coroner. 'It is necessary to have done
with this business tonight.'

The young man smiled. 'I am sorry to have kept you,' he said. 'I went
away, not to evade your summons, but to post to my newspaper an
account of what I suppose I am called back to relate.'

The coroner smiled.

'The account that you posted to your newspaper,' he said, 'differs,
probably, from that which you will give here under oath.'

'That,' replied the other, rather hotly and with a visible flush, 'is as
you please. I used manifold paper and have a copy of what I sent. It was
not written as news, for it is incredible, but as fiction. It may go as a part
of my testimony under oath.'

'But you say it is incredible.'

'That is nothing to you, sir, if I also swear that it is true.'

The coroner was silent for a time, his eyes upon the floor. The men
about the sides of the cabin talked in whispers, but seldom withdrew their
gaze from the face of the corpse. Presently the coroner lifted his eyes and
said: 'We will resume the inquest.'

The men removed their hats. The witness was sworn.

'What is your name?' the coroner asked.

'William Harker.'

'Age?'

'Twenty-seven.'

'You knew the deceased, Hugh Morgan?'

'Yes.'

'You were with him when he died?'

'Near him.'

'How did that happen – your presence, I mean?'

'I was visiting him at his place to shoot and fish. A part of my purpose, however, was to study him and his odd, solitary way of life. He seemed a good model for a character in fiction. I sometimes write stories.'

'I sometimes read them.'

'Thank you.'

'Stories in general – not yours.'

Some of the jurors laughed. Against a sombre background humour shows high lights. Soldiers in the intervals of battle laugh easily, and a jest in the death-chamber conquers by surprise.

'Relate the circumstances of this man's death,' said the coroner. 'You may use any notes or memoranda that you please.'

The witness understood. Pulling a manuscript from his breast-pocket he held it near the candle and turning the leaves until he found the passage that he wanted to read.

2: What May Happen in a Field of Wild Oats

'... The sun had hardly risen when we left the house. We were looking for quail, each with a shotgun, but we had only one dog. Morgan said that our best ground was beyond a certain ridge that he pointed out, and we crossed it by a trail through the *chaparral*. On the other side was comparatively level ground, thickly covered with wild oats. As we emerged from the *chaparral* Morgan was but a few yards in advance. Suddenly we heard, at a little distance to our right and partly in front, a noise as of some animal thrashing about in the bushes, which we could see were violently agitated.

' "We've startled a deer," I said, "I wish we had brought a rifle."

'Morgan, who had stopped and was intently watching the agitated *chaparral*, said nothing, but had cocked both barrels of his gun and was holding it in readiness to aim. I thought him a trifle excited, which surprised me, for he had a reputation for exceptional coolness, even in moments of sudden and imminent peril.

' "Oh, come," I said. "You are are not going to fill up a deer with quail-shot, are you?"

'Still he did not reply; but catching a sight of his face as he turned it slightly towards me I was struck by the intensity of his look. Then I understood that we had serious business in hand, and my first conjecture was that we had "jumped" a grizzly. I advanced to Morgan's side, cocking my piece as I moved.

'The bushes were now quiet and the sounds had ceased, but Morgan was as attentive to the place as before.

' "What is it? What the devil is it?" I asked.

' "The Damned Thing!" he replied, without turning his head. His voice was husky and unnatural. He trembled visibly.

'I was about to speak further, when I observed the wild oats near the place of the disturbance moving in the most inexplicable way. I can hardly describe it. It seemed as if stirred by a streak of wind, which not only bent it, but pressed it down – crushed it so that it did not rise; and this movement was slowly prolonging itself directly towards us.

'Nothing that I had ever seen had affected me so strangely as this unfamiliar and unaccountable phenomenon, yet I am unable to recall any sense of fear. I remember – and tell it here because, singularly enough, I recollected it then – that once in looking carelessly out of an open window I momentarily mistook a small tree close at hand for one of a group of larger trees at a little distance away. It looked the same size as the others, but being more distinctly and sharply defined in mass and detail seemed out of harmony with them. It was a mere falsification of the law of aerial perspective, but it startled, almost terrified me. We so rely upon the orderly operation of familiar natural laws that any seeming suspension of them is noted as a menace to our safety, a warning of unthinkable calamity. So now the apparently causeless movement of the herbage and the slow, undeviating approach of the line of disturbance were distinctly disquieting. My companion appeared actually frightened, and I could hardly credit my senses when I saw him suddenly throw his gun to his shoulder and fire both barrels at the agitated grain! Before the smoke of the discharge had cleared away I heard a loud savage cry – a scream like that of a wild animal – and flinging his gun upon the ground Morgan sprang away and ran swiftly from the spot. At the same instant I was thrown violently to the ground by the impact of something unseen in the smoke – some soft, heavy substance that seemed thrown against me with great force.

'Before I could get upon my feet and recover my gun, which seemed to have been struck from my hands, I heard Morgan crying as if in mortal agony, and mingling with his cries were such hoarse, savage sounds as one hears from fighting dogs. Inexpressibly terrified, I struggled to my feet and looked in the direction of Morgan's retreat; and may Heaven in mercy spare me from another sight like that! At a distance of less than thirty yards was my friend, down on one knee, his head thrown back at a frightful angle, hatless, his long hair in disorder and his whole body in violent movement from side to side, backward and forward. His right arm was lifted and seemed to lack the hand – at least, I could see none. The other arm was invisible. At times, as my memory now reports this extraordinary scene, I could discern but a part of his body; it was as if he had been partly blotted out – I cannot otherwise express it – then a shifting of his position would bring it all into view again.

'All this must have occurred within a few seconds, yet in that time Morgan assumed all the postures of a determined wrestler vanquished by superior weight and strength. I saw nothing but him, and him not always distinctly. During the entire incident his shouts and curses were heard, as if through an enveloping uproar of such sounds of rage and fury as I have never heard from the throat of man or brute!

'For a moment only I stood irresolute, then throwing down my gun I ran forward to my friend's assistance. I had a vague belief that he was suffering from a fit, or some form of convulsion. Before I could reach his side he was down and quiet. All sounds had ceased, but with a feeling of such terror as even these awful events had not inspired I now saw again the mysterious movement of the wild oats, prolonging itself from the trampled area about the prostrate man towards the edge of a wood. It was only when it had reached the wood that I was able to withdraw my eyes and look at my companion. He was dead.'

3: A Man though Naked may be in Rags

The coroner rose from his seat and stood beside the dead man. Lifting an edge of the sheet he pulled it away, exposing the entire body, altogether naked and showing in the candlelight a clay-like yellow. It had, however, broad maculations of bluish black, obviously caused by extravasated blood from contusions. The chest and sides looked as if they had been beaten with a bludgeon. There were dreadful lacerations; the skin was torn in strips and shreds.

The coroner moved round to the end of the table and undid a silk handkerchief which had been passed under the chin and knotted on the top of the head. When the handkerchief was drawn away it exposed what had been the throat. Some of the jurors who had risen to get a better view repented their curiosity and turned away their faces. Witness Harker went to the open window and leaned out across the sill, faint and sick. Dropping the handkerchief upon the dead man's neck the coroner stepped to an angle of the room and from a pile of clothing produced one garment after another, each of which he held up a moment for inspection. All were torn, and stiff with blood. The jurors did not make a closer inspection. They seemed rather uninterested. They had, in truth, seen all this before; the only thing that was new to them being Harker's testimony.

'Gentlemen,' the coroner said, 'we have no more evidence, I think. Your duty has been already explained to you; if there is nothing you wish to ask you may go outside and consider your verdict.'

The foreman rose – a tall, bearded man of sixty, coarsely clad.

'I should like to ask one question, Mr Coroner,' he said. 'What asylum did this yer last witness escape from?'

'Mr Harker,' said the coroner gravely and tranquilly, 'from what asylum did you last escape?'

Harker flushed crimson again, but said nothing, and the seven jurors rose and solemnly filed out of the cabin.

'If you have done insulting me, sir,' said Harker, as soon as he and the officer were left alone with the dead man, 'I suppose I am at liberty to go?'

'Yes.'

Harker started to leave, but paused, with his hand on the door-latch. The habit of his profession was strong in him – stronger than his sense of personal dignity. He turned about and said:

'The book that you have there – I recognize it as Morgan's diary. You seemed greatly interested in it; you read in it while I was testifying. May I see it? The public would like——'

'The book will cut no figure in this matter,' replied the official slipping it into his coat pocket; 'all the entries in it were made before the writer's death.'

As Harker passed out of the house the jury re-entered and stood about the table, on which the now covered corpse showed under the sheet a sharp definition. The foreman seated himself near the candle, produced from his breast-pocket a pencil and scrap of paper and wrote rather laboriously the following verdict, which with various degrees of effort all signed:

'We, the jury, do find that the remains come to their death at the hands of a mountain lion, but some of us thinks, all the same, they had fits.'

4: An Explanation from the Tomb

In the diary of the late Hugh Morgan are certain interesting entries having, possibly, a scientific value as suggestions. At the inquest upon his body the book was not put in evidence; possibly the coroner thought it not worth while to confuse the jury. The date of the first of the entries mentioned cannot be ascertained; the upper part of the leaf is torn away; the part of the entry remaining as follows:

'. . . would run in a half-circle, keeping his head turned always towards the centre, and again he would stand still, barking furiously. At last he ran away into the brush as fast as he could go. I thought at first that he had gone mad, but on returning to the house found no other alteration in his manner than what was obviously due to fear of punishment.

'Can a dog see with his nose? Do odours impress some cerebral centre with images of the thing that emitted them? . . .

'*Sept.* 2 – Looking at the stars last night as they rose above the crest of the ridge east of the house, I observed them successively disappear – from left to right. Each was eclipsed but an instant, and only a few at the same time, but along the entire length of the ridge all that were within a degree or two of the crest were blotted out. It was as if something had passed along between me and them; but I could not see it, and the stars were not thick enough to define its outline. Ugh! don't like this.' ...

Several weeks' entries are missing, three leaves being torn from the book.

'*Sept*. 27 – It has been about here again – I find evidence of its presence every day. I watched again all last night in the same cover, gun in hand, double-charged with buckshot. In the morning the fresh footprints were there, as before. Yet I could have sworn I did not sleep – indeed, I hardly sleep at all. It is terrible, insupportable! If these amazing experiences are real I shall go mad; if they are fanciful I am mad already.

'*Oct*. 3 – I shall not go – it shall not drive me away. No, this is *my* house, *my* land. God hates a coward ...

'*Oct*. 5 – I can stand it no longer; I have invited Harker to pass a few weeks with me – he has a level head. I can judge from his manner if he thinks me mad.

'*Oct*. 7 – I have the solution of the mystery; it came to me last night – suddenly, as by revelation. How simple – how terribly simple!

'There are sounds that we cannot hear. At either end of the scale are notes that stir no chord of that imperfect instrument, the human ear. They are too high or too grave. I have observed a flock of blackbirds occupying an entire tree-top – the tops of several trees – and all in full song. Suddenly – in a moment – at absolutely the same instant – all spring into the air and fly away. How? They could not all see one another – whole tree-tops intervened. At no point could a leader have been visible to all. There must have been a signal of warning or command, high and shrill above the din, but by me unheard. I have observed, too, the same simultaneous flight when all were silent, among not only blackbirds, but other birds – quail, for example, widely separated by bushes – even on opposite sides of a hill.

'It is known to seamen that a school of whales basking or sporting on the surface of the ocean, miles apart, with the convexity of the earth between, will sometimes dive at the same instant – all gone out of sight in a moment. The signal has been sounded – too grave for the ear of the sailor at the masthead and his comrades on the deck – who nevertheless feel its vibrations in the ship as the stones of a cathedral are stirred by the bass of the organ.

'As with sounds, so with colours. At each end of the solar spectrum the chemist can detect the presence of what are known as "actinic" rays. They represent colours – integral colours in the composition of light – which we are unable to discern. The human eye is an imperfect instrument; its range is but a few octaves of the real "chromatic scale." I am not mad; here are colours that we cannot see.

'And, God help me! The Damned Thing is of such a colour!'

A Case of Eavesdropping

Algernon Blackwood

Jim Shorthouse was the sort of fellow who always made a mess of things. Everything with which his hands or mind came into contact issued from such contact in an unqualified and irremediable state of mess. His college days were a mess: he was twice rusticated. His schooldays were a mess: he went to half a dozen, each passing him to the next with a worse character and in a more developed state of mess. His early boyhood was the sort of mess that copy-books and dictionaries spell with a big 'M', and his babyhood – ugh! was the embodiment of howling, yowling, screaming mess.

At the age of forty, however, there came a change in his troubled life, when he met a girl with half a million in her own right, who consented to marry him, and who very soon succeeded in reducing his most messy existence into a state of comparative order and system.

Certain incidents, important and otherwise, of Jim's life would never have come to be told here but for the fact that in getting into his 'messes' and out of them again he succeeded in drawing himself into the atmosphere of peculiar circumstances and strange happenings. He attracted to his path the curious adventures of life as unfailingly as meat attracts flies, and jam wasps. It is to the meat and jam of his life, so to speak, that he owes his experiences; his after-life was all pudding, which attracts nothing but greedy children. With marriage the interest of life ceased for all but one person, and his path became regular as the sun's instead of erratic as a comet's.

The first experience in order of time that he related to me shows that somewhere latent behind his disarranged nervous system there lay psychic perceptions of an uncommon order. About the age of twenty-two – I think after his second rustication – his father's purse and patience had equally given out, and Jim found himself stranded high and dry in a large American city. High and dry! And the only clothes that had no holes in them safely in the keeping of his uncle's wardrobe.

Careful reflection on a bench in one of the city parks led him to the conclusion that the only thing to do was to persuade the city editor of one of the daily journals that he possessed an observant mind and a ready pen, and that he could 'do good work for your paper, sir, as a reporter'. This, then, he did, standing at a most unnatural angle between the editor and the window to conceal the whereabouts of the holes.

'Guess we'll have to give you a week's trial,' said the editor, who, ever on the look-out for good chance material, took on shoals of men in that way and retained on the average one man per shoal. Anyhow it gave Jim Shorthouse the wherewithal to sew up the holes and relieve his uncle's wardrobe of its burden.

Then he went to find living quarters; and in this proceeding his unique characteristics already referred to – what theosophists would call his Karma – began unmistakably to assert themselves, for it was in the house he eventually selected that this sad tale took place.

There are no 'diggings' in American cities. The alternatives for small incomes are grim enough – rooms in a boarding-house where meals are served, or in a room-house where no meals are served – not even breakfast. Rich people live in palaces, of course, but Jim had nothing to do with 'sich-like'. His horizon was bounded by boarding-houses and room-houses; and, owing to the necessary irregularity of his meals and hours, he took the latter.

It was a large, gaunt-looking place in a side street, with dirty windows and a creaking iron gate, but the rooms were large, and the one he selected and paid for in advance was on the top floor. The landlady looked gaunt and dusty as the house, and quite as old. Her eyes were green and faded, and her features large.

'Waal,' she twanged, with her electrifying Western drawl, 'that's the room, if you like it, and that's the price I said. Now, if you want it, why, just say so; and if you don't, why, it don't hurt me any.'

Jim wanted to shake her, but he feared the clouds of long-accumulated dust in her clothes, and as the price and size of the room suited him, he decided to take it.

'Anyone else on this floor?' he asked.

She looked at him queerly out of her faded eyes before she answered.

'None of my guests ever put such questions to me before,' she said; 'but I guess you're different. Why, there's no one at all but an old gent that's stayed here every bit of five years. He's over thar,' pointing to the end of the passage.

'Ah! I see,' said Shorthouse feebly. 'So I'm alone up here?'

'Reckon you are, pretty near,' she twanged out, ending the conversation abruptly by turning her back on her new 'guest', and going slowly and deliberately downstairs.

The newspaper work kept Shorthouse out most of the night. Three times a week he got home at 1 a.m., and three times at 3 a.m. The room proved comfortable enough, and he paid for a second week. His unusual hours had so far prevented his meeting any inmates of the house, and not a sound had been heard from the 'old gent' who shared the floor with him. It seemed a very quiet house.

One night, about the middle of the second week, he came home tired after a long day's work. The lamp that usually stood all night in the hall had burned itself out, and he had to stumble upstairs in the dark. He made considerable noise in doing so, but nobody seemed to be disturbed. The whole house was utterly quiet, and probably everybody was asleep. There were no lights under any of the doors. All was in darkness. It was after two o'clock.

After reading some English letters that had come during the day, and dipping for a few minutes into a book, he became drowsy and got ready for bed. Just as he was about to get in between the sheets, he stopped for a moment and listened. There rose in the night, as he did so, the sound of steps somewhere in the house below. Listening attentively, he heard that it was somebody coming upstairs – a heavy tread, and the owner taking no pains to step quietly. On it came up the stairs, tramp, tramp, tramp – evidently the tread of a big man, and one in something of a hurry.

At once thoughts connected somehow with fire and police flashed through Jim's brain, but there were no sounds of voices with the steps, and he reflected in the same moment that it could only be the old gentleman keeping late hours and tumbling upstairs in the darkness. He was in the act of turning out the gas and stepping into bed, when the house resumed its former stillness by the footsteps suddenly coming to a dead stop immediately outside his own room.

With his hand on the gas, Shorthouse paused a moment before turning it out to see if the steps would go on again, when he was startled by a loud knocking on his door. Instantly, in obedience to a curious and unexplained instinct, he turned out the light, leaving himself and the room in total darkness.

He had scarcely taken a step across the room to open the door, when a voice from the other side of the wall, so close it almost sounded in his ear, exclaimed in German, 'Is that you, father? Come in.'

The speaker was a man in the next room, and the knocking, after all, had not been on his own door, but on that of the adjoining chamber, which he had supposed to be vacant.

Almost before the man in the passage had time to answer in German, 'Let me in at once,' Jim heard someone cross the floor and unlock the door. Then it was slammed to with a bang, and there was audible the sound of footsteps about the room, and of chairs being drawn up to a table and knocking against furniture on the way. The men seemed wholly regardless of their neighbour's comfort, for they made noise enough to waken the dead.

'Serves me right for taking a room in such a cheap hole,' reflected Jim in the darkness. 'I wonder whom she's let the room to!'

The two rooms, the landlady had told him, were originally one. She had put up a thin partition – just a row of boards – to increase her income. The doors were adjacent, and only separated by the massive upright beam between them. When one was opened or shut the other rattled.

With utter indifference to the comfort of the other sleepers in the house, the two Germans had meanwhile commenced to talk both at once and at the top of their voices. They talked emphatically, even angrily. The words 'Father' and 'Otto' were freely used. Shorthouse understood German, but as he stood listening for the first minute or two, an eavesdropper in spite of himself, it was difficult to make head or tail of the talk, for neither would give way to the other, and the jumble of guttural sounds and unfinished sentences was wholly unintelligible. Then very suddenly, both voices dropped together; and after a moment's pause, the deep tones of one of them, who seemed to be the 'father', said, with the utmost distinctness——

'You mean, Otto, that you refuse to get it?'

There was a sound of someone shuffling in the chair before the answer came. 'I mean that I don't know how to get it. It is so much, Father. It is *too* much. A part of it——'

'A part of it!' cried the other, with an angry oath, 'a part of it, when ruin and disgrace are already in the house, is worse than useless. If you can get half you can get all, you wretched fool. Half-measures only damn all concerned.'

'You told me last time –' began the other firmly, but was not allowed to finish. A succession of horrible oaths drowned his sentence, and the father went on, in a voice vibrating with anger——

'You know she will give you anything. You have only been married a few months. If you ask and give a plausible reason you can get all we want and more. You can ask it temporarily. All will be paid back. It will re-establish the firm, and she will never know what was done with it. With that amount, Otto, you know I can recoup all these terrible losses, and in less than a year all will be repaid. But without it ... You must get it, Otto. Hear me, you must. Am I to be arrested for the misuse of trust moneys? Is our honoured name to be cursed and spat on?' The old man choked and stammered in his anger and desperation.

Shorthouse stood shivering in the darkness and listening in spite of himself. The conversation had carried him along with it, and he had been for some reason afraid to let his neighbourhood be known. But at this point he realized that he had listened too long and that he must inform the two men that they could be overheard to every single syllable. So he coughed loudly, and at the same time rattled the handle of his door. It seemed to have no effect, for the voices continued just as loudly as before, the son protesting and the father growing more and more angry. He coughed again persistently, and also contrived purposely in the darkness to tumble against the partition, feeling the thin boards yield easily under his weight, and making a considerable noise in so doing. But the voices went on unconcernedly, and louder than ever. Could it be possible they had not heard?

By this time Jim was more concerned about his own sleep than the morality of overhearing the private scandals of his neighbours, and he went out into the passage and knocked smartly at their door. Instantly, as if by magic, the sounds ceased. Everything dropped into utter silence. There was no light under the door and not a whisper could be heard within. He knocked again, but received no answer.

'Gentlemen,' he began at length, with his lips close to the keyhole and in German, 'please do not talk so loud. I can overhear all you say in the next room. Besides, it is very late, and I wish to sleep.'

He paused and listened, but no answer was forthcoming. He turned the handle and found the door was locked. Not a sound broke the stillness of the night except the faint swish of the wind over the skylight and the creaking of a board here and there in the house below. The cold air of a very early morning crept down the passage, and made him shiver. The silence of the house began to impress him disagreeably. He looked behind him and about him, hoping, and yet fearing, that something would break the stillness. The voices still seemed to ring on in his ears; but that sudden silence, when he knocked at the door, affected him far more unpleasantly than the voices, and put strange thoughts in his brain – thoughts he did not like or approve.

Moving stealthily from the door, he peered over the banisters into the space below. It was like a deep vault that might conceal in its shadows anything that was not good. It was not difficult to fancy he saw an indistinct moving to-and-fro below him. Was that a figure sitting on the stairs peering up obliquely at him out of hideous eyes? Was that a sound of whispering and shuffling down there in the dark halls and forsaken landings? Was it something more than the inarticulate murmur of the night?

The wind made an effort overhead, singing over the skylight, and the door behind him rattled and made him start. He turned to go back to his room, and the draught closed the door slowly in his face as if there were someone pressing against it from the other side. When he pushed it open and went in, a hundred shadowy forms seemed to dart swiftly and silently back to their corners and hiding-places. But in the adjoining room the sounds had entirely ceased, and Shorthouse soon crept into bed, and left the house with its inmates, waking or sleeping, to take care of themselves, while he entered the region of dreams and silence.

Next day, strong in the common sense that the sunlight brings, he determined to lodge a complaint against the noisy occupants of the next room and make the landlady request them to modify their voices at such late hours of the night and morning. But it so happened that she was not to be seen that day, and when he returned from the office at midnight it was, of course, too late.

Looking under the door as he came up to bed he noticed that there was no light, and concluded that the Germans were not in. So much the better. He went to sleep about one o'clock, fully decided that if they came up later and woke him with their horrible noises he would not rest till he had roused the landlady and made her reprove them with that authoritative twang, in which every word was like the lash of a metallic whip.

However, there proved to be no need for such drastic measures, for Shorthouse slumbered peacefully all night, and his dreams – chiefly of the fields of grain and flocks of sheep on the far-away farms of his father's estate – were permitted to run their fanciful course unbroken.

Two nights later, however, when he came home tired out, after a difficult day, and wet and blown about by one of the wickedest storms he had ever seen, his dreams – always of the fields and sheep – were not destined to be so undisturbed.

He had already dozed off in that delicious glow that follows the removal of wet clothes and the immediate snuggling under warm blankets, when his consciousness, hovering on the borderland between sleep and waking, was vaguely troubled by a sound that rose indistinctly from the depths of the house, and, between the gusts of wind and rain, reached his ears with an accompanying sense of uneasiness and discomfort. It rose on the night air with some pretence of regularity, dying away again in the roar of the wind to reassert itself distantly in the deep, brief hushes of the storm.

For a few minutes Jim's dreams were coloured only – tinged, as it were – by this impression of fear approaching from somewhere insensibly upon him. His consciousness, at first, refused to be drawn back from that enchanted region where it had wandered, and he did not immediately awaken. But the nature of his dreams changed unpleasantly. He saw the sheep suddenly run huddled together, as though frightened by the neighbourhood of an enemy, while the fields of waving corn became agitated as though some monster were moving uncouthly among the crowded stalks. The sky grew dark, and in his dream an awful sound came somewhere from the clouds. It was in reality the sound downstairs growing more distinct.

Shorthouse shifted uneasily across the bed with something like a groan of distress. The next minute he awoke, and found himself sitting straight up in bed – listening. Was it a nightmare? Had he been dreaming evil dreams, that his flesh crawled and the hair stirred on his head?

The room was dark and silent, but outside the wind howled dismally and drove the rain with repeated assaults against the rattling windows. How nice it would be – the thought flashed through his mind – if all winds, like the west wind, went down with the sun! They made such fiendish noises at night, like the crying of angry voices. In the daytime they had such a different sound. If only——

Hark! It was no dream after all, for the sound was momentarily growing louder, and its *cause* was coming up the stairs. He found himself speculating feebly what this cause might be, but the sound was still too indistinct to enable him to arrive at any definite conclusion.

The voice of a church clock striking two made itself heard above the wind. It was just about the hour when the Germans had commenced their performance three nights before. Shorthouse made up his mind that if they began it again he would not put up with it for very long. Yet he was already horribly conscious of the difficulty he would have of getting out of bed. The clothes were so warm and comforting against his back. The sound, still steadily coming nearer, had by this time become differentiated from the confused clamour of the elements, and had resolved itself into the footsteps of one or more persons.

'The Germans, hang 'em!' thought Jim. 'But what on earth is the matter with me? I never felt so queer in all my life.'

He was trembling all over, and felt as cold as though he were in a freezing atmosphere. His nerves were steady enough, but he was conscious of a curious sense of malaise and trepidation, such as even the most vigorous men have been known to experience when in the first grip of some horrible and deadly disease. As the footsteps approached this feeling of weakness increased. He felt a strange lassitude creeping over him, a sort of exhaustion, accompanied by a growing numbness in the extremities, and a sensation of dreaminess in the head, as if perhaps the consciousness were leaving its accustomed seat in the brain and preparing to act on another plane. Yet, strange to say, as the vitality was slowly withdrawn from his body, his senses seemed to grow more acute.

Meanwhile the steps were already on the landing at the top of the stairs, and Shorthouse, still sitting upright in bed, heard a heavy body brush past his door and along the wall outside, almost immediately afterwards the loud knocking of someone's knuckles on the door of the adjoining room.

Instantly, though so far not a sound had proceeded from within, he heard, through the thin partition, a chair pushed back and a man quickly cross the floor and open the door.

'Ah! it's you,' he heard in the son's voice. Had the fellow, then, been sitting silently in there all this time, waiting for his father's arrival? To Shorthouse it came not as a pleasant reflection by any means.

There was no answer to this dubious greeting, but the door was closed quickly, and then there was a sound as if a bag or parcel had been thrown on a wooden table and had slid some distance across it before stopping.

'What's that?' asked the son, with anxiety in his tone.

'You may know before I go,' returned the other gruffly. Indeed his voice was more than gruff: it betrayed ill-suppressed passion.

Shorthouse was conscious of a strong desire to stop the conversation before it proceeded any further, but somehow or other his will was not equal to the task, and he could not get out of bed. The conversation went on, every tone and inflexion distinctly audible above the noise of the storm.

In a low voice the father continued. Jim missed some of the words at the beginning of the sentence. It ended with: ' ... but now they've all left, and I've managed to get up to you. You know what I've come for.' There was distinct menace in his tone.

'Yes,' returned the other; 'I have been waiting.'

'And the money?' asked the father impatiently.

No answer.

'You've had three days to get it in, and I've contrived to stave off the worst so far – but tomorrow is the end.'

No answer.

'Speak, Otto! What have you got for me? Speak, my son; for God's sake, tell me.'

There was a moment's silence, during which the old man's vibrating accents seemed to echo through the rooms. Then came in a low voice the answer——

'I have nothing.'

'Otto!' cried the other with passion, 'nothing!'

'I can get nothing,' came almost in a whisper.

'You lie!' cried the other, in a half-stifled voice. 'I swear you lie. Give me the money.'

A chair was heard scraping along the floor. Evidently the men had been sitting over the table, and one of them had risen. Shorthouse heard the bag or parcel drawn across the table, and then a step as if one of the men was crossing to the door.

'Father, what's in that? I must know,' said Otto, with the first signs of determination in his voice. There must have been an effort on the son's part to gain possession of the parcel in question, and on the father's to retain it, for between them it fell to the ground. A curious rattle followed its contact with the floor. Instantly there were sounds of a scuffle. The men were struggling for the possession of the box. The elder man with oaths, and blasphemous imprecations, the other, with short gasps that betokened the strength of his efforts. It was of short duration, and the younger man had evidently won, for a minute later was heard his angry exclamation.

'I knew it. Her jewels! You scoundrel, you shall never have them. It is a crime.'

The elder man uttered a short, guttural laugh, which froze Jim's blood and made his skin creep. No word was spoken, and for the space of ten seconds there was a living silence. Then the air trembled with the sound of a thud, followed immediately by a groan and the crash of a heavy body falling over on to the table. A second later there was a lurching from the table on to the floor and against the partition that separated the rooms. The bed quivered an instant at the shock, but the unholy spell was lifted from his soul and Jim Shorthouse sprang out of bed and across the floor in a single bound. He knew that ghastly murder had been done – the murder by a father of his son.

With shaking fingers but a determined heart he lit the gas, and the first thing in which his eyes corroborated the evidence of his ears was the horrifying detail that the lower portion of the partition bulged un-naturally into his own room. The glaring paper with which it was covered had cracked under the tension and the boards beneath it bent inwards towards him. What hideous load was behind them, he shuddered to think.

All this he saw in less than a second. Since the final lurch against the wall not a sound had proceeded from the room, not even a groan or a footstep. All was still but the howl of the wind, which to his ears had in it a note of triumphant horror.

Shorthouse was in the act of leaving the room to rouse the house and send for the police – in fact his hand was already on the door-knob – when something in the room arrested his attention. Out of the corner of his eyes he thought he caught sight of something moving. He was sure of it, and turning his eyes in the direction, he found he was not mistaken.

Something was creeping slowly towards him along the floor. It was something dark and serpentine in shape, and it came from the place where the partition bulged. He stooped down to examine it with feelings of intense horror and repugnance, and he discovered that it was moving towards him from the *other side* of the wall. His eyes were fascinated, and for the moment he was unable to move. Silently, slowly, from side to side like a thick worm, it crawled forwards into the room beneath his fright-ened eyes, until at length he could stand it no longer and stretched out his arm to touch it. But at the instant of contact he withdrew his hand with a suppressed scream. It was sluggish – and it was warm! and he saw that his fingers were stained with living crimson.

A second more, and Shorthouse was out in the passage with his hand on the door of the next room. It was locked. He plunged forward with all his weight against it, and, the lock giving way, he fell headlong into a room that was pitch dark and very cold. In a moment he was on his feet again and trying to penetrate the blackness. Not a sound, not a movement. Not even the sense of a presence. It was empty, miserably empty!

Across the room he could trace the outline of a window with rain streaming down the outside, and the blurred lights of the city beyond. But the room was empty, appallingly empty; and so still. He stood there, cold as ice, staring, shivering, listening. Suddenly there was a step behind him and a light flashed into the room, and when he turned quickly with his arm up as if to ward off a terrific blow he found himself face to face with the landlady. Instantly the reaction began to set in.

It was nearly three o'clock in the morning, and he was standing there with bare feet and striped pyjamas in a small room, which in the merciful light he perceived to be absolutely empty, carpetless, and without a stick of furniture, or even a window-blind. There he stood staring at the disagreeable landlady. And there she stood too, staring and silent, in a black wrapper, her head almost bald, her face white as chalk, shading a sputtering candle with one bony hand and peering over it at him with her blinking eyes. She looked positively hideous.

'Waal?' she drawled at length, 'I heard yer right enough. Guess you couldn't sleep! Or just prowlin' round a bit – is that it?'

The empty room, the absence of all traces of the recent tragedy, the silence, the hour, his striped pyjamas and bare feet – everything together combined to deprive him momentarily of speech. He started at her blankly without a word.

'Waal?' clanked the awful voice.

'My dear woman,' he burst out finally, 'there's been something awful——' So far his desperation took him, but no further. He positively stuck at the substantive.

'Oh! There hasn't been nothin',' she said slowly still peering at him. 'I reckon you've only seen and heard what the others did. I never can keep folks on this floor long. Most of 'em catch on sooner or later – that is, the ones that's kind of quick and sensitive. Only you being an Englishman I thought you wouldn't mind. Nothin' really happens; it's only thinkin' like.'

Shorthouse was beside himself. He felt ready to pick her up and drop her over the banisters, candle and all.

'Look there,' he said, pointing at her within an inch of her blinking eyes with the fingers that had touched the oozing blood; 'look there, my good woman. Is that only thinking?'

She stared a minute, as if not knowing what he meant.

'I guess so,' she said at length.

He followed her eyes, and to his amazement saw that his fingers were as white as usual, and quite free from the awful stain that had been there ten minutes before. There was no sign of blood. No amount of staring could bring it back. Had he gone out of his mind? Had his eyes and ears played such tricks with him? Had his senses become false and perverted? He dashed past the landlady, out into the passage, and gained his own room in a couple of strides. Whew! . . . the partition no longer bulged. The paper was not torn. There was no creeping, crawling thing on the faded old carpet.

'It's all over now,' drawled the metallic voice behind him. 'I'm going to bed again.'

He turned and saw the landlady slowly going downstairs again, still shading the candle with her hand and peering up at him from time to time as she moved. A black, ugly, unwholesome object, he thought, as she disappeared into the darkness below, and the last flicker of her candle threw a queer-shaped shadow along the wall and over the ceiling.

Without hesitating a moment, Shorthouse threw himself into his clothes and went out of the house. He preferred the storm to the horrors of that top floor, and he walked the streets till daylight. In the evening he told the landlady he would leave the next day, in spite of her assurances that nothing more would happen.

'It never comes back,' she said – 'that is, not after he's killed.'

Shorthouse gasped.

'You gave me a lot for my money,' he growled.

'Waal, it aren't my show,' she drawled. 'I'm no spirit medium. You take chances. Some'll sleep right along and never hear nothin'. Others, like yourself, are different and get the whole thing.'

'Who's the old gentleman? – does he hear it?' asked Jim.

'There's no old gentleman at all,' she answered coolly. 'I just told you that to make you feel easy like in case you did hear anythin'. You were all alone on the floor.

'Say now,' she went on, after a pause in which Shorthouse could think of nothing to say but unpublishable things, 'say now, do tell, did you feel sort of cold when the show was on, sort of tired and weak, I mean, as if you might be going to die?'

'How can I say?' he answered savagely; 'what I felt God only knows.'

'Wall, but He won't tell,' she drawled out. 'Only I was wonderin' how you really did feel, because the man who had that room last was found one morning in bed——'

'In bed?'

'He was dead. He was the one before you. Oh! You don't need to get rattled so. You're all right. And it all really happened, they do say. This house used to be a private residence some twenty-five years ago, and a German family of the name of Steinhardt lived here. They had a big business in Wall Street, and stood way up in things.'

'Ah!' said her listener.

'Oh yes, they did, right at the top, till one fine day it all bust and the old man skipped with the boodle——'

'Skipped with the boodle?'

'That's so,' she said; 'got clear away with all the money, and the son was found dead in his house, committed soocide it was thought. Though there was some as said he couldn't have stabbed himself and fallen in that position. They said he was murdered. The father died in prison. They tried to fasten the murder on him, but there was no motive, or no evidence, or no somethin'. I forget now.'

'Very pretty,' said Shorthouse.

'I'll show you somethin' mighty queer anyways,' she drawled, 'if you'll come upstairs a minute. I've heard the steps and voices lots of times; they don't pheaze me any. I'd just as lief hear so many dogs barkin'. You'll find the whole story in the newspapers if you look it up – not what goes on here, but the story of the Germans. My house would be ruined if they told all, and I'd sue for damages.'

They reached the bedroom, and the woman went in and pulled up the edge of the carpet where Shorthouse had seen the blood soaking in the previous night.

'Look thar, if you feel like it,' said the old hag. Stooping down, he saw a dark, dull stain in the boards that corresponded exactly to the shape and position of the blood as he had seen it.

That night he slept in a hotel, and the following day sought new quarters. In the newspapers on file in his office after a long search he found twenty years back the detailed story, substantially as the woman had said, of Steinhardt & Co.'s failure, the absconding and subsequent arrest of the senior partner, and the suicide, or murder, of the son Otto. The landlady's room-house had formerly been their private residence.

A Home Away from Home

Robert Bloch

The train was late, and it must have been past nine o'clock when Natalie found herself standing, all alone, on the platform before Hightower Station.

The station itself was obviously closed for the night – it was only a way-stop, really, for there was no town here – and Natalie wasn't quite sure what to do. She had taken it for granted that Dr Bracegirdle would be on hand to meet her. Before leaving London she's sent her uncle a wire giving him the time of her arrival. But since the train had been delayed, perhaps he'd come and gone.

Natalie glanced around uncertainly, then noticed the phone booth which provided her with a solution. Dr Bracegirdle's last letter was in her purse, and it contained both his address and his phone number. She had fumbled through her bag and found it by the time she walked over to the booth.

Ringing him up proved a bit of a problem – there seemed to be an interminable delay before the operator made the connection, and there was a great deal of buzzing on the line. A glimpse of the hills beyond the station, through the glass wall of the booth, suggested the reason for the difficulty. After all, Natalie reminded herself, this was West Country⁄ Conditions might be a bit primitive——

'Hello, hello!'

The woman's voice came over the line, fairly shouting above the din. There was no buzzing noise now, and the sound in the background suggested a babble of voices all intermingled. Natalie bent forward and spoke directly and distinctly into the mouthpiece.

'This is Natalie Rivers,' she said. 'Is Dr Bracegirdle there?'

'Whom did you say was calling?'

'Natalie Rivers. I'm his niece.'

'His what, Miss?'

'Niece,' Natalie repeated. 'May I speak to him, please?'

'Just a moment.'

There was a pause, during which the sound of voices in the background seemed amplified, and then Natalie heard the resonant masculine tones, so much easier to separate from the indistinct murmuring.

'Dr Bracegirdle here. My dear Natalie, this is an unexpected pleasure!'

'Unexpected? But I sent you a 'gram from London this afternoon.' Natalie checked herself as she realized the slight edge of impatience which had crept into her voice. 'Didn't it arrive?'

'I'm afraid service is not of the best around here,' Dr Bracegirdle told her, with an apologetic chuckle. 'No, your wire didn't arrive. But apparently you did.' He chuckled again. 'Where are you, my dear?'

'At Hightower Station.'

'Oh, dear. It's in exactly the opposite direction.'

'Opposite direction?'

'From Peterby's. They rang me up just before you called. Some silly nonsense about an appendix – probably nothing but an upset stomach. But I promised to stop round directly, just in case.'

'Don't tell me they still call you for general practice?'

'Emergencies, my dear. There aren't many physicians in these parts. Fortunately, there aren't many patients, either.' Dr Bracegirdle started to chuckle, then sobered. 'Look now. You say you're at the station. I'll just send Miss Plummer down to fetch you in the wagon. Have you much luggage?'

'Only my travel-case. The rest is coming with the household goods, by boat.'

'Boat?'

'Didn't I mention it when I wrote?'

'Yes, that's right, you did. Well, no matter. Miss Plummer will be along for you directly.'

'I'll be waiting in front of the platform.'

'What was that? Speak up, I can hardly hear you.'

'I said I'll be waiting in front of the platform.'

'Oh.' Dr Bracegirdle chuckled once more. 'Bit of a party going on here.'

'Shan't I be intruding? I mean, since you weren't expecting me tonight——'

'Not at all! They'll be leaving before long. You wait for Plummer.'

The phone clicked off and Natalie returned to the platform. In a surprisingly short time, the station wagon appeared and skidded off the road to halt at the very edge of the tracks. A tall, thin grey-haired woman, wearing a somewhat rumpled white uniform, emerged and beckoned to Natalie.

'Come along, my dear,' she called. 'Here, I'll just pop this in back.' Scooping up the bag, she tossed it into the rear of the wagon. 'Now, in with you – and off we go!'

Scarcely waiting for Natalie to close the door after her, the redoubtable

Miss Plummer gunned the motor and the car plunged back on to the road.

The speedometer immediately shot up to seventy, and Natalie flinched. Miss Plummer noticed her agitation at once.

'Sorry,' she said. 'With Doctor out on call, I can't be away too long.'

'Oh, yes, the house-guests. He told me.'

'Did he now?' Miss Plummer took a sharp turn at a crossroads and the tyres screeched in protest, but to no avail. Natalie decided to drown apprehension in conversation.

'What sort of a man is my uncle?' she asked.

'Have you never met him?'

'No. My parents moved to Australia when I was quite young. This is my first trip to England. In fact, it's the first time I've left Canberra.'

'Folks with you?'

'They were in a motor smashup two months ago,' Natalie said. 'Didn't the Doctor tell you?'

'I'm afraid not – you see, I haven't been with him very long.' Miss Plummer uttered a short bark and the car swerved wildly across the road. 'Motor smashup, eh? Some people have no business behind the wheel. That's what Doctor says.'

She turned and peered at Natalie, 'I take it you've come to stay, then?'

'Yes, of course. He wrote me when he was appointed my guardian. That's why I was wondering what he might be like. It's so hard to tell from letters.' The thin-faced woman nodded silently, but Natalie had an urge to confide. 'To tell the truth, I'm just a little bit edgy. I mean, I've never met a psychiatrist before.'

'Haven't you, now?' Miss Plummer shrugged. 'You're quite fortunate. I've seen a few in my time. A bit on the know-it-all side, if you ask me. Though I must say, Dr Bracegirdle is one of the best. Permissive, you know.'

'I understand he has quite a practice.'

'There's no lack of patients for *that* sort of thing,' Miss Plummer observed. 'Particularly amongst the well-to-do. I'd say your uncle has done himself handsomely. The house and all – but you'll see.' Once again the wagon whirled into a sickening swerve and sped forward between the imposing gates of a huge driveway which led towards an enormous house set amidst a grove of trees in the distance. Through the shuttered windows Natalie caught sight of a faint beam of light – just enough to help reveal the ornate facade of her uncle's home.

'Oh, dear,' she muttered, half to herself.

'What is it?'

'The guests – and it's Saturday night. And here I am, all mussed from travel.'

'Don't give it another thought,' Miss Plummer assured her. 'There's no formality here. That's what Doctor told me when I came. It's a home away from home.'

Miss Plummer barked and braked simultaneously, and the station wagon came to an abrupt stop just behind an imposing black limousine.

'Out with you now!' With brisk efficiency, Miss Plummer lifted the bag from the rear seat and carried it up the steps, beckoning Natalie forward with a nod over her shoulder. She halted at the door and fumbled for a key.

'No sense knocking,' she said. 'They'd never hear me.' As the door swung open her observation was amply confirmed. The background noise which Natalie had noted over the tele telephone now formed a formidable foreground. She stood there, hesitant, as Miss Plummer swept forward across the threshold.

'Come along, come along!'

Obediently, Natalie entered, and as Miss Plummer shut the door behind her, blinked with eyes recently unaccustomed to the brightness of the interior.

She found herself standing in a large, somewhat bare hallway. Directly ahead of her was a large staircase; at an angle between the railing and the wall was a desk and chair. To her left, a dark, panelled door – evidently leading to Dr Bracegirdle's private office, for a small brass plate was affixed to it, bearing his name. To her right was a huge open parlor, its windows heavily curtained and shuttered against the night. It was from here that the sounds of sociability echoed.

Natalie started across the hall towards the stairs. As she did so, she caught a glimpse of the parlor. Fully a dozen guests eddied about a large table, talking and gesturing with the animation of close acquaintance – with one another, and with the contents of the lavish array of bottles gracing the table-top. A sudden whoop of laughter indicated that at least one guest had abused the Doctor's hospitality.

Natalie passed the entry hastily, so as not to be observed, then glanced behind her to make sure that Miss Plummer was following with her bag. Miss Plummer was indeed following, but her hands were empty. And as Natalie reached the stairs, Miss Plummer shook her head.

'You didn't mean to go up now, did you?' she murmured. 'Come in and introduce yourself.'

'I thought I might freshen up a bit first.'

'Let me go on ahead and get your room in order. Doctor didn't give me notice, you know.'

'Really, it's not necessary. I could do with a wash——'

'Doctor should be back any moment now. Do wait for him.' Miss Plummer grasped Natalie's arm, and with the same speed and expedition she had bestowed on driving, now steered the girl forward into the lighted room.

'Here's Doctor's niece.' she announced. 'Miss Natalie Rivers, from Australia.'

Several heads turned in Natalie's direction, though Miss Plummer's voice had scarcely penetrated the general conversational din. A short, jolly-looking fat man bobbed towards Natalie, waving a half-empty glass.

'All the way from Australia, eh?' He extended his goblet. 'You must be thirsty. Here, take this – I'll get another.' And before Natalie could reply he turned and plunged back into the group around the table.

'Major Hamilton,' Miss Plummer whispered. 'A dear soul, really. Though I'm afraid he's just a wee bit squiffy.'

As Miss Plummer moved away, Natalie glanced uncertainly at the glass in her hand. She was not quite sure where to dispose of it.

'Allow me.' A tall, grey-haired and quite distinguished-looking man with a black moustache moved forward and took the stemware from between her fingers.

'Thank you.'

'Not at all. I'm afraid you'll have to excuse him. The party spirit, you know.' He nodded, indicating a woman in extreme decolletage chattering animatedly to a group of three laughing men. 'But since it's by way of being a farewell celebration——'

'Ah, there you are!' The short man whom Miss Plummer had identified as Major Hamilton bounced back into orbit around Natalie, a fresh drink in his hand and a fresh smile on his ruddy face. 'I'm back again,' he announced. 'Just like a boomerang, eh?'

He laughed explosively, then paused. 'I say, you *do* have boomerangs in Australia? And blackfellows? Saw quite a bit of you Aussies at Gallipoli. Of course that was some time ago, before *your* time, I daresay——'

'Please, Major.' The tall man smiled at Natalie. There was something reassuring about his presence, and something oddly familiar, too. Natalie wondered where she might have seen him before. She watched while he moved over to the Major and removed the drink from his hand.

'Now see here——' the Major spluttered.

'You've had enough, old boy. And it's almost time for you to go.'

'One for the road——' The Major glanced around, his hands waving in appeal. 'Everyone *else* is drinking!' He made a lunge for his glass but the tall man evaded him. Smiling at Natalie over his shoulder, he drew the Major to one side and began to mutter to him earnestly in low tones. The Major nodded in sudden, drunken placation.

Natalie looked around the room. Nobody was paying the least attention to her except for one elderly woman who sat quite alone on a stool before the piano. She regarded Natalie with a fixed stare that at once emphasized her role as an intruder on a gala scene. Natalie turned away hastily and again caught sight of the woman in decolletage. She suddenly remembered her own desire to change her clothing and peered at the doorway, seeking Miss Plummer. But Miss Plummer was nowhere to be seen.

Walking back into the hall, she peered up the staircase.

'Miss Plummer!' she called.

There was no response.

Then, from out of the corner of her eye, she noted that the door of the room across the hallway was ajar. In fact, it was opening now, quite rapidly, and as Natalie stared, Miss Plummer came backing out of the room, carrying something in her hand. Before Natalie could call out again and attract her attention, she had scurried off down the hallway.

Natalie crossed before the stairs, meaning to follow her, but found herself halting instead before the open doorway.

She gazed in curiously at what was obviously her uncle's consultation room. It was a cozy, book-lined study with heavy, leather-covered furniture grouped before the shelves. The psychiatric couch rested in one corner near the wall and near it was a large mahogany desk. The top of the desk was quite bare, save for a cradle telephone, and a thin brown loop snaking out from it.

Something about the loop disturbed Natalie and before she was conscious of her movement she was inside the room, looking down at the desk-top. Now she recognized the loop, of course: it was the cord from the phone.

And the end had been neatly severed from its connection at the wall.

'Miss Plummer!' Natalie murmured. 'That's what she was carrying – a pair of scissors. But why——?'

'Why not?'

Natalie turned just in time to observe the tall, distinguished-looking man enter the doorway behind her.

'It won't be needed,' he said. 'After all, I *did* tell you it was a farewell celebration.' And he gave a little chuckle.

Again Natalie sensed something strangely familiar about him and this time it came to her. She'd heard the same chuckle over the phone from the depot station.

'But you're playing a joke!' she exclaimed. 'You're Dr Bracegirdle, aren't you?'

'No, my dear.' He shook his head as he moved past her across the room. 'It's just that no one expected you. We were about to leave when your call came. So we had to say *something*.'

There was a moment of silence. Then, 'Where *is* my uncle?' Natalie murmured, at last.

'Over here.'

Natalie found herself standing beside the tall man, gazing down at what lay in a space between the couch and the wall. An instant was all she could bear.

'Messy,' the tall man nodded. 'Of course it was all so sudden, the opportunity, I mean. And then they *would* get into the liquor——'

His voice echoed hollowly in the room and Natalie realized the sounds of the party had died away. She glanced up to see them all standing there in the doorway, watching.

Then their ranks parted and Miss Plummer came quickly into the room, wearing an incongruous fur wrap over the rumpled, ill-fitting uniform.

'Oh my!' she gasped. 'So you found him!'

Natalie nodded and took a step forward. 'You've got to do something,' she said. 'Please!'

'Yes.' But Miss Plummer didn't seem concerned. The others had crowded into the room behind her, and stood staring silently; Natalie turned to them in appeal.

'Don't you see?' she cried. 'It's the work of a madman. He belongs in the asylum!'

'My dear child,' murmured Miss Plummer as she quickly closed and locked the door and the silent starers moved forward. 'This *is* the asylum ...'

The Cat Jumps

Elizabeth Bowen

After the Bentley murder, Rose Hill stood empty two years. Lawns mounted to meadows, white paint peeled from the balconies; the sun, looking more constantly, less fearfully in than sightseers' eyes through the naked windows, bleached the floral wallpapers. The week after the execution, Harold Bentley's legatees had placed the house on the books of the principal agents, London and local. But though sunny, modern and convenient, though so delightfully situate over the Thames valley (above flood level), within easy reach of a golf course, Rose Hill, while frequently viewed, remained unpurchased. Dreadful associations apart, the privacy of the place had been violated; with its terraced garden lily-pond, and pergola cheerfully rose-encrusted the public had been made too familiar. On the domestic scene, too many eyes had burnt the impress of their horror. Moreover, that pearly bathroom, bedroom with wide outlook over a loop of the Thames ... 'The Rose Hill Horror': headlines flashed up at the very sound of the name. 'Oh *no*, dear!' many wives had exclaimed, drawing their husbands from the gate. 'Come away!' they urged, crumpling the agent's order to view as though the house were advancing on them. And husbands came away – with a backward glance at the garage. Funny to think: a chap who was hanged had kept his car there.

The Harold Wrights, however, were not deterred. They had light, bright, shadowless, thoroughly disinfected minds. They believed that they disbelieved in most things but were unprejudiced; they enjoyed frank discussions. They dreaded nothing but inhibitions: they had no inhibitions. They were pious agnostics, earnest for social reform; they explained everything to their children and were annoyed to find their children could not sleep at nights because they thought there was a complex under the bed. They knew all crime to be pathological, and read their murders only in scientific books. They had Vita Glass put into all their windows. No family, in fact, could have been more unlike the mistaken Harold Bentleys.

Rose Hill, from the first glance, suited the Wrights admirably. They were in search of a cheerful week-end house with a nice atmosphere where their friends could join them for frank discussions, and their own and their friends' children 'run wild' during the summer months. Harold Wright, who had a good head, got the agent to knock six hundred off the quoted price of the house. 'That unfortunate affair,' he murmured. Jocelyn commended his inspiration. Otherwise, they did not give the Bentleys another thought.

The Wrights had the floral wallpapers all stripped off and the walls cream-washed; they removed some disagreeably thick pink shades from the electricity, and had the paint renewed inside and out. (The front of the house was bracketed over with balconies, like an overmantel.) Their bedroom mantelpiece, stained by the late Mrs Bentley's cosmetics, had to be scrubbed with chemicals. Also, they had removed from the rock-garden Mrs Bentley's little dog's memorial tablet, with a quotation on it from 'Indian Love Lyrics'. Jocelyn Wright, looking into the unfortunate bath, *the* bath, so square and opulent with its surround of nacreous tiles, said, laughing lightly, she supposed anyone *else* would have had that bath changed. 'Not that that would be possible,' she added; 'the bath's built in ... I've always wanted a built-in bath.'

Harold and Jocelyn turned from the bath to look down at the cheerful river shimmering under a spring haze. All the way down the slope cherry trees were in blossom. Life should be simplified for the Wrights – they were fortunate in their mentality.

After an experimental week-end, without guests or children, only one thing troubled them: a resolute stuffiness, upstairs and down – due, presumably, to the house's having been so long shut up – a smell of unsavoury habitation, of rich cigarette smoke stale in the folds of unaired curtains, of scent spilled on unbrushed carpets; an alcoholic smell – persistent in their perhaps too sensitive nostrils after days of airing, doors and windows open, in rooms drenched thoroughly with sun and wind. They told each other it came from the parquet – they didn't like it, somehow. They had the parquet taken up – at great expense – and put down plain oak floors.

In their practical way, the Wrights now set out to expel, live out, live down, almost (had the word had place in their vocabulary) to 'lay' the Bentleys. Deferred by trouble over the parquet, their occupation of Rose Hill (which should have dated from mid-April) did not begin till the end of May. Throughout a week, Jocelyn had motored from town daily, so that the final installation of themselves and the children was able to coincide with their first week-end party – they asked down five of their friends to warm the house.

That first Friday, everything was auspicious; afternoon sky blue as the garden irises; later, a full moon pendant over the river; a night so warm that, after midnight, their enlightened friends, in pyjamas, could run on the blanched lawns in a state of high though rational excitement. Jane, John and Janet, their admirably spaced-out children, kept awake by the moonlight, hailed their elders out of the nursery skylight. Jocelyn waved to them: they never had been repressed.

The girl Muriel Barker was found looking up the terraces at the house, a shade doubtfully. 'You know,' she said, 'I do rather wonder they don't feel ... *sometimes* ... You know what I mean?'

'No,' replied her companion, a young scientist.

Muriel sighed. 'No one would mind if it had been just a short, sharp shooting. But, it was so ... prolonged. It went on all over the house. Do you remember?' she said timidly.

'No,' replied Mr Cartaret, 'it didn't interest me.'

'Oh, nor me either!' agreed Muriel quickly, but added: 'How he must have hated her! ...'

The scientist, sleepy, yawned frankly and referred her to Krafft Ebing. But Muriel went to bed with *Alice in Wonderland*; she went to sleep with the lights on. She was not, as Jocelyn realized later, the sort of girl to have asked at all.

Next morning was overcast; in the afternoon it rained, suddenly and heavily, interrupting, for some, tennis, for others a pleasant discussion, in a punt, on marriage under the Soviet. Defeated, they all rushed in. Jocelyn went round from room to room, shutting tightly the rain-lashed casements along the front of the house: these continued to rattle; the balconies creaked. An early dusk set in; an oppressive, almost visible moisture, up from the darkening river, pressed on the panes like a presence and slid through the house. The party gathered in the library, round an expansive but thinly burning fire. Harold circulated photographs of modern architecture; they discussed these tendencies. Then Mrs Monkhouse, sniffing, exclaimed: 'Who uses "Trèfle Incarnat"?'

'Now *who*ever would——' her hostess began scornfully. Then from the hall came a howl, a scuffle, a thin shriek. They too sat still; in the dusky library Mr Cartaret laughed out loud. Harold Wright, indignantly throwing open the door, revealed Jane and Jacob rolling at the foot of the stairs biting each other, their faces dark with uninhibited passion. Bumping alternate heads against the foot of the banisters, they shrieked in concord.

'Extraordinary,' said Harold; 'they've never done that before. They have always understood each other so well.'

'I wouldn't do that,' advised Jocelyn, raising her voice slightly; 'you'll hurt your teeth. Other teeth won't grow at once, you know.'

'You should let them find that out for themselves,' disapproved Edward Cartaret, taking up the *New Statesman*. Harold, in perplexity, shut the door on his children, who soon stunned each other to silence.

Meanwhile, Sara and Talbot Monkhouse, Muriel Barker and

Theodora Smith had drawn together over the fire in a tight little knot. Their voices twanged with excitement. By that shock just now, something seemed to have been released. Even Cartaret gave them half his attention. They were discussing *crime passionel*.

'Of course, if that's what they really *want* to discuss ...' thought Jocelyn. But it did seem unfortunate. Partly from an innocent desire to annoy her visitors, partly because the room felt awful – you would have thought fifty people had been there for a week – she went across and opened one of the windows, admitting a pounce of damp wind. They all turned, startled, to hear rain crash on the lead of an upstairs balcony. Muriel's voice was left in forlorn solo: 'Dragged herself ... whining "Harold" ...'

Harold Wright looked remarkably conscious. Jocelyn said brightly, 'Whatever *are* you talking about?' But unfortunately Harold, on almost the same breath, suggested: 'Let's leave that family alone, shall we?' Their friends all felt they might not be asked again. Though they did feel, plaintively, that they had been being natural. However, they disowned Muriel, who, getting up abruptly, said she thought she'd like to go for a walk in the rain before dinner. Nobody accompanied her.

Later, overtaking Mrs Monkhouse on the stairs, Muriel confided: absolutely, she could not stand Edward Cartaret. She could hardly bear to be in the room with him. He seemed so ... cruel. Cold-blooded? No, she meant cruel. Sara Monkhouse, going into Jocelyn's room for a chat (at her entrance Jocelyn started violently) told Jocelyn that Muriel could not stand Edward, could hardly bear to be in a room with him. 'Pity,' said Jocelyn, 'I had thought they might do for each other.' Jocelyn and Sara agreed that Muriel was unrealized: what she ought to have was a baby. But when Sara, dressing, told Talbot Monkhouse that Muriel could not stand Edward, and Talbot said Muriel was unrealized, Sara was furious. The Monkhouses, who never did quarrel, quarrelled bitterly and were late for dinner. They would have been later if the meal itself had not been delayed by an outburst of sex-antagonism between the nice Jacksons, a couple imported from London to run the house. Mrs Jackson, putting everything in the oven, had locked herself into her room.

'Curious,' said Harold, 'the Jacksons' relations to each other always seemed so modern. They have the most intelligent discussions.'

Theodora said she had been re-reading Shakespeare – this brought them point-blank up against Othello. Harold, with titanic force, wrenched round the conversation to Relativity: about this no one seemed to have anything to say but Edward Cartaret. And Muriel, who by some mischance had again been placed beside him, sat deathly, turning down her dark-rimmed eyes. In fact, on the intelligent, sharp-featured faces all round the table, something, perhaps simply a clearness, seemed to be lacking, as though these were wax faces for one fatal instant exposed to a furnace. Voices came out from some dark interiority; in each conversational interchange a mutual vote of no confidence was implicit. You would have said that each personality had been attacked by some kind of decomposition.

'No moon tonight,' complained Sara Monkhouse. Never mind, they would have a cosy evening, they would play paper games, Jocelyn promised.

'If you can see,' said Harold. 'Something seems to be going wrong with the light.'

Did Harold think so? They had all noticed the light seemed to be losing quality, as though a film, smoke-like, were creeping over the bulbs. The light, thinning, darkening, seemed to contract round each lamp into a blurred aura. They had noticed, but, each with a proper dread of his own subjectivity, had not spoken.

'Funny stuff,' Harold said, 'electricity.'

Mr Cartaret could not agree with him.

Though it was late, though they yawned and would not play paper games, they were reluctant to go to bed. You would have supposed a delightful evening. Jocelyn was not gratified.

The library stools, rugs and divans were strewn with Krafft Ebing, Freud, Forel, Weiniger and the heterosexual volume of Havelock Ellis. (Harold had thought it right to install his reference library; his friends hated to discuss without basis.) The volumes were pressed open with paper-knives and small pieces of modern statuary; stooping from one to another, purposeful as a bee, Edward Cartaret read extracts aloud to Harold, to Talbot Monkhouse and to Theodora Smith, who stitched *gros point* with resolution. At the far end of the library, under a sallow drip from a group of electric candles, Mrs Monkhouse and Miss Barker shared an ottoman, spines pressed rigid against the wall. Tensely, one spoke, one listened.

'And these,' thought Jocelyn, leaning back with her eyes shut between the two groups, 'are friends I liked to have in my life. Pellucid, sane ...'

It was remarkable how much Muriel knew. Sara, very much shocked, edged up till their thighs touched. You would have thought the Harold Bentleys had been Muriel's relatives. Surely, Sara attempted, in one's large, bright world one did not think of these things? Practically, they did not exist! Surely Muriel should not ... But Muriel looked at her strangely.

'Did you know,' she said, 'that one of Mrs Bentley's hands was found in the library?'

Sara, smiling a little awkwardly, licked her lip. 'Oh,' she said.

'But the fingers were in the dining-room. He began there.'

'Why isn't he in Broadmoor?'

'That defence failed. He didn't really subscribe to it. He said having done what he wanted was worth anything.'

'Oh!'

'Yes, he was nearly lynched ... She dragged herself upstairs. She couldn't lock any doors – naturally. One maid, her maid, got shut into the house with them; he'd sent all the others away. For a long time everything seemed so quiet: the maid crept out and saw Harold Bentley sitting half-way upstairs, finishing a cigarette. All the lights were full on. He nodded to her and dropped the cigarette through the banisters. Then she saw the ... state of the hall. He went upstairs after Mrs Bentley, saying: "Lucinda!" He looked into room after room, whistling, then he said, "Here we are," and shut a door after him.

'The maid fainted. When she came to it was still going on, upstairs ... Harold Bentley had locked all the garden doors, there were locks even on the french windows. The maid couldn't get out. Everything she touched was ... sticky. At last she broke a pane and got through. As she ran down the garden – the lights were on all over the house – she saw Harold Bentley moving about in the bathroom. She fell right over the edge of a terrace and one of the tradesmen picked her up next day.

'Doesn't it seem odd, Sara, to think of Jocelyn in that bath?'

Finishing her recital, Muriel turned on Sara an ecstatic and brooding look that made her almost beautiful. Sara fumbled with a cigarette; match after match failed her. 'Muriel, you should see a specialist.'

Mutiel held out her hand for a cigarette. 'He put her heart in her hatbox. He said it belonged there?

'You had no right to come here. It was most unfair on Jocelyn. Most ... indelicate.'

Muriel, to whom the word was, properly, unfamiliar, eyed incredulously Sara's lips.

'How dared you come?'

'I thought I might like it. I thought I ought to fulfil myself. I'd never had any experience of these things.'

'Muriel! ...'

'Besides, I wanted to meet Edward Cartaret. Several people said we were made for each other. Now, of course, I shall never marry. Look what comes of it ... I must say Sara, I wouldn't be you or Jocelyn. Shut up all night with a man all alone – I don't know how you dare sleep. I've arranged to sleep with Theodora, and we shall barricade the door. I noticed something about Edward Cartaret the moment I arrived; a kind of insane glitter. He is utterly pathological. He's got instruments in his room, in that black bag. Yes, I looked. Did you notice the way he went on and on about cutting up that cat, and the way Talbot and Harold listened?'

Sara, looking furtively round the room, saw Mr Cartaret making passes over the head of Theodora Smith with a paper-knife. Both appeared to laugh heartily, but in silence.

'Here we are,' said Harold, showing his teeth, smiling.

He stood over Muriel with a siphon in one hand, glass in the other. At this point Jocelyn rising, said she, for one, intended to go to bed.

Jocelyn's bedroom curtains swelled a little over the noisy window. The room was stuffy and – insupportable, so that she did not know where to turn. The house, fingered outwardly by the wind that dragged unceasingly past the walls, was, within, a solid silence: silence heavy as flesh. Jocelyn dropped her wrap to the floor, then watched how its feathered edges crept a little – a draught came in under her bathroom door.

Jocelyn turned in despair and hostility from the strained, pale woman looking at her from her oblong glass. She said aloud: 'There *is* no fear,' then within herself heard this taken up: 'But the death fear, that one is not there to relate! If the spirit, dismembered in agony, dies before the body! If the spirit, in the whole knowledge of its dissolution, drags from chamber to chamber, drops from plane to plane of awareness (as from knife to knife down an oubliette) shedding, receiving agony! Till, long afterwards, death with its little pain is established in the indifferent body.' There was no comfort: death (now at every turn and instant claiming her) was in its every possible manifestation violent death: ultimately she was to be given up to terror.

Undressing, shocked by the iteration of her reflected movements, she flung a towel over the glass. With what desperate eyes of appeal, at Sara's door, she and Sara had looked at each other, clung with their looks – and parted. She could have sworn she heard Sara's bolt slide softly to. But what then, subsequently, of Talbot? And what – she eyed her own bolt, so bright (and for the late Mrs Bentley so ineffective) – what of Harold?

'It's atavistic!' she said aloud, in the dark lit room, and, kicking her slippers away, got into bed. She took *Erewhon* from the rack but lay rigid, listening. As though snatched by a movement, the towel slipped from the mirror beyond her bed-end. She faced the two eyes of an animal in extremity, eyes black, mindless. The clock struck two: she had been waiting an hour.

On the floor, her feathered wrap shivered again all over. She heard the other door of the bathroom very stealthily open, then shut. Harold moved in softly, heavily, knocked against the side of the bath and stood still. He was quietly whistling.

'Why didn't I understand? He must always have hated me. It's tonight he's been waiting for ... *He wanted this house*. His look, as we went upstairs ...'

She shrieked: 'Harold!'

Harold, so softly whistling, remained behind the imperturbable door, remained quite still ... 'He's *listening* for me ...' One pin-point of hope at the tunnel end: to get to Sara, to Theodora, to Muriel. Unmasked, incautious, with a long tearing sound of displaced air, Jocelyn leapt from bed to the door.

But her door had been locked from the outside.

With a strange rueful smile, like an actress, Jocelyn, skirting the foot of the two beds, approached the door of the bathroom. 'At least I have still ... my feet.' For, for some time, the heavy body of Mrs Bentley, tenacious of life, had been dragging itself from room to room. *'Harold!'* she said to the silence, face close to the door.

The door opened on Harold, looking more dreadfully at her than she had imagined. With a quick, vague movement he roused himself from his meditation. Therein he had assumed the entire burden of Harold Bentley. Forces he did not know of assembling darkly, he had faced for untold ages the imperturbable door to his wife's room. She would be there, densely, smotheringly there. She lay like a great cat, always, over the mouth of his life.

The Harolds, superimposed on each other, stood searching the bedroom strangely. Taking a step forward, shutting the door behind him: 'Here we are,' said Harold.

Jocelyn went down heavily. Harold watched.

Harold Wright was appalled. Jocelyn had fainted: Jocelyn never had fainted before. He shook, he fanned, he applied restoratives. His perplexed thoughts fled to Sara – oh, Sara certainly. 'Hi,' he cried, 'Sara!' and successively fled from each to each of the locked passage doors. There was no way out.

Across the passage, a door throbbed to the maniac drumming of Sara Monkhouse. She had been locked in. For Talbot, agonized with solicitude, it was equally impossible to emerge from his dressing-room. Farther down the passage, Edward Cartaret, interested by this nocturnal manifestation, wrenched and rattled his door handle in vain.

Muriel, on her way through the house to Theodora's bedroom, had turned all the keys on the outside, impartially. She did not know which door was Edward Cartaret's. Muriel was a woman who took no chances.

Dearth's Farm

Gerald Bullet

It is really not far: our fast train does it in eighty minutes. But so sequestered is the little valley in which I have made my solitary home that I never go to town without the delicious sensation of poising my hand over a lucky-bag full of old memories. In the train I amuse myself by summoning up some of those ghosts of the past, a past not distant, but sufficiently remote in atmosphere from my present to be invested with a certain sentimental glamour. 'Perhaps I shall meet you – or you.' But never yet have I succeeded in guessing what London held up her sleeve for me. She has that happiest of tricks – without which Paradise will be dull indeed – the trick of surprise. In London, if in no other place, it is the unexpected that happens. For me Fleet Street is the scene *par excellence* of these adventurous encounters, and it was in Fleet Street, three months ago, that I ran across Bailey, of Queens', whom I hadn't seen for five years. Bailey is not his name, nor Queens' his college, but these names will serve to reveal what is germane to my purpose and to conceal the rest.

His recognition of me was instant; mine of him more slow. He told me his name twice; we stared at each other, and I struggled to disguise the blankness of my memory. The situation became awkward. I was the more embarrassed because I feared lest he should too odiously misinterpret my non-recognition of him, for the man was shabby and unshaven enough to be suspicious of an intentional slight. Bailey, Bailey ... now who the devil was Bailey? And then, when he had already made a gesture of moving on, memory stirred to activity.

'Of course, I remember. Bailey. Theosophy. You used to talk to me about theosophy, didn't you? I remember perfectly now.' I glanced at my watch. 'If you're not busy let's go and have tea somewhere.'

He smiled, with a hint of irony in his eyes, as he answered: 'I'm not busy.' I received the uncomfortable impression that he was hungry and with no ordinary hunger, and the idea kept me silent, like an awkward schoolboy, while we walked together to a teashop that I knew.

Seated on opposite sides of the tea-table, we took stock of each other.

He was thin, and his hair greying; his complexion had a soiled unhealthy appearance; the cheeks had sunk in a little, throwing into prominence the high cheekbones above which his sensitive eyes glittered with a new light, a light not of heaven. Compared with the Bailey I now remembered so well, a rather sleek young man with an almost feline love of luxury blossoming like a tropical plant in the exotic atmosphere of his Cambridge rooms, compared with that man this was but a pale wraith. In those days he had been a flaming personality, suited well – too well, for my plain taste – to the highly coloured orientalism that he affected in his mural decorations. And co-existent in him with this lust for soft cushions and chromatic orgies, which repelled me, there was an imagination that attracted me: an imagination delighting in highly coloured metaphysical theories of the universe. These theories, which were as fantastic as *The Arabian Nights*, and perhaps as unreal, proved his academic undoing: he came down badly in his Tripos, and had to leave without a degree. Many a man has done that and yet prospered, but Bailey, it was apparent, hadn't prospered. I made the conventional inquiries, adding, 'It must be six or seven years since we met last.'

'More than that,' said Bailey morosely, and lapsed into silence. 'Look here,' he burst out suddenly, 'I'm going to behave like a cad. I'm going to ask you to lend me a pound note. And don't expect it back in a hurry.'

We both winced a little as the note changed hands. 'You've had bad luck,' I remarked, without, I hope, a hint of pity in my voice. 'What's wrong?'

He eyed me over the rim of his teacup. 'I look a lot older to you, I expect?'

'You don't look very fit,' I conceded.

'No, I don't.' His cup came down with a nervous slam upon the saucer. 'Going grey, too, aren't I?' I was forced to nod agreement. 'Yet, do you know, a month ago there wasn't a grey hair in my head. You write stories, don't you? I saw your name somewhere. I wonder if you could write my story. You may get your money back after all ... By God, that would be funny, wouldn't it!'

I couldn't see the joke, but I was curious about his story. And after we had lit out cigarettes he told it to me, to the accompaniment of a driving storm of rain that tapped like a thousand idiot fingers upon the plate-glass windows of the shop.

2

A few weeks ago, said Bailey, I was staying at the house of a cousin of mine. I never liked the woman, but I wanted free board and lodging, and hunger soon blunts the edge of one's delicacy. She's at least ten years my senior, and all I could remember of her was that she had bullied me when I was a child into learning to read. Ten years ago she married a man named Dearth – James Dearth, the resident owner of a smallish farm in Norfolk, not far from the coast. All her relatives opposed the marriage. Relatives always do. If people waited for the approval of relatives before marrying, the world would be depopulated in a generation. This time it was religion. My cousin's people were primitive and methodical in their religion, as the name of their sect confessed; whereas Dearth professed a universal toleration that they thought could only be a cloak for indifference. I have my own opinion about that, but it doesn't matter now. When I met the man I forgot all about religion: I was simply repelled by the notion of any woman marrying so odd a being. Rather small in build, he possessed the longest and narrowest face I have ever seen on a man of his size. His eyes were set exceptionally wide apart, and the nose, culminating in large nostrils, made so slight an angle with the rest of the face that, seen in profile, it was scarcely human. Perhaps I exaggerate a little, but I know no other way of explaining the peculiar revulsion he inspired in me. He met me at the station in his dogcart, and wheezed a greeting at me. 'You're Mr Bailey, aren't you? I hope you've had an agreeable journey. Monica will be delighted.' This seemed friendly enough, and my host's conversation during that eight-mile drive did much to make me forget my first distaste of his person. He was evidently a man of wide reading, and he had a habit of polite deference that was extremely flattering, especially to me who had had more than my share of the other thing. I was cashiered during the war, you know. Never mind why. Whenever he laughed, which was not seldom, he exhibited a mouthful of very large regular teeth.

Dearth's Farm, to give it the local name, is a place with a personality of its own. Perhaps every place has that. Sometimes I fancy that the earth itself is a personality, or a community of souls locked fast in a dream from which at any moment they may awake, like volcanoes, into violent action. Anyhow, Dearth's Farm struck me as being peculiarly personal, because I found it impossible not to regard its climatic changes as changes of mood. You remember my theory that chemical action is only physical action seen from without? Well, I'm inclined to think in just the same way of every manifestation of natural energy. But you don't want to hear about my fancies. The farmhouse, which is approached by a narrow winding lane from the main road, stands high up in a kind of shallow basin of land, a few acres ploughed, but mostly grass. The countryside has a gentle prettiness more characteristic of the south-eastern counties. On three sides wooded hills slope gradually to the horizon; on the fourth side grassland rises a little for twenty yards and then curves abruptly down. To look through the windows that give out upon this fourth side is to have the sensation of being on the edge of a steep cliff, or at the end of the world. On a still day, when the sun is shining, the place has a languid beauty, an afternoon atmosphere. You remember Tennyson's Lotus Isles, 'in which it seemed always afternoon': Dearth's Farm has something of that flavour on a still day. But such days are rare; the two or three I experienced shine like jewels in the memory. Most often that stretch of fifty or sixty acres is a gathering-ground for all the bleak winds of the earth. They seem to come simultaneously from the land and from the sea, which is six miles away, and they swirl round in that shallow basin of earth, as I have called it, like maddened devils seeking escape from a trap. When the storms were at their worst I used to feel as though I were perched insecurely on a gigantic saucer held a hundred miles above the earth. But I am not a courageous person. Monica, my cousin, found no fault with the winds. She had other fears, and I had not been with her three days before she began to confide them to me. Her overtures were as surprising as they were unwelcome, for that she was not a confiding person by nature I was certain. Her manners were reserved to the point of diffidence, and we had nothing in common save a detestation of the family from which we had both sprung. I suppose you will want to know something of her looks. She was a tall, full-figured woman, handsome for her years, with jet-black hair, a sensitive face, and a complexion almost Southern in its dark colouring. I love beauty and I found pleasure in her mere presence, which did something to lighten for me the gloom that pervaded the house; but my pleasure was innocent enough, and Dearth's watchdog airs only amused me. Monica's eyes – unfathomable pools – seemed troubled whenever they rested on me: whether by fear or by some other emotion I didn't at first know.

She chose her moment well, coming to me when Dearth was out of the house, looking after his men, and I, pleading a headache, had refused to accompany him. The malady was purely fictitious, but I was bored with the fellow's company, and sick of being dragged at his heels like a dog for no better reason than his too evident jealousy afforded.

'I want to ask a kindness of you,' she said. 'Will you promise to answer me quite frankly? I wondered what the deuce was coming, but I promised, seeing no way out of it. 'I want you to tell me,' she went on, 'whether you see anything queer about me, about my behaviour? Do I say or do anything that seems to you odd?'

Her perturbation was so great that I smiled to hide my perception of it. I answered jocularly: 'Nothing at all odd, my dear Monica, except this question of yours. What makes you ask it?'

But she was not to be shaken so easily out of her fears, whatever they were. 'And do you find nothing strange about this household either?'

'Nothing strange at all,' I assured her. 'Your marriage is an unhappy one, but so are thousands of others. Nothing strange about that.'

'What about him?' she said. And her eyes seemed to probe for an answer.

I shrugged my shoulders. 'Are you asking for my opinion of your husband? A delicate thing to discuss.'

'We're speaking in confidence, aren't we!' She spoke impatiently, waving my politeness away.

'Well, since you ask, I don't like him. I don't like his face: it's a parody on mankind. And I can't understand why you threw yourself away on him.'

She was eager to explain. 'He wasn't always like this. He was a gifted man, with brains and an imagination. He still is, for all I know. You spoke of his face – now how would you describe his face, in one word?'

I couldn't help being tickled by the comedy of the situation: a man and a woman sitting in solemn conclave seeking a word by which to describe another man's face, and that man her husband. But her air of tragedy, though I thought it ridiculous, sobered me. I pondered her question for a while, recalling to my mind's eye the long, narrow physiognomy and the large teeth of Dearth.

At last I ventured the word I had tried to avoid. 'Equine,' I suggested. 'Ah!' There was a world of relief in her voice. 'You've seen it, too.'

She told me a queer tale. Dearth, it appears, had a love and understanding of horses that was quite unparalleled. His wife, too, had loved horses and it had once pleased her to see her husband's astonishing power over the creatures, a power which he exercised always for their good. But his benefactions to the equine race were made at a hideous cost to himself, of which he was utterly unaware. Monica's theory was too fantastic even for me to swallow, and I, as you know, have a good stomach for fantasy. You will have already guessed what it was. Dearth was growing, by a process too gradual and subtle for perception, into the likeness of the horses with whom he had so complete sympathy. This was Mrs Dearth's notion of what was happening to her husband. And she pointed out something significant that had escaped my notice. She pointed out that the difference between him and the next man was not altogether, or even mainly, a physical difference. In effect she said: 'If you scrutinize the features more carefully, you will find them to be far less extraordinary than you now suppose. The poison is not in his features. It is in the physical atmosphere he carries about with him: something which infects you with the idea of horses and makes you impose that idea on his appearance, magnifying his facial peculiarities.' Just now I mentioned that in the early days of her marriage Monica had shared his love of horses. Later, of course, she came to detest them only one degree less than she detested her husband. That is saying much. Only a few months before my visit matters had come to a crisis between the two. Without giving any definite reason, she had confessed, under pressure, that he was unspeakably offensive to her; and since then they had met only at meals and always reluctantly. She shuddered to recall that interview, and I shuddered to imagine it. I was no longer surprised that she had begun to entertain doubts of her own sanity.

But this wasn't the worst. The worst was Dandy, the white horse. I found it diffcult to understand why a white horse should alarm her, and I began to suspect that the nervous strain she had undergone was making her inclined to magnify trifles. 'It's his favourite horse,' she said. 'That's as much as saying that he dotes on it to a degree that is unhuman. It never does any work. It just roams the fields by day, and at night sleeps in the stable.' Even this didn't, to my mind, seem a very terrible indictment. If the man was mad on horses, what more natural than this petting of a particular favourite? – a fine animal, too, as Monica herself admitted. 'Roams the fields,' cried my poor cousin urgently. 'Or did until these last few weeks. Lately it has been kept in its stable, day in, day out, eating its head off and working up energy enough to kill us all.' This sounded to me like the language of hysteria, but I waited for what was to follow. 'The day you came, did you notice how pale I looked? I had had a fright. As I was crossing the yard with a pail of separated milk for the calves, that beast broke loose from the stable and sprang at me. Yes, Dandy. He was in a fury. His eyes burned with ferocity. I dodged him by a miracle, dropped the pail, and ran back to the house shrieking for help. When I entered the living-room my hysband feigned to be waking out of sleep. He didn't seem interested in my story, and I'm convinced that he had planned the whole thing.' It was past my understanding how Dearth could have made his horse spring out of a stable and make a murderous attack upon a particular woman, and I said so. 'You don't know him yet,' retorted Monica. 'And you don't know Dandy. Go and look at the beast. Go now, while James is out.'

The farmyard, with its pool of water covered in green slime, its manure and sodden straw, and its smell of pigs, was a place that seldom failed to offend me. But on this occasion I picked my way across the cobble-stones thinking of nothing at all but the homicidal horse that I was about to spy upon. I have said before that I'm not a courageous man, and you'll understand that I stepped warily as I neared the stable. I saw that the lower of the two doors was made fast and with the more confidence unlatched the other.

I peered in. The great horse stood, bolt upright but apparently in a profound sleep. It was, indeed, a fine creature, with no spot or shadow, so far as I could discern, to mar its glossy whiteness. I stood there staring and brooding for several minutes, wondering if both Monica and I were the victims of some astounding hallucination. I had no fear at all of Dandy, after having seen him; and it didn't alarm me when, presently, his frame quivered, his eyes opened, and he turned to look at me. But as I looked into his eyes an indefinable fear possessed me. The horse stared dumbly for a moment, and his nostrils dilated. Although I half-expected him to tear his head out of the halter and prance round upon me, I could not move. I stared, and as I stared, the horse's lips moved back from the teeth in a grin, unmistakably a grin, of malign intelligence. The gesture vividly recalled Dearth to my mind. I had described him as equine, and if proof of the world's aptness were needed, Dandy had supplied that proof.

'He's come back,' Monica murmured to me, on my return to the house. 'Ill, I think. He's gone to lie down. Have you seen Dandy?'

'Yes. And I hope not to see him again.'

But I was to see him again, twice again. The first time was that same night, from my bedroom window. Both my bedroom and my cousin's looked out upon that grassy hill of which I spoke. It rose for a few yards until almost level with the second storey of the house and then abruptly curved away. Somewhere about midnight, feeling restless and troubled by my thoughts, I got out of bed and went to the window to take an airing.

I was not the only restless creature that night. Standing not twenty yards away, with the sky for background, was a great horse. The moonlight made its white flank gleam like silver, and lit up the eyes that stared fixedly at my window.

3

For sixteen days and nights we lived, Monica and I, in the presence of this fear, a fear none the less real for being non-susceptible of definition. The climax came suddenly, without any sort of warning, unless Dearth's idiotic hostility towards myself could be regarded as a warning. The utterly unfounded idea that I was making love to his wife had taken root in the man's mind, and every day his manner to me became more openly vindictive. This was the cue for my departure, with warm thanks for my delightful holiday; but I didn't choose to take it. I wasn't exactly in love with Monica, but she was my comrade in danger and I was reluctant to leave her to face her nightmare terrors alone.

The most cheerful room in that house was the kitchen, with its red-tiled floor, its oak rafters, and its great open fireplace. And when in the evenings the lamp was lit and we sat there, listening in comfort to the everlasting gale that raged round the house, I could almost have imagined myself happy, had it not been for the presence of my reluctant host. He was a skeleton at a feast, if you like! By God, we were a genial party. From seven o'clock to ten we would sit there, the three of us, fencing off silence with the most pitiful of small talk. On this particular night I had been chaffing him gently, though with intention, about his fancy for keeping a loaded rifle hanging over the kitchen mantelpiece;

but at last I sickened of the pastime, and the conversation, which had been sustained only by my efforts, lapsed. I stared at the red embers in the grate, stealing a glance now and again at Monica to see how she was enduring the discomfort of such a silence. The cheap alarum-clock ticked loudly, in the way that cheap alarum-clocks have. When I looked again at Dearth he appeared to have fallen asleep. I say 'appeared', for I instantly suspected him of shamming sleep in order to catch us out. I knew that he believed us to be in love with each other, and his total lack of evidence must have occasioned him hours of useless fury. I suspected him of the most melodramatic intentions: of hoping to see a caress pass between us that would justify him in making a scene. In that scene, as I figured it, the gun over the mantelpiece might play an important part. I don't like loaded guns.

The sight of his closed lids exasperated me into a bitter speech designed for him to overhear. 'Monica, your husband is asleep. He is asleep only in order that he may wake at the chosen moment and pour out the contents of his vulgar little mind upon our heads.'

This tirade astonished her, as well it might. She glanced up, first at me, then at her husband; and upon him her eyes remained fixed. 'He's not asleep,' she said, rising slowly out of her chair.

'I know he's not,' I replied.

By now she was at his side, bending over him. 'No,' she remarked coolly. 'He's dead.'

At those words the wind outside redoubled its fury, and it seemed as though all the anguish of the world was in its wail. The spirit of Dearth's Farm was crying aloud in a frenzy that shook the house, making all the windows rattle. I shuddered to my feet. And in the moment of my rising the wail died away, and in the lull I heard outside the window a sudden sound of feet, of pawing, horse's feet. My horror found vent in a sort of desperate mirth.

'No, not dead. James Dearth doesn't die so easily.'

Shocked by my levity, she pointed mutely to the body in the chair. But a wild idea possessed me, and I knew that my wild idea was the truth. 'Yes,' I said, 'that may be dead as mutton. But James Dearth is outside, come to spy on you and me. Can't you hear him?'

I stretched out my hand to the blind cord. The blind ran up with a rattle, and, pressed against the window, looking in upon us, was the face of the white horse, its teeth bared in a malevolent grin. Without losing sight of the thing for a moment, I backed towards the fire. Monica, divining my intention, took down the gun from its hook and yielded it to my desirous fingers. I took deliberate aim, and shot.

And then, with the crisis over, as I thought, my nerves went to rags. I sat down limply, Monica huddled at my feet; and I knew with a hideous certitude that the soul of James Dearth, violently expelled from the corpse that lay outside the window, was in the room with me, seeking to re-enter that human body in the chair. There was a long moment of agony during which I trembled on the verge of madness, and then a flush came back into the dead pallid cheeks, the body breathed, the eyes opened ... I had just enough strength left to drag myself out of my seat. I saw Monica's eyes raised to mine; I can never for a moment stop seeing them. Three hours later I stumbled into the arms of the stationmaster, who put me in the London train under the impression that I was drunk. Yes, I left alone. I told you I wasn't a courageous man ...

4

Bailey's voice abruptly ceased. The tension in my listening mind snapped, and I came back with a jerk, as though released by a spring, to my seat in the teashop. Bailey's queer eyes glittered across at me for a moment, and then, their light dying suddenly out, they became infinitely weary of me and of all the sorry business of living. A rationalist in grain, I find it impossible to accept the story quite as it stands. Substantially true it may be, probably is, but that it has been distorted by the prism of Bailey's singular personality I can hardly doubt. But the angle of that distortion must remain a matter for conjecture.

No such dull reflections came then to mar my appreciation of the quality of the strange hush that followed his last words. Neither of us spoke. An agitated waitress made us aware that the shop was closing, and we went into the street without a word. The rain was unremitting. I shrank back into the shelter of the porch while I fastened the collar of my mackintosh, and when I stepped out upon the pavement again, Bailey had vanished into the darkness.

I have never ceased to be vexed at losing him, and never ceased to fear that he may have thought the loss not unwelcome to me. My only hope is that he may read this and get into touch with me again, so that I may discharge my debt to him. It is a debt that lies heavily on my conscience – the price of this story, less one pound.

Calling Card

Ramsey Campbell

Dorothy Harris stepped off the pavement and into her hall. As she stooped groaning to pick up the envelopes the front door opened, opened, a yawn that wouldn't be suppressed. She wrestled it shut – she must ask Simon to see to it, though certainly not over Christmas – then she began to open the cards.

Here was Father Christmas, and here he was again, apparently after dieting. Here was a robin like a rosy apple with a beak, and here was an envelope whose handwriting staggered: Simon's and Margery's children, perhaps?

The card showed a church on a snowy hill. The hill was bare except for a smudge of ink. Though the card was unsigned, there was writing within. A Very Happy Christmas And A Prosperous New Year, the message should have said – but now it said A Very Harried Christmas And No New Year. She turned back to the picture, her hands shaking. It wasn't just a smudge of ink; someone had drawn a smeary cross on the hill: a grave.

Though the name on the envelope was a watery blur, the address was certainly hers. Suddenly the house – the kitchen and living room, the two bedrooms with her memories stacked neatly against the walls – seemed far too large and dim. Without moving from the front door she phoned Margery.

'Is it Grandma?' Margery had to hush the children while she said, 'You come as soon as you like, mummy.'

Lark Lane was deserted. An unsold Christmas tree loitered in a shop doorway, a gargoyle craned out from the police station. Once Margery had moved away, the nearness of the police had been reassuring – not that Dorothy was nervous, like some of the old folk these days – but the police station was only a community centre now.

The bus already sounded like a pub. She sat outside on the ferry, though the bench looked and felt like black ice. Lights fished in the Mersey, gulls drifted down like snowflakes from the muddy sky. A whitish object grabbed the rail, but of course it was only a gull. Nevertheless she was glad that Simon was waiting with the car at Woodside.

As soon as the children had been packed off to bed so that Father Christmas could get to work, she produced the card. It felt wet, almost slimy, though it hadn't before. Simon pointed out what she'd overlooked: the age of the stamp. 'We weren't even living there then,' Margery said. 'You wouldn't think they would bother delivering it after sixty years.'

'A touch of the Christmas spirit.'

'I wish they hadn't bothered,' Margery said. But her mother didn't mind now; the addressee must have died years ago. She turned the conversation to old times, to Margery's father. Later she gazed from her bedroom window, at the houses of Bebington sleeping in pairs. A man was creeping about the house, but it was only Simon, laden with presents.

In the morning the house was full of cries of delight, gleaming new toys, balls of wrapping paper big as cabbages. In the afternoon the adults, bulging with turkey and pudding, lolled in chairs. When Simon drove her home that night, Dorothy noticed that the unsold Christmas tree was still there, a scrawny glistening shape at the back of the shop doorway. As soon as Simon left, she found herself thinking about the unpleasant card. She tore it up, then went determinedly to bed.

Boxing Day was her busiest time, what with cooking the second version of Christmas dinner, and making sure the house was impeccable, and hiding small presents for the children to find. She wished she could see them more often, but they and their parents had their own lives to lead.

An insect clung to a tinsel globe on the tree. When she reached out to squash the insect it wasn't there, neither on the globe nor on the floor. Could it have been the reflection of someone thin outside the window? Nobody was there now.

She liked the house best when it was full of laughter, and it would be again soon: 'We'll get a sitter,' Margery promised, 'and first-foot you on New Year's Eve.' She'd used to do that when she had lived at home – she'd waited outside at midnight of the Old Year so as to be the first to cross her mother's threshold. That reminded Dorothy to offer the children a holiday treat. Everything seemed fine, even when they went to the door to leave. 'Grandma, someone's left you a present,' little Denise cried.

Then she cried out, and dropped the package. Perhaps the wind had snatched it from her hands. As the package, which looked wet and mouldy, struck the kerb it broke open. Did its contents scuttle out and sidle away into the dark? Surely that was the play of the wind, which tumbled carton and wrapping away down the street.

Someone must have used her doorway for a wastebin, that was all. Dorothy lay in bed, listening to the wind which groped around the windowless side of the house, that faced on to the alley. She kept thinking

she was on the ferry, backing away from the rail, forgetting that the rail
was also behind her. Her nervousness annoyed her – she was acting like
an old fogey – which was why, next afternoon, she walked to Otterspool
promenade.

Gulls and planes sailed over the Mersey, which was deserted except
for buoys. On the far bank, tiny towns and stalks of factory chimneys
stood at the foot of an enormous frieze of clouds. Sunlight slipped through
to Birkenhead and Wallasey, touching up the colours of microscopic
streets; specks of windows glinted. She enjoyed none of this, for the
slopping of water beneath the promenade seemed to be pacing her.
Worse, she couldn't make herself go to the rail to prove that there was
nothing.

Really, it was heartbreaking. One vicious card and she felt nervous in
her own house. A blurred voice seemed to creep behind the carols on the
radio, lowing out of tune. Next day she took her washing to Lark Lane,
in search of distraction as much as anything.

The Westinghouse Laundromat was deserted. *O O O*, the washing
machines said emptily. There was only herself, and her dervishes of
clothes, and a black plastic bag almost as tall as she was. If someone had
abandoned it, whatever its lumpy contents were, she could see why, for
it was leaking; she smelled stagnant water. It must be a draught that
made it twitch feebly. Nevertheless, if she had been able to turn off her
machine she might have fled.

She mustn't grow neurotic. She still had friends to visit. The following
day she went to a friend whose flat overlooked Wavertree Park. It was
all very convivial – a rainstorm outside made the mince pies more
warming, the chat flowed as easily as the whisky – but she kept glancing
at the thin figure who stood in the park, unmoved by the downpour. The
trails of rain on the window must be lending him their colour, for his skin
looked like a snail's.

Eventually the 68 bus, meandering like a drunkard's monologue, took
her home to Aigburth. No, the man in the park hadn't really looked as
though his clothes and his body had merged into a single greyish mass.
Tomorrow she was taking the children for their treat, and that would
clear her mind.

She took them to the aquarium. Piranhas sank stonily, their sides
glittering like Christmas cards. Toads were bubbling lumps of tar. Finny
humbugs swam, and darting fish wired with light. Had one of the tanks
cracked? There seemed to be a stagnant smell.

In the museum everything was under glass: shrunken heads like sewn
leathery handbags, a watchmaker's workshop, buses passing as though
the windows were silent films. Here was a slum street, walled in by
photographs of despair, real flagstones underfoot, overhung by street-
lamps on brackets. She halted between a grid and a drinking fountain;

she was trapped in the dimness between blind corners, and couldn't see either way. Why couldn't she get rid of the stagnant smell? Grey forlorn faces, pressed like specimens, peered out of the walls. 'Come on, quickly,' she said, pretending that only the children were nervous.

She was glad of the packed crowds in Church Street, even though the children kept letting go of her hands. But the stagnant smell was trailing her, and once, when she grabbed for little Denise's hand, she clutched someone else's, which felt soft and wet. It must have been nervousness which made her fingers seem to sink into the hand.

That night she returned to the aquarium and found she was locked in. Except for the glow of the tanks, the narrow room was oppressively dark. In the nearest tank a large dead fish floated towards her, out of weeds. Now she was in the tank, her nails scrabbling at the glass, and she saw that it wasn't a fish but a snail-coloured hand, which closed spongily on hers. When she woke, her scream made the house sound very empty.

At least it was New Year's Eve. After tonight she could stop worrying. Why had she thought that? It only made her more nervous. Even when Margery phoned to confirm they would first-foot her, that reminded her how many hours she would be on her own. As the night seeped into the house, the emptiness grew.

A knock at the front door made her start, but it was only the Harveys, inviting her next door for sherry and sandwiches. While she dodged a sudden rainstorm, Mr Harvey dragged at her front door, one hand through the letter box, until the latch clicked.

After several sherries Dorothy remembered something she'd once heard. 'The lady who lived next door before me – didn't she have trouble with her son?'

'He wasn't right in the head. He got so he'd go for anyone, even if he'd never met them before. She got so scared of him she locked him out one New Year's Eve. They say he threw himself in the river, though they never found the body.'

Dorothy wished she hadn't asked. She thought of the body, rotting in the depths. She must go home, in case Simon and Margery arrived. The Harveys were next door if she needed them.

The sherries had made her sleepy. Only the ticking of her clock, clipping away the seconds, kept her awake. Twenty past eleven. The splashing from the gutters sounded like wet footsteps pacing outside the window. She had never noticed she could smell the river in her house. She wished she had stayed longer with the Harveys; she would have been able to hear Simon's car.

Twenty to twelve. Surely they wouldn't wait until midnight. She switched on the radio for company. A master of ceremonies was making people laugh; a man was laughing thickly, sounding waterlogged. Was he a drunk in the street? He wasn't on the radio. She mustn't brood; why, she hadn't put out the sherry glasses; that was something to do, to distract her from the intolerably measured counting of the clock, the silenced radio, the emptiness displaying her sounds——

Though the knock seemed enormously loud, she didn't start. They were here at last, though she hadn't heard the car. It was New Year's Day. She ran, and had reached the front door when the phone shrilled. That startled her so badly that she snatched the door open before lifting the receiver.

Nobody was outside – only a distant uproar of cheers and bells and horns – and Margery was on the phone. 'We've been held up, mummy. There was an accident in the tunnel. We'll be over as soon as we can.'

Then who had knocked? It must have been a drunk; she heard him stumbling beside the house, thumping on her window. He'd better take himself off, or she would call Mr Harvey to deal with him. But she was still inside the doorway when she saw the object on her step.

Good God, was it a rat? No, just a shoe, so ancient that it looked stuffed with mould. It wasn't mould, only a rotten old sock. There was something in the sock, something that smelled of stagnant water and worse. She stooped to peer at it, and then she was struggling to close the door, fighting to make the latch click, no breath to spare for a scream. She'd had her first foot, and now – hobbling doggedly alongside the house, its hands slithering over the wall – here came the rest of the body.

The Feet

Mark Channing

Am I, Richard Haldane Bullen, King's Counsel and an Officer of the Crown, a murderer?

Hear the facts and judge for yourself.

I liked my Uncle Harvey, very much. People who didn't know him well, thought him 'queer.' Many collectors of oriental curios *are* queer sort of people, haven't you found that? It is as if something crept out of their curios to inhabit their minds and made them harmless Jekylls and Hydes. They cease to be normal whenever the materialism of the West is overcome by that mysterious Something which seems to exude from almost all Eastern things.

My Uncle Harvey, however, was 'queer' in a strange way. He was afraid of his curios. They dominated his existence. The fact that most of them were gruesome relics, makes this fairly reasonable. I have studied enough psychology to know that. Anyway, I was down from Oxford for the Christmas vacation and Uncle Harvey asked me to dine with him. Now, I have always disliked Bloomsbury. I still do, it depresses me. But because I was fond of the old man and as he had promised to show me his curios – which up to then I had not seen – I accepted the invitation. It was the 22nd of December, I remember, and a damp foggy night.

After dinner we adjourned to his study – his 'Chamber of Horrors,' as he laughingly called it.

As he opened the door of that room, I sensed this 'queerness,' to the point of feeling goose-flesh, all over. It may, of course, have been because he told me that the sombre Indian hangings had come from the Nana Sahib's Palace, at Cawnpore. General Havelock's Highlanders, he said, had torn them down when they wrecked the palace after discovering that awful well, filled to the brim with the bodies of women and children. Mind you, my uncle's study was a cosy room, but its intimacy was – well, stealthy. It was Thug-like. That is, it crept upon you as the Indian Thugs used to creep upon their victims – strangling all sense of happiness with a quick overcoming and an instantaneous merciless domination.

As I have said, I was fond of my Uncle Harvey. I want you to remember that.

Well, as we entered the room, he switched on the lights inside a large cabinet near the fireplace. It was a Victorian bit of furniture, and its glass doors had tightly-pleated, green silk curtains behind them. To me – lighted up and closed as it was – it seemed rather like a house that held some grim secret, which it wished to conceal. That 'queerness' reached out, and literally *grabbed* me, as I opened its doors.

My uncle, who was preparing coffee – he always made his own – looked up as he heard the click of the small key.

'See that big knife with the deep channel running down to its point, Dick? That came from the temple of Kali, in Southern India. It was used in the sacrificing of babies to the goddess ... That tress of hair caked with blood was taken out of the well at Cawnpore after the massacre of 1857 ... The dingy-looking bit of rope by the side of it ——'

'And *these*, Uncle Harvey?' I asked, interrupting him and taking up one of the two circlets of silver ankle-bells. 'What are *these*?' I shook it lightly. I wanted to change the subject, you see.

The bells had a curiously shrill sweet sound, I remember.

'For God's sake put them down!' exclaimed Uncle Harvey.

I glanced at him in astonishment. Banging down the methylated spirit lamp of the coffee machine on to the hammered brass Delhi-work tray over which he was bending, he strode over to me.

'You didn't touch *those* by any chance, did you?' he asked harshly, pointing to two tiny wax models of a woman's feet. They were about an inch long.

As I looked at them, I saw that the artist had evidently made them to resemble feet which had been recently severed from the leg a few inches above the ankle-bones. The shiny redness of the flesh and the whiteness of the splintered bone were horribly realistic. The minute toe-nails were coloured red with henna.

'Good lord, no! I hadn't even noticed them!' I replied. 'What's wrong?' I asked the question because he looked pale and distraught.

'Come and have your coffee, Dick,' he said, gravely, taking me by the arm. This is their story:

'Somewhere in the "sixties," a certain Indian Nawab who had been forced to leave India on account of his savage cruelty to his people, came to live in England. Being as wealthy as Croesus, he brought over with him his harem and a big staff of servants. He wanted to be received in Society, but his reputation for cruelty caused Society to boycott him. He lived absolutely isolated from the civilization in which he had taken refuge. Sinister rumours soon got about. Screams of women were heard at night, and it was said that he murdered several of his women servants. Remember, in the days of which I am speaking an English home was far more a castle than it is today, and as the house was always closely shuttered nobody knew anything for certain. At all events, no less than seven skeletons were dug up in the garden some years later ... That's his picture, hanging over the cabinet you were looking at! Nasty looking fellow, don't you think?'

I turned to look at the oil-painting. My poor old uncle was right. That picture of a tall, bejewelled Indian, with the lean cruel face of a murderous sadist, wasn't the sort of thing I'd care to have in any room of mine!

'When the Nawab died – or was murdered in his turn,' resumed my uncle, 'what was left of his household returned to India and the house was put up for sale.'

'The first people to buy it had not been there a week before their butler was murdered. All the other servants refused to stay in the house. Its next occupants lost their two children *inside* a week, the poor mites were found lying in the hall with their necks broken. Neither the parents nor the doctors thought it was an accident ... How could it have been?'

'Both these tragedies happened within three months. After that, the house remained empty. The Nawab's agents, under orders from his successor, had it cleaned every twelve months. But although the rent was nominal, no one could be found to take it. Doubtless because the workmen and charwomen who cleaned the place swore that each time they came, they found the prints of a woman's small feet in the dust on the carpetless stairs, and also on the marble floor of what used to be the women's apartments. They also maintained that they heard 'sleigh bells' jingling down the passages. None of them ever saw anything, though.'

Now, as my uncle spoke, I distinctly heard the circlet of bells I had been looking at, jingle. I think *he* did, too. I suppose I had laid it down on the edge of its sister anklet and it had slipped.

'Well,' he went on, pretending, I think, not to have heard it, 'then *I* took the house, Dick. *This house.*

'I took it on certain conditions, though. I said I wanted to live in it a week before I would sign the lease. The agents agreed, and as temporary caretakers, put in an Indian who had married a white women. They couldn't get a white man to take on the job, they said.

'Now, as you know, I took over your grandfather's curio business. Then, as now, I believed that strange powers are hidden in certain things. That certain things can be either lucky or unlucky. Well, on the day I was to go into this house a lascar – Indian sailor – came to my shop and asked me to buy from him a wax image of a dancing-girl. It was a beautiful piece of work. They don't make them any more, it's a lost art.

' "Sahib," said the lascar, "buy it! It is from the Temple of Kali. Whoever has it – or even a part of it – in his possession, is under the protection of the goddess. Evil spirits cannot harm him ..."

'I bought the thing – and I remember thinking that it would be a good idea to take it with me when I went to "try-out" this house.

'On the 22nd of December – a year ago today – I arrived with my suitcase. The Indian opened the door. I didin't like the look of him directly I saw him. His eyes had a curious glassy look, which I put down to opium and dismissed him from my mind.

'I found prepared for me the late Nawab's bedroom – a smallish room with carved sandalwood panelling and doors. Beautiful work. I'll show it to you before you go, if you'd like to see it ... It all looked snug and inviting. There was a bright fire burning, and it had been thoroughly cleaned – though, like all other servants of his kind I found, later, that of the three carved sandalwood shelves above the mantelpiece, he had only dusted the two bottom ones ... But I'm tall, and perhaps he couldn't reach the top one.

'Well, one of the first things I did was to stand the image of the dancing-girl on the table under the lamp while I had supper. I wanted to have a good look at her. I'd been too busy to do so before. I had brought a bottle of port and some cold chicken and a couple of books on Eastern Mysticism, and to tell the truth I was rather looking forward to the night.

'That little statue was almost lifelike, Dick!' The enthusiasm of a true collector rang in my uncle's tones. 'Even to the caste mark on her little forehead, every detail was exact, and the colours were so bright she might have been made that very day!

'Now, you may take it from me that I was wide awake. As wide awake as I am now. You may laugh at me if you will – but while I was looking at her I saw a man's thin brown hand, its fingers covered with gorgeous rings, reach over the table, as if to take away the little figure. Whether I was imagining it or not, I snatched up the statue and thrust it hastily into my breast pocket. As I did so, the hand melted into thin air. That's what comes of reading books on Oriental Mysticism! I muttered. And getting up from the table I settled myself in an inviting-looking easy-chair at one side of the fire.

'For an hour or more, nothing happened. Only rats squeaking and scuttering in the wainscoting, and all that ... Then I heard – or thought I heard – a faint moaning, but I decided that it might quite well be a loose shutter swinging in the wind, somewhere.

'I must have dozed, *for I was suddenly wakened by a hand feeling in my breast pocket*. Although the lamp was burning brightly, I could see nothing. But I instinctively grabbed at whatever it was, and my fingers closed round a slim cold wrist.'

My uncle frowned, and for the first time in my life I saw fear in his eyes. And, believe me, to see fear in the eyes of a hard rider to hounds is not a pleasant sight.

'Port and mysticism aren't good for the imagination, Uncle!' I said as cheerily as I could, and gulped down my coffee. The room was getting on my nerves – as strong as they are.

'No, Dick,' retorted my uncle gravely, 'it wasn't imagination. It was something my fingers could hold. A damp, soggy, cold wrist – like the wrist of a corpse ... But it seemed to slip from my fingers. Then I heard the chinking of a nautch-girl's ankle-bells, faintly, on the other side of the door leading into what was the Nawab's harem. Jumping to my feet, I flung open the door. And I found myself looking into the glassy eyes of the Indian caretaker.

' "Did you call, Sahib?" he asked, looking at me with those dead fish-like eyes of his.

'I did some rapid thinking. I've already told you, Dick, that I had taken a dislike to the man. I disliked, still more, finding him where he was at the moment. So I decided to keep him under observation. I bade him come in and sit with me.

'And he came in

'They say this house is haunted,' I said, by way of starting a conversation he was evidently loath to begin.

' "It is true Sahib," he said – and I have never heard anything colder than his voice. "The *Bhoot* (spirit) of a young dancing-girl is in the house. She was the Nawab's favourite. But she fell in love with a young sahib who saw her at the window one day. They were about to elope when the Nawab caught her." '

'And then?' I questioned.

' "Then he cut off her feet – himself, and sent them to the young Englishman." '

My uncle paused a moment and looked towards the cabinet.

'And then, Dick, I swear,' he said to me earnestly, 'that the chinking of those anklet-bells began again – in the other room – but much louder ... They were coming towards me. Whether it was the fog, or whether it was that the caretaker hadn't put enough oil in the lamp, I don't know, but at that moment the room grew darker. Slowly, the door swung open, and the sound of the anklet-bells became shrill and loud.'

My Uncle Harvey paused and mopped his forehead.

'*Then*, Dick,' he said tensely, '*then I saw the feet!*'

As he spoke it seemed to me that the room became darker.

'I saw the feet, I say!' asseverated my uncle. They seemed to have been severed from the leg just above the ankle only a few minutes before! You saw those wax ones? Well, they were like that.' My uncle shuddered ... 'I wish to God I could forget them! I'd be so much happier!' Then he pulled himself together. 'They passed me, and mounted on to the lid of a carved sandal-wood chest inlaid with mother-of-pearl that stood on the opposite side of the fire-place. It's still there! I distinctly saw the fresh

blood glisten in the indented hollows behind the ankle-bones, Dick! ...
They ... *She* seemed to be trying to reach something on the topmost of
the three shelves. I couldn't speak or move. Then that moaning began
again – on the corner where the chest was.

'By a tremendous effort I forced myself to look at my companion.

'He had risen from his chair. No devil in hell could have looked more
evil than he did. I sprang up, oversetting the lamp.

' "Siva! Siva!" I heard myself screaming, in tones as cracked as those
of a man of ninety, "Siva the destroyer is protecting me! You cannot harm
me!"

'As I screamed, he sprang at me, and I leapt from him. I felt his right
hand dart into my breast pocket, seize the statue and drag it out. I only
just managed to clutch at its feet, which broke off in my hand. Then I
fell and must have stunned myself.

'When I came to, the caretaker – a stout Madrassi – was standing at
the table with my morning tea. He seemed to think I had lain down on
the floor to rest.

' "Master will please excuse," he said, "that I did not let him in,
yesterday! But they told me that you had a key, Sahib! Therefore, having
put everything ready, I spent the night at the hospital with my wife. She
died this morning, Sahib." '

My uncle looked at me, as if he suspected I might be amused at his
story. But I wasn't. The misery in his face fairly frightened me.

'The feet of the statue I found clasped in my hand,' he said, slowly.
'There was no trace of the rest of it ... As I sit here, Dick, I swear before
Heaven that I believe those bits of wax are all that stand between me
and the Evil Thing that is still in this house! It may be stupid, and all
that, but I'm convinced that only so long as they are in my possession
am I safe!'

He rose and crossed to the sideboard to mix a 'Doch and Doris.'

I made up my mind, then and there. This fear complex must be
smashed, once and forever. If it weren't smashed, I was convinced he
would go mad. I decided to take away those wax feet, tomorrow I would
tell him that I had done so, and that they had unfortunately been lost.
His obsession would vanish then, I was sure.

Going over to the cabinet I slipped them into my waistcoat pocket and
closed the doors.

'What happened to the man whom you *thought* was the caretaker?' I
asked, casually, as I stood up to go. It was ten to twelve.

My uncle glanced up at the Nawab's picture.

'I suppose he went back to Hell!' he said. And opened the door to go
into the hall.

Coming down the stairs, as though their wearer was running, we both
heard the sound of the anklet-bells.

Instinctively my hand shot to my waistcoat pocket. It was empty.
'The Feet!' gasped my Uncle Harvey.
And fell dead.

Undesirable Guests

William Charlton

Matthew and Julia Brook were a busy couple. They had a house in London and a house in the depths of Derkshire, and travelling between the two would alone have sufficed to keep them occupied. Matthew worked in London as a partner in a firm of investment managers, and the house in Derkshire was a shooting lodge from which he farmed an extensive if not very productive tract of moor. Julia lectured in London on the history of art, and in Derkshire, when the rain stopped, attempted conventional but occasionally saleable landscape paintings. Unemployment, then, was not a problem for them. Neither was childlessness, since they had two young girls of school age and a boy just emerging from babyhood. And they had a full social life. In London they gave and attended many dinner-parties. The remoteness of their Derkshire house was a deterrent to no one but themselves. No sooner had they taken possession of it than friends whom they had not seen for years, settled in places as far away as Hong Kong and Venezuela, came posting back to England to inspect it. As for their relations (and they had plenty of those, on both sides), they seemed to spend the whole year queueing to come, and much bitterness was generated if anyone jumped the queue.

Take, for instance, the Christmas which had just passed. For Christmas itself they had Julia's parents, her unmarried elder sister, and an Italian lady with whom Julia had been at school, who had subsequently married, and then been divorced from, an alcoholic, and who was now recovering from a nervous breakdown. Before this not ideally assorted party they had had Matthew's grandmother, who nearly died of a bad cold, and a modern historian, who made love to their mother's help. The mother's help left in a huff, an annoying thing to happen just before Christmas, but not wholly unexpected, since mother's helps were among the things they almost invariably lost when travelling between London and Derkshire. For the New Year they had been expecting the Fieldings, a congenial family with children the same age as their own, but the Fieldings had called off at the last moment. It was not to be supposed, however, that this would give them several days to themselves, since the demands of their Derkshire neighbours were still unappeased.

When Julia first went from Ladbroke Grove to Derkshire, she imagined that one of the advantages of their country house would be that they would not have any neighbours. She could not have made a greater mistake. The fewness of the local inhabitants in places like Derkshire makes them fasten the more avidly on any pleasant newcomer, and Julia found herself receiving and having to return invitations from a friendly but unsophisticated aboriginal population who all seemed to have the same names, and whose relationship to one another was intensely important to themselves, and very hard for anyone else to master. Thus the Dodsons of Baddlegate were no relation to the Dodsons of The Deane, except that Mrs Dodson of Baddlegate had been a Miss Dodson of The Deane. On the other hand, the Englebys of Stilburn were quite closely related to the Englebys of Hando, but were at feud with them. And the Englebys of Engleby were not in fact the Englebys of Engleby: the impoverished Englebys of Drinkbottle were that. The Englebys of Engleby were another branch of the Stilburn family. As for the Drink-bottles of Dulwick Castle, they were a parvenu family and not really Drinkbottles at all. One thing which Julia clearly understood was that there had been no genuine Drinkbottles since the sixteenth century.

'Don't forget,' said Julia, the morning after they had dispatched her Italian friend, 'that we are having dinner with the Englebys tonight.'

Matthew had forgotten. 'Can't we put them off?'

'We've put them off twice, and they gave us a choice of every day this week.'

Matthew continued with his correspondence.

'Look at that,' he said suddenly, holding out a letter. 'Now we're in real trouble. Now the ceiling's falling in. Seraphim Durness is coming tonight.'

'Oh no! Can't we put him off?'

'Quite impossible. We don't know his address, and anyhow he'll be already on the way.'

'He *can't* be. How *could* Seraphim be so inconsiderate?'

'Look and see for yourself.'

Julia took the letter. Seraphim Durness was an old friend whom Julia, nevertheless, regarded with some mistrust. His name was at once suitable and deceptive. As a boy – Matthew had first known him at school – he had looked like an angel, but already one of the fallen tribe; and his beautiful but reckless appearance was a fair reflection of his personality. From an early age he had formed a habit of doing exactly what he liked. This habit had led to his early departure first from school, subsequently from Oxford, and eventually from England. In recent years he had been heard of in a succession of very out-of-the-way places where, it was

supposed, obstacles to doing what he liked were still few. His letter was
dated from Lima in the first week of December, which suggested it was
not wholly his fault that they had not had more notice.

'My dear Matthew' it began,

'I shall be in England at the end of this month, and I am going up to
visit my aunt at Arven. Could I possibly stay with you on the night of
the 30th? I know you'll be in your beloved Derkshire then, and I know
how Julia's marvellous hospitality can always stretch the house to hold
one or two extra people.

'I am not sure if you heard of my marriage, which was a quiet affair.
Mercedes is with me, and I'm eager for you to meet her ...'

'My God!' said Julia. 'It's not just Seraphim but his wife.'

'Read on,' said Matthew grimly, 'and see what he says about her. You
don't know half of it yet.'

'She looked after me wonderfully last year,' Julia read, 'when I was
sick in the mountains, and I really owe my life to her. Even now, I'm
afraid, you'll find me pretty much of an invalid, but Mercedes gets me
everything I need. I'm sure you will like her. She is an Indian, and knows
more about Indian customs than ever gets into the anthropological
books.'

'No, that's enough,' said Julia, handing back the letter. 'Seraphim's
an invalid, and the wife's an Indian. Do you think she speaks English?'

'Broken Spanish, I expect. But that's all right, my love. You speak
Spanish. You can hear about the Indian customs while she's getting
Seraphim his special food.'

'Special food?' Julia had a horror of visitors who needed special food.
'It doesn't say anything about special food.'

'I thought it was implicit. But perhaps he was referring to urine bottles
or portable oxygen tents. Seraphim must be in a bad way if he describes
himself as an invalid. In fact, I thought his handwriting looked shaky.'

'I don't believe it,' said Julia. 'But look here, Matthew, what about
the Englebys? I don't want to cancel our dinner with them. Why should
we, when the Durnesses come down on us without any warning at all?'

'Well, you needn't. If they're coming at tea-time they can babysit, and
we can let Mrs Dodson off.' Mrs Dodson was the wife of the Brooks'
shepherd, and lived about half a mile away. They had no servants (thanks
to the modern historian) living in the house, but Mrs Dodson held herself
at their disposal when they were in residence.

Days are short in Derkshire at the turn of the year, and today darkness
started to gather immediately after lunch.

'It looks like snow,' said Matthew.

'I don't think so,' said Julia. 'It's very mild.'

'I don't like the colour of the sky,' said Matthew. It was, in fact, an unhealthy greyish-yellow. 'We shall have rain turning to snow when it gets dark. We don't want to go out to the Englebys' and find we can't get back.'

The Brooks' house was at the end of a long, private road, which in turn was at the end of a narrow and indifferent public road running partly across empty moors and partly along a high, unpopulated valley. It was often cut off for several days in winter, but seldom before January. Julia appreciated that there was some risk, but said that they could not cry off their engagement while the temperature was still so high.

'If there's really snow about, the Durnesses will meet it in Dancashire and stay in a hotel, and then we'll have the excuse that we can't leave the children.'

For a while it looked as if this excuse might materialize. Night fell, the hour for tea came and went, and there was no sign of the self-invited guests. In order, however, that they might still be able to attend their dinner if the Durnesses arrived, Matthew and Julia fed their older children, settled Henry, the youngest, for the night, and started to change into evening clothes. They were still changing when they heard the arrival of a car.

One of the reasons why Matthew had been less dismayed than Julia by Seraphim's letter was that he was very curious to see Seraphim's wife. He could remember a fairly rapid succession of women in Seraphim's life, and although they had sometimes been deficient in intelligence, education, breeding, good character and even sanity, they had all been extremely striking to look at. He wondered what oread or primitive, Eve-like figure Seraphim had found in South America.

He was disappointed. Mercedes Durness was a woman of middle age, dressed in black like any respectable South American matron, and she spoke tolerable English. If the blood of the Incas ran in her veins, it showed only in a certain squareness of figure and woodenness of visage. Having shaken hands with Matthew and Julia in a matter-of-fact way, she devoted herself to unpacking the car in which they had arrived and looking after her husband.

As for Seraphim himself, he was indeed something of an invalid. The angelic (or diabolical) light had left him. Julia was in such a hurry to be off, and Mercedes was so much to the fore, that they hardly saw him, but Matthew remarked on his changed looks as they drove away.

'Seraphim looked in very bad form. I've never seen anyone so white.'

'I hope,' said Julia, 'he's not going to collapse on us and be unable to leave tomorrow.' The Brooks were happy to be used as a hotel, but they did not like, as happened all too often, being used as a nursing-home.

'They said they were definitely going on. What did you make of all that stuff they had in their car? It looked as if Seraphim was carrying his coffin round with him.'

'I expect it's the oxygen tent you were telling me about. His wife seemed very efficient at looking after him.'

'Yes, I got the impression she was competent. It makes me happier about leaving the children with them.'

'Had you been worried, then?'

'Well, Seraphim isn't a conspicuously responsible fellow, and you couldn't know what sort of wife he might have picked up, though he did say Mercedes was capable of nursing.'

Julia did not reply, and Matthew glanced at her.

'You look as if you still have reservations.'

'Oh,' she said, 'I'm sure she can cope. It's just that she's so much not Seraphim's type. I suppose it really is Seraphim?'

'What an extraordinary suggestion. Of course it's Seraphim. Who else could it be? But I do wonder what exactly is wrong with him.' Matthew's train of thought was interrupted by snowflakes on the windscreen. 'There you are,' he said. 'The rain's turning to snow.'

'It won't lie,' said Julia. 'Besides, we've got the shovel in the back. You can never get completely stuck if you've got a shovel.'

They had not had time before they left to do more than show their guests where they were sleeping, and explain that there was food on the hot-plates in the dining-room. Their two older children were in bed, and their youngest was already asleep. The dinner set out on the hot-plate was inviting, and would not improve by being kept. It would have been natural, then, for their guests – provided, of course, that they did not require anything special in the way of diet – perhaps after a few minutes in their room, to go to the dining-room and eat. But that was not quite how they acted. Seraphim had emerged from the car an even more decrepit figure than the Brooks, in the darkness of the night and the haste of their departure, had properly realized. He had not gone up with his wife to see their room, but she had deposited him in the hall, where the only sign of life he gave was a low mutter of apology for coming so suddenly and being so ill. When the Brooks had left, Mercedes picked him out of the chair, more like a life-sized doll than a human being, and took him into the kitchen. Not long afterwards, a loud shriek rang through the house.

The two Brooks daughters, Lucy and Amanda, slept in the same room. They had not yet gone to sleep, and this cry alarmed them. It sounded like their brother Henry, of whom they were both very fond, but it did not come from his room, which was a couple of doors away and opened into their parents' bedroom. They wondered what they should do, and, after some consultation, pattered down the passage and looked into Henry's room. He was not there. They turned round to find the visiting lady watching them from the top of the stairs.

'Were you looking for the little boy?' she asked, pleasantly enough. 'He had a bad dream, and I have taken him down to the kitchen to give him some hot milk.'

'May we come too?' asked Amanda, the younger sister.

'No, you would get cold. You must go back to bed. The little boy will be all right in a moment, and then he will go back to bed too.'

The girls returned to their room, but they were not reassured. The cry they had heard had not been the sort of cry a child emits in its sleep: it had the unmistakable urgency of waking terror. Neither was the reason given why they should not come down – that they would get cold in the kitchen – at all convincing.

'I think Henry's hurt himself,' said Lucy.

'The visitors are looking after him,' said Amanda.

But Lucy was nearly nine, and had a sense of responsibility. She was not prepared to leave things in the visitors' hands.

'I think Mummy and Daddy ought to be told.'

'But how can they? They've gone out to a party.'

'We could telephone to them.'

Amanda did not like that suggestion. Ringing up parents at a dinner-party is not something children are encouraged to do. Instead of voicing this real objection, Amanda said: 'The lady told us to go to bed. What if she saw us?'

'She won't see us if we use the telephone in Mummy's room.'

In the end, Lucy brought Amanda to agree to this. They managed to gain the telephone by their parents' bed unobserved, but unfortunately they did not know the right number.

'You must look it up in the book,' said Amanda.

Lucy had never looked up a number before, and she had no real chance. The name Engleby may sound uncommon, but it is not un-common in Derkshire. When Lucy at last found the right page she was confronted by several columns of Englebys, and she did not know to which of them her parents had gone. She tried dialling the first number, but it was not the right one, and in any case she had omitted the dialling code, and therefore received only a dismal whine.

The two girls were discussing what to make of this when they were interrupted by the voice of the visiting lady.

'What, playing with telephones?' she asked reproachfully. 'I thought you were in bed.'

'We were ringing up Mummy.'

'But don't you know that children must never ring up their parents when they are out at parties?'

The girls' faces showed that this shot had gone home.

'But do not look so sad,' the visiting lady said. 'I will make it so that you can play with the telephone, and it will not disturb your parents or cost any money.'

The wire from the telephone ran to a little box on the skirting board under the bed. The visiting lady took the wire and pulled it out of the box as easily as you might pull off a thread that was hanging out of a piece of material. 'Now,' she said, 'you can telephone.'

The lady's movement had frightened the children. 'We don't want to telephone any more,' said Lucy. 'Besides, it won't work now.'

'Yes it will,' said the visiting lady. 'Try it and see.'

'It can't work,' said Amanda, 'because you've broken the wire.'

'Why don't you lift the receiver and try?' the lady repeated.

Reluctantly, Amanda took the receiver off its rest. As soon as she had done so, she heard a voice. It was not like an ordinary voice: more like one of those recorded messages which you tend to get when you ring up the Electricity Board to complain about a power failure. 'Your parents have gone away now,' it said, and there followed a sound like a laugh. Amanda dropped the receiver and started to cry.

'She doesn't like this game,' said Lucy. 'I think we'll go to bed now.'

Even if the children had succeeded in ringing up the right Englebys, they would not have been able to speak to their parents, since their parents were putting to the test Julia's theory that one can never get completely stuck if one has a shovel. The rain had turned to snow with a vengeance, and was being driven across the moors by a howling wind. To begin with, it had merely swirled before their headlights, reducing visiblity to a few yards and forcing them to slow down to twenty, to fifteen, at times to ten miles an hour. But the slower they went, the more time they gave the drifts to build up, and they soon found themselves bumping over ridges of snow and feeling snow scrape the bottom of their car. Eventually they ran into a drift they could not drive through. They got out and put on their boots to start digging. It was extremely cold and the snow was blinding.

'I don't like this,' said Julia.

It would not do for them both to lose heart, and Matthew's spirits rose to the occasion.

'It's a dirty night, but it's fun to be out in it. This drift isn't much. We'll be through it in no time.'

'Do you think we ought to turn back?'

'That would be defeatist.'

'If we don't turn back now, we shan't get back tonight. There'll be no hope of getting back from Stilburn. And then what about the children and the Durnesses?'

'They'll look after each other. Lucy's a sensible girl. But the fact is, I'm not sure we could get back now if we tried. The drifts are piling up all the time, and we're over the highest part of the road now. It would be easier to go on than back.'

Matthew was certainly right on this last point. In another mile or so they would be off the moor and might hope to be below the worst of the snow. Both of them contrasted in their minds the certainty of warmth and hospitality at the Englebys' house with the risk of having to spend the night in their car somewhere between their present position and their home. Such a night could be very unpleasant indeed.

Though perhaps no worse than the night on which Lucy and Amanda were launched. After the episode of the telephone they had returned to their room, but there was no question now of their settling to sleep.

'I wonder when Mummy and Daddy will come back,' said Amanda. 'Let's watch from the window.'

Their room looked down the valley, and on a fine night it was possible to see approaching headlights far away. But tonight, of course, all they could see was snowflakes. After a while they turned away from the window.

'I don't like it here,' said Lucy. 'We don't know these visitors. Let's get dressed and wait for Mummy and Daddy with the Dodsons.'

'What, go out of the house by ourselves?' asked Amanda dubiously.

'We could get out by the back stairs and the kitchen door.'

'What would Mummy say?'

'We'll say we went out because we couldn't get to sleep.'

This was a regular excuse for irregular behaviour at night. Amanda did not criticize it, although it was obviously thin. And neither child made any reference to their brother Henry. They succeeded in getting some clothes on, but not in stealing out by the back stairs. Seraphim was standing outside their door.

'I thought you might not have gone to bed yet,' he said. There was some colour in his cheeks now, and his voice was much stronger than it had been when he arrived. 'How late you stay up. Would you like a game?'

'We were just going to bed now,' said Lucy.

'And why shouldn't you have a game? Your parents won't be back tonight. It's snowing too hard. Have you ever played "Devil in the Dark"?'

'No.'

'It's a game for winter nights. All the lights are put out, and one person is Devil, and has to catch the others. The others try to run away from him. I'll be Devil. You'll find it quite exciting.'

'Mummy doesn't like us playing games after she's said good night to us.'

'Ah, but she won't know, will she, what we do tonight. Besides, it's too late now. My wife is just going to put out the lights.'

He had hardly finished speaking before all the lights went out.

'Now,' came Seraphim's voice, with a laugh, 'which of you can I catch
first?'

The laugh sounded just like the sound they had heard over the telephone. The children started to run.

It was very late when, after digging through many snowdrifts, Matthew
and Julia reached Stilburn. Dinner was over and, in the large hall, lit
by shaded lights, some people were playing cards and others sitting round
the blazing fire. Rupert Engleby came up and greeted them with warmth
and some relief.

'Well done! I rang up to hear if you were coming, but the line must
be down in your part of the country. I couldn't get a ringing sound. You
must be in a dreadful state. There's food waiting for you, but what would
you like to start with? Hot whisky toddy? Ordinary whisky? I'll get some.'

'You'll stay the night with us, of course,' said his wife, who had risen
from the card-table. 'What about the children? Is Mrs Dodson with
them? She'll be able to cope.'

'She'll have to,' said their host, coming up with the whisky. 'You
couldn't possibly get back in this weather.'

Matthew took his glass and drank gratefully and deep. 'As it happened,
the Durnesses, some friends of ours, turned up unexpectedly and are
spending the night. So Mrs Dodson is all right.'

'Is that Lord Durness?' came a voice from one of the card-players, a
stout, very clean-looking man in a green smoking-jacket. Matthew
thought he recognized in him one of their heavier Derkshire neighbours:
a Dodson of The Deane, perhaps, or one of the spurious Drinkbottles.

'Yes, do you know him?'

'I met him in Bolivia last year. An extraordinary fellow. He was living
with a native woman.'

'He seems to have married her. She's with him now.'

'Better him than me. She struck me as a most unattractive lady, and
she had a very queer reputation.'

'Really?' asked Julia. 'What for?'

'You'd never believe it. When I was staying in Cochabamba, the Chief
of Police – who I found a very decent fellow, whatever some people may
say – there's a lot of nonsense gets into the English papers about the
Bolivian police . . .' The spurious Drinkbottle looked round aggressively
to see if anyone would dispute this.

'Go on,' said Matthew. 'What sort of reputation?'

'As I was saying, the Chief of Police told me that one of the chief
troubles they have in the mountain villages is vampirism.'

There was some mirth at this, and the speaker flushed.

'You may laugh, but I can tell you it's no joke to the villagers to have
their children disappearing. Anyhow, this woman was suspected of

having inclinations that way. I dare say there was nothing in it. But if I'd been Durness, I shouldn't have cared to let her get her teeth into me. Ha, ha.'

This time the laughter was confined to the spurious Drinkbottle. It was thought that the joke, though harmless, was a little ill-timed.

Shona and the Water Horse

R. Chetwynd-Hayes

He came down from the moors, a tall lean man with the face of a fallen angel and the haunted look of one who has seen much and forgotten little. It was somewhere between Glenmoriston and Glen Affric that he came upon the little village; a mere huddle of white cottages that clustered round the kirk like a litter of puppies nuzzling the flanks of their mother. He made straight for the manse, a tall, ugly building, with two windows up and two down, with a green door dead centre and an untidy front garden that had not felt the spade or fork for many a year. He hammered on the door with clenched fist, then stood waiting, his eyes fixed on the green panels with a strange intense stare, then when the sould of approaching footsteps told him his summons was about to be answered, looked quickly back over one shoulder at the desolate moorlands.

The door opened and a young girl stood in the opening. She may have been twenty, perhaps younger, with the white skin of a seal-maiden, full moist lips, and black hair that framed her face like a storm-cloud round a mountain peak; large dark eyes surveyed the stranger with cool insolence.

'Well – what is it ye're wanting?'

A hint of the Highland brogue, but education had filed down the consonants to an attractive lilt.

'The minister – I must see him.'

The dark eyes swept down the tall figure, took in at one glance the long, lean, suntanned face, the green jacket to which bits of dried grass clung like cobwebs to a cellar wall, the worn corduroy trousers, the cracked boots.

'Do you suppose his Reverence has nothing better to do than see the likes of you?'

He did not smile, but for a moment the cold grey eyes were lit by a gleam of amusement, then it went, and the girl, despite her self-confidence, involuntarily shuddered.

'A shepherd with such a small flock will find the time.'

'Indeed! And who shall I say has done us the honour of calling?'

'The Water Horse.'

'The – what?'

She began to giggle, then something about the stern, handsome face, the unblinking eyes, made her stop.

'Tell him the Water Horse has words he wishes to speak.'

'Well . . .' She stood reluctantly to one side. 'You had better come in.'

He stood in the small hall and waited while the girl entered a room on the left, closing the door behind her. The murmur of voices came to him, one harsh, impatient, then the girl's, soft, pouring appeasing oil on threatening troubled waters. Presently the door opened and she reappeared, a mischievous smile playing round her lips.

'My father will see you for a few minutes.'

He brushed by her and entered the little room. It smelled of damp, stale tobacco smoke and old books. A little bald-headed man glared up at him from behind a giant desk, then waved a short-fingered hand in the direction of an old padded arm-chair.

'Sit ye down, man. Sit ye down. From what ma daughter tells me, ye're either a madman or a fool, and as I haven't the time to waste on either, say your piece, or be off.'

The stranger lowered his length into the chair, then folded his hands neatly on his flat stomach. A thick, white down covered the backs of his hands, and the minister noticed this peculiarity and frowned.

'Now, who are ye, and what is it you want?'

'I am the Water Horse.'

The minister nodded slowly. 'So you know your Scottish mythology. As I recall there was a Donald MacGregor who had a daughter named Morag, and she found a handsome stranger by the lochside, and being a loose lassie, she put his head on her lap and began to comb his thick black hair.'

It was the stranger's turn to nod.

'And in her comb were fine green strands of weed and grains of silt, and terror entered her soul, for she knew it was the dreaded Water Horse.' The minister smiled grimly. 'A likely tale constructed to keep her father's belt around his waist, but not one likely to find much credence with an educated man life meself.'

'So, you are an educated man, Angus Buchanan.' Again a hint of amusement lit the stranger's eyes. 'You have learnt one set of fables by heart, but deliberately ignored all others. But it is of little consequence to me what you believe. I am the Water Horse.'

'Ye're soft in the head, man.' The Reverend Buchanan leant forward. 'Are you telling me you can change into – what is it? A great black stallion that gallops across the moor on a moonlit night. Aye? Is that what you claim?'

'I cannot cross running water,' the stranger admitted.

'How do you manage then, when you go down into the loch?'

'The waters are still, cool as a maiden's hands, and it is quiet with the great peace, and one can dream away the centuries.'

'Ye're as crazed as a cracked jug, and I'll waste no more time with ye. So get about your business, whatever that might be.'

'But you haven't heard what I have to tell you.'

'Nor do I want to.'

'But you'll hear all the same.'

He rose to his full height and appeared to fill the small room; the Reverend Buchanan looked up and for the first time a flicker of fear made him fall back in his chair. The stranger placed both his hands on the desk and leant forward; the clergyman saw at close quarters the flat planes of his cheeks, the delicate bones, the dark, sinister, handsome face.

'I have come to tell you the devil walks the moor again, and he's looking for a tit-bit to blunt the keen edge of his appetite.'

'The devil!' The clergyman drew out the word 'devil-l-l' as though it had a sweet flavour and he wanted to savour its taste for as long as possible.

'Aye.' The tall figure became upright, and a set of magnificent teeth were bared in a mirthless grin. 'Your old adversary, or a very close relative, or maybe not. Perhaps he is born of men's fears, the outcome of the evil they secretly desire. But he is real enough, and he wants your village; the old, the young, the good, the bad, the blackness, the grey, the white.'

'The devil coming for the village!' Angus Buchanan whispered the words, then he looked up and a sly smile parted his lips. 'But if you are who you say you are, sure you are one of his minions. I seem to remember the Water Horse has two black horns on the top of his black head.'

'I but pluck a single fruit when the desire is on me,' the tall man said quietly, 'but He would consume the entire orchard, trees and all.'

'And what would you have me do?' the minister asked.

'Bolt your doors at sunset and paint a white cross on each panel. Above all, let no one go out on to the moors after nightfall.'

'I canna do it, man.' Mr Buchanan crashed his clenched fist down upon the desk. 'I cannot pamper to superstitious nonsense. This is the twentieth century, not the dark ages, and I'll not make a fool of meself to please a crack-brained stranger, who I'm thinking ought to be locked awa' for his own good.'

'Then you are a fool.' The tall man's face was now harsh, and his eyes blazed with a terrible anger. 'I tell you He will be here before sunset, and you will not know who He is. A traveller begging a bed for the night, a bonny boy with golden hair and laughing eyes, an old woman, a comely maiden, a Stray dog – anyone, anything could be He.'

'I've listened long enough to your blasphemous nonsense.' The clergyman also rose, pushed back his chair and glared at his unwelcome visitor. 'You'll be getting me as crazed as yourself, so awa' with ye.'

'It's the truth I'm telling you.' The stranger's voice rose to a shout. 'The plain truth that is staring you in the face, but you are blinded by ignorance, deafened by stupidity.'

'Get out. I'll no be shouted at and insulted in me own hoose, so out with ye.'

The tall man nodded slowly. 'So be it. I have warned, why I do not know, but hear this. Before the sun rises again, you and all who live in this place will take the long walk, and the black hounds will shepherd you into the shadows.'

He strode to the door, opened it, then walked silently across the hall. At the front door he turned suddenly and saw the girl watching him from the kitchen doorway.

'You are called Shona.' It was a statement of fact, not a question.

She nodded. 'How do you come to know my name?'

'I know. You are one apple He shall not pluck. I will come for you.'

After a while Shona moved slowly to the doorway and stood watching the tall figure as it retreated along the dusty road; her eyes were soft pools of dark wonder, then she raised her voice and called after him.

'You need not bother, I'll no come with you.'

He did not turn his head or give the slightest indication that he had heard her. After a few minutes Shona closed the door and stood with her back leaning against it.

'Sweet God,' she whispered, 'I'll not go with him. I'll not go.'

Night had spread her black mantle across the moors when the Reverend Angus Buchanan sat down to dinner.

'Oh, Lord, we thank you for the food thou hast seen fit to place before us, for which we are truly thankful. Amen.'

Shona repeated, 'Amen', then watched her father take up his knife and fork.

'Father. What did he want?'

'Who?' The minister helped himself to some more boiled beef.

'The man. The tall man.'

Mr Buchanan grunted.

'He was a poor mad creature, thinks he's a Water Horse of all things. Came to tell me the devil's loose on the moors and is coming to eat up the entire village or some such nonsense.'

'The devil loose on the moors?' The girl looked fearfully at the un-curtained windows behind which swirls of mists were wandering like unformed ghosts. 'Do you think he could be?'

'The devil is everywhere,' the parson snapped, 'but not as some horned monster skulking in the heather. Don't ask fool questions.'

'I don't mean the bible devil, but this land has seen so much violence, so much horror spread down over the centuries. Every glen has known the shriek of the murdered, the screams of the ravaged; could not something – someone – have built up over the years? Perhaps in the beginning it might have been a relic of some past race, a different form of life as we know it, a skeleton that is now fleshed with the – excrement of the human mind. That would be the devil, would it not, Father?'

'I'll not have that kind of talk at ma table,' Mr Buchanan roared. 'What's come over you, girl? You sound like that poor mad fool this afternoon. I'm fair ashamed of you, that I am.'

'He said he was the Water Horse,' the girl said softly.

'Aye, and next week he'll say he's Napoleon.'

'Perhaps the Water Horse is a myth founded on fact. There's more water on earth than there is dry land, and I've often wondered why intelligent life did not come from it.'

'Because God in his wisdom decided otherwise,' Mr Buchanan commented dryly. 'Now, if you've finished trying to drive me mad with ye heathen talk, I'll ring for the pudding.'

He rang a little brass cow-bell that stood near to hand, and, almost at once, Flora, a large, raw-boned woman, entered bearing a steaming apple pudding on a silver tray. She placed it before the minister who sniffed appreciatively, then frowned.

'You've forgotten the custard.'

Flora folded her arms.

'I no forget it. The milk curdled. Fresh this morning it was, straight from MacEachern's cow, and now it's only fit to make cheese, which I've no mind to do.'

'But an apple pudding without custard is like a mother without bairns,' the minister complained. 'The milk couldn't have been fresh.'

'I'm telling ye the milk was as fresh as a daisy on a May morning. Ye'll have to eat it the way it was made and that's all there is to it. By-the-by, there's a woman by the kitchen door who wants to know if she can sleep here the night. I said I'd ask ye, and I have.'

'This is not an inn,' Mr Buchanan stated.

'And if it was she'd not have the money to pay, I'm thinking. A poor, starved body by the look of her, a gypo most likely; she'll be content with a blanket in the barn.'

'She seeks ma hospitality,' Mr Buchanan stressed his point by tapping a forefinger on the table, 'and no guest of mine sleeps in the barn. Make up a bed in the room over the stables. It's warm and dry up there, and see the poor soul gets something hot inside her.'

Shona got up and put on her outdoor coat which had been lying on a nearby chair; the minister looked at her with rising indignation.

'And where are you going? Sit down and eat your pudding.'

'I promised to drop in on Sara Edgemont. She's that poorly, and I thought I'd clear up for her, and maybe cook a bit of a meal.'

'She can wait till you've eaten your pudding.'

'I couldn't, Father, honestly. I'm full up.'

She made her escape, ignoring Mr Buchanan's roar of rage, and Flora shrugged while she removed the used plates.

'One word from you and that lassie does as she pleases.'

'Mind ye business, woman,' Mr Buchanan glared at his housekeeper, 'At least she concerns herself with good works, and no gads about like some I could mention.'

'Fat chance she'd have in this forsaken place. It's no wonder the young folk break the apronstrings and are awa' so soon as they're of age.'

When Flora had left the room, the minister laid down his fork and spoon, rose and went over to his armchair, where he sat staring pensively into the fire. Somewhere a dog began to howl, a mournful cry, as though some lost soul were being tormented in a mist-shrouded hell. Mr Buchanan shivered, then leant forward and poked the fire; the flames leapt up, made shadows dance a mad reel across the walls and ceiling, were reflected in the window panes, and the minister found himself looking back over one shoulder.

'Ma nerves,' he muttered. 'I'm getting old.'

He got up and, walking over to his desk, took up his large, black-bound bible, then returned to his chair and opened the volume at the Book of Revelation. He read aloud as was his custom.

'And there was war in heaven: Michael and his angels fought against the dragon; and the dragon fought and his angels.

And prevailed not; nether was their place found any more in heaven.

And the great dragon was cast out, that old serpent called the devil, and Satan, which deceiveth the whole world; he was cast out into the earth, and his angels were cast out with him.'

The Reverend Angus Buchanan closed his bible, then resumed his study of the fire; the dog howled again, and now the cry was taken up by another, and the minister started when the door opened and Shona entered.

'For heaven's sake, lassie, you fair made me jump out of ma skin, creeping in like that. You haven't been long. How is Mrs Edgemont?'

Shona did not answer, but seated herself on a chair opposite and stared at him with bright eyes. Her white skin was paler than usual, and her black hair was beaded with moisture; the full red lips were parted and the smile appeared to have been etched into her face, suggesting some secret knowledge that only she knew. The minister frowned.

'Have you lost your tongue, girl? I asked you, how did you find Mrs Edgemont, and why are you back so early? I thought you were going to cook her a meal.'

She continued to sit perfectly still, but the smile had now taken on a faintly mocking aspect. The fire flared up, then gradually died down until there was only a mass of glowing embers; the minister became aware of an increasing coldness, and he shivered. Outside there was now a growing chorus of howling dogs.

'The fire,' he muttered. 'It's no drawing as it should, and the cold is getting into ma bones.' He seized the poker and stirred the embers; a few solitary sparks shot up the chimney, but the fire still refused to blaze.

'Let me feed it.'

Her voice was only an octave above a whisper, but the minister jerked his head round as though stung by a wasp; the smile was now blatantly mocking, and a hitherto unknown dread made him tremble.

'What do you mean, lassie?'

She rose in one graceful movement, and it seemed that she had suddenly grown lascivious; her dress was strangely loose and appeared reluctant to cover the curves of her breasts. As she moved it slid off one shoulder, and her eyes were now black with an eerie intelligence.

'Give me the – book.'

The night was hideous with the howling of dogs, and wisps of mist were seeping in round the edge of the window; Shona's smile was now a grimace.

'Give me the book.'

She laid one white hand upon the bible, and for a brief second her little finger touched his wrist. A blast of burning ice ran up his arm, his grip slackened and instantly she snatched the bible and tossed it on to the fire. He was so paralysed with terror he could only watch the flames as they licked the tooled leather, then turned the gilt-edged pages first brown, then black.

'You're mad, girl. Mad.'

She laughed. A full, raucous, bellowing laugh, a sound that was not natural to that slender throat, then spinning round on one heel she performed an obscene dance, and her shadow, brought into being by the blazing bible, caracoled across the opposite wall and over the ceiling. Gradually the dance grew more wild; her dress was high up above her waist, and the speechless clergyman saw white thighs, breasts that had escaped from their confinement. Then she suddenly stopped and froze the minister to his chair with a burning stare.

'Who am I, old man? The Incarnate himself? Or a sick dream created by the frustrated desires of a lifetime? Or am I your daughter revealing her true face?'

Mr Buchanan tried to speak before unconsciousness claimed him and he sank into a black pit of unawareness.

'Father. Father.'

Shona was bending over him, a basin was on the table by her side, and a damp cloth was lying on his forehead.

'Father, what is wrong? I couldn't wake you when I came in. Flora,' she said, turning to the housekeeper, 'why is he looking at me like that? Why doesn't he speak?'

'I dinna know, and I don't like the look of him.' Flora shook her head. 'I'm thinking we ought to fetch the doctor.'

'But he was all right when I left, just a little peeved because I went out before eating the pudding.'

She laid her hand on the minister's shoulder, and the effect was terrifying. He twisted wildly as though he had been touched with a hot iron, and his eyes blazed with a light that could have been caused by either anger or fear. He tried to speak, but only succeeded in making a strange hoarse sound that had a ducklike quality, and with his left hand he pushed the girl away so that she fell against the table, upsetting the basin.

'I'll fetch the doctor,' Flora said, backing away while watching the clergyman vainly attempt to rise. 'I dinna like this at all.'

'But what's wrong with him?' Shona was near tears. 'Why does he keep looking at me like that?'

'I canna tell. Perhaps his poor brain is crazed, though more likely he's had a stroke. But one thing's for sure, he canna stand the sight of you.'

Flora fled, and the sound of her retreating footsteps was the rout of sanity. Shona approached the figure that sprawled in the familiar arm-chair and stretched out her hand; the figure writhed, emitted a strangled scream, and Shona withdrew, walking backwards with both hands clasped to trembling lips.

Dr Ross was a short, red-haired man with matching face and bristling moustache. He bustled into the room, dumped his black bag on the table, then sank down on one knee beside the prostrate clergyman.

'What ails you, man, eh? You so hale and hearty, you boast you niver need me services.'

Mr Buchanan made another raucous sound and moved his left hand in the direction of Shona, who gasped as though she had been hit. Doctor Ross frowned.

'There's no need to frighten the lass, she bonny and dutiful as ye weel know. Can ye understand what I am saying?'

Mr Buchanan nodded.

'Then listen carefully. Ye've had a wee stroke, but with rest ye should be as right as rain. Flora and I will make ye up a bed on yon sofa, and Shona, like the good lass she is, will minister to ye. So let's have no more nonsense, or I'll give ye the rough edge of ma tongue.'

The sick man began to jerk his head from side to side, then in an effort to stress his wishes, pointed a trembling finger at Shona. Doctor Ross looked back at her, an expression of growing suspicion on his face.

'Is there aught I should know, Shona?'

'No.' She shook her head. 'I don't understand. When I left him to visit Mrs Edgemont he was finishing his dinner, then when I came back he was like this.'

'You were at Sara Edgemont's all the time? You niver came out and did something that ye Father may have seen?'

'No, I swear. Sara will back me up.'

'Weel, tha's something bothering him, that's for sure. You'd better keep out of his sight till he's more himself. Flora will help me.'

Shona wandered miserably out into the kitchen, where, prompted by some half-formed wish to be of use, she filled the kettle and placed in on the black-iron range, then went over to a cupboard and took out a brown earthenware teapot. The woman was seated by the window, quietly watching her. Shona gave a little cry.

'Who are you?'

'A guest.'

'Oh!' Shona pushed back a strand of hair from her forehead. 'You are the woman that Father said could spend the night in the stable room.'

'I am.' The woman looked up, smiling, her face thin, with a pointed chin and beautiful, slanting green eyes. She had a mass of red hair; so brightly did it shine, Shona thought it looked like red-gold. She said wearily: 'You look so thin.'

'I never get enough to eat.'

'I'm sorry.' Shona looked around with an helpless air. 'Flora should have given you something, but my father has been taken ill, and ...'

'She fed me,' said the woman, 'but not with the food I hunger for.' She got up and moved across the kitchen; her walk was a kind of flowing movement, rather like a snake that has sighted a succulent prey, and her long tapering hands were never still, constantly smoothing the bedraggled dress, fingering any object that came within their grasp: a cup, a knife, eventually Shona herself. The girl involuntarily shrank back when the soft, cold finger caressed her arm, and pleaded plaintively:

'Please don't.'

'But you have such smooth white skin.' The green eyes were but a few inches from her own, and the voice was low, vibrant, stirring up thoughts, desires, that up to then Shona did not realize existed. 'Smooth as a seal-maiden that has played in the waters of some northern sea and has only flirted with the sun. Do you dream, child? You should. Dream of a throne of ice, dream of a star-diamond necklace around your neck, and a moon-ring on your finger, and a laurel of sea-lilies kissing your black hair.'

'Please stop.' Shona pulled her arm free and put the kitchen table between her and the red-haired woman. 'Who are you? What do you want?'

The woman leant against the wall and smiled so very gently.

'For the first – I am known by many names, but for the present you may call me Heandshe!'

'Heandshe!' Shona repeated.

'Yes, I think that describes my present position very neatly. As for the second – I want your white soul.'

'You must be mad,' Shona whispered.

'Who isn't? Madness is a delightful form of sanity. What else would I want but your soul. It will make a pretty plaything. There can be no argument. I must have your soul.'

Flora bustled into the kitchen; she now wore the air of one who has to deal with an exciting crisis, and she brushed Shona aside with an impatient wave of her arm.

'Out of me way, I've got me hands full what with ye poor fether the way he is, and the doctor demanding hot water to make hot compresses or some sich thing.'

'How is he?' Shona asked.

'He seems to be asleep, which should do him a power of good, and I'm going to make meself up a bed next to his in case he needs anything.'

'Can't I help?' Shona pleaded.

'The doctor says you're not to go near him in his present state, and it's best you don't. Now, now, don't carry on so.'

She clasped the sobbing girl in her powerful arms, patting her awkwardly on one shoulder; then suddenly her face was transformed by a ferocious scowl.

'What are you grinning at, you brazen hizzy?'

The red-haired woman sauntered across the room, her hips swinging, a sly smile parting her lips.

'I was thinking – a gazelle in the arms of a she-bear.'

'Awa' with ye to the stables where you belong. I'll no have ye in ma kitchen. And be gone before daybreak or I'll have the law on ye for trespassing.'

'She frightens me,' Shona whispered once the woman had gone. 'Flora, is it true the devil can take any shape?'

'I would'na know, lassie, but if what the old folk say be true, he could. Aye, he could.'

'The Water Horse told Father he was loose on the moors.'

'The Water Horse? I've niver heard sich nonsense.'

'He was tall, with the face of a fallen angel, and Father said he was mad.' Shona sighed and walked over to the window. 'Look how thick the mist has become, I can scarce see across the road. They say the ghosts of Prince Charlie's men go marching across the moors when the mist is thick, and the Grey Dog of Morar goes hunting for lost travellers.' She turned suddenly, her eyes black pools of terror. 'Flora, the devil is in the village . . .'

'Now, now, child, you're upset, and who's to wonder, what with your father struck down, and that gypo woman frightening ye? Why not go to your room and try to sleep? I'll wake you if anything happens.'

'How can I sleep?' She hugged her elbows and bowed her shoulders as though in pain. 'Listen, the dogs have started to howl again. I can understand why old wives say a howling dog foretells a death. It is the most mournful sound under God's sky.'

' 'Tis the mist,' Flora said, 'they canna see clearly, then one starts barking and sets the other off. Come awa' from the window, then go and lie yourself down.'

'I will.' Shona began to walk towards the kitchen door then, when she had reached the table, suddenly stopped. 'You know what I really wish, Flora?'

'No.'

'I wish – I wish I could believe in the Water Horse.'

'But he is a fearsome Kelpie, and he only takes fair form so as to lure honest folk to their doom. You wouldn't want any truck with a great beastie like that.'

'But he wouldn't harm me, Flora. I know he wouldn't. He said he would come back for me.'

'Aye, they all say that.' Flora began to shepherd her out of the kitchen and up the steep stairs. 'You rest yourself and forget all about Water Horses and men that will no come back. They niver do. All the bonny men I've known all said they'd come back, but they didna – na a one.'

She made the girl lie down on her narrow bed, and after removing her shoes, covered her with a blue counterpane, then leant over and kissed the white forehead.

'You should be among bright lights and young folk, not here. The old can be selfish, but the good Lord sees all. Many a curse is a blessing in disguise.'

She crept from the room leaving a small night-light burning by Shona's bed, and the girl lay watching it, deriving a childlike comfort from the tiny flame. The dogs had ceased to howl, but now and again, not far away she heard the deep bay of a hound, and smiled, remembering the legend of the Morar Dog. Then sleep crept up unawares and a dream came into being.

The great black stallion came up from the loch; water streamed from his sable hair, and she saw the two black horns that grew up from the top of his head. She felt no fear as he advanced towards her, rather there was a throbbing joy when he bent his dark head so that she could caress his soft mane.

'I will come for you,' he said, 'and we will dream together beneath the loch.'

Suddenly Shona found herself astride the broad back, clinging with both hands to the black mane, and the wind was singing a wild song as it tried to keep up with them, and all around, from the racing ground to the starlit heavens, came the thudding roar of the Water Horse's pounding hoofs. Louder and louder it grew until the moor shook and the stars trembled against the blue-black sky, and fear rode in on the singing wind.

'The village!' she screamed. 'The village will fall!'

She sat up and the thudding sound was still in her ears, the night-light was trembling, the window shook like some caged thing trying to break free, then with a crash the casements burst open and the milk-white mists poured in. The thudding became a continuous roar, the house shook, a shower of plaster fell from the ceiling, while from beyond the gaping window she could hear the fall of masonry and a rising chorus of screams. She slid from her bed and stumbled to the door; then came a nightmare journey down the trembling stairs, the woodwork emitting a series of protesting groans. They held out until she reached the hall, then collapsed with one last despairing shriek, and Shona saw Flora dragging Mr Buchanan through the study doorway. The floor shook again and Shona had one glimpse of the old man's face; his head was bent backwards between Flora's straddled legs, and his eyes glared their fear and anger as she crouched on the heaving floor. She cried out: 'Father – Father ...' Then the walls caved in, the roof came down and for a while there was only a blessed forgetfulness.

Shona came out into what had been the single, dusty road and looked about her with wide-eyed horror. Every house was a heap of rubble; flames were growing up from some of the ruins like scarlet flowers on the graves of the damned; the wind was singing a dirge as it plucked at her dirt-grimed dress, as though trying to pull her away from this Golgotha. The mist had gone, a great yellow moon gazed down in cold disdain, the stars twinkled like diamonds on black velvet, then the wind finished its song and departed with a final sigh. The ruined village, the surrounding moors, the distant hills, all, save for the crackling flames, were still, silent, eternal. Shona walked to the village boundary; far away, but quite distinct in the bright moonlight, she saw a long file of figures limping with bowed heads towards the horizon. Great black hounds were prowling back and forth on either side, and it seemed she could see a tall woman leading a little old man by the hand, but try as she could Shona felt no grief, no regret.

There was the sound of approaching footsteps and the red-haired woman was walking daintily along the village street, carefully stepping over debris, looking to neither right or left, and as she walked she discarded her tattered dress, reached up and tossed aside the red-gold hair, and it was a tall, slim young man, clad in a black satin suit, who stopped a few feet from the white-skinned girl.

'Ah!' he said softly, 'the stray lamb.'

His hair was as black as a starless night, his eyes were polished emeralds, and his beauty was that of a snake. He laughed softly, and Shona thought of green poison gurgling in tall glasses.

'You may call me "He" now. I am all things to all people.'

'Why did you do it?' she asked.

'You mean – this?' He glanced around the devastated village. 'Had to – no reason – just had to. A mere earth subsidence. They will talk about it for years, and long-haired men with spectacles will explain it away in a single hour. The opposition will get the credit. An act of God.'

'And me?'

'Ah!' He smiled, and his white teeth gleamed like ivory set in pink coral. 'I promised you a throne of ice, and a star diamond, and yes, a moon-ring for your finger. I have never been known to break my word, though I do bend it sometimes.'

He drew closer, placed his arms around her body, and the dust-grimed dress floated away like a leaf falling from a white flower. His mouth was the universe, his eyes eternity, and his lips the doorway to hell. She gave one loud cry.

'Water Horse!'

He released her and laughed.

'The galloping hero, I had forgotten him. Now, where can he be?'

'Here.' The Water Horse stood but a few feet away, still dressed in his green jacket and corduroy trousers. His face was expressionless.

'Ha! An ex-employee. An absconded servant, a dream made from superstition and fear. Is this what you want?'

Shona did not answer, and the Water Horse spoke.

'This is one apple you will not pick.'

He backed away a few steps, and His green eyes were slits of emerald fire.

'I draw my strength from earth, fire and brutality. Would you dare?'

The Water Horse raised his hands.

'My strength comes from the wind and still water. Neither will break. I dare.'

They began to circle each other, both with hands outstretched, fingers curved, moving slowly at first, each one looking for an opening in his adversary's guard before attacking. Then He sprang; a streak of black-ness, and the two figures were locked; hands clawed at throats, bared teeth gleamed white in the moonlight, and the night was hideous with their guttural screams. Shona turned her head away and saw that the burning ruins were now so many heaps of glowing embers; every brick, stone, beam, was bright red, and little spirals of smoke drifted up to the blue-black sky. The two monstrous shadows began to dance across the blackened ground, two great slabs that came together, twisted, parted, elongated, then became squat blobs of pure horror. Shona turned her head and screamed.

He had now a towering giant, all of twelve feet tall; a black face with slanting green eyes, red tapering ears, black curls from which sprouted two red horns. His body was covered with green scales, as also was the thick lashing tail, and His long, red talons were trying to slash his adversary's face. This was how man had always imagined Him; the epitome of horror, the essence of evil, the primeval skeleton fleshed with excrement of the human mind, the great dragon that the gods had thrown out.

And the Water Horse? He was as Shona had dreamed. A mighty black stallion, his sable coat gleaming like the loch in moonlight, his eyes grey mists veiling twin suns, his forelock a figure of white hair that could have well been plucked from the beard of Odin. He reared up on his hindlegs and crashed his hoofs into the face of He – the Incarnate, the Fallen One, the Morning Star; and the Great Dragon fell, twisted over, then leapt on to the black, gleaming back. His taloned feet dug into the heaving flanks, his hands gripped the strong, graceful neck, and with a scream the Water Horse crashed to the ground, then rolled over in an effort to dislodge the fiend on his back. Then he twisted his neck and Shona watched the great teeth sink into the green scaled neck. The Incarnate screamed, a dreadful rasping sound that rang out across the moor, causing grey shadows to go floating over the heather. As the teeth sank deeper, and blood flowed down over the heaving torso, the scream grew fainter, the hideous figure became thinner, and presently the Water Horse released a green and red flecked snake. It writhed into the heather and disappeared from view.

The Water Horse stood for a little while, trembling, drawing great gulps of air through its flaring nostrils, bright red streaks marring the beauty of its sable coat. Then it pawed the ground and gave vent to one mighty roar of triumph. Shona walked very slowly towards him, still a little fearful, but he was as motionless as a great shadow, and her white body stood out against his blackness like a slab of moonlight in a darkened room.

'Let me come with you, Water Horse,' she whispered.

He did not move, and she timidly stroked his head, then her hand went up, gripped his black mane, and in one graceful movement she swung up on to the broad, gleaming back.

The pounding hoofs made the earth tremble, the wind resumed its mad song, the ghosts of the long dead drifted like thistledown across the moor, and the loch shone like a silver tray a little way ahead.

'Oh, Sweet God,' Shona cried, 'what is reality? Who are the dead?'

Man Overboard

Sir Winston Churchill

It was a little after half-past nine when the man fell overboard. The mail steamer was hurrying through the Red Sea in the hope of making up the time which the currents of the Indian Ocean had stolen.

The night was clear, though the moon was hidden behind clouds. The warm air was laden with moisture. The still surface of the waters was only broken by the movement of the great ship, from whose quarter the long, slanting undulations struck out like the feathers from an arrow shaft, and in whose wake the froth and air bubbles churned up by the propeller trailed in a narrowing line to the darkness of the horizon.

There was a concert on board. All the passengers were glad to break the monotony of the voyage and gathered around the piano in the companion-house. The decks were deserted. The man had been listening to the music and joining in the songs, but the room was hot and he came out to smoke a cigarette and enjoy a breath of the wind which the speedy passage of the liner created. It was the only wind in the Red Sea that night.

The accommodation-ladder had not been unshipped since leaving Aden and the man walked out on to the platform, as on to a balcony. He leaned his back against the rail and blew a puff of smoke into the air reflectively. The piano struck up a lively tune and a voice began to sing the first verse of 'The Rowdy Dowdy Boys'. The measured pulsations of the screw were a subdued but additional accompaniment. The man knew the song, it had been the rage at all the music halls when he had started for India seven years before. It reminded him of the brilliant and busy streets he had not seen for so long, but was soon to see again. He was just going to join in the chorus when the railing, which had been insecurely fastened, gave way suddenly with a snap and he fell backwards into the warm water of the sea amid a great splash.

For a moment he was physically too much astonished to think. Then he realized he must shout. He began to do this even before he rose to the surface. He achieved a hoarse, inarticulate, half-choked scream. A startled brain suggested the word, 'Help!' and he bawled this out lustily and with frantic effort six or seven times without stopping. Then he listened.

> 'Hi! hi! clear the way
> For the Rowdy Dowdy Boys.'

The chorus floated back to him across the smooth water for the ship had already completely passed by. And as he heard the music a long stab of terror drove through his heart. The possibility that he would not be picked up dawned for the first time on his consciousness. The chorus started again:

> 'Then – I – say – boys,
> Who's for a jolly spree?
> Rum – tum – tiddley – um,
> Who'll have a drink with me?'

'Help! Help! Help!' shrieked the man, now in desperate fear.

> 'Fond of a glass now and then,
> Fond of a row or noise;
> Hi! hi! clear the way
> For the Rowdy Dowdy Boys!'

The last words drawled out fainter and fainter. The vessel was steaming fast. The beginning of the second verse was confused and broken by the ever-growing distance. The dark outline of the great hull was getting blurred. The stern light dwindled.

Then he set out to swim after it with furious energy, pausing every dozen strokes to shout long wild shouts. The disturbed waters of the sea began to settle again to their rest and the widening undulations became ripples. The aerated confusion of the screw fizzed itself upwards and out. The noise of motion and the sounds of life and music died away.

The liner was but a single fading light on the blackness of the waters and a dark shadow against the paler sky.

At length full realization came to the man and he stopped swimming. He was alone – abandoned. With the understanding the brain reeled. He began again to swim, only now instead of shouting he prayed – mad, incoherent prayers, the words stumbling into one another.

Suddenly a distant light seemed to flicker and brighten.

A surge of joy and hope rushed through his mind. They were going to stop – to turn the ship and come back. And with the hope came gratitude. His prayer was answered. Broken words of thanksgiving rose to his lips. He stopped and stared after the light – his soul in his eyes. As he watched it, it grew gradually smaller. Then the man knew that his fate was certain. Despair succeeded hope; gratitude gave place to curses. Beating the water with his arms, he raved impotently. Foul oaths burst from him, as broken as his prayers – and as unheeded.

The fit of passion passed, hurried by increasing fatigue. He became silent – silent as was the sea, for even the ripples were subsiding into the glassy smoothness of the surface. He swam on mechanically along the track of the ship, sobbing quietly to himself in the misery of fear. And the stern light became a tiny speck, yellower but scarcely bigger than some of the stars, which here and there shone between the clouds.

Nearly twenty minutes passed and the man's fatigue began to change to exhaustion. The overpowering sense of the inevitable pressed upon him. With the weariness came a strange comfort – he need not swim all the long way to Suez. There was another course. He would die. He would resign his existence since he was thus abandoned. He threw up his hands impulsively and sank.

Down, down he went through the warm water. The physical death took hold of him and he began to drown. The pain of that savage grip recalled his anger. He fought with it furiously. Striking out with arms and legs he sought to get back to the air. It was a hard struggle, but he escaped victorious and gasping to the surface. Despair awaited him. Feebly splashing with his hands, he moaned in bitter misery:

'I can't – I must. O God! Let me die.'

The moon, then in her third quarter, pushed out from behind the concealing clouds and shed a pale, soft glitter upon the sea. Upright in the water, fifty yards away, was a black triangular object. It was a fin. It approached him slowly.

His last appeal had been heard.

Superstitious Ignorance

Michael Cornish

Edward tapped his gloved fingers on the leather-covered steering wheel. He stared through the glistening windscreen at the sheen on the bonnet; then at the square houses running away in the half-darkness of the seedy street beyond.

The squat bonnet gleamed with 20th-century superiority over the peeled and grimy façades of the 18th-century villas to either side of the street. Their decayed façades were too ingrained with grime to benefit from the charm of the gaslight – the original Victorian gas lights had survived in that area – which was usually as flattering to such architecture as night club light to female complexions.

'Georgian, I'd say,' Edward said. 'Definitely Georgian.'

His wife Penny stirred beside him in the passenger seat. The big collar of her fawn cashmere coat was turned up, and it pushed out her honey blonde hair a little, but attractively nevertheless. Looking attractive was quite natural to her, and not something studied. The coat, which she had been able to buy at a knock-down price from the people she'd modelled it for, looked marvellous against the black leather upholstery of the Mini-Cooper.

'Yes,' Penny said. 'But my God, look at it.'

'Oh, do try to use your imagination, darling,' Edward said excitedly. 'Just think. A detached Georgian house with a large garden at the back. Eight big rooms and hall. Think of what we could make of it.'

Penny pulled her coat tightly about her, which he resented a little because there was an excellent heater in the car, and until he recognized that it was an instinctive defensive measure against coming to this down-at-heel area at all.

He knew very well in his heart she'd be happy to spend all her life in flats in Chelsea frittering away their modest lump of capital, and that it was only her determination to 'be a good wife' that had steeled her to coming with him in the first place.

'I didn't like that estate agent, darling,' Penny said nervously. 'He did seem so – well, so *shifty*. And vague too. And such a seedy little office.'

Edward laughed indulgently. It made him both exasperated and affectionate to remember that she was still a sucker for any smart exterior, though he'd been quietly trying to open her eyes to the real world for all of the eighteen months he'd known her.

'Oh, come now, Penny my love. He was quite a nice man really. Quite a fine sense of humour if you listened for it. Did you hear how he described negotiating with the little people who own property in this area? "Like dealing with a tankful of eels," he said.'

He saw she wasn't ready to be cajoled out of her nervousness and put his arm round her.

'Now, darling. Just this one house tonight – it shouldn't take more than half an hour – then we can go back. And, seeing that it's Friday night, I'll take you to dinner in the Roman Room. There. What about that?'

She turned her face to him. Her eyes showed a mixture of contrition and delight now that he'd mentioned her favourite place. He kept on smiling, though deep down he was a bit irritated with her for making him resort to such extravagant bribery.

'Besides,' he said. 'It's just because that estate agent's so clueless that he hasn't seen the potential of this area yet. It stands to reason areas like this, only three or four stops on the Tube from the West End, *must* come up. People can't go on paying more and more astronomical prices for houses around the smarter areas, and the rail fares and so on are already driving the long-distance commuters back into town.'

He knew it was all so much repetition, but it seemed to be the only way to do it.

'And what's more, Penny, remember those houses that'd been done up so nicely in the terrace just back around the corner. It's already happening, you see. We just can't afford to miss a chance like this. We'd kick ourselves for ever about it if we did.'

Just for a moment, he saw in his mind's eye the house as it might be: the stucco restored round the windows and the classic door. The door itself could be in natural wood, with coach lamps setting off its delicate, balanced grace. Penny, in the very latest evening gown – she'd surely pick up something just right from her modelling as she always did – in the doorway welcoming the astonished and admiring first-comers to their housewarming.

Penny smiled the sweetest of her private smiles for him, and he knew the enthusiasm that had been in his voice had rekindled her support.

'Oh, Teddy darling, I know you're right. It's just me again. You know you're not to mind.'

He kissed her tenderly and then opened the door and got out to make the most of it before her mood faltered.

He took his big torch out of the side pocket in the door just in case, and then went round to help her out. He shut the door after her briskly, enjoying again the solid musical clunk as the well-made panel fitted as smoothly into place as a folded wing to a falcon's back.

The sound of their feet on the road, then on the pavement, then on the five shallow steps to the front entrance to the house were the only noises to be heard in the quiet and deserted street. Only the light shining dimly here and there through the cheap curtains in the windows of some of the houses, and the old second-hand cars parked intermittently along the roadside, showed that the area was inhabited at all.

The porch light was broken, of course, so the elegant shape of the stucco beneath its peeling, sooty surface paint offered only a sense of desolation and unwelcome now as he groped about with gloved fingers and eyes for signs of a bell. Eventually he found it and pressed it. There was no answering noise from inside: no sound at all.

Penny's patent leather high heel shoes glistened as she moved her feet apprehensively to a new position.

'It's extraordinary, though, that it should be going so cheap if it's as much of a find as you say,' she said quietly as though someone might be listening. 'It does seem ... well ... *fishy*.'

He laughed briskly, establishing the masculine 'no nonsense' note on which they had to see the thing through. He found the door-knocker – obviously a pleasing bit of brass beneath these caked layers of ancient black paint – and banged it sharply several times.

'D'you think anyone's there?' Penny said. 'I don't think the place is occupied after all.'

'Of course there's someone there. The estate agent said there was a sitting tenant, and sitting tenants don't run out unless there's a very good reason. A woman, I think he said, with some kids.'

There was still no sound from inside.

'The point is, Penny darling, for £3,000 this place is a snip, sitting tenant or no sitting tenant. Besides, I'm sure we can winkle her out in no time if we pay her a few hundred to move, and we'll easily be able to do that if we can get this for only £3,000.'

At that moment there was a startling grinding of bolts behind the door and it swung open to present them with a gust of moist and fetid air that was obviously being changed for the first time in months, and a small squat woman in an unspeakably filthy apron. Her face was primitive and olive skinned. Her eyes, so far as Edward could tell in the miserable light of the 30-watt bulb in the hall behind her, were dark and hot with an unfathomable mixture of suspicion, hostility and imperviousness. Her hair was black and parted in the middle, then heaped in an untidy bun at the back of her head. It looked as if it had never been washed, ever.

'Good evening,' Edward said firmly in his best junior management tone. 'Mrs Laristi?'

The woman didn't reply. She watched them as though they were some sort of distant passing show.

'My name's Grafton, and this is my wife. I hope Mr Faithwell at the estate agent's told you we were coming round tonight to look at the house. I gather you know it's up for sale.'

Mrs Laristi spoke at last in a deep, hoarse voice.

'Mr Faidwhell, yes. He been here sometime. Two weeks ago, maybe. He say something or other, I don't know.'

She shrugged, pulling her lips down at the corners.

He decided a firm lead would be the thing to make up for Faithwell's inefficiency. There was no point in letting it go now, as it would be no end of a job getting Penny back here another time. He stepped into the hall past the woman, smiling politely but firmly, and saying, 'Well, we'll be very quick. I promise you, Mrs Laristi, we'll disturb you as little as possible.'

It was then that he noticed the string of kids standing silently behind her. There were four of them and they were all disgustingly filthy. Some had their fingers stuffed in their messy mouths; some worked nervously at the dirty garments at their groins. All stared at him and Penny with their mother's dark-eyed, complex stare.

He took Penny's arm in his to show their solidarity, and looked round the hall, taking in as much as the great plague of shadows left by the 30-watt bulb would allow. The hall was beautifully proportioned, and focused naturally on the swing of the staircase at the end in spite of the peeling wall paper and the hideously blistered and ancient green paint all over the place. The floor was well laid and seemed sound.

'Is no good. This house,' Mrs Laristi said. She shook her head. 'Bad spirits.'

'Bad spirits?' Penny repeated, then blinked at Edward for support. 'I think we'll look in this room first,' Edward said dismissively for answer to both of them.

Somehow the Laristi brood infiltrated past him to stand in a body in front of the door.

'Is our room,' Mrs Laristi said. 'Is for us, for living. Is private.'

'Look,' Edward said reassuringly, 'we won't steal anything or even touch anything. We only want a quick look to see the shape of the room and whether it's structurally OK. You must be sensible, Mrs Laristi. The more fuss you make the longer it'll take, and the longer we'll be here.'

Mrs Laristi watched him for a moment and then shrugged and opened the door, then switched on the dim light. She had been telling the truth. What had presumably once been the kitchen for the whole house was the only room her family apparently used. The old-fashioned iron range built into the wall around the fireplace was in a state of unutterable squalor. The room stank bitterly of urine and filth. There was one massive bed, in which presumably all of them slept, with soiled bedclothes grey and shiny with dirt heaped on it. Clothes and papers and empty and half-empty food containers lay heaped in what remaining space there was. Two cheap wooden chairs were the only other pieces of furniture in the room.

Three or four mangy fox-faced cats suddenly shot from under the bed and out between his legs to disappear somewhere into the house.

'Yes,' Edward said. 'Thank you, I think we've seen enough of that room.'

'It's becoming a little more obvious why it's only three thousand,' Penny muttered to him breathlessly; she had been holding her breath in Mrs Laristi's room.

Edward walked across to the other side of the hall and reached for the handle of the nearest door, glad that he had kept his gloves on, and thinking that there was no future in playing too much deference to the woman, because she didn't own the place anyway.

But Mrs Laristi suddenly moved with unexpected speed to push past in front of him, reeking of old cooking grease and bodily staleness.

'Ah, Dios, wait . . . wait! For other rooms first it must be done, it must be done.' She rolled her eyes upwards, crossed herself and muttered on while she went through a series of genuflections and then some weird and distinctively pagan-looking gestures in front of the door. To Edward's amazement, all the children imitated her movement as best they could behind her.

'How depressing,' Penny said weakly beside him. She had turned her head a little so that her nose was against the big turned-up cashmere collar. He squeezed her waist to reassure her.

When she had finished, Mrs Laristi opened the door fearfully and peered hesitantly beyond it as though it might at any moment be necessary to bolt. Edward stepped in after her and switched on the light, which once again proved to be a bare 30-watt bulb. There was nothing unpleasant to see in the room beyond its dirtiness. Obviously it wasn't even used now. And it stank of cats. Otherwise, there were some old and rotted armchairs, a bare iron bedframe, and a lot of old newspapers and magazines and empty cans scattered about – presumably when the chaos became too much in her room she simply shifted the excess in here.

Edward made himself miss all this and see the potential of the beautiful casement windows at either end. Above, he saw to his delight, there was a fine moulded ceiling that certainly looked as though it was the work of real craftsmen, and was more or less intact apart from the dirt. There was a sort of arch in the middle of the room to indicate that it could be used as two if necessary, and fine wood fireplace surrounds in each section. His heart leaped with new resolution about the house as he went out.

'Yes,' he said, rubbing his gloved hands together. 'And now let's move on. Shall we see the room opposite?'

Mrs Laristi burst into speech again.

'This house no good. Not glad. Is evil presences. Is old evil thing, maybe murder, I don't know. Very evil things live here. No good for you.'

'I'm afraid ghosts are allergic to me,' he said, enjoying his archness the more because he knew it would be meaningless to her. 'They just vanish away wherever I go.'

Mrs Laristi looked at him suspiciously and sniffed.

Edward said: 'Now I think we'll have a look in this room opposite.'

He moved to the door on the opposite side of the hall, but once again Mrs Laristi and her troop of silent children sprang ahead of him and went through their weird and muddled ritual.

'Oh, Teddy darling, I don't like this. It's so strange, what're they doing?'

'Don't take any notice of the silly old troll. She thinks going through all this corny mumbo jumbo is going to frighten us off the house. Really, I ask you, it's too absurd for words! It makes you want to laugh out loud.'

Mrs Laristi had stopped now and looked round at them with hostility, suspicious about their whispering. From her face it looked as though she thought they had been planning to murder her.

'What nice children you have, Mrs Laristi,' Penny said reassuringly. 'It must be so jolly, all being together in a group like that. So nice for playing.' She produced a semblance of her social laugh, and Edward squeezed her hand in gratitude for the effort she had made.

Mrs Laristi looked at her children as though Penny had reminded her of an enemy. She turned on her children suddenly and began shouting at the youngest and hitting him for no apparent reason. The child immediately started to scream, and then one of the elder children began to attack its mother. She turned on it too with gusto, until she had eventually subdued them both.

Penny put her hand behind Edward's arm and they watched with more disgust than embarrassment this flurry of near-animal turmoil. When it was over Edward opened the door and strode firmly into the room. The light didn't work and he had to use his torch. This room was completely bare, and had only one casement window. It didn't run the whole length of the house like the room opposite. The air in it was damp and clammy and cold. There was a strange smell about that wasn't quite so recognizable this time. There was something more to it than just dirt and staleness and cats. Something familiar and rather disturbing. Not quite drains or mustiness. Something else.

'What's that funny smell, Penny darling?'

But Penny had taken out the little handkerchief soaked in Worth perfume she kept in her handbag and was dabbing it to her nose, so presumably she had managed to avoid it altogether.

Edward walked across the room, puzzling over the smell, listening to his feet echoing on the boards. He pulled absent-mindedly at a piece of peeled wallpaper exposed by the steely finger of light from his torch; still the smell meant nothing to him.

'Now, upstairs,' Mrs Laristi said, pressing them with sudden vigour. 'Many rooms upstairs.'

They trooped up the bare shadowy stairs which pirouetted round to face a narrow landing. The landing was in complete darkness. Edward switched on his torch and swung it about. There seemed to be rather nice panelling in the form of a dado on both walls, although it was of course ruined at present by countless layers of horrible old paint. Possibly that might have saved it from the worm, though: that was a consoling thought worth remembering.

'Of course,' he said to Penny in a strong, conversational tone, 'you have to remember this area was something of a little health spa right outside the City of London when all these nice houses were built. That accounts for the expensive and tasteful workmanship. This house probably belonged to a rich merchant; probably his little showpiece in the country. It seems odd to think of it like that now, doesn't it?'

These rooms,' Mrs Laristi said. 'Bad rooms. Cold and not good. You wait for me make it done for you go in.'

She and her children then went into her ritual once again before she would let them into any of the rooms. Edward found, to his intense irritation, that his common sense was being eroded slowly by the repetition of her muddled yet strangely disturbing performance. The inept support from her children added to its macabre effect now instead of making it more ridiculous, as he had expected. He began to feel uneasy, and this made him furious with her and all the more determined to overcome the puerile weakness in him that was susceptible to such rubbish.

The rooms he went into with Penny were not in so bad a state as those downstairs, though they too were suffering from long neglect. They were all completely empty, and had obviously not even been entered, let alone used, more than once or twice in decades. The ancient and filthy wallpaper had not been changed since Victorian times. There were thick layers of dirt on the pleasantly shaped windows, some of which had broken panes with pieces of wood tacked over them.

The two rooms which had been the principal bedrooms had excellent ceilings in the same style as the downstairs main rooms, and really attractive fireplace surrounds disfigured by chocolate paint. As far as he could tell from the beam of his torch – none of the lights was working, of course – there were no tell-tale signs of a leaky roof above the ceilings either.

'There's something eerie about these rooms,' Penny muttered. 'They're so – well, so *deserted*. It's as though as much living as ought to be done in them has been done already. They're . . . well – sort of empty tombs. Aren't they?'

'Oh, don't be silly,' he said shortly, because something of the same feeling had come to him – simply as a result of the Laristis' repeated absurdities, he knew very well. 'All houses are like this before anything's been done to them. You've got to look at them with what can be done in your mind, not just take them as they are.'

She didn't reply, and he knew he had upset her, but he hardened himself against it. Everything he had seen so far had confirmed the potential of the place, and he damned well wasn't going to be jockeyed out of it by female pressure, even if Penny's was being added to the Laristi woman's for the time being. He'd soon shake her out of that when he got her to the Roman Room.

'Is evil, this house,' Mrs Laristi chose that moment to chip in again, watching him with her black eyes, which looked in the gloom of the landing like the source of all the darkness in the house. 'Sometimes,' she said, 'there is terrible cries and shrieks. There is horror that frightens my little ones so they cannot sleep or eat for days. They sick for days.'

'Oh, for God's sake, that's enough of this drivel,' Edward burst out. 'We've had quite enough ignorance and folly for now. What kind of fools d'you think we are? We're not taken in by that sort of thing, don't you see. If we like the house we'll buy it whatever you say, and we'll probably even give you a whole lot of money to find somewhere else to live you'll like better. Now let us see the rest of it without any more fuss.'

Mrs Laristi's face went wooden. Behind her, the small faces of her children watched him, their eyes glittering like rats' eyes in the shadows.

Mrs Laristi shrugged.

'You have seen all. Is no more to see.'

'Oh really,' Edward said, regretting his outburst now as a sign of being rattled. 'Now listen, Mrs Laristi. I know there's another room downstairs which you deliberately avoided showing me. The room at the back opposite side to the long living room. I shan't go until we've seen it. Now come on.'

He led the way imperiously down the stairs, the beam of his torch a sword blade cutting the gloom aside. He could hear Penny's high heels following, then the multiple trample of the Laristi horde.

He strode straight to the door which he knew led to the room Mrs Laristi had been keeping from him. She jostled furiously in front of him once again and put her revolting hands on his dark crombie overcoat, pushing him away from the door.

'Ah no, no,' she shrieked, 'is the evil room, the evil room! You must not go in for fear of death . . . ah Dios, Dios!'

To his surprise, Edward saw that she was genuinely terrified now. Her face was as lifeless as dough, her black eyes bright with panic.

'This room is where big evil in the house is living. There is terrible sounds in this room, always. Maybe old murder there, maybe many murders, maybe worse. There is terrible things come out at night to make evil in the house. Oh, Madre de Dios.'

'Oh, Teddy,' Penny's voice was thin as water. 'Let's leave it and go ... please, please. Surely this one room doesn't matter now when we've seen so many.'

'Nonsense!' Edward almost shouted. 'Superstitious nonsense! I'm not surprised there're terrible noises with those revolting cats having the run of the place. For God's sake let's behave like intelligent adults instead of a lot of snivelling savages.'

He gripped Penny's arm roughly to bring her to her senses and then swept Mrs Laristi and her children aside with the hand in which he held his big torch. He pushed at the door, but it was locked. Fortunately the woman had left the key in the lock. He turned it and flung the door open, pulling Penny firmly inside with him so that the beginning would be over before there was time to think.

He almost laughed with the pathos of it when he looked round in the room. It was big and harmless and empty. It was almost cheerful with the moonlight pouring in through the pleasing french windows that gave on to the long garden beyond. Of course, the garden was bound to be a wilderness now, but perhaps some good plants had survived and could be trimmed into shape again. And, unsurprisingly, the glass in the french windows was mostly broken.

The only sound was the voices of the Laristis gabbling away at their mumbo jumbo outside, louder than ever because of her panic.

The room was really very nice indeed, with perhaps the best ceiling of all, though the wallpaper was in ruins again. The only odd thing about it was the smell, which was once again very much the same smell as in the other adjoining room which he'd been in at the beginning, and which had perplexed him then.

He walked forward with Penny across the room, sniffing at the smell, knowing at the back of his mind that there was something important about it, while he played his torch on the intricacies of the ceiling.

At that moment a cat scuttled from a dark corner and out of the broken french window, and the floor cracked and gave way beneath them. Penny's thin, elastic scream coincided with the sensation of their falling, and then unconsciousness came and hit him like a giant fist.

Agonizing pain in his legs brought him to, he didn't know how long afterwards. At the same moment the smell he had been worrying about the moment before the accident leaped forward to reveal itself in his mind. It was the vile smell of the hideous, insidious fungus that swallows houses alive like a python. It was *Merulius Lacrymans*. Dry rot.

He tried to move, but the pain in his legs leaped, making him scream. He realized his trousers were warm and wet, and that he was already faint from loss of blood. He groped with his hands and found he was lying on heaps of rubble and broken brick. They must have fallen through to some deep foundations beneath the house.

Panic at the thought of Penny shot through him. He called her name and groped about in the darkness for her. His hand came in contact with the familiar softness of her cashmere coat. He sobbed with relief and grasped her for comfort, in spite of the pain.

But she didn't respond. When his fingers found her face he knew why. Her head was right over, her neck broken. She was dead.

Then the sound of the key turning in the lock in the door above somewhere and the noise of the Laristis gabbling their charms came to him dimly, showing him that he couldn't have been unconscious for long.

He cried out for help, but the pain in the effort turned into a scream. The only answer was increased gabbling from the Laristis. It dawned on him suddenly that she would take their disappearance merely as the work of the evil she imagined to be in control of the room. Any cries she heard would only confirm in her mind that something awful had happened to them because of it. He knew for certain she'd do nothing about it.

His thoughts flew to the estate agent, Faithwell. Surely he'd do something.

But there was little hope of anything from an inefficient and listless fellow like that. He'd take the fact that they didn't contact him again as a sign that they weren't interested in the house; if he remembered them at all.

And it was Friday night. Nobody would miss them until Monday at the earliest, when they'd see he hadn't turned up at the office ...

Tears sprang to his eyes; tears of fury at Mrs Laristi and the superstition that was now inevitably going to be the death of him, too. He put his head on Penny's sweet-smelling cashmere coat and wept with fury, and with weakness through his rapid loss of blood, which he did not know how to stop.

The Dead Smile

F. Marion Crawford

1

Sir Hugh Ockram smiled as he sat by the open window of his study, in the late August afternoon, and just then a curiously yellow cloud obscured the low sun, and the clear summer light turned lurid, as if it had been suddenly poisoned and polluted by the four vapours of a plague. Sir Hugh's face seemed, at best, to be made of fine parchment drawn skin-tight over a wooden mask, in which two eyes were sunk out of sight, and peered from far within through crevices under the slanting, wrinkled lids, alive and watchful like two toads in their holes, side by side and exactly alike. But as the light changed, then a little yellow glare flashed in each. Nurse Macdonald said once that when Sir Hugh smiled he saw the faces of two women in hell – two dead women he had betrayed. (Nurse Macdonald was a hundred years old.) And the smile widened, stretching the pale lips across the discoloured teeth in an expression of profound self-satisfaction, blended with the most unforgiving hatred and contempt for the human doll. The hideous disease of which he was dying had touched his brain. His son stood beside him, tall, white, and delicate as an angel in a primitive picture, and though there was deep distress in his violet eyes as he looked at his father's face, he felt the shadow of that sickening smile stealing across his own lips and parting them and drawing them against his will. And it was like a bad dream, for he tried not to smile and smiled the more. Beside him, strangely like him in her wan, angelic beauty, with the same shadowy golden hair, the same sad violet eyes, the same luminously pale face, Evelyn Warburton rested one hand upon his arm. And as she looked into her uncle's eyes, and could not turn her own away, she knew that the deathly smile was hovering on her own red lips, drawing them tightly across her little teeth, while two bright tears ran down her cheeks to her mouth, and dropped from the upper to the lower lip while she smiled– and the smile was like the shadow of death and the seal of damnation upon her pure, young face.

'Of course,' said Sir Hugh very slowly, and still looking out at the trees, 'if you have made up your mind to be married, I cannot hinder you, and I don't suppose you attach the smallest importance to my consent——'

'Father!' exclaimed Gabriel reproachfully.

'No, I do not deceive myself,' continued the old man, smiling terribly. 'You will marry when I am dead, though there is a very good reason why you had better not – why you had better not,' he repeated very emphatically, and he slowly turned his toad eyes upon the lovers.

'What reason?' asked Evelyn in a frightened voice.

'Never mind the reason, my dear. You will marry just as if it did not exist.' There was a long pause. 'Two gone,' he said, his voice lowering strangely, 'and two more will be four – all together – for ever and ever, burning, burning, burning bright.'

At the last words his head sank slowly back, and the little glare of the toad eyes disappeared under the swollen lids, and the lurid cloud passed from the westering sun, so that the earth was green again and the light pure. Sir Hugh had fallen asleep, as he often did in his last illness, even while speaking.

Gabriel Ockram drew Evelyn away, and from the study they went out into the dim hall, softly closing the door behind them, and each audibly drew breath, as though some sudden danger had been passed. They laid their hands each in the others, and their strangely-alike eyes met in a long look, in which love and perfect understanding were darkened by the secret terror of an unknown thing. Their pale faces reflected each other's fear.

'It is his secret,' said Evelyn at last. 'He will never tell us what it is.'

'If he dies with it,' answered Gabriel, 'let it be on his own head!'

'On his head!' echoed the dim hall. It was a strange echo, and some were frightened by it, for they said that if it were a real echo it should repeat everything and not give back a phrase here and there, now speaking, now silent. But Nurse Macdonald said that the great hall would never echo a prayer when an Ockram was to die, though it would give back curses ten for one.

'On his head!' it repeated quite softly, and Evelyn started and looked round.

'It is only the echo,' said Gabriel, leading her away.

They went out into the late afternoon light, and sat upon a stone seat behind the chapel, which was built across the end of the east wing. It was very still, not a breath stirred, and there was no sound near them. Only far off in the park a song-bird was whistling the high prelude to the evening chorus.

'It is very lonely here,' said Evelyn, taking Gabriel's hand nervously, and speaking as if she dreaded to disturb the silence. 'If it were dark, I should be afraid.'

'Of what? Of me?' Gabriel's sad eyes turned to her.

'Oh no! How could I be afraid of you? But of the old Ockrams – they say they are just under our feet here in the north vault outside the chapel, all in their shrouds, with no coffins, as they used to bury them.'

'As they always will – as they will bury my father, and me. They say an Ockram will not lie in a coffin.'

'But it cannot be true – these are fairy tales – ghost stories!' Evelyn nestled nearer to her companion, grasping his hand more tightly, and the sun began to go down.

'Of course. But there is a story of old Sir Vernon, who was beheaded for treason under James II. The family brought his body back from the scaffold in an iron coffin with heavy locks, and they put it in the north vault. But even afterwards, whenever the vault was opened to bury another of the family, they found the coffin wide open, and the body standing upright against the wall, and the head rolled away in a corner, smiling at it.'

'As Uncle Hugh smiles?' Evelyn shivered.

'Yes, I suppose so,' answered Gabriel, thoughtfully. 'Of course I never saw it, and the vault has not been opened for thirty years – none of us have died since then.'

'And if – if Uncle Hugh dies – shall you——' Evelyn stopped, and her beautiful thin face was quite white.

'Yes. I shall see him laid there too – with his secret, whatever it is.' Gabriel sighed and pressed the girl's little hand.

'I do not like to think of it,' she said unsteadily. 'O Gabriel, what can the secret be? He said we had better not marry – not that he forbade it – but he said it so strangely, and he smiled – ugh!' Her small white teeth chattered with fear, and she looked over her shoulder while drawing still closer to Gabriel. 'And, somehow, I felt it in my own face——'

'So did I,' answered Gabriel in a low, nervous voice. 'Nurse Macdonald——' He stopped abruptly.

'What? What did she say?'

'Oh – nothing. She has told me things – they would frighten you, dear. Come, it is growing chilly.' He rose, but Evelyn held his hand in both of hers, still sitting and looking up into his face.

'But we shall be married, just the same – Gabriel! Say that we shall!'

'Of course, darling – of course. But while my father is so very ill, it is impossible——'

'O Gabriel, Gabriel dear! I wish we were married now!' cried Evelyn in sudden distress. 'I know that something will prevent it and keep us apart.'

'Nothing shall!'

'Nothing?'

'Nothing human,' said Gabriel Ockram, as she drew him down to her. And their faces, that were so strangely alike, met and touched – and

Gabriel knew that the kiss had a marvellous savour of evil, but on
Evelyn's lips it was like the cool breath of a sweet and mortal fear. And
neither of them understood, for they were innocent and young. Yet she
drew him to her by her lightest touch, as a sensitive plant shivers and
waves its thin leaves, and bends and closes softly upon what it wants, and
he let himself be drawn to her willingly, as he would if her touch had been
deadly and poisonous; for she strangely loved that half voluptuous breath
of fear and he passionately desired the nameless evil something that
lurked in her maiden lips.

'It is as if we loved in a strange dream,' she said.

'I fear the waking,' he murmured.

'We shall not wake, dear – when the dream is over it will have
already turned into death, so softly that we shall not know it. But until
then——'

She paused, and her eyes sought his, and their faces slowly came
nearer. It was as if they had thoughts in their red lips that foresaw and
foreknew the deep kiss of each other.

'Until then——' she said again, very low, and her mouth was nearer
to his.

'Dream – till then,' murmured his breath.

2

Nurse Macdonald was a hundred years old. She used to sleep sitting
all bent together in a great old leathern arm-chair with wings, her feet
in a bag footstool lined with sheepskin, and many warm blankets
wrapped about her, even in summer. Beside her a little lamp always
burned at night by an old silver cup, in which there was something to
drink.

Her face was very wrinkled, but the wrinkles were so small and fine
and near together that they made shadows instead of lines. Two thin locks
of hair, that was turning from white to a smoky yellow again, were drawn
over her temples from under her starched white cap. Every now and then
she woke, and her eyelids were drawn up in tiny folds like little pink silk
curtains, and her queer blue eyes looked straight before her through doors
and walls and worlds to a far place beyond. Then she slept again, and
her hands lay one upon the other on the edge of the blanket, the thumbs
had grown longer than the fingers with age, and the joints shone in the
low lamplight like polished crab-apples.

It was nearly one o'clock in the night, and the summer breeze was
blowing the ivy branch against the panes of the window with a hushing
caress. In the small room beyond, with the door ajar, the girl-maid who
took care of Nurse Macdonald was fast asleep. All was very quiet. The

old woman breathed regularly, and her indrawn lips trembled each time as the breath went out, and her eyes were shut.

But outside the closed window there was a face, and violet eyes were looking steadily at the ancient sleeper, for it was like the face of Evelyn Warburton, though there were eighty feet from the sill of the window to the foot of the tower. Yet the cheeks were thinner than Evelyn's, and as white as a gleam, and her eyes stared, and the lips were not red with life, they were dead and painted with new blood.

Slowly Nurse Macdonald's wrinkled eyelids folded themselves back, and she looked straight at the face at the window while one might count ten.

'Is it time?' she asked in her little old, far-away voice.

While she looked the face at the window changed, for the eyes opened wider and wider till the white glared all round the bright violet, and the bloody lips opened over gleaming teeth, and stretched and widened and stretched again, and the shadow golden hair rose and streamed against the window in the night breeze. And in answer to Nurse Macdonald's question came the sound that freezes the living flesh.

That low moaning voice that rises suddenly, like the scream of storm, from a moan to a wail, from a wail to a howl, from a howl to the fear-shriek of the tortured dead – he who had heard knows, and he can bear witness that the cry of the banshee is an evil cry to hear alone in the deep night. When it was over and the face was gone, Nurse Macdonald shook a little in her great chair, and still she looked at the black square of the window, but there was nothing more there, nothing but the night, and the whispering ivy branch. She turned her head to the door that was ajar, and there stood the girl in her white gown, her teeth chattering with fright.

'It is time, child,' said Nurse Macdonald. 'I must go to him, for it is the end.'

She rose slowly, leaning her withered hands upon the arms of the chair, and the girl brought her a woollen gown and a great mantle, and her crutch-stick, and made her ready. But very often the girl looked at the window and was unjointed with fear, and often Nurse Macdonald shook her head and said words which the maid could not understand.

'It was like the face of Miss Evelyn,' said the girl at last, trembling.

But the ancient woman looked up sharply and angrily, and her queer blue eyes blared. She held herself by the arm of the great chair with her left hand, and lifted up her crutch-stick to strike the maid with all her might. But she did not.

'You are a good girl,' she said, 'but you are a fool. Pray for wit, child, pray for wit – or else find service in another house than Ockram Hall. Bring the lamp and help me under my left arm.

The crutch-stick clacked on the wooden floor, and the low heels of the woman's slippers clappered after her in slow triplets, as Nurse Macdonald got towards the door. And down the stairs each step she took was a labour in itself, and by the clacking noise the waking servants knew that she was coming, very long before they saw her.

No one was sleeping now, and there were lights and whisperings and pale faces in the corridors near Sir Hugh's bedroom, and now someone went in, and now someone came out, but everyone made way for Nurse Macdonald, who had nursed Sir Hugh's father more than eighty years ago.

The light was soft and clear in the room. There stood Gabriel Ockram by his father's bedside, and there knelt Evelyn Warburton, her hair lying like a golden shadow down her shoulders, and her hands clasped nervously together. And opposite Gabriel, a nurse was trying to make Sir Hugh drink. But he would not, and though his lips were parted, his teeth were set. He was very, very thin and yellow now, and his eyes caught the light sideways and were as yellow coals.

'Do not torment him,' said Nurse Macdonald to the woman who held the cup. 'Let me speak to him, for his hour is come.'

'Let her speak to him,' said Gabriel in a dull voice.

So the ancient woman leaned to the pillow and laid the feather-weight of her withered hand, that was like a brown moth, upon Sir Hugh's yellow fingers, and she spoke to him earnestly, while only Gabriel and Evelyn were left in the room to hear.

'Hugh Ockram,' she said, 'this is the end of your life; and as I saw you born, and saw your father born before you, I am come to see you die. Hugh Ockram, will you tell me the truth?'

The dying man recognised the little far-away voice he had known all his life, and he very slowly turned his yellow face to Nurse Macdonald; but he said nothing. Then she spoke again.

'Hugh Ockram, you will never see the daylight again. Will you tell the truth?'

His toad-like eyes were not dull yet. They fastened themselves on her face.

'What do you want of me?' he asked, and each word struck hollow on the last. 'I have no secrets. I have lived a good life.'

Nurse Macdonald laughed – a tiny, cracked laugh, that made her old head bob and tremble a little, as if her neck were on a steel spring. But Sir Hugh's eyes grew red, and his pale lips began to twist.

'Let me die in peace,' he said slowly.

But Nurse Macdonald shook her head, and her brown, moth-like hand left his and fluttered to his forehead.

'By the mother that bore you and died of grief for the sins you did, tell me the truth!'

Sir Hugh's lips tightened on his discoloured teeth.

'Not on earth,' he answered slowly.

'By the wife who bore your son and died heart-broken, tell me the truth!'

'Neither to you in life, nor to her in eternal death.'

His lips writhed, as if the words were coals between them, and a great drop of sweat rolled across the parchment of his forehead. Gabriel Ockram bit his hand as he watched his father die. But Nurse Macdonald spoke a third time.

'By the woman whom you betrayed, and who waits for you this night, Hugh Ockram, tell me the truth!'

'It is too late. Let me die in peace.'

The writhing lips began to smile across the set yellow teeth, and the toad eyes glowed like evil jewels in his head.

'There is time,' said the ancient woman. 'Tell me the name of Evelyn Warburton's father. Then I will let you die in peace.'

Evelyn started back, kneeling as she was, and stared at Nurse Macdonald, and then at her uncle.

'The name of Evelyn's father?' He repeated slowly, while the awful smile spread upon his dying face.

The light was growing strangely dim in the great room. As Evelyn looked, Nurse Macdonald's crooked shadow on the wall grew gigantic. Sir Hugh's breath came thick, rattling in his throat, as death crept in like a snake and choked it back. Evelyn prayed aloud, high and clear.

Then something rapped at the window, and she felt her hair rise upon her head in a cool breeze, as she looked around in spite of herself. And when she saw her own white face looking in at the window, and her own eyes staring at her through the glass, wide and fearful, and her own hair streaming against the pane, and her own lips dashed with blood, she rose slowly from the floor and stood rigid for one moment, till she screamed once and fell back into Gabriel's arms. But the shriek that answered hers was the fear-shriek of the tormented corpse, out of which the soul cannot pass for shame of deadly sins, though the devils fight in it with corruption, each for their due share.

Sir Hugh Ockram sat upright in his death-bed, and saw and cried aloud:

'Evelyn!' His harsh voice broke and rattled in his chest as he sank down. But still Nurse Macdonald tortured him, for there was a little life left in him still.

'You have seen the mother as she waits for you, Hugh Ockram. Who was this girl Evelyn's father? What was his name?'

For the last time the dreadful smile came upon the twisted lips, very slowly, very surely now, and the toad eyes glared red, and the parchment face glowed a little in the flickering light. For the last time words came.

'They know it in hell.'

Then the glowing eyes went out quickly, the yellow face turned waxen pale, and a great shiver ran through the thin body as Hugh Ockram died.

But in death he still smiled, for he knew his secret and kept it still, on the other side, and he would take it with him, to lie with him for ever in the north vault of the chapel where the Ockrams lie uncoffined in their shrouds – all but one. Though he was dead, he smiled, for he had kept his treasure of evil truth to the end, and there was none left to tell the name he had spoken, but there was all the evil he had not undone left to bear fruit.

As they watched – Nurse Macdonald and Gabriel, who held Evelyn still unconscious in his arms while he looked at the father – they felt the dead smile crawling along their own lips – the ancient crone and the youth with the angel's face. Then they shivered a little, and both looked at Evelyn as she lay with her head on his shoulder, and, though she was very beautiful, the same sickening smile was twisting her mouth too, and it was like the foreshadowing of a great evil which they could not understand.

But by and by they carried Evelyn out, and she opened her eyes and the smile was gone. From far away in the great house the sound of weeping and crooning came up the stairs and echoed along the dismal corridors, for the women had begun to mourn the dead master, after the Irish fashion, and the hall had echoes of its own all that night, like the far-off wail of the banshee among forest trees.

When the time was come they took Sir Hugh in his winding-sheet on a trestle bier, and bore him to the chapel and through the iron door and down the long descent to the north vault, with tapers, to lay him by his father. And two men went in first to prepare the place and came back staggering like drunken men, and white, leaving their lights behind them.

But Gabriel Ockram was not afraid, for he knew. And he went in alone and saw that the body of Sir Vernon Ockram was leaning upright against the stone wall, and that his head lay on the ground near by with the face turned up, and the dried leathern lips smiled horribly at the dried-up corpse, while the iron coffin, lined with black velvet, stood open on the floor.

Then Gabriel took the thing in his hands, for it was very light, being quite dried by the air of the vault, and those who peeped in from the door saw him lay it in the coffin again, and it rustled a little, like a bundle of reeds, and sounded hollow as it touched the sides and the bottom. He also placed the head upon the shoulders and shut down the lid, which fell to with a rusty spring that snapped.

After that they laid Sir Hugh beside his father, with the trestle bier on which they had brought him, and they went back to the chapel.

But when they saw one another's faces, master and men, they were all smiling with the dead smile of the corpse they had left in the vault, so that they could not bear to look at one another until it had faded away.

3

Gabriel Ockham became Sir Gabriel, inheriting the baronetcy with the half-ruined fortune left by his father, and still Evelyn Warburton lived at Ockram Hall, in the south room that had been hers ever since she could remember anything. She could not go away, for there were no relatives to whom she could have gone, and besides there seemed to be no reason why she should not stay. The world would never trouble itself to care what the Ockrams did on their Irish estates, as it was long since the Ockrams had asked anything of the world.

So Sir Gabriel took his father's place at the dark old table in the dining-room, and Evelyn sat opposite to him, until such time as their mourning should be over, and they might be married at last. And meanwhile their lives went on as before, since Sir Hugh had been a hopeless invalid during the last year of his life, and they had seen him but once a day for the little while, spending most of their time together in a strangely perfect companionship.

But though the late summer saddened into autumn, and autumn darkened into winter, and storm followed storm, and rain poured on rain through the short days and the long nights, yet Ockram Hall seemed less gloomy since Sir Hugh had been laid in the north vault beside his father. And at Christmastide Evelyn decked the great hall with holly and green boughs, and huge fires blazed on every hearth. Then the tenants were all bidden to a New Year's dinner, and they ate and drank well, while Sir Gabriel sat at the head of the table. Evelyn came in when the port wine was brought, and the most respected of the tenants made a speech to propose her health.

It was long, he said, since there had been a Lady Ockram. Sir Gabriel shaded his eyes with his hand and looked down at the table, but a faint colour came into Evelyn's transparent cheeks. But, said the grey-haired farmer, it was longer still since there had been a Lady Ockram so fair as the next was to be, and he gave the health of Evelyn Warburton.

Then the tenants all stood up and shouted for her, and Sir Gabriel stood up likewise, beside Evelyn. And when the men gave the last and loudest cheer of all there was a voice not theirs, above them all, higher, fiercer, louder – a scream not earthly, shrieking for the bride of Ockram Hall. And the holly and the green boughs over the great chimney-piece shook and slowly waved as if a cool breeze were blowing over them. But the men turned very pale, and many of them sat down their glasses, but others let them fall upon the floor for fear. And looking into one another's faces, they were all smiling strangely, a dead smile, like dead Sir Hugh's. One cried out words in Irish, and the fear of death was suddenly upon them all so that they fled in panic, falling over one another like wild beasts in the burning forest, when the thick smoke runs along the flame, and the tables were overset, and drinking glasses and bottles were broken in heaps, and the dark red wine crawled like blood upon the polished floor.

Sir Gabriel and Evelyn stood alone at the head of the table before the wreck of the feast, not daring to turn to see each other, for each knew that the other smiled. But his right arm held her and his left hand clasped her right as they stared before them, and but for the shadows of her hair one might not have told their two faces apart. They listened long, but the cry came not again, and the dead smile faded from their lips, while each remembered that Sir Hugh Ockram lay in the north vault, smiling in his winding-sheet, in the dark, because he had died with his secret.

So ended the tenants' New Year's dinner. But from that time on Sir Gabriel grew more and more silent, and his face grew even paler and thinner than before. Often without warning and without words, he would rise from his seat, as if something moved him against his will, and he would go out into the rain or the sunshine to the north side of the chapel, and sit on the stone bench, staring at the ground as if he could see through it, and through the vault below, and through the white winding-sheet in the dark, to the dead smile that would not die.

Always when he went out in that way Evelyn came out presently and sat beside him. Once, too, as in summer, their beautiful faces came suddenly near, and their lids drooped, and their red lips were almost joined together. But as their eyes met, they grew wide and wild, so that the white showed in a ring all round the deep violet, and their teeth chattered, and their hands were like hands of corpses, each in the other's for the terror of what was under their feet, and of what they knew but could not see.

Once, also, Evelyn found Sir Gabriel in the Chapel alone, standing before the iron door that led down to the place of death, and in his hand there was the key to the door, but he had not put it in the lock. Evelyn drew him away, shivering, for she had also been driven in waking dreams to see that terrible thing again, and to find out whether it had changed since it had lain there.

'I'm going mad, Sir,' said Gabriel, covering his eyes with his hand as he went with her. 'I see it in my sleep, I see it when I am awake – it draws me to it, day and night – and unless I see it I shall die!'

'I know,' answered Evelyn, 'I know. It is as if threads were spun from it, like a spider's, drawing us down to it.' She was silent for a moment, and then she stared violently and grasped his arm with a man's strength, and almost screamed the words she spoke. 'But we must not go there!' she cried. 'We must not go!'

Sir Gabriel's eyes were half shut, and he was not moved by the agony on her face.

'I shall die, unless I see it again,' he said, in a quiet voice not like his own. And all that day and that evening he scarcely spoke, thinking of it, always thinking, while Evelyn Warburton quivered from head to foot with a terror she had never known.

She went alone, on a grey winter's morning, to Nurse Macdonald's room in the tower, and sat down beside the great leathern easy-chair, laying her thin white hand upon the withered fingers.

'Nurse,' she said, 'what was it that Uncle Hugh should have told you, that night before he died? It must have been an awful secret — and yet, though you asked him, I feel somehow that you know it, and that you know why he used to smile so dreadfully.'

The old woman's head moved slowly from side to side.

'I only guess — I shall never know,' she answered slowly in her cracked little voice.

'But what do you guess? Who am I? Why did you ask who my father was? You know I am Colonel Warburton's daughter, and my mother was Lady Ockram's sister, so that Gabriel and I are cousins. My father was killed in Afghanistan. What secret can there be?'

'I do not know. I can only guess.'

'Guess what?' asked Evelyn imploringly, and pressing the soft withered hands, as she leaned forward. But Nurse Macdonald's wrinkled lids dropped suddenly over her queer blue eyes, and her lips shook a little with her breath, as if she were asleep.

Evelyn waited. By the fire the Irish maid was knitting fast, and the needles clicked like three of four clocks ticking against each other. And the real clock on the wall solemnly ticked alone, checking off the seconds of the woman who was a hundred years old, and had not many days left. Outside the ivy branch beat the window in the wintry blast, as it had beaten against the glass a hundred years ago.

Then as Evelyn sat there she felt again the waking of a horrible desire — the sickening wish to go down, down to the thing in the north vault, and to open the winding-sheet, and see whether it had changed, and she held Nurse Macdonald's hands as if to keep herself in her place and fight against the appalling attraction of the evil dead.

But the old cat that kept Nurse Macdonald's feet warm, lying aways on the bag footstool, got up and stretched itself, and looked up into Evelyn's eyes, while its back arched, and its tail thickened and bristled, and its ugly pink lips drew back in a devilish grin, showing its sharp teeth. Evelyn stared at it, half fascinated by its ugliness. Then the creature suddenly put out one paw with all its claws spread, and spat at the girl, and all at once the grinning cat was like the smiling corpse far down below, so that Evelyn shivered down to her small feet and covered her face with her free hand lest Nurse Macdonald should wake and see the dead smile there, for she could feel it.

The old woman had already opened her eyes again, and she touched her cat with the end of her crutch-stick, whereupon its back went down and its tail shrunk, and it sidled back to its place in the bag footstool. But its yellow eyes looked up sideways at Evelyn, between the slits of its lids.

'What is it that you guess, nurse?' asked the young girl again.

'A bad thing – a wicked thing. But I dare not tell you, lest it might not be true, and the very thought should blast your life. For if I guess right, he meant that you should not know, and that you two should marry, and pay for his old sin with your soul.'

'He used to tell us that we ought not to marry——'

'Yes – he told you that, perhaps – but it was as if a man put poisoned meat before a starving beast, and said "do not eat" but never raised his hand to take the meat away. And if he told you that you should not marry, it was because he hoped you would, for of all men living or dead, Hugh Ockram was the falsest man that ever told a cowardly lie, and the cruellest that ever hurt a weak woman, and the worst that ever loved a sin.'

'But Gabriel and I love each other,' said Evelyn very sadly.

Nurse Macdonald's old eyes looked far away, at sights seen long ago, and that rose in the grey winter air amid the mists of an ancient youth.

'If you love, you can die together,' she said very slowly. 'Why should you live, if it is true? I am a hundred years old. What has life given me? The beginning is fire, the end is a heap of ashes, and between the end and the beginning lies all the pain in the world. Let me sleep, since I cannot die.'

Then the old woman's eyes closed again, and her head sank a little lower upon her breast.

So Evelyn went away and left her asleep, with the cat asleep on the bag footstool; and the young girl tried to forget Nurse Macdonald's words, but she could not, for she heard them over and over again in the wind, and behind her on the stairs. And as she grew sick with fear of the frightful unknown evil to which her soul was bound, she felt a bodily something pressing her, and pushing her, and forcing her on, and from the other side she felt the threads that drew her mysteriously, and when she shut her eyes, she saw in the chapel behind the altar, the low iron door through which she must pass to go to the thing.

And as she lay awake at night, she drew the sheet over her face, lest she should see shadows on the wall beckoning her and the sound of her own warm breath made whisperings in her ears, while she held the mattress with her hands, to keep from getting up and going to the chapel. It would have been easier if there had not been a way thither through the library, by a door which was never locked. It would be fearfully easy to take her candle and go softly through the sleeping house. And the key of the vault lay under the altar behind a stone that turned. She knew the little secret. She could go alone and see.

But when she thought of it, she felt her hair rise on her head, and first she shivered so that the bed shook, and then the horror went through her in a cold thrill that was agony again, like myriads of icy needles, boring into her nerves.

4

The old clock in Nurse Macdonald's tower struck midnight. From her room she could hear the creaking chains and weights in their box in the corner of the staircase, and overheard the jarring of the rusty lever that lifted the hammer. She had heard it all her life. It struck eleven strokes clearly and then came the twelfth, with a dull half stroke, as though the hammer were too weary to go on, and had fallen asleep against the bell.

The old cat got up from the bag footstool and stretched itself, and Nurse Macdonald opened her ancient eyes and looked slowly round the room by the dim light of the night lamp. She touched the cat with her crutch-stick, and it lay down upon her feet. She drank a few drops from her cup and went to sleep again.

But downstairs Sir Gabriel sat straight up as the clock struck, for he had dreamed a fearful dream of horror, and his heart stood still, till he awoke at its stopping, and it beat again furiously with his breath, like a wild thing set free. No Ockram had ever known fear waking, but sometimes it came to Sir Gabriel in his sleep.

He pressed his hands on his temples as he sat up in bed, and his hands were icy cold, but his head was hot. The dream faded far, and in its place there came the sick twisting of his lips in the dark that would have been a smile. Far off, Evelyn Warburton dreamed that the dead smile was on her mouth, and awoke, starting with a little moan, her face in her hands shivering.

But Sir Gabriel struck a light and got up and began to walk up and down his great room. It was midnight, and he had barely slept an hour, and in the north of Ireland the winter nights are long.

'I shall go mad,' he said to himself, holding his forehead. He knew that it was true. For weeks and months the possession of the thing had grown upon him like a disease, till he could think of nothing without thinking first of that. And now all at once it outgrew his strength, and he knew that he must be its instrument or lose his mind – that he must do the deed he hated and feared, if he could fear anything, or that something would snap in his brain and divide him from life while he was yet alive. He took the candlestick in his hand, the old-fashioned heavy candlestick that had always been used by the head of the house. He did not think of dressing, but went as he was, in his silk nightclothes and his slippers, and he opened the door. Everything was very still in the great old house. He shut the door behind him and walked noiselessly on the carpet through the long corridor. A cool breeze blew over his shoulder and blew the flame of his candle straight out from him. Instinctively he stopped and looked round, but all was still, and the upright flame burned steadily. He walked on, and instantly a strong draught was behind him, almost extinguishing the light. It seemed to blow him on his way, ceasing whenever he turned, coming again when he went on – invisible, icy.

Down the great staircase to the echoing hall he went, seeing nothing but the flame of the candle standing away from him over the guttering wax, while the cold wind blew over his shoulder and through his hair. On he passed through the open door into the library, dark with old books and carved bookcases, on through the door in the shelves, with painted shelves on it, and the imitated backs of books, so that one needed to know where to find it – and it shut itself after him with a soft click. He entered the low-arched passage, and though the door was shut behind him and fitted tightly in its frame, still the cold breeze blew the flame forward as he walked. And he was not afraid, but his face was very pale, and his eyes were wide and bright, looking before him, seeing already in the dark air the picture of the thing beyond. But in the chapel he stood still, his hand on the little turning stone tablet in the back of the stone altar. On the tablet were engraved words, '*Clavis sepulchri Clarissimorum Dominorum De Ockram*' – ('the key to the vault of the most illustrious lord of Ockram.') Sir Gabriel paused and listened. He fancied that he heard a sound far off in the great house where all had been so still, but it did not come again. Yet he waited at the last, and looked at the low iron door. Beyond it, down the long descent, lay his father uncoffined, six months dead, corrupt, terrible in his clinging shroud. The strangely preserving air of the vault could not yet have done its work completely. But on the thing's ghastly features, with their half-dried, open eyes, there would still be the frightful smile with which the man had died – the smile that haunted——

As the thought crossed Sir Gabriel's mind, he felt his lips writhing, and he struck his own mouth in wrath with the back of his hand so fiercely that a drop of blood ran down his chin and another, and more, falling back in the gloom upon the chapel pavement. But still his bruised lips twisted themselves. He turned the tablet by the simple secret. It needed no safer fastening, for had each Ockram been confined in pure gold, and had the door been wide, there was no a man in Tyrone brave enough to go down to the place, saving Gabriel Ockram himself, with his angel's face and his thin, white hands, and his sad unflinching eyes. He took the great gold key and set it into the lock of the iron door, and the heavy, rattling noise echoed down the descent beyond like footsteps, as if a watcher had stood behind the iron and were running away within, with heavy dead feet. And though he was standing still, the cool wind was from behind him, and blew the flame of the candle against the iron panel. He turned the key.

Sir Gabriel saw that his candle was short. There were new ones on the altar, with long candlesticks and he lit one, and left his own burning on the floor. As he set it down on the pavement his lip began to bleed again, and another drop fell upon the stones.

He drew the iron door open and pushed it back against the chapel wall, so that it should not shut of itself, while he was within, and the horrible draught of the sepulchre came up out of the depths in his face, foul and dark. He went in, but though the fetid air met him, yet the flame of the tall candle was blown straight from him against the wind while he walked down the easy incline with steady steps, his loose slippers slapping the pavement as he trod.

He shaded the candle with his hand, and his fingers seemed to be made of wax and blood as the light shone through them. And in spite of him the unearthly draught forced the flame forward, till it was blue over the black wick, and it seemed as if it must go out. But he went straight on, with shining eyes.

The downward passage was wide, and he could not always see the walls by the struggling light, but he knew when he was in the place of death by the larger, drearier echo of his steps in the greater space and by the sensation of a distant blank wall. He stood still, almost enclosing the flame of the candle in the hollow of his hand. He could see a little, for his eyes were growing used to the gloom. Shadowy forms were outlined in the dimness, where the biers of the Ockrams stood crowded together, side by side, each with its straight, shrouded corpse, strangely preserved by the dry air, like the empty shell that the locust sheds in summer. And a few steps before him he saw clearly the dark shape of headless Sir Vernon's iron coffin, and he knew that nearest to it lay the thing he sought.

He was as brave as any of those dead men had been, and they were his fathers, and he knew that sooner or later he should lie there himself, beside Sir Hugh, slowly drying to a parchment shell. But he was still alive, and he closed his eyes a moment, and three great drops stood on his forehead.

Then he looked again, and by the whiteness of the winding-sheet he knew his father's corpse, for all the others were brown with age; and, moreover, the flame of the candle was blown towards it. He made four steps till he reached it, and suddenly the light burned straight and high, shedding a dazzling yellow glare upon the fine linen that was all white, save over the face, and where the joined hands were laid on the breast. And at those places ugly stains had spread, darkened with outlines of the

features and of the tight-clasped fingers. There was a frightful stench of
drying death.

As Sir Gabriel looked down, something stirred behind him, softly at
first, then more noisily, and something fell to the stone floor with a dull
thud and rolled up to his feet; he started back, and saw a withered head
lying almost face upward on the pavement, grinning at him. He felt the
cold sweat standing on his face, and his heart beat painfully.

For the first time in all his life that evil thing which men call fear was
getting hold of him, checking his heart-strings as a cruel driver checks
a quivering horse, clawing at his backbone with icy hands, lifting his hair
with freezing breath climbing up and gathering in his midriff with leaden
weight.

Yet presently he bit his lip and bent down, holding the candle in one
hand, to lift the shroud back from the head of the corpse with the other.
Slowly he lifted it. Then it clove to the half-dried skin of the face, and
his hand shook as if someone had struck him on the elbow, but half in
fear and half in anger at himself, he pulled it, so that it came away with
a little ripping sound. He caught his breath as he held it, not yet throwing
it back, and not yet looking. The horror was working in him, and he felt
that old Vernon Ockram was standing up in his iron coffin, headless, yet
watching him with the stump of his severed neck.

While he held his breath he felt the dead smile twisting his lips. In
sudden wrath at his own misery, he tossed the death-stained linen backward, and looked at last. He ground his teeth lest he should shriek aloud.

There it was, the thing that haunted him, that haunted Evelyn
Warburton, that was like a blight on all that came near him.

The dead face was blotched with dark stains, and the thin, grey hair
was matted about the discoloured forehead. The sunken lids were half
open, and the candle light gleamed on something foul where the toad eyes
had lived.

But yet the dead thing smiled, as it had smiled in life; the ghastly lips
were parted and drawn wide and tight upon the wolfish teeth, cursing
still, and still defying hell to do its worst – defying, cursing, and always
and for ever smiling alone in the dark.

Sir Gabriel opened the winding-sheet where the hands were, and the
blackened, withered fingers were closed upon something stained and
mottled. Shivering from head to foot, but fighting like a man in agony
for his life, he tried to take the package from the dead man's hold. But
as he pulled at it the claw-like fingers seemed to close more tightly, and
when he pulled harder the shrunken hands and arms rose from the corpse
with a horrible look of life following his motion – then as he wrenched
the sealed packet loose at last, the hands fell back into their place still
folded.

He set down the candle on the edge of the bier to break the seals from the stout paper. And, kneeling on one knee, to get a better light, he read what was within, written long ago in Sir Hugh's queer hand.

He was no longer afraid.

He read how Sir Hugh had written it all down that it might perchance be a witness of evil and of his hatred; how he had loved Evelyn Warburton, his wife's sister; and how his wife had died of a broken heart with his curse upon her, and how Warburton and he had fought side by side in Afghanistan, and Warburton had fallen; but Ockram had brought his comrade's wife back a full year later, and little Evelyn, her child, had been born in Ockram Hall. And next, how he had wearied of the mother, and she had died like her sister with his curse on her. And then, how Evelyn had been brought up as his niece, and how he had trusted that his son Gabriel and his daughter, innocent and unknowing, might love and marry, and the souls of the women he had betrayed might suffer another anguish before eternity was out. And, last of all, he hoped that some day, when nothing could be undone, the two might find his writing and live on, not daring to tell the truth for their children's sake and the world's word, man and wife.

This he read, kneeling beside the corpse in the north vault, by the light of the altar candle; and when he had read it all, he thanked God aloud that he had found the secret in time. But when he rose to his feet and looked down at the dead face it was changed, and the smile was gone from it for ever, and the jaw had fallen a little, and the tired, dead lips were relaxed. And then there was a breath behind him and close to him, not cold like that which had blown the flame of the candle as he came, but warm and human. He turned suddenly.

There she stood, all in white, with her shadowy golden hair – for she had risen from her bed and had followed him noiselessly, and had found him reading, and had herself read over his shoulder. He started violently when he saw her, for his nerves were unstrung – and then he cried out her name in the still place of death:

'Evelyn!'

'My brother!' she answered, softly and tenderly, putting out both hands to meet his.

Georgy Porgy

Roald Dahl

Without in any way wishing to blow my own trumpet, I think that I can claim to being in most respects a moderately well-matured and rounded individual. I have travelled a good deal. I am adequately read. I speak Greek and Latin. I dabble in science. I can tolerate a mildly liberal attitude in the politics of others. I have compiled a volume of notes upon the evolution of the madrigal in the fifteenth century. I have witnessed the death of a large number of persons in their beds; and in addition, I have influenced, at least I hope I have, the lives of quite a few others by the spoken word delivered from the pulpit.

Yet in spite of all this, I must confess that I have never in my life – well, how shall I put it? – I have never really had anything much to do with women.

To be perfectly honest, up until three weeks ago I had never so much as laid a finger on one of them except perhaps to help her over a stile or something like that when the occasion demanded. And even then I always tried to ensure that I touched only the shoulder or the waist or some other place where the skin was covered, because the one thing I never could stand was actual contact between my skin and theirs. Skin touching skin, my skin, that is, touching the skin of a female, whether it were leg, neck, face, hand, or merely finger, was so repugnant to me that I invariably greeted a lady with my hands clasped firmly behind my back to avoid the inevitable handshake.

I could go further than that and say that any sort of physical contact with them, even when the skin wasn't bare, would disturb me considerably. If a woman stood close to me in a queue so that our bodies touched, or if she squeezed in beside me on a bus seat, hip to hip and thigh to thigh, my cheeks would begin burning like mad and little prickles of sweat would start coming out all over the crown of my head.

This condition is all very well in a schoolboy who has just reached the age of puberty. With him it is simply Dame Nature's way of putting on the brakes and holding the lad back until he is old enough to behave himself like a gentleman. I approve of that.

But there was no reason on God's earth why I, at the ripe old age of thirty-one, should continue to suffer a similar embarrassment. I was well trained to resist temptation, and I was certainly not given to vulgar passions.

Had I been even the slightest bit ashamed of my own personal appearance, then that might possibly have explained the whole thing. But I was not. On the contrary, and though I say it myself, the fates had been rather kind to me in that regard. I stood exactly five and a half feet tall in my stockinged feet, and my shoulders, though they sloped downward a little from the neck, were nicely in balance with my small neat frame. (Personally, I've always thought that a little slope on the shoulder lends a subtle and faintly aesthetic air to a man who is not overly tall, don't you agree?) My features were regular, my teeth were in excellent condition (protruding only a smallish amount from the upper jaw), and my hair, which was an unusually brilliant ginger-red, grew thickly all over my scalp. Good heavens above, I had seen men who were perfect shrimps in comparison with me displaying an astonishing aplomb in their dealings with the fairer sex. And oh, how I envied them! How I longed to do likewise – to be able to share in a few of those pleasant little rituals of contact that I observed continually taking place between men and women – the touching of hands, the peck on the cheek, the linking of arms, the pressure of knee against knee or foot against foot under the dining-table, and most of all, the full-blown violent embrace that comes when two of them join together on the floor – for a dance.

But such things were not for me. Alas, I had to spend my time avoiding them instead. And this, my friends, was easier said than done, even for a humble curate in a small country region far from the fleshpots of the metropolis.

My flock, you understand, contained an inordinate number of ladies. There were scores of them in the parish, and the unfortunate thing about it was that at least sixty per cent of them were spinsters, completely untamed by the benevolent influence of holy matrimony.

I tell you I was jumpy as a squirrel.

One would have thought that with all the careful training my mother had given me as a child, I should have been capable of taking this sort of thing well in my stride; and no doubt I would have done if only she had lived long enough to complete my education. But alas, she was killed when I was still quite young.

She was a wonderful woman, my mother. She used to wear huge bracelets on her wrists, five or six of them at a time, with all sorts of things hanging from them and tinkling against each other as she moved. It didn't matter where she was, you could always find her by listening for the noise of those bracelets. It was better than a cowbell. And in the evenings she used to sit on the sofa in her black trousers with her feet tucked up underneath her, smoking endless cigarettes from a long black holder. And I'd be crouching on the floor, watching her.

'You want to taste my martini, George?' she used to ask.

'Now stop it, Clare,' my father would say. 'If you're not careful you'll stunt the boy's growth.'

'Go on,' she said. 'Don't be frightened of it. Drink it.'

I always did everything my mother told me.

'That's enough,' my father said. 'He only has to know what it tastes like.'

'Please don't interfere, Boris. This is *very* important.'

My mother had a theory that nothing in the world should be kept secret from a child. Show him everything. Make him *experience* it.

'I'm not going to have any boy of mine going around whispering dirty secrets with other children and having to guess about this thing and that simply because no one will tell him.'

Tell him everything. Make him listen.

'Come over here, George, and I'll tell you what there is to know about God.'

She never read stories to me at night before I went to bed; she just 'told' me things instead. And every evening it was something different.

'Come over here, George, because now I'm going to tell you about Mohammed.'

She would be sitting on the sofa in her black trousers with her legs crossed and her feet tucked up underneath her, and she'd beckon to me in a queer languorous manner with the hand that held the long black cigarette-holder, and the bangles would start jingling all the way up her arm.

'If you must have a religion I suppose Mohammedanism is as good as any of them. It's all based on keeping healthy. You have lots of wives, and you mustn't ever smoke or drink.'

'Why mustn't you smoke or drink, Mummy?'

'Because if you've got lots of wives you have to keep healthy and virile.'

'What is virile?'

'I'll go into that tomorrow, my pet. Let's deal with one subject at a time. Another thing about the Mohammedan is that he never never gets constipated.'

'Now, Clare,' my father would say, looking up from his book. 'Stick to the facts.'

'My dear Boris, you don't know anything about it. Now if only *you* would try bending forward and touching the ground with your forehead morning, noon, and night every day, facing Mecca, you might have a bit less trouble in that direction yourself.'

I used to love listening to her, even though I could only understand about half of what she was saying. She really was telling me secrets, and there wasn't anything more exciting than that.

'Come over here, George, and I'll tell you precisely how your father makes his money.'

'Now, Clare, that's quite enough.'

'Nonsense, darling. Why make a *secret* of it with the child? He'll only imagine something much much worse.'

I was exactly ten years old when she started giving me detailed lectures on the subject of sex. This was the biggest secret of them all, and therefore the most enthralling.

'Come over here, George, because now I'm going to tell you how you came into this world, right from the very beginning.'

I saw my father glance up quietly, and open his mouth wide the way he did when he was going to say something vital, but my mother was already fixing him with those brilliant shining eyes of hers, and he went slowly back to his book without uttering a sound.

'Your poor father is embarrassed,' she said, and she gave me her private smile, the one that she gave nobody else, only to me – the one-sided smile where just one corner of her mouth lifted slowly upward until it made a lovely long wrinkle that stretched right up to the eye itself, and became a sort of wink-smile instead.

'Embarrassment, my pet, is the one thing that I want you never to feel. And don't think for a moment that your father is embarrassed only because of *you*.'

My father started wriggling about in his chair.

'My God, he's even embarrassed about things like that when he's alone with me, his own wife.'

'About things like what?' I asked.

At that point my father got up and quietly left the room.

I think it must have been about a week after this that my mother was killed. It may possibly have been a little later, ten days or a fortnight, I can't be sure. All I know is that we were getting near the end of this particular series of 'talks' when it happened; and because I myself was personally involved in the brief chain of events that led up to her death, I can still remember every single detail of that curious night just as clearly as if it were yesterday. I can switch it on in my memory any time I like and run it through in front of my eyes exactly as though it were the reel of a cinema film; and it never varies. It always ends at precisely the same place, no more and no less, and it always begins in the same peculiarly sudden way, with the screen in darkness, and my mother's voice somewhere above me, calling my name:

'George! Wake up, George, wake up!'

And then there is a bright electric light dazzling in my eyes, and right from the very centre of it, but far away, the voice is still calling me:

'George, wake up and get out of bed and put your dressing-gown on! Quickly! You're coming downstairs. There's something I want you to see.'

Come on, child, come on! Hurry up! And put your slippers on. We're
going outside.'

'Outside?'

'Don't argue with me, George. Just do as you're told.' I am so sleepy
I can hardly see to walk, but my mother takes me firmly by the hand
and leads me downstairs and out through the front door into the night
where the cold air is like a sponge of water in my face, and I open my
eyes wide and see the lawn all sparkling with frost and the cedar tree with
its tremendous arms standing black against a thin small moon. And
overhead a great mass of stars is wheeling up into the sky.

We hurry across the lawn, my mother and I, her bracelets all jingling
like mad and me having to trot to keep up with her. Each step I take
I can feel the crisp frosty grass crunching softly underfoot.

'Josephine has just started having her babies,' my mother says. 'It's a
perfect opportunity. You shall watch the whole process.'

There is a light burning in the garage when we get there, and we go
inside. My father isn't there, nor is the car, and the place seems huge and
bare, and the concrete floor is freezing cold through the soles of my
bedroom slippers. Josephine is reclining on a heap of straw inside the low
wire cage in one corner of the room – a large blue rabbit with small pink
eyes that watch us suspiciously as we go towards her. The husband, whose
name is Napoleon, is now in a separate cage in the opposite corner, and
I notice that he is standing up on his hind legs scratching impatiently at
the netting.

'Look!' my mother cries. 'She's just having the first one! It's almost
out!'

We both creep closer to Josephine, and I squat down beside the cage
with my face right up against the wire. I am fascinated. Here is one rabbit
coming out of another. It is magical and rather splendid. It is also very
quick.

'Look how it comes out all neatly wrapped up in its own little
cellophane bag!' my mother is saying.

'And just look how she's taking care of it now! The poor darling doesn't
have a face-flannel, and even if she did she couldn't hold it in her paws,
so she's washing it with her tongue instead.'

The mother rabbit rolls her small pink eyes anxiously in our direction,
and then I see her shifting position in the straw so that her body is between
us and the young one.

'Come round the other side,' my mother says. 'The silly thing has
moved. I do believe she's trying to hide her baby from us.'

We go round the other side of the cage. The rabbit follows us with her
eyes. A couple of yards away the buck is prancing madly up and down,
clawing at the wire.

'Why is Napoleon so excited?' I ask.

'I don't know, dear. Don't you bother about him. Watch Josephine.
I expect she'll be having another one soon. Look how carefully she's
washing that little baby! She's treating it just like a human mother treats
hers! Isn't it funny to think that I did almost exactly the same sort of thing
to you once?' The big blue doe is still watching us, and now, again, she
pushes the baby away with her nose and rolls slowly over to face the other
way. Then she goes on with her licking and cleaning.

'Isn't it wonderful how a mother knows instinctively just what she has
to do?' my mother says. 'Now you just imagine, my pet, that the baby
is *you*, and Josephine is *me* – wait a minute, come back over here again
so you can get a better look.'

We creep back around the cage to keep the baby in view.

'See how she's fondling it and kissing it all over! There! She's *really*
kissing it now, isn't she! Exactly like me and you!'

I peer closer. It seems a queer way of kissing to me.

'Look!' I scream. 'She's eating it!'

And sure enough, the head of the baby rabbit is now disappearing
swiftly into the mother's mouth.

'Mummy! Quick!'

But almost before the sound of my scream has died away, the whole
of that tiny pink body has vanished down the mother's throat.

I swing quickly around, and the next thing I know I'm looking straight
into my own mother's face, not six inches above me, and no doubt she
is trying to say something or it may be that she is too astonished to say
anything, but all I see is the mouth, the huge red mouth opening wider
and wider until it is just a great big round gaping hole with a black centre,
and I scream again, and this time I can't stop. Then suddenly out come
her hands, and I can feel her skin touching mine, the long cold fingers
closing tightly over my fists, and I jump back and jerk myself free and
rush blindly out into the night. I run down the drive and through the
front gates, screaming all the way, and then, above the noise of my own
voice I can hear the jingle of bracelets coming up behind me in the dark,
getting louder and louder as she keeps gaining on me all the way down
the long hill to the bottom of the lane and over the bridge on to the main
road where the cars are streaming by at sixty miles an hour with headlights blazing.

Then somewhere behind me I hear a screech of tyres skidding on the
road surface, and then there is silence, and I notice suddenly that the
bracelets aren't jingling behind me any more.

Poor Mother.

If only she could have lived a little longer.

I admit that she gave me a nasty fright with those rabbits, but it wasn't
her fault, and anyway queer things like that were always happening
between her and me. I had come to regard them as a sort of toughening

process that did me more good than harm. But if only she could have lived long enough to complete my education, I'm sure I should never have had all that trouble I was telling you about a few minutes ago.

I want to get on with that now. I didn't mean to begin talking about my mother. She doesn't have anything to do with what I originally started out to say. I won't mention her again.

I was telling you about the spinsters in my parish. It's an ugly word, isn't it – spinsters? It conjures up the vision either of a stringy old hen with a puckered mouth or of a huge ribald monster shouting around the house in riding-breeches. But these were not like that at all. They were a clean, healthy, well-built group of females, the majority of them highly bred and surprisingly wealthy, and I feel sure that the average unmarried man would have been gratified to have them around.

In the beginning, when I first came to the vicarage, I didn't have too bad a time. I enjoyed a measure of protection, of course, by reason of my calling and my cloth. In addition, I myself adopted a cool dignified attitude that was calculated to discourage familiarity. For a few months, therefore, I was able to move freely among my parishioners, and no one took the liberty of linking her arm in mine at a charity bazaar, or of touching my fingers with hers as she passed me the cruet at suppertime. I was very happy. I was feeling better than I had in years. Even that little nervous habit I had of flicking my earlobe with my forefinger when I talked began to disappear.

This was what I call my first period, and it extended over approximately six months. Then came trouble.

I suppose I should have known that a healthy male like myself couldn't hope to evade embroilment indefinitely simply by keeping a fair distance between himself and the ladies. It just doesn't work. If anything it has the opposite effect.

I would see them eyeing me covertly across the room at a whist drive, whispering to one another, nodding, running their tongues over their lips, sucking at their cigarettes, plotting the best approach, but always whispering, and sometimes I overheard snatches of their talk – 'What a shy person ... he's just a trifle nervous, isn't he ... he's much too tense ... he needs companionship ... he wants loosening up ... we must teach him how to relax.' And then slowly, as the weeks went by, they began to stalk me. I knew they were doing it. I could feel it happening although at first they did nothing definite to give themselves away.

That was my second period. It lasted for the best part of a year and was very trying indeed. But it was paradise compared with the third and final phase.

For now, instead of sniping at me sporadically from far away, the attackers suddenly came charging out of the wood with bayonets fixed. It was terrible, frightening. Nothing is more calculated to unnerve a man than the swift unexpected assault. Yet I am not a coward. I will stand my ground against any single individual of my own size under any circumstances. But this onslaught, I am now convinced, was conducted by vast numbers operating as one skilfully co-ordinated unit.

The first offender was Miss Elphinstone, a large woman with moles. I had dropped in on her during the afternoon to solicit a contribution towards a new set of bellows for the organ, and after some pleasant conversation in the library she had graciously handed me a cheque for two guineas. I told her not to bother to see me to the door and I went out into the hall to get my hat. I was about to reach for it when all at once – she must have come tip-toeing up behind me – all at once I felt a bare arm sliding through mine, and one second later her fingers were entwined in my own, and she was squeezing my hand hard, in out, in out, as though it were the bulb of a throat-spray.

'Are you really so Very Reverend as you're always pretending to be?' she whispered.

Well!

All I can tell you is that when that arm of hers came sliding in under mine, it felt exactly as though a cobra was coiling itself around my wrist. I leaped away, pulled open the front door, and fled down the drive without looking back.

The very next day we held a jumble sale in the village hall (again to raise money for the new bellows), and towards the end of it I was standing in a corner quietly drinking a cup of tea and keeping an eye on the villagers crowding round the stalls when all of a sudden I heard a voice beside me saying, 'Dear me, what a hungry look you have in those eyes of yours.' The next instant a long curvaceous body was leaning up against mine and a hand with red fingernails was trying to push a thick slice of coconut cake into my mouth.

'Miss Prattley,' I cried. 'Please!'

But she'd got me up against the wall and with a teacup in one hand and a saucer in the other I was powerless to resist. I felt the sweat breaking out all over me and if my mouth hadn't quickly become full of the cake she was pushing into it, I honestly believe I would have started to scream.

A nasty incident, that one; but there was worse to come.

The next day it was Miss Unwin. Now Miss Unwin happened to be a close friend of Miss Elphinstone's *and* of Miss Prattley's, and this of course should have been enough to make me very cautious. Yet who would have thought that she of all people, Miss Unwin, that quiet gentle little mouse who only a few weeks before had presented me with a new hassock exquisitely worked in needlepoint with her own hands, who would have thought that *she* would ever have taken a liberty with anyone? So when she asked me to accompany her down to the crypt to show her the Saxon murals, it never entered my head that there was devilry afoot. But there was.

I don't propose to describe that encounter; it was too painful. And the ones which followed were no less savage. Nearly every day from then on, some new outrageous incident would take place. I became a nervous wreck. At times I hardly knew what I was doing. I started reading the burial service at young Gladys Pitcher's wedding. I dropped Mrs Harris's new baby into the font during the christening and gave it a nasty ducking. An uncomfortable rash that I hadn't had in over two years reappeared on the side of my neck, and that annoying business with my earlobe came back worse than ever before. Even my hair began coming out in my comb. The faster I retreated, the faster they came after me. Women are like that. Nothing stimulates them quite so much as a display of modesty or shyness in a man. And they become doubly persistent if underneath it all they happen to detect – and here I have a most difficult confession to make – if they happen to detect, as they did in me, a little secret gleam of longing shining in the backs of the eyes.

You see, actually I was mad about women.

Yes, I know. You will find this hard to believe after all that I have said, but it was perfectly true. You must understand that it was only when they touched me with their fingers or pushed up against me with their bodies that I became alarmed. Providing they remained at a safe distance, I could watch them for hours on end with the same peculiar fascination that you yourself might experience in watching a creature you couldn't bear to touch – an octopus, for example, or a long poisonous snake. I loved the smooth white look of a bare arm emerging from a sleeve, curiously naked like a peeled banana. I could get enormously excited just from watching a girl walk across the room in a tight dress; and I particularly enjoyed the back view of a pair of legs when the feet were in rather high heels – the wonderful braced-up look behind the knees, with the legs themselves very taut as though they were made of strong elastic stretched out almost to breaking-point, but not quite. Sometimes, in Lady Birdwell's drawing-room, sitting near the window on a summer's afternoon, I would glance over the rim of my teacup towards the swimming pool and become agitated beyond measure by the sight of a little patch of sunburned stomach bulging between the top and bottom of a two-piece bathing-suit.

There is nothing wrong in having thoughts like these. All men harbour them from time to time. But they did give me a terrible sense of guilt. Is it me, I kept asking myself, who is unwittingly responsible for the shameless way in which these ladies are now behaving? Is it the gleam in my eye (which I cannot control) that is constantly rousing their passions and egging them on? Am I unconsciously giving them what is sometimes known as the come-hither signal every time I glance their way? Am I?

Or is this brutal conduct of theirs inherent in the very nature of the female?

I had a pretty fair idea of the answer to this question, but that was not good enough for me. I happen to possess a conscience that can never be consoled by guesswork; it has to have proof. I simply had to find out who was really the guilty party in this case – me or them, and with this object in view, I now decided to perform a simple experiment of my own invention, using Snelling's rats.

A year or so previously I had had some trouble with an objectionable choirboy named Billy Snelling. On three consecutive Sundays this youth had brought a pair of white rats into church and had let them loose on the floor during my sermon. In the end I had confiscated the animals and carried them home and placed them in a box in the shed at the bottom of the vicarage garden. Purely for humane reasons I had then proceeded to feed them, and as a result, but without any further encouragement from me, the creatures began to multiply very rapidly. The two became five, and the five became twelve.

It was at this point that I decided to use them for research purposes. There were exactly equal numbers of males and females, six of each, so that conditions were ideal.

I first isolated the sexes, putting them into two separate cages, and I left them like that for three whole weeks. Now a rat is a very lascivious animal, and any zoologist will tell you that for them this is an inordinately long period of separation. At a guess I would say that one week of enforced celibacy for a rat is equal to approximately one year of the same treatment for someone like Miss Elphinstone or Miss Prattley; so you can see that I was doing a pretty fair job in reproducing actual conditions.

When the three weeks were up, I took a large box that was divided across the centre by a little fence, and I placed the females on one side and the males on the other. The fence consisted of nothing more than three single strands of naked wire, one inch apart, but there was a powerful electric current running through the wires.

To add a touch of reality to the proceedings, I gave each female a name. The largest one, who also had the longest whiskers, was Miss Elphinstone. The one with a short thick tail was Miss Prattley. The smallest of them all was Miss Unwin, and so on. The males, all six of them, were ME.

I now pulled up a chair and sat back to watch the result.

All rats are suspicious by nature, and when I first put the two sexes together in the box with only the wire between them, neither side made a move. The males stared hard at the females through the fence. The females stared back, waiting for the males to come forward. I could see that both sides were tense with yearning. Whiskers quivered and noses twitched and occasionally a long tail would flick sharply against the wall of the box.

After a while, the first male detached himself from his group and advanced gingerly towards the fence, his belly close to the ground. He touched a wire and was immediately electrocuted. The remaining eleven rats froze, motionless.

There followed a period of nine and a half minutes during which neither side moved; but I noticed that while all the males were now staring at the dead body of their colleague, the females had eyes only for the males.

Then suddenly Miss Prattley with the short tail could stand it no longer. She came bounding forward, hit the wire, and dropped dead.

The males pressed their bodies closer to the ground and gazed thoughtfully at the two corpses by the fence. The females also seemed to be quite shaken, and there was another wait, with neither side moving.

Now it was Miss Unwin who began to show signs of impatience. She snorted audibly and twitched a pink mobile nose-end from side to side, then suddenly she started jerking her body quickly up and down as though she were doing pushups. She glanced round at her remaining four companions, raised her tail high in the air as much as to say, 'Here I go, girls,' and with that she advanced briskly to the wire, pushed her head through it, and was killed.

Sixteen minutes later, Miss Foster made her first move. Miss Foster was a woman in the village who bred cats, and recently she had had the effrontery to put up a large sign outside her house in the High Street, saying FOSTER'S CATTERY. Through long association with the creatures she herself seemed to have acquired all their most noxious characteristics, and whenever she came near me in a room I could detect, even through the smoke of her Russian cigarette, a faint but pungent aroma of cat. She had never struck me as having much control over her baser instincts, and it was with some satisfaction, therefore, that I watched her now as she foolishly took her own life in a last desperate plunge towards the masculine sex.

A Miss Montgomery-Smith came next, a small determined woman who had once tried to make me believe that she had been engaged to a bishop. She died trying to creep on her belly under the lowest wire, and I must say I thought this a very fair reflection upon the way in which she lived her life.

And still the five remaining males stayed motionless, waiting.

The fifth female to go was Miss Plumley. She was a devious one who was continually slipping little messages addressed to me into the collection bag. Only the Sunday before, I had been in the vestry counting the money after morning service and had come across one of them tucked inside a folded ten shilling note. *Your poor throat sounded hoarse today during the sermon*, it said. *Let me bring you a bottle of my own cherry pectoral to soothe it down. Most affectionately, Eunice Plumley.*

Miss Plumley ambled slowly up to the wire, sniffed the centre strand with the tip of her nose, came a fraction too close, and received two hundred and forty volts of alternating current through her body.

The five males stayed where they were, watching the slaughter.

And now only Miss Elphinstone remained on the feminine side.

For a full half-hour neither she nor any of the others made a move. Finally one of the males stirred himself slightly, took a step forward, hesitated, thought better of it, and slowly sank back into a crouch on the floor.

This must have frustrated Miss Elphinstone beyond measure, for suddenly, with eyes blazing, she rushed forward and took a flying leap at the wire. It was a spectacular jump and she nearly cleared it; but one of her hind legs grazed the top strand, and thus she also perished with the rest of her sex.

I cannot tell you how much good it did me to watch this simple and, though I say it myself, this rather ingenious experiment. In one stroke I had laid open the incredibly lascivious, stop-at-nothing nature of the female. My own sex was vindicated; my own conscience was cleared. In a trice, all those awkward little flashes of guilt from which I had continually been suffering lew out of the window. I felt suddenly very strong and serene in the knowledge of my own innocence.

For a few moments I toyed with the absurd idea of electrifying the black iron railings that ran around the vicarage garden; or perhaps just the gate would be enough. Then I would sit back comfortably in a chair in the library and watch through the window as a read Misses Elphinstone and Prattley and Unwin came forward one after the other and paid the final penalty for pestering an innocent male.

Such foolish thoughts!

What I must actually do now, I told myself, was to weave around me a sort of invisible electric fence constructed entirely out of my own personal moral fibre. Behind this I would sit in perfect safety while the enemy, one after another, flung themselves against the wire.

I would begin by cultivating a brusque manner. I would speak crisply to all women, and refrain from smiling at them I would no longer step back a pace when one of them advanced upon me. I would stand my ground and glare at her, and if she said something that I considered suggestive, I would make a sharp retort.

It was in this mood that I set off the very next day to attend Lady Birdwell's tennis party.

I was not a player myself, but her ladyship had graciously invited me to drop in and mingle with the guests when play was over at six o'clock. I believe she thought that it lent a certain tone to a gathering to have a clergyman present, and she was probably hoping to persuade me to repeat the performance I gave the last time I was there, when I sat at the piano for a full hour and a quarter after supper and entertained the guests with a detailed description of the evolution of the madrigal through the centuries.

I arrived at the gates on my cycle promptly at six o'clock and pedalled up the long drive towards the house. This was the first week of June, and the rhododendrons were massed in great banks of pink and purple all the way along on either side. I was feeling unusually blithe and dauntless. The previous day's experiment with rats had made it impossible now for anyone to take me by surprise. I knew exactly what to expect and I was armed accordingly. All around me the little fence was up.

'Ah, good evening, Vicar,' Lady Birdwell cried, advancing upon me with both arms outstretched.

I stood my ground and looked her straight in the eye. 'How's Birdwell?' I said. 'Still up in the city?'

I doubt whether she had ever before in her life heard Lord Birdwell referred to thus by someone who had never even met him. It stopped her dead in her tracks. She looked at me queerly and didn't seem to know how to answer.

'I'll take a seat if I may,' I said, and walked past her towards the terrace where a group of nine or ten guests were settled comfortably in cane chairs, sipping their drinks. They were mostly women, the usual crowd, all of them dressed in white tennis clothes, and as I strode in among them my own sober black suiting seemed to give me, I thought, just the right amount of separateness for the occasion.

The ladies greeted me with smiles. I nodded to them and sat down in a vacant chair, but I didn't smile back.

'I think perhaps I'd better finish my story another time,' Miss Elphinstone was saying. 'I don't believe the vicar would approve.' She giggled and gave me an arch look. I knew she was waiting for me to come out with my usual little nervous laugh and to say my usual little sentence about how broadminded I was; but I did nothing of the sort. I simply raised one side of my upper lip until it shaped itself into a tiny curl of contempt (I had practised in the mirror that morning), and then I said sharply, in a loud voice, '*Mens sana in corpore sano*.'

'What's that?' she cried. 'Come again, Vicar.'

'A clean mind in a healthy body,' I answered. 'It's a family motto.'

There was an odd kind of silence for quite a long time after this. I could see the women exchanging glances with one another, frowning, shaking their heads.

'The vicar's in the dumps,' Miss Foster announced. She was the one who bred cats. 'I think the vicar needs a drink.'

'Thank you,' I said, 'but I never imbibe. You know that.'

'Then do let me fetch you a nice cooling glass of fruit cup?'

This last sentence came softly and rather suddenly from someone just

behind me, to my right, and there was a note of such genuine concern
in the speaker's voice that I turned round.

I saw a lady of singular beauty whom I had met only once before,
about a month ago. Her name was Miss Roach, and I remembered that
she had struck me then as being a person far out of the usual run. I had
been particularly impressed by her gentle and reticent nature; and the
fact that I had felt comfortable in her presence proved beyond doubt that
she was not the sort of person who would try to impinge herself upon me
in any way.

'I'm sure you must be tired after cycling all that distance,' she was
saying now.

I swivelled right round in my chair and looked at her carefully. She
was certainly a striking person – unusually muscular for a woman, with
broad shoulders and powerful arms and a huge calf bulging on each leg.
The flush of the afternoon's exertions was still upon her, and her face
glowed with a healthy red sheen.

'Thank you so much, Miss Roach,' I said, 'but I never touch alcohol
in any form. Maybe a small glass of lemon squash ...'

'The fruit cup is only made of fruit, Padre.'

How I loved a person who called me 'Padre'. The word has a military
ring about it that conjures up visions of stern discipline and officer rank.

'Fruit cup?' Miss Elphinstone said. 'It's harmless.'

'My dear man, it's nothing but vitamin C,' Miss Foster said.

'Much better for you than fizzy lemonade,' Lady Birdwell said.
'Carbon dioxide attacks the lining of the stomach.'

'I'll get you some,' Miss Roach said, smiling at me pleasantly. It was
a good open smile, and there wasn't a trace of guile or mischief from one
corner of the mouth to the other.

She stood up and walked over to the drink table. I saw her slicing an
orange, then an apple, then a cucumber, then a grape, and dropping the
pieces into a glass. Then she poured in a large quantity of liquid from
a bottle whose label I couldn't quite read without my spectacles, but I
fancied that I saw the name JIM on it, or TIM, or PIM, or some such word.

'I hope there's enough left,' Lady Birdwell called out. 'Those greedy
children of mine do love it so.'

'Plenty,' Miss Roach answered, and she brought the drink to me and
set it on the table.

Even without tasting it I could easily understand why children adored
it. The liquid itself was dark amber-red and there were great hunks of
fruit floating around among the ice cubes; and on top of it all, Miss Roach
had placed a sprig of mint. I guessed that the mint had been put there
specially for me, to take some of the sweetness away and to lend a touch
of grown-upness to a concoction that was otherwise so obviously for
youngsters.

'Too sticky for you, Padre!'

'It's delectable,' I said, sipping it. 'Quite perfect.'

It seemed a pity to gulp it down quickly after all the trouble Miss Roach had taken to make it, but it was so refreshing I couldn't resist.

'Do let me make you another!'

I liked the way she waited until I had set the glass on the table, instead of trying to take it out of my hand.

'I wouldn't eat the mint if I were you,' Miss Elphinstone said.

'I'd better get another bottle from the house,' Lady Birdwell called out. 'You're going to need it, Mildred.'

'Do that,' Miss Roach replied. 'I drink gallons of the stuff myself,' she went on, speaking to me. 'And I don't think you'd say that I'm exactly what you might call emaciated.'

'No indeed,' I answered fervently. I was watching her again as she mixed me another brew, noticing how the muscles rippled under the skin of the arm that raised the bottle. Her neck also was uncommonly fine when seen from behind; not thin and stringy like the necks of a lot of these so-called modern beauties, but thick and strong with a slight ridge running down either side where the sinews bulged. It wasn't easy to guess the age of a person like this, but I doubted whether she could have been more than forty-eight or nine.

I had just finished my second big glass of fruit cup when I began to experience a most peculiar sensation. I seemed to be floating up out of my chair, and hundreds of little warm waves came washing in under me, lifting me higher and higher. I felt as buoyant as a bubble, and everything around me seemed to be bobbing up and down and swirling gently from side to side. It was all very pleasant, and I was overcome by an almost irresistible desire to break into song.

'Feeling happy?' Miss Roach's voice sounded miles and miles away, and when I turned to look at her, I was astonished to see how near she really was. She, also, was bobbing up and down.

'Terrific,' I answered. 'I'm feeling absolutely terrific.'

Her face was large and pink, and it was so close to me now that I could see the pale carpet of fuzz covering both her cheeks, and the way the sunlight caught each tiny separate hair and made it shine like gold. All of a sudden I found myself wanting to put out a hand and stroke those cheeks of hers with my fingers. To tell the truth, I wouldn't have objected in the least if she had tried to do the same to me.

'Listen,' she said softly. 'How about the two of us taking a little stroll down the garden to see the lupins?'

'Fine,' I answered. 'Lovely. Anything you say.'

There is a small Georgian summer-house alongside the croquet lawn in Lady Birdwell's garden, and the very next thing I knew, I was sitting inside it on a kind of chaise-longue and Miss Roach was beside me. I was still bobbing up and down, and so was she, and so, for that matter, was the summer-house, but I was feeling wonderful. I asked Miss Roach if she would like me to give her a song.

'Not now,' she said, encircling me with her arms and squeezing my chest against hers so hard that it hurt.

'Don't,' I said, melting.

'That's better,' she kept saying. 'That's much better, isn't it?'

Had Miss Roach or any other female tried to do this sort of thing to me an hour before, I don't quite know what would have happened. I think I would probably have fainted. I might even have died. But here I was now, the same old me, actually relishing the contact of those enormous bare arms against my body! Also – and this was the most amazing thing of all – I was beginning to feel the urge to reciprocate.

I took the lobe of her left ear between my thumb and forefinger, and tugged it playfully.

'Naughty boy,' she said.

I tugged harder and squeezed it a bit at the same time. This roused her to such a pitch that she began to grunt and snort like a hog. Her breathing became loud and stertorous.

'Kiss me,' she ordered.

'What?' I said.

'Come on, kiss me.'

At that moment, I saw her mouth. I saw this great mouth of hers coming slowly down on top of me, starting to open, and coming closer and closer, and opening wider and wider; and suddenly my whole stomach began to roll right over inside me and I went stiff with terror.

'No!' I shrieked. 'Don't! Don't, Mummy, don't!'

I can only tell you that I had never in all my life seen anything more terrifying than that mouth. I simply could not *stand* it coming at me like that. Had it been a red-hot iron someone was pushing into my face I wouldn't have been nearly so petrified, I swear I wouldn't. The strong arms were around me, pinning me down so that I couldn't move, and the mouth kept getting larger and larger, and then all at once it was right on top of me, huge and wet and cavernous, and the next second – I was inside it.

I was right inside this enormous mouth, lying on my stomach along the length of the tongue, with my feet somewhere around the back of the throat; and I knew instinctively that unless I got myself out again at once I was going to be swallowed alive – just like that baby rabbit. I could feel my legs being drawn down the throat by some kind of suction, and quickly I threw up my arms and grabbed hold of the lower front teeth and held on for dear life. My head was near the mouth-entrance, and I could actually look right out between the lips and see a little patch of the world outside – sunlight shining on the polished wooden floor of the summerhouse, and on the floor itself a gigantic foot in a white tennis shoe.

I had a good grip with my fingers on the edge of the teeth, and in spite of the suction, I was managing to haul myself up slowly towards the daylight when suddenly the upper teeth came down on my knuckles and started chopping away at them so fiercely I had to let go. I went sliding back down the throat, feet first, clutching madly at this and that as I went, but everything was so smooth and slippery I couldn't get a grip. I glimpsed a bright flash of gold on the left as I slid past the last of the molars, and then three inches farther on I saw what must have been the uvula above me, dangling like a thick red stalactite from the roof of the throat. I grabbed at it with both hands but the thing slithered through my fingers and I went on down.

I remember screaming for help, but I could barely hear the sound of my own voice above the noise of the wind that was caused by the throat-owner's breathing. There seemed to be a gale blowing all the time, a queer erratic gale that blew alternately very cold (as the air came in) and very hot (as it went out again).

I managed to get my elbows hooked over a sharp fleshy ridge – I presume the epiglottis – and for a brief moment I hung there, defying the suction and scrabbling with my feet to find a foothold on the wall of the larynx; but the throat gave a huge swallow that jerked me away, and down I went again.

From then on, there was nothing else for me to catch hold of, and down and down I went until soon my legs were dangling below me in the upper reaches of the stomach, and I could feel the slow powerful pulsing of peristalsis dragging away at my ankles, pulling me down and down and down ...

Far above me, outside in the open air, I could hear the distant babble of women's voices:

'It's not true ...'

'But my dear Mildred, how awful ...'

'The man must be mad ...'

'Your poor mouth, just look at it ...'

'A sex maniac ...'

'A sadist ...'

'Someone ought to write to the bishop ...'

And then Miss Roach's voice, louder than the others, swearing and screeching like a parakeet:

'He's damn lucky I didn't kill him, the little bastard! ... I said to him, listen, I said, if ever I happen to want any of my teeth extracted, I'll go to a dentist, not to a goddam vicar ... It isn't as though I'd given him any encouragement either! ...'

'Where is he now, Mildred?'

'God knows. In the bloody summer-house, I suppose.'
'Hey girls, let's go and root him out!'

Oh dear, oh dear. Looking back on it all now, some three weeks later, I don't know how I ever came through the nightmare of that awful afternoon without taking leave of my senses.

A gang of witches like that is a very dangerous thing to fool around with, and had they managed to catch me in the summer-house right then and there when their blood was up, they would as likely as not have torn me limb from limb on the spot.

Either that, or I should have been frog-marched down to the police station with Lady Birdwell and Miss Roach leading the procession through the main street of the village.

But of course they didn't catch me.

They didn't catch me then, and they haven't caught me yet, and if my luck continues to hold, I think I've got a fair chance of evading them altogether – or anyway for a few months, until they forget about the whole affair.

As you might guess, I am having to keep entirely to myself and to take no part in public affairs or social life. I find that writing is a most salutary occupation at a time like this, and I spend many hours each day playing with sentences. I regard each sentence as a little wheel, and my ambition lately has been to gather several hundred of them together at once and to fit them all end to end, with the cogs interlocking, like gears, but each wheel a different size, each turning at a different speed. Now and again I try to put a really big one right next to a very small one in such a way that the big one, turning slowly, will make the small one spin so fast that it hums. Very tricky, that.

I also sing madrigals in the evenings, but I miss my own harpsichord terribly.

All the same, this isn't such a bad place, and I have made myself as comfortable as I possibly can. It is a small chamber situated in what is almost certainly the primary section of the duodenal loop, just before it begins to run vertically downward in front of the right kidney. The floor is quite level – indeed it was the first level place I came to during that horrible descent down Miss Roach's throat – and that's the only reason I managed to stop at all. Above me, I can see a pulpy sort of opening that I take to be the pylorus, where the stomach enters the small intestine (I can still remember some of those diagrams my mother used to show me), and below me, there is a funny little hole in the wall where the pancreatic duct enters the lower section of the duodenum.

It is all a trifle bizarre for a man of conservative tastes like myself. Personally I prefer oak furniture and parquet flooring. But there is anyway one thing here that pleases me greatly, and that is the walls. They are lovely and soft, like a sort of padding, and the advantage of this is that I can bounce up against them as much as I wish without hurting myself.

There are several other people about, which is rather surprising, but thank God they are every one of them males. For some reason or other, they all wear white coats, and they bustle around pretending to be very busy and important. In actual fact, they are an uncommonly ignorant bunch of fellows. They don't even seem to realize where they *are*. I try to tell them, but they refuse to listen. Sometimes I get so angry and frustrated with them that I lose my temper and start to shout; and then a sly mistrustful look comes over their faces and they begin backing slowly away, and saying, 'Now then. Take it easy. Take it easy, Vicar, there's a good boy. Take it easy.'

What sort of talk is that?

But there is one oldish man – he comes in to see me every morning after breakfast – who appears to live slightly closer to reality than the others. He is civil and dignified, and I imagine he is lonely because he likes nothing better than to sit quietly in my room and listen to me talk. The only trouble is that whenever we get on to the subject of our whereabouts, he starts telling me that he's going to help me to escape. He said it again this morning, and we had quite an argument about it.

'But can't you see,' I said patiently, 'I don't *want* to escape.'

'My dear Vicar, why ever not?'

'I keep telling you – because they're all searching for me outside.'

'Who?'

'Miss Elphinstone and Miss Roach and Miss Prattley and all the rest of them.'

'What nonsense.'

'Oh yes they are! And I imagine they're after *you* as well, but you won't admit it.'

'No, my friend, they are not after me.'

'Then may I ask precisely what you are doing down here?'

A bit of a stumper for him, that one. I could see he didn't know how to answer it.

'I'll bet you were fooling around with Miss Roach and got yourself swallowed up just the same as I did. I'll bet that's exactly what happened, only you're ashamed to admit it.'

He looked suddenly so wan and defeated when I said this that I felt sorry for him.

'Would you like me to sing you a song?' I asked.

But he got up without answering and went quietly out into the corridor.

'Cheer up,' I called after him. 'Don't be depressed. There is always some balm in Gilead.'

Woodman's Knot

Mary Danby

Sandra Morrison met Daniel Carne at the fun fair, which came to Durringford every summer and filled the field behind the Co-op with lights and shrieking and the smell of fried onions.

She had just won herself a goldfish, by throwing ping-pong balls into a goldfish bowl, and was walking past the rifle range, carrying the fish in a plastic, water-filled bag, when he put down his rifle and stepped backwards, bumping into her and making her drop the goldfish. The water poured out of the bag. By the time he had picked up the stranded fish, pop-eyed and gasping in the palm of his hand, and carried it back to the stall for some water, it had died.

He tried to win her another, but failed.

'It doesn't matter,' she said. 'I didn't really want it anyway.'

They walked through the fair together, and Sandra hoped people would think he was her boyfriend. He was extremely tall – at least six foot six – and he was broad, too. A real hunk of a fellow, with curly blond hair and a tanned, outdoor skin. His face, if not handsome, was pleasant enough, with greenish-blue eyes, a solemn mouth and a wide, fairly short nose. She thought he must be about twenty-six: quite old for her really. Not that she was bothered by that; after all, at seventeen she was hardly a child.

'You here alone?' he asked, as they paused to watch the bumper cars.

'I'm meeting a friend,' Sandra explained, 'from the hairdresser's where I work, but she doesn't seem to have turned up.'

'Live round here?'

Sandra nodded. 'Got a room down Eastham Street. My parents are abroad – Hong Kong actually.' She never liked admitting that her mother had long since run away and left her, or that her father was serving a ten-year prison sentence – somewhere in Yorkshire, she believed.

'Fancy a coffee?' asked Daniel. He smiled, showing regular white teeth.

That night, he took her home to Eastham Street and surprised her by soberly shaking hands with her by the front gate. She felt a little disappointed, but honoured, too. He respected her.

The next day, they met at the bus station and he took her for a ride on the back of his motorcycle. He had brought a spare helmet for her, which showed thoughtfulness. Sandra felt the bike surge beneath her, her heart surged with an unfamiliar, exciting emotion. She held him tightly, enjoying the feeling of his big, solid body encircled by her arms. She pressed her face against his broad back and thought she could be falling in love.

During the next few weeks, they spent quite some time in each other's company. Daniel wasn't much of a talker, but she did manage to find out a few things about him. He had once been married, when he was very young, and had a little girl called Eleanora – Ellie – who lived with him and his sister Katryn. He seemed reluctant to say much about his marriage, but it seemed his wife had gone away. Probably she had run off with another, like Sandra's mother had done. Sandra hated her for that. Poor Daniel. How he, too, must have suffered.

Daniel and his brothers, cousins and uncles worked together to make wooden furniture. They had their own business. 'You never heard of Carne chairs?' he asked her. She hadn't.

He lived in Woodman's Knot, a few miles out of the town, with all the other members of his family. It sounded like some kind of commune. 'I'll take you there, if you like,' he said.

The following Sunday he fetched her on his bike. She was wearing her best dress and had washed her straight, dark hair that morning, so that it gleamed in the summer sun.

'You're looking nice, then,' he said politely.

He wore light blue jeans with a wine-red, vest-like top. It showed off his well-muscled shoulders. Sandra thought he could probably squeeze her to death if he chose. She could think of worse ways to go.

They left the main road and took a track that went through the middle of a dense forest – Woodman's Knot, he told her, turning his head slightly. After a number of twists and bends, they reached a wide clearing. Sandra was surprised to find herself surrounded by at least twenty houses – except that they weren't really houses. Some were large trailers, complete with steps and porches and their own small gardens. Some were wooden sheds, some were made from concrete blocks, and there was an old Nissen hut which appeared to be the workshop, for there were a number of tables and chairs at different stages of construction standing outside its open doors. From inside, she could hear sounds of woodworking, and round the back there seemed to be some kind of generator throbbing away. A large, plain-sided van stood under the trees.

She climbed off the bike, and Daniel wheeled it into a corrugated-iron shelter, leaving it alongside two other motorbikes, several bicycles, a pram and an old black Austin saloon.

Several people were coming out to see the stranger, and they smiled at Sandra from their doorsteps. Children stopped playing, and dogs came bounding forward. But Daniel took Sandra firmly by the arm and led her to the largest of the trailers. 'First,' he said, 'you have to meet Aunt Marietta.'

Sandra had heard about Aunt Marietta. She was his great-grandfather's sister, and was a hundred and six years old. Sandra had never met anyone so old before. She expected to find someone frail and trembly, with papery skin and watery eyes, propped up on cushions, with a crocheted shawl around her shoulders. But Aunt Marietta was quite a shock. She had a wrinkled face, but she stood up straight and strong, without using a stick, and the hand that took Sandra's was as firm as a young man's.

'My dear,' she said, and her voice was rich and rounded, 'welcome to Woodman's Knot. Welcome to our homestead.' She had an accent that sounded slightly foreign.

'Thank you, Miss Carne,' said Sandra, almost curtseying.

'You'll call me Aunt Marietta.' It was a command. 'I may not have a pretty face now, but at least I have a pretty name, eh?' She chuckled. 'You know, Daniel has told me quite a lot about you. It is pleasing. Yes. We are happy to accept you.' She smiled kindly at Sandra's confused expression. 'It's all right, my dear. We Carnes like to share each other's pleasures – and our little sadnesses, too. So we do not choose for ourselves alone. We choose for all the Carnes. Now, Daniel will take you around and introduce you to the family. You will have tea with me at half past four.'

'What did she mean?' asked Sandra as they left the old lady's trailer. 'All that about choosing.'

'She just likes us all to be friends,' said Daniel, taking her arm again. 'Don't mind her.'

The rest of the Carne family consisted of Daniel's father, Stephen – a genial, quiet giant of a man, whose eloquence was more in the strength of his huge arms than in his speech – his brothers, Nico and Ben, his warm-voiced sister Katryn, his Aunt Greta and Uncles Hugo and Leo, his Great-aunt Bella and Great-uncle Julius, and numerous cousins, nephews and nieces. They were all tall and well-built – a formidable team. And there was Daniel's daughter, Ellie, six years old, who stood in front of Sandra and looked up at her with unblinking blue eyes set like gemstones in her soft, freckled face.

'Are you going to marry my daddy?' she asked unnervingly.

Sandra gave an awkward little laugh, but Daniel came quickly to the rescue. He put an arm around Sandra's shoulders and said to Ellie: 'Wait and see, Little Miss Curious.'

Sandra's stomach seemed to lurch within her. Did this mean he might be considering her for his wife? Was that what Aunt Marietta had been talking about? She looked about her, at the warm, friendly faces of the Carnes, happy together in their tight little community. Working together. Helping each other. Sharing. She thought of her cold bedsitting-room in Eastham Street, and the greasy fishcakes her landlady dished up four times a week, her job at 'Hair Today', with Mr Tony endlessly bossing her about. Most of all, though, she thought of Daniel Carne, of his tenderness, his strength, and how much she wanted him.

For the whole of the following week, they didn't see each other. Daniel was away selling furniture, driving around the country with samples of their hand-crafted pieces and taking order from shopkeepers. It was fine, strong furniture, as sturdy as the men who made it, and much in demand among those who were trying to bring to their homes a look of the farmhouse kitchen. The best seller was the Carne rocker, and Daniel collected a good number of orders for this graceful beechwood showpiece.

'There's this new place in Birmingham – a furniture emporium, they call it – wants thirty rockers. And that's just one order,' Daniel told Sandra the following Saturday. They were sitting together in a small café, drinking Coca-Cola out of cans.

'That's nice.'

Sandra was so happy to see him again. Now she could ask him all the questions that had been gradually forming in her mind all week as she shampooed and blow-dried and cleaned basins and swept up little piles of hair.

'Daniel –' she began.

'If they can sell those, and I think they can, they'll be wanting more,' he interrupted eagerly. 'We'll be working round the clock.'

Sandra thought: He won't be able to spare the time to see me. He's trying to tell me kindly. 'Oh ...' she said. 'Well ...'

'So it seemed to me,' he went on, taking her hand across the table. 'you'd be better off coming to live at Woodman's Knot.'

He was looking down. She couldn't see his eyes. What did he mean?

'The thing is, girl, I'm hoping you might be wanting to marry me.'

Later on, when she tried to remember how she felt when he proposed, all that came to her was a sensation of everything around her feeling insubstantial – the floor beneath her feet, the chair she was sitting on. Of course, she had said yes, and they had gone together to the jewellery shop in the market to buy a ring that was as like a diamond as anything she'd ever seen.

'Where shall we get married?' she had asked. 'St Andrew's, by the Town Hall? Or the Register Office?'

But she should have guessed. The Carnes had a custom for weddings, too. Daniel's Uncle Hugo was to be the minister, having been born on

Midsummer Night. For some reason, this gave him a special religious status in the family, and, from the way Daniel spoke about it, Sandra could tell he thought Uncle Hugo a far more worthy person to conduct the ceremony than the Reverend Cumberside at St Andrew's. And that was good enough for her, but she did worry about the legal side – the fact that Daniel had been married before, and she might lose her rights to a pension, that her children could be illegitimate.

Daniel laughed at her. 'You won't need to worry yourself about any of that,' he said. 'Just you trust me.'

So she did, and that night she went to bed late and, not drawing the curtains, lay looking out at the stars as she sang herself to sleep.

There seemed no point in waiting. Sandra gave a week's notice to Mr Tony and her landlady, neither of whom seemed too concerned about her leaving, and packed up her belongings in two suitcases. Before she went, she called in on her friend Ruth, a plump, plain girl of about thirty, who rented a room in the same house. Ruth worked at the Durringford Public Library. She was quiet and reserved, but friendly, too, and always ready to listen.

'Good luck, Sandra,' she said now. 'I'm glad you've found a proper family to belong to.'

She waved cheerfully out of the window when Daniel came to fetch Sandra in the old black Austin.

On the way to Woodman's Knot, Sandra asked the question she had been saving all week.

'Daniel . . .?'

'Yes, girl?' He stretched out a hand and rested it on hers.

'Daniel – why didn't Aunt Marietta marry? Or Katryn? Or your Aunt Greta – your Great-aunt Bella? Or any of them? Don't they like men?'

He laughed, a deep, comfortable laugh. 'Bless your heart, of course they do. They love 'em.' He paused, smiling. 'At least, that's what they say.'

'Then why on earth . . .?'

'It's an old family tradition. Carne girls never marry. Never have. But don't think they mind. It's the way of it, that's all.'

'Then Ellie won't ever? And if we – if we had a – a little girl . . .?'

'She'd be a Carne. Just like all the rest.'

There seemed nothing else Sandra could say. The tradition seemed a very strange one – it made her feel somehow uneasy – but she had to admit that none of the Carne women looked too unhappy with their lot. Perhaps they were fulfilled in other ways, like nuns.

'Can I ask you something else?'

Daniel took his hand off hers to change gear, then replaced it on the steering-wheel. 'Fire away, then,' he said lightly.

It was difficult, trying to talk to him about his private life. Still, if they were going to be married, they ought to be able to be open with each other.

Ellie's mother went away – you told me that. Did you – did you love her?'

There was silence for a few seconds.

'Yes. Yes, I loved her.'

Sandra almost wished she hadn't asked. She felt now in some kind of competition with the first wife.

'Why did she go, then? Please, Daniel, I don't want to pry, but you must see that I've got to know.'

'It was for the best,' he said slowly. 'It's not easy to understand, but it was what was right, see?'

'Not really.' Sandra bit her lip, trying to find the sense of it.

She was about to ask him why none of his brothers' wives were around, nor, come to think of it, any other married women, but he had turned off into the wood now and they were almost at the clearing.

Abruptly, as if on impulse, he stopped the car and switched off the engine.

'Sandra,' he said slowly, turning to her and putting an arm around her. 'You're marrying a Carne. We're a very old family – centuries old – and we've always done things our own way. There'll be things you wonder at and things that seem like they've just been put there to puzzle you. But don't you be bothered by any of it. Just you be a good wife to me – and a good mother, when the time comes – and I'll take care of you. Right?'

It was a long speech for him. She sat quiet, feeling lost and lonely.

'All right, girl?' He had both arms around her now, and suddenly he was kissing her, and his kisses were filled with longing and passion. Eventually he drew away from her and re-started the engine.

She relaxed back into her seat, smiling to herself. She was warm again, confident now. He wanted her. Everything would be all right. As they drove into the clearing, she was bold enough to ask: 'Love me?'

Daniel chuckled. 'You bet.'

'Me, too.' And then they were engulfed by the family, who swept her away to Aunt Greta's caravan, where she was to live until her wedding in two days' time.

The men stood on one side of the clearing, the women on the other. From her place behind old Aunt Marietta, Sandra could just see Uncle Hugo, bulky in a long, loose, red garment, and, beyond him, the crowd of men. Somewhere behind them was Daniel, waiting to be led forward. Nervously, she stroked her white silk shift with its broad border of crimson roses – a Carne heirloom, they had told her. Completely covering her head was a fine muslin veil.

'Excited?' whispered Katryn, a tall, reassuring presence at her side.

She nodded and gulped a little, wondering if she would find the words she had so carefully practised, when the time came to speak them.

Uncle Hugo's voice went on: '... For the Flesh lusteth against the Spirit, and the Spirit against the Flesh ... and on the Day of Days wilt there be the Fulfilment of the Word ... Come forth for the Joining, ye that will be joined.'

Sandra felt hands pushing her, and stumbled to the front of the crowd. Opposite her stood Daniel, also wearing a white silk shift, only his was undecorated. He looked very serious. They went together to stand before Uncle Hugo, who held up a large, ornately-carved dagger on a black velvet cushion.

Sandra glanced apprehensively at Daniel, but he squeezed her hand encouragingly.

'Daniel Carne, do you stand before me?' asked Uncle Hugo in a deep voice.

'Before you all,' said Daniel.

'Sandra Morrison, do you stand before me?'

'Before you all,' she answered in a small voice, aware that everyone was listening with great care.

'Do you kiss the blade of the Carnes? Do you sever thereby all ties outside the family? Do you swear to be true members of the family till you do part in death?'

'We do.' Daniel and Sandra both kissed the dagger blade.

'Cleave, then, one to the other, and be fruitful, so that the Word may be fulfilled.'

Sandra knew what the Word was – it was the creed of the Carnes, everything they believed in, Katryn had said.

She and Daniel then recited together: 'And our fruit shall find succour, and there will be life for generation unto generation, according to the Word.'

'Daniel, take thou Sandra. Sandra, take thou Daniel. The Joining is done.'

Solemnly, they turned to each other and, as was the proper custom, Daniel lifted the veil from her face and embraced her.

It was all over. Sandra was now Mrs Daniel Carne.

Ellie came running up with a posy of flowers, and people brought from their huts and trailers all manner of good food and drink for the wedding feast. It was a time of great happiness.

That night, in the smart blue caravan that was to be their home, they lay together and talked for a while. He was Sandra's first proper lover.

When the talking was over, he was more than she could ever have wished for.

She was very happy at Woodman's Knot. While Daniel spent his days cutting down trees and taking his turn in the workshop, Sandra learnt her various duties: tending the kitchen garden, helping to look after the children, cooking, washing clothes – in a big iron tub with a paddle you had to turn by hand – and keeping the caravan neat and pretty for Daniel when he came home to her each evening.

Once a week, she and her sister-in-law Katryn were given a lift by one of the men into Durringford, to buy supplies. She liked to do this – it made her feel she was still a little in touch with what she thought of as the 'real' world. She hadn't watched television or listened to the radio since going to live in Woodman's Knot, nor had she read a newspaper. She lived in almost total isolation from outside news. But as the months went by, she found herself lulled deeper and deeper into the insular rhythm of the Carne community, until it was a struggle to remind herself that there had ever been anything else.

And then she became pregnant. It was wonderful at first. Daniel was endearingly tender towards her and proud that she was what he called 'bearing'. Little Ellie fetched and carried for her, telling her she mustn't get tired. As she sat in her porch on the rocking-chair Daniel had given her as a wedding present, cosily knitting baby clothes, Aunt Marietta would come and sit with her, sometimes, to keep her company. The old lady talked about the importance of good food and sleep, so that she would produce a healthy baby – a boy, Aunt Marietta was sure. A fine new Carne to carry on the family traditions.

Once, Sandra had asked her what it was like to be a Carne woman, never marry or have children herself, and she had answered, in that rich, oddly-accented voice: 'But we feel no loss, my dear. There are always children for us to care for. Yes, I think perhaps we are the lucky ones.'

Katryn, who was big-boned, handsome, demonstrative young woman, would have made an excellent mother, Sandra thought. She was very capable, and was a great help to Sandra, making little outfits for the baby, renovating an old pram and painting the little rocker cot that Stephen Carne had made in the workshop for his new grandchild. There seemed such a lot to do. The baby would be born in June, according to Daniel's Aunt Greta, who was looking after Sandra during her pregnancy and who would act as midwife when the time came for 'the pains', as Aunt Marietta put it.

All through the winter they took good care of her, telling her to wrap herself up against the cold, escorting her across the clearing in case she should slip on some ice, bringing her tempting, nourishing meals, as if she were an invalid. When the first primroses appeared, she was as ready to cast off their attentions as she cast off their knitted shawls. Once or twice she tried to assert her independence, but she could see that it distressed them. They were so sure that they knew best.

On one of their weekly trips to Durringford – that, at least, they still allowed her – Sandra and Katryn stopped at a tea-shop for a snack. Apart from a few items to come from the supermarket, they had finished their shopping. They had a pleasant few minutes over their coffee and biscuits and were about to leave when a girl in a red woolly hat came in and sat at the table next to them. She saw Sandra and gave a smile of recognition.

Sandra smiled back. 'It's Ruth,' she told Katryn. 'You know the girl who had the room next to me in Eastham Street. Works at the library. Shall I ask her to join us?'

Katryn stood up. 'No,' she said, fastening her coat, 'don't do that. You go and sit with her for a bit while I go and finish the shopping. It won't take me long.'

Always so kind. Always so helpful. Sandra sometimes sourly wondered how she'd ever managed life without Katryn.

Ruth was pleased about the baby, and wanted to know how Sandra was getting on at Woodman's Knot. Sandra had told her a little about the Carne family before she had left Eastham Street, and now she was able to paint a much fuller picture.

'It certainly sounds friendly there,' said Ruth. 'Are you really happy, then?'

'Oh, yes,' said Sandra. 'At least ... I used to be.'

'Not now?' asked Ruth.

Sandra turned the pepper-pot round and round on the table. 'It's the baby,' she said after a while. 'Something to do with my baby. They won't treat me like a normal person. I mean, it's nice to be fussed over, but they're behaving as if I was going to give birth to the heir to the throne. They keep watching me.'

'What about Daniel?' said Ruth. 'Does he fuss over you, too?'

Sandra shook her head. 'That's just it,' she said quietly. 'He used to. It was ... well, just terrific. But now ...'

'He's cooled off? Some men are like that when their wives are pregnant, you know. It'll be all right later.'

'No,' said Sandra, 'it isn't that. He says it's another of their funny traditions. He – he almost avoids me. We haven't been alone together for weeks. It's as if I were – unclean, somehow.' She blinked as tears came into her eyes. 'He's moved out of our caravan, Ruth. His aunt is living with me now. She says it'll be that way right up till the weaning time. But I don't know if I can stand it much longer, really I don't.'

Ruth took her hand across the table. 'How long to go, then, till the baby's born?'

Sandra sniffled. 'Twelve weeks.'

'Well then, not too bad. And another few months after that and he'll come back to you. It's one of those things that has to be accepted, when you marry into that sort of family. You can't change it. And you do love Daniel, don't you?'

'Oh, yes.'

'Then you'll have to learn to take him for what he is.'

'I suppose so,' said Sandra, blowing her nose. 'But they're a very peculiar family, Ruth, really they are. I mean, none of the Carne girls ever marry, and when the men find wives they seem to go away after a while. I don't understand.'

'I shouldn't try, then,' Ruth said comfortably. 'Just you get on and have that baby and leave them to deal with their silly customs. I dare say there's no harm in it at all. Oh look, here's your friend.'

Sandra pushed back her chair. 'I must go,' she said. 'Thanks, Ruth. I mean, for letting me tell you.' She smiled staunchly. 'It's not too bad really, I expect. I probably exaggerate.'

'Shall we meet again some time?' suggested Ruth.

'I – I don't know,' said Sandra, looking over to where Katryn stood patiently in the doorway of the tea-shop, laden with bags. 'It might be difficult. I come shopping every week, though, so perhaps we'll see each other.'

'Take care, then,' said Ruth.

On the way home, Katryn positioned herself between Sandra and Daniel, who was driving the big van.

'Is she nice, your friend from the library?' asked Katryn. 'You seemed to be having a good chat.'

'Yes,' said Sandra. 'She's a very understanding sort of person.'

Without taking his eyes off the road, Daniel said: 'Now then, girl, you've got enough people to be understanding at home, without having to go gossiping to others.'

'I wasn't gossiping,' objected Sandra.

Katryn put a hand on her arm. 'Of course you weren't,' she said soothingly, 'but I do think you ought to be resting more, not rushing about Durringford every week. You're looking quite tired. She is, isn't she, Daniel? Best to stay at home until the little one comes.'

Suddenly Sandra *felt* tired. She knew it was useless to try and overrule their wishes. They were so big, so powerful. All right, then. She'd do as they said, like a good little girl, and when it was all over she and Daniel could be together again. One thing she was sure about, though. This first baby would be her last.

Having decided to do it all their way, to be their puppet, she found the next few weeks quite enjoyable. True, she missed Daniel, the closeness they had once shared, but his obvious approval of her new acquiescence was a great deal better than his previous coolness. Although he was still careful not to touch her, he seemed more relaxed in her company, and even brought her presents sometimes – a bunch of primroses, a little doll he had carved. It represented motherhood, he told her, but she didn't like it very much. It had no face. He laughed and said that was because he wasn't much of a carver.

When the pains came, Aunt Greta came to her caravan and brewed herbal tea, which Sandra was made to drink, even though it made her feel slightly sick. Katryn was by her bed, holding her hand, but the other women were left outside. Now and then, she thought she could hear them chanting in low voices, but the herbal tea made her head swim, and she couldn't understand what they were saying.

She asked for Daniel, but Katryn said: 'No, this is a time for women,' and Aunt Greta said: 'Keep your mind on the pain, dear. Push it away.'

At that moment, Aunt Marietta came into the caravan, carrying a small basket. She smiled and nodded encouragingly at the sweating, moaning Sandra, then sat in the rocking-chair, gazing attentively at the scene.

'Come along, Sandra dear,' said Aunt Greta. 'I believe I can see the little one's head.'

As a final wave of pain came and went, Sandra opened her eyes to see Aunt Marietta bending down over the bed, sprinkling something out of the basket and muttering: 'Roderick . . . Roderick Carne.'

'What . . .?' said Sandra, trying to sit up.

Katryn put a hand on her shoulder and gently pushed her back on to the pillow.

'It's all right,' said Aunt Greta. 'Look – it's a boy you've given us.' She held up a red, wet, wrinkled creature, which immediately began to cry loudly.

'There,' she said, handing the baby to Sandra. 'Take him. His name is Roderick.'

'But . . .' Sandra looked down at the tiny, screwed-up face. 'I – I wanted to call him Jason.'

'I'm afraid you're too late, dear,' said Aunt Greta. 'He has already been named.'

Aunt Marietta, who was about to leave the caravan, paused and stirred the contents of her basket with her hand. 'Powdered woodruff,' she explained. 'It's called "blood-cup", hereabouts. We always use it for naming. Can you smell it, my dear? Like new-mown hay, isn't it?'

'Give me the baby, Sandra,' said Katryn. 'You should have some rest, now.'

Roderick was a typical Carne, strong, huge, healthy and perfectly formed, with pale gold hair and his father's greeny-blue eyes. He was very contented, and lay happily in his pram outside the caravan, cooing up at the sky all day. Very often, Daniel could be seen wheeling him around the clearing, talking quietly to him and letting him clutch at his outstretched finger.

Sandra adored him. He was everything to her, the core of her existence. When she held him to her breast it was, for her, a kind of completion. He couldn't, of course, be to her what Daniel had been, but somehow that didn't matter so much now.

Daniel was very kind to her, very attentive and solicitous, but she could tell he was more interested in the baby than her. Perhaps it was his defence against this custom of estrangement. Perhaps, when she stopped feeding the baby, he would be as ardent and loving as before.

Meanwhile, all the women of the family were eager to help her look after Roderick, and she sat back and allowed herself to enjoy all the fuss they made of her. Motherhood seemed to be an especially honourable estate within the Carne family.

October came, and it would soon be Daniel's birthday. Sandra had by now become used to letting the others do her shopping, but she wanted to buy something special for Daniel – something to show that her love had held firm through this time of trial, that indicated her readiness to welcome him back. She had been saving up the allowance he gave her, and there was enough to buy him a silver identity bracelet – something he said he had always wanted. She would have their initials engraved on it, his and hers, intertwined. Katryn insisted on accompanying her to Durringford to buy it, as if she needed a nanny, Sandra thought.

While Katryn went to the ironmonger's for some paraffin, Sandra chose Daniel's present and gave an order for the engraving. With a few minutes to spare before she was due to meet Katryn, she wandered down the High Street, inspecting the dresses in the shop windows – all the clothes she never seemed to buy nowadays. Most of her things were made one of Daniel's cousins. They were very nice, but she did miss the fun of shopping.

Outside Woolworth's, someone touched her arm. She turned.

'Ruth!'

The older girl smiled. 'How are you, Sandra? I've been wondering. I've looked for you around town, but ...'

'I haven't been in for a while. I've got my baby now. Roderick.'

'There's a fancy name,' said Ruth.

Sandra blushed slightly. 'Yes, I know.'

'But you're looking good,' Ruth went on. 'Is – is everything all right now?'

'Fine.' Sandra nodded. 'Yes, it's all right.' Because it would be, very soon. She knew it would.

'Oh,' said Ruth, feeling in the pocket of her jacket. 'There's something ... Perhaps I shouldn't now, but ...' She found a piece of paper, folded into a small square. 'I saw it in an encyclopaedia. Copied it out. I've had it in my pocket for ages, thinking I might see you. Months ago it was, someone rang up the library to ask when Carnegie Hall was built, and when I looked it up, well, on the same page there was this. I don't think it means anything at all – a bit of a joke now – but I thought there might once have been some link ... Maybe I shouldn't give it to you, though. I don't want you all upset over nothing.'

Sandra laughed and snatched the paper from her hand. 'I'll never know till I read it, will I?'

Ruth shrugged. 'Look, I'm late,' she said. 'I have to go. Promise me you won't take it too seriously.'

'Promise.'

As her friend hurried off, Sandra turned away and went to stand in the entrance of a shop, where she read the tidily written paragraph on the piece of paper. '*Carneads*,' was the heading.

'A nomadic European tribe,' she read, 'which, in the belief that it could create a race of great physical strength, weaned its children on their mothers' flesh. Their way of life took on a religious significance, and included the practice of celibacy in females born to the tribe. After a number of notorious murder trials in the 18th century, including that of Julio Carne, sentenced to death in Zurich in 1756 for the murder of four young women, the tribe appears to have dissipated and died out. (The name *Carnead* presumably derives from a number of European words meaning "flesh".)'

She dropped the piece of paper and stood absolutely still for a moment. Then her hands began to tremble, and she thrust them into her pockets. The encyclopaedia was wrong. The day of the Carneads was not over. They lived on, in Woodman's Knot. She was sure. This was no over-working of her imagination. It all fitted so horribly well.

'Are you coming?'

She heard a car horn. The old black Austin had pulled up a few yards away, and Katryn was calling to her. Nico Carne was at the wheel.

'Yes, coming.' She climbed in the back and pulled her arms around herself, hugging. Smile. Act normally. Did you get what you wanted? Oh, yes, thank you – did you? Keep going. Don't show fear. Tonight, after dark, put Roderick in his pram and run. Run through the woods. Away. Anywhere. Tell someone. The police. How long till the baby would be weaned? She didn't know. She'd left that to Them. Soon, though, surely. Her milk was barely enough for him now. Tonight, then, Perhaps without the pram. Perhaps she should just carry him. Quicker. Quieter. Please God he won't make a noise.

She shied away from thinking about details, but her mind kept drag-ging her back. How did they do it? How could you feed a tiny baby on flesh? Mince it and boil it? Make a nourishing soup? Was that what became of Daniel's first wife, when Ellie was a baby? All the other wives? Was that how the body she so adored, the strong, firm muscles that had held her so lovingly, were once nourished? She felt sick.

'Could you open a window?' she asked.

Katryn turned round, concerned. 'Feeling bad?' she asked. 'Oh dear, that won't do.'

How could they keep the flesh for long enough? Did they freeze it, dry it, smoke it – pickle it in brine?

'Drive more slowly, Nico,' said Katryn. 'She's gone quite pale.'

When they reached Woodman's Knot, Sandra walked unsteadily to the caravan and up the steps. Inside, she could hear Aunt Greta crooning to the baby. Trying to control the hate and trepidation she knew must show in her face, she opened the door.

'Oh –' Her eyes opened wide. 'What are you doing?'

Aunt Greta looked up and smiled. 'Why, feeding our baby, of course.'

'He doesn't have a bottle, Aunt Greta,' protested Sandra. 'He's *my* baby and *I* feed him. Here – give him to me!' The panic arose in her. She couldn't still it.

'Hello, girl.'

It was Daniel's voice. He stood behind her, filling the doorway with his big, handsome body, filling her mind with terror and loathing. He stepped forward, put his hands on her rigid shoulders, and kissed her quickly on the mouth. Then he was gone, and his place was taken by his two brothers, Nico and Ben. As Sandra stood shaking, powerless with fear, they each grasped one of her arms and took her to stand in front of her baby.

'Roderick!' she whimpered, then one of them put his huge, rough hand over her mouth. It smelled of linseed oil.

She struggled and kicked out at them, but they held her fast. Then Aunt Marietta came, and Sandra knew that the fight was over.

'Drink this,' said Aunt Marietta, holding up a beaker of something pale and pungent, 'and there will be no fear of what is to come. Do it for Roderick Carne – for your fine, strong boy.'

Sandra drank, and was glad of the two men supporting her, or she would have fallen to the floor. Aunt Marietta began one of her vaguely Biblical chants, about the spirit and the flesh and the blood that shall flow from generation unto generation, according to the Word. And Sandra saw without emotion the gleam of a knife-blade among the folds of her skirt, and watched as Aunt Marietta made circles with it in the air before her face. It was the dagger she had kissed on her wedding day. And when the moment came, and the dagger descended, the baby turned irritably from his bottle and began to cry.

'Ah, bless the hungry little fellow,' said Aunt Greta, rocking him. 'He wants his mother.'

The Lodger in Room 16

David Dixon

There was something rather odd about the lodger in Room 16, and Mr Feith didn't think he could stand any more of it.

Right now, he was stooped at the keyhole of his next-door neighbour like a huge, bald-headed bird looking for worms, but all he could see was the corner of a crude, hefty, wooden table which told him nothing it had not told him on many previous inspections. His innate timidity restricted his investigations to the daylight hours when he knew the lodger must be out, and it was only during these hours that he tried the door. It was always locked.

A little later, Mr Feith left the lodging-house in a very determined frame of mind. He walked briskly in a district of empty warehouses and dilapidated buildings. Evening was drawing in. The streets were always deserted after dark, due jointly to marauding packs of vandals and a strange series of disappearances which had plagued the area for years. This suited Mr Feith perfectly.

He had on a black overcoat two sizes too big for him, and which he seldom took off, and pebble-glass spectacles that magnified his eyes to look like slugs wallowing darkly in axle-grease. He was panting, for he tended always to walk faster than he was fit for. It was trying to rain.

Mr Feith had a rolled-up newspaper under an arm when he returned to the lodging-house some ten minutes later. A bar of yellow light beneath the door under the ground-floor stairs betrayed the presence of the landlord within. Mr Feith delivered one startling rap on the door with a knuckle.

'Go away,' commanded a muffled voice.

Mr Feith stood his ground. He waited two whole minutes patiently, then delivered a second stunning rap on the door.

There followed a muffled curse, and the door was snatched open. The landlord glared down at the bent, bird-like figure before him, whose spectacles reflected the light of the room to look like dim headlamps in its face.

'Well?' he barked impatiently.

Mr Feith insinuated himself into the room, which was packed to the ceiling with a scruffy and rusty collection of junk. The landlord shut the door with unnecessary loudness as Mr Feith explained his visit.

'I wish to speak with you, Mr Moule, about certain disturbances on the top floor which are making my stay here difficult.'

'I haven't the time for it,' snapped the landlord. 'If I remember correctly, Mr Feith, you took that room on the understanding that if it wasn't to your satisfaction you'd find another elsewhere. That's my understanding of the matter, Mr Feith. And I'll thank you to remember that you demanded that room and made a nuisance of yourself about it after I'd told you them rooms up there wasn't for letting. And I'll thank you to remember that I didn't show you the top floor or offer you a room anywhere. You found it yourself.'

'Nevertheless, Mr Moule, these disturbances must stop,' said Mr Feith with determination. 'I don't know what Number 16 is up to, but I think that as the landlord you should be concerned about it. I believe that something is being wilfully and maliciously destroyed in there at night, sometimes as much as three times a week, sir. There seems to be a crank-handled device in there which sounds to me rusty, Mr Moule, and the machine's task involves a sound that I can only describe as that of crunching sticks. Crunching sticks, Mr Moule, is as near as I can describe it.'

In fact, it was intolerable. The disturbances always lasted about forty-five minutes and were thunderous, the shuddering noise seeming to interfere with every atom of Mr Feith's body. They could occur on any night and at any hour after dark. Mr Feith feared most of all those that happened in the small hours, when his sleep would be troubled by appalling dreams, and he would wake in a cold sweat in the dark and find himself listening to that infernally chilling sound: the scraping, ponderous turn of the crank-handle and the sound of crunching sticks. The paranoid degree of anxiety that he felt at these times seemed to bring him to the brink of insanity.

'Is that all you wanted to say, Mr Feith?'

'Indeed, I believe I hardly need say more to arouse your professional concern, Mr Moule.'

'Then, no doubt, you'll be anxious to leave,' said the landlord, turning to the door. 'Let's not go poking our nose into other people's business, Mr Feith. The man in Number 16 works in a local cemetery and would not be pleased at your interest in his affairs, I've no doubt. You took that room on the understanding that if you had any complaints you'd find another elsewhere. My advice is to do just that.'

'But wait a moment——' Mr Feith protested.

'Now, now,' said the landlord, helping him out through the door, 'that's all I got to say on the matter, and that's that.'

Back in his room with the door locked, Mr Feith stood at his window thoughtfully. The view here was cluttered with archaic roofs and chimneys of various sizes and shapes, and part of a cinema could be seen amidst them, its neon signs lighting up his face dimly pink, then blue, then pink again.

After trying the crossword, Mr Feith took his *Daily Telegraph* apart and changed some of the old newspaper sheets on his bed with it. He worked by the glow of the cinema signs, for he liked to save on electricity.

He went to bed much later with a sick lump of dread in his stomach and slept fitfully all night. The house remained tomb-like in its silence, however, and this was not what Mr Feith had expected. The following morning he rose in a very grim mood, for the constant dread of nights was becoming insufferable. Though the disturbances were by no means regular, the lapses between them never exceeded five nights, and last night had been the fifth. He would have to look forward to a disturbance all over again, this time with the certainty of no reprieve. Mr Feith was furious. He brushed his teeth venomously in the fourth-floor bathroom and, after a wrathful shave, emerged in the gloomy corridor with small pieces of pink lavatory paper pressed on his bleeding jowls.

The fact that the man worked among the dead and committed God knew what crimes after dark did not frighten Mr Feith a bit now that he was angry. When he got back to his room he wrote out a very stiff note in which he advised the recipient that should the disturbances continue he would have no further recourse but to notify the police. He slipped the note under the door of Number 16 and waited perfunctorily for signs of response, but of course there were none. He tried the door, but it was locked.

He then left the lodging-house to pick up his dole money, for it was Thursday. He bore a plastic carrier bag that contained library books due for replacement.

It was dark when he returned, and it was trying to rain again.

Behind the lodging-house was a pitch-dark cobbled square; it lay by the side of a road that fortunately was well enough lit. On the other side of the road to the square, Mr Feith emerged from a beaten path that was crowded by trees and wild vegetation. The bank of verdure at his right screened a cemetery of considerable age, reputedly, though it couldn't be connected with his next-door neighbour since it had been abandoned to riotous vegetation long ago. The soil here smelt overpoweringly rich and nutritious, and the wild weeds beyond the trees were gigantic, with stems as thick as Mr Feith's wrists.

Walking briskly, Mr Feith disappeared into the square, where he met with something of an accident, for he had forgotten that the dustbins belonging to the buildings on the three sides of the square were always strung across its centre. He had formally complained of this to the landlord on many occasions, for it constituted a danger at night. He had even been able to describe a lodger whom he believed guilty of placing the obstruction, a small, mad-looking skeleton of a man with shrivelled eyes and a dry, cynical voice, who, in the summer, always walked down to the newsagent's in overcoat, pyjamas and slippers.

Mr Feith's collision was thunderous. He was just getting the hang of his prostrate circumstances when a sash-window slammed open up above. The light of the obscured streetlamp nearest the square flooded over a wall and illuminated a double-barrelled shotgun as it peered furtively out of a window halfway up the back of one of the lodging-houses. The dry, hairless head of Mr Feith's dustbin suspect appeared cautiously behind the weapon. 'Who goes there?' it barked.

Mr Feith conveyed his identity and circumstances with restrained exasperation, and announced that he would deliver a written complaint to the landlord about the dustbins.

'You leave them bloody dustbins be,' the old man retorted with hostility. 'I saw someone coming out by that old cemetery down there just now, Mr Feet, and I've got this 'ere notion maybe it was you. You keep well away from that place, that's my advice to you.'

Having by now regathered his library books and repositioned his spectacles, Mr Feith remained politely to inquire what the devil the madman was talking about.

'If you can't take advice without asking bloody questions all the time you don't bloody well deserve any. I bin 'ere a long time, Mr Feet, and I got a sharp eye in me 'ead. That there is the Devil's graveyard, and woe betide any man what gets 'isself buried in it.'

Mr Feith assured the old man that he had no intention of being interred there.

'You just 'ope and pray that that may be the case, and God be thanked,' said the old man darkly, 'for there is a great evil at large in this godless neighbourhood, with folks being nicked outer their very beds o'night these many years,' he added, crossing himself feverishly.

'And what does this devil look like, then?' Mr Feith inquired contemptuously. 'Does he have horns like the books have it, and a tail?'

' 'E don't look 'ealthy, Mr Feet,' said the old man with a shudder, 'and that's no exaggeration. 'E's horribly fat and grey. 'E looks rotten, Mr Feet, soft and rotten like an over-ripe plum. And then there's 'is 'ead.'

'What's wrong with that?'

'I don't like to think on it,' said the old man with horror. 'You keep well away from that place, that's my advice to you. You'll be good enough to set that dustbin up before you go, else I'll not rest peaceful in me bed tonight.'

Mr Feith couldn't stand this old man, whose personal abandon and madness represented the very depths of human degradation. Indeed, it was only with a nauseous taste in his mouth that he was able to associate with anybody reduced to living in a house of this quality.

He was fortunate with the timing of the disturbance that night. Instead of having to wait up half the night in order to avoid having his sleep poisoned with it, he had to listen to it somewhat before midnight, while the cinema lights were still on. The sound began with a familiar scraping screech of what Mr Feith took to be a crank-handle. This continued at brief, regular intervals, punctuating the ceaseless, muffled, crunching sticks noise which then commenced.

Thereafter, Mr Feith's room was filled and ravaged by the physical presence of noise. The dust on the floor rose up and hung like a ground mist over the floorboards. Mr Feith found it hard to believe that nobody beneath heard this racket, and once again the inevitable question rose in the thunder: what on earth was his neighbour doing in there? Even through the rubber soles of his slippers he could feel the boards throb in rhythm with the activity in the next room; the vibration would deaden his ankles soon into an unaccountable numbness, and the dust would scour his lungs.

In exasperation, Mr Feith did something he had often thought of doing before, but, in the dark hours, had always lacked the character for. He took almost two minutes to turn the key in his door as noiselessly as possible, and crept down the corridor to the door of Room 16. The sound here was so quiet that until he reached the door he suspected that it might have stopped. The door glowed dimly around its edges and at the keyhole. Mr Feith stooped and applied an eye to the keyhole.

The light within was tremulous, and its unsteadiness seemed to increase and subside with the scraping turn of the crank-handle. Mr Feith thought it might be that of a candle, and wondered why his neighbour didn't use his electricity.

The view was dominated by the corner of the crude table, as was to be expected, but Mr Feith's attention was drawn by something else, something that he couldn't quite get the hang of at first. It overhung the edge of the table a little and seemed to be of an apricot hue with bluish discolouring; it was badly crumpled. Mr Feith thought it might be made of some kind of flexible rubber. It wobbled and vibrated with the same throbbing rhythm as that of the unseen candle, and it sometimes advanced jerkily down over the edge of the table, which seemed to strain to the same rhythm, though it appeared to be stoutly made.

Mr Feith wondered if the rubber thing might be some kind of long-sleeved glove, since he suspected that he could make out the fingers, but as the sleeve grew longer and longer, he became doubtful; he didn't like the texture of it at all. He remained long enough to watch the scene shudder and strain once more, and to see the rubber oddity on the table make one further jerky reach for the bottom of his field of view, then he rose to go.

Unfortunately, he applied his weight to the door-handle, for his back was not what it had been. When his weight was at its greatest, he lost his grip. The handle made a thunderous clunk in its housing, and Mr Feith found to his stunned alarm that the door stood six inches ajar. It opened to the left, so that he could see nothing of his neighbour, but it was clear that his neighbour was aware of his presence and had stopped work. Mr Feith could hear quite plainly now the slow, wheezing respiration of the man inside, who sounded grotesquely fat, and bronchial. Mr Feith had never previously heard so much as a footstep of him. It occurred to him that he might enter and communicate his grievances in person, and it was no doubt this very idea which precipitated his hasty retreat, in which he cared little for the racket he made. He locked his door hastily and drew his armchair against it.

He stood by his window, perhaps because it presented a comforting token of egress. While waiting, his dimly blue, then pink, then blue face was frozen with apprehension. After a few minutes, however, the grinding scrape of the crank-handle announced the resumption of his neighbour's mysterious labours, and Mr Feith opened his window to let in some fresh air.

The following day, he descended the dark stairflights in a very determined frame of mind indeed.

'What the devil do you want now?' the landlord snarled, snatching open his door.

'I wish to speak to you about that man in Room 16,' said Mr Feith firmly. He tried to insinuate himself into the landlord's room, but physical obstruction on the latter's part kept him out. Mr Feith could see dozens of food-mixers in their boxes stacked up amongst the cluttered junk within. Mr Moule was in the habit of receiving at regular intervals – usually at night – large consignments of cassette-radios, watches and other valuables of this kind, and furtive men visited him frequently. Mr Feith had never been in any doubt but that Mr Moule had business of dark merit and doubtful honour on the side.

'I think I already told you to keep your nose out of his affairs, Mr Feith, and if you had any brains you wouldn't forget it so easy.'

Mr Feith was determined not be offended. 'As I was going to say, this man started a disturbance last night and I looked through the keyhole and observed candle-light in the room.'

Mr Feith proceeded to describe what he had seen through the keyhole. He didn't mention how he had accidentally opened the door, nor the threatening note he had rashly delivered, which now weighed so heavily on his peace of mind.

'I suspect that something is being wilfully and maliciously destroyed in there at night, and I submit, Mr Moule, that it must stop. I suggest we take a key upstairs, the pair of us, and have a look inside.'

'I don't have a key to Number 16,' said the landlord.

Mr Feith couldn't hide his astonishment. 'Do you mean to say that you haven't a spare key to one of your own rooms, Mr Moule?'

'I do,' enunciated the landlord. Mr Feith became uncomfortably aware of one particular eye, rheumy and bloodshot, bulging at him belligerently. 'The man in Number 16 is no lodger of mine, Mr Feith. He came with the house and is none of my business or yours.'

'I don't believe I understand, Mr Moule——'

'I couldn't care less, Mr Feith.'

Mr Feith thought of something else. 'And that's another thing. Why is it that you're prepared to do the rounds for everybody – knocking on their doors for their rent money – while I have to come down here to pay mine? This seems a little unfair, doesn't it?'

'I never go on the top floor, Mr Feith, and don't plan to change me habits. I don't need any trouble around here, for reasons you'll no doubt understand, and I'd advise you to keep your nose to yourself it it's a cheap roof over your head you want. That's all I got to say on it, and that's that.'

Back on the top floor, Mr Feith stooped to the keyhole of Room 16, but all he could see was the corner of the table in the gloom. The strange rubber thing had gone.

Then he tried the door, and something unexpected happened. It opened. The room seemed to have been left for his inspection. He opened the door wider and stepped to the threshold of the room. A timid peer revealed the occupant to be absent.

The object that stole his attention was the table in the middle of the room, or, at least, the filthy machinery that it supported. Apart from this the room was little furnished. There was a battered wardrobe at one end, and curtains of grimy cobwebs hung on each side of the little window; the thick carpet of dust was badly scuffed around the table. There was a reek of old sacks and God knew what else in the room.

The sight of the mangle made Mr Feith feel ill. It was bolted on the table excessively, and the table was extensively strutted underneath with iron-work and itself was bolted to the floor. The rollers were almost as big as dustbins; one of them was set into the table with only about three inches protruding, while the height of the other appeared to be adjustable. An adjustable flap of rubber hung against the upper roller on the output side, covering the gap beneath. A badly stained gutter ran round the far side of the table at an angle, and a battered filthy-looking bucket stood underneath its end, covered with a ragged scrap of matting. The whole contraption was perhaps the most repulsive thing that he had ever seen.

Gingerly, Mr Feith entered the room.

The electric lighting consisted of stripped wires hanging uselessly in cobwebs from a hole in the ceiling, and Mr Feith supposed that the furry mass of cobwebs by the wardrobe must be the slot meter. The wardrobe contained a dirty pile of sacks and two slugs. It also contained dozens of crudely-fashioned wax-like objects that resembled the half-used candle he found under a window, a misshapen oddity welded on to an enamel plate in its own wax. There was a primitive tinder-box on the window-sill with blobs of dirt all over it.

Mr Feith could see no sign of his threatening note anywhere. He wondered why he had been allowed in, or if the occupant had simply slipped up. Outside, it was raining hard. The monotonous murmurs and mutterings of it had been a constant companion for Mr Feith all morning.

He looked idly out the window. Though he couldn't see very clearly through the rain patterns on the glass, the flat grey wash of the courtyard and the green of the trees beyond were discernible. Sometimes even these were obliterated when sudden gusts of wind lashed the back of the house with rain.

Mr Feith began to suspect that, through the rivulets of water on the glass, he could make out an unexpected form near the trees by the abandoned cemetery. He pressed his nose against the glass and peered into the rain. He could hardly see much better, and the condensation on this side of the glass caused by his breath wasn't helping much. It was unquestionably a man. He looked bloodless, large and repulsively fat, and seemed to have something black and shiny – perhaps an oilskin – in one mushy-looking hand. Mr Feith did not think the head should look as mushy and featureless as it did. He became overwhelmed with a giddy sickness at the sight of the man.

The man was gazing up the back of the house, and the possibility that he was aware of Mr Feith's peering at him from the window of Room 16 could not be discounted.

Mr Feith ducked out of sight. Perhaps he was being imaginative, but if the mysterious man in Room 16 looked like anything, surely he would look like that thing outside, like some kind of maggot that crawled out of the soil to commit obscene crimes amongst humanity at night. Mr Feith believed that he had been discovered in his snooping by the very man who occupied the room.

Perhaps it had been the smell in the room, or perhaps Mr Feith was over-reacting, but for the rest of that day he felt very ill indeed, and confined himself to his room with the door locked. His illness seemed if anything to worsen as night drew in. He had seated himself on the square of hardboard that served to protect his backside from the vicious springs of his gutted armchair. He sat like this until late into the night, unable to move, the cold dampness of the climate drenching him to the bones.

Late that night, Mr Feith was roused from his stupor by the sound of a slow, heavy tread on the top of the stairs, and a vaguely familiar wheezing noise. Mr Feith listened, barely breathing, as the tread proceeded down the landing, the wheezing sound getting louder. It passed Room 16 and came towards the only other door at this end: that of Mr Feith.

The tread stopped outside Mr Feith's door, and nothing could be heard for a bit except the wheezing. Mr Feith, in the neon-lit gloom of his room, remained frozen where he sat, numbed with terror and dismay.

His visitor then began to grope on the surface of the door; the sound of this was horribly soft and unmethodical. Soon the door-handle was struck a couple of times, then turned. As the door strained and cracked behind him, Mr Feith shrieked without restraint. Rotten bits of wood spat out from around the lock and scattered on the floor, and as the door split asunder, a sickening stench of wet soil and dead cats invaded the room.

In common with Mr Feith's life, his disappearance passed unnoticed by the world in which he lived. His screams wandered along all the dark corridors of the house for over a minute, but no one stirred: Some fifty minutes later, the tread of a descender could have been heard on the stairs, and a bronchial wheezing, which some of the lodgers might have noticed before in the house. But nobody reported it to the police. A suspicious lodger on the ground floor might have been able to furnish the police with a description of the descender, since the hall light, unlike those of the upper corridors and stairs, was kept in serviceable order, and it remained switched on, day and night. But the hall was deserted when the man on the stairs arrived.

No one was there to see the descender in such detail, or to smell the appalling reek of corruption that hung about him. And no one was there to connect the screams with the hideous burden that he had slung over his shoulder: a filthy oilskin sack, which had in it something half as massive and heavy, something that filled the sack like laundry, and bobbed up and down rather flabbily on his back as he made his way out.

The Adventure of the Speckled Band

Sir Arthur Conan Doyle

In glancing over my notes of the seventy-odd cases in which I have during the last eight years studied the methods of my friend Sherlock Holmes, I find many tragic, some comic, a large number merely strange, but none commonplace; for, working as he did rather for the love of his art than for the acquirement of wealth, he refused to associate himself with any investigation which did not tend towards the unusual, and even the fantastic. Of all these varied cases, however, I cannot recall any which presented more singular features than that which was associated with the well-known Surrey family of the Roylotts of Stoke Moran. The events in question occurred in the early days of my association with Holmes, when we were sharing rooms as bachelors, in Baker Street. It is possible that I might have placed them upon record before, but a promise of secrecy was made at the time, from which I have only been freed during the last month by the untimely death of the lady to whom the pledge was given. It is perhaps as well that the facts should now come to light, for I have reasons to know there are widespread rumours as to the death of Dr Grimesby Roylott which tend to make the matter even more terrible than the truth.

It was early in April, in the year '83, that I woke one morning to find Sherlock Holmes standing, fully dressed, by the side of my bed. He was a late riser as a rule, and, as the clock on the mantelpiece showed me that it was only a quarter past seven, I blinked up at him in some surprise, and perhaps just a little resentment, for I was myself regular in my habits.

'Very sorry to knock you up, Watson,' said he, 'but it's the common lot this morning. Mrs Hudson has been knocked up, she retorted upon me, and I on you.'

'What is it, then? A fire?'

'No, a client. It seems that a young lady has arrived in a considerable state of excitement, who insists upon seeing me. She is waiting now in the sitting-room. Now, when young ladies wander about the Metropolis at this hour of the morning, and knock sleepy people up out of their beds, I presume that it is something very pressing which they have to communicate. Should it prove to be an interesting case, you would, I am sure, wish to follow it from the outset. I thought at any rate that I should call you, and give you the chance.'

'My dear fellow, I would not miss it for anything.'

I had no keener pleasure than in following Holmes in his professional investigations, and in admiring the rapid deductions, as swift as intuitions, and yet always founded on a logical basis, with which he unravelled the problems which were submitted to him. I rapidly threw on my clothes, and was ready in a few minutes to accompany my friend down to the sitting-room. A lady dressed in black and heavily veiled, who had been sitting in the window, rose as we entered.

'Good morning, madam,' said Holmes cheerily. 'My name is Sherlock Holmes. This is my intimate friend and associate, Dr Watson, before whom you can speak as freely as before myself. Ha, I am glad to see that Mrs Hudson has had the good sense to light the fire. Pray draw up to it, and I shall order you a cup of hot coffee, for I observe that you are shivering.'

'It is not cold which makes me shiver,' said the woman in a low voice, changing her seat as requested.

'What then?'

'It is fear, Mr Holmes. It is terror.' She raised her veil as she spoke, and we could see that she was indeed in a pitiable state of agitation, her face all drawn and grey, with restless, frightened eyes, like those of some hunted animal. Her features and figure were those of a woman of thirty, but her hair was shot with premature grey, and her expression was weary and haggard. Sherlock Holmes ran her over with one of his quick, all-comprehensive glances.

'You must not fear,' said he soothingly, bending forward and patting her forearm. 'We shall soon set matters right, I have no doubt. You have come in by train this morning, I see.'

'You know me, then?'

'No, but I observe the second half of a return ticket in the palm of your left glove. You must have started early, and yet you had a good drive in a dog-cart, along heavy roads, before you reached the station.'

The lady gave a violent start, and stared in bewilderment at my companion.

'There is no mystery, my dear madam,' said he, smiling. 'The left arm of your jacket is spattered with mud in no less than seven places. The marks are perfectly fresh. There is no vehicle save a dog-cart which throws up mud in that way, and then only when you sit on the left-hand side of the driver.'

'Whatever your reasons may be, you are perfectly correct,' said she. 'I started from home before six, reached Leatherhead at twenty past, and came in by the first train to Waterloo. Sir, I can stand this strain no longer, I shall go mad if it continues. I have no one to turn to – none, save only one, who cares for me, and he, poor fellow, can be of little aid. I have heard of you, Mr Holmes; I have heard of you from Mrs Farintosh, whom you helped in the hour of her sore need. It was from her that I had your address. Oh, sir, do you not think you could help me too, and at least throw a little light through the dense darkness which surrounds me? At present it is out of my power to reward you for your services, but in a month or two I shall be married, with the control of my own income, and then at least you shall not find me ungrateful.'

Holmes turned to his desk, and unlocking it, drew out a small case-book which he consulted.

'Farintosh,' said he. 'Ah, yes, I recall the case; it was concerned with an opal tiara. I think it was before your time, Watson. I can only say, madam, that I shall be happy to devote the same care to your case as I did to that of your friend. As to reward, my profession is its reward; but you are at liberty to defray whatever expenses I may be put to, at the time which suits you best. And now I beg that you will lay before us everything that may help us in forming an opinion upon the matter.'

'Alas!' replied our visitor. 'The very horror of my situation lies in the fact that my fears are so vague, and my suspicions depend so entirely upon small points, which might seem trivial to another, that even he to whom of all others I have a right to look for help and advice looks upon all that I tell him about it as the fancies of a nervous woman. He does not say so, but I can read it from his soothing answers and averted eyes. But I have heard, Mr Holmes, that you can see deeply into the manifold wickedness of the human heart. You may advise me how to walk amid the dangers which encompass me.'

'I am all attention, madam.'

'My name is Helen Stoner, and I am living with my stepfather, who is the last survivor of one of the oldest Saxon families in England, the Roylotts of Stoke Moran, on the western border of Surrey.'

Holmes nodded his head. 'The name is familiar to me,' said he.

'The family was at one time among the richest in England, and the estate extended over the borders into Berkshire in the north, and Hamp-shire in the west. In the last century, however, four successive heirs were of a dissolute and wasteful disposition, and the family ruin was eventually completed by a gambler, in the days of the Regency. Nothing was left, save a few acres of ground and the two-hundred-year-old house, which is itself crushed under a heavy mortgage. The last squire dragged out his existence there, living the horrible life of an aristocratic pauper; but his only son, my stepfather, seeing that he must adapt himself to the new conditions, obtained an advance from a relative, which enabled him to take a medical degree, and went out to Calcutta, where, by his pro-fessional skill and his force of character, he established a large practice.

In a fit of anger, however, caused by some robberies which had been perpetrated in the house, he beat his native butler to death, and narrowly escaped a capital sentence. As it was, he suffered a long term of imprisonment, and afterwards returned to England a morose and disappointed man.

'When Dr Roylott was in India he married my mother, Mrs Stoner, the young widow of Major-General Stoner, of the Bengal Artillery. My sister Julia and I were twins, and we were only two years old at the time of my mother's remarriage. She had a considerable sum of money, not less than a thousand a year, and this she bequeathed to Dr Roylott entirely whilst we resided with him, with a provision that a certain annual sum should be allowed to each of us in the event of our marriage. Shortly after our return to England my mother died – she was killed eight years ago in a railway accident near Crewe. Dr Roylott then abandoned his attempts to establish himself in practice in London, and took us to live with him in the ancestral house at Stoke Moran. The money which my mother had left was enough for all our wants, and there seemed no obstacle to our happiness.

'But a terrible change came over our stepfather about this time. Instead of making friends and exchanging visits with our neighbours, who had at first been overjoyed to see a Roylott of Stoke Moran back in the old family seat, he shut himself up in his house, and seldom came out save to indulge in ferocious quarrels with whoever might cross his path. Violence of temper approaching to mania has been hereditary in the men of the family, and in my stepfather's case it had, I believe, been intensified by his long residence in the tropics. A series of disgraceful brawls took place, two of which ended in the police-court, until at last he became the terror of the village, and the folks would fly at his approach, for he is a man of immense strength, and absolutely uncontrollable in his anger.

'Last week he hurled the local blacksmith over a parapet into a stream, and it was only by paying over all the money that I could gather together that I was able to avert another public exposure. He had no friends at all save the wandering gipsies, and he would give these vagabonds leave to encamp upon the few acres of bramble-covered land which represent the family estate, and would accept in return the hospitality of their tents, wandering away with them sometimes for weeks on end. He has a passion also for Indian animals, which are sent over to him by a correspondent, and he has at this moment a cheetah and a baboon, which wander freely over his grounds, and are feared by the villagers almost as much as their master.

'You can imagine from what I say that my poor sister Julia and I had no great pleasure in our lives. No servant would stay with us, and for a long time we did all the work of the house. She was but thirty at the time of her death, and yet her hair had already begun to whiten, even as mine has.'

'Your sister is dead, then?'

'She died just two years ago, and it is of her death that I wish to speak to you. You can understand that, living the life which I have described, we were little likely to see anyone of our own age and position. We had, however, an aunt, my mother's maiden sister, Miss Honoria Westphail, who lives near Harrow, and we were occasionally allowed to pay short visits at this lady's house. Julia went there at Christmas two years ago, and met there a half-pay Major of Marines, to whom she became engaged. My stepfather learned of the engagement when my sister returned, and offered no objection to the marriage; but within a fortnight of the day which had been fixed for the wedding, the terrible event occurred which has deprived me of my only companion.'

Sherlock Holmes had been leaning back in his chair with his eyes closed, and his head sunk in a cushion, but he half-opened his lids now, and glanced across at his visitor.

'Pray be precise as to details,' said he.

'It is easy for me to be so, for every event of that dreadful time is seared into my memory. The manor house is, as I have already said, very old, and only one wing is now inhabited. The bedrooms in this wing are on the ground floor, the sitting-rooms being in the central block of the buildings. Of these bedrooms, the first is Dr Roylott's, the second my sister's, and the third my own. There is no communication between them, but they all open out into the same corridor. Do I make myself plain?'

'Perfectly so.'

'The windows of the three rooms open out upon the lawn. The fatal night Dr Roylott had gone to his room early, though we knew that he had not retired to rest, for my sister was troubled by the smell of the strong Indian cigars which it was his custom to smoke. She left her room, therefore, and came into mine, where she sat for some time, chatting about her approaching wedding. At eleven o'clock she rose to leave me, but she paused at the door and looked back.

'"Tell me, Helen," said she, "have you ever heard anyone whistle in the dead of the night?"

'"Never," said I.

'"I suppose that you could not possibly whistle yourself in your sleep?"

'"Certainly not. But why?"

'"Because during the last few nights I have always, about three in the morning, heard a low clear whistle. I am a light sleeper, and it has awakened me. I cannot tell where it came from – perhaps from the next room, perhaps from the lawn. I thought that I would just ask you whether you had heard it."

'"No, I have not. It must be those wretched gipsies in the plantation."

'"Very likely. And yet if it were on the lawn I wonder that you did not hear it also."

'"Ah, but I sleep more heavily than you."

'"Well, it is of no great consequence at any rate," she smiled back at me, closed my door, and a few moments later I heard her key turn in the lock.'

'Indeed,' said Holmes. 'Was it your custom always to lock yourselves in at night?'

'Always.'

'And why?'

'I think that I mentioned to you that the Doctor kept a cheetah and a baboon. We had no feeling of security unless our doors were locked.'

'Quite so. Pray proceed with your statement.'

'I could not sleep that night. A vague feeling of impending misfortune impressed me. My sister and I, you will recollect, were twins, and you know how subtle are the links which bind two souls which are so closely allied. It was a wild night. The wind was howling outside, and the rain was beating and splashing against the windows. Suddenly, amidst all the hubbub of the gale, there burst forth the wild scream of a terrified woman. I knew that it was my sister's voice. I sprang from my bed, wrapped a shawl round me, and rushed into the corridor. As I opened my door I seemed to hear a low whistle, such as my sister described, and a few moments later a clanging sound, as if a mass of metal had fallen. As I ran down the passage my sister's door was unlocked, and revolved slowly upon its hinges. I stared at it horror-stricken, not knowing what was about to issue from it. By the light of the corridor lamp I saw my sister appear at the opening, her face blanched with terror, her hands groping for help, her whole figure swaying to and fro like that of a drunkard. I ran to her and threw my arms round her, but at that moment her knees seemed to give way and she fell to the ground. She writhed as one who is in terrible pain, and her limbs were dreadfully convulsed. At first I thought that she had not recognized me, but as I bent over her she suddenly shrieked out in a voice which I shall never forget, "O, my God! Helen! It was the band! The speckled band!' There was something else which she would fain have said, and she stabbed with her finger into the air in the direction of the Doctor's room, but a fresh convulsion seized her and choked her words. I rushed out, calling loudly for my stepfather, and I met him hastening from his room in his dressing-gown. When he reached my sister's side she was unconscious, and though he poured brandy down her throat, and sent for medical aid from the village, all efforts were in vain, for she slowly sank and died without having recovered her consciousness. Such was the dreadful end of my beloved sister.'

'One moment,' said Holmes; 'are you sure about this whistle and metallic sound? Could you swear to it?'

'That was what the county coroner asked me at the inquiry. It is my strong impression that I heard it, and yet among the crash of the gale, and the creaking of an old house, I may possibly have been deceived.'

'Was your sister dressed?'

'No, she was in her nightdress. In her right hand was found the charred stump of a match, and in her left a match-box.'

'Showing that she had struck a light and looked about her when the alarm took place. That is important. And what conclusions did the coroner come to?'

'He investigated the case with great care, for Dr Roylott's conduct had long been notorious in the county, but he was unable to find any satisfactory cause of death. My evidence showed that the door had been fastened upon the inner side, and the windows were blocked by old-fashioned shutters with broad iron bars, which were secured every night. The walls were carefully sounded, and were shown to be quite solid all round, and the flooring was also thoroughly examined, with the same result. The chimney is wide, but is barred up by four large staples. It is certain, therefore, that my sister was quite alone when she met her end. Besides, there were no marks of any violence upon her.'

'How about poison?'

'The doctors examined her for it, but without success.'

'What do you think that this unfortunate lady died of, then?'

'It is my belief that she died of pure fear and nervous shock, though what it was which frightened her I cannot imagine.'

'Were there gipsies in the plantation at the time?'

'Yes, there are nearly always some there.'

'Ah, and what did you gather from this allusion to a band – a speckled band?'

'Sometimes I have thought that it was merely the wild talk of delirium, sometimes that it may have referred to some band of people, perhaps to these very gipsies in the plantation. I do not know whether the spotted handkerchiefs which so many of them wear over their heads might have suggested the strange adjective which she used.'

Holmes shook his head like a man who is far from being satisfied.

'These are very deep waters,' said he; 'pray go on with your narrative.'

'Two years have passed since then, and my life has been until lately lonelier than ever. A month ago, however, a dear friend, whom I have known for many years, has done me the honour to ask my hand in marriage. His name is Armitage – Percy Armitage – the second son of Mr Armitage, of Crane Water, near Reading. My stepfather has offered no opposition to the match, and we are to be married in the course of the spring. Two days ago some repairs were started in the west wing of the building, and my bedroom wall has been pierced, so that I have had to move into the chamber in which my sister died, and to sleep in the very bed in which she slept. Imagine, then, my thrill of terror when last night, as I lay awake, thinking over her terrible fate, I suddenly heard in the silence of the night the low whistle which had been the herald of her own death. I sprang up and lit the lamp, but nothing was to be seen in the room. I was too shaken to go to bed again, however, so I dressed, and as soon as it was daylight I slipped down, got a dog-cart at the Crown Inn, which is opposite, and drove to Leatherhead, from whence I have come on this morning, with the one object of seeing you and asking your advice.'

'You have done wisely,' said my friend. 'But have you told me all?'

'Yes, all.'

'Miss Roylott, you have not. You are screening your stepfather.'

'Why, what do you mean?'

For answer Holmes pushed back the frill of back lace which fringed the hand that lay upon our visitor's knee. Five little livid spots, the marks of four fingers and a thumb, were printed upon the white wrist.

'You have been cruelly used,' said Holmes.

The lady coloured deeply, and covered over her injured wrist. 'He is a hard man,' she said, 'and perhaps he hardly knows his own strength.'

There was a long silence, during which Holmes leaned his chin upon his hands and stared into the crackling fire.

'This is very deep business,' he said at last. 'There are a thousand details which I should desire to know before I decide upon our course of action. Yet we have not a moment to lose. If we were to come to Stoke Moran today, would it be possible for us to see over these rooms without the knowledge of your stepfather?'

'As it happens, he spoke of coming into town today upon some most important business. It is probable that he will be away all day, and that there would be nothing to disturb you. We have a housekeeper now, but she is old and foolish, and I could easily get her out of the way.'

'Excellent. You are not averse to this trip, Watson?'

'By no means.'

'Then we shall both come. What are you going to do yourself?'

'I have one or two things which I would wish to do now that I am in town. But I shall return by the twelve o'clock train, so as to be there in time for your coming.'

'And you may expect us early in the afternoon. I have myself some small business matters to attend to. Will you not wait and breakfast?'

'No, I must go. My heart is lightened already since I have confided my trouble to you. I shall look forward to seeing you again this afternoon. She dropped her thick black veil over her face, and glided from the room.

'And what do you think of it all, Watson?' asked Sherlock Holmes, leaning back in his chair.

'It seems to me to be a most dark and sinister business.'

'Dark enough and sinister enough.'

'Yet if the lady is correct in saying that the flooring and walls are sound, and that the door, window and chimney are impassable, then her sister must have been undoubtedly alone when she met her mysterious end.'

'What becomes, then, of these nocturnal whistles, and what of the very peculiar words of the dying woman?'

'I cannot think.'

'When you combine the ideas of whistles at night, the presence of a band of gipsies who are on intimate terms with this old doctor, the fact that we have every reason to believe that the doctor has an interest in preventing his stepdaughter's marriage, the dying allusion to a band, and finally, the fact that Miss Helen Stoner heard a metallic clang, which might have been caused by one of these metal bars which secured the shutters falling back into its place, I think there is good ground to think that the mystery may be cleared along those lines.'

'But what, then, did the gipsies do?'

'I cannot imagine.'

'I see many objections to any such a theory.'

'And so do I. It is precisely for that reason that we are going to Stoke Moran this day. I want to see whether the objections are fatal, or if they may be explained away. But what, in the name of the devil!'

The ejaculation had been drawn from my companion by the fact that our door had been suddenly dashed open, and that a huge man framed himself in the aperture. His costume was a peculiar mixture of the professional and of the agricultural, having a black top hat, a long frock-coat, and a pair of high gaiters, with a hunting-crop swinging in his hand. So tall was he that his hat actually brushed the cross-bar of the doorway, and his breadth seemed to span it across from side to side. A large face, seared with a thousand wrinkles, burned yellow with the sun and marked with every evil passion, was turned from one to the other of us, while his deep-set, bile-shot eyes, and the high, thin, fleshless nose gave him somewhat the resemblance to a fierce old bird of prey.

'Which of you is Holmes?' asked this apparition.

'My name, sir, but you have the advantage of me,' said my companion quietly.

'I am Dr Grimesby Roylott, of Stoke Moran.'

'Indeed, Doctor,' said Holmes blandly. 'Pray take a seat.'

'I will do nothing of the kind. My stepdaughter has been here. I have traced her. What has she been saying to you?'

'It is a little cold for the time of the year,' said Holmes.

'What has she been saying to you?' screamed the old man furiously.

'But I have heard that the crocuses promise well,' continued my companion imperturbably.

'Ha! You put me off, do you?' said our new visitor, taking a step forward, and shaking his hunting-crop. 'I know you, you scoundrel! I have heard of you before. You are Holmes the meddler.'

My friend smiled.

'Holmes the busybody!'

His smile broadened.

'Holmes the Scotland-yard Jack-in-office.'

Holmes chuckled heartily. 'Your conversation is most entertaining,' said he. 'When you go out close the door, for there is a decided draught.'

'I will go when I have had my say. Don't you dare to meddle with my affairs. I know that Miss Stoner has been here – I traced her! I am a dangerous man to fall foul of! See here.' He stepped swiftly forward, seized the poker, and bent it into a curve with his huge brown hands.

'See that you keep yourself out of my grip,' he snarled, and, hurling the twisted poker into the fireplace, he strode out of the room.

'He seems a very amiable person,' said Holmes, laughing. 'I am not quite so bulky, but if he had remained I might have shown him that my grip was not much more feeble than his own.' As he spoke he picked up the steel poker, and with a sudden effort straightened it out again.

'Fancy his having the insolence to confound me with the official detective force! This incident gives zest to our investigation, however, and I only trust that our little friend will not suffer from her imprudence in allowing this brute to trace her. And now, Watson, we shall order breakfast, and afterwards I shall walk down to Doctors' Commons, where I hope to get some data which may help us in this matter.'

It was nearly one o'clock when Sherlock Holmes returned from his excursion. He held in his hand a sheet of blue paper, scrawled over with notes and figures.

'I have seen the will of the deceased wife,' said he. 'To determine its exact meaning I have been obliged to work out the present prices of the investments with which it is concerned. The total income, which at the time of the wife's death was little short of £1,100, is now through the fall in agricultural prices not more than £750. Each daughter can claim an income of £250, in case of marriage. It is evident, therefore, that if both girls had married this beauty would have had a mere pittance, while even one of them would cripple him to a serious extent. My morning's work has not been wasted, since it has proved that he has the very strongest motives for standing in the way of anything of the sort. And now, Watson, this is too serious for dawdling, especially as the old man is aware that we are interesting ourselves in his affairs, so if you are ready we shall call a cab and drive to Waterloo. I should be very much obliged if you would slip your revolver into your pocket. An Eley's No. 2 is an excellent argument with gentlemen who can twist steel pokers into knots. That and a tooth-brush are, I think, all that we need.'

At Waterloo we were fortunate in catching a train for Leatherhead, where we hired a trap at the station inn, and drove for four or five miles through the lovely Surrey lanes. It was a perfect day, with a bright sun and a few fleecy clouds in the heavens. The trees and wayside hedges were just throwing out their first green shoots, and the air was full of the pleasant smell of the moist earth. To me at least there was a strange contrast between the sweet promise of the spring and this sinister quest upon which we were engaged. My companion sat in front of the trap, his arms folded, his hat pulled down over his eyes, and his chin sunk upon his breast, buried in the deepest thought. Suddenly, however, he started, tapped me on the shoulder, and pointed over the meadows.

'Look there!' said he.

A heavily-timbered park stretched up in a gentle slope, thickening into a grove at the highest point. From amidst the branches there jutted out the grey gables and high rooftree of a very old mansion.

'Stoke Moran?' said he.

'Yes, sir, that be the house of Dr Grimesby Roylott,' remarked the driver.

'There is some building going on there,' said Holmes; 'that is where we are going.'

'There's the village,' said the driver, pointing to a cluster of roofs some distance to the left; 'but if you want to get to the house, you'll find it shorter to go over this stile, and so by the foot-path over the fields. There it is, where the lady is walking.'

'And the lady, I fancy, is Miss Stoner,' observed Holmes, shading his eyes. 'Yes, I think we had better do as you suggest.'

We got off, paid our fare, and the trap rattled back on its way to Leatherhead.

'I thought it as well,' said Holmes, as we climbed the stile, 'that this fellow should think we had come here as architects, or on some definite business. It may stop his gossip. Good afternoon, Miss Stoner. You see that we have been as good as our word.'

Our client of the morning had hurried forward to meet us with a face which spoke her joy. 'I have been waiting so eagerly for you,' she cried, shaking hands with us warmly. 'All has turned out splendidly. Dr Roylott has gone to town, and it is unlikely that he will be back before evening.'

'We have had the pleasure of making the Doctor's acquaintance,' said Holmes, and in a few words he sketched out what had occurred. Miss Stoner turned white to the lips as she listened.

'Good heavens!' she cried, 'he has followed me, then.'

'So it appears.'

'He is so cunning that I never know when I am safe from him. What will he say when he returns?'

'He must guard himself, for he may find that there is someone more cunning than himself upon his track. You must lock yourself from him tonight. If he is violent, we shall take you away to your aunt's at Harrow. Now, we must make the best use of our time, so kindly take us at once to the rooms which we are to examine.'

The building was of grey, lichen-blotched stone, with a high central portion, and two curving wings, like the claws of a crab, thrown out on each side. In one of these wings the windows were broken, and blocked with wooden boards, while the roof was partly caved in, a picture of ruin. The central portion was in little better repair, but the right-hand block was comparatively modern, and the blinds in the windows, with the blue smoke curling up from the chimneys, showed that this was where the family resided. Some scaffolding had been erected against the end wall, and the stonework had been broken into, but there were no signs of any workmen at the moment of our visit. Holmes walked slowly up and down the ill-trimmed lawn, and examined with deep attention the outsides of the windows.

'This, I take it, belongs to the room in which you used to sleep, the centre one to your sister's, and the one next to the main building to Dr Roylott's chamber?'

'Exactly so. But I am now sleeping in the middle one.'

'Pending the alterations, as I understand. By the way, there does not seem to be any very pressing need for repairs at that end wall.'

'There were none. I believe that it was an excuse to move me from my room.'

'Ah! that is suggestive. Now, on the other side of this narrow wing runs the corridor from which these three rooms open. There are windows in it, of course?'

'Yes, but very small ones. Too narrow for anyone to pass through.'

'As you both locked your doors at night, your rooms were unapproachable from that side. Now, would you have the kindness to go into your room, and to bar your shutters.'

Miss Stoner did so, and Holmes, after a careful examination through the open window, endeavoured in every way to force the shutter open, but without success. There was no slit through which a knife could be passed to raise the bar. Then with his lens he tested the hinges, but they were of solid iron, built firmly into the massive masonry. 'Hum!' said he, scratching his chin in some perplexity, 'my theory certainly presents some difficulty. No one could pass these shutters if they were bolted. Well, we shall see if the inside throws any light upon the matter.'

A small side-door led into the whitewashed corridor from which the three bedrooms opened. Holmes refused to examine the third chamber, so we passed at once to the second, that in which Miss Stoner was now sleeping, and in which her sister had met her fate. It was a homely little room, with a low ceiling and a gaping fire-place, after the fashion of old country houses. A brown chest of drawers stood in one corner, a narrow white-counterpaned bed in another, and a dressing-table on the left-hand side of the window. These articles, with two small wickerwork chairs, made up all the furniture in the room, save for a square of Wilton carpet in the centre. The boards round and the panelling of the walls were brown, worm-eaten oak, so old and discoloured that it may have dated from the original building of the house. Holmes drew one of the chairs into a corner and sat silent, while his eyes travelled round and round and up and down, taking in every detail of the apartment.

'Where does that bell communicate with?' he asked at last, pointing to a thick bell-rope which hung down beside the bed, the tassel actually lying upon the pillow.

'It goes to the housekeeper's room.'

'It looks newer than the other things?'

'Yes, it was only put there a couple of years ago.'

'Your sister asked for it, I suppose?'

'No, I never heard of her using it. We used always to get what we wanted for ourselves.'

'Indeed, it seemed unnecessary to put so nice a bell-pull there. You will excuse me for a few minutes while I satisfy myself as to this floor.' He threw himself down upon his face with his lens in his hand, and crawled swiftly backwards and forwards, examining minutely the cracks between the boards. Then he did the same with the woodwork with which the chamber was panelled. Finally he walked over to the bed and spent some time in staring at it, and in running his eye up and down the wall. Finally he took the bell-rope in his hand and gave it a brisk tug.

'Why, it's a dummy,' said he.

'Won't it ring?'

'No, it is not even attached to a wire. This is very interesting. You can see now that it is fastened to a hook just above where the little opening of the ventilator is.'

'How very absurd! I never noticed that before.'

'Very strange!' muttered Holmes, pulling at the rope. 'There are one or two very singular points about this room. For example, what a fool a builder must be to open a ventilator in another room, when, with the same trouble, he might have communicated with the outside air!'

'That is also quite modern,' said the lady.

'Done about the same time as the bell-rope,' remarked Holmes.

'Yes, there were several little changes carried out about that time.'

'They seem to have been of a most interesting character – dummy bell-ropes, and ventilators which do not ventilate. With your permission, Miss Stoner, we shall now carry our researches into the inner apartment.'

Dr Grimesby Roylott's chamber was larger than that of his step-daughter, but was as plainly furnished. A camp bed, a small wooden shelf full of books, mostly of a technical character, an arm-chair beside the bed, a plain wooden chair against the wall, a round table, and a large iron safe were the principal things which met the eye. Holmes walked slowly round and examined each and all of them with the keenest interest.

'What's in here?' he asked, tapping the safe.

'My stepfather's business papers.'

'Oh! you have seen inside, then!'

'Only once, some years ago. I remember that it was full of papers.'

'There isn't a cat in it, for example?'

'No. What a strange idea!'

'Well, look at this!' He took up a small saucer of milk which stood on the top of it.

'No; we don't keep a cat. But there is a cheetah and a baboon.'

'Ah, yes, of course! Well, a cheetah is just a big cat, and yet a saucer of milk does not go very far in satisfying its wants, I dare say. There is one point which I should wish to determine.' He squatted down in front of the wooden chair, and examined the seat of it with the greatest attention.

'Thank you. That is quite settled,' said he, rising and putting his lens in his pocket. 'Hullo! here is something interesting!'

The object which had caught his eye was a small dog lash hung on one corner of the bed. The lash, however, was curled upon itself, and tied so as to make a loop of whipcord.

'What do you make of that, Watson?'

'It's a common enough lash. But I don't know why it should be tied.'

'That is not quite so common, is it? Ah, me! it's a wicked world, and when a clever man turns his brain to crime it is the worst of all. I think that I have seen enough now, Miss Stoner, and, with your permission, we shall walk out upon the lawn.'

I had never seen my friend's face so grim, or his brow so dark, as it was when we turned from the scene of this investigation. We had walked several times up and down the lawn, neither Miss Stoner nor myself liking to break in upon his thoughts before he roused himself from his reverie.

'It is very essential, Miss Stoner,' said he, 'that you should absolutely follow my advice in every respect.'

'I shall most certainly do so.'

'The matter is too serious for any hesitation. Your life may depend upon your compliance.'

'I assure you that I am in your hands.'

'In the first place, both my friend and I must spend the night in your room.'

Both Miss Stoner and I gazed at him in astonishment.

'Yes, it must be so. Let me explain. I believe that that is the village inn over there?'

'Yes, that is the "Crown."'

'Very good. Your windows would be visible from there?'

'Certainly.'

'You must confine yourself to your room, on pretence of a headache, when your stepfather comes back. Then when you hear him retire for the night, you must open the shutters of your window, undo the hasp, put your lamp there as a signal to us, and then withdraw with everything which you are likely to want into the room which you used to occupy. I have no doubt that, in spite of the repairs, you could manage there for one night.'

'Oh, yes, easily.'

'The rest you will leave in our hands.'

'But what will you do?'

'We shall spend the night in your room, and we shall investigate the cause of this noise which has disturbed you.'

'I believe, Mr Holmes, that you have already made up your mind,' said Miss Stoner, laying her hand upon my companion's sleeve.

'Perhaps I have.'

'Then for pity's sake tell me what was the cause of my sister's death.'

'I should prefer to have clearer proofs before I speak.'

'You can at least tell me whether my own thought is correct, and if she died from some sudden fright.'

'No, I do not think so. I think that there was probably some more tangible cause. And now, Miss Stoner, we must leave you, for if Dr Roylott returned and saw us, our journey would be in vain. Goodbye, and be brave, for if you will do what I have told you, you may rest assured that we shall soon drive away the dangers that threaten you.'

Sherlock Holmes and I had no difficulty in engaging a bedroom and sitting-room at the Crown Inn. They were on the upper floor, and from our window we could command a view of the avenue gate, and of the inhabited wing of Stoke Moran manor house. At dusk we saw Dr Grimesby Roylott drive past, his huge form looming up beside the little figure of the lad who drove him. The boy had some slight difficulty in undoing the heavy iron gates, and we heard the hoarse roar of the Doctor's voice, and saw the fury with which he shook his clenched fists at him. The trap drove on, and a few minutes later we saw a sudden light spring up among the trees as the lamp was lit in one of the sitting-rooms.

'Do you know, Watson,' said Holmes, as we sat together in the gathering darkness, 'I have really some scruples as to taking you tonight. There is a distinct element of danger.'

'Can I be of assistance?'

'Your presence might be invaluable.'

'Then I shall certainly come.'

'It is very kind of you.'

'You speak of danger. You have evidently seen more in these rooms than was visible to me.'

'No, but I fancy that I may have deduced a little more. I imagine that you saw all that I did.'

'I saw nothing remarkable save the bell-rope, and what purpose that could answer I confess is more than I can imagine.'

'You saw the ventilator, too?'

'Yes, but I do not think that it is such a very unusual thing to have a small opening between two rooms. It was so small that a rat could hardly pass through.'

'I knew that we should find a ventilator before ever we came to Stoke Moran.'

'My dear Holmes!'

'Oh, yes, I did. You remember in her statement she said that her sister could smell Dr Roylott's cigar. Now, of course, that suggests at once that there must be a communication between the two rooms. It could only be a small one, or it would have been remarked upon at the coroner's inquiry. I deduced a ventilator.'

'But what harm can there be in that?'

'Well, there is at least a curious coincidence of dates. A ventilator is made, a cord is hung, and a lady who sleeps in the bed dies. Does not that strike you?'

'I cannot as yet see any connection.'

'Did you observe anything very peculiar about that bed?'

'No.'

'It was clamped to the floor. Did you ever see a bed fastened like that before?'

'I cannot say that I have.'

'The lady could not move her bed. It must always be in the same relative position to the ventilator and to the rope – for so we may call it, since it was clearly never meant for a bell-pull.'

'Holmes,' I cried, 'I seem to see dimly what you are hitting at. We are only just in time to prevent some subtle and horrible crime.'

'Subtle enough and horrible enough. When a doctor does go wrong he is the first of criminals. He has nerve and he has knowledge. Palmer and Pritchard were among the heads of their profession. This man strikes even deeper, but I think, Watson, that we shall be able to strike deeper still. But we shall have horrors enough before the night is over: for goodness' sake let us have a quiet pipe, and turn our minds for a few hours to something more cheerful.'

About nine o'clock the light among the trees was extinguished, and all was dark in the direction of the manor house. Two hours passed slowly away, and then suddenly, just at the stroke of eleven, a single bright light shone out right in front of us.

'That is our signal,' said Holmes, springing to his feet; 'it comes from the middle window.'

As we passed out he exchanged a few words with the landlord, explaining that we were going on a late visit to an acquaintance, and that it was possible that we might spend the night there. A moment later we were out on the dark road, a chill wind blowing in our faces, and one yellow light twinkling in front of us through the gloom to guide us on our sombre errand.

There was little difficulty in entering the grounds, for unrepaired breaches gaped in the old park wall. Making our way among the trees, we reached the lawn, crossed it, and were about to enter through the window, when out from a clump of laurel bushes there darted what seemed to be a hideous and distorted child, who threw itself on the grass with writhing limbs, and then ran swiftly across the lawn into the darkness.

'My God!' I whispered, 'did you see it?'

Holmes was for the moment as startled as I. His hand closed like a vice upon my wrist in his agitation. Then he broke into a low laugh, and put his lips to my ear.

'It is a nice household,' he murmured, 'that is the baboon.'

I had forgotten the strange pets which the Doctor affected. There was a cheetah, too; perhaps we might find it upon our shoulders at any moment. I confess that I felt easier in my mind when, after following Holmes's example and slipping off my shoes, I found myself inside the bedroom. My companion noiselessly closed the shutters, moved the lamp on to the table, and cast his eyes round the room. All was as we had seen it in the day-time. Then, creeping up to me and making a trumpet of his hand, he whispered into my ear again so gently that it was all that I could do to distinguish the words:

'The least sound would be fatal to our plans.'

I nodded to show that I had heard.

'We must sit without a light. He would see it through the ventilator.'

I nodded again.

'Do not go to sleep; your very life may depend upon it. Have your pistol ready in case we should need it. I will sit on the side of the bed, and you in that chair.'

I took out my revolver and laid it on the corner of the table.

Holmes had brought up a long thin cane, and this he placed upon the bed beside him. By it he laid the box of matches and the stump of a candle. Then he turned down the lamp and we were left in darkness.

How shall I ever forget that dreadful vigil! I could not hear a sound, not even the drawing of a breath, and yet I knew that my companion sat open-eyed, within a few feet of me, in the same state of nervous tension in which I was myself. The shutters cut off the least ray of light, and we waited in absolute darkness. From outside came the occasional cry of a night-bird, and once at our very window a long drawn, cat-like whine, which told us that the cheetah was indeed at liberty. Far away we could hear the deep tones of the parish clock, which boomed out every quarter of an hour. How long they seemed, those quarters! Twelve o'clock, and one, and two, and three, and still we sat waiting silently for whatever might befall.

Suddenly there was the momentary gleam of a light up in the direction of the ventilator, which vanished immediately, but was succeeded by a strong smell of burning oil and heated metal. Some one in the next room had lit a dark lantern. I heard a gentle sound of movement, and then all was silent once more, though the smell grew stronger. For half an hour I sat with straining ears. Then suddenly another sound became audible – a very gentle, soothing sound, like that of a small jet of steam escaping continually from a kettle. The instant that we heard it, Holmes sprang from the bed, struck a match, and lashed furiously with his cane at the bell-pull.

'You see it, Watson?' he yelled. 'You see it?'

But I saw nothing. At the moment when Holmes struck the light I heard a low, clear whistle, but the sudden glare flashing into my weary eyes made it impossible for me to tell what it was at which my friend lashed so savagely. I could, however, see that his face was deadly pale, and filled with horror and loathing.

He had ceased to strike, and was gazing up at the ventilator, when suddenly there broke from the silence of the night the most horrible cry to which I have ever listened. It swelled up louder and louder, a hoarse yell of pain and fear and anger all mingled in the one dreadful shriek. They say that away down in the village, and even in the distant parsonage, that cry raised the sleepers from their beds. It struck cold to our hearts, and I stood gazing at Holmes, and he at me, until the last echoes of it had died away into the silence from which it rose.

'What can it mean?' I gasped.

'It means that it is all over,' Holmes answered. 'And perhaps, after all, it is for the best. Take your pistol, and we shall enter Dr Roylott's room.'

With a grave face he lit the lamp, and led the way down the corridor. Twice he struck at the chamber door without any reply from within. Then he turned the handle and entered, I at his heels, with the cocked pistol in my hand.

It was a singular sight which met our eyes. On the table stood a dark lantern with the shutter half open, throwing a brilliant beam of light upon the iron safe, the door of which was ajar. Beside this table, on the wooden chair, sat Dr Grimesby Roylott, clad in a long grey dressing-gown, his bare ankles protruding beneath, and his feet thrust into red heelless Turkish slippers. Across his lap lay the short stock with the long lash which we had noticed during the day. His chin was cocked upwards, and his eyes were fixed in a dreadful rigid stare at the corner of the ceiling. Round his brow he had a peculiar yellow band, with brownish speckles, which seemed to be bound tightly round his head. As we entered he made neither sound nor motion.

'The band! the speckled band!' whispered Holmes.

I took a step forward. In an instant his strange headgear began to move, and there reared itself from among his hair the squat diamond-shaped head and puffed neck of a loathsome serpent.

'It was a swamp adder!' cried Holmes – 'the deadliest snake in India. He has died within ten seconds of being bitten. Violence does, in truth, recoil upon the violent, and the schemer falls into the pit which he digs for another. Let us thrust this creature back into its den, and we can then remove Miss Stoner to some place of shelter, and let the county police know what has happened.'

As he spoke he drew the dog whip swiftly from the dead man's lap, and throwing the noose round the reptile's neck, he drew it from its horrid perch, and carrying it at arm's length, threw it into the iron safe, which he closed upon it.

Such are the true facts of the death of Dr Grimesby Roylott, of Stoke Moran. It is not necessary that I should prolong a narrative which has already run to too great a length, by telling how we broke the sad news to the terrified girl, how we conveyed her by the morning train to the care of her good aunt at Harrow, of how the slow process of official inquiry came to the conclusion that the Doctor met his fate while indiscreetly playing with a dangerous pet. The little which I had yet to learn of the case was told me by Sherlock Holmes as we travelled back next day.

'I had,' said he, 'come to an entirely erroneous conclusion, which shows, my dear Watson, how dangerous it always is to reason from insufficient data. The presence of the gipsies, and the use of the word "band," which was used by the poor girl, no doubt, to explain the appearance which she had caught a horrid glimpse of by the light of her match, were sufficient to put me upon an entirely wrong scent. I can only claim the merit that I instantly reconsidered my position when, however, it became clear to me that whatever danger threatened an occupant of the room could not come either from the window or the door. My attention was speedily drawn, as I have already remarked to you, to this ventilator, and to the bell-rope which hung down to the bed. The discovery that this was a dummy, and that the bed was clamped to the floor, instantly gave rise to the suspicion that the rope was there as a bridge for something passing through the hole, and coming to the bed. The idea of a snake instantly occurred to me, and when I coupled it with my knowledge that the Doctor was furnished with a supply of creatures from India, I felt that I was probably on the right track. The idea of using a form of poison which could not possibly be discovered by any chemical test was just such a one as would occur to a clever and ruthless man who had had an Eastern training. The rapidity with which such a poison would take effect would also, from his point of view, be an advantage. It would be a sharp-eyed coroner indeed who could distinguish the two little dark punctures which would show where the poison fangs had done their work. Then I thought of the whistle. Of course, he must recall the snake before the morning light revealed it to the victim. He had trained it, probably by the use of the milk which we saw, to return to him when summoned. He would put it through the ventilator at the hour that he thought best, with the certainty that it would crawl down the rope, and land on the bed. It might or might not bite the occupant, perhaps she might escape every night for a week, but sooner or later she must fall a victim.

'I had come to these conclusions before ever I had entered his room. An inspection of his chair showed me that he had been in the habit of standing on it, which, of course, would be necessary in order that he should reach the ventilator. The sight of the safe, the saucer of milk, and the loop of whipcord was enough to finally dispel any doubts which may have remained. The metallic clang heard by Miss Stoner was obviously caused by her father hastily closing the door of his safe upon its terrible occupant. Having once made up my mind, you know the steps which I took in order to put the matter to the proof. I heard the creature hiss, as I have no doubt that you did also, and I instantly lit the light and attacked it.'

'With the result of driving it through the ventilator.'

'And also with the result of causing it to turn upon its master at the other side. Some of the blows of my cane came home, and roused its snakish temper, so that it flew upon the first person it saw. In this way I am no doubt indirectly responsible for Dr Grimesby Roylott's death, and I cannot say that it is likely to weigh very heavily upon my conscience.'

When Morning Comes

Elizabeth Fancett

The Right Honourable Sir William Wellborn smiles to himself as he riffles through his papers. They rustle softly in the darkness. He looks around the empty House – home of the law-makers, society's protectors, the orderers of good. He is proud to be their leader. But then, it was his birthright. All the Wellborns had been law-makers, leaders, men of vision.

He had been particularly pleased with today. The House had been more than usually impressed with his oratory, his qualities of leadership had been never more apparent or appreciated. There were still the old die-hards, of course, clinging to their decrepit ideas of democracy. But things were changing rapidly. *He* was changing them. Life was changing, the old orders passing. And his Bill would go through. He was sure of that.

He frowns, remembering something, shrugs it away. He switches off the small light over his desk. The shadows crawl close, night deepens. He listens to the dark silence.

What? For a moment ... he'd thought ... Just so! He'd *thought* – imagined – as he'd imagined it before. He was tired, he would go home. He hesitates. Or should he stay and think it out; now, while it was still fresh in his mind, and then forget it? He switches on the light again.

Let's see now, what had he been saying when he'd heard – thought he'd heard – something? It had been somewhere towards the end of his speech – he couldn't exactly remember where. Was it before or after his summing up? Or had it been? ...

He sits down, trying to remember ...

The House had been hushed, tense, hanging on his words ...

'We all know that the Abortion Act is not working as it should. And, as it stands, it never will! Most of the medical profession, and the Church – though, thank God, the Church carries little weight these days – continue to oppose and obstruct it in every way. My Bill is designed precisely to overcome this opposition. Abortion should be made legally binding on all doctors; not only to ensure abortions for all who wish them, but also, where circumstances justify it, to enforce in cases where those forbidden to procreate insist on breaking the compulsory contraception law!'

There had been a general murmur in the House, a stirring of uneasiness.

Had it been then? No. It had come later, when the House was hushed again, all eyes and minds fastened on him as he concluded his speech.

'We *must* prevent irresponsible and selfish parents from bringing into our world the unfit and the surplus human beings who can contribute nothing to our society except further problems and disasters. Mankind must be thinned out before the best are crowded out, as weeds crowd out the good plants. Is that what we want – a world of weeds?'

It had been then that he'd heard – no, *thought* he'd heard it. Like a ripple in his brain, a shadow moving across his mind – a voice, a word, repeated once ... twice ... softly: 'Herod,' it had said. 'Herod. Herod.'

He had looked over to where his only strong opponent sat, the Bishop Duval. Duval was the only churchman left in the Common House of Law-makers, tolerated chiefly for his age and his long standing as a Member. But he still had power in the Church. Duval, he remembered, had called him that very word in the early stages of the Bill.

'Herod!' he had thundered out at him. 'Slaughterer of innocents! Slayer of the unborn!'

But today, Duval had been strangely silent. As if he'd given up the fight, or as if ...

A slight breeze murmurs through the high window. The great curtains flap. A small sound, but startling. Wellborn is startled, then angry with himself. He was a fool to stay here, remembering! And yet ...

He remembers the Grey Man, sitting alone in the visitors' gallery, as he had every day throughout the debate. An old man, grey-suited, grey-haired, grey-faced. He knew him? No. And yet something familiar about the old man ... his face ...

He sits in the darkness.

Remembering.

Remembering the Grey Man.

Duval groans softly as he recalls the day – the dreadful day. He should have spoken up, tried once more to stem this terrible tide of power. But he had been silent throughout the day's proceedings. Today, with this infamous Bill nearing its final stages, he had been voiceless, letting evil be done, while that arrogant Wellborn rushed through yet another Bill of murder!

He groans aloud. He was an old man, worn out. He was a broken voice crying in the terrible wilderness, an ancient reed bent low by the icy winds of change.

But yesterday, he had tried ...

'The House well knows my views on abortion!' he had thundered. 'And on every other law this glorified social welfare worker has forced – or tried to force – upon this House and our nation! I have sat heartsick, helpless, despairing, while he has put before you evil upon evil. Selective marriage, wedlock forbidden to the unfit – you balked at that – but what did he offer in its place? Compulsory contraception for the so-called unfit! And you passed that. You allowed abortion by consent, because *he* pushed it. You refused its abolition, because *he* pleaded for it – despite irrefutable evidence that the medical profession and the country as a whole were against it and considered it evil. Now – compulsory abortion! State murder! Are you going to allow that?'

He had looked around the silent House.

'How many of us,' he had asked, 'here in this House, in this world, would be alive if abortion had prevailed in our parents' day? *We* were allowed to be born, conceived in love, permitted to live, to grow. Will you deny to others what we ourselves were given – the precious gift of life – the gift to *be*?'

He might have swayed them then if he'd remained calm. But for a moment his eyes had met Wellborn's, saw the contempt in them, for himself and for all he represented.

'Can't you see,' he had thundered out at them, 'can't any of you see the way this man's power is growing? What next will he ask for? I'll tell you what next – euthanasia! First, death by relatives' consent, then death by compulsion. He won't be content with saying who shall come into this world, he'll want to say when we shall go out of it. When to kill off the old, the feeble, like sick dogs, regardless of their right to live out their God-given span. And it won't stop there! He'll dispatch anyone – *anyone* – who doesn't fit in with social or world requirements, who makes a mess of his blueprint for that mythical, marvellous world his mind envisages.

'In the plain-speaking words of which the Right Honourable Sir William Wellborn is so fond – if *he* had been aborted over forty years ago this world would have gone a long way to becoming the finer place he wishes it to be!'

He had turned then on Wellborn.

'In the Name of God and all creation, who – what – do you think you are? You're not God! You're not even a man!'

There had been uproar then in the House, voices protesting, a few approving.

'Order! Order!' cried the Speaker. 'I *will* have order!'

Instantly, the House had quietened. Not because of the Speaker, but of Wellborn, who stood there, magnificently unperturbed by the fracas, quietly smiling.

Duval shudders at the memory, sees again that striking figure, so sure,

so confident in his power. He hears his voice – calm, cool, ignoring
Duval's outburst, ignoring *him*.

'Pass the law to fit the circumstances,' he had said in his firm clear
voice. 'This you have always done. Now we need *this* law. We might never
have to enforce it, but we need it. Yes, it is hard. But what is our
alternative? Is it not better to do the deed *before* rather than *after* birth?
We can – we *must* – prevent more illegal births to those forbidden to
procreate. We can – we *must* – prevent births of the unfit; the malformed,
the idiots, the uneducable. We can – we *must* – stem the tide of surplus
human beings who threaten to engulf the rapidly dwindling spaces of this
earth.

'This is mankind's sole remedy, his long-term defence, and ultimately
his glory!'

Wellborn's hated voice bites deep into his mind. How to stop him?
How to? ...

He hears a light rapping on his door. Who would call so late?

'Come!' he says.

The door opens. Duval stares at his visitor, trying to place him. Then
as old eyes meet, gnarled hands grip in greeting. Duval has remembered.

'Morney! It *is* Morney! Sit down, old friend, sit down! There is much
to be said between us.'

The Grey Man sits.

Impatiently, Wellborn puts the papers in his case, closes it. He would go
home. Another hard day tomorrow. Anyway, this was ridiculous. He
hadn't heard a thing – not a whisper, not a sound – but the echo of his
own voice when he had finished speaking.

He frowns, not liking the thought engendered. His own voice? His –
conscience? Nonsense! Heart and mind, he is for this Bill. It is *his* baby.
He smiles at the apt phrase. It had been he who had pushed through the
original Bill. He had always advocated it, fought for it, upheld it whenever it seemed threatened with abolition.

He grins suddenly in the darkness. Was he not known by the Press as
'Abortion Bill?' He was pleased with the tag. And he was keeping up with
the family tradition. Yes, no doubt about it – he was a born leader, and
the House knew it. His grin deepens. Not bad for a man of his years, for
one who——

He tenses, listening. Then ... just then? ... He shakes himself angrily.
He had heard nothing – neither then, nor before! It had been – well –
an echo of Duval's outburst perhaps, lingering somewhere in the
chambers of his own mind. He mustn't let that confounded churchman
get him ...

His thoughts cease suddenly. Distinctly, clearly, he hears it. It is the
same voice. It whispers out to him from the crawling shadows, from the

thick blackness of the vast, empty House. Now, as before, a word –
repeated once ... twice ... softly ...
   'Herod,' it says. 'Herod. Herod.'

   'And that's the story of the Wellborns to date,' says Duval grimly. 'True
to pattern, eh?'
   'How did he get such power?' Morney's grey eyes are grave, troubled.
'One man – how does one man like him get such power? And in so short
a time!'
   'God knows!' groans Duval. 'It just seemed to happen, that's all. Six
years ago there was no Wellborn on the political scene. Suddenly, there
he was. And soon, a good many people who would have been – were not!'
   'Where did he come from?' asks Morney.
   'Tasmania, I presume. Soon after he was born, his mother took him
there. I wish to God he'd stayed there, died there!' Duval looks curiously
at Morney. 'But you know more about him than I do. You brought him
into the world.'
   Morney's face becomes greyer, his eyes avoid Duval's. He says slowly:
'That's why I've come to see you.' He pauses, forcing himself to look at
Duval.
   'What if I were to tell you' – Morney's voice thickens – 'that the Right
Honourable Sir William Wellborn – does not exist?'

   The small light is a comfortless speck in the enveloping gloom. But he
is glad of it. He can barely see the great doors through which he must
pass to leave the Chamber. They seem a long way from him.
   He is not afraid. Merely curious. But he is glad of the light. It helps
him to think, to reason this out. He hadn't heard it – not really, not
consciously ...
   Again the voice: 'Herod.'
   And again: 'Herod, Herod.'
   A rush of rage overcomes him. He wheels angrily, calling out to the
darkness.
   'Duval, is that you?'
   Silence. Nothing.
   'How's it fixed, Duval? Hidden microphones ... in the rafters, behind
the curtains ... the visitors' gallery?' He laughs harshly, mockingly. 'A
little old, aren't you, for such damn silly tricks! How did you get them up
there, for God's sake? Or perhaps your angels helped you! Trying to make
me believe it's heavenly voices – voices of vengeance, eh? Eh, Duval?'
   He feels better, now that he knows. Of course it was Duval – though
how he worked it God knows! – playing a senile trick, a last desperate
measure to scare him. Scare *him* – Wellborn! A ludicrous ruse, the old
fool! When the House heard about this, Duval would be finished.

But a thought still nags at him. *How* was it worked? A recording, timed for periodic 'haunting'? Or was Duval here, in the House . . . somewhere . . . in the darkness?

His voice – raw, harsh, tears, at the silence:

'It won't work, churchman! This is Wellborn you're dealing with . . . "Abortion Bill" . . . remember? To hell with you and your damned tricks! To hell with you and your damned morals!'

Silence. Nothing.

'That's *my* voice, Duval, *my* voice! Do you hear? This House is filled with my voice, with my laws! With *me*!'

He stops abruptly, appalled at his own screeching. He listens. Nothing. Not even his own breathing can he hear. The air is dead, the darkness dead.

For the first time in his life, he is suddenly, icily afraid.

He begins to walk – unsteadily, gropingly, towards the doors, holding on to the seat edges as he goes.

Quarter of the way . . . slowly . . . slowly . . . Now by the Speaker's rostrum . . . a little farther . . . He pauses. The visitors' gallery is high above him – where the Grey Man sat today . . . and yesterday . . .

The grey face moves across his mind, like a half-formed vision, as seen through eyes that sleep – but do not sleep. His thoughts race ahead of his heartbeat, until his heart knocks louder on his mind. Not far from the doors . . . *Now!* He reaches out to touch them. He stops. *Is* stopped. A barrier before and around him. Nothing that he can see or feel or know – but it is there, in the darkness.

The fear grows in him. He stands stricken, in a limbo of terror, in a black void, in a cage of nothingness that is a steel trap around him.

He is cold, yet sweat pours from him like rivulets from a rain-drenched tree, He *is* a tree – not a man – a living being capable of rational thought, self-governed, moved by his own will! He, the maker of laws, was subject now to other laws to which he gave no credence. His mind struggles, fighting to surface, until gradually conscious thought returns.

'Wait!' his mind says. 'This will pass . . . just a while . . . Wait!'

It was something in *him*, he decides. He alone was responsible for this temporary paralysis. Self-hypnosis – something like that. It was nothing he could not control. If he gave it thought, he could countermand it. He would!

His will says: 'Move! Walk!' His mind demands it. But his body does not obey.

'Move!' screams his mind. He tries to echo the scream in his throat, but his mouth will not move either. He sweats, struggles, and while he struggles, his mind and will straining against alien forces, the silence breaks in a wave of whispered sounds. From the great domed ceiling, from the high corners of the vast Chamber, growing louder, nearer – one voice, one cry: 'Herod! Herod! Herod!'

The great doors are flung open. Light from the outer chamber rushes in upon him. Instantly, he feels that he is free. He stumbles towards the open doors, almost into the arms of the astonished caretaker.

'Sir William! I heard shouting ... I thought – Sir William, what is it? Are you ill?'

He brushes the man aside, hurries from the gloomy Chamber, through the reassuringly lighted outer room, into the fresh, clear, open wideness of the night.

Morney quails before Duval's grave, shocked eyes.

'I know it was wrong,' he says, 'but she begged me to do it. She was afraid how her husband would react if his son, his heir, were deformed.'

'Deformed?'

'The chances were high. She'd been taking certain drugs, without my knowledge.'

'So you refused it life because it *might* be deformed?' Duval's voice is stern, uncompromising. He studies Morney's sad, grey face. Then, more gently, he asks: 'And was it?'

'No ... at least ... not very much.' Morney's voice is unsteady. 'The left foot had just three toes.'

'Dear God!' groans Duval. 'To lose one's life – for so little!'

'A small defect, yes,' says Morney. 'But it was too much for a Wellborn – the high born! She considered the abortion justified.'

'And you?'

'No. But – she was a wealthy and influential woman. Had I refused, she could have ruined me.'

'Supposing,' asks Duval slowly, 'the child *had* been born malformed – would you have destroyed it?'

'God! No!' cries Morney, shocked.

Ah, such indignation! thinks Duval sadly. But what is the difference? Before or after birth – it was still a living child. It was still murder! But he does not say these things. He knows that Morney has divined his thoughts.

'But why,' asks Duval, 'the *pretence* of birth?'

'Without an heir, the Wellborn estate would have been forfeit to the Government.'

'But there could have been other children!'

'No. The abortion put paid to that.'

'And Lord Wellborn – how did you explain to him?'

'A miscarriage.'

'And the false registration of birth – did he know of that?'

'No. He died soon after the child ... died. Lady Wellborn kept to the house until the time when the child would have been born. Then I registered the birth and helped in other ways to establish belief in her son's existence. I set up the management of the estate, then she closed the house and left for Tasmania, ostensibly taking the child with her.'

'So,' says Duval grimly, 'for thirty-four years she lived out a lie, on money that was not rightfully hers.'

'It was a *penal* law,' protests Morney, 'that left a childless widow penniless when her husband died! Morally, the money was hers, the estate hers!'

'*Morally?*' Duval's mouth twists in an ironic smile.

Morney takes his meaning. He sighs heavily. 'She died,' he says softly, 'regretting it. I lived regretting it.'

Duval looks at him curiously. '*Where* did you live? As I remember, you yourself left the country soon after Lady Wellborn.'

Morney nods. 'She paid me well for my services. I – put every penny into a home for the malformed in – well, it doesn't matter where. It was a grim, lonely place, but I did what I could for them ... a kind of atonement for' – he stumbles – 'for murder.'

The word is out. It lies between them in the heavy silence, Morney's grey face becomes greyer, older. Duval's heart twists with compassion for this man.

'What's done is done!' he says briskly. 'But it is not too late to do something about this impostor.' He frowns. 'How could he have known about the abortion, that there was no heir to the Wellborn estate? None but yourself and Lady Wellborn knew about it, yet immediately she died he took over the estate and entered politics – just as the real Wellborn would have done – if he had lived.'

Morney turns desperate eyes towards him. 'Tell me, Duval, have I – could I – have altered destiny? If the real Wellborn had been allowed to live – might things have been different? I mean ... all those who were killed before birth because of this impostor's law ... all those who were not even conceived – would these have known life – if I had let him live?'

Duval hesitates, seeing the grey tortured face, the haunted eyes. He says: 'I doubt it – I doubt it very much. You know as well as I do that it is a tradition with the Wellborns to ensure a good world – for *their* kind Their family motto is "Who cannot be well born shall not *be* born!" ... and "The unfit shall not conceive!" ... and "The useless shall die!" ' He laughs, without humour, dryly, harshly. 'The motto gets longer with each succeeding Wellborn. No – alive or dead – born or aborted – the Right Honourable Sir William Wellborn would have been true to the faith of his fathers!'

He is quiet for a moment, appalled by his own words. He didn't really believe that. The laws of heredity were not that rigid. Men's souls were not necessarily patterns of the past, a man's spirit was not the blueprint of his ancestors. Maybe – who knows – if the real Wellborn had lived – so many would not have died!

But he is glad that he has said it. Some of the greyness departs from Morney's face. The load has been lightened, the guilt does not cut so cruel, so deep.

'What shall we do?' he asks.

Duval's eyes harden. 'Tomorrow, in the height of his power, in his moment of triumph, we'll strike him down! By the time we've finished with him, he'll wish he'd never been born!' He hesitates, looks at Morney. 'I will need you. Will you come?'

'I will come,' says Morney. 'It is time – *my* time . . . and his!'

'We can do this quietly, Morney. Not for his sake . . . but for yours.' Morney's eyes are grateful with relief.

Duval looks at the clock. 'Stay here tonight. Tomorrow, we'll get to the House early . . . he's always there first. We'll face him with it. He'll get out of politics . . . and the country . . . faster than he came in! Once again, the Right Honourable Sir William Wellborn is due for a disappearance – and this time he won't be coming back!'

He stands uncertainly beside his car. His legs tremble still. He decides to walk, give himself time to explain the inexplicable – for explanation there must be.

His steps make lonely echoes on the night pavements. He casts no shadow, for the quiet streets are dark. He walks alone in a silent world . . . thinking . . . thinking . . .

Gradually his heartbeat steadies in the crisp sweetness of the air, his legs feel part of him once more. He is almost himself again.

He turns suddenly, and wonders why. He had heard nothing. He sees nothing. He walks on, angry with himself.

He has reached a decision. Tomorrow, when the Bill was law, he would take a holiday – it was all he needed. He was fit – always had been – as far back as he could remember . . . He frowns. There had been those periods when his memory played him up . . . and there had been dreams . . . disturbing dreams . . . Signs of strain, he could see that now. He should have heeded the warning. Well, he would now.

Meanwhile . . . a good night's sleep . . . that's all he wanted to see him through the following day. His mind turns to Duval. Have to do something about that damned churchman! It would be tricky, for he had quite a following in high places – heaven, mostly! He grins delightedly at his joke. The old fool had been right though – euthanasia *was* his next move. And Duval would be one of the first to go!

He walks on . . . thinking . . . planning . . .

It felt good, the night – the clear air, the crisp lonely streets. Felt good to walk alone, as if he owned it all – the street, the houses, the people, the city. They were his, in a way. He had made them what they were, and many cities like this one. He had improved people's lives. And his influence was spreading. His laws, his ideas, were being adopted by other countries. There was more food, more work, more leisure, more *room* – because there were fewer *people*. It was the Wellborn answer – always had been. But it had taken *him* to get things this far.

He breathes deeply, drinking in the night. Yes it was good to be alive!

He comes to a row of mean, tightly packed little houses. They would go soon, he'd see to that! At least his compulsory contraception law had considerably lessened overcrowding in this area, raised the general level of living. Take this place, for instance. It would be swarming with poor, underfed children – imbeciles some of them – uneducable most of them. Misfits, drains on the community.

He draws level with the first house. Its grubby-curtained windows reflect dully in the cold starlight. He passes it . . . and the next . . . before the sound reaches him.

A soft sighing, a low lamenting, riffles through the silence. He stops, listens, straining to catch it, so faint it is. As he listens, it loudens, rises in pitch, grows in volume, a collective cry of mourning, of human misery, of grief and despair. It strikes at his heart, chilling it, stopping it. Would no one hear it . . . waken . . . come out of their houses? Surely they must hear it – such wailing, such . . .

He remembers suddenly that the houses are empty, their owners evicted months ago. A sullen, low-class group, all of them subject to the compulsory contraception laws which none had dared to break.

A memory forces itself into his mind – something Duval had said in one of his diatribes. Something about Rachel . . . a voice? . . . 'A voice in Rama was heard, lamentation and great mourning; Rachel bewailing her children and would not be comforted because they are not.' BECAUSE THEY ARE NOT!

He moves away from the houses, striding swiftly, as if he would walk away from his thoughts, from the sound. He walks desperately, blindly, forcing his mind into blankness, until the row of houses is far behind him. But the sound follows – the moaning, the crying, the . . . lamentation . . . He is almost running now, running without thought, except one – to be home.

He stops. The last wail has died away. Silence all about him. Deep silence. The streets are void. Blackness. Everywhere blackness.

Then a sound.

A footfall. Soft as a flake of snow upon snow. But he hears it clearly in the empty soundless night. He turns. No one.

He urges on. Nearing home now. He sees the iron gates, his driveway, the distant light in the house porch.

Again the sound. He turns. Something small, something grey . . . no, not grey ... no colour at all, really. No form either. It was nothing! He reaches for the gates, opens them, slips inside. His feet scrunch on gravel – a heartening, homely sound. He begins to walk. Stops. *Is* stopped. A barrier before and around him. Nothing that he can see or feel or know. But it is there, as before. Like a steel trap.

'Who is it? Who is it?' He calls out, but he cannot hear his voice – only the silence, sees only the blackness, the empty soundless blackness. He tastes the panic in his mouth, does desperate battle with it. He *will* keep calm, sane ... he *will!*

Suddenly the darkness is full of shadows – grey shadows ... no ... no colour at all, really ... and no form that he can recognize. They are coming out at him from the blackness, a throng of moving, gliding nebulous shapes that are shadow, shadows that are shapes.

Something detaches itself from the greyish mass ... something small, very small ... so very small.

His heart beats in his dried-up throat. Something speaks, yet does not speak. But he hears.

'Come! Come! Come!'

He thinks he is running, but he is not running. He is borne through dark streets like a rush of wind in the still air, past silent, sleeping houses, by the black waters of the river, in a scurry of time that has no part with time.

A huge dark shape stabs the sky above him. He stands before the House. He is alone. All is darkness. Nothing but quiet darkness.

He waits ...

And something that is very small moves in the darkness, and a voice that is not a voice says: 'Come!' And he has no time for thought ... no time for terror ... no time ...

Now he has time for terror. He is aware of himself, of where he is. He stands *within* the House! How? How? How? And why?

Pale moonlight shafts through the high windows. He looks about him, at the emptiness, the silence. Yet he is conscious of movement, of life ... somewhere ... all around him, close-packed in vast emptiness, filling every speck of space with life ... crowding him ... suffocating ...

He tries to fling himself to the floor, but a force unseen, unfelt, holds him upright.

'Who are you? Why am I here?' he wants to shout, but he does not. Anger, pride, assert themselves, smothering his fear. He would not speak with ghosts, with non-existent things! He'd be damned if he would! But then ... His fear returns. Might he not be damned if he *didn't*?

Anger again overcomes him. That he, Sir William Wellborn, should even *think* of damnation and ghosts! He'd had dreams before. They passed. Morning brought its relief and release. Patience. This dream will pass. Like the others ...

Sound breaking silence. A voice ... a familiar word: 'Herod.' He shouts then: 'Let me see you! Let me see you!'

Silence. An eternity of moment, then: 'You see us! You see us!' A clear voice, ringing, echoing ... and another ... and another ... voice upon voice, from every part of the great House.

His head spins this way ... that way ... up ... down ... around, as each voice takes up the cry: 'You see us! You see us!'

And he sees!

His trembling hand goes to his forehead, as if he would brush this nightmare from his sleeping eyes. But his eyes do not sleep. They look ... see ...

They hang suspended in air, like tiny curled clouds floating in a void. They drift lower, nearer ... to *him*. They pass before him, above and behind him, until they are a cage about him. And he sees into the transparent, tiny curled clouds.

Yet still his mind says: 'Wait! It will pass ... fade away with the night. Soon be over ... when morning comes!'

Then he hears the voice that is not a voice, that speaks yet does not speak, and it is as the sound of many whispers, saying: 'These are the womb-dwellers, the womb-dwellers, the unborn. These are they who were and are not, who lived, but had no chance to live! Look well on these who are slain in the womb!'

'Slain in the womb! Slain in the womb!' The sound fills his ears, his head, as from the mass of clouds about him the phantom foetus take up the cry. Then the voices cease. They drift away from him, melting into the shadows.

Revulsion mingles with his terror as others take their place – tiny, grotesque parodies of human form that swirl in clouds around him.

Again, the voice that is not a voice. 'These are the malformed, the cripples, the idiots. These are the unfit, who wanted to live, but are not. Look well on these who wanted to live!'

There is a violence upon him. 'To live?' he mocks. 'You're dead, you're dead, you're *dead*. You don't exist because you're not *fit* to live!'

'Not fit to live! Not fit to live!' The wailing chills the anger in him. He stands, like a stone, waiting for it to cease, for *them* to pass.

And, as before, in silence they fade, and the darkness is filled with larger shadows and from the mass something moves forward, stands before him. Light shines through it, yet it has shape – perfect human shape, full-grown – and it is beautiful and he cannot look upon it. Its voice, too, is beautiful, clear-toned, ringing: 'We are the unconceived – who never were and will never be. Among us are the great ones, whom the world never knew and never will know. They are the world's lost heritage, her glory that never was and will not be. Among us, too, are the souls that wait to be conceived, but do not know if they await in vain.'

He laughs: high, crackled, desperate laughter. He cannot hear his laughter, and he is glad. That *proves* it is a dream! He would cheat them – yes, even in his dreams he could, *would* prove himself the master!

'Wait then –wait for ever!' he screams. 'Wait for bodies that will never come, because *I* won't let them come! Mourn then for bodies lost, because *I* killed – I, Herod ...' He chokes. No, not Herod ... he hadn't meant to say that ... not even in a dream! 'I, Wellborn, will go on preventing them, preventing you, from peopling our world! There'll be others never born – many others! This world is not for you! Not for the freaks, the idiots, the cripples, the fools! You can't come into ii as you like, taking our food, our jobs, cramming our country, sharing our wealth, stealing our happiness! There's no room for you! No room, no room!'

'No room, no room!' they chorus in echoing cry.

He shouts above them, lashing out in savage oratory: 'Who cares what – or how many – great men may be lost!'

'Who cares? Who cares?' they echo.

'We have to take that chance – we *take* that chance – we will *always* take that chance!' Familiar words – which formed some of his answers to Duval—— Of course! All this was his doing!

'Duval!' he cries. 'He sent you, didn't he! Sent you into my dreams to torment me, to curse me, to cause me to waken sweating, trembling, conscience-stricken! Well, I'll waken all right – but not sweating, trembling, conscience-stricken! I'll waken tomorrow and come to this House, and you'll be gone, and I'll get my way and they'll pass my law and there's nothing – *nothing* – that you or that meddling churchman can do about it! And it won't be a dream! When morning comes – you'll see, you'll see! My word stays, my law stays – because *I* live! *You* don't! Do you hear me, ghosts of the unborn? YOU DON'T EXIST! YOU NEVER WERE! Just figures in my dream ... ghosts in a living man's dream!'

His voice fades, trailing in the still air. He is alone. He is exultant. He has banished them from his dream—— *Dream?* He had *heard* his own voice! He fights his panic. So what? One *could* actually talk – shout – in a dream, especially a vivid dream such as this. Patience! he tells himself. All he had to do was wait until morning ... wait until morning ...

The House lies hushed, empty, in the deep night. He waits for the dream to end, that he may drift in quiet sleep towards the inevitable dawn.

Something in the shadows moves. He groans, shudders. The dream is not yet over. A voice calls out of the shadows: 'You are nothing! You never were! Like us, you are nothing!'

Ice grips his heart as he breathes in the cry.

'One of us! One of us! One of us!'

His head spins this way, that way, all around, as the clamour and the crying grows. He flings wide his arms, flaying the dark emptiness around him.

'No! No! I *am*! I live! It is *you* who are nothing!'

His voice thunders out, filling the House with its sound and its fury. Abruptly, the clamour and the crying ceases. Not an echo remains. He is alone. In silence. In darkness. Even the moon has bowed before the night.

And the darkness and the nothingness move in upon him. He is seized by a mighty force that lifts and sweeps him upwards ...

He stands on the edge of the visitors' gallery, high above the House. Aware of himself and yet not aware, alive and yet not alive. He waits as if before Creation, when all was nothing and earth a void and darkness was upon the face of the deep.

The moonlight trembles through the windows and they come and fill the House before him. Host upon host of them – shapes that are shadows, shadows that are shapes, formless yet having form. And the womb-clouds, transparent in moonlight, fill the air above them and hang, unmoving, in the stillness.

Now he no longer sees them. For there is a wall around him – soft, yielding but impenetrable; a wall he has no desire to break or reach beyond, so safe is he in its warm and gentle bounds. A calmness dwells within him, and a peace, that has no part with sleep.

And he is not ready for the tearing, rushing sound that breaks him from the soft warm darkness and rips him into terror.

Sudden light spills in upon him, and in its centre – a face – the face of the Grey Man. There is steel in the moonlight ... terror ... death ...

Grey eyes, grey face, looming larger, nearer ... moonlight on steel ... grey face ... grey eyes ...

Steel.

Moonlight.

Steel.

'Come!' says the voice that is not a voice.

He cannot hear it.

But he comes.

They stand in the outer chamber of the House, in the early morning quietness.

Morney glances uncertainly at Duval.

'He *will* be there?'

'Sure to be. This is his great day!' Duval's voice is grim, but he is uneasy. He does not want to feel triumph over a foe about to fall.

'Duval.' Morney speaks softly, divining his feelings, his thoughts. 'Let *me* see him! After all, it *was* my guilt that made it possible.'

Duval hesitates. 'What will you tell him?'

'The truth.'

'Very well.' His voice is gruff with relief. 'I'll wait here.'

Morney pushes open one of the great doors, closes it quickly behind him.

Duval waits, his eyes fastened on the closed doors. A thought disturbs him. What if the man is violent? What if the doctor—— His unease grows. He pushes open the door, enters the Chamber.

He stops. Morney is kneeling beside something on the floor beneath the visitors' gallery – something crumpled, sprawled ...

'Morney!'

The doctor looks up. He is trembling violently.

'Is he – dead?' asks Duval quietly.

Morney does not answer.

'In the Name of God, man – what is it?'

Morney shakes his head. 'Not in the Name of God, Duval! Not in *His* name!'

Duval does not know the doctor's voice. It is thick, strange – as though he were someone else. It spurs Duval to his side.

'Have you examined him?'

Morney gets up quickly as Duval approaches, stands between him and the crumpled heap on the floor.

'Yes ... yes, he's – dead!'

'Don't blame yourself for this, Morney! He couldn't have known that you were about to end his masquerade.'

'No. He couldn't have known.'

Duval looks at him closely, curiously. It was still not Morney's voice. And his face was as if death had touched him also. He tries to move past him, but Morney puts out a pleading hand.

'No, Duval! Don't touch him! He's – been dead some time ... the soul has surely gone!'

Duval is gently reproachful. 'We cannot say that. No one knows how long the soul remains with the body. I must give him conditional absolution.'

'Absolution?' Morney laughs, and – like his voice – the laughter is not his. 'The innocent need no absolution!'

'The innocent!' Duval stares at him. 'Hardly that, Morney! Penitent, perhaps, in those last few seconds before he——' He glances briefly up at the visitors' gallery, then gently but firmly sets the trembling doctor aside.

Duval is kneeling now, pulling apart the coat that Wellborn had worn yesterday in the House. A crushed and twisted body, a battered, bloody head stove in by the violent fall – these he had been prepared to see, and the soul that might be in them, to forgive.

But these things he does not see. Just bands of linen, yellow-aged, incongruous in the midst of the crumpled, empty clothing.

Duval is very still. The blessing of heaven is in his hands and his heart, but in his mind, in his soul – a strange and awful knowledge of the living powers of hell.

His fingers touch the linen bands. Slowly, and with dread, he sets them aside. Morney scarcely breathes beside him, so still is he. Then:

'A long time,' says Morney. 'Dead ... a long, long time ...'

Duval looks down at what his trembling hands have uncovered.

Something small, so very small – so very, very small.

And on the little left foot of the tiny withered body – just three toes. Just three toes.

The Girl From Tomango

Rick Ferreira

In the bright coolness of the hotel room, Sinclair scrambled madly out of the wilted linen suit and the sweat-soaked shirt. He stepped into a pair of shorts that he found after a minute of frantic fumbling in the open suitcase on the bed. He reached for his sun-glasses and thrust his feet into his sandals, begrudging the time it took to secure the straps. And all he could hear, above the sighing of the coconut trees that filled the room, was the sing-song voice of the young man at the reception desk below:

'She worked here, did you say? Now, let me see. Lily Carew? Oh, yes. the pretty, light-skinned girl. She left suddenly, sir. Just like that. Got a job with the film company, I expect. Must be in Hollywood right now having a big time. We all said she was better looking than that *Carmen Jones* girl. We all said——'

Then there was his own voice, cutting the flow off: 'She couldn't have. I worked on that film location. She didn't leave Tomango. At least, not with us ...' And the sudden, arch, all-knowing look. 'Then *you* must be the gentleman who wrote the letters. The ones we returned to London. Oh, yes. Now I remember your face, sir. You left before the others. That's why I couldn't place you at first.'

So Lily had disappeared.

But Tomango was a tiny island and she had said that the hotel job was simply wonderful. The job of a lifetime, in fact. 'Meeting all the movie stars in the flesh. I love waiting on them! And they say nice things to me, too ...'

Yet she had gone, damn it. But *where*?

Sinclair found a beach shirt and slipped it on, ignoring the buttons. He stepped out on to the verandah, then ran down the flight of wooden stairs to the second verandah below. He jumped the last two steps that led directly to the beach. The white sand, the blue line of sea breaking into gentle foam, the clump of wind-tossed palms, the flamingos moving stiff-leggedly a few feet away – the stinging brightness went out of the picture when he slipped on the sun-glasses. And suddenly the bone-chilling dampness of London seemed a lot farther than a jet-flight away.

Then Sinclair saw the boat.

It lay on its side, looking flatter and wider than he remembered, with the sail-pole bare and jutting out at an angle. A dark old man was sitting in the boat's shadow, the fishing-net he was mending criss-crossing his widespread legs. A pair of trousers, tattered and just over knee-length, was the only thing he wore.

Everything was the same as it had been on that other day. Everything. Only the sun seemed fiercer, brighter, if that were possible.

He could feel the sweat gathering at his hairline and his heart started a slow heavy pounding. The dark old man didn't look up, even when Sinclair's shadow fell across the net and the lower half of his body. He cleared his throat, and when nothing happened at that, Sinclair said: 'Excuse me ...'

The old man looked up then and he knew he hadn't made a mistake. The sun-dried face was like dark polished oak but the eyes were surprisingly clear and young-looking. There wasn't the slightest flicker of recognition in them. But Sinclair still said: 'You do remember me, don't you?'

'Lots of white men come and go on Tomango now. All the same to me.' The young eyes in the old face went back to the net and the mending. 'You want to hire the boat?'

'Yes,' Sinclair said, watching the old man closely. 'I would like to take a trip to Turk Island.' A trickle of sweat came rolling down his cheek, bringing a taste of salt to the corner of his mouth. 'It's a tiny place about half an hour's sail from here. Just sand and coconut trees. You have to take your own water ...'

'Me don't go there. Nobody ever go there. There is bad spirit on Turk Island.' The old man threaded a ball of twine through a diamond-shaped space in the net. 'There is Friday Island. Very nice. No bad spirits. I take you there?'

Sinclair sank on one knee and his face was now level with the old man's.

'*You* took me to Turk Island a month ago. I was staying at the hotel – the one back there. I was with a unit making a film. I ... I had arranged to meet a friend on Turk Island. I stayed the night on the island and you came back for me the next day. I came back alone because my ... my friend wanted to wait until it was dark when some other boat would fetch her back here.' He wanted to grab the net and tug it free from the slow-moving hands. He wanted the old man to look at *him*. 'Now, do you remember? Do *you*?'

The old man looked up then.

'Dis friend ... so she a woman, eh?' The eyes were clear and questioning, like a child's. But the voice was only mildly curious. 'What she look like?'

'She was slim and brown,' Sinclair said. 'And ... and very lovely.' How else could one describe Lily – with the wind in her tumbling russet hair, the brown eyes shining, her laughter bubbling over with the sheer joy of living? 'You must remember my trip. A month isn't that long. I need someone to tell me that I didn't just dream her up . . .'

'To some . . . a month is like all the years.' The old man looked down at his hands and the net. 'Yes, Mista. I remember you . . . taking you there and bringin' you back. But why she not come and go with you?'

Patience. That was all that it needed. Sinclair took a deep breath.

'She arranged that someone else would take her to the island and bring her back . . .' Lily, smiling in the firelight of that night. The smooth brown arms reaching out, eagerly and unashamed. 'She said that everyone would gossip here if we left and came back together. Someone else did take her to Turk Island and bring her back. But *who*? And how do I find him?'

The old man shook his head.

'No one got there but me.' He paused and looked up. Not at Sinclair, but out to the flamingos with their pink feet deep in the blue-white foam. 'Then how she come and go from there? *How* she do that, Mista?'

Sinclair took the sun-glasses off, for the sweat had run right down and streaked the lenses. The heat and the light hammered at his naked eyes. 'Look,' he said. 'Please help me. *Please*. I'm really trying to find this girl. No one seems to know where she's gone. That morning you brought me back from Turk Island there was a telegram for me at the hotel. It told me to catch the next plane leaving for London. I . . . I write the stories that are made into motion pictures. *Movies*. My bosses needed me to work on a story back in London.'

The old man nodded gravely as if he fully understood the mad hectic world that gave Sinclair a living. He was still looking out into the endless space of sea and hot sky: 'Dis girl? You love her, then?'

Baring one's heart to an old native on a West Indian beach wasn't exactly the kind of thing one did with ease. Yet Sinclair found himself saying: 'Yes. I . . . I would like to marry her and take her back to London with me. I never did get the chance to tell her that. I finally said it in the letters I wrote her, but they came back – unopened. She had left her job at the hotel.' Now he couldn't stop himself. Somehow the empty beach seemed the right place for confessing, and the old man's quiet attentiveness made it almost the normal thing to do.

'I *had* to come back at the first chance I got. I just can't forget her. It's as simple as that . . .' Lily laughing. Her whole glorious brown body shaking in merriment. Like the evening on Turk Island when some insect had bitten him. 'Please help. There must be someone who——'

The old man dragged his eyes back slowly.

'Me. I loved her, too. But too much. Too much . . .'

Sinclair flattened a hand on the hot sand to steady himself. He said: '*You?* Why? What – what was she to you?'

'I was her Pa!'

The glare made it hard for Sinclair to focus his eyes. '*Was?* Is – is she dead?' He could feel himself beginning to shake as he forced the words out. 'But *how? When?*'

The old man nodded, slowly too. 'She dead, yes. No one go to Turk Island but me. I take her there first – then *you*, Mista. That day I bring you back – I never go again to Turk Island. Lily no swim. When she was little girl she hate water to wet her hair. Lily no swim . . .'

Sinclair forced himself upright and the beach was just a blast of bright colour and the gently-lapping tide was suddenly roaring and crashing like full-size breakers.

'My God! You must be mad. You *must* be . . .'

But the old man was looking up at him, clear-eyed, head shaking sadly.

'She was bad. All bad – like her Portuguese Ma. A long time I took her to Turk Island to meet many men. And after, always I bring her back here. She like men, but Lily, she no like to marry.' The old man shook his head again. 'De day I take you to her, I say, "Dis is last time, Lily, *last time*. I warning you . . ."'

The sun still glared, but suddenly there was no heat to it at all. The sweat on Sinclair's face and chest had gone icy cold. 'I – I'll fetch the police. God. You had no right——'

'All de right in de world. It was a Pa to do it. Who else? I give her time – but she was bad. All bad. Like she Ma . . .'

'You bastard! You murdering bastard——'

'And she died bad, Mista. I see that she pay for she sins dat way. De first day her mouth is bone-dry and de cramps in de belly is all de time, no stoppin'. De next day the sun crack-up her lip like knife-cuts and she drag herself under the coconut trees. She croakin' like a bull-frog now and de lips gettin' bigger and bigger. Her eyes too watery to see if de boat is comin' but she keep clawin' at de coconut tree to stand up and look——'

He had to stop him. He *had* to. Sinclair crashed down on the old man, knocking the ball of twine from the thickly corded hands, his own seeking blindly for the long, reedy neck.

His feet got tangled in the net, then he slipped and crashed heavily on the thin curve of the boat, knocking the wind out of his enraged lungs, scraping his left arm on the roughness of peeling paint. He stayed a moment, panting, flat against the boat, and the sweat was flowing more generously than ever. 'De waiter from de hotel, he coming this way . . .' From the old man's tone it could have been a tired comment on the heat.

Sinclair turned his head to look.

A stocky white-coated figure was almost on them. The black moon-round face split into a white grin and there wasn't a streak of sweat on it. 'Will you come in the hotel for lunch, sir? Or you taking a boat trip so you want a pack-lunch, sir? The manager want to know, sir ...'

Sinclair stared at the waiter, his rage ebbing now, leaving a dull anger like a nagging toothache. He knew he *had* to do something. He took a deep breath. 'Yes, I'm going for a sail. I've just been arranging it. Make it three bottles of mineral water and – and some fruit. I ought to be back by tea-time.' Sinclair was standing upright now and behind him he could feel that the old man was on his feet too, already busy with preparations for the trip. 'Make it as quick as you can. I'll see you this evening when I get back ...'

'Right, sir!'

The waiter was streaking back to the hotel, was already halfway there, when Sinclair turned to the old man. The net had been neatly bundled with the ball of twine lying on top of it and the old man was now in the boat, adjusting the sail-pole, moving with the easy agility of someone half his age. That Sinclair remembered, too, from the other time. He watched the old man until the hate in his eyes burned a response, for the old man stopped, turned his head, and said, still calm: 'What you hope to find, Mista?'

'*Lily!*' Sinclair said. 'Christ, man – she could still be alive. She could have found water and food of some sort. There must be water on the island; your bloody weather isn't always perfect. It *rains*, remember? Then there's the possibility that she could have been taken off by some passing boat – in spite of what you say ...'

The old man cut him short by saying again, 'No one go to Turk Island but me. Nobody.' The oddly young eyes met his. 'Rain fall, yes, but on dat island it make frog-water right away. All slimy and green, not for drinking, even if you dying for water. Only water for frogs ...' The old man got nimbly out of the boat, bent and pushed, and the shallow shell moved easily, came flat and upright, and in a moment the surf was washing creamily against the prow, the stern still anchoring the boat to the sand.

Sinclair said nothing more to the old man after that. They waited, the old man sitting placidly on the boat's edge, while Sinclair gazed impatiently back at the hotel through the sun-glasses he had been forced to slip on again. The the waiter came in sight, a blob of hurrying white, then soon just a few yards away, hugging a straw carrier-bag that was a plug for the local cottage-industry. 'All here, sir. Three bottles of de mineral. Slices of pineapple an' bits of cold chicken. That okay, sir?'

'Fine! Thank you – and be sure that I see you around this evening, will you?'

'Yes, *sir!*' The waiter shot a bright glance at the silent old man. 'You take good care of de gentleman, Ramos. You hear?' The waiter grinned whitely at them both, then turned and went streaking back to the shade of the verandahs.

Ramos? So that was the old man's name ...

'Okay, Ramos.' Sinclair said curtly. 'We are going to bring Lily back to Tomango.' He stepped in, holding the straw-bag. The old man pushed the boat deep into the surf and, with that surprising agility, hopped on board too. Sinclair settled himself in the prow, the bag at his feet, watching the old man smoothly run the sail up then move to the tiller, and in a minute they had caught the hot wind and were tacking out of the sheltered bay in a wide sweeping curve, heading for the open sea – a sea that glinted like blue glass and was almost as smooth.

He watched the old man, seething at the placid unconcern, at the sureness with which everything was done. A killer – no! A *would-be* killer. Yet the old man sat there, at the tiller, with the serenity of a child unconscious of sin. Sinclair could have lunged at him once again but he was wary of just being afloat; never quite happy in boats, large or small. And boats didn't come much smaller than this one. Then suddenly he remembered——

'*Coconuts*! Of course – the coconuts! They're filled with water and that white fleshy meat. Lily could shin up a tree, couldn't she? They do it all day on Tomango. That's enough to keep her alive. She'll be *alive*, I know she'll be——'

Sinclair stopped then, for the curiously clear eyes had come around to meet his hooded ones and there was something in them ... 'You no see that though the coconut trees all got nice leaves, fresh and green, all the nuts is *dead* nuts? All de nuts dry up long before they grow full and big.' Pity was what the eyes mirrored. 'That time you go by night, eh? You no see the bad part of Turk Island. And you must remember 'bout the *carrion crabs* ...'

The sun was hammering at his bare head, draping his shoulders like a hot towel, yet Sinclair was suddenly shivering again. 'What? – What sort of crabs?'

The old man shook his head. 'We no talk 'bout that.'

'Oh, we will! We will *talk*, you murdering bastard. And we'll find Lily very much alive. *I just know that she is* ...' Quicksilver, resourceful, laughing Lily ... no spooky island could snuff out that animal vitality. Sinclair took a deep breath, hoping to calm his suddenly queasy stomach. 'Okay, Ramos. Just forget about your damn crabs and get us to the island. On that trip we did it in less than half an hour ...' Or was it just the high excitement of anticipated love-making that had made the trip seem short, sending the boat skimming through the sudden dusk of that unforgettable evening? *Lily! Darling Lily! I'm on my way to bring you back* ...

But the old man was saying, loudly now, high above the swell of water: 'They big as turtles but they hide until there is something dead. They no eat flesh of the living. Never, Mista! But the moment you dead, they *know*. Then they come marching out, all in rows and rows. They get to the body and then they arrange it. Like Christ on the cross. First, they pin de hands and the legs down with big claws that break off easy – the special claws for pinning down de body to de place. Then they use the real ripping claws to tear at de flesh when they get down to de eating ...' Sudden alarm flared in the clear eyes when Sinclair stood up, shakily, making the light boat rock furiously. 'You want to pitch us in de sea, Mista? Sit down, Mista! Look – we very near Turk Island now ...' The old man locked the tiller under a dark armpit, his hands reaching out to steady the boat. He said softly, 'You may be right, Mista. Lily – she's alive, perhaps. More than perhaps. She is a clever, clever girl ...' He took away an oak-coloured hand to gesture. 'Look, Mista. You just look over your shoulder ...'

Sinclair sat down then and looked.

Turk Island was a swaying green smudge on his right, a smudge that grew more definite and vividly green with every passing second. Then they were tacking smoothly around a rocky headland and the glassy blue of the sea was suddenly trapped in the small still lagoon; that, too, he remembered. The old man lowered the sail and produced an oar, exactly as before, in the dark of that other evening. But now it was eye-searing sunlight, and Sinclair was suddenly aware of the odd feature that he had overlooked on his first trip – that Turk Island was utterly and unnaturally *silent*.

The sand stretched away, white and unmarked, into a thick line of coconut trees that neither thrashed nor whispered, as they did, perpetually, in the high winds of Tomango. But here, no winds blew, no brilliant flash of bird-feathers, no chatter of monkeys, no squawk from the parrots. Nothing but sunlight and the strange dead silence. Sinclair sat in the gently bobbing boat, stunned with utter disbelief that it had been like this, too, that other time – and yet he had noticed nothing. But then there had been the all-pervading need to possess Lily ...

And in the silence, the old man paddle-steered the boat on to the beach and sprang over the side. 'Very quiet, eh?' He stood ankle-deep in the blue water and held out a hand to Sinclair. 'We look, Mista. But we no look for long. Dis is a bad, bad place ...'

Sinclair stood up, ignoring the hand, fixing his sun-glasses on the old man's face. 'I'd better find her alive, Ramos. I'd start praying if I were——'

He stopped then, for he had seen something that transfixed him with blazing joy. High up the beach, on the thick snake-like roots of the coconut trees, Lily stood waiting, the gay pattern of the caftan-type dress she'd worn, bright against the expanse of white sand. Waiting, too weak to run to meet him – *but alive*!

'Lily! *Lily* ...'

Sinclair tumbled out of the boat, fell flat in the clear blue water, picked himself up, then, dripping but exhilarant, he struck at Ramos as the old man moved to block his path. 'Get away you fool! Lily! She's *there* – in the trees. Can't you see?' But Sinclair was running now, a shambling, skidding kind of run, his eyes riveted to that beckoning dress. At last, he was stumbling over the contorted uncovered roots of the coconut trees, among the crackling dead branches, and then he reached her.

Only it was Lily's dress and not Lily. Pinned high on the knotty trunks with a few huge thorns ... just a flag of distress that no wind stirred, a futile signal that no one had seen. He reached up and ripped it down and the fabric tore loudly in the unnatural stillness. Sinclair was very near to sobbing. Then—— 'Lily! Thank God ...'

For this time it was *her*.

The mass of coppery hair caught the sun's glare, deep in the grove of palms. Her head was propped high on a twisted root and he wasn't too late. He stumbled nearer and nearer as the gloom deepened, then he fell almost on top of her. 'Lily! *Darling* ...' Sinclair reached out for her hair, rippling gently as she restlessly turned her head and his hand went deep in the soft mass – and then he shrieked with sudden pain. His fingers had instantly been pricked by a thousand red-hot needles. Too late, he saw the mass of busy ants that were giving the constant motion to Lily's hair, as it streamed out and over the giant root!

And Lily—— Oh God! *Lily* ...

Beyond the glorious hair, her white, fleshless bones now lay spread-eagled as the *crabs* must have pinned her. The skeleton hands and feet were each wearing the grotesque ornament of a great curving claw, half buried in the sandy soil. Sinclair struggled up, waving a burning hand in agony, and looked down into the grinning skull, framed by the coppery, moving hair. Then he found that he was running – and sobbing as he ran; that he was now free of the coconut-grove and making for the boat. That a voice, hoarse with hate, was shouting close to his ear, 'Ramos! You murdering bastard! I'm going to——'

Ramos turned. He had been bending over by the boat and, when the old man faced him, across the rapidly narrowing beach, Sinclair could see that he was clutching a huge stone, his lean arms tensed with holding it high, ready to smash it down on him. But Sinclair didn't care. He was younger, stronger, and his hate propelled him on like a bullet from a gun. 'You're joining her, Ramos! I'll be leaving you dead for those damn crabs ...'

But Sinclair was just a few yards away when the old man dropped the stone into the water of the lagoon and started walking, very slowly, towards him.

Sinclair stumbled for a moment, in sheer surprise, then he was in reaching distance and he threw himself on Ramos and his hands closed over the old man's throat – over an Adam's apple big as a half-swallowed plum. He started squeezing, madly, mercilessly, and Ramos never made a move to fight back. For one crazy moment, before the young-looking eyes started rolling, popping, Sinclair caught a look in them that could only be described as *joyous*. He even thought that when the old man tried to croak out something, in the first few seconds, the words sounded oddly like: 'We all bad. *All bad, M-i-s-t-a* ...'

Sinclair couldn't be sure. He couldn't be sure of anything he did in those few minutes. He only knew that he took his hands away when the harsh croaking finally stopped, and Ramos sagged, lifeless, against him. Then Sinclair was looking down at the dark, thin-stick body, lying with the curious awkwardness of an abandoned puppet, an arm under the chest, the head with its bulging eyes and lolling tongue, pointing past his trembling feet, up to the rise of white sand and the grove of coconut trees ...

He was still staring at the thing at his feet, panting, the sweat running off him in a salty tide, when Sinclair heard the first sound on the island that *he* hadn't made. A curious swishing, scraping sound, like sand being shifted by a hundred busy shovels. He thought he knew then what he would see – even before he turned his head sharply and looked in the direction where the old man's eyes were blankly watching them advance ...

But the size and colour of the crabs held Sinclair rooted, and staring in utter disbelief.

A myriad scrabbling claws were propelling their huge shiny black shells in a slittering, skidding run across the white sand. Line upon armoured black line, the carrion crabs were pouring endlessly out from the roots of the sheltering palms, heading for the thing at his feet, in a mad, famished rush ...

The hoarse voice was again shrieking in his ear as Sinclair turned and ran for the safety of the open lagoon and the boat.

'No! Oh, Christ – No!'

He splashed into the warm blue water and pushed madly at the boat to get it completely clear of the sand, for Ramos had beached it half in and half out of the water. He kept on frantically pushing for a full sweating minute, but he couldn't budge it; the boat didn't move, not even an inch. Sobbing and gasping, Sinclair finally threw himself over the side and looked in.

The blue, clear water splashed softly inside, filling the boat, giving it the look of an exotically-shaped bath-tub. The straw basket lay, half submerged, still holding the broken glass of the three smashed bottles, with the bits of food bobbing gently, like edible soft toys. He knew then what Ramos had been doing with the huge stone – the stone that had never meant to be used as a weapon of defence. Only of destruction.

Sinclair stared into the boat for what seemed a long, long time.

Then, still thigh-deep in the water, he finally turned and looked back up the beach. He didn't want to, but some irresistible force twisted his throbbing head so that he could look at the carrion crabs doing their grisly work.

The old man had already been neatly spread-eagled, four great claws pinning his hands and feet to the hot white sand – and Sinclair had turned at the very moment when the eating had begun. With the first sound of tearing flesh he caught the hideous stench of the giant crabs, like that of an unhosed slaughter-house in the heat of high summer.

He sank slowly into the blue water, resting his head on the useless boat, then cried like a lost child. For he knew that he would remain lost for as long as he remained alive. No rescuing boat would sail into the still lagoon. In the end, though, he knew that he would be found.

The carrion crabs would *know*, to the very second, just when to set out in search of him ...

Dog or Demon?

Theo Gift

'The following pages came into my hands shortly after the writer's death. He was a brother officer of my own, had served under me with distinction in the last Afghan campaign, and was a young man of great spirit and promise. He left the army on the occasion of his marriage with a very beautiful girl, the daughter of a Leicestershire baronet; and I partially lost sight of him for some little time afterwards. I can, however, vouch for the accuracy of the principal facts herein narrated, and of the story generally; the sad fate of the family having made a profound impression, not only in the district in Ireland where the tragedy occurred, but throughout the country.

'(Signed) WILLIAM J. PORLOCK,
'Lieut.-Col.,——Regt.

'*The Currah, Co. Kildare.*'

At last she is dead!

It came to an end today: all that long agony, those heart-rending cries and moans, the terrified shuddering of that poor, wasted body, the fixed and maddened glare, more awful for its very unconsciousness. Only this very day they faded out and died one by one, as death crept at last up the tortured and emaciated limbs, and I stood over my wife's body, and tried to thank God for both our sakes that it was all over.

And yet it was I who had done it. I who killed her – not meaningly or of intent (I will swear that), not even so that the laws of this earth can punish me; but truly, wilfully all the same; of my own brutal, thoughtless selfishness. I put it all down in my diary at the time. I tear out the pages that refer to it now, and insert them here, that when those few friends who still care for me hear of the end they may know how it came about.

June 10th, 1878. Castle Kilmoyle, Kerry – Arrived here today with K. after a hard battle to get away from Lily, who couldn't bear me going, and tried all manner of arguments to keep me from leaving her.

'What have *you* to do with Lord Kilmoyle's tenants?' she would keep on asking. 'They owe no rent to you. Oh, Harry, do let them alone and stay here. If you go with him you'll be sure to come in for some of the ill-feeling that already exists against himself; and I shall be so miserably anxious all the time. Pray don't go.'

I told her, however, that I must; first, because I had promised, and men don't like going back from their word without any cause; and secondly, because Kilmoyle would be desperately offended with me if I did. The fact is, I hadn't seen him for three years till we met at that tennis-party at the Fitz Herbert's last week; and when he asked me if I would like to run over for a week's fishing at his place in Ireland, and help him to enforce the eviction of a tenant who declined either to pay for the house he lived in or leave it, I accepted with effusion. It would be a spree. I had nothing to do, and I really wanted a little change and waking up. As for Lily, her condition naturally makes me rather nervous and fanciful at present, and to have me dancing attendance on her does her more harm than good. I told her so, and asked her, with half a dozen kisses, if she'd like to tie me to her apron-string altogether. She burst out crying, and said she would! There is no use in reasoning with the dear little girl at present. She is better with her sisters.

June 12th – We have begun the campaign by giving the tenant twenty-four hours' notice to quit or pay. Kilmoyle and I rode down with the bailiff to the cottage, a well-built stone one in the loveliest glen ever dreamt of out of fairyland, to see it served ourselves. The door was shut and barred, and as no answer save a fierce barking from within responded to our knocks, we were beginning to think that the tenant had saved us the trouble of evicting him by decamping of his own accord, when, on crossing round the side of the house where there was a small unglazed window, we came in full view of him, seated as coolly as possible beside a bare hearthstone, with a pipe in his mouth and a big brown dog between his knees. His hair, which was snow-white, hung over his shoulders, and his face was browned to the colour of mahogany by exposure to sun and wind; but he might have been carved out of mahogany too for all the sign of attention that he gave while the bailiff repeated his messages, until Kilmoyle, losing patience, tossed a written copy of the notice into him through the open window, with a threat that, unless he complied with it, he would be smoked out of the place like a rat; after which we rode off, followed by a perfect pandemonium of barks and howls from the dog, a lean and hideous mongrel, who seemed to be only held by force from flying at our throats.

We had a jolly canter over the hills afterwards, selected the bit of river that seemed most suitable for our fishing on the morrow; and wound up the day with a couple of bottles of champagne at dinner, after which Kilmoyle was warmed up into making me an offer which I accepted on the spot – i.e., to let me have the identical cottage we had been visiting rent free, with right of shooting and fishing, for two years, on condition only of my putting and keeping it in order for that time. I wonder what Lily will say to the idea. She hates Ireland almost as much as Kilmoyle's tenants are supposed to hate him, but really it would cost mighty little to make a most picturesque little place of the cabin in question, and I believe we should both find it highly enjoyable to run down here for a couple of months' change in the autumn, after a certain and much-looked-forward-to event is well over.

June 19th – The job is done, and the man out; and Kilmoyle and I shook hands laughingly today over our victory as he handed me the key in token of my new tenantship. It has been rather an exciting bit of work, however; for the fellow – an illconditioned old villain, who hasn't paid a stiver of rent for the last twelve months, and only a modicum for the three previous years – *wouldn't* quit; set all threats, persuasions, and warnings at defiance, and simply sat within his door with a loaded gun in his hand, and kept it pointed at anyone who tried to approach him. In the end, and to avoid bloodshed, we had to smoke him out. There was nothing else for it, for though we took care that none of the neighbours should come near the house with food, he was evidently prepared to starve where he was rather than budge an inch; and on the third day, Donovan, the bailiff, told Kilmoyle that if he didn't want it to come to that, he must have in the help either of the 'peelers' or a bit of smoke.

Kilmoyle vowed he wouldn't have the peelers anyhow. He had said he'd put the man out himself, and he'd do it; and the end of it was, we first had the windows shuttered up from outside, a sod put in the chimney, and then the door taken off its hinges while the tenant's attention was momentarily distracted by the former operations. Next, a good big fire of damp weeds which had been piled up outside was set alight, and after that there was nothing to do but wait.

It didn't take long. The wind was blowing strongly in the direction of the house, and the dense volume of thick, acrid smoke would have driven me out in about five minutes. As for the tenant, he was probably more hardened on th subject of atmosphere generally, for he managed to stand it for nearly half an hour, and until Kilmoyle and I were almost afraid to keep it up lest he should let himself be smothered out of sheer obstinacy. Just as I was debating, however, whether I wouldn't brave his gun, and make a rush for him at all costs, nature or vindictiveness got the better of his perversity; a dark figure staggered through the stifling vapour to the door, fired wildly in the direction of Kilmoyle (without hitting him, thank God!), and then dropped, a miserable object, purple with suffocation and black with smoke, upon the threshold, whence some of the keepers dragged him out into the fresh air and poured a glass of whisky down his throat, just too late to prevent his fainting away.

Five minutes later the fire was out, the windows opened, and two stalwart Scotch keepers put in charge of the dwelling, while Kilmoyle and I went home to dinner, and the wretched old man, who had given us so much trouble for nothing, was conveyed in a handcart to the village by some of his neighbours, who had been looking on from a distance, and beguiling the time by hooting and groaning at us.

'Who wants the police in these cases?' said Kilmoyle triumphantly. 'To my mind, Glennie, it's mere cowardice to send for those poor fellows to enforce orders we ought to be able to carry out for ourselves, and so get them into odium with the whole neighbourhood. We managed this capitally by ourselves – and, upon my word, I couldn't help agreeing heartily with him. Indeed, the whole affair had gone off with only one trifling accident, and that was no one's fault but the tenant's.

It seems that for the last two days his abominable dog had been tied up in a miserable little pigsty a few yards from the house, Donovan having threatened him that if the brute flew at or bit anyone it would be shot instantly. Nobody was aware of this, however, and unforntunately, when the bonfire was at its height, a blazing twig fell on the roof of this little shelter and set it alight; the clouds of smoke which were blowing that way hiding what had happened until the wretched animal inside was past rescue; while even its howls attracted no attention, from the simple fact that not only it, but a score of other curs belonging to the neighbours round had been making as much noise as they could from the commencement of the affair.

Now, of course, we hear that the evicted tenant goes about swearing that we deliberately and out of malice burnt his only friend alive, and calling down curses on our heads in consequence. I don't think we are much affected by them, however. Why didn't he untie the poor brute himself? ...

June 22nd – A letter from Lady Fitz Herbert, Lily's eldest sister, telling me she thinks I had better come back at once! L. not at all well, nervous about me, and made more, instead of less so, by my account of our successful raid. What a fool I was to write it! I thought she would be amused; but the only thing now is to get back as quickly as possible, and I started this morning, Kilmoyle driving me to the station. We were bowling along pretty fast, when, as we turned a bend in the road, the horse swerved suddenly to one side, and the off-wheel of the trap went over something with that sickening sort of jolt, the meaning of which some of us know, by experience, and which made Kilmoyle exclaim:

'Good heavens, we've run over something!'

Fortunately nothing to hurt! Nothing but the carcase of a dead dog, whose charred and blackened condition would have sufficiently identified it with the victim of Tuesday's bonfire, even if we had not now perceived its late owner seated among the heather near the roadside, and occupied in pouring forth a string of wailing sounds, which might have

been either prayers or curses for aught we could tell; the while he waved
his shaggy white head and brown claw-like hands to and fro in unison.
I yelled at him to know why he had left his brute of a dog there to upset
travellers, but he paid no attention, and did not seem to hear, and as we
were in a hurry to catch the train we could not afford to waste words on
him, but drove on.

June 26th. Holly Lodge, West Kensington – This day sees me the proud
father of a son and heir, now just five hours old, and, though rather too
red for beauty, a very sturdy youngster, with a fine pair of lungs of his
own. Lily says she is too happy to live, and as the dread of losing her has
been the one thought of the last twenty-four hours, it is a comfort to know
from the doctor that this means she has got through it capitally, and is
doing as well as can be expected. Thank God for all His mercies!

July 17th – Lily has had a nasty fright this evening, for which I hope
she won't be any worse. She was lying on a couch out in the veranda for
the first time since her convalescence, and I had been reading to her till
she fell asleep, when I closed the book, and leaving the bell beside her
in case she should want anything, went into my study to write letters. I
hadn't been there for half an hour, however, when I was startled by a
cry from Lily's voice and a sharp ringing of the bell, which made me fling
open the study window and dart round to the veranda at the back of the
house. It was empty, but in the drawing-room within, Lily was standing
upright, trembling with terror and clinging to her maid, while she tried
to explain to her that there was *someone* hidden in the veranda or close
by, though so incoherently, owing to the state of agitation she was in, that
it was not until I and the man-servant had searched veranda, garden,
and outbuildings, and found nothing, that I was even able to understand
what had frightened her.

It appeared then that she had suddenly been awakened from sleep by
the pressure of a heavy hand on her shoulder, and a hot breath – so close,
it seemed as if someone were about to whisper in her ear – upon her cheek.
She started up, crying out, 'Who's that? What is it?' but was only
answered by a hasty withdrawal of the pressure, and the pit-pat of heavy
but shoeless feet retreating through the dusk to the further end of the
veranda. In a sudden access of ungovernable terror she screamed out,
sprang to her feet, ringing the bell as she did so, and rushed into the
drawing-room, where she was fortunately joined by her maid, who had
been passing through the hall when the bell rang.

Well, as I said, we searched high and low, and not a trace of any
intruder could we find; nay, not even a stray cat or dog, and we have
none of our own. The garden isn't large, and there is neither tree nor
shrub in it big enough to conceal a boy. The gate leading into the road
was fastened inside, and the wall is too high for easy climbing; while the
maid having been in the hall, could certify that no one had passed out

through the drawing-room. Finally I came to the conclusion that the whole affair was the outcome of one of those very vivid dreams which sometimes come to us in the semi-conscious moment between sleep and waking; and though Lily, of course, wouldn't hear of such an idea, for a long while, I think even she began to give into it after the doctor had been sent for, and had pronounced it the only rational one, and given her a composing draught before sending her off to bed. At present she is sleeping soundly, but it has been a disturbing evening, and I'm glad it's over.

September 20th – Have seen Dr C— today, and he agrees with me – that there is nothing for it but change and bracing air. He declares the fright Lily had in July must have been much more serious than we imagined, and that she has never got over it. She *seemed* to do so. She was out and about after her confinement as soon as other people; but I remember now her nerves seemed gone from the first. She was always starting, listening, and trembling without any cause, except that she appeared in constant alarm lest something should happen to the baby; and as I took that to be a common weakness with young mothers over their first child, I'm afraid I paid no attention to it. We've a very nice nurse for the boy, a young Irish-woman named Bridget McBean (not that she's ever seen Ireland herself, but her parents came from there, driven by poverty to earn their living elsewhere, and after faithfully sending over every farthing they could screw out of their own necessities to 'the ould folks at home', died in the same poverty here). Bridget is devoted to the child, and as long as he is in her care Lily generally seems easy and peaceful. Otherwise (and some strange instinct seems to tell her when this is the case) she gets nervous at once, and is always restless and uneasy.

Once she awoke with a scream in the middle of the night, declaring, 'Something was wrong with the baby. Nurse had gone away and left it; she was sure of it!' To pacify her I threw on my dressing-gown and ran up to the nursery to see; and, true enough, though the boy was all right and sound asleep, Nurse was absent, having gone up to the cook's room to get something for her toothache. She came back the next moment, and I returned to satisfy Lily, but she would scarcely listen to me.

'Is it *gone*?' she asked. 'Was the nursery door open? Oh, if it had been! Thank God, you were in time to drive the thing down. But how – how could it have got into the house?'

'*It*? What?' I repeated, staring.

'The dog you passed on the stairs. I saw it as it ran past the door – *a big black dog!*'

'My dear, you're dreaming. I passed no dog; nothing at all.'

'Oh, Harry, didn't you see it then? I did, though it went by so quietly. Oh, is it in the house still?'

I seized the candle, went up and down stairs and searched the whole house thoroughly; but again found nothing. The fancied dog must have been a shadow on the wall only, and I told her so pretty sharply; yet on two subsequent occasions when, for some reason or another, she had the child's cot put beside her own bed at night, I was woke by finding her sitting up and shaking with fright, while she assured me that something – *some animal* – had been trying to get into the room. She could hear its breathing distinctly as it scratched at the door to open it! Dr C— is right. Her nerves are clearly all wrong, and a thorough change is the only thing for her. How glad I am that the builder writes me my Kerry shooting-box is finished! We'll run over there next week ...

September 26th, The Cabin, Kilmoyle Castle, Kerry – Certainly this place is Paradise after London, and never did I imagine that by raising the roof so as to transform a garret into a large, bright attic, quite big enough for a nursery, throwing out a couple of bay windows into the two rooms below, and turning an adjoining barn into a kitchen and servants' room, this cottage could ever have been made into such a jolly little box. As for Lily, she's delighted with it, and looks ever so much better already. Am getting my guns in order for tomorrow, anticipating a pleasant day's shooting.

September 27th – Here's an awful bother! Bridget has given warning and declares she will leave today! It seems she knew her mother came from Kerry, and this morning she has found out that the old man who lived in this very cottage was her own grandfather, and that he died of a broken heart within a week of his eviction, having first called down a solemn curse on Kilmoyle and me, and all belonging to us, in this world and the next. They also say that he managed to scoop out a grave for his dog, and bury it right in front of the cabin door; and now Bridget is alternately tearing her hair for ever having served under her 'grandfather's murth-erer', and weeping over the murderer's baby the while she packs her box for departure. That wouldn't matter so much, though it's awfully un-pleasant; for the housekeeper at the Castle will send us someone to mind the boy till we get another nurse; but the disclosure seems to have driven Lily as frantic as Bridget. She entreated me with tears and sobs to give up the cabin, and take her and baby back to England before 'the curse could fall upon us', and wept like one brokenhearted when I told her she must be mad even to suggest such a thing after all the expense I had been to. All the same, it's a horrid nuisance. She has been crying all day, and if this fancy grows on her the change will do her no good, and I shan't know what to do. I'm sorry I was cross to her, poor child, but I was rather out of sorts myself, having been kept awake all night by the ceaseless mournful howling of some unseen cur. Besides, I'm bothered about Kilmoyle. He arranged long ago to be here this week; but the bailiff says he has been ill and is travelling, and speaks in a mysterious way as if the illness were D.T. I hope not! I had no idea before that my old chum was even addicted to drink. Anyhow, I won't be baulked of a few days shooting, at all events, and perhaps by that time Lily will have calmed down.

October 19th, The Castle—It is weeks since I opened this, and I only do so now before closing it for ever. I shall never dare to look at it again after writing down what I must today. I did go out for my shooting on the morning after my last entry, and my wife, with the babe in her arms, stood at the cabin door to see me off. The sunlight shone full on them – on the tearstains still dark under her sweet blue eyes, and the downy head and tiny face of the infant on her breast. But she smiled as I kissed my hand to her. I shall never forget that – the last smile that *ever* . . . The woman we had brought with us as servant told me the rest. She said her mistress went on playing with the child in the sunshine till it fell asleep and then laid it in its cot inside, and sat beside it rocking it. By-and-by, however, the maid went in and asked her to come and look at something that was wrong with the new kitchen arrangements, and Lily came out with her. They were in the kitchen about ten minutes, when they heard a wail from the cabin, and both ran out. Lily was first, and cried out:

'Oh, Heaven! Look! what's *that* – that great dog, *all black and burnt-looking*, coming out of the house? Oh, my baby! My baby!'

The maid saw no dog, and stopped for an instant to look round for it, letting her mistress run on. Then she heard one wild shriek from within – such a shriek as she had never heard in all her life before – and followed. She found Lily lying senseless on the floor, and in the cradle the child – stone dead! Its throat had been torn open by some savage animal, and on the bedclothes and the fresh white matting covering the floor were the blood-stained imprints of a dog's feet!

That was three weeks ago. It was evening when I came back; came back to hear my wife's delirious shrieks piercing the autumn twilight – those shrieks which, from the moment of her being roused from the merciful insensibility which held her for the first hours of her loss, she has never ceased to utter. We have moved her to the Castle since then; but I can hear them now. She has never regained consciousness once. The doctors fear she never will.

And she never did! That last entry in my diary was written two years ago. For two years my young wife, the pretty girl who loved me so dearly, and whom I took from such a happy home, has been a raving lunatic – obliged to be guarded, held down, and confined behind high walls. They have been my own walls, and I have been her keeper. The doctors wanted me to send her to an asylum; said it would be for her good, and on that I consented; but she grew so much worse there, her frantic struggles and shrieks for me to come to her, to 'save her from the dog, to keep it off', were so incessant and heart-rending that they sent for me; and I have never left her again. God only knows what that means; what the horror and agony of those two years, those ceaseless, piteous cries for her child, *our* child, those agonized entreaties to me 'not to go with Kilmoyle; to take her away, away'; those – oh! how have I ever borne it! ...

Today it is over. She is dead; and – I scarce dare leave her even yet! Never once in all this time have I been tempted to share the horrible delusion which, beginning in a weak state of health, and confirmed by the awful coincidence of our baby's death, upset my darling's brain; and yet now – now that it is over, I feel as if the madness which slew her were coming on me also. As she lay dying last night, and I watched by her alone, I seemed to hear a sound of snuffling and scratching at the door outside, as though some animal were there. Once, indeed, I strode to it and threw it open, but there was nothing – nothing but a dark, fleeting shadow seen for one moment, and the sound of soft, unshod feet going pit, pat, pit, pat, upon the stairs as they retreated downwards. It was but fancy; my own heartbeats, as I knew; and yet – yet if the women who turned me out an hour ago should have left her alone – if that sound *now* –

Here the writing came to an abrupt end, the pen lying in a blot across it. At the inquest held subsequently the footman deposed that he heard his master fling open the study door, and rush violently upstairs to the death-chamber above. A loud exclamation, and the report of a pistol-shot followed almost immediately; and on running to the rescue he found Captain Glennie standing inside the door, his face livid with horror, and the revolver in his outstretched hand still pointed at a corner of the room on the other side of the bier, the white covering on which had in one place been dragged off and torn. Before the man could speak, however, his master turned round to him, and exclaiming:

'Williams, *I have seen it*! It was there! *On her*! Better this than a madhouse! There is no other escape,' put the revolver to his head, and fired. He was dead ere even the servant could catch him.

The Yellow Wallpaper

Charlotte Perkins Gilman

It is very seldom that mere ordinary people like John and myself secure ancestral halls for the summer.

A colonial mansion, a hereditary estate, I would say a haunted house, and reach the height of romantic felicity – but that would be asking too much of fate!

Still I will proudly declare that there is something queer about it.

Else, why should it be let so cheaply? And why have stood so long untenanted?

John laughs at me, of course, but one expects that in marriage.

John is practical in the extreme. He has no patience with faith, an intense horror of superstition, and he scoffs openly at any talk of things not to be felt and seen and put down in figures.

John is a physician, and *perhaps* – (I would not say it to a living soul of course, but this is dead paper and a great relief to my mind) – *perhaps* that is one reason I do not get well faster.

You see, he does not believe I am sick!

And what can one do?

If a physician of high standing, and one's own husband, assures friends and relatives that there is really nothing the matter with one but temporary nervous depression – a slight hysterical tendency – what is one to do?

My brother is also a physician, and also of high standing, and he says the same thing.

So I take phosphates or phosphites – whichever it is – and tonics, and journeys, and air, and exercise, and am absolutely forbidden to 'work' until I am well again.

Personally I disagree with their ideas.

Personally I believe that congenial work, with excitement and change, would do me good.

But what is one to do?

I did write for a while in spite of them; but it *does* exhaust me a good deal – having to be so sly about it, or else meet with heavy opposition.

I sometimes fancy that in my condition if I had less opposition and more society and stimulus – but John says the very worst thing I can do is to think about my condition, and I confess it always makes me feel bad.

So I will let it alone and talk about the house.

The most beautiful place! It is quite alone, standing well back from the road, quite three miles from the village. It makes me think of English places that you read about, for there are hedges, and walls and gates that lock, and lots of separate little houses for the gardeners and people.

There is a *delicious* garden! I never saw such a garden – large and shady, full of box-bordered paths, and lined with long grape-covered arbours with seats under them.

There were greenhouses, too, but they are all broken now.

There was some legal trouble, I believe, something about the heirs and co-heirs; anyhow, the place has been empty for years.

That spoils my ghostliness, I am afraid; but I don't care – there is something strange about the house – I can feel it.

I even said so to John one moonlight evening, but he said what I felt was a *draught*, and shut the window.

I get unreasonably angry with John sometimes. I'm sure I never used to be so sensitive. I think it is due to this nervous condition.

But John says if I feel so I shall neglect proper self-control; so I take pains to control myself – before him, at least, and that makes me very tired.

I don't like our room a bit. I wanted one downstairs that opened on the piazza and had roses all over the window, and such pretty, old-fashioned chintz hangings! but John would not hear of it.

He said there was only one window and not room for two beds, and no near room for him if he took another.

He is very careful and loving, and hardly lets me stir without special direction.

I have a schedule prescription for each hour in the day; he takes all care from me, and so I feel basely ungrateful not to value it more.

He said we came here solely on my account, that I was to have perfect rest and all the air I could get. 'Your exercise depends on your strength, my dear,' said he, 'and your food somewhat on your appetite; but air you can absorb all the time.' So we took the nursery at the top of the house.

It is a big, airy room, the whole floor nearly, with windows that look all ways, and air and sunshine galore. It was nursery first and then playground and gymnasium, I should judge; for the windows are barred for little children, and there are rings and things in the walls.

The paint and paper look as if a boys' school had used it. It is stripped off – the paper – in great patches all around the head of my bed, about as far as I can reach, and in a great place on the other side of the room low down. I never saw a worse paper in my life.

One of those sprawling flamboyant patterns committing every artistic sin.

It is dull enough to confuse the eye in following, pronounced enough to constantly irritate, and provoke study, and when you follow the lame, uncertain curves for a little distance they suddenly commit suicide – plunge off at outrageous angles, destroy themselves in unheard-of contradictions.

The colour is repellent, almost revolting: a smouldering, unclean yellow, strangely faded by the slow-turning sunlight.

It is a dull yet lurid orange in some places, a sickly sulphur tint in others.

No wonder the children hated it! I should hate it myself if I had to live in this room long.

There comes John, and I must put this away – he hates to have me write a word.

We have been here two weeks, and I haven't felt like writing before, since that first day.

I am sitting by the window now, up in this atrocious nursery, and there is nothing to hinder my writing as much as I please, save lack of strength.

John is away all day, and even some nights when his cases are serious.

I am glad my case is not serious!

But these nervous troubles are dreadfully depressing.

John does not know how much I really suffer. He knows there is no *reason* to suffer, and that satisfies him.

Of course it is only nervousness. It does weigh on me so not to do my duty in any way!

I meant to be such a help to John, such a real rest and comfort, and here I am a comparative burden already!

Nobody would believe what an effort it is to do what little I am able – to dress and entertain, and order things.

It is fortunate Mary is so good with the baby. Such a dear baby!

And yet I *cannot* be with him, it makes me so nervous.

I suppose John never was nervous in his life. He laughs at me so about this wallpaper!

At first he meant to repaper the room, but afterwards he said that I was letting it get the better of me, and that nothing was worse for a nervous patient than to give way to such fancies.

He said that after the wallpaper was changed it would be the heavy bedstead, and then the barred windows, and then that gate at the head of the stairs, and so on.

'You know the place is doing you good,' he said, 'and really, dear, I don't care to renovate the house just for a three months' rental.'

'Then do let us go downstairs,' I said, 'there are such pretty rooms there.'

Then he took me in his arms and called me a blessed little goose, and said he would go down the cellar if I wished, and would have it white-washed into the bargain.

But he is right enough about the beds and windows and things.

It is as airy and comfortable a room as anyone need wish, and of course, I would not be so silly as to make him uncomfortable just for a whim.

I'm really getting quite fond of the big room, all but that horrid paper.

Out of one window I can see the garden, those mysterious deep-shaded arbours, the riotous old-fashioned flowers, and bushes and gnarly trees.

Out of another I get a lovely view of the bay and a little private wharf belonging to the estate. There is a beautiful shaded lane that runs down there from the house. I always fancy I see people walking in these numerous paths and arbours, but John has cautioned me not to give way to fancy in the least. He says that with my imaginative power and habit of story-making a nervous weakness like mine is sure to lead to all manner of excited fancies, and that I ought to use my will and good sense to check the tendency. So I try.

I think sometimes that if I were only well enough to write a little it would relieve the press of ideas and rest me.

But I find I get pretty tired when I try.

It is so discouraging not to have any advice and companionship about my work. When I get really well John says we will ask Cousin Henry and Julia down for a long visit; but he says he would as soon put fireworks in my pillow-case as to let me have those stimulating people about now.

I wish I could get well faster.

But I must not think about that. This paper looks to me as if it *knew* what a vicious influence it had!

There is a recurrent spot where the pattern lolls like a broken neck and two bulbous eyes stare at you upside-down.

I got positively angry with the impertinence of it and the everlasting-ness. Up and down and sideways they crawl, and those absurd, unblink-ing eyes are everywhere. There is one place where two breadths didn't match, and the eyes go all up and down the line, one a little higher than the other.

I never saw so much expression in an inanimate thing before, and we all know how much expression they have!

I used to lie awake as a child and get more entertainment and terror out of blank walls and plain furniture than most children could find in a toy-store.

I remember what a kindly wink the knobs of our big old bureau used to have, and there was one chair that always seemed like a strong friend.

I used to feel that if any of the other things looked too fierce I could always hop into that chair and be safe.

The furniture in this room is no worse than inharmonious, however, for we had to bring it all from downstairs. I suppose when this was used as a playroom they had to take the nursery things out, and no wonder! I never saw such ravages as the children have made here.

The wallpaper, as I said before, is torn off in spots, and it sticketh closer than a brother – they must have had perseverance as well as hatred.

Then the floor is scratched and gouged and splintered, the plaster itself is dug out here and there, and this great heavy bed, which is all we found in the room, looks as if it had been through the wars.

But I don't mind it a bit – only the paper.

There comes John's sister. Such a dear girl as she is, and so careful of me! I must not let her find me writing.

She is a perfect, an enthusiastic housekeeper, and hopes for no better profession. I verily believe she thinks it is the writing which made me sick!

But I can write when she is out, and see her a long way off from these windows.

There is one that commands the road, a lovely, shaded, winding road, and one that just looks off over the country. A lovely country, too, full of great elms and velvet meadows.

This wallpaper has a kind of sub-pattern in a different shade, a particularly irritating one, for you can only see it in certain lights, and not clearly then.

But in the places where it isn't faded, and where the sun is just so, I can see a strange, provoking, formless sort of figure, that seems to sulk about that silly and conspicuous front design.

There's sister on the stairs!

Well, the Fourth of July is over! The people are all gone and I am tired out. John thought it might do me good to see a little company, so we just had Mother and Nellie and the children down for a week.

Of course I didn't do a thing. Jennie sees to everything now.

But it tired me all the same.

John says if I don't pick up faster he shall send me to Weir Mitchell in the fall.

But I don't want to go there at all. I had a friend who was in his hands once, and she says he is just like John and my brother, only more so!

Besides, it is such an undertaking to go so far.

I don't feel as if it was worth while to turn my hand over for anything, and I'm getting dreadfully fretful and querulous.

I cry at nothing, and cry most of the time.

Of course I don't when John is here, or anybody else, but when I am alone.

And I am alone a good deal just now. John is kept in town very often by serious cases, and Jennie is good and lets me alone when I want her to.

So I walk a little in the garden or down that lovely lane, sit on the porch under the roses, and lie down up here a good deal.

I'm getting really fond of the room in spite of the wallpaper. Perhaps *because* of the wallpaper.

It dwells in my mind so!

I lie here on this great immovable bed – it is nailed down, I believe – and follow that pattern about by the hour. It is as good as gymnastics, I assure you, I start, we'll say, at the bottom, down in the corner over there where it has not been touched, and I determine for the thousandth time that I *will* follow that pointless pattern to some sort of a conclusion.

I know a little of the principles of design, and I know this thing was not arranged on any laws of radiation, or alternation, or repetition, or symmetry, or anything else that I ever heard of.

It is repeated, of course, by the breadths, but not otherwise.

Looked at in one way, each breadth stands alone, the bloated curves and flourishes – a kind of 'debased Romanesque' with *delirium tremens* – go waddling up and down in isolated columns of fatuity.

But, on the other hand, they connect diagonally, and the sprawling outlines run off in great slanting waves of optic horror, like a lot of wallowing seaweeds in full chase.

The whole thing goes horizontally, too, at least it seems so, and I exhaust myself in trying to distinguish the order of its going in that direction.

They have used a horizontal breadth for a frieze, and that adds wonderfully to the confusion.

There is one end of the room where it is almost intact, and there, when the cross-lights fade and the low sun shines directly upon it, I can almost fancy radiation, after all – the interminable grotesques seem to form around a common centre and rush off in headlong plunges of equal distraction.

It makes me tired to follow it. I will take a nap, I guess.

I don't know why I should write this.

I don't want to.

I don't feel able.

And I know John would think it absurd. But I *must* say what I feel and think in some way – it is such a relief!

But the effort is getting to be greater than the relief.

Half the time now I am awfully lazy, and lie down ever so much.

John says I mustn't lose my strength, and has me take cod-liver oil and lots of tonics and things, to say nothing of ale and wine and rare meat.

Dear John! He loves me very dearly, and hates to have me sick. I tried to have a real earnest reasonable talk with him the other day, and tell him how I wished he would let me go and make a visit to Cousin Henry and Julia.

But he said I wasn't able to go, nor able to stand it after I got there; and I did not make out a very good case for myself, for I was crying before I had finished.

It is getting to be a great effort for me to think straight. Just this nervous weakness, I suppose.

And dear John gathered me up in his arms, and just carried me upstairs and laid me on the bed, and sat by me and read to me till he tired my head.

He said I was his darling and his comfort and all he had, and that I must take care of myself for his sake, and keep well.

He says no one but myself can help me out of it, that I must use my will and self-control and not let my silly fancies run away with me.

There's one comfort, the baby is well and happy, and does not have to occupy this nursery with the horrid wallpaper.

If we had not used it that blessed child would have! What a fortunate escape! Why, I wouldn't have a child of mine, an impressionable little thing, live in such a room for worlds.

I never thought of it before, but it is lucky that John kept me here, after all. I can stand it so much easier than a baby, you see.

Of course I never mention it to them any more – I am too wise – but I keep watch of it all the same.

There are things in that paper that nobody knows but me, or ever will.

Behind that outside pattern the dim shapes get clearer every day.

It is always the same shape, only very numerous.

And it is like a woman stooping down and creeping about behind that pattern. I don't like it a bit. I wonder – I begin to think – I wish John would take me away from here!

It is so hard to talk with John about my case, because he is so wise, and because he loves me so.

But I tried it last night.

It was moonlight. The moon shines in all around, just as the sun does.

I hate to see it sometimes, it creeps so slowly, and always comes in by one window or another.

John was asleep and I hated to waken him, so I kept still and watched the moonlight on that undulating wallpaper till I felt creepy.

The faint figure behind seemed to shake the pattern, just as if she wanted to get out.

I got up softly and went to feel and see if the paper *did* move, and when I came back John was awake.

'What it is, little girl?' he said. 'Don't go walking about like that – you'll get cold.'

I thought it was a good time to talk, so I told him that I really was not gaining here, and that I wished he would take me away.

'Why, darling!' said he, 'our lease will be up in three weeks, and I can't see how to leave before. The repairs are not done at home, and I cannot possibly leave town just now. Of course if you were in any danger I could and would, but you really are better, dear, whether you can see it or not. I am a doctor, dear, and I know. You are gaining flesh and colour, your appetite is better. I feel really much easier about you.'

'I don't weigh a bit more,' said I, 'nor as much; and my appetite may be better in the evening, when you are here, but it is worse in the morning, when you are away.'

'Bless her little heart!' said he with a big hug; 'she shall be as sick as she pleases. But now let's improve the shining hours by going to sleep, and talk about it in the morning.'

'And you won't go away?' I asked gloomily.

'Why, how can I, dear? It is only three weeks more and then we will take a nice little trip of a few days while Jennie is getting the house ready. Really, dear, you are better!'

'Better in body, perhaps——' I began, and stopped short, for he sat up straight and looked at me with such a stern, reproachful look that I could not say another word.

'My darling,' said he, 'I beg of you, for my sake and for our child's sake, as well as for your own, that you will never for one instant let that idea enter your mind! There is nothing so dangerous, so fascinating, to a temperament like yours. It is a false and foolish fancy. Can you not trust me as a physician when I tell you so?'

So of course I said no more on that score, and we went to sleep before long. He thought I was asleep first, but I wasn't – I lay there for hours trying to decide whether that front pattern and the back pattern really did move together or separately.

On a pattern like this, by daylight, there is a lack of sequence, a defiance of law, that is a constant irritant to a normal mind.

The colour is hideous enough, and unreliable enough, and infuriating enough, but the pattern is torturing.

You think you have mastered it, but just as you get well under way in following, it turns a back somersault, and there you are. It slaps you in the face, knocks you down, and tramples upon you. It is like a bad dream.

The outside pattern is a florid arabesque, reminding one of a fungus. If you can imagine a toadstool in joints, an interminable string of toadstools, budding and sprouting in endless convolutions – why, that is something like it.

That is, sometimes!

There is one marked peculiarity about this paper, a thing nobody seems to notice but myself, and that is that it changes as the light changes.

When the sun shoots in throught the east window – I always watch for that first long, straight ray – it changes so quickly that I never can quite believe it.

That is why I watch it always.

By moonlight – the moon shines in all night when there is a moon – I wouldn't know it was the same paper.

At night in any kind of light, in twilight, candlelight, lamplight, and worst of all by moonlight, it becomes bars! The outside pattern, I mean, and the woman behind it is as plain as can be.

I didn't realize for a long time what the thing was that showed behind – that dim sub-pattern – but now I am quite sure it is a woman.

By daylight she is subdued, quiet. I fancy it is the pattern that keeps her so still. It is so puzzling. It keeps me quiet by the hour.

I lie down ever so much now. John says it is good for me, and to sleep all I can.

Indeed, he started the habit by making me lie down for an hour after each meal.

It is a very bad habit, I am convinced, for, you see, I don't sleep.

And that cultivates deceit, for I don't tell them I'm awake – oh, no!

The fact is, I am getting a little afraid of John.

He seems very queer sometimes, and even Jennie has an inexplicable look.

It strikes me occasionally, just as a scientific hypothesis, that perhaps it is the paper!

I have watched John when he did not know I was looking, and come into the room suddenly on the most innocent excuses, and I've caught him several times *looking at the paper*! And Jennie too. I caught Jennie with her hand on it once.

She didn't know I was in the room, and when I asked her in a quiet, a very quiet voice, with the most restrained manner possible, what she was doing with the paper she turned around as if she had been caught stealing, and looked quite angry – asked me why I should frighten her so!

Then she said that the paper stained everything it touched, and that she had found yellow smooches on all my clothes and John's, and she wished we would be more careful!

Did not that sound innocent? But I know she was studying that pattern, and I am determined that nobody shall find it out but myself!

Life is very much more exciting now than it used to be. You see I have something more to expect, to look forward to, to watch. I really do eat better, and am more quiet than I was.

John is so pleased to see me improve! He laughed a little the other day, and said I seemed to be flourishing in spite of my wallpaper.

I turned it off with a laugh. I had no intention of telling him that it was *because* of the wallpaper – he would make fun of me. He might even want to take me away.

I don't want to leave now until I have found it out. There is a week more, and I think that will be enough.

I'm feeling ever so much better! I don't sleep much at night, for it is so interesting to watch developments; but I sleep a good deal in the daytime.

In the daytime it is tiresome and perplexing.

There are always new shoots on the fungus, and new shades of yellow all over it. I cannot keep count of them, though I have tried conscientiously.

It is the strangest yellow, that wallpaper! It makes me think of all the yellow things I ever saw – not beautiful ones like buttercups, but old foul, bad yellow things.

But there is something else about that paper – the smell! I noticed it the moment we came into the room, but with so much air and sun it was not bad. Now we have had a week of fog and rain, and whether the windows are open or not the smell is here.

It creeps all over the house,

I find it hovering in the dining-room, skulking in the parlour, hiding in the hall, lying in wait for me on the stairs.

It gets into my hair.

Even when I go to ride, if I turn my head suddenly and surprise it – there is that smell!

Such a peculiar odour, too! I have spent hours in trying to analyse it, to find what it smelled like.

It is not bad – at first, and very gentle, but quite the subtlest, most enduring odour I ever met.

In this damp weather it is awful. I wake up in the night and find it hanging over me.

It used to disturb me at first. I thought seriously of burning the house – to reach the smell.

But now I am used to it. The only thing I can think of that it is like is the *colour* of the paper – a yellow smell!

There is a very funny mark on this wall, low down, near the mopboard. A streak that runs around the room. It goes behind every piece of furniture, except the bed, a long, straight even *smooch*, as if it had been rubbed over and over.

I wonder how it was done and who did it, and what they did it for. Round and round and round – round and round and round – it makes me dizzy!

I really have discovered something at last.

Through watching so much at night, when it changes so, I have finally found out.

The front pattern *does* move – and no wonder. The woman behind shakes it!

Sometimes I think there are a great many women behind, and sometimes only one, and she crawls around fast, and her crawling shakes it all over.

Then in the very bright spots she keeps still, and in the very shady spots she just takes hold of the bars and shakes them hard.

And she is all the time trying to climb through. But nobody could climb through that pattern – it strangles so; I think that is why is has so many heads.

They get through, and then the pattern strangles them off and turns them upside-down, and makes their eyes white!

If those heads were covered or taken off it would not be half so bad.

I think that woman gets out in the daytime!

And I'll tell you why – privately – I've seen her!

I can see her out of every one of my windows!

It is the same woman, I know, for she is always creeping, and most women do not creep by daylight.

I see her in that long shaded lane, creeping up and down. I see her in those dark grape arbours, creeping all around the garden.

I see her on that long road under the trees, creeping along, and when a carriage comes she hides under the blackberry vines.

I don't blame her a bit. It must be very humiliating to be caught creeping by daylight!

I always lock the door when I creep by daylight. I can't do it at night, for I know John would suspect something at once.

And John is so queer, now, that I don't want to irritate him. I wish he would take another room! Besides, I don't want anybody to get that woman out at night but myself.

I often wonder if I could see her out of all the windows at once.

But, turn as fast as I can, I can only see out of one at one time.

And though I always see her she *may* be able to creep faster than I can turn!

I have watched her sometimes away off in the open country, creeping as fast as a cloud shadow in a high wind.

If only that top pattern could be gotten off from the under one! I mean to try it, little by little.

I have found out another funny thing, but I shan't tell it this time! It does not do to trust people too much.

There are only two more days to get this paper off, and I believe John is beginning to notice. I don't like the look in his eyes.

And I heard him ask Jennie a lot of professional questions about me. She had a very good report to give.

She said I slept a good deal in the daytime.

John knows I don't sleep very well at night, for all I'm so quiet!

He asked me all sorts of questions, too, and pretended to be very loving and kind.

As if I couldn't see through him!

Still, I don't wonder he acts so, sleeping under this paper for three months.

It only interests me, but I feel sure John and Jennie are secretly affected by it.

Hurrah! This is the last day, but it is enough. John is to stay in town overnight, and won't be out until this evening.

Jennie wanted to sleep with me – the sly thing! – but I told her I should undoubtedly rest better for a night all alone.

That was clever, for really I wasn't alone a bit! As soon as it was moonlight, and that poor thing began to crawl and shake the pattern, I got up and ran to help her.

I pulled and she shook, I shook and she pulled, and before morning we had reeled off yards of that paper.

A strip about as high as my head and half around the room.

And then when the sun came and that awful pattern began to laugh at me I declared I would finish it today!

We go away tomorrow, and they are moving all my furniture down again to leave things as they were before.

Jennie looked at the wall in amazement, but I told her merrily that I did it out of pure spite at the vicious thing.

She laughed and said she wouldn't mind doing it herself, but I must not get tired.

How she betrayed herself that time!

But I am here, and no person touches this paper but me – not *alive*!

She tried to get me out of the room – it was too patent! But I said it was so quiet and empty and clean now that I believed I would lie down again and sleep all I could; and not to wake me even for dinner – I would call when I woke.

So now she is gone, and the servants are gone, and the things are gone, and there is nothing left but that great bedstead nailed down, with the canvas mattress we found on it.

We shall sleep downstairs tonight, and take the boat home tomorrow.

I quite enjoy the room, now it is bare again.

How those children did tear about here!

This bedstead is fairly gnawed!

But I must get to work.

I have locked the door and thrown the key down into the front path.

I don't want to go out, and I don't want to have anybody come in, till John comes.

I want to astonish him.

I've got a rope up here that even Jennie did not find. If that woman does get out, and tries to get away, I can tie her!

But I forgot I could not reach far without anything to stand on!

This bed will *not* move!

I tried to lift and push it until I was lame, and then I got so angry I bit off a little piece at one corner – but it hurt my teeth.

Then I peeled off all the paper I could reach standing on the floor. It sticks horribly and the pattern just enjoys it! All those strangled heads and bulbous eyes and waddling fungus growths just shriek with derision!

I am getting angry enough to do something desperate. To jump out of the window would be admirable exercise, but the bars are too strong even to try.

Besides, I wouldn't do it. Of course not. I know well enough that a step like that is improper and might be misconstrued.

I don't like to *look* out of the windows even – there are so many of those creeping women, and they creep so fast.

I wonder if they all come out of that wallpaper, as I did?

But I am securely fastened now by my well-hidden rope – you don't get *me* out in the road there!

I suppose I shall have to get back behind the pattern when it comes night, and that is hard!

It is so pleasant to be out in this great room and creep around as I please!

I don't want to go outside. I won't, even if Jennie asks me to.

For outside you have to creep on the ground, and everything is green instead of yellow.

But here I can creep smoothly on the floor, and my shoulder just fits in that long smooch around the wall, so I cannot lose my way.

Why, there's John at the door!

It is no use, young man, you can't open it!

How he does call and pound!

Now he's crying for an axe.

It would be a shame to break down that beautiful door!

'John, dear!' said I in the gentlest voice, 'the key is down by the front steps, under a plantain leaf!'

That silenced him for a few moments.

Then he said – very quietly indeed, 'Open the door, my darling!'

'I can't,' said I. 'The key is down by the front door, under a plantain leaf!'

And then I said it again, several times, very gently and slowly, and said it so often that he had to go and see, and he got it, of course, and came in. He stopped short by the door.

'What is the matter?' he cried. 'For God's sake, what are you doing?'

I kept on creeping just the same, but I looked at him over my shoulder.

'I've got out at last,' said I, 'in spite of you and Jennie! And I've pulled off most of the paper, so you can't put me back!'

Now why should that man have fainted? But he did, and right across my path by the wall, so that I had to creep over him every time!

Gibbet Lane

Anthony Gittins

They walked together down the road with a purposeful but laboured stride which, in addition to their farcically large and elaborate rucksacks (every pastime has its panache), marked them as town-dwellers on a week-end hike.

Their movements and pace, schooled to a pavement scuttle, lacked rhythm. They fatigued themselves much more by swinging fast downhill than by plodding uphill, and their long periods of silence were due to this fatigue, and not to any absorption or even interest in the scenery.

Conclusive proof that they came from the noisome intestines of a large town was afforded by their pale faces and a complete ignorance of the purpose of gate-fasteners. And as they were in Surrey (where the country timidly begins south of the latitude through Guildford), and as they expected any and every farmhouse to supply them with tea ('we're quite willing to pay'), and as they behaved with a transatlantic disregard for other people's property, it was evident that they were Londoners.

The taller one, who had a wart (described by his mother as a birth-mark and by his father as a damned pimple) on his forehead and sheepish eyes, was a Mr Gollen, aged thirty-two, and he worked in the Chancery Lane office of the Belladonna Insurance Company. His friend, Mr Pounceby, aged thirty-seven, had a large head and rather short hair, and also worked in the Chancery Lane office of the Belladonna Insurance Company. They both had the unimpressionable and sceptical nature common to all insurance agents, and also that deficiency of imagination which is normal in business men.

In fine, they were stolid creatures; material in outlook; daring jesters at the expense of the League of Nations ('damned old mothers' meeting,' Mr Pounceby would say); no less daring in their censure of politicians ('start every war, they do,' Mr Gollen would observe); and raucously contemptuous of the supernatural ('ghosts? All bosh and eyewash!' they would chorus disdainfully).

It is particularly important to remember that they were so scornful about psychic phenomena. Had they been windy old men, or neurotics, or journalists, no genuine authority could have attached to this story of theirs.

They had just, for the fourth time, unsuccessfully requested tea at a farmhouse.

'Frightfully unsociable people round here,' remarked Mr Pounceby, as they trudged on, their huge limp rucksacks likening them to parched camels searching for an oasis.

'Yes, frightfully,' agreed Mr Gollen. 'Dash it all, you'd think they'd be jolly glad to make a tanner out of two cups of tea.'

'Or two cups of tea out of tanner – I mean, tannin,' rejoined Mr Pounceby wittily.

'I wish I could think of things like that as quickly as you do, George,' said Mr Gollen with intense admiration. 'You know, you ought to write a play. I'll bet you could do that Noel Coward sort of dialogue as easy as pat.'

'Oh, I don't know,' said the gratified Mr Pounceby, desperately cranking his mind in the hope of churning out another witticism. But it was like winding an empty sausage-machine. Nothing emerged. He did try a pun on 'Coward' and 'pat', but even in his own eyes it was a dismal failure, so he hastily revived their original topic.

'No, they're not so hospitable as people in Town,' he declared, just as if he were in the habit of dropping into houses in, say, the Cromwell Road and offering the residents threepence for a cup of tea. 'Hullo, there's someone ahead, up by that signpost. We'll ask him where the nearest pub is.'

They covered the intervening distance in silence.

The man who stood near the old, discoloured signpost, occasionally swiping with his stick at the long grass, had a pale, oval face with bright eyes set in dark pits and a thin, curved nose which came forth like an unexpected challenge from his meek and otherwise regular features.

He was about fifty, and wore a brown tweed shooting hat (back to front) with a small feather in one side, very old breeches and dull green stockings, a soiled white cotton scarf tied round his neck and tucked into his faded yellow corduroy waistcoat, and a comparatively new, heather-mixture Norfolk jacket. The clothes did not hang well on him: it was as if, at one time and another, he had been given each garment by a different employer, for they were oddly contrasted and all of better material than probably he himself could afford.

Altogether, with his rough apparel and sensitive features, he cut an unusual figure. He might have been a poet forced to earn his living on the land, and would, indeed, have been less conspicuous at the Café Royal than he was here.

Mr Pounceby, however, was not of this opinion.

'Typical countryman,' he remarked as they approached.

'Yes,' agreed Mr Gollen, wishing that he had been the first to make this astute observation. 'Shall I ask him, or will you?'

Mr Pounceby said he would. He straightened his back and tried to look as if he had walked thirty miles that day and was enjoying it, whereas he had only walked seven and was loathing it. 'Which is the way to the nearest public house?' he called out.

The man stopped swiping at the grass with his stick and looked at them. Before replying he deftly decapitated a small clump of rushes. 'There's one at Felday,' he said.

'Which way's that? Oh, I see it's on the signpost,' said Mr Pounceby.

'If you go by that signpost,' rejoined the man, 'it'll be the English Channel you'll reach before Felday. It swings round with the wind. See?' He grasped it with one hand and twisted it. 'Now it's right.'

'Thanks,' said Mr Gollen.

'Not that it'll help you any better, even now, to find Felday,' said the man, 'if you're strange to these parts.' He began chewing a reed. 'I see you are,' he added.

This huffed Mr Pounceby, who, though proud of being a townee, always hoped to pass unidentified as such in the country because, as he candidly confessed, 'they'll do much more for you, you know, if they think you're one of their sort'. Unfortunately he always failed to pass as 'one of their sort' because he believed that, to do in Rome as the Romans do, it was only necessary to wear a toga and sandals.

'Isn't it rather a waste of the taxpayers' money,' he said, 'to put up signposts which are of no use?'

'Squire's orders. Nothing to do with the taxpayers,' replied the man. 'Very few people use this lane, anyway.'

And in his tone there was something which implied that the lane was rarely frequented, not because it was out of the way but because it had an unpleasant history.

He threw away the reed he had been chewing, and moved the post again until it was upright. Then he noted the shadow which it cast. The sun was disappearing behind a muddle of dark clouds, and the dim, attenuated shadow struck the base of an oak in the opposite hedge. 'Ten minutes to five,' he observed. 'You've got about a mile and a half to go.'

'Well, thanks,' said Mr Gollen again, for he was no conversationalist at the best of times, and having noticed the lowering sky he was anxious to reach shelter before it rained.

He shook hands with the man and moved towards the lane, which was little more than a path, leading to Felday.

Mr Pounceby also awarded the stranger a handshake, and at the same time was about to express his thanks when (and Mr Pounceby afterwards remained positive on this point) the man said:

'I'll come some of the way with you.'

'Well, thanks very much,' said Mr Pounceby, and caught up with his friend Gollen, while the man fell into step on the outside of Mr Pounceby.

'There's a use for everything, you see,' said the man. (Gollen and Pounceby, appalled by the prospect of another mile and a half, had abruptly subsided into one of their periodic silences). 'Take that signpost. As a signpost it's useless. It should say how far it is to Felday. It should say that this lane's called Gibbet Lane. It should quite reasonably always point in the same direction. It doesn't do any of these things. But all the same it's a pretty good sort of sundial.'

He spoke swiftly, smoothly, giving scant opportunity for question or comment.

'When poor old Jasey had such a terrible fright up here – over a year ago, that was – I thought it was that signpost that did it. Until I got home I did, anyway. Jasey's my dog – red setter. It does look a bit queer in this dull light, don't you think?'

Mr Pounceby glanced back over his shoulder.

'Come on,' growled Mr Gollen, who was concerned about the rapidly darkening sky.

'Like a gallows, rather,' added the man, without waiting for a reply. 'Actually, there was a gallows there once. The last man they hanged on it was a farmer named Colter – James Colter. Case of wife murder. Two hours after he was dead they found he was innocent. The next morning the gibbet was down – struck by lightning, some said. But there were six people in the neighbourhood who swore they'd seen James Colter during the night.'

He paused for a moment. Low in the sky the last pale strand of the sun disappeared, and a small, unexpected wind murmured a requiem in the trees. Then there was silence. The man's voice became more subdued.

'That's why this lane is called Gibbet Lane, and, whatever people may say, there's something mighty queer about it. I never bring Jasey up here now, but I often wonder what he could tell about that afternoon he took fright up here.

'It was like this. We were walking together down this lane. Jasey was two or three yards in front of me. Mind you, he isn't a nervous dog, and never has been. But he suddenly stopped dead and looked round. His eyes were focused about where I was, but he didn't seem to see me. God only knows what did catch his eye, for I've never seen such fear in the look of beast or man as I did then. The hair on his back went straight up, and he began edging away as if hell and all the devils were there.

'I clicked my finger two or three times and called out quietly, but it didn't have any effect. Then he let out a yell and bolted. My God, how he bolted! He went slap down this lane faster than a greyhound could have done, I reckon, and howling all the way.'

The man nodded ahead to where the gable of a farmhouse was visible.

The window under the gable faced up the lane, which was dead straight and, for the most part, hemmed in by high rocky banks, as if it had once been the bed of a stream. There was no grass, no plant life, no vegetation at all on either bank. It was a sombre gully, and shadows were now huddling into the crannies and fissures of its barren sides.

'That's where I used to live, with my sister. It's empty now. My sister died last March. Well, Jasey was back there in a flash and had jumped the gate into the yard before my sister had time to run downstairs and open it for him. You see, she'd not only heard him coming but had been looking out of her bedroom window – that's the one you can see from here – when he'd started behaving so queerly. She'd seen it all.

'A couple of minutes later I got back, wondering whether that queer-looking signpost had had anything to do with it or whether the dog had seen something strange. It's said they're more susceptible than human beings to – well, to anything psychic. They can sense the presence of death, too. Anyway, I asked my sister what her opinion was. She said: "Oh, he must have taken fright at some noise. If you'd been with him at the moment . . ."'

' "But I was with him," I said. "Just behind him."'

' "*With* him? When he bolted?" '

' "Yes. In fact, I was with him all the way down until he ran off like that." '

'My sister looked at me rather curiously, and asked if I'd been drinking. She knew very well, though, that I never do drink, and I told her so. She fixed her eyes very queerly on me, then.

' "I saw you come some of the way down," she said. "Then I attended to something in the room. When I looked out again I . . . Dick, I'm frightened," she said suddenly, and caught hold of my arm. "You're telling me the truth, aren't you? Swear to me you were in the lane when . . ."'

' "Nancy," I said, "I give you my oath that I was with the dog every step of the way till he bolted from me. Why do you ask?"'

'She went very white then, and I thought she was going to faint. "I don't understand it!" she cried. "I can see every inch of that lane from my window, and as God's my witness I swear there was not a soul in it when Jasey took fright. The dog was absolutely alone!"'

'You can imagine what a shock that gave me,' continued the man after a moment's pause. 'For I remembered that the dog had been looking where I was, and yet . . . yet,' he said very slowly, 'there was something about me – shall I say, something *in* me – so horrible that it sent an animal half-mad with fear. It's the sort of thing that can easily turn a man's reason, isn't it, if he thinks about it . . . much?'

At this point the man stopped abruptly, and Mr Pounceby, more perturbed than he cared to show, realized that the story was at an end.

He realized also, with genuine uneasiness, that they were now walking down the very lane where this peculiar incident had taken place. At that moment he wished he was miles from the spot. Subsequently, he wished most emphatically that he had never gone down the lane at all. It served him as a perennial topic of conversation, of course, but the whole of that afternoon's experience was one that he would never have voluntarily undergone again.

'What a remarkable thing!' he said, mastering his uneasiness.

'What's remarkable?' asked Mr Gollen, speaking for the second time since leaving the signpost.

They passed into gloomy shadows formed by a dark conspiracy of elms and the failing afternoon light. Westward, the rain was already sheeting the skyline.

'Why, the story this gentleman has just told us,' retorted Mr Pounceby.

Mr Gollen looked about him with a perplexed frown, and then stared very hard at his friend. 'What the dickens d'you mean?' he demanded in bewilderment. 'What story? What gentleman?'

Mr Pounceby glanced sharply to his right, stopped dead; and remained as rigid as if he had just awoken from a nightmare. His mouth sagged open; his skin turned the colour of chalk.

'My God!' he exclaimed. And again, slowly, almost in a whisper: 'My ... God!'

He wheeled round and peered up the dim perspective of the lane.

Beside the signpost, which stood gauntly against a dado of pale clouds, was a man – an indistinct but recognizable figure – swiping with a stick at the long grass.

An hour later, the two of them were in the pub at Felday, and had related their experience to the barman. Mr Pounceby was still considerably shaken.

Outside, the rain was sousing every inch of ground, and mists had descended as if to hold unholy communion with the deep cold lake among the pines.

'Grindlay,' said the barman, and spelt it out. 'Mr Oliver Grindlay – that's who it was. It's a mercy he'd gone when you went back. Why? Because that story about him and the dog is true, every word. It turned him up pretty bad – he's never been the same man since. And if he knew that something of the sort had happened again today ...

'We don't talk about it much in these parts. It was a Grindlay, you know, that murdered James Colter's wife and had Colter hanged for it on that spot where the signpost is now. That's another queer thing, the way Mr Grindlay is always up alone by that signpost. Seems to sort of fascinate him.

'You can't explain these things, though, and it's my belief that it's wisest
not to think about 'em. But there's some would like to know – though they don't care to hang about Gibbet Lane and find out,' said the barman slowly – 'just what that dog of his saw which sent him hell-for-leather back home, pretty near stark mad with fear.'

Mr Pounceby, who was paler than usual, glanced at his own blurred reflection in the dark, rain-slashed window.

'I shouldn't,' he said, and ordered two more double whiskies.

A Question of Conscience

Catherine Gleason

'Of course we must have a revolution.' Miles Myres gently banged the pub table with his fist for emphasis. 'The ruling classes have us by the throat, and look at the mess they've made of the country.'

'But it's changing slowly, isn't it?' said Diana doubtfully. 'I mean, everybody's got so liberal over the last twenty years or so, compared with ——'

'That's just the people in power paying lip-service to ideals they ignore. A sop for the gullible and their own consciences – the system's basically the same. All the great social changes have come about through violent action. The hunger marchers, the suffragettes ... we'll all be old before we get a decent form of true Socialism, if ever, by conventional means. We need to seize the land, turf out the hidebound traditionalists in Parliament and replace them with people who know what it's all about.'

'Well, making people be socialist sounds a bit arbitrary to me,' argued Diana. 'How can you tell that your sort of government wouldn't be even more repressive than the one we've got now? Like the Communist one in Russia, or ——'

'Oh, Di, you've missed the whole point.' With a grimace of mock despair, Miles drained his glass, stood up and kissed her briefly. 'Got to go now. My train's due in ten minutes. Don't forget to read the Alexander Berkman.'

'See you Monday,' she said without enthusiasm.

Miles swung out of the pub and made for the railway station across the road. He caught his train easily enough and settled into an empty compartment.

After a few moments' hesitation he unwound the college scarf from his neck and stuffed it into his overnight bag, then began to read 'The Politics of Experience' by way of light relief from the tedium of the journey.

Miles did not expect his tedium to be much relieved at the end of it, either. He was spending the weekend with his Uncle Roland, a recidivist whose ideals and pleasures were rooted in the culture of the eighteenth century. Or so his mother had told him; Uncle Roland had refused to have anything to do with his mother, or with Miles, until Miles was twenty-one, after the death of Miles's father twelve years ago, saying that he 'had no time for matrons and brats'.

Knowing his close-handedness, Miles's mother had suspected that Roland Myres was afraid that he would have to help support them financially. If this was the case, he needn't have worried, as Mrs Myres had managed competently with her salary and the proceeds of her husband's investments.

There was also the question of his roistering, country-squire habits. Miles yawned and set down his book, watching the lush, flat countryside passing the window as the train ambled on. Perhaps he and his mother had been too conventionally respectable to suit his uncle's tastes.

Then, by way of a twenty-first birthday present, a letter had arrived from Roland Myres saying that he had willed his estate to his nephew in default of other living relatives, and that he would like to see what kind of a man Miles had become.

Pound signs had momentarily lit up in their eyes, and then Miles had recalled his principles and reflected that the country hall would make an excellent hostel for derelicts, or a hippy-style commune, not to mention pop festivals in the summer. He was left with the tiresome problem of pleasing Uncle Roland to secure the estate.

Miles entirely disapproved of what he had heard about his uncle. He had no time for 'fascists', as he termed that type of reactionary; they did not believe in the inherent kindliness, the essential compassion, the merciful brotherhood of mankind, as he did.

Come the Revolution they should all be lined up and shot.

On the other hand, Miles reminded himself, he was a pacifist. Strange how evil begot evil, and aggression brought out one's worst instincts. Uneasily, he conceded that Roland Myres was probably widely misunderstood, and a victim of Society just as much as anybody else. Perhaps he, Miles, could change his uncle's ideas, make him see the light, as it were.

Property is robbery, warned his conscience.

Don't for goodness' sake blow it now, warned his mother.

Miles sighed and resumed his book. In a couple of hours the train idled into a tiny country station called Fayton, but unaccountably pronounced Fayn. Miles handed in his ticket and was accosted by a sad little man in an overcoat which looked too big for him.

'Mr Miles? I'm Norton, sir. Mr Myres sent me to meet you.' And the old man touched his cap and made to take Miles's case.

'It's all right, I'll manage that. It's very heavy.'

'As you wish, sir.' Norton's lined face remained impassive, but Miles had the feeling that he was relieved. 'The car's this way.'

He led Miles towards an ancient Bentley parked at an awkward angle on the narrow lane outside the station. A laughing couple leapt into a sports car behind theirs, reversed noisily and prepared to overtake them. Norton made heavy going of starting the Bentley and selecting first gear, while Miles watched the couple enviously. They were due for a brighter weekend than he.

As the sports car passed, it whisked against the wing of the big car with a scraping noise. Immediately, Norton switched off the engine and jumped out, waving his arms and shouting at the driver, who waved back with a derisive gesture favoured by soldiers and horsemen before accelerating away down the lane.

'The careless young devil, see what he's done! Mr Myres'll be furious! You saw it, sir, didn't you? It wasn't my fault!'

'Don't get upset, Norton, it's only a scratch.' Miles was puzzled by the disproportionate anxiety of the old man's reaction; he looked close to tears, and his hands were shaking with distress.

'But you'll tell him, won't you, sir? You'll tell him it wasn't my fault!'

'Yes, of course. It's only taken an inch of paint off, in any case. Look, would you like me to drive? You're much too agitated.'

'No thank you, sir. I'll be all right.' Muttering to himself, Norton climbed back into the car and began a steady crawl towards Fayton House.

Miles had the weird sensation of leaving behind the twentieth century as they rolled ponderously through black iron gates set in a high surrounding wall, and over half a mile of driveway to Uncle Roland's home.

'Miles, my boy, how are you?' His uncle was at the front door of his handsome, rambling old house to greet him. 'I expect a glass of sherry would go down rather well after your gruelling journey, especially the last bit, eh? Come on in.'

The latter remarks were shouted over the din of a fearsome barking and howling from somewhere round the side of the house. Miles had not known that his uncle was fond of dogs.

He returned the greetings, accepted the offer of sherry gratefully, and was promptly shown inside. A wide, curving staircase stood at the far end of a spacious hall, from which half a dozen rooms led off into the depths of the house. Uncle Roland pushed open the door of one of these and ushered his nephew in.

'This is the drawing-room. Now, sherry.' He poured two glasses from a crystal decanter and joined Miles, who was admiring the view from the bay window. Then he set down the drinks and put his hands on Miles's shoulders, turning him towards the light, and examined his face carefully.

'H'm. You're a Myres all right, but there's a bit of your mother's side. Can't be helped. Well, how was your journey?'

Miles told him, meanwhile assessing his uncle's appearance. There was certainly a family resemblance; Miles had the same somewhat protruberant eyes and thick lips, and the sparse, sandy hair. On the other hand he emphatically did not have his uncle's huge bulk and coarse purplish complexion, mottled with broken veins.

He tried to glaze over the accident with the sports car and the Bentley, but his uncle interrupted.

'So that old fool Norton managed to get it scratched again, did he? You old fool,' he remarked with casual scorn to Norton, who had made an untimely entrance and, on hearing his name mentioned, was hovering nervously near the door. 'You'll have to go.'

'There was nothing Norton could have done, Uncle,' protested Miles, beginning to see why the old man had been so terrified over the incident.

'Is that so? Very well, we'll let it pass this time,' said Uncle Roland with an indulgent laugh.

'Yes, sir. Thank you, sir. You're not needing anything at the moment? Right then, sir.' Norton closed the door quietly behind him.

Miles could never understand how one man could bear to be another's servant, and Norton was obviously miserable and frightened of his employer.

'Why doesn't he leave?' Miles demanded.

Uncle Roland shrugged. 'He's near retirement age, so who would take him on? Besides, he's been here fifty years. He's the only one who'll live in, as a matter of fact. The cook and the cleaning woman come in every day from the village, and so does Hodges, who looks after the dogs. Now, if you've finished your drink, come and see your room. Most of the house is shut off, you know. Too big for one person really ...'

Still talking, he walked out of the drawing-room and across the hall to the stairs.

'I expect you're quite lonely here sometimes,' said Miles, trudging up the steep staircase. 'I mean, just you and – oh! My God!'

He clutched the banister rail in shock as, rounding a bend in the stairs, he saw a face looming close to his. It was only a mirror placed at a dim spot on the curve of the wall, so that little light reached it, but the image of the person approaching was rendered grey and ghostly, and Miles's heart skipped rapidly in the couple of seconds it took for his reason to provide the explanation.

His uncle roared with laughter. 'It catches everyone like that! Had a fellow to stay last month and he came up in the dark – chap damn' near had a heart attack!'

Gritting his teeth into a grin to accompany Uncle Roland's hilarity, Miles followed him up to a small, neat bedroom.

'In answer to your question – no, I don't get lonely. Plenty of sportsmen hereabouts, and there's a filly down in the village who can be persuaded to accommodate one in ... various ways, some quite unusual.'

His uncle treated him to a man-to-man leer, and, receiving no response, went on briskly:

'Well – I'll leave you to unpack. Let Norton know if you need anything, and dinner's in about half an hour.'

Miles was glad to be alone. He fought down a sense of increasing dislike. This man was, after all, a blood relation, though nothing like the mild, kind father he remembered.

The conversation over dinner, during which Uncle Roland ate and drank voraciously, did nothing to change his opinion. Roland Myres was reactionary to a degree normally encountered only in students' theories, or nightmares.

'What are you studying at that university of yours?' he wanted to know.

'My course,' said Miles importantly, 'comprises History of Politics, Ecology, Sociology and Law.'

'What, no brain surgery?' His uncle clapped his hands to his paunch and laughed uproariously. 'My, no wonder educational standards have dropped since the War. And what do you intend to do with your smattering of politics, law and so forth?'

'Hardly a smattering, Uncle,' replied Miles angrily. 'It's a four-year course, you know.'

'As long as that?' Roland Myres spluttered, then checked himself. 'Well, well. I'm sure the degree of erudition you'll acquire will be ample for making your way in the kind of society your peers want. Good old Sunday-supplement stuff for everyone, including the dustmen, eh? If the economy'll stand it.'

'Not at all,' retorted Miles heatedly. 'Our generation doesn't care for material possessions and antiquated conventions ——' He was about to launch into his celebrated antiparent speech, including material drawn from sources as diverse as Lenin and Kerouac, but his uncle stopped him with a wave of his hand.

'Two things your generation really are capable of,' he remarked wearily, wiping his bulbous eyes, 'are self-deception and chop logic. Now, come outside and see the animals. There's enough light left.'

'The animals' turned out to be two fine hunters, which flattened their ears as their master approached, and four savage-looking crossbred greyhounds in a compound adjacent to the stable.

'All in excellent sporting condition, eh, Hodges?'

'Oh yes, sir. And the dogs are in fine fettle for tomorrow.' Hodges, a small, whining man, gave an oily smile and patted one of the horses.

'Do you keep them for guard dogs?' asked Miles, nodding towards the compound.

'Well, for coursing mostly. But we turn 'em loose at night, and I wouldn't like to be the burglar who tries to break into Fayton House, what, Hodges?'

'No, I wouldn't.' Hodges doubled up briefly with sycophantic laughter.

'I let them out every night before I go home, and lock them up first thing in the morning, you see, sir,' he told Miles. 'They're bred with a strain of Dobermann pinscher, see. Killers, they are.'

'But what if a tramp gets in during the night?' asked Miles, horrified. 'Or a child, or someone from the village?'

'Not much likelihood of that, sir.'

'Do you ride?' asked Uncle Roland, turning abruptly back towards the house.

'I'm afraid not.'

'Well, never mind. There's some coursing tomorrow afternoon, and you can look around the village. Would you like another drink before you turn in?'

'No thanks, I'm rather tired.'

'Very well. Good night.'

They parted in unspoken but mutual contempt.

The following day was traumatic for the sensitive, town-bred Miles. He was woken by a commotion in the yard beneath his window; it was his uncle thrashing one of the hunters.

'Got to remind 'em who's boss,' he said afterwards, by way of explanation.

Later that morning in Fayton Village, his uncle raised his hand again, perhaps for the same reason, to a cowering girl. He did not actually strike her, because he saw Miles approaching, and hastily changed his violent gesture to a paternal pat on the head; but the girl looked abnormally terrified.

'Run along now,' he told her as Miles came closer. 'Poor thing, she's simple. Afraid of her own shadow.'

This incident disgusted Miles, but he made no comment.

They had come down to the village for a pub lunch before the afternoon's sport, and his uncle had slipped out while Miles was ordering food. When Uncle Roland had been missing for half an hour, Miles went in search of him, and interrupted the episode with the village girl, the 'filly' presumably.

That afternoon was one of the worst he had ever spent. He knew vaguely what coursing hares was all about, but seeing the animals painfully and inevitably killed by swift, savage dogs provoked the same reaction as had his first and last bullfight; he went off on his own and was quietly sick. It was the sight of his uncle's face as much as the slaughter that nauseated him. Alight with cruel enjoyment, the red-veined eyes popping from the flushed, purplish face, and the fleshy lips open with coarse shouts or slack with sensual excitement, Uncle Roland epitomized everything that was depressing, ugly and depraved about mankind – the easy sadism, the crass, bloated animalism that rent the precious, thin veneer of civilization.

'Did you enjoy it?' asked Uncle Roland on the way home. 'My dogs were splendid, don't you think?'

'Splendid dogs,' echoed Miles automatically.

'The secret is to starve them beforehand, you know.'

'Really,' said Miles.

In the quiet of his room, Miles scolded himself for not having taken his uncle to task over his inhuman behaviour. And for not getting out of this unwholesome environment immediately. But then, he argued, his objections would be unlikely to change his uncle's lifestyle, so why bother? He could not admit to himself that, besides real fear, he felt a kind of horrified fascination for his repulsively brash relative.

Over dinner that evening, Uncle Roland asked for a potted version of Miles's convictions. He gave it listlessly, in all its revolutionary glory, while Uncle Roland put away colossal amounts of food and wine.

'Then I gather you didn't approve of this afternoon's sport?' asked his uncle, when he had finished.

'No. I think all life is sacred.'

'And I think,' said his uncle, 'that you young radicals are totally impractical. Chop it down regardless, whatever it is, if it's older than you – that's your philosophy in a nutshell. And what have you got to replace the current "system", or whatever word is fashionable jargon at the moment? Well, you don't quite know. Result: Chaos. If you ask me, young fellow,' he said, pushing back his chair, 'your kind are the middle-class equivalent of soccer thugs and street vandals – mindlessly destructive. Discipline, you need self-discipline at the least. Bring back capital punishment as a deterrent, and the birch, and half this country's problems would be solved.'

Why not? thought Miles dully. And thumbscrews and the rack and the whole bloodstained caboodle? He said nothing.

'Well, I'm off now. I'm sure you can amuse yourself better than I can. Spot of cockfighting, I think, and then a visit to my lady friend.'

'Cockfighting's illegal, isn't it?'

'Of course. But you can always get to see a bit if you know the right people. I wish you a fond goodnight.'

Roland Myres stood up and walked out of the room, and presently Miles heard the front door slam. He sat over the remains of the meal until Norton came to clear away.

'Thanks for standing up for me over the car, sir.'

'That's OK, Norton. – I say, you're not well.'

The old man was swaying slightly as he reached for the dishes from the table.

'Oh, I'm all right, sir. Bit of a cold, I think.' Norton was shivering and pale, his forehead shiny with sweat.

'I should go to bed straight away if I were you.'

'I can't, sir.' Norton put down the tray he was carrying and rubbed his temples. 'Mr Myres has forgotten his key again. I'll have to wait up to let him in when he gets out of the car. It's the dogs you see, sir. It could be dangerous if he has to wait about at the front door, like.'

'Well, that's no problem. I'll let him in.'

The old man's face lit up. 'Oh, would you, sir? Fact is, I took some aspirin and a whisky, and I'm not sure I can stay awake. I'd be really grateful.'

'That's quite all right. You go to bed, Norton, and I'll let him in.'

And so it was arranged.

After Norton's departure, Miles took a bottle of whisky and a jug of water into the drawing-room and settled down to wait for his uncle.

Twelve o'clock, one o'clock, half past one. Miles was halfway down his bottle and the room was beginning to sway slightly by the time the Bentley purred up the drive and its headlights swept the curtains.

Miles hurried into the hall. He could hear his uncle crooning some drunken song, slamming the car door, staggering up the front steps, fumbling for his keys.

Miles's hand reached for the latch.

'Norton? Norton, f'gotten me blasted keys. Hurry up with the door, damn you.'

Miles withdrew his hand and stood frowning, considering. He was an idealistically-committed activist, wasn't he? His uncle was a cruel, re-actionary boor. Why should he, Miles, help to preserve such a creature?

'Norton! What's the matter with you, man? Open this door im-mediately!'

After all, his uncle's death would be no loss to anybody. He was a crass capitalist of the worst kind. Miles rocked a little on his heels, savouring an obscure sense of pleasurable power.

'Norton! Norton, let me in! The dogs will be here soon – Norton, open the door!' His uncle's bombastic tone had changed to one of panicky pleading.

A sense of perverse excitement reared up somewhere in Miles's mind. Another man's life depended on his whim.

He smiled slightly. Oh well, better do the decent thing. Reluctantly he stretched out his hand to the latch; again he paused.

The seconds that followed were the longest of Miles's life. His emotions were a jumble of conflicting urges and desires.

'Norton, the dogs! I can see the dogs! For the love of God, man ——'
The words died in a scream of animal terror.

It was too late.

Catherine Gleason

Miles ran into the drawing-room and switched off the light. He hurried to the bay window and lifted the heavy curtain.

Outside in the moonlight, his uncle was running for his life towards the stable, and after him loped two lithe, sinister forms, moving with easy grace as if some instinct told them that for this prey there was no escape. Miles watched breathlessly as the ravening hounds fastened on the staggering form of Ronald Myres, pulled him screaming to the ground and tore into the twitching body with all the viciousness their master had cultivated so carefully.

Miles saw the kill to the end, only turning away when the dogs developed a savage tugging game with the corpse. His palms were damp with excitement and he was breathing heavily.

The snarling, rending sounds still ringing in his ears, he quietly crossed the hall to the stairs. *His* hall, *his* stairs; it was all his property now.

It was my fault entirely, officer, he mentally rehearsed. Norton wasn't feeling well and I told him to go to bed, that I would wait up and let my uncle in. I'm afraid I fell asleep ... No, I didn't hear anything. Yes, it's a dreadful thing – I can hardly believe it – but I did tell him, you know, that it wasn't wise to let the dogs roam loose at night ...

He smiled to himself as he began to climb the stairs. The story was foolproof, surely?

Then, in the half-light, came an unspeakable shock. A ghastly face suddenly loomed before him, a familiar, bloated face with gloating, distended eyes, full of animal satisfaction, the thick, loose lips still smirking in sadistic excitement.

Choking back a scream, Miles clung to the banister, his head spinning and his heart labouring in a state of nauseated, paralysed terror.

It took him some minutes to recognize his reflection in the mirror.

The Basket Chair

Winston Graham

Whiteleaf had his first coronary when he was staying with his niece Agnes and her husband Roy Paynter. He came through it, as of course he fully expected he would. When a healthy man is struck down with a near fatal blow it is as if he has walked into a brick wall in the dark; he is brought up starkly against the realization of his own mortality, and there is nothing to cushion the psychological shock. But Julian Whiteleaf had lived so closely with his own mortality for so long that a heart attack was just another obstacle to be carefully surmounted and added to his list of battle scars. No doubt this attitude of mind had helped him to stay alive when probability was not on his side.

But this was a nasty business, so painful and so disabling. It was hospital for three weeks and then it would be another four at least in Agnes's house before he was well enough to go home. The doctor had been a little reluctant to let him out of hospital, but Whiteleaf badly wanted to leave and Agnes had had some training as a nurse and said she could manage, as Roy was out all day. She was a highly efficient woman.

Although she was his only surviving relative Whiteleaf had never really cared for Agnes. She was a childless, stocky, formidable woman of forty, who made ends meet on Roy's inadequate salary and found time and money for endless good works. Yet whether it was the Red Cross or the Women's Institute or the Homebound Club, every good deed was performed with the same grim patient efficiency, so that joy was noticeably lacking from the occasion. Far better, Whiteleaf thought – and had sometimes said – if she took a paid job of her own to supplement the family income; but this advice was not appreciated.

So in some ways he would have been happy enough to stay another week or so in hospital; but as he had opted out of the Health Service some time ago it saved a great deal of money to leave, and anyway he rather thought Agnes liked making the effort to prove her devotion.

Another four weeks with Agnes, mainly confined to his bed, was a daunting prospect. But the time would pass. Whiteleaf was a great reader, and Agnes brought a portable radio up to his bedroom. He would have time to ruminate, time to rest. At sixty-five one became philosophical.

He had had an interesting life, and it bore looking back on. Born above a small bookshop in Bloomsbury, he had been vaguely literary from an early age, but his talents had lain in the unprofitable fields for which Bloomsbury in the 'thirties offered so much scope. Apart from helping in his father's bookshop, he had worked on two Fabian magazines, then had been assistant editor on a Theosophist newspaper which shortly folded up; he had reviewed and done freelance work, had dabbled in Spiritualism, and then become secretary to the Society for Psychoneural Research. Here he met Mrs Melanie Buxton who financed the society, and had become her lover.

At this stage the war had come and he had found himself a reluctant soldier entering a world which had almost no physical or psychological resemblance to the ingrown, rather intense, fringe-intellectual world he had inhabited before. For a while the fresh air and the hard life did him good. He strengthened and broadened and mellowed under it. But in 1943 he was invalided out, having been twice seriously wounded in the desert and having contracted asthma and a kidney complaint from which he would suffer for the rest of his life.

To his surprise he found himself a rich man. Mrs Melanie Buxton, who was twenty years older than he was, had just died, and she left the bulk of her personal fortune – about £200,000 – to Julian Whiteleaf, 'to help him continue in the paths of research to which we are both devoted.'

Whiteleaf sold the bookshop, which he had also just inherited, and at forty years of age settled down to the existence of a quiet, ailing, dilettante. He never went back to live in Bloomsbury but bought himself a pleasant service flat in Hurlingham and never moved again. There was no one to oversee his interpretation of Mrs Buxton's will, but to fulfil the spirit of the bequest he kept the society in being with a tiny office and a secretary and continued to review books and write articles on paranormal phenomena. So, gradually, he had become something of an authority. Once or twice he helped to conduct inquiries into so-called haunted houses. He continued to dabble in Theosophy. He was known as a fair-minded commentator on the spiritualist scene. He was neither a committed believer nor a scoffing sceptic. Editors of national newspapers, confronted with an unusual book which did not quite fit into any of the recognized slots, would say: 'Oh, send it to Whiteleaf; see what he makes of it.'

He never married. His experiences with Mrs Buxton had satisfied him, and his ill-health after the war was a sufficient disincentive to extreme physical effort.

He joined a good London club and had many friendly acquaintances there or among those with interests like his own; but he had no real friends. He did not feel the lack of them. He looked at life through books. He was a precise, quiet man, sandy and rather small, who spoke without moving his lips. He lived very much within his income and never gave money away, except £20 to his niece each Christmas.

His visits to her were annual and largely a duty. She was the daughter of his sister who had died in the 'fifties, and blood, he supposed, etc. ... but it was really rather an effort. He would, he knew, have made an excuse to stop the visits before this, had it not been for her husband Roy, who had a responsible but dead-end and underpaid job on the railways, and who, apart from being a nice inoffensive chap for whom Whiteleaf felt some sympathy at having married Agnes, also appealed to the other interest in Whiteleaf's life, which was the steam-engine.

This was the topic of conversation four nights out of the seven that Whiteleaf usually came to spend with them, especially when Agnes was out on some charitable mission; and sometimes at the week-end the two men would go to the railway museum, which was only a few miles away, and study the old locomotives and compare notes. It was a bond. And when he was dangerously ill two years ago after a gall-bladder operation, Roy had come up to London each week-end to see him and had brought up old catalogues and lists of engines from the days of steam, which he had been able to borrow from the local files.

Now that Whiteleaf was convalescing in their house and for a lengthy period, he felt he should pay them something for his keep, and he offered them £5 a week which Agnes accepted – grudgingly, he thought. But it would be a considerable help to them, he well knew, and not to be sniffed at, his weekly cheque. Agnes spent no more time on him than she would have done on her unpaid good works. The doctor called daily and Agnes took his blood pressure night and morning when she gave him his pills. And a starvation diet. His £5 was, all profit.

Convalescence is a strange experience. Whiteleaf was used to it, but 'every time', he wrote in his diary a couple of days after he came back from hospital, 'it presents a new face. It is as if the mind during serious illness concentrates all its energies on survival; but once the crisis is past it relaxes. It even relaxes its normal vigilance and controls – so that strange fancies, wayward concepts, take a hold that in normal times of health they would never begin to do. Nerves are on edge, imagination gets loose, temper frays as if one were a child again. Why snap at Agnes over the fire in my room. She so obviously is doing her best. Why allow oneself to think so much about the basket chair?'

Whiteleaf's diary was the one thing he had kept to all his life. Very often he wrote in it thoughts which later were useful to him when reviewing books or writing articles. He had been glad to get back to it when the doctor's prohibition was removed, and to fill in the empty days.

He had always done this after his operations, even calling on the nurses to help him. This time happily there had been no unconsciousness, only great pain and then forced immobility.

'Of course,' he wrote two days after that, 'one wonders how far all paranormal phenomena are explained in this way. And in this context, what does "explained" mean? "Imagination gets loose," I see I wrote overleaf. But how do we separate illusion from reality? We define reality as something which because it is apprehended by the majority of men is therefore assumed to exist. But does consensus of opinion necessarily prove the positive of any theory of reality? Still less therefore can it disprove the negative. Galileo believed that the earth moved round the sun. His was the scientific eye, perceiving what others could not see. May not the psychic eye perceive another area of truth at present hidden from the rest of us?'

'Is something worrying you, Uncle?' Roy asked that evening when he was sitting with him after supper.

'No. Why?'

'You keep staring at the fireplace as if something didn't please you.'

'Not at all. Nothing is worrying me. But in fact I was looking at that chair on the other side beside the lamp.'

'That one? What about it?'

'It's new, isn't it? I mean new to you? Since my last visit.'

'We've had it about a year. Agnes bought it at a sale. It's a bit of a rickety old thing but it's very comfortable. You'll be able to try it in another week or so.'

'It looks seventy or eighty years old to me.'

'Maybe. But it's *strong*. The frame's strong. Like iron. It's quite heavy to lift. I think Agnes paid a pound for it. About this film . . .'

They returned to discussing *La Bête Humaine*, which Whiteleaf had seen thirty years ago and considered the best film about railways ever made. Roy had never seen it and wanted to. There were copies in France, and being in railways he might be able to pull a string or two. He also knew the proprietor of the local cinema who, between alternate bingo nights, was always willing to risk a bit of something way-out. He preferred sex or horror films, but if the French film were offered to him to show for a couple of nights without rental charge he would certainly agree to show it.

But it would cost money to bring it over and to put it on. It was no good Ron trying to do anything unless he knew Uncle Julian would bear the cost. Uncle Julian was doubtful, discouraging: he'd want to know a lot more about what he was letting himself in for before he even considered it. They discussed it for a long time and came as near an argument as they ever got, Roy pressing and Whiteleaf hedging away.

After Roy had gone Agnes came in and settled him down for the night.

It was diuretic pills in the morning and potassium pills at night, and she gave him these now and saw his inhaler was within reach, threw some slack coal on the fire, which kept it in most of the night but almost extinguished it as a provider of heat, and then stood by the bed, square and uncompromising, and asked him if he wanted anything more.

He said no and she kissed his forehead perfunctorily and left. It was eleven o'clock. He read for a few minutes and then put out the light and composed himself for sleep. The room and the house were very quiet. Roy and Agnes were separated from him by the bathroom and the box room, and their movements could not be heard. In the distance a diesel train hooted. It was a lonely sound.

Then the basket chair creaked as if someone had just sat down in it.

'I think,' said Dr Abrahams, 'you might have stayed in another week. Are you moving about too much?'

'No. Only once or twice a day, with my niece's help, just as you advised.'

'He never has need to stir a finger otherwise,' said Agnes uncompromisingly.

'Well, the electrocardiograms are satisfactory. But why aren't you sleeping?'

'I do well enough when I get off, but it takes an hour or two to – compose myself.'

'He sleeps in the afternoon,' Agnes said. 'I expect that takes the edge off. I can *never* sleep at night if I have a nap after lunch.'

'The breathing all right?'

'No worse than usual. I always need the inhaler a few times.'

After the doctor had gone, Agnes came back and found Whiteleaf writing in his diary.

'You shouldn't do that,' she said. 'It tires you. Dr Abrahams was asking me if you were worried about something. I said not so far as I know.'

'Not so far as I know either. Tell me, Agnes, about that basket chair. Roy says you bought it in a sale.'

Agnes looked rather peculiar. 'Yes. Why? What's wrong with it?'

'Nothing at all. But what sale?'

'Oh, it was that big house about a mile out of Swindon. D'you remember it? No, you won't, I don't expect.'

'D'you mean Furze Hall?'

'No. Beyond that. There was a Miss Covent lived there, all by herself with only one servant. It had thirty-four rooms. Fantastic. She was eighty when she died.'

'What made you go?'

'Oh, it was advertised. Carol Elliot wanted a few things – you know, from down the road – so I went with her. It was an awful old place; she'd let it go to ruin, this Miss Covent: all the roofs leaked, I should think; it's being pulled down. Most of the furniture was junk but it went very cheap. I paid a pound for the chair and a pound for that bookcase in the hall and two pounds for four kitchen mats and——'

Agnes went on about her bargains and then switched to some other subject, which Whiteleaf ignored.

'Did you know anything about it?' he asked presently. 'About the house where you bought those things?'

'The Covents' place? Well, of course, I'd never been *in* before. Hardly anyone had. It was like something out of Boris Karloff, I can tell you. The old lady must have been bats, living there alone. There was some story Carol Elliot was telling me about it but I didn't pay much attention.

'Ask her sometime.'

'Carol? Yes, I'll ask her. But why?'

'I'm interested in old places. You know my interests.'

'Well, I never heard it was *haunted*, if that's what you mean. Don't you like the chair? I can take it out.'

'No, leave it where it is. I like old things.'

'Well, it's comfy, I can tell you that. I always enjoy sitting in it when I come to see you last thing.'

When she had gone Whiteleaf continued in his diary: 'Recorded and authenticated "possession" of small items of furniture is relatively rare and has no reliable weight of testimony behind it such as the "possession" of houses has. The poltergeist one accepts, because one has to accept it. Beyond that there is only reasonable cause to believe and reasonable cause to doubt. In the case of a chair . . .' He wrote no more that evening.

The following day he began a new entry. 'Is this the hallucination of illness or the clearer perception of convalescence? It is certainly a very peculiar shape. That high rounded back. It is a half-way style, reminiscent of one of the old hooded hall chairs of the 18th Century. Why does someone or something appear to sit in it every night when I am trying to sleep? And am I right in supposing sometimes that I can hear breathing and footsteps? Odd that in all these years of interest and study this should be the first possibly psychic event that has ever happened to me . . .'

The next evening Agnes said: 'I saw Carol today. It is a funny story about the Covents. Of course she's lived here all her life and we've only been here ten years. She says it was before her time but her mother often spoke of it.'

'Spoke of what?' Whiteleaf asked.

'Well, it's not a very nice story, Uncle. It won't upset you to talk about it?'

'I'm not made of cotton wool,' he said impatiently. 'In any case, how can something that presumably happened years ago have any effect? I'm allowed to read the daily papers, aren't I?'

'Yes, well, yes...' Agnes plucked at her lip. 'Well, Carol says they were a young married couple, the Covents, during World War One. He was in the Battle of the Somme and was blown up and hideously disfigured. Apparently spent a couple of years in hospital and they then let him out. I suppose plastic surgery wasn't much help in those days...'

'No, it was in an experimental stage.'

'So they hadn't done him any good. He was still terrible to look at, and when he came home he never went out of the house but used to sit by the fire all day reading and thinking. His wife used to go out and do all the shopping, etc., Carol's mother says, and that way she met another man and had an affair with him. Somehow or other Captain Covent discovered this, and it must have turned his brain because she suddenly stopped going shopping and everyone thought they had gone away...'

Whiteleaf felt his heart give a slight excited lurch. 'Interesting.'

'After a few weeks someone got suspicious and they broke into the house and there they were, both dead, one on either side of the empty fireplace. Apparently he'd tied her to a chair and then sat down opposite her and watched her starve to death. Then he cut his own throat. That's what the doctors said. It was a big sensation in the 'twenties.'

'Very interesting,' said Whiteleaf.

'Well, horrible I say. They hadn't any children so the property came to his eldest sister and she took it over and lived there until last year. I tell you the house would have given me the creeps without any funny stories.'

Silence fell and the door downstairs banged.

'That's Roy,' said Agnes. 'I'll get him to shift that chair tonight, just so that it won't worry you.'

'Not at all,' said Whiteleaf. 'Leave it just where it is.'

Agnes shivered. 'Don't tell Roy. He's superstitious about these things.'

Whiteleaf shifted himself up the bed. 'D'you realize I remember the First World War?'

'Do you, Uncle? Yes, I suppose you do. But you'd be very young.'

'I well remember celebrating the Armistice. I was thirteen at the time. It never occured to me that that I should have to fight in another war myself.'

When she had gone downstairs to get Roy his tea, Whiteleaf wrote just one sentence in his diary. 'I wonder if this chair, this basket chair was the one Captain Covent sat in? Or was it hers?'

That night, although he was still not sure about the breathing, he was quite certain about the footsteps. The creaking of the chair as someone sat in it began about ten minutes or so after he was left alone and went on for a little while with faint furtive creaks. They were very faint but very distinct as someone stirred in the chair. Then also quite distinctly there was the soft pad of footsteps, about six or seven, moving away from the chair towards the door. They did not reach the door. They stopped half-way and were heard no more. Presently the creaking died away.

It is surprising what tension is generated by the supernatural. One can write about it. One can attend spiritualist séances. One can even visit haunted houses and still remain detached, scientific, aloof. But in a silent bedroom, entirely alone, with only this wayward wandering spirit for company, Julian Whiteleaf felt himself screwing up to meet some crisis that he greatly feared but could not imagine. It was clearly not doing his health much good or aiding his recovery. The whole thing was strikingly interesting; but he would have to take care, to take great care, to find some means of rationalizing this experience so that he could regain his detachment. Only his diary helped.

'Supposing,' he wrote, 'that I am *not* the victim of a sick man's hallucination and that for some reason I have become clairaudient. (The "some reason" could well be the rare combination of my hypersensitive perceptions during convalescence and the presence of a chair with such an evil aura, amounting to "possession".) Supposing that, then is there any resolution or solution of the situation in which I find myself? Is there any *progress* in this nightly occurrence? Is there a likelihood that I may become clairvoyant too? (And in the circumstances would I wish to be? Hardly!) Why are there only six or seven steps, and why do they always move towards the door?'

That night there were exactly the same number of steps but they were quite audible now, a soft firm footfall, measured but fading at the usual spot.

Whiteleaf never kept his light on, but Agnes had lent him her electric clock, which had an illuminated face, so that when one's eyes were accustomed to the dark one could just see about the room. And tonight a pale blue flame was flickering in the fire, so this helped. But sitting up in bed, Whiteleaf wished there had been no such fire, for the flame conjured up movements about the old chair. He thought: insanity is not evil, yet it so often wears the same guise. Covent must have been insane, driven insane by his own mutilated face rather than by jealousy of his wife. Only an insane man could tie a woman to a chair and watch her starve to death. I must examine that chair more closely. There may even be signs of where the rope has frayed the frame.

It was four o'clock in the morning before he fell asleep.

Dr Abrahams said to Agnes: 'Your uncle is not making the progress that I'd hoped for. His blood pressure is up a little and his breathing is not too satisfactory. If this goes on we'll get him back in hospital.'

'It's just as you like,' said Agnes. 'I always help him when he gets out of bed, and we're careful he doesn't overdo it. I keep the fire going all day and night to help his asthma.'

'Of course he uses that inhaler too much: I've told him to go easy on it, but it would be unwise to take it away; he has come to depend on it. One is between the devil and the deep sea.'

'I'll watch him,' said Agnes. 'But he *is* difficult. Strong-minded. He'd fight before he went back to hospital.'

'That's what I'm afraid of,' said Abrahams.

While they were downstairs talking, Whiteleaf was up and examining the chair, as he had done once before when left to himself. As Roy had said, it was a strangely heavy chair for one made principally of cane. The framework was of a thin rounded wood like bamboo but enormously hard. You couldn't make any indentation in it with a fruit knife. There was a number of stains on the seat under the cushion: they could have been bloodstains: impossible without forensic equipment to tell. Whiteleaf had never sat in the chair and did not want to do so now. He felt he might have been sitting on something that should not be there. Only Agnes sat on it, in the evenings, and he had been tempted more than once to ask her not to.

He hastily climbed back into bed as he heard her feet on the stairs.

Later he wrote: 'I get the feeling that someone or something is trying to escape. To escape from the bondage of the chair. (Not surprising, perhaps, in view of its history!) But something more than just that – otherwise why the steps? It's as if the body rotted away long ago but the spirit is still attached to the scene of its suffering and still striving to get away. The footsteps always move towards the door. If they ever reached the door, would something go out? This I could accept more readily were this the actual room in which the tragedy took place. Yet perhaps in the room in which this *did* happen, there *were* only eight steps from chair to door. Perhaps after the tragedy the chair was not moved for years and this "possession", this spirit, became bound for ever to a routine of "escape" each night. Even so it does *not* escape: it repeats for ever the ghastly ritual. Could it now in this new situation really escape for ever if the footsteps could reach this door? How to encourage them?'

It was the follwoing day that he had the idea. Agnes, with her passion for cleanliness, was scouring his room as she did every day, and when she moved the basket chair to vacuum under it he suddenly called to her not to put it back.

Frowning she switched off the vacuum and listened.

'Don't put the chair back there. Put it – put it just by the dressing-table, just to the left of the dressing-table. I think I fancy it over there.'

She did not move. 'What's the matter, Uncle? Doesn't the furniture suit you? I do my best, you know.'

'You do very well,' he said. 'I'm not complaining, but if you move the chair by the dressing-table it will give me a better view of the fire.'

She stared. 'I don't see how it can. The fire ...' She stopped and shrugged. 'Oh, well, it makes no difference to me. If that's your fancy. *Where* d'you want it?'

'Over there. A bit farther. That's a good place for it there, I think.'

'D'you want me to move this other chair over? Make more room for the commode.'

'Er – no. No, just leave that. Thank you, Agnes.' He began to say something more but she had switched on the vacuum again.

He didn't really mind because he was counting the steps. At the most the chair was now seven from the door.

'An experiment,' he wrote in his diary. 'Possibly nothing will come of it. Possibly I shall have interfered with the "possession" altogether. Or possibly the footsteps will reach the door and something will *go out*.'

He spent the rest of the day quietly reading an old book on the Great Western Railway which Roy had brought him. This, he thought, was one of the sagas of our time. The wonderful Castle locomotives that set up records seventy years ago which have never been broken. The 4-4-0's that preceded them. The Cities and the Kings ... He wished he could concentrate. He wished, perhaps, that he had agreed to pay the expense of having that old film over, even though it dealt with French railways and French engines. They were indeed majestic in their own right. The great snorting locomotives of the Train Bleu, of the Orient Express, with their strange pulsating beat even when they are at rest ... He wished he could concentrate.

Roy was out that evening at a social affair, Masonic or Rotary or something, so he did not see him. Agnes came up as usual, and, in spite of its uncustomary position, she sat in the basket chair. It was on the tip of his tongue to ask her not to; but again he refrained, partly because he was afraid of her uncomprehending stare, with its half implication that Uncle must be going a bit peculiar, and partly because her having been in the chair had not affected the manifestation on earlier nights.

She stayed longer than normal, talking about some work she was doing for refugees, and he listened impatiently, longing for her to be gone. She stayed in fact until Roy came in, by which time it was nearly midnight; then she gave the fire an unsympathetic poke, thumped his pillow, saw that he had enough water for the night, gave him her perfunctory kiss and was gone.

Roy had come straight upstairs, and the house soon settled. Whiteleaf's heart was thumping. To try to ease it, he began to compose the article he would write for one of the psychic papers on his experiences with a basket chair. One of the psychic papers? But possibly *The Guardian* would print it, or even *The Times*. It all depended upon the end, upon the resolution. It all depended on what happened tonight. In a way it was a triumph, that a man so involved as he had been all his life in paranormal phenomena, should at this late stage *experience* it in the most exciting moment of his life. The trouble was it wasn't over yet; he was in the middle of it; and the final experience, if there was one, was yet to come.

The fire was burning a little brighter tonight; Agnes had forgotten to bring up as much slack as usual, and this, with the help of the clock, gave adequate light – though dim. He could see all but the corners of the room. The chair in its new position was not so clearly outlined as it had been by the fire: it looked taller, still more hump-backed, like a man without a head. It cast a faint shadow on the wall behind that did not look quite its own.

The creaking was late coming tonight. He had thought it might not come at all. Always it began with a fairly definite over-all creaking such as would occur when Mrs Covent first sat in it. Then it would be silent except for the faint creaks that broke out whenever she moved. There was no sign of her struggling, as she must have struggled before she became too weak. Perhaps it was her dying that one heard. And the footsteps were the release of her spirit, moving away.

Yet always towards the door. Now they would reach the door. Perhaps – who knew – he would see something go out.

They began. They were slower and heavier tonight. Every step was distinct, seemed to shake the room, measured itself with a thumping of his heart. He sat up sharply in bed, straining to the darker side of the room to see if he could see anything. A flickering flame from the fire, just like that other night, brought shadows to life in the silent room.

The footsteps reached five, reached six and appeared to hesitate. They were at the door. A seventh and then the fire did play tricks, for he saw the door quiver and begin to open. He screwed up his eyes, one hand pulling at the skinny flesh around his throat.

But there was no mistake. He *was* seeing something. The door was literally *opening* to allow something to go out. He could feel the difference in the air. The door was wide and something must be going out.

Then he twisted round in the bed, clutching at the rail behind him, trying to get up, to move away, to get out of bed and scream. Because round the door a hideous deformed face was appearing with one eye, and the flesh drawn up and scarred, and a gash where the mouth should have been, and no recognizable nose.

It was clear then – quite clear – that moving the chair was not enabling Mrs Covent to go out. Captain Covent was coming in.

'It was always a possibility, of course,' said Dr Abrahams. 'The pulmonary oedema was an added complication. But I'm disappointed. He gave one the impression of great tenacity – great physical tenacity, I mean;

such men can often endure more than ordinary people and yet recover
and live to a great age.'

'Well, I can tell you it gave me the shock of my life,' said Agnes, drying
her eyes. 'I came in at half past seven as usual, and *there* he was half out
of bed and clutching his throat. He seemed all right when I left him. We
were a bit later than usual – about twelve it would be. I never heard a
thing in the night. But he'd such an *expression* on his face.'

'He's been dead some hours. He probably died soon after you left him.
I think the expression is due to the nature of the complaint: a sudden great
pain, shortness of breath, no doubt he was trying to call you.'

'He had a bell there,' said Roy. 'It was on the table. Just there on the
table. I'd have heard if he'd rung. I always sleep light.'

'Yes, well, there it is, there it is. His condition had been vaguely
unsatisfactory all last week, without there being anything one could
necessarily pick on. I take it you're his nearest relatives?'

'His only relatives,' said Agnes. 'But he was well known in his circle.
I think there will be a fair number of people at the funeral.'

There was a fair number of people at the funeral. Representatives of
societies with long names and short membership lists, club friends who
had known Whiteleaf for a long time, one or two newspaper men,
nominees from charities which had benefited in the past, some of Agnes's
friends. It was a fine day, and the ceremony passed off well. After it, after
a discreet interval, after a quiet period of mourning Agnes and Roy
burned the diary which had first put the idea into their heads. By
discreetly opening it each afternoon while Uncle Julian was asleep, Agnes
had been able to keep in touch with the progression of his thoughts.

At the same time they burned a rubber mask of humourously unpleasant appearance which Roy had bought in the toy department of a
big store and painted and altered to look more hideous. There seemed
no particular reason to burn the mop with which Agnes had bumped
nightly on the ceiling beneath Uncle Julian's bedroom. Nor did they
bother to burn the basket chair which Agnes had bought in a jumble sale
and whose cane had the peculiarity of reacting with creaks and clicks
about fifteen minutes after a person had been sitting in it, a peculiarity
they had not noticed until Uncle Julian had drawn attention to it in his
diary. It seemed a pity, Agnes said, to destroy a useful chair.

That spring they had their first real holiday for ten years. They went
to the South of France for two weeks. Roy had considered giving up his
railway job, but for the moment he was keeping it to see how much Uncle
Julian's invested income brought in. On the way back from the South
of France they spent two days in Paris, and Roy made inquiries about
the film he was interested in. Later that year in Swindon he intended to
give a private showing to his interested friends of *La Bête Humaine*.

The Tsanta in the Parlour

Stephen Grendon

After seven years of profound silence – surely a length of time sufficiently long to have encouraged hope for the worst – Ernest Ambler made it plain to his uncle, Theophilus, that he was not, after all, dead – 'lost in the wilds of South America,' as he put it, but not permanently. His letter was followed by his peace-offering, and no doubt, the old man reflected pessimistically, his peace-offering would in all probability shortly be followed by Ernest himself, and there would begin once more the problem of waiting upon Ernest's better nature just long enough to allow his real self to assert control, after which Ernest would need to be packed off to some remote place all over again.

Full circle. Circles, rather.

'I may very well be a crusty old curmudgeon,' said Theophilus to the single servant who waited upon him in his gloomy old house on Main Street in the Southern town of Euphoria, 'but naturally, *I* couldn't believe it, could I? No, of course not,' he went on, replying to his question as he had replied to his own questions for half a century gone by, 'nor do I need Ernest to remind me. What a curse on my old bones! To have to deal with Ernest once, twice, thrice – and God knows how many times! Get his room ready, Fulton. And what was in that box? I noticed you took the stamps off for your cousin's girl – I hope her collection is growing.'

'It is, Mr Ambler. Very much. Thanks to you partly.'

'The box, Fulton.'

'Yes, sir. A small object.'

'Yes, it was, wasn't it! Oh, forgive me – you meant its contents. I referred to the box. My error. A small object, eh? What kind of object?'

'It was a shrivelled something. Rubbery.'

'Where is it?'

'Over on the mantel. I thought perhaps it was meant to belong with your collection of ivory and ebony pieces.'

Theophilus Ambler meandered over to look at his nephew's peace-offering. He was a tall, thin man, but not cadaverous so much as anaemic-looking, still able despite his seventy-odd years, and only a little absent-minded. He put on his pince-nez and peered.

The peace-offering stood between an ivory elephant and an ebony rook, looming larger than either. Brown, shrivelled, rubbery indeed, with a resemblance to a monkey's head; it was not nice to touch. He swept it off the mantel in the palm of his hand and held it forth into the sunlight streaming through the french windows.

'Ernest will never change,' he said. 'I suppose he would call in a sense of humour.'

'What is it, Mr Ambler?'

'Damn it, man – you might have seen it for yourself. It's a human head, shrunken of course. Probably Jivaro in origin. They call these things tsantas. There are still head-hunters down there, I suspect. It doesn't seem to be Ernest's head, though. Much too dark. An Indian, probably.'

'It's an odd gift, isn't it?'

'Only Ernest would think of it. And what the devil I'm to do with it, I don't know.'

'No one would notice it among those pieces, sir. That's why I put it there.'

Ambler smiled and replaced it. 'Good enough. Now let me have his letter again.'

'I think it's in the pocket of your robe, sir.'

'Oh, yes. So it is.' He took it out and read it slowly, aloud, while Fulton stood in almost obsequious attention. ' "Dear Uncle Theophilus, Like a bad penny, I am turning up again. It now seems quite possible that I may be in the States again within a few weeks or months – events will determine that – and I should like to see you, naturally. I hope all is forgiven. Under separate cover, I am sending you a little curio which you might like. I picked it up not so long ago and thought of you immediately. My best wishes.' Humph! Best wishes, indeed. That is an ambiguous letter, in my opinion. But, of course, Ernest never wrote anything straightforward in his life – or spoke it, either. How long ago was it written? Three weeks. I suppose we can expect him any day.'

'I'm afraid so,' agreed Fulton.

Fulton drifted out of the room and Theophilus was left alone. He made a determined effort to put the unpleasant thought of his nephew from his mind, and settled down to read. But Ernest persisted. Ernest, who had never been a very pleasant child, and who had made life miserable for practically everyone, relative or friend, with whom he had been associated. And how long will it be before I have to get him out of another scrape? he wondered. He was really getting too well along in years for that sort of thing, he felt. Not really doddering yet, of course, but still – no longer young. And Ernest, who must now be well into his forties, was old enough by this time to know what responsibilities meant. But he knew in his heart that Ernest would never be old enough for that.

In the night the house creaked and groaned in the wind; rafters cracked and the bushes around the old building whispered in the hushing night air. Theophilus Amber went to his bed not long after sundown, and Fulton went shortly thereafter. The old house was thus quickly lulled in darkness, and the sounds it made were long familiar. Mice scuttered in the attic, making their intimate small patterings; Theophilus had come to welcome them; he slept to their footsteps, and no creak or crack or groan invaded his sleep.

But this night a new sound flowed through the house.

Theophilus woke to it at last. He lay for a while listening, and decided finally that it must be Fulton talking in his sleep. Or grumbling. He sighed and waited for the sound to subside.

But it did not subside. So Theophilus dragged himself out of bed, got into his slippers and dressing-gown in the dark, puttered over to a candle, lit it, and held it before him to light his way into the hall. He went down to Fulton's room, opened the door, and looked in. Fulton's face caught the flickering candlelight.

Theophilus listened.

No sound. Nothing whatever from Fulton.

Fulton lay in peaceful sleep, as quiet as a tired child. And a child he is sometimes, reflected Theophilus wearily, withdrawing again and closing the door.

He stood there in the shadowed hall, listening.

Certainly there was a voice somewhere. Since it was not Fulton's, it must belong to someone else. A faint prickle of perturbation made itself evident. No one else should be in the house, and the sound came from inside; the wind would have whipped breath away from anyone beyond the walls.

Thoughtfully, Theophilus blew out the candle. He felt somewhat more secure in darkness without the light to offer himself as a target for any possible invader. Ah, but who would invade the house? And for what? For there was nothing of value in any part of it. And what potential burglar would announce himself so carelessly?

The darkness enfolded him, the darkness enclosed him in an uncertain security.

He went noiselessly back along the hall to the head of the stairs. The sound came from below, steadily. Ah, but what was it? A muttering – or a tittering – a shrill gibberish – or an incoherent series of mouthings, scarcely human. And yet, now and then, it seemed, there were guttural words.

Ambler listened, straining himself to detach and isolate recognizable sounds.

And presently, slowly, word by word, fragments of a sentence fell into his consciousness, and he put them together painstakingly, while the darkness pressed about him with false security.

'Een ... thees ... house ... ees ... Meestaire Amblair ...'

The darkness concealed menace, the terrible muttering from below gave birth to alarm. Ambler was not afraid, but he was not inclined to dare the unknown without weapons and without some knowledge of what he might face. He felt instinctively that something dreadful lurked in the darkness below.

'Bite,' said the gibbering voice. 'Bite,' came the muttering. 'Bite,' rose out of the incoherent sounds from below.

'Een ... thees ... house,' it said again.

And what a horrible tittering sound! How primitive! thought Ambler in some confusion. His confusion was, however, controlled. He made no betraying sound; whatever it was, menaced him, he was sure.

The silence which fell was as sudden as it was unexpected. It made Theophilus Ambler even more uncomfortable than the sounds. But what came after was even worse in that sentient darkness.

A new sound now, an incredible sound.

Someone weeping, someone sobbing!

Ambler stood there listening unbelievingly. What in God's name had got into the house? He felt his skin scrawl; he felt something gnawing at the pit of his stomach; he felt in turmoil, in a wretchedness of undefined fear and a kind of sick loathing, for the sound was so piteous that it was revolting.

The sound of grief diminished, fell away, was gone, and the silence came.

In a little while the familiar signatures of the old house began once more, serenely – the creaking and cracking and groaning, the wind's hush-hush at the eaves, the comfort of mice scampering above overhead.

Theophilus Ambler retreated noiselessly to his room, where he sat for a long time listening, listening and wondering, before he brought himself to put off his slippers and dressing-gown and return to bed.

He considered inquiring next morning to Fulton whether he had heard anything in the night, but thought better of it. If Fulton had heard, he would find some opportunity to mention it; if he had not, there was no need to alarm him. That would come soon enough, if the experience persisted.

Nevertheless, Theophilus Ambler made a thorough search of the old house. He turned up several articles which had been lost for years, but nothing at all to show up that anyone had got into the house during the night. Every door and every window remained locked, just as they had been at bedtime the previous night. Moreover, nothing whatever was in any way disturbed. Could it have been that one of the Negroes from the other side of town had got drunk and wandered into the neighbourhood, finding himself a corner somewhere outside the house from which the sounds, despite the tearing wind, had reached into and through the walls? But no, hardly; that was stretching the bounds of probability too far. Yet it was undeniable that the sounds he had heard in the night might very well have been made by a black.

Theophilus sat for some time in the horsehair-furnished parlour, ostensibly reading, but secretly pondering the problem. With each hour that passed, his perplexity grew. More than once, he gazed meditatively over at that curious peace offering of Ernest's, and at last he went to bring it out into a strong light so that he could examine it closely. Was it his imagination, or was the thing damp?

He looked at it closely.

It had once been a fine head, he decided. Almost Nordic, save for its dark skin and the cut of the mouth. He fingered it judiciously. It seemed that some kind of teeth had been put into it. Very sharp, too. The jaws seemed firm enough. He replaced it on the mantel; his improbable theory was clearly untenable, and he was left more puzzled than ever.

Several times during that day, he found himself regarding the Jivaro head with mixed emotions, uppermost among which was the impulse to rid himself of the object with summary dispatch.

He waited for night with some apprehension.

That night he lay in his dark bedroom at the head of the stairs waiting for untoward sounds, for no wind filled the old house with the familiar noises to which Theophilus had been so long accustomed. The clock struck nine, the clock struck ten, the clock struck eleven. Outside, the town grew quiet towards midnight as the streets emptied and the last late crowd from the last picture-show dispersed.

Inside the old house on Main Street the voice began again.

Theophilus rose at once; he had not undressed, but had only put on his gown, in one pocket of which he had taken care to place a small pistol. He had put out a strong-beamed flashlight, feeling more secure with it in his hand than candles; and, so armed, he set out from his room, walking with every caution to the head of the stairs and slowly, slowly down, step by step, careful to make no sound.

The voice gibbered in the darkness; the voice complained, argued, cried – a horrible cacophony in the black well below.

Near the bottom of the stairs, Theophilus paused. The atmosphere of menace around him was thick, unpleasant, cloying. Once again, there were audible words, disjointed, almost meaningless.

'Head ... of ... stairs ... room ... een ... these ... house ... een ...

third ... night ...' And again gibberish, horribly intermingled with sounds of grief.

And what was to be made of that?

The sounds came from the parlour, beyond any question.

Mustering his courage, Theophilus tiptoed down the hall towards the old-fashioned portieres which marked the entrance to the parlour. In the silence which held the house, the sounds seemed twice and three times as loud as they were, so that at any moment Theophilus expected a distraught Fulton to appear at the head of the stairs. But there was no betrayal from above.

He stood before the closed portieres listening. He heard a constant muttering, and, paying careful attention, he detected a pattern of gutturals. Words, certainly. But not English. Words in some alien language. Phonetic, he decided; probably primitive, with now and then an English word. It struck him as very odd that the heavy accent of the English words was so similar to the less obvious accent Ernest had affected when last he had visited in Euphoria.

His impulse was to retreat, but he would not yield to it.

He did the second-best thing; he effected a compromise. Rather than enter the parlour, he made a small parting of the portieres at the level of his eyes, thrust his flashlight into the opening and, focusing the beam on the mantel, switched it on.

The ivory and ebony figures sprang into being – and the dark brown head, agleam as with perspiration there. It seemed to Theophilus Ambler that there was a burning of tiny eyes, a movement of the shrunken lips. But the instant the light flashed forth, the sounds from within the room ceased.

There was nothing.

But wait – ! The head was not where he had put it. When last he had put it down, it was left standing next to an ivory knight; now it stood before a teakwood box – fully a foot and a half away. Could Fulton have moved it? Hardly. Even if he had taken it up, he would have replaced it precisely where it had been.

What then? The possibilities which occurred to him were not comforting. Theophilus was not unimaginative, but he was not inclined to accept the products of his imagination too readily. He looked across the room to the figures illuminated by his flash flashlight's beam. He could not rid himself of the conviction that one among them gazed back, with malevolence.

He snapped off the light and withdrew, allowing the portieres to close before him. He waited.

Nothing happened.

He was vaguely disconcerted; he had expected the gibbering and muttering to begin again, but no, no untoward sound came out of the parlour. Indeed, the room and the house were as one might expect them to be in the dead of the night.

Theophilus walked back to the stairs. There he waited a while longer. Nothing took place, no unaccountable sound invaded the darkness.

He went slowly up the stairs in the dark, with every step expecting to hear that weird voice again. But he heard nothing; all was as before, except that Fulton was snoring. He's lying on his back again, thought Theophilus. He turned at the head of the stairs and looked back down into the well of black. He had a momentary feeling that someone watched him; he thought he saw a vague, shadowy figure, neck to toes – without a head; but he blinked and it was gone.

More shaken that he cared to admit to himself, he re-entered his room. He considered blocking the door with the heavy easy chair in his room, but stoutly refused to give way to a fear so nebulous as that he now entertained. Just to be on the safe side, however, he slipped his pistol under his pillow, and presently he slept after a fashion.

The morning brought more than another day. It brought Ernest Ambler, looking, if possible, more dissipated than ever, with bags under his eyes, and smoulding fire, like a fever inside. He was of medium height, stoop-shouldered, and, one might have said, hawk-like in his appearance, except that it did injustice to a noble family of birds. His face was not so much prepossessing as it was fascinating in a revolting way. He looked, and often acted, like a character out of a painting by Felicien Rops, quite as if he had practised every known major vice and quite a few minor ones.

Theophilus found his nephew at breakfast when the old man descended.

Ernest shot him an unsteady glance. 'Hello, Uncle Theo,' he said with false heartiness. 'You're looking uncommonly well.'

Theophilus growled an acknowledgement. 'And you're looking seedy, if I must say so. Puffy.'

'It was a long trip.'

'I'll bet it was. How'd you make it? In steerage?'

Ernest set forth his trip in patience. He made it commendably short. He had been working among the Jivaro Indians. He had sent a sample of their work, but apparently it had not yet arrived.

'I got it,' said Theophilus shortly.

Ernest seemed manifestly surprised. 'Oh,' he said. 'Oh, you did.' He licked his lips. 'But surely, not very long ago, eh?'

'Two days ago.'

'Then this is actually the . . . the third day you've had it, isn't it?'

A stupid question, thought Theophilus. Small wonder he tittered after it. Still had that disgusting accent too.

'How the devil did you get along with the Indians, Ernest? Or can you speak their language?'

'I learned it. And I taught some of them English. Oh, I taught them a lot of things, and they taught me. That head I sent you – I can do that sort of thing myself now. And a lot of others.'

'Equally reprehensible, no doubt.'

Ernest frowned angrily. 'You would think so.'

'I know the precedents,' answered Theophilus curtly. 'How long are you planning on staying?'

'Oh, not too long. A week or two, maybe. Then I must go back. I've got quite a reputation among those Indians.'

'I can imagine.'

'You'll find it hard to believe, but they think I'm a big medicine-man – the equivalent of an African witch-doctor, no less.'

He was gloating. He was actually proud of what the Jivaros thought. Theophilus repressed a shudder.

'Congratulations,' he said dryly. 'And tell me, Ernest, that head you sent me. Did it take you very long?'

'Oh, no, just ...' Ernest caught himself and glared at the old man. 'What do you mean?'

'What did you think I meant?' countered Theophilus blandly.

Ernest swallowed. 'You always think the worst of me,' he muttered.

'Ah, and whose fault is that?' Theophilus got up, leaning above his nephew. He had scarcely touched his coffee, but he no longer had any appetite for it. 'If you're staying, Ernest, you take the room next to mine. I have to tell you, though – there appears to be somebody else in the house, besides Fulton and me. You'll find out about that in good time.'

Ernest stared after him with narrowed eyes.

Theophilus was profoundly disturbed. He read his nephew's eyes. He read hope, hate, avarice; he read more. And how curiously Ernest had spoken! He was not cringing, as he had formerly done; he was not apologizing or begging; his was an attitude of watchful waiting, an almost irrepressible gloating straying from behind his feverish eyes.

Theophilus continued to be upset at intervals throughout the day. So did Fulton, what with the way in which Ernest presumed to order him about. Ernest managed to surcharge the already troubled atmosphere of the house on Main Street with an explosive chaos. Moreover, as evening approached, Ernest began to get extremely fidgety, and at last, immediately after supper, rose and left the house, mumbling that he would be back later, and no one needed to be waiting up for him – as if anyone intended to do so.

'The front door will be left open,' said Theophilus. And it would be just like Ernest to come in in the midst of a soliloquy from that thing in the parlour, he thought. He half hoped he would do so.

But that night advanced without the disturbance of the past two nights. Theophilus listened for hours. When at last the clock struck eleven, he was tense with listening. He heard the murmur of wind in the trees, the creaking of the house, the scuttering of mice – and, a quarter past the hour, a terrific clatter on the front porch, followed by an assault on the door, which opened and closed, and permitted Theophilus to hear a succession of unsteady footsteps advancing down the hall.

Ernest – and drunk. Theophilus sighed. He might have expected that. He got up, pulling on his dressing-gown. He opened the door of his room and stood there, waiting, listening to Ernest stumbling through the hall, up the stairs. He hoped that Ernest would find his own room.

That hope, however, was not destined to be fulfilled. Seeing the open door, Ernest came into his uncle's room, lurched across to the bed, and flung himself on it. Disgusted, Theophilus walked over and touched him on the shoulder. Ernest looked warily around, bleary-eyed. Seeing Theophilus, his eyes, opened wide and closed again, tightly.

'Go 'way,' he muttered thickly. 'Never wash 'fraid 'v you 'live, n' 'fraid 'v you dead. Go 'way.'

Was it worth it? Theophilus wondered. If left alone, Ernest might go to sleep in a matter of seconds; if not, he might become obstreperous and insistently difficult. He stood there for a moment, feeling the chill of the night through his dressing-gown; then he gave up, and went out, leaving the door ajar, so that he might hear if Ernest got up again. He could as easily sleep next door, in the room assigned to Ernest, as in his own, much as he disliked being routed from his own warm bed.

He got into Ernest's bed, profoundly hoping that he might be able now to sleep without interruption for what remained of the night.

He was.

He woke up just as Fulton found him. Fulton, much agitated, his hands almost palsied. He woke quickly.

'Mr Ambler, sir – Mr Ernest's on your bed.'

'Yes, of course. I let him.'

'I'm afraid he's ill, sir.'

'Drunk, damn him! Just plain beastly drunk.'

Fulton looked apologetically dubious. 'But the blood,' he said faintly.

'Blood?' echoed Theophilus.

He got up, forgetting his dressing-gown, and walked in his nightshirt as fast as he was able down the hall to his own room.

Fulton had not exaggerated. There was quite a bit of blood emanating apparently from some puffy wounds on Ernest's neck. Ernest himself was dead; of that there was not the shadow of a doubt. His neck was

torn and lacerated but not fatally, to Theophilus Ambler's untrained
eye.

'Call somebody,' he said to Fulton.

'The undertaker?' ventured Fulton.

'And the sheriff, too. They'll want to ask questions. They always do.'

The sheriff came and asked a good many questions, particularly after
a report from the county coroner was in. Ernest Ambler had died of
poison, evidently administered through the wounds in his neck. Curare.
A poison well-known to certain Indian tribes of South America. As for
the wounds in his neck – clearly bites of some kind. Perhaps rats. What
did Mr Theophilus Ambler know about it?

Theophilus was not of much help. But for the fact that he had not a
shred of motive for wanting his nephew out of the way, it might have gone
very badly for him and for Fulton. As it was, the absence of evidence
failed to constitute anything positive. Two or three times it was on the
tip of his tongue to say something about that strange tsanta on the mantel,
but he wisely forebore; he might escape a barred cell for a padded one.

At the first opportunity, however, he examined the bloodstains on the
stairs which the men from the sheriff's office had found; there were not
many, and they ended half-way down the stairs. He went into the
parlour. The tsanta stood on the very edge of the shelf. There was a red-
brown smear at one corner of its mouth. Theophilus had not a doubt but
that, if he sent away the pointed 'teeth' from that monkey-like head, he
would find the source of the curare which had killed Ernest.

He had an understandable reluctance to do so.

But something would have to be done about the thing on the mantel.
For the time being it could stay where it was – but not for long.

Within a fortnight the mail brought in a letter sent to Theophilus Ambler
by the American consul at Cuenca, Ecuador. Did Mr Ambler have in
his possession a shrunken Jivaro head, recently acquired? And if so, would
he send it post-haste to the consulate? The consul was sorry, but he had
been plagued by a Jivaro woman who had told him a long rigmarole and
given him no rest until he sent to inquire. Her husband, whose headless
body had been discovered in the garden behind a small house once
occupied by Ernest Ambler, who had gone from there, had been murdered by someone – according to her, by Ambler, who had – so she told
the consul she had learned from her husband's spectre – performed
certain ancient rites in sorcery over the head and dispatched it to a place
in America to do a deed, after which the head would be returned. Now
the ghost of the dead Indian appeared nightly to his wife, weeping and
clamouring for his head. It was absurd, it was ridiculous, but the consul
hoped that Mr Theophilus Ambler knew how difficult a consul's life
could be and might understand.

Theophilus understood very well indeed. The tsanta had been sent to do a deed – on the third night in the room at the head of the stairs. The incorrigible Ernest had counted on the tsanta's earlier arrival. Fortunately, Theophilus was in a position to appreciate the irony of the situation, however incredible.

He took no chances with the tsanta. He packed it carefully and sent it by air to the American consulate at Cuenca.

The Frogwood Roundabout

Roy Harrison

It was the summer of 1914 when the travelling fair came to Frogwood.
It came suddenly, it came overnight; no sight nor sound nor rumour, but
one morning it was there – on Frogwood Common – big and bright and
brash and shiny, glittering with paint and polish, and raucous with the
cries of barkers and Italians selling ice cream and Cockneys selling eels
and gipsies selling fortunes: *'Your Destiny Is In The Stars!'* *'The Lady Zela
Sees All!'* And in the middle of the common, on the edge of the ice cream
stalls and the lemonade stalls and the shooting-galleries and the barrel-
organs and the gipsy tents, was the giant roundabout, blazing red, with
its plunging horses – white, cream-coloured, black and cream, black and
white, red mouths and white manes – and all the while, as the roundabout turned and the horses plunged up and down, the steam-organ
brayed out music.

And everybody was there, even the soldiers from the camp three miles
away; pale, moustached and cocky in their khaki uniforms. The little
boys gaped at them admiringly; the girls and young women eyed them
either with a different kind of admiration or with a half-suppressed,
foreboding shiver.

Jack and Alicia and Georgie sidled and pushed and squeezed their way
through the crowds, deafened by the music, shoved every way they
turned, hot and excited, desperately wanting to buy everything on the
stalls, win every coconut at the coconut-shy, ride on that huge and
hurtling roundabout, and never ever have to go home.

Alicia jumped and spun round as a voice bellowed in her ear, 'Come
on now, ladies and gents, come on now! Come on, little lady, you're
jumpy as a kitten, don't be shy!' This, with an impudent wink at Alicia,
who went red. She heard Georgie giggle behind her. 'I'm not going to
eat you, little lady; I wouldn't dream of eating such a pretty little lady
as you!' The man smashed his big brawny hands together. 'Ladies and
gents, you won't see the like of this again, not in your lifetimes you won't!
We don't stay, we're on our way, from dawn to dusk to break of day! We
ride faster than Time itself, we ride for ever! That's right, ladies and

gents,' he went on, as someone guffawed, 'a ride on our roundabout is the ride of a lifetime, a ride to last you till Judgement Day! The world is changing, the world is in a hurry, so come on, come on! Like the bad penny and the bad cloth, we're not here today and gone tomorrow, we're here today and gone tonight! Tomorrow we'll be in London, next week in Paris, the week after that, Berlin! Ladies and gents, you won't see the like again, you won't see ——'

Jack pulled Alicia's arm as the man went on shouting his incantation. 'Come on, Alicia, for heaven's sake. Those London fellows just want to take every penny you're got. And did you ever hear such stuff as that chap's spouting! Let's get some lemonade; I'm so dry I could drink a bucketful.'

'But we want to go on the roundabout, we want to go on the round-about!' Georgie wailed anxiously, hanging on to Alicia's other arm as the three of them pushed and stumbled and pushed again through the noisy village crowd.

'Oh stop pulling, Jack, you'll tear my dress,' Alicia said. 'I don't think we can afford to go on the roundabout, Georgie; you know Mother only gave us so much.'

Georgie started whimpering. 'I want to go on the roundabout, you *said* we could go on the roundabout!'

'We'll go and ask the man how much it costs,' said Jack, who prided himself on being practical. 'Then we'll know. But I'm having some lemonade first.'

So Jack had two glasses of lemonade, and Alicia had to buy Georgie an ice cream cornet almost half as big as himself, and Jack and Alicia went on the coconut-shy – and lost; and tried the shooting gallery – and lost; and then Jack said, 'Let's have some brandysnaps.' But they had no more money.

And for a while they wandered disconsolately around; and the barkers were shouting; and the barrel-organs were playing; and Mrs Corbett, who owned the Frogwood grocery shop, was sitting huge and happy in a cheap flowered dress, gobbling jellied eels and shaking with laughter at something Bert Daniels, the Frogwood barber, was telling her. Jack paused to stare half-enviously at some soldiers jostling, cursing and laughing round the fortune-teller's tent. And on the roundabout the Frogwood children were whooping and yelling as they hurtled round and round on the plunging, painted horses, and the steam-organ brayed out 'Goodbye Dolly Gray' and 'Any Old Iron'.

It wasn't much fun, just watching; and it wasn't much fun just to go home.

But the man working the roundabout seemed to be the same man who had teased Alicia before; at any rate, he shouted, as the roundabout shuddered to a halt – and children piled off and others got on – 'Come on, little lady, come on, young gents! Faster than Time itself, the ride of a lifetime, we ride for ever and we never stop! No more money? But wouldn't you like to ride if you could, eh?' And he laughed in a way that was somehow very unpleasant.

Alicia looked up at the horses, now motionless on their poles. They were all different colours, but they all had bright red mouths and big brutal teeth and solid brutal hooves, and they seemed to be grinning, row after row of them. She knew they were only made of wood, but she was suddenly afraid of them. They looked as if they could come alive any minute, biting, bucking, trampling, brawling.

'No money, young gents, little lady? I'll make you an offer, and when I make anyone an offer I keep to it! Come out here at nine o'clock – at nine o'clock, mind you – and you can ride the roundabout for nothing! Free, gratis, and for nothing!'

'But we have to be in bed by then,' said Jack, hesitantly. 'And besides, it's very kind of you, but ——'

'Free, gratis, and for nothing!' the man said, as if he hadn't heard. 'How you get here is your problem, young master. Far be it from me to put ideas into young persons' heads. Faster than Time itself we ride; we never stop! Free, gratis, and for nothing; by tomorrow we won't be here, and we'll never be back! Free ——' The music started braying out again, and the roundabout began to turn, and his words were lost, and the three children looked at each other.

'A free ride?' said Alicia. 'But it'll be dark. And Father would never ——'

The roundabout was hurtling round, and the horses were rising and plunging and champing, faster and faster, and the music was brawling, and all the children of Frogwood were yelling, and the horses plunged and grinned, plunged and grinned, and it would soon be dark, and it would soon be tomorrow.

Jack thought it strange that none of these other children, most of whom they knew, had taken the least bit of notice of what the man had said. Not even Philip Myers, who was for ever cadging sweets; not even that awful Maisie Simmons, who was always yelling like a boy, and had holes in her knickers. None of them. They behaved as if they just hadn't heard.

Clouds scudded over the swaying trees which surrounded Frogwood Common. People were drifting away; only the soldiers remained. It was getting late; it was getting colder. Georgie sucked the last few flakes and blobs of his ice cream cornet. Back home their father was reading the paper and talking cryptically about soldiers, and 'fatal decisions', and people who threw bombs at people, and Austria – a country which apparently didn't have a sea coast but was full of forests. Jack fell into a daydream, full of learning, hardly noticing the supper Mother put before them. It would be school tomorrow.

And after the children went to bed they stayed awake in their room, ready to put on shoes and coats when it was late enough. And a brief rain fell like a rushing of leaves, and it grew darker outside the window, and, on the common, sky and clouds and trees merged into a whispering, blue-grey wetness. Out there the roundabout waited; the grinning, painted horses waited.

Jack, Alicia and Georgie dressed and slipped out of the house, very very carefully, very cautiously, soundlessly latching the door, scurrying round the side of the house, and up on to the common. And there was the roundabout and there was the man waiting in the damp grass.

'Come on little lady, come on young gents! The ride of a lifetime, the ride that lasts for ever, and all for free!'

Georgie began to cry. 'I don't want to ride for ever, not for ever!'

'Hush Georgie, you're just tired. The man's only teasing you,' said Alicia soothingly.

And Jack said, 'It's really very good of you.'

'Up we go then!' said the man, a sudden harsh note of indifference in his voice, and jumped on to the roundabout. The children got on and climbed upon their horses; Alicia trying to overcome that needle-sharp tingle of fear at the sight of her horse's white, grinning, powrful teeth and blood-red mouth.

'Ready?' cried the man, and the roundabout started to turn. No lights, no music, just the roundabout turning, slowly at first, on the shadowy common; very slowly, then faster, then faster and faster; and the man was chanting in his barker's voice, chanting horrible words that didn't seem to make sense, 'Everybody's getting on, everybody's getting on! Here today, gone tonight, more next week, gone the week after! Time is spinning past; every second, every day, every year! The times are in a hurry, the world is moving faster!'

Georgie burst out crying, 'I want to go home, I want to go home!' But the roundabout was now hurtling round so fast that the common could not be seen, Frogwood could not be seen; it was all that the children could do to hold on to their horses. And the terrible voice went on, higher and louder, resounding all around them, more like the voice of a machine now than the voice of a man, 'Ladies and gents, you won't see the like again; times come, times go, but we go faster and faster!' And the horses screamed and plunged, reared and plunged, and Alicia clung screaming. Jack's face was a white spinning blur, clenched and sobbing. The terrifying mechanical voice brayed, echoing as if in laughter, 'You can't get off now, you can't get off now!' And the roundabout spun and spun, faster than Time itself.

Blood rained from the skies, dying men bled to death in the mud, guns boomed like thunder. Factory chimneys belched. Men lay shot dead in the streets. Dynamos pounded. Bombs exploded in city blocks,

reducing them to rubble. Revolvers barked. Mobs tore women to
death.

The roundabout hurtled at dizzying speed. There was nothing outside
any more; only the plunging, laughing, screaming horses. Only Mother
was there, for an instant, terribly upset, sobbing and wailing, 'Where are
my children? Where are my children?'

Death screeched and gestured on a square in Nuremberg. The
chimneys of Dachau and Buchenwald were transfigured with light and
fire, and the souls of millions blew out like snowflakes falling back into
space. Cars whizzed along the roads. Mrs Corbett's grocery shop was
replaced by a supermarket. Frogwood became a suburb. A mushroom
cloud blossomed white in the sky to the shivering cry of a gong and high
tinkling strings like children's voices. 'Every home should have one,'
voices said with a sneer. 'You can't afford to be without one.'

Plunging, biting, kicking, their jaws wide with laughter, the horses
roared on. And outside the roundabout the night was a black whirlwind;
the blood road in Alicia's ears, and she saw they were not alone on the
roundabout. For on every horse were scores of children, children with
arms and legs like sticks, bodies with tightly wrapped ribs, huge heads
and blank, staring, terrified eyes. Korea wept, India stared, Egypt
moaned, and Africa screamed in a dream of blood. And somewhere in
the night a voice sobbed on and on, 'Mummy I want to go home.
Mummy, Mummy I want to go home!'

And the night never ended, and the Frogwood roundabout flew faster
and faster.

The Beast with Five Fingers

W. F. Harvey

The story, I suppose, begins with Adrian Borlsover, whom I met when I was a little boy and he an old man. My father had called to appeal for a subscription, and before he left, Mr Borlsover laid his right hand in blessing on my head. I shall never forget the awe in which I gazed up at his face and realized for the first time that eyes might be dark and beautiful and shining, and yet not able to see.

For Adrian Borlsover was blind.

He was an extraordinary man, who came of an eccentric stock. Borlsover sons for some reason always seemed to marry very ordinary women; which perhaps accounted for the fact that no Borlsover had been a genius, and only one Borlsover had been mad. But they were great champions of little causes, generous patrons of odd sciences, founders of querulous sects, trustworthy guides to the bypath meadows of erudition.

Adrian was an authority on the fertilization of orchids. He had held at one time the family living at Borlsover Conyers, until a congenital weakness of the lungs obliged him to seek a less rigorous climate in the sunny south-coast watering-place where I had seen him. Occasionally he would relieve one or other of the local clergy. My father described him as a fine preacher, who gave long and inspiring sermons from what many men would have considered unprofitable texts. 'An excellent proof,' he would add, 'of the truth of the doctrine of direct verbal inspiration.'

Adrian Borlsover was exceedingly clever with his hands. His penmanship was exquisite. He illustrated all his scientific papers, made his own woodcuts, and carved the reredos that is at present the chief feature of interest in the church at Borlsover Conyers. He had an exceedingly clever knack in cutting silhouettes for young ladies and paper pigs and cows for little children, and made more than one complicated wind-instrument of his own devising.

When he was fifty years old Adrian Borlsover lost his sight. In a wonderfully short time he adapted himself to the new conditions of life. He quickly learnt to read Braille. So marvellous indeed was his sense of touch, that he was still able to maintain his interest in botany. The mere passing of his long supple fingers over a flower was sufficient means for its identification, though occasionally he would use his lips. I have found several letters of his among my father's correspondence; in no case was there anything to show that he was afflicted with blindness, and this in spite of the fact that he exercised undue economy in the spacing of lines. Towards the close of his life Adrian Borlsover was credited with powers of touch that seemed almost uncanny. It has been said that he could tell at once the colour of a ribbon placed between his fingers. My father would neither confirm nor deny the story.

Adrian Borlsover was a bachelor. His elder brother, Charles, had married late in life, leaving one son, Eustace, who lived in the gloomy Georgian mansion at Borlsover Conyers, where he could work undisturbed in collecting material for his great book on heredity.

Like his uncle, he was a remarkable man. The Borlsovers had always been born naturalists, but Eustace possessed in a special degree the power of systematizing his knowledge. He had received his university education in Germany; and then, after post-graduate work in Vienna and Naples, had travelled for four years in South America and the East, getting together a huge store of material for a new study into the processes of variation.

He lived alone at Borlsover Conyers with Saunders, his secretary, a man who bore a somewhat dubious reputation in the district, but whose powers as a mathematician, combined with his business abilities, were invaluable to Eustace.

Uncle and nephew saw little of each other. The visits of Eustace were confined to a week in the summer or autumn – tedious weeks, that dragged almost as slowly as the bath-chair in which the old man was drawn along the sunny sea-front. In their way the two men were fond of each other, though their intimacy would, doubtless, have been greater, had they shared the same religious views. Adrian held to the old-fashioned evangelical dogmas of his early manhood; his nephew for many years had been thinking of embracing Buddhism. Both men possessed, too, the reticence the Borlsovers had always shown, and which their enemies sometimes called hypocrisy. With Adrian it was a reticence as to the things he had left undone; but with Eustace it seemed that the curtain which he was so careful to leave undrawn hid something more than a half-empty chamber.

Two years before his death Adrian Borlsover developed, unknown to himself, the not uncommon power of automatic writing. Eustace made the discovery by accident. Adrian was sitting reading in bed, the forefinger of his left hand tracing the Braille characters, when his nephew noticed that a pencil the old man held in his right hand was moving slowly along the opposite page. He left his seat in the window and sat down beside the bed. The right hand continued to move, and now he could see plainly that they were letters and words which it was forming.

'Adrian Borlsover,' wrote the hand, 'Eustace Borlsover, Charles Borlsover, Francis Borlsover, Sigismund Borlsover, Adrian Borlsover, Eustace Borlsover, Saville Borlsover. B for Borlsover. Honesty is the Best Policy. Beautiful Belinda Borlsover.'

'What curious nonsense!' said Eustace to himself.

'King George ascended the throne in 1760,' wrote the hand. 'Crowd, a noun of multitude; a collection of individuals. Adrian Borlsover, Eustace Borlsover.'

'It seems to me,' said his uncle, closing the book, 'that you had much better make the most of the afternoon sunshine and take your walk now.'

'I think perhaps I will,' Eustace answered as he picked up the volume. 'I won't go far, and when I come back, I can read to you those articles in *Nature* about which we were speaking.'

He went along the promenade, but stopped at the first shelter, and, seating himself in the corner best protected from the wind, he examined the book at leisure. Nearly every page was scored with a meaningless jumble of pencil-marks; rows of capital letters, short words, long words, complete sentences, copy-book tags. The whole thing, in fact, had the appearance of a copy-book, and, on a more careful scrutiny, Eustace thought that there was ample evidence to show that the handwriting at the beginning of the book, good though it was, was not nearly so good as the handwriting at the end.

He left his uncle at the end of October with a promise to return early in December. It seemed to him quite clear that the old man's power of automatic writing was developing rapidly, and for the first time he looked forward to a visit that would combine duty with interest.

But on his return he was at first disappointed. His uncle, he thought, looked older. He was listless, too, preferring others to read to him and dictating nearly all his letters. Not until the day before he had left had Eustace an opportunity of observing Adrian Borlsover's new-found faculty.

The old man, propped up in bed with pillows, had sunk into a light sleep. His two hands lay on the coverlet. His left hand tightly clasping his right. Eustace took an empty manuscript-book and placed a pencil within reach of the fingers of the right hand. They snatched at it eagerly, then dropped the pencil to loose the left hand from its restraining grasp.

'Perhaps to prevent interference I had better hold that hand,' said Eustace to himself, as he watched the pencil. Almost immediately it began to write.

'Blundering Borlsovers, unnecessarily unnatural, extraordinarily eccentric, culpably curious.'

'Who are you?' asked Eustace in a low voice.

'Never you mind,' wrote the hand of Adrian.

'Is it my uncle who is writing?'

'O my prophetic soul, mine uncle!'

'Is it anyone I know?'

'Silly Eustace, you'll see me very soon.'

'When shall I see you?'

'When poor old Adrian's dead.'

'Where shall I see you?'

'Where shall you not?'

Instead of speaking his next question, Eustace wrote it. 'What is the time?'

The fingers dropped the pencil and moved three or four times across the paper. Then, picking up the pencil, they wrote: 'Ten minutes before four. Put your book away, Eustace. Adrian mustn't find us working at this sort of thing. He doesn't know what to make of it, and I won't have poor old Adrian disturbed. Au revoir!'

Adrian Borlsover awoke with a start.

'I've been dreaming again,' he said; 'such queer dreams of leaguered cities and forgotten towns. You were mixed up in this one, Eustace, though I can't remember how. Eustace, I want to warn you. Don't walk in doubtful paths. Choose your friends well. Your poor grandfather . . .'

A fit of coughing put an end to what he was saying, but Eustace saw that the hand was still writing. He managed unnoticed to draw the book away. 'I'll light the gas,' he said, 'and ring for tea.' On the other side of the bed-curtain he saw the last sentences that had been written.

'It's too late, Adrian,' he said. 'We're friends already, aren't we, Eustace Borlsover?'

On the following day Eustace left. He thought his uncle looked ill when he said goodbye, and the old man spoke despondently of the failure his life had been.

'Nonsense, uncle,' said his nephew. 'You have got over your difficulties in a way not one in a hundred thousand would have done. Everyone marvels at your splendid perseverance in teaching your hand to take the place of your lost sight. To me it's been a revelation of the possibilities of education.'

'Education,' said his uncle dreamily, as if the word had started a new train of thought. 'Education is good so long as you know to whom and for what purpose you give it. But with the lower orders of men, the base and more sordid spirits, I have grave doubts as to its results. Well, good-bye, Eustace; I may not see you again. You are a true Borlsover, with all the Borlsover faults. Marry, Eustace. Marry some good, sensible girl. And if by any chance I don't see you again, my will is at my solicitors. I've not left you any legacy, because I know you're well provided for; but I thought you might like to have my books. Oh, and there's just one other thing. You know, before the end people often lose control over themselves and make absurd requests. Don't pay any attention to them, Eustace. Goodbye!' and he held out his hand. Eustace took it. It remained in his a fraction of a second longer than he had expected and gripped him with a virility that was surprising. There was, too, in its touch a subtle sense of intimacy.

'Why, uncle,' he said, 'I shall see you alive and well for many long years to come.'

Two months later Adrian Borlsover died.

'Eustace Borlsover was in Naples at the time. He read the obituary notice in the *Morning Post* on the day announced for the funeral.

'Poor old fellow!' he said. 'I wonder whether I shall find room for all his books.'

The question occurred to him again with greater force when, three days later, he found himself standing in the library at Borlsover Conyers, a huge room built for use and not for beauty in the year of Waterloo by a Borlsover who was an ardent admirer of the great Napoleon. It was arranged on the plan of many college libraries, with tall projecting bookcases forming deep recesses of dusty silence, fit graves for the old hates of forgotten controversy, the dead passions of forgotten lives. At the end of the room, behind the bust of some unknown eighteenth-century divine, an ugly iron corkscrew stair led to a shelf-lined gallery. Nearly every shelf was full.

'I must talk to Saunders about it,' said Eustace. 'I suppose that we shall have to have the billiard-room fitted up with bookcases.'

The two men met for the first time after many weeks in the dining-room that evening.

'Hallo!' said Eustace, standing before the fire with his hands in his pockets. 'How goes the world, Saunders? Why these dress togs?' He himself was wearing an old shooting-jacket. He did not believe in mourning, as he had told his uncle on his last visit; and, though he usually went in for quiet-coloured ties, he wore this evening one of an ugly red, in order to shock Morton, the butler, and to make them thrash out the whole question of mourning for themselves in the servants' hall. Eustace was a true Borlsover. 'The world,' said Saunders, 'goes the same as usual, confoundedly slow. The dress togs are accounted for by an invitation from Captain Lockwood to bridge.'

'How are you getting there?'

'There's something the matter with the car, so I've told Jackson to drive me round in the dogcart. Any objection?'

'O dear me, no! We've had all things in common for far too many years for me to raise objections at this hour of the day.'

'You'll find your correspondence in the library,' went on Saunders. 'Most of it I've seen to. There are a few private letters I haven't opened.

There's also a box with a rat or something inside it that came by the
evening post. Very likely it's the six-toed beast Terry was sending us to
cross with the four-toed albino. I didn't look because I didn't want to
mess up my things; but I should gather from the way it's jumping about
that it's pretty hungry.'

'Oh, I'll see to it,' said Eustace, 'while you and the captain earn an
honest penny.'

Dinner over and Saunders gone, Eustace went into the library.
Though the fire had been lit, the room was by no means cheerful.

'We'll have all the lights on, at any rate,' he said, as he turned the
switches. 'And, Morton,' he added, when the butler brought the coffee,
'get me a screwdriver or something to undo this box. Whatever the
animal is, he's kicking up the deuce of a row. What is it? Why are you
dawdling?'

'If you please, sir, when the postman brought it, he told me that they'd
bored the holes in the lid at the post office. There were no breathing holes
in the lid, sir, and they didn't want the animal to die. That is all,
sir.'

'It's culpably careless of the man, whoever he was,' said Eustace, as
he removed the screws, 'packing an animal like this in a wooden box with
no means of getting air. Confound it all! I meant to ask Morton to bring
me a cage to put it in. Now I suppose I shall have to get one myself.'

He placed a heavy book on the lid from which the screws had been
removed, and went into the billiard-room. As he came back into the
library with an empty cage in his hand, he heard the sound of something
falling, and then of something scuttling along the floor.

'Bother it! The beast's got out. How in the world am I to find it again
in this library?'

To search for it did indeed seem hopeless. He tried to follow the sound
of the scuttling in one of the recesses, where the animal seemed to be
running behind the books in the shelves; but it was impossible to locate
it. Eustace resolved to go on quietly reading. Very likely the animal might
gain confidence and show itself. Saunders seemed to have dealt in his
usual methodical manner with most of the correspondence. There were
still the private letters.

What was that? Two sharp clicks and the lights in the hideous candel-
abras that hung from the ceiling suddenly went out.

'I wonder if something has gone wrong with the fuse,' said Eustace,
as he went to the switches by the door. Then he stopped. There was a
noise at the other end of the room, as if something was crawling up the
iron corkscrew stair. 'If it's gone into the gallery,' he said, 'well and good.'
He hastily turned on the lights, crossed the room, and climbed up the
stair. But he could see nothing. His grandfather had placed a little gate
at the top of the stair, so that children could run and romp in the gallery

without fear of accident. This Eustace closed, and, having considerably narrowed the circle of his search, returned to his desk by the fire.

How gloomy the library was! There was no sense of intimacy about the room. The few busts that an eighteenth-century Borlsover had brought back from the grand tour might have been in keeping in the old library. Here they seemed out of place. They made the room feel cold in spite of the heavy red damask curtains and great gilt cornices.

With a crash two heavy books fell from the gallery to the floor; then, as Borlsover looked, another, and yet another.

'Very well. You'll starve for this, my beauty!' he said. 'We'll do some little experiments on the metabolism of rats deprived of water. Go on! Chuck them down! I think I've got the upper hand.' He turned once more to his correspondence. The letter was from the family solicitor. It spoke of his uncle's death, and of the valuable collection of books that had been left to him in the will.

'There was one request [he read] which certainly came as a surprise to me. As you know, Mr Adrian Borlsover had left instructions that his body was to be buried in as simple a manner as possible at Eastbourne. He expressed a desire that there should be neither wreaths nor flowers of any kind, and hoped that his friends and relatives would not consider it necessary to wear mourning. The day before his death we received a letter cancelling these instructions. He wished the body to be embalmed (he gave us the address of the man we were to employ – Pennifer, Ludgate Hill), with orders that his right hand should be sent to you, stating that it was at your special request. The other arrangements about the funeral remained unaltered.'

'Good Lord,' said Eustace, 'what in the world was the old boy driving at? And what in the name of all that's holy is that?'

Someone was in the gallery. Someone had pulled the cord attached to one of the blinds, and it had rolled up with a snap. Someone must be in the gallery, for a second blind did the same. Someone must be walking round the gallery, for one after the other the blinds sprang up, letting in the moonlight.

'I haven't got to the bottom of this yet,' said Eustace, 'but I will do, before the night is very much older;' and he hurried up the corkscrew stair. He had just got to the top, when the lights went out a second time, and he heard again the scuttling along the floor. Quickly he stole on tiptoe in the dim moonshine in the direction of the noise, feeling, as he went, for one of the switches. His fingers touched the metal knob at last. He turned on the electric light.

About ten yards in front of him, crawling along the floor, was a man's hand. Eustace stared at it in utter amazement. It was moving quickly in the manner of a geometer caterpillar, the fingers humped up one moment, flattened out the next; the thumb appeared to give a crablike motion to the whole. While he was looking, too surprised to stir, the hand disappeared round the corner. Eustace ran forward. He no longer way it, but he could hear it, as it squeezed its way behind the books on one of the shelves. A heavy volume had been displaced. There was a gap in the row of books, where it had got in. In his fear lest it should escape him again, he seized the first book that came to his hand and plugged it into the hole. Then, emptying two shelves of their contents, he took the wooden boards and propped them up in front to make his barrier double sure.

'I wish Saunders was back,' he said; 'one can't tackle this sort of thing alone.' It was after eleven, and there seemed little likelihood of Saunders returning before twelve. He did not dare to leave the shelf unwatched, even to run downstairs to ring the bell. Morton, the butler, often used to come round about eleven to see that the windows were fastened, but he might not come. Eustace was thoroughly unstrung. At last he heard steps down below.

'Morton!' he shouted. 'Morton!'

'Sir?'

'Has Mr Saunders got back yet?'

'Not yet, sir.'

'Well, bring me some brandy, and hurry up about it. I'm up in the gallery, you duffer.'

'Thanks,' said Eustace, as he emptied the glass. 'Don't go to bed yet, Morton. There are a lot of books that have fallen down by accident. Bring them up and put them back in their shelves.'

Morton had never seen Borlsover in so talkative a mood as on that night. 'Here,' said Eustace, when the books had been put back and dusted, 'you might hold up these boards for me, Morton. That beast in the box got out, and I've been chasing it all over the place.'

'I think I can hear it chawing at the books, sir. They're not valuable, I hope? I think that's the carriage, sir; I'll go and call Mr Saunders.'

It seemed to Eustace that he was away for five minutes, but it could hardly have been more than one, when he returned with Saunders. 'All right, Morton, you can go now. I'm up here, Saunders.'

'What's all the row?' asked Saunders, as he lounged forward with his hands in his pockets. The luck had been with him all the evening. He was completely satisfied, both with himself and with Captain Lockwood's taste in wines. 'What's the matter? You look to me to be in an absolutely blue funk.'

'That old devil of an uncle of mine,' began Eustace – 'Oh, I can't explain it all. It's his hand that's been playing Old Harry all the evening. But I've got it cornered behind these books. You've got to help me to catch it.'

'What's up with you, Eustace? What's the game?'

'It's no game, you silly idiot! If you don't believe me, take out one of those books and put your hand in and feel.'

'All right,' said Saunders; 'but wait till I've rolled up my sleeve. The accumulated dust of centuries, eh?' He took off coat, knelt down, and thrust his arm along the shelf.

'There's something there right enough,' he said. 'It's got a funny, stumpy end to it, whatever it is, and nips like a crab. Ah! no, you don't!' He pulled his hand out in a flash. 'Shove in a book quickly. Now it can't get out.'

'What was it?' asked Eustace.

'Something that wanted very much to get hold of me. I felt what seemed like a thumb and forefinger. Give me some brandy.'

'How are we to get it out of there?'

'What about a landing-net?'

'No good. It would be too smart for us. I tell you, Saunders, it can cover the ground far faster than I can walk. But I think I see how we can manage it. The two books at the ends of the shelf are big ones, that go right back against the wall. The others are very thin. I'll take out one at a time, and you slide the rest along, until we have it squashed between the end two.'

It certainly seemed to be the best plan. One by one as they took out the books, the space behind grew smaller and smaller. There was something in it that was certainly very much alive. Once they caught sight of fingers feeling for a way of escape. At last they had it pressed between the two big books.

'There's muscle there, if there isn't warm flesh and blood,' said Saunders, as he held them together. 'It seems to be a hand right enough, too. I suppose this is a sort of infectious hallucination. I've read about such cases before.'

'Infectious fiddlesticks!' said Eustace, his face white with anger; 'bring the thing downstairs. We'll get it back into the box.'

It was not altogether easy, but they were successful at last. 'Drive in the screws,' said Eustace; 'we won't run any risks. Put the box in this old desk of mine. There's nothing in it that I want. Here's the key. Thank goodness there's nothing wrong with the lock.'

'Quite a lively evening,' said Saunders. 'Now let's hear more about your uncle.'

They sat up together until early morning. Saunders had no desire for sleep. Eustace was trying to explain and to forget; to conceal from himself a fear that he had never felt before – the fear of walking alone down the long corridor to his bedroom.

'Whatever it was,' said Eustace to Saunders on the following morning, 'I propose that we drop the subject. There's nothing to keep us here for the next ten days. We'll motor up to the Lakes and get some climbing.'

'And see nobody all day, and sit bored to death with each other every night. Nor for me, thanks. Why not run up to town? Run's the exact word in this case, isn't it? We're both in such a blessed funk. Pull yourself together, Eustace, and let's have another look at the hand.'

'As you like,' said Eustace; 'there's the key.'

They went into the library and opened the desk. The box was as they had left it on the previous night.

'What are you waiting for?' asked Eustace.

'I am waiting for you to volunteer to open the lid. However, since you seem to funk it, allow me. There doesn't seem to be the likelihood of any rumpus this morning at all events.' He opened the lid and picked out the hand.

'Cold?' asked Eustace.

'Tepid. A bit below blood heat by the feel. Soft and supple too. If it's the embalming, it's a sort of embalming I've never seen before. Is it your uncle's hand?'

'Oh yes, it's his all right,' said Eustace. 'I should know those long thin fingers anywhere. Put it back in the box, Saunders. Never mind about the screws. I'll lock the desk, so that there'll be no chance of its getting out. We'll compromise by motoring up to town for a week. If we can get off soon after lunch, we ought to be at Grantham or Stamford by night.'

'Right,' said Saunders, 'and tomorrow – oh, well, by tomorrow we shall have forgotten all about this beastly thing.'

If, when the morrow came, they had not forgotten, it was certainly true that at the end of the week they were able to tell a very vivid ghost-story at the little supper Eustace gave on Hallow E'en.

'You don't want us to believe that it's true, Mr Borlsover? How perfectly awful!'

'I'll take my oath on it, and so would Saunders here; wouldn't you, old chap?'

'Any number of oaths,' said Saunders. 'It was a long thin hand, you know, and it gripped me just like that.'

'Don't, Mr Saunders! Don't! How perfectly horrid! Now tell us another one, do! Only a really creepy one, please.'

'Here's a pretty mess!' said Eustace on the following day, as he threw a letter across the table to Saunders. 'It's your affair, though. Mrs Merrit, if I understand it, gives a month's notice.'

'Oh, that's quite absurd on Mrs Merrit's part,' replied Saunders. 'She doesn't know what she's talking about. Let's see what she says.'

'Dear Sir [he read]. This is to let you know that I must give you a month's notice as from Tuesday, the 13th. For a long time I've felt the place too big for me; but when Jane Parfit and Emma Laidlaw go off with scarcely as much as an "If you please", after frightening the wits out of the other girls, so that they can't turn out a room by themselves or walk alone down the stairs for fear of treading on half-frozen toads or hearing it run along the passages at night, all I can say is that it's no place for me. So I must ask you, Mr Borlsover, sir, to find a new housekeeper, that has no objection to large and lonely houses, which some people do say, not that I believe them for a minute, my poor mother always having been a Wesleyan, are haunted.

> 'Yours faithfully,
> 'ELIZABETH MERRIT.

'P.S. – I should be obliged if you would give my respects to Mr Saunders. I hope that he won't run any risks with his cold.'

'Saunders,' said Eustace, 'you've always had a wonderful way with you in dealing with servants. You mustn't let poor old Merrit go.'

'Of course she shan't go,' said Saunders. 'She's probably only angling for a rise in salary. I'll write to her this morning.'

'No. There's nothing like a personal interview. We've had enough of town. We'll go back tomorrow, and you must work your cold for all its worth. Don't forget that it's got on to the chest, and will require weeks of feeding up and nursing.'

'All right; I think I can manage Mrs Merrit.'

But Mrs Merrit was more obstinate than he had thought. She was very sorry to hear of Mr Saunders's cold, and how he lay awake all night in London coughing; very sorry indeed. She'd change his room for him gladly and get the south room aired, and wouldn't he have a hot basin of bread and milk last thing at night? But she was afraid that she would have to leave at the end of the month.

'Try her with an increase of salary,' was the advice of Eustace.

It was no use. Mrs Merrit was obdurate, though she knew of a Mrs Goddard, who had been housekeeper to Lord Gargrave, who might be glad to come at the salary mentioned.

'What's the matter with the servants, Morton?' asked Eustace that evening, when he brought the coffee into the library. 'What's all this about Mrs Merrit wanting to leave?'

'If you please, sir, I was going to mention it myself. I have a confession to make, sir. When I found your note, asking me to open that desk and take out the box with the rat, I broke the lock, as you told me, and was glad to do it, because I could hear the animal in the box making a great noise, and I thought it wanted food. So I took out the box, sir, and got a cage, and was going to transfer it, when the animal got away.'

'What in the world are you talking about? I never wrote any such note.'

'Excuse me, sir; it was the note I picked up here on the floor on the day you and Mr Saunders left. I have it in my pocket now.'

It certainly seemed to be in Eustace's handwriting. It was written in pencil, and began somewhat abruptly.

'Get a hammer, Morton,' he read, 'or some other tool and break open the lock in the old desk in the library. Take out the box that is inside. You need not do anything else. The lid is already open. Eustace Borlsover.'

'And you opened the desk?'

'Yes, sir; and, as I was getting the cage ready, the animal hopped out.'

'What animal?'

'The animal inside the box, sir.'

'What did it look like?'

'Well, sir, I couldn't tell you,' said Morton, nervously. 'My back was turned, and it was half way down the room when I looked up.'

'What was its colour?' asked Saunders. 'Black?'

'Oh no, sir; a greyish white. It crept along in a very funny way, sir. I don't think it had a tail.'

'What did you do then?'

'I tried to catch it; but it was no use. So I set the rat-traps and kept the library shut. Then that girl, Emma Laidlaw, left the door open when she was cleaning, and I think it must have escaped.'

'And you think it is the animal that's been frightening the maids?'

'Well no, sir, not quite. They said it was – you'll excuse me, sir – a hand that they saw. Emma trod on it once at the bottom of the stairs. She thought then it was a half-frozen toad, only white. And then Parfit was washing up the dishes in the scullery. She wasn't thinking about anything in particular. It was close on dusk. She took her hands out of the water and was drying them absent-minded like on the roller towel, when she found she was drying someone else's hand as well, only colder than hers.'

'What nonsense!' exclaimed Saunders.

'Exactly, sir; that's what I told her; but we couldn't get her to stop.'

'You don't believe all this?' said Eustace, turning suddenly towards the butler.

'Me, sir? Oh no, sir! I've not seen anything.'

'Nor heard anything?'

'Well, sir, if you must know, the bells do ring at odd times, and there's nobody there when we go; and when we go round to draw the blinds of a night, as often as not somebody's been there before us. But, as I says to Mrs Merrit, a young monkey might do wonderful things, and we all know that Mr Borlsover has had some strange animals about the place.'

'Very well, Morton, that will do.'

'What do you make of it?' asked Saunders, when they were alone. 'I mean of the letter he said you wrote.'

'Oh, that's simple enough,' said Eustace. 'See the paper it's written on? I stopped using that paper years ago, but there were a few odd sheets and envelopes left in the old desk. We never fastened up the lid of the box before locking it in. The hand got out, found a pencil, wrote this note, and shoved it through the crack on to the floor, where Morton found it. That's plain as daylight.'

'But the hand couldn't write!'

'Couldn't it? You've not seen it do the things I've seen.' And he told Saunders more of what had happened at Eastbourne.

'Well,' said Saunders, 'in that case we have at least an explanation of the legacy. It was the hand which wrote, unknown to your uncle, that letter to your solicitor bequeathing itself to you. Your uncle had no more to do with that request than I. In fact, it would seem that he had some idea of this automatic writing and feared it.'

'Then if it's not my uncle, what is it?'

'I suppose some people might say that a disembodied spirit had got your uncle to educate and prepare a little body for it. Now it's got into that little body and is off on its own.'

'Well, what are we to do?'

'We'll keep our eyes open,' said Saunders, 'and try to catch it. If we can't do that, we shall have to wait till the bally clockwork runs down. After all, if it's flesh and blood, it can't live for ever.'

For two days nothing happened. Then Saunders saw it sliding down the banister in the hall. He was taken unawares and lost a full second before he started in pursuit, only to find that the thing had escaped him. Three days later Eustace, writing alone in the library at night, saw it sitting on an open book at the other end of the room. The fingers crept over the page, as if it were reading; but before he had time to get up from his seat, it had taken the alarm, and was pulling itself up the curtains. Eustace watched it grimly, as it hung on to the cornice with three fingers and flicked thumb and forefinger at him in an expression of scornful derision.

'I know what I'll do,' he said. 'If I only get it into the open, I'll set the dogs on to it.'

He spoke to Saunders of the suggestion.

'It's a jolly good idea,' he said; 'only we won't wait till we find it out of doors. We'll get the dogs. There are the two terriers and the under-keeper's Irish mongrel, that's on to rats like a flash. Your spaniel has not got spirit enough for this sort of game.'

They brought the dogs into the house, and the keeper's Irish mongrel chewed up the slippers, and the terriers tripped up Morton, as he waited at table; but all three were welcome. Even false security is better than no security at all.

For a fortnight nothing happened. Then the hand was caught, not by the dogs, but by Mrs Merrit's grey parrot. The bird was in the habit of periodically removing the pins that kept its seed- and water-tins in place, and of escaping through the holes in the side of the cage. When once at liberty, Peter would show no inclination to return, and would often be about the house for days. Now, after six consecutive weeks of captivity, Peter had again discovered a new way of unloosing his bolts and was at large, exploring the tapestried forests of the curtains and singing songs in praise of liberty from cornice and picture-rail.

'It's no use your trying to catch him,' said Eustace to Mrs Merrit, as she came into the study one afternoon towards dusk with a step-ladder. 'You'd much better leave Peter alone. Starve him into surrender, Mrs Merrit; and don't leave bananas and seed about for him to peck at when he fancies he's hungry. You're far too soft-hearted.'

'Well, sir, I see he's right out of reach now on that picture-rail; so, if you wouldn't mind closing the door, sir, when you leave the room, I'll bring his cage in tonight and put some meat inside it. He's that fond of meat, though it does make him pull out his feathers to suck the quills. They *do* say that if you cook——'

'Never mind, Mrs Merrit,' said Eustace, who was busy writing; 'that will do; I'll keep an eye on the bird.'

For a short time there was silence in the room.

'Scratch poor Peter,' said the bird. 'Scratch poor old Peter!'

'Be quiet, you beastly bird!'

'Poor old Peter! Scratch poor Peter; do!'

'I'm more likely to wring your neck, if I get hold of you.' He looked up at the picture-rail, and there was the hand, holding on to a hook with three fingers, and slowly scratching the head of the parrot with the fourth. Eustace ran to the bell and pressed it hard; then across to the window, which he closed with a bang. Frightened by the noise, the parrot shook its wings preparatory to flight, and, as it did so, the fingers of the hand got hold of it by the throat. There was a shrill scream from Peter, as he fluttered across the room, wheeling round in circles that ever descended, borne down under the weight that clung to him. The bird dropped at last quite suddenly, and Eustace saw fingers and feathers rolled into an inextricable mass on the floor. The struggle abruptly ceased, as finger and thumb squeezed the neck; the bird's eyes rolled up to show the whites, and there was a faint, half-choked gurgle. But, before the fingers had time to loose their hold, Eustace had them in his own.

'Send Mr Saunders here at once,' he said to the maid who came in answer to the bell. 'Tell him I want him immediately.'

Then he went with the hand to the fire. There was a ragged gash across the back, where the bird's beak had torn it, but no blood oozed from the wound. He noted with disgust that the nails had grown long and discoloured.

'I'll burn the beastly thing,' he said. But he could not burn it. He tried to throw it into the flames, but his own hands, as if impelled by some old primitive feeling, would not let him. And so Saunders found him, pale and irresolute, with the hand still clasped tightly in his fingers.

'I've got it at last,' he said, in a tone of triumph.

'Good, let's have a look at it.'

'Not when it's loose. Get me some nails and a hammer and a board of some sort.'

'Can you hold it all right?'

'Yes, the thing's quite limp; tired out with throttling poor old Peter, I should say.'

'And now,' said Saunders, when he returned with the things, 'what are we going to do?'

'Drive a nail through it first, so that it can't get away. Then we can take our time over examining it.'

'Do it yourself,' said Saunders. 'I don't mind helping you with guinea-pigs occasionally, when there's something to be learned, partly because I don't fear a guinea-pig's revenge. This thing's different.'

'Oh, my aunt!' he giggled hysterically, 'look at it now.' For the hand was writhing in agonized contortions, squirming and wriggling upon the nail like a worm upon the hook.

'Well,' said Saunders, 'you've done it now. I'll leave you to examine it.'

'Don't go, in heaven's name! Cover it up, man; cover it up! Shove a cloth over it! Here!' and he pulled off the antimacassar from the back of a chair and wrapped the board in it. 'Now get the keys from my pocket and open the safe. Chuck the other things out. Oh, Lord, it's getting itself into frightful knots! Open it quick!' He threw the thing in and banged the door.

'We'll keep it there till it dies,' he said. 'May I burn in hell, if I ever open the door of that safe again.'

Mrs Merrit departed at the end of the month. Her successor, Mrs Handyside, certainly was more successful in the management of the servants. Early in her rule she declared that she would stand no nonsense, and gossip soon withered and died.

'I shouldn't be surprised if Eustace married one of these days,' said Saunders. 'Well, I'm in no hurry for such an event. I know him far too well for the future Mrs Borlsover to like me. It will be the same old story again; a long friendship slowly made – marriage – and a long friendship quickly forgotten.'

But Eustace did not follow the advice of his uncle and marry. Old habits crept over and covered his new experience. He was, if anything, less morose, and showed a great inclination to take his natural part in country society.

Then came the burglary. The men, it was said, broke into the house by way of the conservatory. It was really little more than an attempt, for they only succeeded in carrying away a few pieces of plate from the pantry. The safe in the study was certainly found open and empty, but, as Mr Borlsover informed the police inspector, he had kept nothing of value in it during the last six months.

'Then you're lucky in getting off so easily, sir,' the man replied. 'By the way they have gone about their business I should say they were experienced cracksmen. They must have caught the alarm when they were just beginning their evening's work.'

'Yes,' said Eustace, 'I suppose I am lucky.'

'I've no doubt,' said the inspector, 'that we shall be able to trace the men. I've said that they must have been old hands at the game. The way they got in and opened the safe shows that. But there's one little thing that puzzles me. One of them was careless enought not to wear gloves, and I'm bothered if I know what he was trying to do. I've traced his finger-marks on the new varnish on the window-sashes in every one of the downstairs rooms. They are very distinctive ones too.'

'Right hand or left or both?' asked Eustace.

'Oh, right every time. That's the funny thing. He must have been a foolhardy fellow, and I rather think it was him that wrote that.' He took out a slip of paper from his pocket. 'That's what he wrote, sir: "I've got out, Eustace Borlsover, but I'll be back before long." Some jailbird just escaped, I suppose. It will make it all the easier for us to trace him. Do you know the writing, sir?'

'No,' said Eustace. 'It's not the writing of anyone I know.'

'I'm not going to stay here any longer,' said Eustace to Saunders at luncheon. 'I've got on far better during the last six months than I expected, but I'm not going to run the risk of seeing that thing again. I shall go up to town this afternoon. Get Morton to put my things together, and join me with the car at Brighton on the day after tomorrow. And bring the proofs of those two papers with you. We'll run over them together.'

'How long are you going to be away?'

'I can't say for certain, but be prepared to stay for some time. We've stuck to work pretty closely through the summer, and I for one need a holiday. I'll engage the rooms at Brighton. You'll find it best to break the journey at Hitchin. I'll wire to you there at the "Crown" to tell you the Brighton address.'

The house he chose at Brighton was in a terrace. He had been there before. It was kept by his old college gyp, a man of discreet silence, who was admirably partnered by an excellent cook. The rooms were on the first floor. The two bedrooms were at the back, and opened out of each other. 'Mr Saunders can have the smaller one, though it is the only one with a fire-place,' he said. 'I'll stick to the larger of the two, since it's got a bath-room adjoining. I wonder what time he'll arrive with the car.'

Saunders came about seven, cold and cross and dirty. 'We'll light the fire in the dining-room,' said Eustace, 'and get Prince to unpack some of the things while we are at dinner. What were the roads like?'

'Rotten. Swimming with mud, and a beastly cold wind against us all day. And this is July. Dear Old England!'

'Yes,' said Eustace, 'I think we might do worse than leave Old England for a few months.'

They turned in soon after twelve.

'You oughtn't to feel cold, Saunders,' said Eustace, 'when you can afford to sport a great fur-lined coat like this. You do yourself very well, all things considered. Look at those gloves, for instance. Who could possibly feel cold when wearing them?'

'They are far too clumsy, though, for driving. Try them on and see'; and he tossed them through the door on to Eustace's bed and went on with his unpacking. A minute later he heard a shrill cry of terror. 'Oh, Lord,' he heard, 'it's in the glove! Quick, Saunders, quick!' Then came a smacking thud. Eustace had thrown it from him. 'I've chucked it into the bath-room,' he gasped; 'it's hit the wall and fallen into the bath. Come now, if you want to help.' Saunders, with a lighted candle in his hand, looked over the edge of the bath. There it was, old and maimed, dumb and blind, with a ragged hole in the middle, crawling, staggering, trying to creep up the slippery sides, only to fall back helpless.

'Stay there,' said Saunders. 'I'll empty a collar-box or something, and we'll jam it in. It can't get out while I'm away.'

'Yes, it can,' shouted Eustace. 'It's getting out now; it's climbing up the plug-chain. – No, you brute, you filthy brute, you don't! – Come back, Saunders; it's getting away from me. I can't hold it; it's all slippery. Curse its claws! Shut the window, you idiot! It's got out!' There was the sound of something dropping on to the hard flag-stones below, and Eustace fell back fainting.

For a fortnight he was ill.

'I don't know what to make of it,' the doctor said to Saunders. 'I can only suppose that Mr Borlsover has suffered some great emotional shock. You had better let me send someone to help you nurse him. And by all means indulge that whim of his never to be left alone in the dark. I would keep a light burning all night, if I were you. But he *must* have more fresh air. It's perfectly absurd, this hatred of open windows.'

Eustace would have no one with him but Saunders. 'I don't want the other man,' he said. 'They'd smuggle it in somehow. I know they would.'

'Don't worry about it, old chap. This sort of thing can't go on indefinitely. You know I saw it this time as well as you. It wasn't half so active. It won't go on living much longer, especially after that fall. I heard it hit the flags myself. As soon as you're a bit stronger, we'll leave this place, not bag and baggage, but with only the clothes on our backs, so that it won't be able to hide anywhere. We'll escape it that way. We won't give any address, and we won't have any parcels sent after us. Cheer up, Eustace! You'll be well enough to leave in a day or two. The doctor says I can take you out in a chair tomorrow.'

'What have I done?' asked Eustace. 'Why does it come after me? I'm no worse than other men. I'm no worse than you, Saunders; you know I'm not. It was you who was at the bottom of that dirty business in San Diego, and that was fifteen years ago.'

'It's not that, of course,' said Saunders. 'We are in the twentieth century, and even the parsons have dropped the idea of your old sins finding you out. Before you caught the hand in the library, it was filled with pure malevolence – to you and all mankind. After you spiked it through with that nail, it naturally forgot about other people and concentrated its attention on you. It was shut up in that safe, you know, for nearly six months. That gives you plenty of time for thinking of revenge.'

Eustace Borlsover would not leave his room, but he thought there must be something in Saunder's suggestion of a sudden departure from Brighton. He began rapidly to regain his strength.

'We'll go on the first of September,' he said.

The evening of the thirty-first of August was oppressively warm. Though at midday the windows had been wide open, they had been shut an hour or so before dusk. Mrs Prince had long since ceased to wonder at the strange habits of the gentlemen on the first floor. Soon after their arrival she had been told to take down the heavy window curtains in the two bedrooms, and day by day the rooms had seemed to grow more bare. Nothing was left lying about.

'Mr Borlsover doesn't like to have any place where dirt can collect,' Saunders had said as an excuse. 'He likes to see into all the corners of the room.'

'Couldn't I open the window just a little?' he said to Eustace that evening. 'We're simply roasting in here, you know.'

'No, leave well alone. We're not a couple of boarding-school misses fresh from a course of hygiene lectures. Get the chess-board out.'

They sat down and played. At ten o'clock Mrs Prince came to the door with a note. 'I am sorry I didn't bring it before,' she said, 'but it was left in the letter-box.'

'Open it, Saunders, and see if it wants answering.'

It was very brief. There was neither address nor signature.

'Will eleven o'clock tonight be suitable for our last appointment?'

'Who is it from?' asked Borlsover.

'It was meant for me,' said Saunders. 'There's no answer, Mrs Prince,' and he put the paper into his pocket.

'A dunning letter from a tailor; I suppose he must have got wind of our leaving.'

It was a clever lie, and Eustace asked no more questions. They went on with their game.

On the landing outside Saunders could hear the grandfather's clock whispering the seconds, blurting out the quarter-hours.

'Check,' said Eustace. The clock struck eleven. At the same time there was a gentle knocking on the door; it seemed to come from the bottom panel.

'Who's there?' asked Eustace.

There was no answer.

'Mrs Prince, is that you?'

'She is up above,' said Saunders; 'I can hear her walking about the room.'

'Then lock the door; bolt it too. Your move, Saunders.'

While Saunders sat with his eyes on the chess-board, Eustace walked over to the window and examined the fastenings. He did the same in Saunders's room, and the bath-room. There were no doors between the three rooms, or he would have shut and locked them too.

'Now, Saunders,' he said, 'don't stay all night over your move. I've had time to smoke one cigarette already. It's bad to keep an invalid waiting. There's only one possible thing for you to do. What was that?'

'The ivy blowing against the window. There, it's your move now, Eustace.'

'It wasn't the ivy, you idiot! It was someone tapping at the window'; and he pulled up the blind. On the outer side of the window, clinging to the sash, was the hand.

'What is that it's holding?'

'It's a pocket-knife. It's going to try to open the window by pushing back the fastener with the blade.'

'Well, let it try,' said Eustace. 'Those fasteners screw down; they can't be opened that way. Anyhow, we'll close the shutters. It's your move, Saunders, I've played.'

But Saunders found it impossible to fix his attention on the game. He could not understand Eustace, who seemed all at once to have lost his fear. 'What do you say to some wine?' he asked. 'You seem to be taking things coolly, but I don't mind confessing that I'm in a blessed funk.'

'You've no need to be. There's nothing supernatural about that hand, Saunders. I mean it seems to be governed by the laws of time and space. It's not the sort of thing that vanishes into thin air or slides through oaken doors. And since that's so, I defy it to get in here. We'll leave the place in the morning. I for one have bottomed the depths of fear. Fill your glass, man! The windows are all shuttered; the door is locked and bolted. Pledge me my Uncle Adrian! Drink, man! What are you waiting for?'

Saunders was standing with his glass half raised. 'It can get in,' he said hoarsely; 'it can get in! We've forgotten. There's the fire-place in my bedroom. It will come down the chimney.'

'Quick!' said Eustace, as he rushed into the other room; 'we haven't a minute to lose. What can we do? Light the fire, Saunders. Give me a match, quick!'

'They must be all in the other room. I'll get them.'

'Hurry, man, for goodness sake! Look in the bookcase! Look in the bath-room! Here, come and stand here; I'll look.'

'Be quick!' shouted Saunders. 'I can hear something!'

'Then plug a sheet from your bed up the chimney. No, here's a match!' He had found one at last, that had slipped into the crack in the floor.

'Is the fire laid? Good, but it may not burn. I know – the oil from that old reading-lamp and this cotton wool. Now the match, quick! Pull the sheet away, you fool! We don't want it now.'

There was a great roar from the grate, as the flames shot up. Saunders had been a fraction of a second too late with the sheet. The oil had fallen on to it. It, too, was burning.

'The whole place will be on fire!' cried Eustace, as he tried to beat out the flames with a blanket. 'It's no good! I can't manage it. You must open the door, Saunders, and get help.'

Saunders ran to the door and fumbled with the bolts. The key was stiff in the lock. 'Hurry,' shouted Eustace, 'or the heat will be too much for me.' The key turned in the lock at last. For half a second Saunders stopped to look back. Afterwards he could never be quite sure as to what he had seen, but at the time he thought that something black and charred was creeping slowly, very slowly, from the mass of flames towards Eustace Borlsover. For a moment he thought of returning to his friend; but the noise and the smell of the burning sent him running down the passage, crying: 'Fire! Fire!' He rushed to the telephone to summon help and then back to the bath-room – he should have thought of that before – for water. As he burst into the bed-room there came a scream of terror which ended suddenly, and then the sound of a heavy fall.

This is the story which I heard on successive Saturday evenings from the senior mathematical master at a second-rate suburban school. For Saunders has had to earn a living in a way which other men might reckon less congenial than his old manner of life. I had mentioned by chance the name of Adrian Borlsover, and wondered at the time why he changed the conversation with such unusual abruptness. A week later Saunders began to tell me something of his own history; sordid enough, though shielded with a reserve I could well understand, for it had to cover not only his failings, but those of a dead friend. Of the final tragedy he was at first especially loath to speak; and it was only gradually that I was able to piece together the narrative of the preceding pages. Saunders was reluctant to draw any conclusions. At one time he thought that the fingered beast had been animated by the spirit of Sigismund Borlsover, a sinister eighteenth-century ancestor, who, according to legend, built and worshipped in the ugly pagan temple that overlooked the lake. At another time Saunders believed the spirit to belong to a man whom Eustace had once employed as a laboratory assistant, 'a black-haired, spiteful little brute,' he said, 'who died cursing his doctor, because the fellow couldn't help him to live to settle some paltry score with Borlsover.'

From the point of view of direct contemporary evidence Saunders's story is practically uncorroborated. All the letters mentioned in the narrative were destroyed, with the exception of the last note which Eustace received, or rather which he would have received, had not Saunders intercepted it. That I have seen myself. The handwriting was thin and shaky, the handwriting of an old man. I remember the Greek 'e' was used in 'appointment'. A little thing that amused me at the time was that Saunders seemed to keep the note pressed between the pages of his Bible.

I had seen Adrian Borlsover once. Saunders I learnt to know well. It was by chance, however, and not by design, that I met a third person of the story, Morton, the butler. Saunders and I were walking in the Zoological Gardens one Sunday afternoon, when he called my attention to an old man who was standing before the door of the Reptile house.

'Why, Morton,' he said, clapping him on the back, 'how is the world treating you?'

'Poorly, Mr Saunders,' said the old fellow, though his face lighted up at the greeting. 'The winters drag terribly nowadays. There don't seem no summers or springs.'

'You haven't found what you were looking for, I suppose?'

'No, sir, not yet; but I shall some day. I always told them that Mr Borlsover kept some queer animals.'

'And what is he looking for?' I asked, when we had parted from him.

'A beast with five fingers,' said Saunders. 'This afternoon, since he has been in the Reptile House, I suppose it will be a reptile with a hand. Next week it will be a monkey with practically no body. The poor old chap is a born materialist.'

The Voice in the Night

William Hope Hodgson

It was a dark, starless night. We were becalmed in the Northern Pacific. Our exact position I do not know; for the sun had been hidden during the course of a weary, breathless week, by a thin haze which had seemed to float above us, about the height of our mastheads, at whiles descending and shrouding the surrounding sea.

With there being no wind, we had steadied the tiller, and I was the only man on deck. The crew, consisting of two men and a boy, were sleeping forrard in their den; while Will – my friend, and the master of our little craft – was aft in his bunk on the port side of the little cabin.

Suddenly, from out of the surrounding darkness, there came a hail: 'Schooner, ahoy!'

The cry was so unexpected that I gave no immediate answer, because of my surprise.

It came again – a voice curiously throaty and inhuman, calling from somewhere upon the dark sea away on our port broadside:
'Schooner, ahoy!'

'Hullo!' I sung out, having gathered my wits somewhat. 'What are you? What do you want?'

'You need not be afraid,' answered the queer voice, having probably noticed some trace of confusion in my tone. 'I am only an old – man.'

The pause sounded oddly; but it was only afterwards that it came back to me with any significance.

'Why don't you come alongside, then?' I queried somewhat snappishly; for I liked not his hinting at my having been a trifle shaken.

'I – I – can't. It wouldn't be safe. I——' The voice broke off, and there was silence.

'What do you mean?' I asked, growing more and more astonished. 'Why not safe? Where are you?'

I listened for a moment; but there came no answer. And then, a sudden indefinite suspicion, of I knew not what, coming to me, I stepped swiftly to the binnacle, and took out the lighted lamp. At the same time, I knocked on the deck with my heel to waken Will. Then I was back at the side, throwing the yellow funnel of light out into the silent immensity beyond our rail. As I did so, I heard a slight, muffled cry, and then the sound of a splash, as though someone had dipped oars abruptly. Yet I cannot say that I saw anything with certainty; save, it seemed to me, that with the first flash of the light, there had been something upon the waters, where now there was nothing.

'Hullo, there!' I called. 'What foolery is this!'

But there came only the indistinct sounds of a boat being pulled away into the night.

Then I heard Will's voice, from the direction of the after scuttle:

'What's up, George?'

'Come here, Will!' I said.

'What is it?' he asked, coming across the deck.

I told him the queer things which had happened. He put several questions; then, after a moment's silence, he raised his hands to his lips, and hailed:

'Boat, ahoy!'

From a long distance away, there came back to us a faint reply, and my companion repeated his call. Presently, after a short period of silence, there grew on our hearing the muffled sound of oars; at which Will hailed again.

This time there was a reply:

'Put away the light.'

'I'm damned if I will,' I muttered; but Will told me to do as the voice bade, and I shoved it down under the bulwarks.

'Come nearer,' he said, and the oar-strokes continued. Then, when apparently some half-dozen fathoms distant, they again ceased.

'Come alongside,' exclaimed Will. 'There's nothing to be frightened of aboard here!'

'Promise that you will not show the light?'

'What's to do with you,' I burst out, 'that you're so infernally afraid of the light?'

'Because——' began the voice, and stopped short.

'Because what?' I asked, quickly.

Will put his hand on my shoulder.

'Shut up a minute, old man,' he said in a low voice. 'Let me tackle him.'

He leant over the rail.

'See here, Mister,' he said, 'this is a pretty queer business, you coming upon us like this, right out in the middle of the blessed Pacific. How are we to know what sort of hanky-panky trick you're up to? You say there's only one of you. How are we to know, unless we get a squint at you – eh? What's your objection to the light, anyway?'

As he finished, I heard the noise of the oars again, and then the voice came; but now from a greater distance, and sounding extremely hopeless and pathetic.

'I am sorry – sorry! I would not have troubled you, only I am hungry, and – so is she.'

The voice died away, and the sound of the oars, dipping irregularly, was borne to us.

'Stop!' sung out Will. 'I don't want to drive you away. Come back! We'll keep the light hidden, if you don't like it.'

He turned to me:

'It's a damned queer rig, this; but I think there's nothing to be afraid of?'

There was a question in his tone, and I replied.

'No, I think the poor devil's been wrecked around here, and gone crazy.'

The sound of the oars drew nearer.

'Shove that lamp back in the binnacle,' said Will; then he leaned over the rail, and listened. I replaced the lamp, and came back to his side. The dipping of the oars ceased some dozen yards distant.

'Won't you come alongside now?' asked Will in an even voice. 'I have had the lamp put back in the binnacle.'

'I – I cannot,' replied the voice. 'I dare not come nearer. I dare not even pay you for the – provisions.'

'That's all right,' said Will, and hesitated. 'You're welcome to as much as grub as you can take——' Again he hesitated.

'You are very good,' exclaimed the voice. 'May God, who understands everything, reward you——' It broke off huskily.

'The – the lady?' said Will, abruptly, 'Is she——'

'I have left her behind upon the island,' came the voice.

'What island?' I cut in.

'I know not its name,' returned the voice. 'I would to God——!' it began, and checked itself as suddenly.

'Could we not send a boat for her?' asked Will at this point.

'No!' said the voice, with extraordinary emphasis. 'My God! No!' There was a moment's pause; then it added, in a tone which seemed a merited reproach:

'It was because of our want I ventured—— Because her agony tortured me.'

'I am a forgetful brute,' exclaimed Will. 'Just wait a minute, whoever you are, and I will bring you up something at once.'

In a couple of minutes he was back again, and his arms were full of various edibles. He paused at the rail.

'Can't you come alongside for them?' he asked.

'No – I *dare not*,' replied the voice, and it seemed to me that in its tones I detected a note of stifled craving – as though the owner hushed a mortal desire. It came to me then in a flash, that the poor old creature out there in the darkness, was *suffering* for actual need of that which Will held in his arms; and yet, because of some unintelligible dread, refraining from dashing to the side of our little schooner, and receiving it. And with the lightning-like conviction, there came the knowledge that the Invisible was not mad; but sanely facing some intolerable horror.

'Damn it, Will!' I said, full of many feelings, over which predominated a vast sympathy. 'Get a box. We must float off the stuff to him in it.'

This we did – propelling it away from the vessel, out into the darkness, by means of a boat-hook. In a minute, a slight cry from the Invisible came to us, and we knew that he had secured the box.

A little later, he called out a farewell to us, and so heartful a blessing, that I am sure we were the better for it. Then, without more ado, we heard the ply of oars across the darkness.

'Pretty soon off,' remarked Will, with perhaps just a little sense of injury.

'Wait,' I replied. 'I think somehow he'll come back. He must have been badly needing that food.'

'And the lady,' said Will. For a moment he was silent; then he continued:

'It's the queerest thing ever I've tumbled across, since I've been fishing.'

'Yes,' I said, and fell to pondering.

And so the time slipped away – an hour, another, and still Will stayed with me; for the queer adventure had knocked all desire for sleep out of him.

The third hour was three parts through, when we heard again the sound of oars across the silent ocean.

'Listen!' said Will, a low note of excitement in his voice.

'He's coming, just as I thought,' I muttered.

The dipping of the oars grew nearer, and I noted that the strokes were firmer and longer. The food had been needed.

They came to a stop a little distance off the broadside, and the queer voice came again to us through the darkness:

'Schooner, ahoy!'

'That you?' asked Will.

'Yes,' replied the voice. 'I left you suddenly; but – but there was great need.'

'The lady?' questioned Will.

'The – lady is grateful now on earth. She will be more grateful soon in – in heaven.'

Will began to make some reply, in a puzzled voice; but became confused, and broke off short. I said nothing. I was wondering at the curious pauses, and, apart from my wonder, I was full of a great sympathy.

The voice continued:

'We – she and I, have talked, as we shared the result of God's tenderness and yours——'

Will interposed; but without coherence.

'I beg of you not to – to belittle your deed of Christian charity this night,' said the voice. 'Be sure that it has not escaped His notice.'

It stopped, and there was a full minute's silence. Then it came again:

'We have spoken together upon that which – which has befallen us. We had thought to go out, without telling any, of the terror which has come into our – lives. She is with me in believing that tonight's happenings are under a special ruling, and that it is God's wish that we should tell you all that we have suffered since – since——'

'Yes?' said Will, softly.

'Since the sinking of the *Albatross*.'

'Ah!' I exclaimed, involuntarily. 'She left Newcastle for 'Frisco some six months ago, and hasn't been heard of since.'

'Yes,' answered the voice. 'But some few degrees to the North of the line she was caught in a terrible storm, and dismasted. When the day came, it was found that she was leaking badly, and, presently, it falling to a calm, the sailors took to the boats, leaving – leaving a young lady – my fiancée – and myself upon the wreck.

'We were below, gathering together a few of our belongings, when they left. They were entirely callous, through fear, and when we came up upon the decks, we saw them only as small shapes afar off upon the horizon. Yet we did not despair, but set to work and constructed a small raft. Upon this we put such few matters as it would hold, including a quantity of water and some ship's biscuit. Then, the vessel being very deep in the water, we got ourselves on to the raft, and pushed off.

'It was later, when I observed that we seemed to be in the way of some tide or current, which bore us from the ship at an angle; so that in the course of three hours, by my watch, her hull became visible to our sight, her broken masts remaining in view for a somewhat longer period. Then, towards evening, it grew misty, and so through the night. The next day we were still encompassed by the mist, the weather remaining quiet.

'For four days, we drifted through this strange haze, until, on the evening of the fourth day, there grew upon our ears the murmur of breakers at a distance. Gradually it became plainer, and, somewhat after midnight, it appeared to sound upon either hand at no very great space. The raft was raised upon a swell several times, and then we were in smooth water, and the noise of the breakers was behind.

'When the morning came, we found that we were in a sort of great lagoon; but of this we noticed little at the time; for close before us, through the enshrouding mist, loomed the hull of a large sailing-vessel. With one accord, we fell upon our knees and thanked God; for we thought that here was an end to our perils. We had much to learn.

'The raft drew near to the ship, and we shouted on them, to take us aboard; but none answered. Presently, the raft touched the side of the vessel, and, seeing a rope hanging downwards, I seized it and began to climb. Yet I had much ado to make my way up, because of a kind of grey, lichenous fungus, which had seized upon the rope, and which blotched the side of the ship, lividly.

'I reached the rail, and clambered over it, on to the deck. Here, I saw that the decks were covered, in great patches, with the grey masses, some of them rising into nodules several feet in height; but at the time, I thought less of this matter than of the possibility of there being people aboard the ship. I shouted; but none answered. Then I went to the door below the poop deck. I opened it, and peered in. There was a great smell of staleness, so that I knew in a moment that nothing living was within, and with the knowledge, I shut the door quickly; for I felt suddenly lonely.

'I went back to the side, where I had scrambled up. My – my sweetheart was still sitting quietly upon the raft. Seeing me look down, she called up to know whether there were any aboard of the ship. I replied that the vessel had the appearance of having been long deserted; but that if she would wait a little I would see whether there was anything in the shape of a ladder, by which she could ascend to the deck. Then we would make a search through the vessel together. A little later, on the opposite side of the decks, I found a rope side-ladder. This I carried across, and a minute afterwards, she was beside me.

'Together, we explored the cabins and apartments in the after-part of the ship; but nowhere was there any sign of life. Here and there, within the cabins themselves, we came across odd patches of that queer fungus; but this, as my sweetheart said, could be cleansed away.

'In the end, having assured ourselves that the after portion of the vessel was empty, we picked our ways to the bows, between the ugly grey nodules of that strange growth; and here we made a further search, which told us that there was indeed none aboard but ourselves.

'This being now beyond any doubt, we returned to the stern of the ship, and proceeded to make ourselves as comfortable as possible. Together, we cleared out and cleaned two of the cabins; and after that, I made examination whether there was anything eatable in the ship. This I soon found was so, and thanked God in my heart for His goodness. In addition to this, I discovered the whereabouts of the freshwater pump, and having fixed it, I found the water drinkable, though somewhat unpleasant to the taste.

'For several days, we stayed aboard the ship, without attempting to get to the shore. We were busily engaged in making the place habitable.

Yet even thus early, we became aware that our lot was even less to be desired than might have been imagined; for though, as a first step, we scraped away the odd patches of growth that studded the floors and walls of the cabins and saloons, yet they returned almost to their original size within the space of twenty-four hours, which not only discouraged us, but gave us a feeling of vague unease.

'Still, we would not admit ourselves to be beaten, so set to work afresh, and not only scraped away the fungus, but soaked the places where it had been with carbolic, a can-full of which I had found in the pantry. Yet, by the end of the week, the growth had returned in full strength, and, in addition, it had spread to other places, as though our touching it had allowed germs from it to travel elsewhere.

'On the seventh morning, my sweetheart woke to find a small patch of it growing on her pillow, close to her face. At that, she came to me, so soon as she could get her garments upon her. I was in the galley at the time, lighting the fire for breakfast.

' "Come here, John," she said, and led me aft. When I saw the thing upon her pillow, I shuddered, and then and there we agreed to go right out of the ship and see whether we could not fare to make ourselves more comfortable ashore.

'Hurriedly, we gathered together our few belongings, and even among these, I found that the fungus had been at work; for one of her shawls had a little lump of it growing near the edge. I threw the whole thing over the side, without saying anything to her.

'The raft was still alongside; but it was too clumsy to guide, and I lowered down a small boat that hung across the stern, and in this we made our way to the shore. Yet, as we drew near to it, I became gradually aware that here the vile fungus, which had driven us from the ship, was growing riot. In places it rose into horrible, fantastic mounds, which seemed almost to quiver, as with a quiet life, when the wind blew across them. Here and there, it took on the forms of vast fingers, and in others it just spread out flat and smooth and treacherous. Odd places, it appeared as grotesque stunted trees, seeming extraordinarily kinked and gnarled – the whole quaking vilely at times.

'At first, it seemed to us that there was no single portion of the surrounding shore which was not hidden beneath the masses of the hideous lichen; yet, in this, I found we were mistaken; for somewhat later, coasting along the shore at a little distance, we descried a smooth white patch of what appeared to be fine sand, and there we landed. It was not sand. What it was, I do not know. All that I have observed, is that upon it, the fungus will not grow; while everywhere else, save where the sand-like earth wanders oddly, pathwise, amid the grey desolation of the lichen, there is nothing but loathsome greyness.

'It is difficult to understand how cheered we were to find one place that was absolutely free from the growth, and here we deposited our belongings. Then we went back to the ship for such things as it seemed to us we should need. Among other matters, I managed to bring ashore with me one of the ship's sails, with which I constructed two small tents, which, though exceedingly rough-shaped, served the purposes for which they were intended. In these, we lived and stored our various necessities, and thus for a matter of some four weeks, all went smoothly and without particular unhappiness. Indeed, I may say with much of happiness – for – for we were together.

'It was on the thumb of her right hand, that the growth first showed. It was only a small circular spot, much like a little grey mole. My God! how the fear leapt to my heart when she showed me the place. We cleaned it, between us, washing it with carbolic and water. In the morning of the following day, she showed her hand to me again. The grey thing had returned. For a little while, we looked at one another in silence. Then, still wordless, we started again to remove it. In the midst of the operation, she spoke suddenly.

' "What's that on the side of your face, Dear!" Her voice was sharp with anxiety. I put my hand up to feel.

' "There! Under the hair by your ear. – A little to the front a bit." My finger rested upon the place, and then I knew.

' "Let us get your thumb done first," I said. And she submitted, only because she was afraid to touch me until it was cleansed. I finished washing and disinfecting her thumb, and then she turned to my face. After it was finished, we sat together and talked awhile of many things; for there had come into our lives sudden, very terrible thoughts. We were, all at once, afraid of something worse than death. We spoke of loading the boat with provisions and water, and making our way out on to the sea; yet we were helpless, for many causes, and – and the growth had attacked us already. We decided to stay. God would do with us what was His will. We would wait.

'A month, two months, three months passed, and the places grew somewhat, and there had come others. Yet we fought so strenuously with the fear, that its headway was but slow, comparatively speaking.

'Occasionally, we ventured off to the ship for such stores as we needed. There, we found that the fungus grew persistently. One of the nodules on the maindeck became soon as high as my head.

'We had now given up all thought or hope of leaving the island. We had realized that it would be unallowable to go among healthy humans with the thing from which we were suffering.

'With this determination and knowledge in our minds, we knew that we should have to husband our food and water; for we did not know, at that time, but that we should possibly live for many years.

'This reminds me that I have told you that I am an old man. Judged by years this is not so. But – but——'

He broke off; then continued somewhat abruptly:

'As I was saying, we knew that we should have to use care in the matter of food. But we had no idea then how little food there was left, of which to take care. It was a week later, that I made the discovery that all the other bread tanks – which I had supposed full – were empty, and that (beyond odd tins of vegetables and meat, and some other matters) we had nothing on which to depend, but the bread in the tank which I had already opened.

'After learning this, I bestirred myself to do what I could, and set to work at fishing in the lagoon; but with no success. At this, I was somewhat inclined to feel desperate, until the thought came to me to try outside the lagoon, in the open sea.

'Here, at times, I caught odd fish; but so infrequently, that they proved of but little help in keeping us from the hunger which threatened. It seemed to me that our deaths were likely to come by hunger, and not by the growth of the thing which had seized upon our bodies.

'We were in this state of mind when the fourth month wore out. Then I made a very horrible discovery. One morning, a little before midday, I came off from the ship, with a portion of the biscuits which were left. In the mouth of her tent, I saw my sweetheart sitting, eating something.

' "What is it, my dear?" I called out as I leapt ashore. Yet, on hearing my voice, she seemed confused, and, turning, slyly threw something towards the edge of the little clearing. It fell short, and, a vague suspicion having arisen in me, I walked across and picked it up. It was a piece of the grey fungus.

'As I went to her, with it in my hand, she turned deadly pale; then a rose red.

'I felt strangely dazed and frightened.

' "My dear! My dear!" I said, and could say no more. Yet, at my words, she broke down and cried bitterly. Gradually, as she calmed, I got from her the news that she had tried it the preceding day, and – and liked it. I got her to promise on her knees not to touch it again, however great our hunger. After she had promised, she told me that the desire for it had come suddenly, and that, until the moment of desire, she had experienced nothing towards it, but the most extreme repulsion.

'Later in the day, feeling strangely restless, and much shaken with the thing which I had discovered, I made my way along one of the twisted paths – formed by the white, sand-like substance – which led among the fungoid growth. I had, once before, ventured along there; but not to any great distance. This time, being involved in perplexing thought, I went much further than hitherto.

'Suddenly, I was called to myself, by a queer hoarse sound on my left. Turning quickly, I saw that there was movement among an extraordinarily shaped mass of fungus, close to my elbow. It was swaying uneasily, as though it possessed life of its own. Abruptly, as I stared, the thought came to me that the thing had a grotesque resemblance to the figure of a distorted human creature. Even as the fancy flashed into my brain, there was a slight, sickening noise of tearing, and I saw that one of the branch-like arms was detaching itself from the surrounding grey masses, and coming towards me. The head of the thing – a shapeless grey ball, inclined in my direction. I stood stupidly, and the vile arm brushed across my face. I gave out a frightened cry, and ran back a few paces. There was a sweetish taste upon my lips, where the thing had touched me. I licked them, and was immediately filled with an inhuman desire. I turned and seized a mass of the fungus. Then more, and – more. I was insatiable. In the midst of devouring, the remembrance of the morning's discovery swept into my mazed brain. It was sent by God. I dashed the fragment I held, to the ground. Then, utterly wretched and feeling a dreadful guiltiness, I made way back to the little encampment.

'I think she knew, by some marvellous intuition which love must have given, so soon as she set eyes on me. Her quiet sympathy made it easier for me, and I told her of my sudden weakness; yet omitted to mention the extraordinary thing which had gone before. I desired to spare her all the unnecessary terror.

'But, for myself, I had added an intolerable knowledge, to breed an incessant terror in my brain; for I doubted not but that I had seen the end of one of those men who had come to the island in the ship in the lagoon; and in that monstrous ending, I had seen our own.

'Thereafter, we kept from the abominable food, though the desire for it had entered into our blood. Yet, our drear punishment was upon us; for, day by day, with monstrous rapidity, the fungoid growth took hold of our poor bodies. Nothing we could do would check it materially, and so – and so – we who had been human, became—— Well, it matters less each day. Only – only we had been man and maid!

'And day by day, the fight is more dreadful, to withstand the hunger-lust for the terrible lichen.

'A week ago we ate the last of the biscuit, and since that time I have caught three fish. I was out here fishing tonight, when your schooner drifted upon me out of the mist. I hailed you. You know the rest, and may God, out of His great heart, bless you for your goodness to a – a couple of poor outcast souls.'

There was the dip of an oar – another. Then the voice came again, and for the last time, sounding through the slight surrounding mist, ghostly and mournful.

'God bless you! Goodbye!'

'Goodbye,' we shouted together, hoarsely, our hearts full of many emotions.

I glanced about me. I became aware that the dawn was upon us.

The sun flung a stray beam across the hidden sea; pierced the mist dully, and lit up the receding boat with a gloomy fire. Indistinctly, I saw something nodding between the oars. I thought of a sponge – a great, grey nodding sponge—— The oars continued to ply. They were grey – as was the boat – and my eyes searched a moment vainly for the conjunction of hand and oar. My gaze flashed back to the – head. It nodded forward as the oars went backward for the stroke. Then the oars were dipped, the boat shot out of the patch of light, and the – the thing went nodding into the mist.

The Ash-Tree

M. R. James

Everyone who has travelled over Eastern England knows the smaller country-houses with which it is studded – the rather dank little buildings, usually in the Italian style, surrounded with parks of some eighty to a hundred acres. For me they have always had a very strong attraction: with the grey paling of split oak, the noble trees, the meres with their reed-beds, and the line of distant woods. Then, I like the pillared portico – perhaps stuck on to a red-brick Queen Anne house which has been faced with stucco to bring it into line with the 'Grecian' taste of the end of the eighteenth century; the hall inside, going up to the roof, which hall ought always to be provided with a gallery and a small organ. I like the library, too, where you may find anything from a Psalter of the thirteenth century to a Shakespeare quarto. I like the pictures, of course; and perhaps most of all I like fancying what life in such a house was when it was first built, and in the piping times of landlords' prosperity, and not least now, when, if money is not so plentiful, taste is more varied and life quite as interesting. I wish to have one of these houses, and enough money to keep it together and entertain my friends in it modestly.

But this is a digression. I have to tell you of a curious series of events which happened in such a house as I have tried to describe. It is Castringham Hall in Suffolk. I think a good deal has been done to the building since the period of my story, but the essential features I have sketched are still there – Italian portico, square block of white house, older inside than out, park with fringe of woods, and mere. The one feature that marked out the house from a score of others is gone. As you looked at it from the park, you saw on the right a great old ash-tree growing within half a dozen yards of the wall, and almost or quite touching the building with its branches. I suppose it had stood there ever since Castringham ceased to be a fortified place, and since the moat was filled in and the Elizabethan dwelling-house built. At any rate, it had wellnigh attained its full dimensions in the year 1690.

In that year the district in which the Hall is situated was the scene of a number of witch-trials. It will be long, I think, before we arrive at a

just estimate of the amount of solid reason – if there was any – which lay
at the root of the universal fear of witches in old times. Whether the
persons accused of this offence really did imagine that they were possessed
of unusual powers of any kind; or whether they had the will at least, if
not the power, of doing mischief to their neighbours; or whether all the
confessions, of which there are so many, were extorted by the mere
cruelty of the witch-finders – these are questions which are not, I fancy,
yet solved. And the present narrative gives me pause. I cannot altogether
sweep it away as mere invention. The reader must judge for himself.

Castringham contributed a victim to the *auto-da-fé*. Mrs Mothersole
was her name, and she differed from the ordinary run of village witches
only in being rather better off and in a more influential position. Efforts
were made to save her by several reputable farmers of the parish. They
did their best to testify to her character, and showed considerable anxiety
as to the verdict of the jury.

But what seems to have been fatal to the woman was the evidence of
the then proprietor of Castringham Hall – Sir Matthew Fell. He deposed
to having watched her on three different occasions from his window, at
the full of the moon, gathering sprigs 'from the ash-tree near my house.'
She had climbed into the branches, clad only in her shift, and was cutting
off small twigs with a peculiarly curved knife, and as she did so she seemed
to be talking to herself. On each occasion Sir Matthew had done his best
to capture the woman, but she had always taken alarm at some accidental
noise he had made, and all he could see when he got down to the garden
was a hare running across the park in the direction of the village.

On the third night he had been at the pains to follow at his best speed,
and had gone straight to Mrs Mothersole's house; but he had had to wait
a quarter of an hour battering at her door, and then she had come out
very cross, and apparently very sleepy, as if just out of bed; and he had
no good explanation to offer of his visit.

Mainly on this evidence, though there was much more of a less striking
and unusual kind from other parishioners, Mrs Mothersole was found
guilty and condemned to die. She was hanged a week after the trial, with
five or six more unhappy creatures, at Bury St Edmunds.

Sir Matthew Fell, then Deputy-Sheriff, was present at the execution.
It was a damp, drizzly March morning when the cart made its way up
the rough grass hill outside Northgate, where the gallows stood. The
other victims were apathetic or broken down with misery; but Mrs
Mothersole was, as in life so in death, of a very different temper. Her
'poysonous Rage,' as a reporter of the time puts it, 'did so work upon the
Bystanders – yea, even upon the Hangman – that it was constantly
affirmed of all that saw her that she presented the living Aspect of a mad
Divell. Yet she offer'd no Resistance to the Officers of the Law; only she
looked upon those that laid Hands upon her with so direfull and venom-

ous an Aspect that – as one of them afterwards assured me – the meer
Thought of it preyed inwardly upon his Mind for six Months after.'

However, all that she is reported to have said was the seemingly
meaningless words: 'There will be guests at the Hall.' Which she repeated
more than once in an undertone.

Sir Matthew Fell was not unimpressed by the bearing of the woman.
He had some talk upon the matter with the Vicar of his parish, with
whom he travelled home after the assize business was over. His evidence
at the trial had not been very willingly given; he was not specially infected
with the witch-finding mania, but he declared, then and afterwards, that
he could not give any other account of the matter than that he had given,
and that he could not possibly have been mistaken as to what he saw.
The whole transaction had been repugnant to him, for he was a man who
liked to be on pleasant terms with those about him; but he saw a duty
to be done in this business, and he had done it. That seems to have been
the gist of his sentiments, and the Vicar applauded it, as any reasonable
man must have done.

A few weeks after, when the moon of May was at the full, Vicar and
Squire met again in the park, and walked to the Hall together. Lady Fell
was with her mother, who was dangerously ill, and Sir Matthew was
alone at home; so the Vicar, Mr Crome, was easily persuaded to take a
late supper at the Hall.

Sir Matthew was not very good company this evening. The talk ran
chiefly on family and parish matters, and, as luck would have it, Sir
Matthew made a memorandum in writing of certain wishes or intentions
of his regarding his estates, which afterwards proved exceedingly useful.

When Mr Crome thought of starting for home, about half-past nine
o'clock, Sir Matthew and he took a preliminary turn on the gravelled
walk at the back of the house. The only incident that struck Mr Crome
was this: they were in sight of the ash-tree which I described as growing
near the windows of the building, when Sir Matthew stopped and said:

'What is that that runs up and down the stem of the ash? It is never
a squirrel? They will all be in their nests by now.'

The Vicar looked and saw the moving creature, but he could make
nothing of its colour in the moonlight. The sharp outline, however, seen
for an instant, was imprinted on his brain, and he could have sworn, he
said, though it sounded foolish, that, squirrel or not, it had more than
four legs.

Still, not much was to be made of the momentary vision, and the two
men parted. They may have met since then, but it was not for a score
of years.

Next day Sir Matthew Fell was not downstairs at six in the morning,
as was his custom, nor at seven, nor yet at eight. Hereupon the servants
went and knocked at his chamber door. I need not prolong the descrip-

tion of their anxious listenings and renewed batterings on the panels. The door was opened at last from the outside, and they found their master dead and black. So much you have guessed. That there were any marks of violence did not at the moment appear; but the window was open.

One of the men went to fetch the parson, and then by his directions rode on to give notice to the coroner. Mr Crome himself went as quick as he might to the Hall, and was shown to the room where the dead man lay. He has left some notes among his papers which show how genuine a respect and sorrow was felt for Sir Matthew, and there is also this passage, which I transcribe for the sake of the light it throws upon the course of events, and also upon the common beliefs of the time:

'There was not any the least Trace of an Entrance having been forc'd to the Chamber: but the Casement stood open, as my poor Friend would always have it in this Season. He had his Evening Drink of small Ale in a silver vessel of about a pint measure, and tonight had not drunk it out. This Drink was examined by the Physician from Bury, a Mr Hodgkins, who could not, however, as he afterwards declar'd upon his Oath, before the Coroner's quest, discover that any matter of a venomous kind was present in it. For, as was natural, in the great Swelling and Blackness of the Corpse, there was talk made among the Neighbours of Poyson. The Body was very much Disorder'd as it laid in the Bed, being twisted after so extream a sort as gave too probable Conjecture that my worthy Friend and Patron had expir'd in great Pain and Agony. And what is as yet unexplain'd, and to myself the Argument of some Horrid and Artfull Designe in the Perpetrators of this Barbarous Murther, was this, that the Women which were entrusted with the laying-out of the Corpse and washing it, being both sad Persons and very well Respected in their Mournfull Profession, came to me in a great Pain and Distress both of Mind and Body, saying, what was indeed confirmed upon the first View, that they had no sooner touch'd the Breast of the Corpse with their naked Hands than they were sensible of a more than ordinary violent Smart and Acheing in their Palms, which, with their whole Forearms, in no long time swell'd so immoderately, the Pain still continuing, that, as afterwards proved, during many weeks they were forc'd to lay by the exercise of their Calling; and yet no mark seen on the Skin.

'Upon hearing this, I sent for the Physician, who was still in the House, and we made as carefull a Proof as we were able by the Help of a small Magnifying Lens of Crystal of the condition of the Skinn on this Part of the Body: but could not detect with the Instrument we had any Matter of Importance beyond a couple of small Punctures or Pricks, which we then concluded were the Spotts by which the Poyson might be introduced, remembering that Ring of *Pope Borgia*, with other known Specimens of the Horrid Art of the Italian Poysoners of the last age.

'So much is to be said of the Symptoms seen on the Corpse. As to what

I am to add, it is meerly my own Experiment, and to be left to Posterity to judge whether there be anything of Value therein. There was on the Table by the Beddside a Bible of the small size, in which my Friend – punctuall as in Matters of less Moment, so in this more weighty one – used nightly, and upon his First Rising, to read a sett Portion. And I taking it up – not without a Tear duly paid to him which from the Study of this poorer Adumbration was now pass'd to the contemplation of its great Originall – it came into my Thoughts, as at such moments of Helplessness we are prone to catch at any the least Glimmer that makes promise of Light, to make trial of that old and by many accounted Superstitious Practice of drawing the *Sortes*: of which a Principall Instance, in the case of his late Sacred Majesty the Blessed Martyr King *Charles* and my Lord *Falkland*, was now much talked of. I must needs admit that by my Trial not much Assistance was afforded me: yet, as the Cause and Origin of these Dreadful Events may hereafter be search'd out, I set down the Results, in the case it may be found that they pointed the true Quarter of the Mischief to a quicker Intelligence than my own.

'I made, then, three trials, opening the Book and placing my Finger upon certain Words: which gave in the first these words, from Luke xiii. 7, *Cut it down*: in the second, Isaiah xiii. 20, *It shall never be inhabited*; and upon the third Experiment, Job xxxix. 30, *Her young ones also suck up blood*.'

This is all that need be quoted from Mr Crome's papers. Sir Matthew Fell was duly coffined and laid into the earth, and his funeral sermon, preached by Mr Crome on the following Sunday, has been printed under the title of 'The Unsearchable Way; or, England's Danger and the Malicious Dealings of Antichrist,' it being the Vicar's view, as well as that most commonly held in the neighbourhood, that the Squire was the victim of a recrudescence of the Popish Plot.

His son, Sir Matthew the second, succeeded to the title and estates. And so ends the first act of the Castringham tragedy. It is to be mentioned, though the fact is not surprising, that the new Baronet did not occupy the room in which his father had died. Nor, indeed, was it slept in by anyone but an occasional visitor during the whole of his occupation. He died in 1735, and I do not find that anything particular marked his reign, save a curiously constant mortality among his cattle and live-stock in general, which showed a tendency to increase slightly as time went on.

Those who are interested in the details will find a statistical account in a letter to the *Gentleman's Magazine* of 1772, which draws the facts from the Baronet's own papers. He put an end to it at last by a very simple expedient, that of shutting up all his beasts in sheds at night, and keeping no sheep in his park. For he had noticed that nothing was ever attacked that spent the night indoors. After that the disorder confined itself to wild birds, and beasts of chase. But as we have no good account of the symptoms, and as all-night watching was quite unproductive of any clue,

I do not dwell on what the Suffolk farmers called the 'Castringham sickness.'

The second Sir Matthew died in 1735, as I said, and was duly succeeded by his son, Sir Richard. It was in his time that the great family pew was built out on the north side of the parish church. So large were the Squire's ideas that several of the graves on that unhallowed side of the building had to be disturbed to satisfy his requirements. Among them was that of Mrs Mothersole, the position of which was accurately known, thanks to a note on a plan of the church and yard, both made by Mr Crome.

A certain amount of interest was excited in the village when it was known that the famous witch, who was still remembered by a few, was to be exhumed. And the feeling of surprise, and indeed disquiet, was very strong when it was found that, though her coffin was fairly sound and unbroken, there was no trace whatever inside it of body, bones, or dust. Indeed, it is a curious phenomenon, for at the time of her burying no such things were dreamt of as resurrection-men, and it is difficult to conceive any rational motive for stealing a body otherwise than for the uses of the dissecting-room.

The incident revived for a time all the stories of witch-trials and of the exploits of the witches, dormant for forty years, and Sir Richard's orders that the coffin should be burnt were thought by a good many to be rather foolhardy, though they were duly carried out.

Sir Richard was a pestilent innovator, it is certain. Before his time the Hall had been a fine block of the mellowest red brick; but Sir Richard had travelled in Italy and become infected with the Italian taste, and, having more money than his predecessors, he determined to leave an Italian palace where he had found an English house. So stucco and ashlar masked the brick; some indifferent Roman marbles were planted about in the entrance-hall and gardens; a reproduction of the Sibyl's temple at Tivoli was erected on the opposite bank of the mere; and Castringham took on an entirely new, and, I must say, a less engaging, aspect. But it was much admired, and served as a model to a good many of the neighbouring gentry in after-years.

One morning (it was in 1754) Sir Richard woke after a night of discomfort. It had been windy, and his chimney had smoked persistently, and yet it was so cold that he must keep up a fire. Also something had so rattled about the window that no man could get a moment's peace. Further, there was the prospect of several guests of position arriving in the course of the day, who would expect sport of some kind, and the inroads of the distemper (which continued among his game) had been lately so serious that he was afraid for his reputation as a game-preserver. But what really touched him most nearly was the other matter of his sleepless night. He could certainly not sleep in that room again.

That was the chief subject of his meditations at breakfast, and after it he began a systematic examination of the rooms to see which would suit his notions best. It was long before he found one. This had a window with an eastern aspect and that with a northern; this door the servants would be always passing, and he did not like the bedstead in that. No, he must have a room with a western look-out, so that the sun could not wake him early, and it must be out of the way of the business of the house. The housekeeper was at the end of her resources.

'Well, Sir Richard,' she said, 'you know that there is but one room like that in the house.'

'Which may that be?' said Sir Richard.

'And that is Sir Matthew's – the West Chamber.'

'Well, put me in there, for there I'll lie tonight,' said her master. 'Which way is it? Here, to be sure'; and he hurried off.

'Oh, Sir Richard, but no one has slept there these forty years. The air has hardly been changed since Sir Matthew died there.'

Thus she spoke, and rustled after him.

'Come, open the door, Mrs Chiddock. I'll see the chamber, at least.'

So it was opened, and, indeed, the smell was very close and earthy. Sir Richard crossed to the window, and, impatiently, as was his wont, threw the shutters back, and flung open the casement. For this end of the house was one which the alterations had barely touched, grown up as it was with the great ash-tree, and being otherwise concealed from view.

'Air it, Mrs Chiddock, all today, and move my bed-furniture in the afternoon. Put the Bishop of Kilmore in my old room.'

'Pray, Sir Richard,' said a new voice, breaking in on this speech, 'might I have the favour of a moment's interview?'

Sir Richard turned round and saw a man in black in the doorway, who bowed.

'I must ask your indulgence for this intrusion, Sir Richard. You will, perhaps, hardly remember me. My name is William Crome, and my grandfather was Vicar here in your grandfather's time.'

'Well, sir,' said Sir Richard, 'the name of Crome is always a passport to Castringham. I am glad to renew a friendship of two generations' standing. In what can I serve you? for your hour of calling – and, if I do not mistake you, your bearing – shows you to be in some haste.'

'That is no more than the truth, sir. I am riding from Norwich to Bury St Edmunds with what haste I can make, and I have called in on my way to leave with you some papers which we have but just come upon in looking over what my grandfather left at his death. It is thought you may find some matters of family interest in them.'

'You are mighty obliging, Mr Crome, and, if you will be so good as to follow me to the parlour, and drink a glass of wine, we will take a first look at these same papers together. And you, Mrs Chiddock, as I said, be about airing this chamber ... Yes, it is here my grandfather died ... Yes, the tree, perhaps, does make the place a little dampish ... No; I do not wish to listen to any more. Make no difficulties, I beg. You have your orders – go. Will you follow me, sir?'

They went to the study. The packet which young Mr Crome had brought – he was then just become a Fellow of Clare Hall in Cambridge, I may say, and subsequently brought out a respectable edition of Polyaenus – contained among other things the notes which the old Vicar had made upon the occasion of Sir Matthew Fell's death. And for the first time Sir Richard was confronted with the enigmatical *Sortes Biblicae* which you have heard. They amused him a good deal.

'Well,' he said, 'my grandfather's Bible gave one prudent piece of advice – *Cut it down*. If that stands for the ash-tree, he may rest assured I shall not neglect it. Such a nest of catarrhs and agues was never seen.'

The parlour contained the family books, which, pending the arrival of a collection which Sir Richard had made in Italy, and the building of a proper room to receive them, were not many in number.

Sir Richard looked up from the paper to the bookcase.

'I wonder,' says he, 'whether the old prophet is there yet? I fancy I see him.'

Crossing the room, he took out a dumpy Bible, which, sure enough, bore on the flyleaf the inscription: 'To Matthew Fell, from his Loving Godmother, Anne Aldous, 2 September, 1659.'

'It would be no bad plan to test him again, Mr Crome. I will wager we get a couple of names in the Chronicles. H'm! what have we here? "Thou shalt seek me in the morning, and I shall not be." Well, well! Your grandfather would have made a fine omen of that, hey? No more prophets for me! They are all in a tale. And now, Mr Crome, I am infinitely obliged to you for your packet. You will, I fear, be impatient to get on. Pray allow me – another glass.'

So with offers of hospitality, which were genuinely meant (for Sir Richard thought well of the young man's address and manner), they parted.

In the afternoon came the guests – the Bishop of Kilmore, Lady Mary Hervey, Sir William Kentfield, etc. Dinner at five, wine, cards, supper, and dispersal to bed.

Next morning Sir Richard is disinclined to take his gun with the rest. He talks with the Bishop of Kilmore. This prelate, unlike a good many of the Irish Bishops of his day, had visited his see, and, indeed, resided there for some considerable time. This morning, as the two were walking along the terrace and talking over the alterations and improvements in the house, the Bishop said, pointing to the window of the West Room:

'You could never get one of my Irish flock to occupy that room, Sir Richard.'

'Why is that, my lord? It is, in fact, my own.'

'Well, our Irish peasantry will always have it that it brings the worst of luck to sleep near an ash-tree, and you have a fine growth of ash not two yards from your chamber window. Perhaps,' the Bishop went on, with a smile, 'it has given you a touch of its quality already, for you do not seem, if I may say it, so much the fresher for your night's rest as your friends would like to see you.'

'That, or something else, it is true, cost me my sleep from twelve to four, my lord. But the tree is to come down tomorrow, so I shall not hear much more from it.'

'I applaud your determination. It can hardly be wholesome to have the air you breathe strained, as it were, through all that leafage.'

'Your lordship is right there, I think. But I had not my window open last night. It was rather the noise that went on – no doubt from the twigs sweeping the glass – that kept me open-eyed.'

'I think that can hardly be, Sir Richard. Here – you see it from this point. None of these nearest branches even can touch your casement unless there were a gale, and there was none of that last night. They miss the panes by a foot.'

'No, sir, true. What, then, will it be, I wonder, that scratched and rustled so – ay, and covered the dust on my sill with lines and marks?'

At last they agreed that the rats must have come up through the ivy. That was the Bishop's idea, and Sir Richard jumped at it.

So the day passed quietly, and night came, and the party dispersed to their rooms, and wished Sir Richard a better night.

And now we are in his bedroom, with the light out and the Squire in bed. The room is over the kitchen, and the night outside still and warm, so the window stands open.

There is very little light about the bedstead, but there is a strange movement there; it seems as if Sir Richard were moving his head rapidly to and fro with only the slightest possible sound. And now you would guess, so deceptive is the half-darkness, that he had several heads, round and brownish, which move back and forward, even as low as his chest. It is a horrible illusion. Is it nothing more? There! something drops off the bed with a soft plump, like a kitten, and is out of the window in a flash; another – four – and after that there is quiet again.

'Thou shalt seek me in the morning, and I shall not be.'

As with Sir Matthew, so with Sir Richard – dead and black in his bed!

A pale and silent party of guests and servants gathered under the window when the news was known. Italian poisoners, Popish emissaries, infected air – all these and more guesses were hazarded, and the Bishop of Kilmore looked at the tree, in the fork of whose lower boughs a white tom-cat was crouching, looking down the hollow which years had gnawed in the trunk. It was watching something inside the tree with great interest.

Suddenly it got up and craned over the hole. Then a bit of the edge on which it stood gave way, and it went slithering in. Everyone looked up at the noise of the fall.

It is known to most of us that a cat can cry; but few of us have heard, I hope, such a yell as came out of the trunk of the great ash. Two or three screams there were – the witnesses are not sure which – and then a slight and muffled noise of some commotion or struggling was all that came. But Lady Mary Hervey fainted outright, and the housekeeper stopped her ears and fled till she fell on the terrace.

The Bishop of Kilmore and Sir William Kentfield stayed. Yet even they were daunted, though it was only at the cry of a cat; and Sir William swallowed once or twice before he could say:

'There is something more than we know of in that tree, my lord. I am for an instant search.'

And this was agreed upon. A ladder was brought, and one of the gardeners went up, and, looking down the hollow, could detect nothing but a few dim indications of something moving. They got a lantern, and let it down by a rope.

'We must get at the bottom of this. My life upon it, my lord, but the secret of these terrible deaths is there.'

Up went the gardener again with the lantern, and let it down the hole cautiously. They saw the yellow light upon his face as he bent over, and saw his face struck with an incredulous terror and loathing before he cried out in a dreadful voice and fell back from the ladder – where, happily, he was caught by two of the men – letting the lantern fall inside the tree.

He was in a dead faint, and it was some time before any word could be got from him.

By then they had something else to look at. The lantern must have broken at the bottom, and the light in it caught upon dry leaves and rubbish that lay there, for in a few minutes a dense smoke began to come up, and then flame; and, to be short, the tree was in a blaze.

The bystanders made a ring at some yards' distance, and Sir William and the Bishop sent men to get what weapons and tools they could; for, clearly, whatever might be using the tree as its lair would be forced out by the fire.

So it was. First, at the fork, they saw a round body covered with fire – the size of a man's head – appear very suddenly, then seem to collapse and fall back. This, five or six times; then a similar ball leapt into the air and fell on the grass, where after a moment it lay still. The Bishop went as near as he dared to it, and saw – what but the remains of an enormous spider, veinous and seared! And, as the fire burned lower down, more terrible bodies like this began to break out from the trunk, and it was seen that these were covered with greyish hair.

All that day the ash burned, and until it fell to pieces the men stood about it, and from time to time killed the brutes as they darted out. At last there was a long interval when none appeared, and they cautiously closed in and examined the roots of the tree.

'They found,' says the Bishop of Kilmore, 'below it a rounded hollow place in the earth, wherein were two or three bodies of these creatures that had plainly been smothered by the smoke; and, what is to me more curious, at the side of this den, against the wall, was crouching the anatomy or skeleton of a human being, with the skin dried upon the bones, having some remains of black hair, which was pronounced by those that examined it to be undoubtedly the body of a woman, and clearly dead for a period of fifty years.'

The Dancing-Partner

Jerome K. Jerome

'This story,' commenced MacShaugnassy, 'comes from Furtwangen, a small town in the Black Forest. There lived there a very wonderful old fellow named Nicholau Geibel. His business was the making of mechanical toys, at which work he had acquired an almost European reputation. He made rabbits that would emerge from the heart of a cabbage, flop their ears, smooth their whiskers, and disappear again; cats that would wash their faces, and mew so naturally that dogs would mistake them for real cats, and fly at them; dolls, with phonographs concealed within them, that would raise their hats and say, "Good morning; how do you do?" and some that would even sing a song.

'But he was something more than a mere mechanic; he was an artist. His work was with him a hobby, almost a passion. His shop was filled with all manner of strange things that never would, or could, be sold – things he had made for the pure love of making them. He had contrived a mechanical donkey that would trot for two hours by means of stored electricity, and trot, too, much faster than the live article, and with less need for exertion on the part of the driver; a bird that would shoot up into the air, fly round and round in a circle, and drop to earth at the exact spot from where it started, a skeleton that, supported by an upright iron bar, would dance a hornpipe; a life-size lady doll that could play the fiddle; and a gentleman with a hollow inside who could smoke a pipe and drink more lager beer than any three average German students put together, which is saying much.

'Indeed, it was the belief of the town that old Geibel could make a man capable of doing everything that a respectable man need want to do. One day he made a man who did too much, and it came about in this way:

'Young Doctor Follen had a baby, and the baby had a birthday. Its first birthday put Doctor Follen's household into somewhat of a flurry, but on the occasion of its second birthday, Mrs Doctor Follen gave a ball in honour of the event. Old Geibel and his daughter Olga were among the guests.

'During the afternoon of the next day some three or four of Olga's bosom friends, who had also been present at the ball, dropped in to have a chat about it. They naturally fell to discussing the men, and to criticizing their dancing. Old Geibel was in the room, but he appeared to be absorbed in his newspaper, and the girls took no notice of him.

' "There seem to be fewer men who can dance at every ball you go to," said one of the girls.

' "Yes, and don't the ones who can, give themselves airs," said another; "they make quite a favour of asking you."

' "And how stupidly they talk," added a third. "They always say exactly the same things: 'How charming you are looking tonight.' 'Do you often go to Vienna? Oh, you should, it's delightful.' 'What a charming dress you have on.' 'What a warm day it has been.' 'Do you like Wagner?' I do wish they'd think of something new."

' "Oh, I never mind how they talk," said a fourth. "If a man dances well he may be a fool for all I care."

' "He generally is," slipped in a thin girl, rather spitefully.

' "I go to a ball to dance," continued the previous speaker, not noticing the interruption. "All I ask of a partner is that he shall hold me firmly, take me round steadily, and not get tired before I do."

' "A clockwork figure would be the thing for you," said the girl who had interrupted.

' "Bravo!" cried one of the others, clapping her hands, "what a capital idea!"

' "What's a capital idea?" they asked.

' "Why, a clockwork dancer, or, better still, one that would go by electricity and never run down."

'The girls took up the idea with enthusiasm.

' "Oh, what a lovely partner he would make," said one; "he would never kick you, or tread on your toes."

' "Or tear your dress," said another.

' "Or get out of step."

' "Or get giddy and lean on you."

' "And he would never want to mop his face with his handkerchief. I do hate to see a man do that after every dance."

' "And wouldn't want to spent the whole evening in the supper-room."

' "Why, with a phonograph inside him to grind out all the stock remarks, you would not be able to tell him from a real man," said the girl who had first suggested the idea.

' "Oh yes, you would," said the thin girl, "he would be so much nicer."

'Old Geibel had laid down his paper, and was listening with both his ears. On one of the girls glancing in his direction, however, he hurriedly hid himself again behind it.

'After the girls were gone, he went into his workshop, where Olga heard him walking up and down, and every now and then chuckling to himself; and that night he talked to her a good deal about dancing and dancing men – asked what they usually said and did – what dances were most popular – what steps were gone through, with many other questions bearing on the subject.

'Then for a couple of weeks he kept much to his factory, and was very thoughtful and busy, though prone at unexpected moments to break into a quiet low laugh, as if enjoying a joke that nobody else knew of.

'A month later another ball took place in Furtwangen. On this occasion it was given by old Wenzel, the wealthy timber merchant, to celebrate his niece's betrothal, and Geibel and his daughter was again among the invited.

'When the hour arrived to set out, Olga sought her father. Not finding him in the house, she tapped at the door of his workshop. He appeared in his shirt-sleeves, looking hot but radiant.

' "Don't wait for me," he said, "you go on. I'll follow you. I've got something to finish." '

'As she turned to obey he called after her, "Tell them I'm going to bring a young man with me – such a nice young man, and an excellent dancer. All the girls will like him." Then he laughed and closed the door.

'Her father generally kept his doings secret from everybody, but she had a pretty shrewd suspicion of what he had been planning, and so, to a certain extent, was able to prepare the guests for what was coming. Anticipation ran high, and the arrival of the famous mechanist was eagerly awaited.

'At length the sound of wheels was heard outside, followed by a great commotion in the passage, and old Wenzel himself, his jolly face red with excitement and suppressed laughter, burst into the room and announced in stentorian tones:

' "Herr Geibel – and a friend." '

'Herr Geibel and his "friend" entered, greeted with shouts of laughter and applause, and advanced to the centre of the room.

' "Allow me, ladies and gentlemen," said Herr Geibel, "to introduce you to my friend, Lieutenant Fritz. Fritz, my dear fellow, bow to the ladies and gentlemen." '

'Geibel placed his hand encouragingly on Fritz's shoulder, and the lieutenant bowed low, accompanying the action with a harsh clicking noise in his throat, unpleasantly suggestive of a death rattle. But that was only a detail.

' "He walks a little stiffly" (old Geibel took his arm and walked him forward a few steps. He certainly did walk stiffly), "but then walking is not his forte. He is essentially a dancing man. I have only been able to teach him the waltz as yet, but at that he is faultless. Come, which of you ladies may I introduce him to as a partner. He keeps perfect time; he never gets tired; he won't kick you or tread on your dress; he will hold you as firmly as you like, and go as quickly or as slowly as you please; he never gets giddy; and he is full of conversation. Come, speak up for yourself, my boy."

'The old gentleman twisted one of the buttons at the back of his coat, and immediately Fritz opened his mouth, and in thin tones that appeared to proceed from the back of his head, remarked suddenly, "May I have the pleasure?" and then shut his mouth again with a snap.

'That Lieutenant Fritz had made a strong impression on the company was undoubted, yet none of the girls seemed inclined to dance with him. They looked askance at his waxen face, with its staring eyes and fixed smile, and shuddered. At last old Geibel came to the girl who had conceived the idea.

' "It is your own suggestion, carried out to the letter," said Geibel, "an electric dancer. You owe it to the gentleman to give him a trial."

'She was a bright, saucy little girl, fond of a frolic. Her host added his entreaties, and she consented.

'Herr Geibel fixed the figure to her. Its right arm was screwed round her waist, and held her firmly; its delicately jointed left hand was made to fasten itself upon her right. The old toy-maker showed her how to regulate its speed, and how to stop it, and release her.

' "It will take you round in a complete circle," he explained, "be careful that no one knocks against you, and alters its course."

'The music struck up. Old Geibel put the current in motion, and Annette and her strange partner began to dance.

'For a while everyone stood watching them. The figure performed its purpose admirably. Keeping perfect time and step, and holding its little partner tight clasped in an unyielding embrace, it revolved steadily, pouring forth at the same time a constant flow of squeaky conversation, broken by brief intervals of grinding silence.

' "How charming you are looking tonight," it remarked in its thin, far-away voice. "What a lovely day it has been. Do you like dancing? How well our steps agree. You will give me another, won't you? Oh, don't be so cruel. What a charming gown you have on. Isn't waltzing delightful? I could go on dancing for ever – with you. Have you had supper?"

'As she grew more familiar with the uncanny creature, the girl's nervousness wore off, and she entered into the fun of the thing.

' "Oh, he's just lovely," she cried, laughing, "I could go on dancing with him all my life."

'Couple after couple now joined them, and soon all the dancers in the room were whirling round behind them. Nicholaus Geibel stood looking on, beaming with childish delight at his success.

'Old Wenzel approached him, and whispered something in his ear. Geibel laughed and nodded, and the two worked their way quietly towards the door.

' "This is the young people's house tonight," said Wenzel, so soon as they were outside; "you and I will have a quiet pipe and a glass of hock, over in the counting-house."

'Meanwhile the dancing grew more fast and furious. Little Annette loosened the screw regulating her partner's rate of progress, and the figure flew round with her, swifter and swifter. Couple after couple dropped out exhausted, but they only went the faster, till at length they remained dancing alone.

'Madder and madder became the waltz. The music lagged behind: the musicians, unable to keep pace, ceased, and sat staring. The younger guests applauded, but the older faces began to grow anxious.

' "Hadn't you better stop, dear?" said one of the women. "You'll make yourself so tired."

'But Annette did not answer.

' "I believe she's fainted," cried out a girl who had caught sight of her face as it was swept by.

'One of the men sprang forward and clutched at the figure, but its impetus threw him down on to the floor, where its steel-cased feet laid bare his cheek. The thing evidently did not intend to part with its prize easily.

'Had anyone retained a cool head, the figure, one cannot help thinking, might easily have been stopped. Two or three men acting in concert might have lifted it bodily off the floor, or have jabbed it into a corner. But few human heads are capable of remaining cool under excitement. Those who are not present think how stupid must have been those who were; those who are reflect afterwards how simple it would have been to do this, that, or the other, if only they had thought of it at the time.

'The women grew hysterical. The men shouted contradictory directions to one another. Two of them made a bungling rush at the figure, which had the result of forcing it out of its orbit in the centre of the room, and sending it crashing against the walls and furniture. A stream of blood showed itself down the girl's white frock, and followed her along the floor. The affair was becoming horrible. The women rushed screaming from the room. The men followed them.

'One sensible suggestion was made: "Find Geibel – fetch Geibel."

'No one had noticed him leave the room, no one knew where he was. A party went in search of him. The others, too unnerved to go back into the ball-room, crowded outside the door and listened. They could hear the steady whir of the wheels upon the polished floor as the thing spun round and round; the dull thud as every now and again it dashed itself and its burden against some opposing object and ricocheted off in a new direction.

'And everlastingly it talked in that thin ghostly voice, repeating over and over the same formula: "How charming you are looking tonight.

What a lovely day it has been. Oh, don't be so cruel. I could go on dancing for ever – with you. Have you had supper?"

'Of course they sought for Geibel everywhere but where he was. They looked in every room in the house, then they rushed of in a body to his own place, and spent precious minutes in waking up his deaf old house-keeper. At last it occurred to one of the party that Wenzel was missing also, and then the idea of the counting-house across the yard presented itself to them, and there they found him.

'He rose up, very pale, and followed them; and he and old Wenzel forced their way through the crowd of guests gathered outside, and entered the room, and locked the door behind them.

'From within there came the muffled sound of low voices and quick steps, followed by a confused scuffling noise, then silence, then the low voices again.

'After a time the door opened, and those near it pressed forward to enter, but old Wenzel's broad shoulders barred the way.

' "I want you – and you, Bekler," he said, addressing a couple of the older men. His voice was calm, but his face was deadly white. "The rest of you, please go – get the women away as quickly as you can."

'From that day old Nicholau Geibel confined himself to the making of mechanical rabbits, and cats that mewed and washed their faces.'

Jordan

Glyn Jones

I am worried. Today when I cut my chin with my white-handled razor, I didn't bleed. That was the way Danny's shaving went. Danny was my friend. Together we had a spell working the fairs and markets out there in that country where there was nothing but farms and chapels. It was a sort of uncivilized place. I had invented a good line, a special cube guaranteed to keep the flies off the meat, and Danny had his little round boxes of toothpaste. This toothpaste he scraped off a big lump of wet batter, a few pounds of it, greenish in colour and with a bad smell, it stood on a tin plate and sometimes Danny would sell it as corn cure. So as to gather a crowd around his trestle he used to strip down to his black tights and walk about with a fifty-six pound solid iron weight hanging by a short strap from his teeth. This was to show what wonderful teeth you would have if you used Danny's toothpaste. It was only when he was doing this that you ever saw any colour in Danny's face. The colour came because he did the walking about upside down, he was on his hands doing it with his black stockings in the air.

Danny was thin and undersized. If I made a joke about his skinny legs he would lower his lids offended and say, 'Don't be so personal.' He was very touchy. His tights were coms dyed black and they looked half empty, as though large slices had been cut off from inside them. He had a fine, half half-starved face, very thin and leathery, like a sad cow. There was only one thing wrong with his face and that was the ears. Danny's ears were big and yellow, and they stood out at right angles to his head. From the front they looked as though they had been screwed into his skull, and one had been screwed in a lot farther than the other. His straight carrot hair was very long and thick and brushed back over his head. When he scuffled about on his bandy arms with that half hundredweight dangling from his teeth, his mop opened downwards off his scalp as though it was on a hinge, and bumped along the cobblestones. He was very proud of his teeth. He thought so much of them he never showed them to anyone. Nobody ever saw Danny grinning.

My own line was that special cube I had invented to keep the flies off the meat. I used to soften down a few candles and shape the grease into dices with my fingers. Then I put one or two of these white dices on a cut of meat on my trestle in the middle of the market crowds. There were always plenty of fat flies and bluebottles buzzing about in those markets, what with the boiled sweet stalls and the horse-droppings, but you never saw one perching on my meat with the white cubes on it. This wasn't because the flies didn't like candle-grease but because under the meat-plate I had a saucer of paraffin oil.

One night Danny and I were sitting on the bed in our lodging house. The place was filthy and lousy and we were catching bugs on our needles off the walls and roasting them to death one by one in the candle flame. Danny was bitter. The fair had finished but the farmers had kept their hands on their ha'pennies. And the weather was bad, very wet and gusty and cold all the time. Danny said we were pioneers. He said these farmers were savages, they didn't care about having filthy teeth, or eating their food fly-blown. He was very downhearted. He hadn't had much to eat for a few days and between the noisy bursting of the bugs his empty belly crowed. I was downhearted too. We had to get money from somewhere to pay for our lodgings and a seat in the horsebrake drawing out of town the next morning. I asked Danny to come out into the town to see what we could pick up but he wouldn't. At first he said it was too cold. Then he said he had got to darn his tights and his stockings. In the end I went by myself.

The town had been newly wetted with another downpour and Danny was right about the cold. As I walked up the dark empty main street I could feel the wind blowing into the holes in my boots. Everywhere was closed up and silent and deserted. I looked in at the Bell and the Feathers and the Glyndwr, but they were all empty. From the swing door of the Black Horse I saw inside a big broad-shouldered man sitting down by himself in the bar. Apart from him the bar was deserted. He was by the fire and his back was towards me. I knew bumming a drink out of him would be as easy as putting one hand in the other. I knew this because he had a red wig on coming down over the collar of his coat, and a man who wears a wig is lonely.

On the table in front of the man I could see a glass of whisky and in his hand was a little black book. He was singing a hymn out of it in Welsh. It was sad, a funeral hymn, but very determined. I stood by the door of the empty bar and listened. The man seemed huge in the neck and across the shoulders, and every time he moved all the flesh on him seemed to begin to tremble. If he kept dead still he stopped trembling. I went in past him and stood the other side of the table by the fire.

When I got round to the front of this man something snapped like a carrot inside me. He face was hideous. The flesh of it looked as though it had been torn apart into ribbons and shoved together again anyhow back on to the bones. Long white scars ran glistening through the purple skin like ridges of gristle. Only his nose had escaped. This was huge and dark and full of holes, it curved out like a big black lump of wood with the worm in it. He was swarthy, as though he was sitting in a bar of shadow, and I looked up to see if perhaps a roof-beam had come between him and the hanging oil-lamp lighting the bar. There wasn't a hair on him, no moustache or eyebrows, but his wig was like the bright feathers of a red hen. It started a long way back, half-way up his scalp, and the gristly scars streamed down over his forehead and cheekbones from under it. He had a tidy black suit on and a good thick-soled boot with grease rubbed in. The other leg was what looked like a massive iron pipe blocked up at the end with a solid wooden plug. It came out on to the hearth from the turn-up of his trousers.

It is best to tell the tale when you haven't got any cash to put on the counter. When I began to talk to him by the fire I tucked my feet under the settle and said I was a salesman. Although Danny and I could put all our belongings in a tobacco-box, I soon had a fine range of second-hand goods for sale. The man closed his little book to listen. He told me he was Jordan, man-servant to the old doctor of the town. I took a polished piece of rabbit's backbone out of my waistcoat pocket and passed it over to him. It looked like a small cow's skull, complete with horns. He examined it slowly, trembling all the time. He had huge soft hands and his finger-nails were as green as grass. I told him he could keep it. He called for whisky for both of us.

As I drank my whisky I enjoyed thinking what I had for sale. I had a little harmonium, portable, very good for Welsh hmyns, perfect except for a rip in the bellows; a new invention that would get a cork out of a bottle – like that!; a nice line in leather purses, a free gift presented with each one – a brass watch-key, number eight, or a row of glass-headed pins; a pair of solid leather knee-boots, just the thing for him because they were both for the same leg. The man's eyes were small, they looked half closed up, and he watched me hard without moving them all the time. In the heat of the fire a strong smell came off him. It was a damp clinging smell, clammy, like the mildewed corner of some old church, up there behind the organ where they keep the bier. At last he bent forward and held his smashed face close to mine. I stopped talking. He trembled and said softly, 'I am interested in buying only one thing.'

Somehow I felt mesmerized, I couldn't say anything. I am not often like that. I lifted my eyebrows.

Jordan didn't answer. His little eyes slid round the empty bar. Then he moved his lips into a word that staggered me. I stared at him. For a minute by the blazing bar fire I went cold as clay. He nodded his head and made the same mouthing of his smashed face as before. The word he shaped out was, 'Corpses'.

There was dead silence between us. The clock in the bar echoed loudly, like a long-legged horse trotting down an empty street. But I let my face go into a twist and I squeezed a tear into the end of my eye. I crossed myself and offered the serving man the body of my brother. I had buried him, I remembered, a week ago come tomorrow.

Jordan took his hat and stick out of the corner. The stick was heavy, with a lot of rope wound round it, and the black hat had a wide brim. When he stood up he was like a giant rising above me. He was much bigger even than I thought. He looked down hard at the little bone I had given him and then threw it on the back of the fire. We went out into the street. As we walked along, his iron leg bumped on the pavement and made a click-clicking noise like a carried bucket. He would show me where to bring the corpse and I was to come between midnight and daybreak.

We walked together out of the town into the country. It was pitch dark and soon the way was through wet fields. It was still cold but I didn't feel it any more. Jordan had this peg leg but he was big, and I sweated keeping up with him. He trembled all the time as he walked but his shaking didn't make you think he was weak. He was like a powerful machine going full force and making the whole throbbing engine-house tremble to the foundations with its power. I trotted behind him breathless. He was so busy singing the Welsh burial hymn that he didn't drop a word to me all the way.

At last we came to a gate across the lane we were following. There was a farm-house beyond it, all in darkness. Jordan stopped singing and shouted, twice. There was no reply. He started singing again. He poised himself on his iron leg and his walking stick and gave the gate a great kick with his good foot. It fell flat. We found ourselves going at full speed across a farmyard. A heavy sheepdog ran out of the shadows barking and showing a fringe of teeth. He looked huge and fierce enough to tear us in pieces. Jordan didn't pause and I kept close behind him. The dog changed his gallop into a stiff-legged prowl, and he filled his throat with a terrible snarl. Then suddenly he sprang straight at Jordan's throat. As he rose in the air Jordan hit him a ringing crack on the head with his stick. He used both hands to bring it down. The dog dropped to the pebbles of the yard passing a contented sigh. He didn't move again. Jordan put his good foot on him and brought the stick down on his head again and again. He went on doing this, his sad hymn getting louder and louder, until the dog's brains came out. I went cold in my sweat to hear him. At last he wiped the handle of the stick in the grass of the hedge and went on down the lane, singing.

We came in sight of the lights of a big house. 'That's the place,' he said. 'Bring it round to the back door. Good night.'

He went off into the darkness like a giant in his broad-brimmed hat.

I wiped the sweat off my head. After he had disappeared I could hear his hymn and his leg clicking for a long time. His hymn was slow and sad, but it didn't make me unhappy at all. It frightened the life out of me.

On the way back to the town I kicked the dead dog into the ditch.

Danny never let his job slide off his back. As I climbed up the stairs of our lodging house I came face to face with two eyes watching me through the upright bars of the top landing banister. It was Danny dawdling about on his hands, practising. I had a lot of trouble persuading him to be a corpse. All had had to do was pretend to be dead and to let me and the blackman on the landing below carry him out to the doctor's house. Then when we were paid and everybody in the house was asleep he could get out of one of the downstairs windows. We would be waiting for him. We would leave the town by the first brake in the morning. It was safe as houses. Nothing could go wrong. At last Danny agreed.

At midnight the three of us set out for Jordan's house. We were me, Danny and Marky. Marky was a half-caste cheapjack, a long thin shiny man the colour of gunmetal, selling fire-damaged remnants and bankrupt stock and that. He used to dribble and paw you at close quarters but he would do anything you asked him for tuppence or thruppence. We walked through the fields carrying a rolled up sack and my trestle until we came in sight of the house Jordan had shown me. Danny stripped to his coms under a tree and hid his clothes. He put on an old cream-flannel nightgown Marky had brought out of stock. Then we sewed him in the sack and put him on the planks of my trestle. It was pitch dark and cold, with the small rain drizzling down again as fine as pepper.

The doctor's house was all in darkness. We went round to the little pointed wooden door at the back of the garden. I whispered to Danny to ask if he was all right. There were two answers, Danny's teeth chattering and the uproar of dogs howling and barking inside the garden. I had never thought about dogs. What were we going to do?

At once I heard the click of the leg the other side of the wall and Jordan's voice speaking. 'Down, Farw. Down, Angau,' he growled. The narrow pointed door was thrown open, and suddenly we saw Jordan. He was stripped naked to the half and he had left off his wig. He looked so huge, so powerful and ugly in the doorway, with his swelling nose and his fleshy body all slashed, I almost let go of our load with fright. And behind him the hounds, three of them, black and shaggy and big as ponies, yelped and barked and bayed and struggled to get past him to attack us. Jordan spoke sharply to them and at last we were able to carry Danny into the garden. He was as light on the boards as a bag of hay. Jordan spoke only to the dogs. He made a sign and led us hobbling along the pebble path across the yard towards some dark out-houses. The three hounds paced whining beside us, sniffing all the time at the sack and spilling their dribble.

The room we went into smelt like a stable. It was dim and empty but there was an oil-lamp hanging from a nail in a low beam. We laid Danny across some feed-boxes under this lamp. Jordan stood back by the stable door with the whimpering dogs while we were doing it, watching us all the time. I could feel his eyes burning into my back. His skin was very dark and his chest bulged up into bip paps resting above his powerful folded arms. But all his body was torn with terrible wounds like his face. Long shining scars like the glistening veins you see running through the rocks of a cliff-face spread in all directions over his flesh. His bald head had a large dome on it and that was covered with scars too. His whole body gleamed down to his waist, the drizzle had given him a high shine like the gloss of varnish.

We left Danny lying on the boards across the feed-boxes and came back up to the door to ask for our money. Jordan didn't reply. Instead he took a large clasp-knife out of the pocket in the front of his trousers and opened it. Then, ordering the dogs to stay, he went past us and bumped over to where Danny was lying in his sack. He seemed to take a long time to get there. There was dead silence. As he went from us we could see a black hole in his back you could put your fist into. My skin prickled. Marky's eyes rolled with the dogs sniffing him and he began to paw the air. I looked round and saw a hay-fork with a stumpy leg in the corner. Jordan turned round under the lamp and looked back at us. The blade of the open knife trembled in his hand. He turned again and cut open the sewing in the sack above Danny's face. I could hardly breathe. Danny was so white under the hanging lamp I thought he was really dead. My hair stirred. Danny's teeth showed shining in his open mouth, and in the lamplight falling right down upon them the whites of his half-opened eyes glistened. He was pale and stiff, as if he had already begun to rot. Jordan bent over, gazing down at him, with the knife in his hand, the lamp spreading a shine over the skin of his wet back. I was frightened, but if Danny's teeth chattered or his belly crowed I was willing to use the pitchfork to get us out. At last Jordan turned. He spoke for the first time.

'He is a good corpse,' he said.

'He is my brother,' I told him.

'Where did you get him from?'

'I dug him up.'

He nodded. He left the knife open on the feed-box and came over to us. Putting his hand again into his front pocket he brought out a large lump of wadding. This he opened and in the middle lay three gold sovereigns. He passed the coins over to me with his huge trembling hands and motioned us out roughly. He went back and blew out the oil-lamp and we left Danny alone there in the darkness. Jordan locked the stable

door and the hounds trotted round us growling as we left the garden
through the little door.

'Good night,' said Jordan.

'Good night, brother,' I said.

We walked about in the fields, trying to keep warm, waiting for the
time to go back to get Danny out. Marky had gone icy cold. I was
worried, especially about those dogs. I wished I had a drop of drink inside
my. When we thought everything would be quiet again we went back
to see if it was safe to give Danny the whistle. I threw my coat over the
bottle-glass stuck on top of the garden wall and climbed up. I could see
a candle lit in a downstairs window of the doctor's house and by its light
Jordan moved about inside the room in his nightshirt and nightcap.
Presently his light disappeared and all was in darkness.

An owl in a tree close by started screeching. Marky was frightened and
climbed up on to the garden wall to be near me. There was no sign of
Jordan's dogs in the garden. It was bitterly cold up there on top of the
wall without our coats on. The wind was lazy, it went right through us
instead of going round. It had stopped raining again. There was a moon
now but it was small and a long way off, very high up in the sky, and
shrunken enough to go into your cap.

We waited a long time shivering and afraid to talk. Marky's eyes were
like glass marbles. At last I saw something moving in the shadows by the
stable. My heart shot up hot into my throat. Marky caught hold of me
trembling like a leaf. A figure in white began to creep along the wall. It
was Danny. He must have got out through one of the stable windows.
I whistled softly to him and at that there was uproar. The three hounds
came bounding across the yard from nowhere, making straight for Danny,
baying and snarling like mad. I didn't know what to do for the moment
with fright. The dogs were almost on top of him. Danny sprang on to his
hands and began trotting towards them. His black legs waved in the air
and his nightshirt fell forward and hung down to the ground over his
head. The dogs stopped dead when they saw him. Then they turned
together and galloped away into the shadows howling with fright. When
Danny reached the wall we grabbed him firmly by the ankles and pulled
him up out of the garden at one pluck. We were not long getting back
to our lodging house. The next morning we paid our landlord and the
brake driver with one of the sovereigns we had had off Jordan.

I didn't have any luck. All the rest of the summer it was still wet and there
were hardly any flies. I tried selling elephant charms, very lucky, guaranteed, but the harvest failed and in the end I couldn't even give them
away. Danny got thinner and thinner and more quiet. He was like a rush.
He had nothing to say. There never was much in his head except the roots
of his hair. Having been a corpse was on his mind. And he was like a real

corpse to sleep with, as cold as ice and all bones. He lost interest even in standing on his hands.

We visited a lot of towns that held fairs but without much luck. One market day we were sitting in a coffee tavern. It was a ramshackle place built of wooden planks put up for the market day in a field behind the main street. The floor was only grass and the tables and benches stood on it. You could get a plate of peas and a cup of tea there cheap. Danny didn't care about food now even when we had it. Because it was market day this coffee tavern was crowded. It was very close inside, enough to make you faint, and the wasps were buzzing everywhere. All the people around us were jabbering Welsh and eating food out of newspapers.

Presently, above the noise, I heard a bumping and clicking sound in the passage. I felt as though a bath-full of icy water had shot over me inside my clothes. I looked round but there was no way to escape. Then I heard the funeral hymn. In a minute Jordan was standing in the entrance of the coffee tavern. He was huge, bigger than ever, a doorful. In one hand was his roped-up stick and in the other his black hymn-book. His broad-brimmed hat was on his head, but instead of his wig he had a yellow silk handkerchief under it with the corners knotted. He stopped singing and stood in the doorway looking round for an empty seat. A man from our table just then finished his peas and went out. Jordan saw the empty place and hobbled in. We couldn't escape him. He came clicking through the eating crowd like an earthquake and sat down at our table opposite us.

At first I didn't know what to do. Danny had never seen Jordan and was staring down at the grease floating on his tea. I tried to go on leading the peas up to my mouth on my spoon but I could hardly do it. Jordan was opposite, watching me. He could see I was shaking. I pretended to fight the wasps. I could feel his bright bunged-up eyes on me all the time. He put his arms in a ring on the table and leaned over towards me. I was spilling the peas in my fright. I couldn't go on any longer. I lowered my spoon and looked at him. He was so hideous at close quarters I almost threw up. The big black block of his nose reached out at me, full of worm-holes, and the rest of his face looked as though it had been dragged open with hooks. But he was smiling.

'Jordan,' I said, although my tongue was like a lump of cork. 'Mr Jordan.'

He nodded. 'You've come back,' he said. 'Where have you been keeping?'

The whole coffee tavern seemed to be trembling with his movements. I felt as though I was in the stifling loft of some huge pipe-organ, with the din coming out full blast and all the hot woodwork in a shudder. His question had me stammering. I told him I had been busy. My business kept me moving, I travelled about a lot. The wooden building around

me felt suffocating, airless as a glasshouse. I glanced at Danny. He looked
as though he had been tapped and all his blood run off. Even his yellow
ears had turned chalky.

Jordan nodded again, grinning his terrible grin. 'The chick born in hell
returns to the burning,' he said. All the time he watched me from under
the front knot of his yellow handkerchief. He ignored Danny althogether.
His eyes were small, but they looked as though each one had had a good
polish before being put into his head.

'Our bargain was a good one,' he went on, still smiling. 'Very good.
It turned out well.'

I was afraid he would hear my swallow at work, it sounded loud even
above the jabbering. 'I am glad,' I said, 'I did my best. I always do my
best.'

'My master was pleased,' he said. He leaned farther forward and
beckoned me towards him. I bent my head to listen and his wooden nose
was up touching my ear. 'A splendid corpse,' he whispered. 'Inside, a
mass of corruption. Tumours and malignant growths. Exactly what my
master needed. Cut up beautifully, it did.'

There was a loud sigh from Danny. When I turned to look at him he
wasn't there. He had gone down off his bench in a heap on the grass.
People all round got up from their tables and crowded round. Some of
them waved their arms and shouted. 'Give him air,' they said, 'he's
fainted. Give him air.' For a minute I forgot all about Jordan. I told the
people Danny was my friend. They carried him out of the coffee tavern
and laid him on the grass at the side of the road. 'Loosen his neck,'
somebody said, and his rubber breast and collar were snatched off
showing his black coms underneath. The crowd came on like flies round
jam. At last Danny opened his eyes. Someone brought him a glass of
water out of the coffee tavern. He sat up, bowed his shoulders and put
his hands over his face as though he was crying. I spotted something then
I had never noticed before. There was a big bald hole in his red hair at
the top of his head. He looked sickly. But before long he could stand
again. I pushed his breast and collar into my pocket and took him back
to our lodging house. I looked round but I couldn't see Jordan at all in
the crowd. Danny was in bed for a week. He was never the same again.
For one thing if he cut himself shaving he didn't bleed. The only thing
that came out of the cut was a kind of yellow water.

Before the year was out I had buried Danny. It was wild weather and
he caught a cold standing about half-naked in his tights in the fairs and
markets. He took to his bed in our lodgings. Soon he was light-headed
and then unconscious. Every night I sat by him in our bedroom under
the roof with the candle lit listening to his breathing.

One night I dropped off to sleep in the chair and he woke me up screaming. He dreamt Jordan was trying to chop his hands off to make him walk on the stumps. I was terrified at the noise he made. The candle went out and the roar of the wind sawing at the roof of the house was deafening. My heart was thumping like a drum as I tried to relight the candle. I couldn't stop Danny screaming. A few minutes later he died with a yell. Poor Danny. Being a corpse was too much for him. He never struggled out from under the paws of his memories.

The next night the man from the parish came. He asked me if I wasn't ashamed to bury my friend like that. He meant that Danny hadn't had a shave for a week. In the candle-light he had a bright copper beard and he wasn't quite so much like a cow. When the man had gone I started to shave the corpse. It was hard doing it by candle-light. High up on the cheek-bone I must have done something wrong, I must have cut him, because he opened one of his eyes and looked hard at me with it. I was more careful after that. I didn't want to open that vein they say is full of lice.

The morning of the funeral I borrowed a black tie off our landlord. I bummed a wreath on strap. It was very pretty. It was a lot of white flowers on wires made into the shape of a little arm-chair. In the bars of the back was a card with the word 'Rest' on it done in forget-me-nots. Danny always liked something religious like that.

There was nobody in the funeral except the parson and me and two gravediggers. It was a bad day in autumn and very stormy. The long grass in the graveyard was lying down smooth under the flow of the wind. There was some willow trees around the wall all blown bare except for a few leaves sticking to the thin twigs like hair-nits. The parson in his robes was a thin man but he looked fat in the wind. As he gabbled the service the big dried-up leaves blown along the path scratched at the gravel with webbed fingers, like cut-off hands. I wanted to run away. When Danny was in the earth the gravediggers left. The parson and I sang a funeral hymn. The wind was roaring. As we were singing I heard another voice joining in in the distance. It was faint. I had been waiting for it. I didn't need to look round. I knew the sound of the voice and the clicking leg. They came closer and closer. Soon the voice was deafening, the sad hymn roaring like a waterfall beside me. Jordan came right up and stood between me and the parson, touching me. For shaking he was like a giant tree hurling off the storm. His little black book was in his hand. Even in the wind I could smell the strong mouldiness that came off him, clammy as grave-clay. He was bigger than ever. The brim of his black hat was spread out like a roof over my head. As he stood beside me he seemed to be absorbing me. He put his arm with the night-stick in his hand around my shoulders. I felt as though I was gradually disappearing inside his huge body. The ground all around me melted, the path began to flow faster and faster past my feet like a rushing river. I tried to shout out in my terror. I fainted.

When I came round the parson was beside me. We were sitting on the heap of earth beside Danny's open grave. I was as wet as the bed of the river with fright. When I spoke to the parson about Jordan he humoured me. That was a fortnight ago. Yesterday when I cut myself shaving I didn't bleed. All that came out of the cut was a drop or two of yellow water. I won't be long now. I am finished. I wouldn't advise anybody to try crossing Jordan.

The Thing in the Cellar

David H. Keller

It was a huge cellar, entirely out of proportion to the size of the house above it. The owner admitted that it was probably built for a distinctly different kind of structure from that which rose above it. Probably the first house had been burned and poverty had caused a diminution of the dwelling erected to take its place.

A winding stone stairway connected the cellar with the kitchen. Round the base of this series of steps successive owners of the house had placed their firewood, winter vegetables and junk. The junk had gradually been pushed back till it rose, head high, in a barricade of uselessness. What was behind that barricade no one knew and no one cared. For some hundreds of years no one had crossed it to penetrate to the black reaches of the cellar behind it.

At the top of the steps, separating the kitchen from the cellar, was a stout oaken door. This door was, in a way, as peculiar and out of relation to the rest of the house as the cellar. It was a strange kind of door to find in a modern house, and certainly a most unusual door to find in the inside of the house – thick, stoutly built, dextrously rabbeted together, with huge wrought iron hinges and a lock that looked as though it came from Castle Despair. Separating a house from the outside world, such a door would be excusable; swinging between kitchen and cellar it seemed peculiarly inappropriate.

From the earliest months of his life, Tommy Tucker seemed unhappy in the kitchen. In the front parlour, in the formal dining-room, and especially on the first floor of the house, he acted like a normal, healthy child; but carry him to the kitchen and he began at once to cry. His parents, being plain people, ate in the kitchen save when they had company. Being poor, Mrs Tucker did most of her work, though occasionally she had a charwoman in to do the extra Saturday cleaning, and thus much of her time was spent in the kitchen. And Tommy stayed with her, at least as long as he was unable to walk. Much of the time he was decidedly unhappy.

When Tommy learned to crawl, he lost no time in leaving the kitchen.

No sooner was his mother's back turned than the little fellow crawled as fast as he could for the doorway opening into the front of the house, the dining-room and the parlour. Once away from the kitchen he seemed happy; at least he ceased to cry. On being returned to the kitchen, his howls so thoroughly convinced the neighbours that he had colic, that more than one bowl of catnip and sage tea was brought to his assistance.

It was not until the boy learned to talk that the Tuckers had any idea as to what made him cry so hard when he was in the kitchen. In other words, the baby had to suffer for many months before he obtained at least a little relief, and even when he told his parents what was the matter they were absolutely unable to comprehend. This is not to be wondered at, because they were both hard-working, rather simple-minded persons.

What they finally learned from their little son was this: that if the cellar door was shut and securely fastened with the heavy iron lock, Tommy could at least eat a meal in peace; if the door was simply closed but not locked, he shivered with fear but kept quiet; but if the door was open, if even the slightest streak of black showed that it was not tightly shut, then the little three-year-old would scream himself to the point of exhaustion, especially if his tired father refused him permission to leave the kitchen.

Playing in the kitchen, the child developed two interesting habits. Rags, scraps of paper and splinters of wood were continually being pushed under the thick oak door to fill the space between the door and the sill. Whenever Mrs Tucker opened the door there was always some trash there, placed by her son. It annoyed her, and more than once the little fellow was thrashed for this conduct, but punishment acted in no way as a deterrent. The other habit was as singular. Once the door was closed and locked, he would rather boldly walk up to it and caress the old lock. Even when he was so small that he had to stand on tiptoe to touch it with the tips of his fingers he would touch it with slow caressing strokes; later on, as he grew, he used to kiss it.

His father, who only saw the boy at the end of the day, decided that there was no sense in such conduct, and in his masculine way tried to break the lad of his foolishness. There was, of necessity, no effort on the part of the boy's hard-working parent to understand the psychology behind his son's conduct. All that the man knew was that his little son was acting in a way that was decidedly queer.

Tommy loved his mother and was willing to do anything he could to help her in the household tasks, but one thing he would not do, and never did do, and that was to fetch and carry between the house and the cellar. If his mother opened the door, he would run screaming from the room, and he never returned voluntarily till he was assured that the door was closed.

He never explained why he acted as he did. In fact, he refused to talk about it, at least to his parents, and that was just as well, because had he done so, they would simply have been more positive than ever that there was something wrong with their only child. They tried, in their own way, to break the child of his unusual habits; failing to change him at all, they decided to ignore his peculiarities.

That is, they ignored them until he became six years old and the time came for him to go to school. He was a sturdy little chap by that time, and more intelligent than the usual boys beginning in the primer class. Mr Tucker was, at times, proud of him; the child's attitude towards the cellar door was the one thing most disturbing to the father's pride. Finally, nothing would do but that the Tucker family should call on the local physician. It was an important event in the life of the Tuckers; so important that it demanded the wearing of Sunday clothes and all that sort of thing.

'The matter is just this, Dr Hawthorn,' said Mr Tucker in a somewhat embarrassed manner. 'Our little Tommy is old enough to start school but he behaves childish in regard to our cellar, and the missus and I thought you could tell us what to do about it. It must be his nerves.'

'Ever since he was a baby,' continued Mrs Tucker, taking up the thread of the conversation where her husband has paused, 'Tommy has had a great fear of the cellar. Even now, big boy that he is, he does not love me enough to fetch and carry for me through that door and down those steps. It is not natural for a child to act as he does, and what with chinking the cracks with rags and kissing the lock, he drives me to the point where I fear he may become daft-like as he grows older.'

The doctor, eager to satisfy new customers, and dimly remembering some lectures on the nervous system received when he was a medical student, asked some general questions, listened to the boy's heart, examined his lungs and looked at his eyes and finger-nails. At last he commented,

'Looks like a fine healthy boy to me.'

'Yes, all except the cellar door,' said father.

'Has he ever been sick?'

'Naught but fits once or twice when he cried himself blue in the face,' answered the mother.

'Frightened?'

'Perhaps. It was always in the kitchen.'

'Suppose you go out and let me talk to Tommy by myself.'

And there sat the doctor, very much at his ease, and the little six-year-old boy very uneasy.

'Tommy, what is there in the cellar that you're afraid of?'

'I don't know.'

'Have you ever seen it?'

'No, sir.'

'Ever heard it? Smelt it?'

'No, sir.'

'Then how do you know there is something there?'

'Because.'

'Because what?'

'Because there is.'

That was as far as Tommy would go, and at last his seeming obstinacy annoyed the physician even as it had for several years annoyed Mr Tucker. He went to the door and called the parents into the room.

'He thinks there is something down in the cellar,' he stated.

The Tuckers simply looked at each other.

'That's foolish,' commented Mr Tucker.

' 'Tis just a plain cellar with junk and firewood and cider barrels in it,' added Mrs Tucker. 'Since we moved into that house I have not missed a day without going down those stone steps and I know there is nothing there. But the lad has always screamed when the door was open. I recall now that since he was a child in arms he has always screamed when the door was open.'

'He thinks there is something there,' said the doctor.

'That is why we brought him to you,' replied the father. 'It's the child's nerves. Perhaps feetida or something will calm him.'

'I will tell you what to do,' advised the doctor. 'He thinks there is something there. Just as soon as he finds he is wrong and there is nothing there, he will forget about it. He has been humoured too much. What you want to do is to open that cellar door and make him stay by himself in the kitchen. Nail the door open so that he cannot close it. Leave him alone there for an hour, and then go and laugh at him and show him how silly it was for him to be afraid of an empty cellar. I will give you some nerve and blood tonic, and that will help, but the big thing is to show him that there is nothing to be afraid of.'

On the way back to the Tucker home, Tommy broke away from his parents. They caught him after an exciting chase and kept him between them for the rest of the way home. Once in the house he disappeared, and was found in the guest-room under the bed. The afternoon being already spoiled for Mr Tucker, he determined to keep the child under observation for the rest of the day. Tommy ate no supper, in spite of the urgings of the unhappy mother. The dishes were washed, the evening paper read, the evening pipe smoked; and then, and only then, did Mr Tucker take down his tool box and get out a hammer and some long nails.

'And I am going to nail the door open, Tommy, so you cannot close it, as that was what the doctor said, Tommy, and you are to be a man and stay here in the kitchen alone for an hour, and we will leave the lamp a-burning and then, when you find there is naught to be afraid of, you will be well and a real man and not something for a man to be ashamed of being the father of.'

But at the last, Mrs Tucker kissed Tommy and cried and whispered to her husband not to do it, and to wait till the boy was larger; but nothing was to do except to nail the thick door open, so it could not be shut, and leave the boy there alone with the lamp burning and the dark open space of the doorway to look at with eyes that grew as hot and burning as the flame of the lamp.

That same day Dr Hawthorn took supper with a classmate of his, a man who specialized in psychiatry, and who was particularly interested in children. Hawthorn told Johnson about his newest case, the little Tucker boy, and asked him for his opinion. Johnson frowned.

'Children are odd, Hawthorn. Perhaps they are like dogs. It may be their nervous system is more acute than in the adult. We know that our eyesight is limited, also our hearing and smell. I firmly believe there are forms of life which exist in such a form that we can neither see, hear nor smell them. Fondly we delude ourselves into the fallacy of believing that they do not exist because we cannot prove their existence. This Tucker lad may have a nervous system that is peculiarly acute. He may dimly appreciate the existence of something in the cellar which is unappreciable to his parents. Evidently there is some basis in this fear of his. Now I am not saying that there is anything in the cellar. In fact, I suppose that it is just an ordinary cellar, but this boy, since he was a baby, has thought that there was something there, and that is just as bad as though there actually were. What I would like to know is what makes him think so. Give me the address and I will call tomorrow and have a talk with the little fellow.'

'What do you think of my advice?'

'Sorry, old man, but I think it was perfectly rotten. If I were you, I would step round there on my way home and prevent them from following it. The little fellow may be badly frightened. You see, he evidently thinks there is something there.'

'But there isn't.'

'Perhaps not. No doubt he is wrong, but he thinks so.'

It all worried Dr Hawthorn so much that he decided to take his friend's advice. It was a cold night, a foggy night, and the physician felt cold as he tramped along the streets. At last he came to the Tucker house. He remembered now that he had been there once before, long years ago, when little Tommy Tucker came into the world. There was a light in the front window and in no time at all Mr Tucker came to the door.

'I have come to see Tommy,' said the doctor.

'He is back in the kitchen,' replied the father.

'He gave one cry but since then he has been quiet,' sobbed the wife.

'If I had let her have her way she would have opened the door, but

I said to her, "Mother, now is the time to make a man out of our Tommy." And I guess he knows by now that there was naught to be afraid of. Well, the hour is up. Suppose we go and get him and put him to bed?'

'It has been a hard time for the little child,' whispered the wife.

Carrying the candle, the man walked ahead of the woman and the doctor and at last opened the kitchen door. The room was dark.

'Lamp has gone out,' said the man. 'Wait till I light it.'

'Tommy! Tommy!' called Mrs Tucker.

But the doctor ran to where a white form was stretched on the floor. Sharply he called for more light. Trembling, he examined all that was left of little Tommy. Twitching, he looked down the open space into the cellar. At last he turned to Tucker and Tucker's wife.

'Tommy – Tommy's been hurt,' he stammered. 'I guess he's dead.'

The mother threw herself on the floor and picked up the torn, mutilated thing that had been only a little while ago her little Tommy.

The man took his hammer and drew out the nails and closed the door and locked it, and then drove in a long spike to reinforce the lock. Then he took hold of the doctor's shoulders and shook him.

'What killed him, Doctor? What killed him?' he shouted into Hawthorn's ear.

The doctor looked at him bravely in spite of the fear in his throat.

'How do I know, Tucker?' he replied. 'How do I know? Didn't you tell me that there was nothing there? Nothing down there? In the cellar?'

Suffer the Little Children

Stephen King

Miss Sidley was her name, and teaching was her game.

She was a small woman who had to reach on tiptoes to write on the highest level of the blackboard, which she was doing now. Behind her, none of the children giggled or whispered or munched on secret sweets held in cupped hands. They knew Miss Sidley too well. Miss Sidley knew instinctively who was chewing gum at the back of the room, who had a beanshooter in his pocket, who wanted to go to the bathroom to trade baseball cards rather than use the facilities. Like God, she seemed to know everything all at once.

She was greying, and the brace she wore to support her failing back was lined clearly against her print dress. Small, constantly suffering, gimlet-eyed woman. But they feared her. Her tongue was a school-yard legend. The eyes, when turned on a giggler or a whisperer, could turn the stoutest knees to water.

Now, writing the day's list of spelling words on the slate, she reflected that the success of her long teaching career could be summed and checked and proven by this one everyday action. She could turn her back on her pupils in confidence.

'Vacation,' she said, pronouncing the word as she wrote it in her firm, no-nonsense script. 'Edward, you will please use the word *vacation* in a sentence.'

'I went on a vacation to New York City,' Edward piped. Then, as Miss Sidley had taught, he repeated the word carefully. 'Vay-cay-shun.'

'Very good, Edward.' She began the next word.

She had her little tricks, of course; success, she firmly believed, depended as much upon taking note of little things as it did upon the big ones. She applied the principle constantly in the classroom, and it never failed.

'Jane,' she said quietly.

Jane, who had been furtively perusing her Reader, looked up guiltily.

'Close that book right now, please.' The book shut; Jane looked pale, hating eyes at Miss Sidley's back. 'And you will stay for fifteen minutes after the final bell.'

Jane's lips trembled. 'Yes, Miss Sidley.'

One of her little tricks was the careful use of her glasses. The whole class was reflected to her in their thick lenses and she had always been thinly amused by their guilty frightened faces when she caught them at their nasty little games.

Now she saw a phantomish, distorted Robert in the first row wrinkle his nose. She did not speak. Robert would hang himself if given just a little more rope.

'Tomorrow,' she pronounced clearly. 'Robert, you will please use the word tomorrow in a sentence.' Robert frowned over the problem. The classroom was hushed and sleepy in the late September sun. The electric clock over the door buzzed a rumour of three o'clock dismissal just a half-hour away and the only thing that kept young heads from drowsing over their spellers was the silent, ominous threat of Miss Sidley's back.

'I am waiting, Robert.'

'Tomorrow a bad thing will happen,' Robert said. The words were perfectly innocuous, but Miss Sidley, with the seventh sense that all strict disciplinarians have, could sense a double meaning.

'Too-mor-row,' Robert finished. His hands were folded neatly on the desk, and he wrinkled his nose again. He also smiled a tiny side-of-the-mouth smile. Miss Sidley was suddenly unaccountably sure Robert knew her little trick with the glasses.

Very well.

She began to write the next word with no comment of commendation for Robert, letting her straight body speak its own message. She watched carefully with one eye. Soon Robert would stick out his tongue or make that disgusting finger gesture, just to see if she really knew what he was doing. Then he would be punished.

The reflection was small, ghostly, and distorted. And she had all but the barest corner of her eye on the word she was writing.

Robert changed.

She caught just a corner of it, just a frightening glimpse of Robert's face changing into something . . . different.

She whirled around, face white, barely noticing the protesting stab of pain in her back.

Robert looked at her blandly, questioningly. His hands were neatly folded. The first signs of an afternoon cowlick showed at the back of his head. He did not look frightened.

I have imagined it, she thought. I was looking for something, and when there was nothing, I just made something up. However——

'Robert?' she asked. She had meant to be authoritative; the unspoken demand for confession. It did not come out that way.

'Yes, Miss Sidley?' His eyes were a very dark brown, like the mud at the bottom of a slow-running stream.

'Nothing.'

She turned back to the board and a little whisper ran through the class.

'Be *quiet!*' her voice snapped. She turned again and faced them. 'Another sound and we will all stay after school with Jane!' She addressed the whole class, but looked particularly at Robert. He looked back with a child-like I-didn't-do-it innocence.

She turned to the board and began to write, not looking out of the corners of her glasses. The last half-hour dragged, and it seemed that Robert gave her a strange look on the way out. A look that said, *we have a secret, don't we?*

It wouldn't get out of her mind.

It seemed to be stuck like a tiny string of roast beef between two molars, a small thing, actually, but feeling as big as a cinderblock.

She sat down to her solitary dinner at five, poached eggs on toast, still thinking about it. She knew she was getting older and accepted the knowledge calmly. She was not going to be one of those old lady schoolteachers dragged kicking and screaming from their classrooms at the age of retirement. They reminded her of gamblers emotionally unable to leave the tables while they were losing. But *she* was not losing. She had always been a winner.

She looked down at her poached egg.

Hadn't she?

She thought of the well-scrubbed faces in her third grade classroom, and found Robert's face superimposed over them.

She got up and switched on a light.

Later, just before dropping off to sleep, Robert's face floated in front of her, smiling unpleasantly in the darkness behind her lids. The face began to change——

But before she saw exactly what it was changing into, she dropped off to sleep.

Miss Sidley spent an unrestful night and the next day her temper was short. She waited, almost hoped for a whisperer, a giggler, or perhaps even a note-passer. But the class was quiet – very quiet. They all stared at her unresponsively, and it seemed that she could feel the weight of their eyes on her like blind, crawling ants.

Now stop! she told herself sternly. She paused, controlling an urge to bite her lip. She was acting like a skittish girl just out of Seminary.

Again the day seemed to drag, and she believed she was more relieved than her charges when the dismissal bell rang. The children lined up in orderly rows at the door, boys and girls by height, hands dutifully linked.

'Dismissed,' she said, and listened sourly as they shrieked down the hall and into the bright sunlight.

What was it? It was bulbous. It shimmered and it changed and it stared at me, yes, stared and grinned and it wasn't a child at all. It was old and it was evil and——

'Miss Sidley?'

Her head jerked up; a little *oh!* hiccupped involuntarily from her throat.

It was Mr Hanning. He smiled apologetically. 'Didn't mean to disturb you.'

'Quite all right,' she said, more curtly than she had intended. What had she been thinking? What was wrong with her?

'Would you mind checking the paper towels in the girls' lavatory?'

'Surely.' She got up, placing her hands against the small of her back.

Mr Hanning looked at her sympathetically. Save it, she thought. The old maid is not amused. Or even interested.

She brushed by Mr Hanning and started down the hall to the girls' lavatory. A capering group of small boys, carrying scratched and pitted baseball equipment, grew silent at the sight of her and leaked out the door, where their cries began again.

Miss Sidley looked after them resentfully, reflecting that children had been different in her day. Not more polite – children have never had time for that – and not exactly more respectful of their elders; it was a kind of hypocrisy that had never been there before. A smiling quietness around adults that had never been there before. A kind of quiet contempt that was upsetting and unnerving. As if they were ...

Hiding behind masks.

She pushed the thought away and went into the lavatory.

It was a small, tiled room with frosted glass windows, shaped like an L. The toilets were ranged along one bar, the sinks along both sides of the shorter bar.

As she checked along the paper towel containers, she caught a glimpse of her face in one of the mirrors and was startled into looking at it more closely.

God.

There was a look that hadn't been there two days before, a frightened, watching look. With sudden shock she realized that the tiny, blurred reflection in her glasses coupled with Robert's pale, respectful face had gotten inside her and was festering.

The door opened and she heard two girls come in, giggling secretly about something. She was about to turn the corner and walk out past them when she heard her own name. She turned back to the washbowls and began checking the towel holders again.

'And then he——'

Soft giggles.

'She knows, but——'

More giggles, soft and sticky as melting soap.

'Miss Sidley is——'
Stop it! Stop that noise!
By moving slightly she could see their shadows, made fuzzy and ill-defined by the diffuse light filtering through the frosted windows, holding on to each other with girlish glee.
Another thought crawled up out of her mind.
They knew she was there.
Yes, they did, the little bitches. They knew.
She would shake them. Shake them until their teeth rattled and their giggles turned to wails and she would make them admit that they knew, they knew, they——
The shadows changed.
They seemed to elongate, to flow like dripping tallow, taking on strange, hunched shapes that made Miss Sidley cringe back against the porcelain washstands, her heart swelling in her chest.
But they went on giggling.
The voiced changed, no longer girlish, now sexless and soulless, and quite, quite evil. A slow, turgid sound of mindless humour that flowed around the corner to her like river mud.
She stared at the hunched shadows and suddenly screamed at them. The scream went on and on, swelling in her head until it attained a pitch of lunacy. And then she fainted. The giggling, like the laughter of demons, followed her down into darkness.
She could not, of course, tell them the truth.
Miss Sidley knew this even as she opened her eyes and looked up at the anxious faces of Mr Hanning and Mrs Crossen. Mrs Crossen was holding a bottle of sharp smelling stuff under her nose. Mr Hanning turned around and told the two little girls who were looking curiously at Miss Sidley to go on home now, please.
They both smiled at her, slow, we-have-a-secret smiles, and went out.
Very well. She would keep their secret. For a while. She would not have people thinking her insane. She would not have them thinking that the first feelers of senility had touched her early. She would play their game. Until she could expose their nastiness and rip it out. By the roots.
'I'm afraid I slipped,' she said calmly, sitting up and ignoring the excruciating pain in her back. 'A patch of wetness.'
'This is awful,' Mr Hanning said. 'Terrible. Are you——'
'Did the fall hurt your back, Emily?' Mrs Crossen interrupted. Mr Hanning looked at her gratefully.
Miss Sidley got up, her spine screaming in her body.
'No,' she said. 'In fact, something seems to have snapped back into place. It actually feels better.'
'We can send for a——' Mr Hanning began.

'No physician necessary. I'll just go on home.' Miss Sidley smiled at him coolly.

'I'll get you a taxi.'

'I always take the bus,' Miss Sidley said. She walked out.

Mr Hanning sighed and looked at Mrs Crossen. 'She *does* seem more like herself——'

The next day Miss Sidley kept Robert after school. He did nothing, so she simply accused him falsely. She felt no qualms; he was a monster, not a little boy. And she would make him admit it.

Her back was in agony. She realized Robert knew; he expected that would help him. But it wouldn't. That was another of her little advantages. Her back had been a constant pain to her for the last twelve years, and there had been times when it had been this bad – well, almost as bad – as this.

She closed the door, shutting the two of them in.

For a moment she stood still, training her gaze on Robert. She waited for him to drop his eyes. He didn't. He gazed back at her, and presently a little smile began to play around the corners of his mouth.

'Why are you smiling, Robert?' she asked softly.

'I don't know.' Robert went on smiling.

'Tell me, please, Robert.'

Robert said nothing. He went on smiling.

The outside sounds of children at play were far off, distant, dreamy. Only the hypnotic buzz of the wall clock was real.

'There's quite a few of us,' Robert said suddenly, as if he were commenting on the weather.

It was Miss Sidley's turn to be silent.

'Eleven right here in this school.' Robert went on smiling his small smile.

Quite evil, she thought, amazed. Very, incredibly evil.

'Please don't lie,' she said clearly. 'Lies only make things worse.'

Robert's smile grew wider; it became vulpine. 'Do you want to see me change, Miss Sidley?' he asked. 'Would you like to see it right out?'

Miss Sidley felt a nameless chill. 'Go away,' she said curtly. 'And bring your mother and father to school with you tomorrow. We'll get this business straightened out.' There. On solid ground again. She waited for his face to crumble, waited for the tears and the pleas to relent.

Robert's smile grew wider. He showed his teeth. 'It will be just like Show and Tell, won't it, Miss Sidley? Robert – the *other* Robert – he liked Show and Tell. He's still hiding 'way, 'way down in my head.' The smile curled at the corners of his mouth like charring paper. 'Sometimes he runs around . . . it itches. He wants me to let him out.'

'Go away,' Miss Sidley said numbly. The buzzing of the clock seemed very loud.

Robert changed.

His face suddenly ran together like melting wax, the eyes flattening and spreading like knife-struck egg yolks, nose widening and yawning, mouth disappearing. The head elongated, and the hair was suddenly not hair but straggling, twitching growths.

Robert began to chuckle.

The slow, cavernous sound came from what had been his nose, but the nose was eating into the lower half of his face, nostrils meeting and merging into a central blackness like a huge, shouting mouth.

Robert got up, still chuckling, and behind it all she could see the last shattered remains of the other Robert, howling in maniac terror, screeching to be let out.

She ran.

She fled screaming down the corridor, and the few late-leaving pupils turned to look at her with large and uncomprehending eyes.

Mr Hanning jerked open his door and looked out just as Miss Sidley plunged through the wide glass front doors, a wild, waving scarecrow silhouetted against the bright September sky.

He ran after her, Adam's apple bobbing convulsively 'Miss Sidley! *Miss Sidley!*'

Robert came out of the classroom and watched curiously.

Miss Sidley neither heard nor saw. She clattered down the walk and across the sidewalk and into the streets with her screams trailing behind her like banners. There was a huge, blatting horn and then the bus was looming over her, the bus driver's face a plaster mask of fear. Air brakes whined and hissed like dragons in flight.

Miss Sidley fell, and the huge wheels shuddered to a smoking stop just eight inches from her frail, brace-armoured body. She lay shuddering on the pavement, hearing the crowd gather around her.

She turned over and the children were staring down at her. They were ringed in a tight little circle, like mourners around an open grave. And at the head of the grave was Robert, his little face sober and solemn, ready to read the death rites and shovel the first spade of dirt over her face.

From far away, the bus driver's shaken babble: '. . . crazy or somethin' . . . my God, another half a foot . . .'

Miss Sidley stared numbly at the children. Their shadows covered her and blocked out the sun. Their faces were impassive. Some of them were smiling little secret smiles, and Miss Sidley knew that soon she would begin to scream again.

Then Mr Hanning broke their tight noose and shooed them away.

Miss Sidley began to sob weakly.

She did not go back to her third grade for a month. She told Mr Hanning calmly that she had not been feeling herself, and Mr Hanning suggested that she go to a reputable, ah, doctor, and discuss the matter with him. Miss Sidley agreed that this was the only sensible and rational course. She also said that if the school board wished her resignation she would tender it immediately, although it would hurt her very much. Mr Hanning, looking uncomfortable, said he doubted if that would be necessary.

The upshot of the matter was that Miss Sidley went back to her class in late October, once again ready to play the game and now knowing how to play it.

For the first week she let things go on as ever. It seemed the whole class now regarded her with hostile, shielded eyes. Robert smiled distantly at her from his first-row seat, and she did not have the courage to take him to task.

Once, while on playground duty, Robert walked over to her, holding a dodgem ball, smiling. 'There's more of us now,' he said. 'Lots, lots more.' A girl on the jungle gym looked across the playground at them and smiled, as if she had heard.

Miss Sidley smiled serenely, refusing to remember the face changing, mutating: 'Why, Robert, whatever do you mean?'

But Robert only continued smiling and went back to his game. Miss Sidley knew the time had come.

She brought the gun to school in her handbag.

It had been her brother Jim's. He had taken it from a dead German shortly after the Battle of the Bulge. Jim had been gone ten years now. She had not opened the box that held the gun in more years than that, but when she did it was still there, gleaming dully. The four clips of shells were still in the box, too, and she loaded carefully the way Jim had showed her once.

She smiled pleasantly at her class; at Robert in particular. Robert smiled back and she could see the murky alienness swimming just below his skin, muddy, full of filth.

She never cared wondering just what was impersonating Robert, but she wished she knew if the real Robert was still inside. She did not wish to be a murderess. She decided that the real Robert must have died or gone insane, living inside the dirty, crawling thing that had chuckled at her in the classroom and sent her screaming into the street. So even if he was still alive, putting him out of his misery would be a mercy.

'Today we're going to have a Test,' Miss Sidley said.

The class did not groan or shift apprehensively; they merely looked at her. She could feel their eyes, like weights. Heavy, smothering.

'It's a very special Test. I will call you down to the mimeographing room one by one and give you your Test. Then you may have a candy and go home for the day. Won't that be nice?'

They smiled empty smiles and said nothing.

'Robert, will you come first?'

Robert got up, smiling his little smile. He wrinkled his nose quite openly at her. 'Yes, Miss Sidley.'

Miss Sidley took her bag and they went down the empty, echoing corridor together, past the sleepy buzz of reciting classes coming from behind closed doors.

The mimeograph room was at the far end of the hall, past the lavatories. It had been soundproofed two years ago; the big machine was very old and very noisy.

Miss Sidley closed the door behind them and locked it.

'No one can hear you,' she said calmly. She took the gun from her bag. 'You or the gun.'

Robert smiled innocently. 'There are lots of us, though. Lots more than here.' He put one small scrubbed hand on the paper-tray of the mimeograph machine. 'Would you like to see me change, Miss Sidley?'

Before she could speak, the change began. Robert's face began to melt and shimmer into the grotesqueness beneath, and Miss Sidley shot him. Once. In the head.

He fell back against the paper-lined shelves and slid down to the floor, a little dead boy with a round black hole above the right eye.

He looked very pathetic.

Miss Sidley stood over him, breathing hard. Her scrawny cheeks were livid.

The huddled figure didn't move.

It was human.

It was Robert.

No!

It was all in your mind, Emily. All in your mind.

No! No, no, *no!*

She went back up to the room and began to lead them down, one by one. She killed twelve of them and would have killed them all if Mrs Crossen hadn't come down for a package of composition paper.

Mrs Crossen's eyes got very big; one hand crept up and clutched her mouth. She began to scream and she was still screaming when Miss Sidley reached her and put a hand on her shoulder. 'It had to be done, Margaret,' she said sadly to the screaming Mrs Crossen. 'It's terrible, but it had to. They are all monsters. I found out.'

Mrs Crossen stared at the gay-clothed little bodies scattered around the mimeograph and continued to scream.

The little girl whose hand Miss Sidley was holding began to cry steadily and monotonously.

'Change,' Miss Sidley said. 'Change for Mrs Crossen. Show her it had to be done.'

The girl continued to weep uncomprehendingly.

'Damn you, *change!*' Miss Sidley screamed. 'Dirty bitch, dirty, crawl-

ing, filthy unnatural *bitch!* Change! God damn you, *change!*' She raised
the gun. The little girl cringed, and then Mrs Crossen was on her like
a cat, and Miss Sidley's back gave way.

No trial.

The papers screamed for a trial, bereaved parents swore hysterical
oaths against Miss Sidley, and the city sat back on its haunches in numb
shock——

——*Twelve children!*

The State Legislature called for more stringent teacher examination
tests, Summer Street School closed for a week of mourning, and Miss
Sidney went quietly to an antiseptic madhouse in the next state. She was
put in deep analysis, given the most modern drugs, introduced into daily
work-therapy sessions. A year later, under strictly controlled conditions,
Miss Sidley was put in an experimental encounter-therapy situation.

Buddy Jenkins was his name, psychiatry was his game.

He sat behind a one-way glass with a clipboard, looking into a room
which had been outfitted as a nursery. On the far wall, the cow was
jumping over the moon and the mouse was halfway up the clock. Miss
Sidley sat in her wheelchair with a story book, surrounded by a group
of soft, trusting, totally mindless retarded children. They smiled at her
and drooled and touched her with small wet fingers while attendants at
the next window watched for the first sign of an aggressive move.

For a time Buddy thought she responded well. She read aloud, stroked
a girl's head, picked up a small boy when he fell over a toy block. Then
she seemed to see something which disturbed her; a frown creased her
brow and she looked away from the children.

'Take me away, please,' Miss Sidley said, softly and tonelessly, to no
one in particular.

And so they took her away. Buddy Jenkins watched the children watch
her go, their eyes wide and empty, but somehow deep. One smiled, and
another put his fingers in his mouth slyly. Two little girls clutched each
other and giggled.

That night Miss Sidley cut her throat with a bit of broken mirror-glass,
and Buddy Jenkins began to watch the children.

The Pond

Nigel Kneale

It was deeply scooped from a corner of the field, a green stagnant hollow with thorn bushes on its banks.

From time to time something moved cautiously beneath the prickly branches that were laden with red autumn berries. It whistled and murmured coaxingly.

'Come, come, come, come,' it whispered. An old man, squatting frog-like on the bank. His words were no louder than the rustling of the dry leaves above his head. 'Come now. Sssst – ssst! Little dear – here's a bit of meat for thee.' He tossed a tiny scrap of something into the pool. The weed rippled sluggishly.

The old man sighed and shifted his position. He was crouching on his haunches, because the bank was damp.

He froze.

The green slime had parted on the far side of the pool. The disturbance travelled to the bank opposite, and a large frog drew itself half out of the water. It stayed quite still, watching; then with a swift crawl it was clear of the water. Its yellow throat throbbed.

'Oh! – little dear,' breathed the old man. He did not move.

He waited, letting the frog grow accustomed to the air and slippery earth. When he judged the moment to be right, he made a low grating noise in his throat.

He saw the frog listen.

The sound was subtly like the call of its own kind. The old man paused, then made it again.

This time the frog answered. It sprang into the pool, sending the green weed slopping, and swam strongly. Only its eyes showed above the water. It crawled out a few feet distant from the old man and looked up the bank, as if eager to find the frog it had heard.

The old man waited patiently. The frog hopped twice, up the bank.

His hand was moving, so slowly that it did not seem to move, towards the handle of the light net at his side. He gripped it, watching the still frog.

Suddenly he struck.

A sweep of the net, and its wire frame whacked the ground about the frog. It leaped frantically, but was helpless in the green mesh.

'Dear! Oh, my dear!' said the old man delightedly.

He stood with much difficulty and pain, his foot on the thin rod. His joints had stiffened and it was some minutes before he could go to the net. The frog was still struggling desperately. He closed the net round its body and picked both up together.

'Ah, big beauty!' he said. 'Pretty. Handsome fellow, you!'

He took a darning needle from his coat lapel and carefully killed the creature through the mouth, so that its skin would not be damaged; then put it in his pocket.

It was the last frog in the pond.

He lashed the water with the handle, and the weed swirled and bobbed: there was no sign of life now but the little flies that flitted on the surface.

He went across the empty field with the net across his shoulder, shivering a little, feeling that the warmth had gone out of his body during the long wait. He climbed a stile, throwing the net over in front of him, to leave his hands free. In the next field, by the road, was his cottage.

Hobbling through the grass with the sun striking a long shadow from him, he felt the weight of the dead frog in his pocket, and was glad.

'Big beauty!' he murmured again.

The cottage was small and dry, and ugly and very old. Its windows gave little light, and they had coloured panels, dark-blue and green, that gave the rooms the appearance of being under the sea.

The old man lit a lamp, for the sun had set; and the light became more cheerful. He put the frog on a plate, and poked the fire, and when he was warm again, took off his coat.

He settled down close beside the lamp and took a sharp knife from the drawer of the table. With great care and patience, he began to skin the frog.

From time to time he took off his spectacles and rubbed his eyes. The work was tiring; also the heat from the lamp made them sore. He would speak aloud to the dead creature, coaxing and cajoling it when he found his task difficult. But in time he had the skin neatly removed, a little heap of tumbled, slippery film. He dropped the stiff stripped body into a pan of boiling water on the fire, and sat again, humming and fingering the limp skin.

'Pretty,' he said. 'You'll be so handsome.'

There was a stump of black soap in the drawer and he took it out to rub the skin, with the slow, over-careful motion that showed the age in his hand. The little mottled thing began to stiffen under the curing action. He left it at last and brewed himself a pot of tea, lifting the lid of the simmering pan occasionally to make sure that the tiny skull and bones were being boiled clean without damage.

Sipping his tea, he crossed the narrow living-room. Well away from the fire stood a high table, its top covered by a square of dark cloth supported on a frame. There was a faint smell of decay.

'How are you, little dears?' said the old man.

He lifted the covering with shaky scrupulousness. Beneath the wire support were dozens of stuffed frogs.

All had been posed in human attitudes; dressed in tiny coats and breeches to the fashion of an earlier time. There were ladies and gentlemen and bowing flunkeys. One, with lace at his yellow, waxen throat, held a wooden wine-cup. To the dried forepaw of its neighbour was stitched a tiny glassless monocle, raised to a black button eye. A third had a midget pipe pressed into its jaws, with a wisp of wool for smoke. The same coarse wool, cleaned and shaped, served the ladies for their miniature wigs; they wore long skirts and carried fans.

The old man looked proudly over the stiff little figures.

'You, my lord – what are you doing, with your mouth so glum?' His fingers prised open the jaws of a round-bellied frog dressed in satins; shrinkage must have closed them. 'Now you can sing again, and drink up!'

His eyes searched the banqueting, motionless party.

'Where now——? Ah!'

In the middle of the table three of the creatures were fixed in the attitudes of a dance.

The old man spoke to them. 'Soon we'll have a partner for the lady there. He'll be the handsomest of the whole company, my dear, so don't forget to smile at him and look your prettiest!'

He hurried back to the fireplace and lifted the pan; poured off the steaming water into a bucket.

'Fine, shapely brain-box you have.' He picked with his knife, cleaning the tiny skull. 'Easy does it.' He put it down on the table, admiringly; it was like a transparent flake of ivory. One by one he found the delicate bones in the pan, knowing each for what it was.

'Now, little duke, we have all of them that we need,' he said at last. 'We can make you into a picture indeed. The beau of the ball. And such an object of jealousy for the lovely ladies!'

With wire and thread he fashioned a stiff little skeleton, binding in the bones to preserve the proportions. At the top went the skull.

The frog's skin had lost its earlier flaccidness. He threaded a needle, eyeing it close to the lamp. From the table drawer he now brought a loose wad of wool. Like a doctor reassuring his patient by describing his methods, he began to talk.

'This wool is coarse. I know, little friend. A poor substitute to fill that skin of yours, you may say: wool from the hedges, snatched by the thorns from a sheep's back.' He was pulling the wad into tufts of the size he required. 'But you'll find it gives you such a springiness that you'll thank me for it. Now, carefully does it——'

With perfect concentration he worked his needle through the skin, drawing it together round the wool with almost untraceable stitches.

'A piece of lace in your left hand, or shall it be a quizzing-glass?' With tiny scissors he trimmed away a fragment of skin. 'But wait – it's a dance and it is your right hand that we must see, guiding the lady.'

He worked the skin precisely into place round the skull. He would attend to the empty eye-holes later.

Suddenly he lowered his needle.

He listened.

Puzzled, he put down the half-stuffed skin and went to the door and opened it.

The sky was dark now. He heard the sound more clearly. He knew it was coming from the pond. A far-off, harsh croaking, as of a great many frogs.

He frowned.

In the wall cupboard he found a lantern ready trimmed, and lit it with a flickering splinter. He put on an overcoat and hat, remembering his earlier chill. Lastly he took his net.

He went very cautiously. His eyes saw nothing at first, after working so close to the lamp. Then, as the croaking came to him more clearly and he grew accustomed to the darkness, he hurried.

He climbed the stile as before, throwing the net ahead. This time, however, he had to search for it in the darkness tantalized by the sounds from the pond. When it was in his hand again, he began to move stealthily.

About twenty yards from the pool he stopped and listened.

There was no wind and the noise astonished him. Hundreds of frogs must have travelled through the fields to this spot; from other water where danger had arisen, perhaps, or drought. He had heard of such instances.

Almost on tiptoe he crept towards the pond. He could see nothing yet. There was no moon, and the thorn-bushes hid the surface of the water.

He was a few paces from the pond when, without warning, every sound ceased.

He froze again. There was absolute silence. Not even a watery plop or splashing told that one frog out of all those hundreds had dived for shelter into the weed. It was strange.

He stepped forward, and heard his boots brushing the grass.

He brought the net up across his chest, ready to strike if he saw anything move. He came to the thorn bushes, and still heard no sound.

Yet, to judge by the noise they had made, they should be hopping in dozens from beneath his feet.

Peering, he made the throaty noise which had called the frog that afternoon. The hush continued.

He looked down at where the water must be. The surface of the pond, shadowed by the bushes, was too dark to be seen. He shivered, and waited.

Gradually, as he stood, he became aware of a smell.

It was wholly unpleasant. Seemingly it came from the weed, yet mixed with the vegetable odour was one of another kind of decay. A soft, oozy bubbling accompanied it. Gases must be rising from the mud at the bottom. It would not do to stay in this place and risk his health.

He stooped, still puzzled by the disappearance of the frogs, and stared once more at the dark surface. Pulling his net to a ready position, he tried the throaty call for the last time.

Instantly he threw himself backwards with a cry.

A vast, belching bubble of foul air shot from the pool. Another gushed up past his head; then another. Great patches of slimy weed were flung high among the thorn branches.

The whole pond seemed to boil.

He turned blindly to escape, and stepped into the thorns. He was in agony. A dreadful slobbering deafened his ears: the stench overcame his senses. He felt the net whipped from his hand. The icy weeds were wet on his face. Reeds lashed him.

Then he was in the midst of an immense, pulsating softness that yielded and received and held him. He knew he was shrieking. He knew there was no one to hear him.

An hour after the sun had risen, the rain slackened to a light drizzle.

A policeman cycled slowly on the road that ran by the cottage, shaking out his cape with one hand, and half-expecting the old man to appear and call out a comment on the weather. Then he caught sight of the lamp, still burning feebly in the kitchen, and dismounted. He found the door ajar, and wondered if something was wrong.

He called to the old man. He saw the uncommon handiwork lying on the table as if it had been suddenly dropped; and the unused bed.

For half an hour the policeman searched in the neighbourhood of the cottage, calling out the old man's name at intervals, before remembering the pond. He turned towards the stile.

Climbing over it, he frowned and began to hurry. He was disturbed by what he saw.

On the bank of the pond crouched a naked figure.

The policeman went closer. He saw it was the old man on his haunches;

his arms were straight; the hands resting between his feet. He did not move as the policeman approached.

'Hallo, there!' said the policeman. He ducked to avoid the thorn bushes catching his helmet. 'This won't do, you know. You can get into trouble——'

He saw green slime in the old man's beard, and the staring eyes. His spine chilled. With an unprofessional distaste, he quickly put out a hand and took the old man by the upper arm. It was cold. He shivered, and moved the arm gently.

Then he groaned and ran from the pond.

For the arm had come away at the shoulder: reeds and green water-plants and slime tumbled from the broken joint.

As the old man fell backwards, tiny green stitches glistened across his belly.

The Graveyard Rats

Henry Kuttner

Old Masson, the caretaker of one of Salem's oldest and most neglected cemeteries, had a feud with the rats. Generations ago they had come up from the wharves and settled in the graveyard, a colony of abnormally large rats, and when Masson had taken charge after the inexplicable disappearance of the former caretaker, he decided that they must go. At first he set traps for them and put poisoned food by their burrows, and later he tried to shoot them, but it did no good. The rats stayed, multiplying and overrunning the graveyard with their ravenous hordes.

They were large, even for the *mus decumanus*, which sometimes measures fifteen inches in length, exclusive of the naked pink and grey tail. Masson had caught glimpses of some as large as good-sized cats, and when, once or twice, the grave-diggers had uncovered their burrows, the malodorous tunnels were large enough to enable a man to crawl into them on his hands and knees. The ships that had come generations ago from distant ports to the rotting Salem wharves had brought strange cargoes.

Masson wondered sometimes at the extraordinary size of these burrows. He recalled certain vaguely disturbing legends he had heard since coming to ancient, witch-haunted Salem – tales of a moribund, inhuman life that was said to exist in forgotten burrows in the earth. The old days, when Cotton Mather had hunted down the evil cults that worshipped Hecate and the dark Magna Mater in frightful orgies, had passed; but dark gabled houses still leaned perilously towards each other over narrow cobbled street, and blasphemous secrets and mysteries were said to be hidden in subterranean cellars and caverns, where forgotten pagan rites were still celebrated in defiance of law and sanity. Wagging their grey heads wisely, the elders declared that there were worse things than rats and maggots crawling in the unhallowed earth of the ancient Salem cemeteries.

And then, too, there was this curious dread of the rats. Masson disliked and respected the ferocious little rodents, for he knew the danger that lurked in their flashing, needle-sharp fangs; but he could not understand the inexplicable horror which the oldsters held for deserted, rat-infested houses. He had heard vague rumours of ghoulish beings that dwelt far underground, and that had the power of commanding the rats, marshalling them like horrible armies. The rats, the old men whispered, were messengers between this world and the grim and ancient caverns far below Salem. Bodies had been stolen from graves for nocturnal subterranean feasts, they said. The myth of the Pied Piper is a fable that hides a blasphemous horror, and the black pits of Avernus have brought forth hell-spawned monstrosities that never venture into the light of day.

Masson paid little attention to these tales. He did not fraternize with his neighbours, and, in fact, did all he could to hide the existence of the rats from intruders. Investigation, he realized, would undoubtedly mean the opening of many graves. And while some of the gnawed, empty coffins could be attributed to the activities of the rats, Masson might find it difficult to explain the mutilated bodies that lay in some of the coffins.

The purest gold is used in filling teeth, and this gold is not removed when a man is buried. Clothing, of course, is another matter; for usually the undertaker provides a plain broadcloth suit that is cheap and easily recognizable. But gold is another matter; and sometimes, too, there were medical students and less reputable doctors who were in need of cadavers, and not over-scrupulous as to where these were obtained.

So far Masson has successfully managed to discourage investigation. He had fiercely denied the existence of the rats, even though they sometimes robbed him of his prey. Masson did not care what happened to the bodies after he had performed his gruesome thefts, but the rats inevitably dragged away the whole cadaver through the hole they gnawed in the coffin.

The size of these burrows occasionally worried Masson. Then, too, there was the curious circumstance of the coffins always being gnawed open at the end, never at the side or top. It was almost as though the rats were working under the direction of some impossibly intelligent leader.

Now he stood in an open grave and threw a last sprinkling of wet earth on the heap beside the pit. It was raining, a slow, cold drizzle that for weeks had been descending from soggy black clouds. The graveyard was a slough of yellow, sucking mud, from which the rain-washed tombstones stood up in irregular battalions. The rats had retreated to their burrows, and Masson had not seen one for days. But his gaunt, unshaved face was set in frowning lines; the coffin on which he was standing was a wooden one.

The body had been buried several days earlier, but Masson had not dared to disinter it before. A relative of the dead man had been coming to the grave at intervals, even in the drenching rain. But he would hardly come at this late hour, no matter how much grief he might be suffering, Masson thought, grinning wryly. He straightened and laid the shovel aside.

From the hill on which the ancient graveyard lay he could see the lights of Salem flickering dimly through the downpour. He drew a flashlight from his pocket. He would need light now. Taking up the spade, he bent and examined the fastenings of the coffin.

Abruptly he stiffened. Beneath his feet he sensed an unquiet stirring and scratching, as though something were moving within the coffin. For a moment a pang of superstitious fear shot through Masson, and then rage replaced it as he realized the significance of the sound. The rats had forestalled him again!

In a paroxysm of anger Masson wrenched at the fastenings of the coffin. He got the sharp edge of the shovel under the lid and pried it up until he could finish the job with his hands. Then he sent the flashlight's cold beam darting down into the coffin.

Rain spattered against the white satin lining; the coffin was empty. Masson saw a flicker of movement at the head of the case, and darted the light in that direction.

The end of the sarcophagus had been gnawed through, and a gaping hole led into darkness. A black shoe, limp and dragging, was disappearing as Masson watched, and abruptly he realized that the rats had forestalled him by only a few minutes. He fell on his hands and knees and made a hasty clutch at the shoe, and the flashlight incontinently fell into the coffin and went out. The shoe was tugged from his grasp, he heard a sharp, excited squealing, and then he had the flashlight again and was darting its light into the burrow.

It was a large one. It had to be, or the corpse could not have been dragged along it. Masson wondered at the size of the rats that could carry away a man's body, but the thought of the loaded revolver in his pocket fortified him. Probably if the corpse had been an ordinary one Masson would have left the rats with their spoils rather than venture into the narrow burrow, but he remembered an especially fine set of cuff-links he has observed, as well as a stickpin that was undoubtedly a genuine pearl. With scarcely a pause he clipped the flashlight to his belt and crept into the burrow.

It was a tight fit, but he managed to squeeze himself along. Ahead of him in the flashlight's glow he could see the shoes dragging along the wet earth of the bottom of the tunnel. He crept along the burrow as rapidly as he could, occasionally barely able to squeeze his lean body through the narrow walls.

The air was overpowering with its musty stench of carrion. If he could not reach the corpse in a minute, Masson decided, he would turn back. Belated fears were beginning to crawl, maggot-like, within his mind, but greed urged him on. He crawled forward, several times passing the mouth of adjoining tunnels. The walls of the burrow were damp and slimy, and twice lumps of dirt dropped behind him. The second time he paused and screwed his head around to look back. He could see nothing, of course, until he had unhooked the flashlight from his belt and reversed it.

Several clods lay on the ground behind him, and the danger of his position suddenly became real and terrifying. With thoughts of a cave-in making his pulse race, he decided to abandon the pursuit, even though he had now almost overtaken the corpse and the invisible things that pulled it. But he had overlooked one thing: the burrow was too narrow to allow him to turn.

Panic touched him briefly, but he remembered a side tunnel he had just passed, and backed awkwardly along the tunnel until he came to it. He thrust his legs into it, backing until he found himself able to turn. Then he hurriedly began to retrace his way, although his knees were bruised and painful

Agonizing pain shot through his leg. He felt sharp teeth sink into his flesh, and kicked out frantically. There was a shrill squealing and the scurry of many feet. Flashing the light behind him, Masson caught his breath in a sob of fear as he saw a dozen great rats watching him intently, their slitted eyes glittering in the light. They were great misshapen things, as large as cats, and behind them he caught a glimpse of a dark shape that stirred and moved swiftly aside into the shadow; and he shuddered at the unbelievable size of the thing.

The light had held them for a moment, but they were edging closer, their teeth dull orange in the pale light. Masson tugged at his pistol, managed to extricate it from his pocket, and aimed carefully. It was an awkward position, and he tried to press his feet into the soggy sides of the burrow so that he should not inadvertently send a bullet into one of them.

The rolling thunder of the shot deafened him, for a time, and the clouds of smoke set him coughing. When he could hear again and the smoke had cleared, he saw that the rats were gone. He put the pistol back and began to creep swiftly along the tunnel, and then with a scurry and a rush they were upon him again.

They swarmed over his legs, biting and squealing insanely, and Masson shrieked horribly as he snatched for his gun. He fired without aiming, and only luck saved him from blowing a foot off. This time the rats did not retreat so far, but Masson was crawling as swiftly as he could along the burrow, ready to fire again at the first sound of another attack.

There was patter of feet and he sent the light stabbing back of him. A great grey rat paused and watched him. Its long ragged whiskers twitched, and its scabrous, naked tail was moving slowly from side to side. Masson shouted and the rat retreated.

He crawled on, pausing briefly, the black gap of a side tunnel at his elbow, as he made out a shapeless huddle on the damp clay a few yards ahead. For a second he thought it was a mass of earth that had been dislodged from the roof, and then he recognized it as a human body.

It was a brown and shrivelled mummy, and with a dreadful un-believing shock Masson realized that it was moving.

It was crawling towards him, and in the pale glow of the flashlight the man saw a frightful gargoyle face thrust into his own. It was the passion-less, death's-head skull of a long-dead corpse, instinct with hellish life; and the glazed eyes swollen and bulbous betrayed the thing's blindness. It made a faint groaning sound as it crawled towards Masson, stretching its ragged and granulated lips in a grin of dreadful hunger. And Masson was frozen with abysmal fear and loathing.

Just before the Horror touched him, Masson flung himself frantically into the burrow at his side. He heard a scrambling noise at his heels, and the thing groaned dully as it came after him. Masson, glancing over his shoulder, screamed and propelled himself desperately through the narrow burrow. He crawled along awkwardly, sharp stones cutting his hands and knees. Dirt showered into his eyes, but he dared not pause even for a moment. He scrambled on, gasping, cursing, and praying hysteri-cally.

Squealing triumphantly, the rats came at him, horrible hunger in their eyes. Masson almost succumbed to their vicious teeth before he succeeded in beating them off. The passage was narrowing, and in a frenzy of terror he kicked and screamed and fired until the hammer clicked on an empty shell. But he had driven them off.

He found himself crawling under a great stone, embedded in the roof, that dug cruelly into his back. It moved a little as his weight struck it, and an idea flashed into Masson's fright-crazed mind. If he could bring down the stone so that it blocked the tunnel!

The earth was wet and soggy from the rains, and he hunched himself half upright and dug away at the dirt around the stone. The rats were coming closer. He saw their eyes glowing in the reflection of the flash-light's beam. Still he clawed frantically at the earth. The stone was giving. He tugged at it and it rocked in its foundation.

A rat was approaching – the monster he had already glimpsed. Grey and leprous and hideous it crept forward with its orange teeth bared, and in its wake came the blind dead thing, groaning as it crawled. Masson gave a last frantic tug at the stone. He felt it slide downward, and then he went scrambling along the tunnel.

Behind him the stone crashed down, and he heard a sudden frightful shriek of agony. Clods showered upon his legs. A heavy weight fell on his feet and he dragged them free with difficulty. The entire tunnel was collapsing!

Gasping with fear, Masson threw himself forward as the soggy earth collapsed at his heels. The tunnel narrowed until he could barely use his hands and legs to propel himself; he wriggled forward like an eel and suddenly felt satin tearing beneath his clawing fingers, and then his head crashed against something that barred his path. He moved his legs, discovering that they were not pinned under the collapsed earth. He was lying flat on his stomach, and when he tried to raise himself he found that the roof was only a few inches from his back. Panic shot through him.

When the blind horror had blocked his path, he had flung himself desperately into a side tunnel, a tunnel that had no outlet. He was in a *coffin*, an empty coffin into which he had crept through the hole the rats had gnawed in its end!

He tried to turn on his back and found that he could not. The lid of the coffin pinned him down inexorably. Then he braced himself and strained at the coffin lid. It was immovable, and even if he could escape from the sarcophagus, how could he claw his way up through five feet of hard packed earth?

He found himself gasping. It was dreadfully fetid, unbearably hot. In a paroxysm of terror he ripped and clawed at the satin until it was shredded. He made a futile attempt to dig with his feet at the earth from the collapsed burrow that blocked his retreat. If he were only able to reverse his position he might be able to claw his way through to air ... air ...

White-hot agony lanced through his breast, throbbed in his eyeballs. His head seemed to be swelling, growing larger and larger; and suddenly he heard the exultant squealing of the rats. He began to scream insanely but could not drown them out. For a moment he thrashed about hysterically within his narrow prison, and then he was quiet, gasping for air. His eyelids closed, his blackened tongue protruded, and he sank down into the blackness of death with the mad squealing of the rats dinning in his ears.

Thurnley Abbey

Perceval Landon

Three years ago I was on my way out to the East, and, as an extra day in London was of some importance, I took the Friday evening mail train to Brindisi instead of the usual Thursday morning Marseilles express. Many people shrink from the long forty-eight-hour train journey through Europe, and the subsequent rush across the Mediterranean on the nineteen-knot *Isis* or *Osiris*; but there is really very little discomfort on either the train or the mail-boat, and unless there is actually nothing for me to do, I always like to save the extra day and a half in London before I say goodbye to her for one of my longer tramps. This time – it was early, I remember in the shipping season, probably about the beginning of September – there were few passengers, and I had a compartment in the P. and O. Indian express to myself all the way from Calais. All Sunday I watched the blue waves dimpling the Adriatic, and the pale rosemary along the cuttings; the plain white towns, with their flat roofs and their bold 'duomos,' and the grey-green gnarled olive orchards of Apulia. The journey was just like any other. We ate in the dining-car as often and as long as we decently could. We slept after luncheon; we dawdled the afternoon away with yellow-backed novels; sometimes we exchanged platitudes in the smoking-room, and it was there that I met Alastair Colvin.

Colvin was a man of middle height, with a resolute, well-cut jaw; his hair was turning grey; his moustache was sun-whitened, otherwise he was clean-shaven – obviously a gentleman, and obviously also a preoccupied man. He had no great wit. When spoken to, he made the usual remarks in the right way, and I daresay he refrained from banalities only because he spoke less than the rest of us; most of the time he buried himself in the Wagon-lit Company's time-table, but seemed unable to concentrate his attention on any one page of it. He found that I had been over the Siberian railway, and for a quarter of an hour he discussed it with me. Then he lost interest in it, and rose to go to his compartment. But he came back again very soon, and seemed glad to pick up the conversation again.

Of course this did not seem to me to be of any importance. Most

travellers by train become a trifle infirm of purpose after thirty-six hours'
rattling. But Colvin's restless way I noticed in somewhat marked contrast
with the man's personal importance and dignity; especially ill-suited was
it to his finely made large hand with strong, broad, regular nails and its
few lines. As I looked at his hand I noticed a long, deep, and recent scar
of ragged shape. However, it is absurd to pretend that I thought anything
was unusual. I went off at five o'clock on Sunday afternoon to sleep away
the hour or two that had still to be got through before we arrived at
Brindisi.

Once there, we few passengers transhipped our hand baggage, verified
our berths – there were only a score of us in all – and then, after an aimless
ramble of half an hour in Brindisi, we returned to dinner at the Hotel
International, not wholly surprised that the town had been the death of
Virgil. If I remember rightly, there is a gaily painted hall at the International – I do not wish to advertise anything, but there is no other place
in Brindisi at which to await the coming of the mails – and after dinner
I was looking with awe at a trellis overgrown with blue vines, when
Colvin moved across the room to my table. He picked up *Il Secolo*, but
almost immediately gave up the pretence of reading it. He turned
squarely to me and said:

'Would you do me a favour?'

One doesn't do favours to stray acquaintances on continental expresses
without knowing something more of them than I knew of Colvin. But I
smiled in a non-committal way, and asked him what he wanted. I wasn't
wrong in part of my estimate of him; he said bluntly:

'Will you let me sleep in your cabin on the *Osiris*?' And he coloured
a little as he said it.

Now, there is nothing more tiresome than having to put up with a
stable-companion at sea, and I asked him rather pointedly:

'Surely there is room for all of us?' I thought that perhaps he had been
partnered off with some mangy Levantine, and wanted to escape from
him at all hazards.

Colvin, still somewhat confused, said: 'Yes; I am in a cabin by myself.
But you would do me the greatest favour if you would allow me to share
yours.'

This was all very well, but, besides the fact that I always sleep better
when alone, there had been some recent thefts on board English liners,
and I hesitated, frank and honest and self-conscious as Colvin was. Just
then the mail-train came in with a clatter and a rush of escaping steam,
and I asked him to see me again about it on the boat when we started.
He answered me curtly – I suppose he saw the mistrust in my manner
– 'I am a member of White's.' I smiled to myself as he said it, but I
remembered in a moment that the man – if he were really what he
claimed to be, and I make no doubt that he was – must have been sorely

put to it before he urged the fact as a guarantee of his respectability to a total stranger at a Brindisi hotel.

That evening, as we cleared the red and green harbour-lights of Brindisi, Colvin explained. This is his story in his own words.

'When I was travelling in India some years ago, I made the acquaintance of a youngish man in the Woods and Forests. We camped out together for a week and I found him a pleasant companion. John Broughton was a light-hearted soul when off duty, but a steady and capable man in any of the small emergencies that continually arise in that department. He was liked and trusted by the natives, and though a trifle over-pleased with himself when he escaped to civilization at Simla or Calcutta, Broughton's future was well assured in Government service, when a fair sized estate was unexpectedly left to him, and he joyfully shook the dust of the Indian plains from his feet and returned to England. For five years he drifted about London. I saw him now and then. We dined together about every eighteen months, and I could trace pretty exactly the gradual sickening of Broughton with a merely idle life. He then set out on a couple of long voyages, returned as restless as before, and at last told me that he had decided to marry and settle down at his place, Thurnley Abbey, which had long been empty. He spoke about looking after the property and standing for his constituency in the usual way. Vivien Wilde, his fiancée, had, I suppose, begun to take him in hand. She was a pretty girl with a deal of fair hair and rather an exclusive manner; deeply religious in a narrow school, she was still kindly and high-spirited, and I thought that Broughton was in luck. He was quite happy and full of information about his future.

'Among other things, I asked him about Thurnley Abbey. He confessed that he hardly knew the place. The last tenant, a man called Clarke, had lived in one wing for fifteen years and seen no one. He had been a miser and a hermit. It was the rarest thing for a light to be seen at the Abbey after dark. Only the barest necessities of life were ordered, and the tenant himself received them at the side-door. His one half-caste manservant, after a month's stay in the house, had abruptly left without warning, and had returned to the Southern States. One thing Broughton complained bitterly about: Clarke had wilfully spread the rumour among the villagers that the Abbey was haunted, and had even condescended to play childish tricks with spirit-lamps and salt in order to scare trespassers away at night. He had been detected in the act of his tomfoolery, but the story spread, and no one, said Broughton, would venture near the house except in broad daylight. The hauntedness of Thurnley Abbey was now, he said with a grin, part of the gospel of the countryside, but he and his young wife were going to change all that. Would I propose myself any time I liked? I, of course, said I would, and equally, of course, intended to do nothing of the sort without a definite invitation.

'The house was put in thorough repair, though not a stick of the old furniture and tapestry were removed. Floors and ceilings were relaid: the roof was made watertight again, and the dust of half a century was scoured out. He showed me some photographs of the place. It was called an Abbey, though as a matter of fact it had been only the infirmary of the long-vanished Abbey of Closter some five miles away. The larger part of this building remained as it had been in pre-Reformation days, but a wing had been added in Jacobean times, and that part of the house had been kept in something like repair by Mr Clarke. He had in both the ground and first floors set a heavy timber door, strongly barred with iron, in the passage between the earlier and the Jacobean parts of the house, and had entirely neglected the former. So there had been a good deal of work to be done.

'Broughton, whom I saw in London two or three times about this period, made a deal of fun over the positive refusal of the workmen to remain after sundown. Even after the electric light had been put into every room, nothing would induce them to remain, though, as Broughton observed, electric light was death on ghosts. The legend of the Abbey's ghosts had gone far and wide, and the men would take no risks. They went home in batches of five and six, and even during the daylight hours there was an inordinate amount of talking between one and another, if either happened to be out of sight of his companion. On the whole, though nothing of any sort or kind had been conjured up even by their heated imaginations during their five months' work upon the Abbey, the belief in ghosts was rather strengthened than otherwise in Thurnley because of the men's confessed nervousness, and local tradition declared itself in favour of the ghost of an immured nun.

"Good old nun!" said Broughton.

'I asked him whether in general he believed in the possibility of ghosts, and, rather to my surprise, he said that he couldn't say he entirely disbelieved in them. A man in India had told him one morning in camp that he believed that his mother was dead in England, as her vision had come to his tent the night before. He had not been alarmed, but had said nothing, and the figure vanished again. As a matter of fact, the next possible dak-walla brought on a telegram announcing the mother's death. "There the thing was," said Broughton. But at Thurnley he was practical enough. He roundly cursed the idiotic selfishness of Clarke, whose silly antics had caused all the inconvenience. At the same time, he couldn't refuse to sympathize to some extent with the ignorant workmen. "My own idea," said he, "is that if a ghost ever does come in one's way, one ought to speak to it."

'I agreed. Little as I knew of the ghost world and its conventions, I had always remembered that a spook was in honour bound to wait to be spoken to. It didn't seem much to do, and I felt that the sound of one's own voice would at any rate reassure oneself as to one's wakefulness. But there are few ghosts outside Europe – few, that is, that a white man can see – and I had never been troubled with any. However, as I have said, I told Broughton that I agreed.

'So the wedding took place, and I went to it in a tall hat which I bought for the occasion, and the new Mrs Broughton smiled very nicely at me afterwards. As it had to happen, I took the Orient Express that evening and was not in England again for nearly six months. Just before I came back I got a letter from Broughton. He asked if I could see him in London or come to Thurnley, as he thought I should be better able to help him than anyone else he knew. His wife sent a nice message to me at the end, so I was reassured about at least one thing. I wrote from Budapest that I would come and see him at Thurnley two days after my arrival in London, and as I sauntered out of the Pannonia into the Kerepesi Utcza to post my letters, I wondered of what earthly service I could be to Broughton. I had been out with him after tiger on foot, and I could imagine few men better able at a pinch to manage their own business. However, I had nothing to do, so after dealing with some small accumulations of business during my absence, I packed a kit-bag and departed to Euston.

'I was met by Broughton's great limousine at Thurnley Road Station, and after a drive of nearly seven miles we echoed through the sleepy streets of Thurnley village, into which the main gates of the park thrust themselves, splendid with pillars and spread-eagles and tom-cats rampant atop of them. I never was a herald, but I know that the Broughtons have the right to supporters – Heaven knows why! From the gates a quadruple avenue of beech-trees led inwards for a quarter of a mile. Beneath them a neat strip of fine turf edged the road and ran back until the poison of the dead beech-leaves killed it under the trees. There were many wheel-tracks on the road, and a comfortable little pony trap jogged past me laden with a country parson and his wife and daughter. Evidently there was some garden party going on at the Abbey. The road dropped away to the right at the end of the avenue, and I could see the Abbey across a wide pasturage and a broad lawn thickly dotted with guests.

'The end of the building was plain. It must have been almost mercilessly austere when it was first built, but time had crumbled the edges and toned the stone down to an orange-lichened grey wherever it showed behind its curtain of magnolia, jasmine, and ivy. Farther on was the three-storied Jacobean house, tall and handsome. There had not been the slightest attempt to adapt the one to the other, but the kindly ivy had glossed over the touching-point. There was a tall flèche in the middle of the building, surmounting a small bell-tower. Behind the house there rose the mountainous verdure of Spanish chestnuts all the way up the hill.

'Broughton had seen me coming from afar, and walked across from his other guests to welcome me before turning me over to the butler's care. This man was sandy-haired and rather inclined to be talkative. He could, however, answer hardly any questions about the house: he had, he said, only been there three weeks. Mindful of what Broughton had told me, I made no enquiries about ghosts, though the room into which I was shown might have justified anything. It was a very large low room with oak beams projecting from the white ceiling. Every inch of the walls, including the doors, was covered with tapestry, and a remarkably fine Italian fourpost bedstead, heavily draped, added to the darkness and dignity of the place. All the furniture was old, well made, and dark. Underfoot there was a plain green pile carpet, the only new thing about the room except the electric-light fittings and the jugs and basins. Even the looking-glass on the dressing-table was an old pyramidal Venetian glass set in heavy repoussé frame of tarnished silver.

'After a few minutes' cleaning up, I went downstairs and out upon the lawn, where I greeted my hostess. The people gathered there were of the usual country type, all anxious to be pleased and roundly curious as to the new master of the Abbey. Rather to my surprise, and quite to my pleasure, I rediscovered Glenham, whom I had known well in old days in Barotseland: he lived quite close, as, he remarked with a grin, I ought to have known. "But," he added, "I don't live in a place like this." He swept his hand to the long, low lines of the Abbey in obvious admiration, and then, to my intense interest, muttered beneath his breath, "Thank God!" He saw that I had overheard him, and turning to me said decidedly, "Yes, 'thank God' I said, and I meant. I wouldn't live at the Abbey for all Broughton's money."

' "But surely," I demurred, "you know that old Clarke was discovered in the very act of setting light to his bug-a-boos?"

'Glenham shrugged his shoulders. "Yes, I know about that. But there is something wrong with the place still. All I can say is that Broughton is a different man since he has lived here. I don't believe that he will remain much longer. But – you're staying here? – well, you'll hear all about it tonight. There's a big dinner, I understand." The conversation turned off to old reminiscences, and Glenham soon after had to go.

'Before I went to dress that evening I had twenty minutes' talk with Broughton in his library. There was no doubt that the man was altered, gravely altered. He was nervous and fidgety, and I found him looking at me only when my eye was off him. I naturally asked him what he wanted of me. I told him I would do anything I could, but that I couldn't conceive what he lacked that I could provide. He said with a lustreless smile that there was, however, something, and that he would tell me the following morning. It struck me that he was somehow ashamed of himself, and perhaps ashamed of the part he was asking me to play. However, I dismissed the subject from my mind and went up to dress in my palatial room. As I shut the door a draught blew out of the Queen of Sheba from the wall, and I noticed that the tapestries were not fastened to the wall at the bottom. I have always held very practical views about spooks, and it has often seemed to me that the slow waving in firelight of loose tapestry upon a wall would account for ninety-nine per cent of the stories one hears. Certainly the dignified undulation of this lady with her attendants and huntsmen – one of whom was untidily cutting the throat of a fallow deer upon the very steps on which King Solomon, a grey-faced Flemish nobleman with the order of the Golden Fleece, awaited his fair visitor – gave colour to my hypothesis.

'Nothing much happened at dinner. The people were very much like those of the garden party. A young woman next me seemed anxious to know what was being read in London. As she was far more familiar than I with the most recent magazines and literary supplements, I found salvation in being myself instructed in the tendencies of modern fiction. All true art, she said, was shot through and through with melancholy. How vulgar were the attempts at wit that marked so many modern books! From the beginning of literature it had always been tragedy that embodied the highest attainment of every age. To call such works morbid merely begged the question. No thoughtful man – she looked sternly at me through the steel rim of her glasses – could fail to agree with me. Of course, as one would, I immediately and properly said that I slept with Pett Ridge and Jacobs under my pillow at night, and that if "Jorrocks" weren't quite so large and cornery, I would add him to the company. She hadn't read any of them, so I was saved – for a time. But I remember grimly that she said that the dearest wish of her life was to be in some awful and soul-freezing situation of horror, and I remember that she dealt hardly with the hero of Nat Paynter's vampire story, between nibbles at her brown-bread ice. She was a cheerless soul, and I couldn't help thinking that if there were many such in the neighbourhood, it was not surprising that old Glenham had been stuffed with some nonsense or other about the Abbey. Yet nothing could well have been less creepy than the glitter of silver and glass, and the subdued lights and cackle of conversation all round the dinner-table.

'After the ladies had gone I found myself talking to the rural dean. He was a thin, earnest man, who at once turned the conversation to old Clarke's buffooneries. But, he said, Mr Broughton had introduced such a new and cheerful spirit, not only into the Abbey, but, he might say, into the whole neighbourhood, that he had great hopes that the ignorant superstitions of the past were from henceforth destined to oblivion. Thereupon his other neighbour, a portly gentleman of independent

means and position, audibly remarked "Amen," which damped the rural
dean, and we talked of partridges past, partridges present, and pheasants
to come. At the other end of the table Broughton sat with a couple of his
friends, red-faced hunting men. Once I noticed that they were discussing
me, but I paid no attention to it at the time. I remembered it a few hours
later.

'By eleven all the guests were gone, and Broughton, his wife, and I were
alone together under the fine plaster ceiling of the Jacobean drawing-
room. Mrs Broughton talked about one or two of the neighbours, and
then, with a smile, said that she knew I would excuse her, shook hands
with me, and went off to bed. I am not very good at analysing things,
but I felt that she talked a little uncomfortably and with a suspicion of
effort, smiled rather conventionally, and was obviously glad to go. These
things seem trifling enough to repeat, but I had throughout the faint
feeling that everything was not square. Under the circumstances, this was
enough to set me wondering what on earth the service could be that I
was to render – wondering also whether the whole business were not some
ill-advised jest in order to make me come down from London for a mere
shooting-party.

'Broughton said little after she had gone. But he was evidently
labouring to bring the conversation round to the so-called haunting of
the Abbey. As soon as I saw this, of course I asked him directly about
it. He then seemed at once to lose interest in the matter. There was no
doubt about it: Broughton was somehow a changed man, and to my mind
he had changed in no way for the better. Mrs Broughton seemed no
sufficient cause. He was clearly very fond of her, and she of him. I
reminded him that he was going to tell me what I could do for him in
the morning, pleaded my journey, lighted a candle, and went upstairs
with him. At the end of the passage leading into the old house he grinned
weakly and said, "Mind, if you see a ghost, do talk to it; you said you
would." He stood irresolutely a moment and then turned away. At the
door of his dressing-room he paused once more: "I'm here," he called
out, "if you should want anything. Good night," and he shut his door.

'I went along the passage to my room, undressed, switched on a lamp
beside my bed, read a few pages of the *Jungle Book*, and then, more than
ready for sleep, turned the light off and went fast asleep.

'Three hours later I woke up. There was not a breath of wind outside.
There was not even a flicker of light from the fireplace. As I lay there,
an ash tinkled slightly as it cooled, but there was hardly a gleam of the
dullest red in the grate. An owl cried among the silent Spanish chestnuts
on the slope outside. I idly reviewed the events of the day, hoping that
I should fall off to sleep again before I reached dinner. But at the end
I seemed as wakeful as ever. There was no help for it. I must read my

Jungle Book again till I felt ready to go off, so I fumbled for the pear at the end of the cord that hung down inside the bed, and I switched on the bedside lamp. The sudden glory dazzled me for a moment. I felt under my pillow for my book with half-shut eyes. Then, growing used to the light, I happened to look down to the foot of my bed.

'I can never tell you really what happened then. Nothing I could ever confess in the most abject words could even faintly picture to you what I felt. I know that my heart stopped dead and my throat shut automatically. In one instinctive movement I crouched back up against the head-boards of the bed, staring at the horror. The movement set my heart going again, and the sweat dripped from every pore. I am not a particularly religious man, but I had always believed that God would never allow any supernatural appearance to present itself to man in such a guise and in such circumstances that harm, either bodily or mental, could result to him. I can only tell you that at that moment both my life and my reason rocked unsteadily on their seats.'

The other *Osiris* passengers had gone to bed. Only he and I remained leaning over the starboard railing, which rattled uneasily now and then under the fierce vibration of the over-engined mail-boat. Far over, there were the lights of a few fishing-smacks riding out the night, and a great rush of white combing and seething water fell out and away from us overside.

At last Colvin went on:

'Leaning over the foot of my bed, looking at me, was a figure swathed in a rotten and tattered veiling. This shroud passed over the head, but left both eyes and the right side of the face bare. It then followed the line of the arm down to where the hand grasped the bed-end. The face was not entirely that of a skull, though the eyes and the flesh of the face were totally gone. There was a thin, dry skin drawn tightly over the features, and there was some skin left on the hand. One wisp of hair crossed the forehead. It was perfectly still. I looked at it, and it looked at me, and my brains turned dry and hot in my head. I had still got the pear of the electric lamp in my hand, and I played idly with it; only I dared not turn the light out again. I shut my eyes, only to open them in a hideous terror the same second. The thing had not moved. My heart was thumping, and the sweat cooled me as it evaporated. Another cinder tinkled in the grate, and a panel creaked in the wall.

'My reason failed me. For twenty minutes, or twenty seconds, I was able to think of nothing else but this awful figure, till there came, hurtling through the empty channels of my senses, the remembrance that Broughton and his friends had discussed me furtively at dinner. The dim possibility of its being a hoax stole gratefully into my unhappy mind, and once there, one's pluck came creeping back along a thousand tiny veins. My first sensation was one of blind unreasoning thankfulness that my brain was going to stand the trial. I am not a timid man, but the best of us needs some human handle to steady him in time of extremity, and in this faint but growing hope that after all it might be only a brutal hoax, I found the fulcrum that I needed. At last I moved.

'How I managed to do it I cannot tell you, but with one spring towards the foot of the bed I got within arm's-length and struck out one fearful blow with my fist at the thing. It crumbled under it, and my hand was cut to the bone. With the sickening revulsion after my terror, I dropped half-fainting across the end of the bed. So it was merely a foul trick after all. No doubt the trick had been played many a time before; no doubt Broughton and his friends had had some large bet among themselves as to what I should do when I discovered the gruesome thing. From my state of abject terror I found myself transported into an insensate anger. I shouted curses upon Broughton. I dived rather than climbed over the bed-end on to the sofa. I tore at the robed skeleton – how well the whole thing had been carried out, I thought – I broke the skull against the floor, and stamped upon its dry bones. I flung the head away under the bed, and rent the brittle bones of the trunk in pieces. I snapped the thin thigh-bones across my knee, and flung them in different directions. The shin-bones I set up against a stool and broke with my heel. I raged like a Berserker against the loathly thing, and stripped the ribs from the back-bone and slung the breastbone against the cupboard. My fury increased as the work of destruction went on. I tore the frail rotten veil into twenty pieces, and the dust went up over everything, over the clean blotting-paper and the silver inkstand. At last my work was done. There was but a raffle of broken bones and strips of parchment and crumbling wool. Then, picking up a piece of the skull – it was the cheek and temple bone of the right side, I remember – I opened the door and went down the passage to Broughton's dressing-room. I remember still how my sweat-dripping pyjamas clung to me as I walked. At the door I kicked and entered.

'Broughton was in bed. He had already turned the light on and seemed shrunken and horrified. For a moment he could hardly pull himself together. Then I spoke. I don't know what I said. Only I know that from a heart full and over-full with hatred and contempt, spurred on by shame of my own recent cowardice, I let my tongue run on. He answered nothing. I was amazed at my own fluency. My hair still clung lankily to my wet temples, my hand was bleeding profusely, and I must have looked a strange sight. Broughton huddled himself up at the head of the bed just as I had. Still he made no answer, no defence. He seemed preoccupied with something besides my reproaches, and once or twice moistened his lips with his tongue. But he could say nothing, though he moved his hands now and then, just as a baby who cannot speak moves its hands.

'At last the door into Mrs Broughton's room opened and she came in, white and terrified. "What is it? What is it? Oh, in God's name! what is it?" she cried again and again, and then she went up to her husband and sat on the bed in her night-dress, and the two faced me. I told her what the matter was. I spared her husband not a word for her presence there. Yet he seemed hardly to understand. I told the pair that I had spoiled their cowardly joke for them. Broughton looked up.

' "I have smashed the foul thing into a hundred pieces," I said. Broughton licked his lips again and his mouth worked. "By God!" I shouted, "it would serve you right if I thrashed you within an inch of your life. I will take care that not a decent man or woman of my acquaintance ever speaks to you again. And there," I added, throwing the broken piece of the skull upon the floor beside his bed, "there is a souvenir for you, of your damned work tonight!"

'Broughton saw the bone, and in a moment it was his turn to frighten me. He squealed like a hare caught in a trap. He screamed and screamed till Mrs Broughton, almost as bewildered as myself, held on to him and coaxed him like a child to be quiet. But Broughton – and as he moved I thought that ten minutes ago I perhaps looked as terribly ill as he did – thrust her from him, and scrambled out of the bed on to the floor, and still screaming put out his hand to the bone. It had blood on it from my hand. He paid no attention to me whatever. In truth I said nothing. This was a new turn indeed to the horrors of the evening. He rose from the floor with the bone in his hand, and stood silent. He seemed to be listening. "Time, time, perhaps," he muttered, and almost at the same moment fell at full length on the carpet, cutting his head against the fender. The bone flew from his hand and came to rest near the door. I picked Broughton up, haggard and broken, with blood over his face. He whispered hoarsely and quickly, "Listen, listen!" We listened.

'After ten seconds' utter quiet, I seemed to hear something. I could not be sure, but at last there was no doubt. There was a quiet sound as of one moving along the passage. Little regular steps came towards us over the hard oak flooring. Broughton moved to where his wife sat, white and speechless, on the bed, and pressed her face into his shoulder.

'Then, the last thing that I could see as he turned the light out, he fell forward with his own head pressed into the pillow of the bed. Something in their company, something in their cowardice, helped me, and I faced the open doorway of the room, which was outlined fairly clearly against the dimly lighted passage. I put out one hand and touched Mrs Broughton's shoulder in the darkness. But at the last moment I too failed. I sank on my knees and put my face in the bed. Only we all heard. The footsteps came to the door, and there they stopped. The piece of bone was lying a yard inside the door. There was a rustle of moving stuff, and the thing was in the room. Mrs Broughton was silent: I could hear Broughton's voice praying, muffled in the pillow: I was cursing my own cowardice. Then the steps moved out again on the oak boards of the passage, and I heard the sounds dying away. In a flash of remorse I went to the door and looked out. At the end of the corridor I thought I saw something that moved away. A moment later the passage was empty. I stood with my forehead against the jamb of the door almost physically sick.

'"You can turn the light on," I said, and there was an answering flare. There was no bone at my feet. Mrs Broughton had fainted. Broughton was almost useless, and it took me ten minutes to bring her to. Broughton only said one such thing worth remembering. For the most part he went on muttering prayers. But I was glad afterwards to recollect that he had said that thing. He said in a colourless voice, half as a question, half as a reproach, "You didn't speak to her."

'We spent the remainder of the night together. Mrs Broughton actually fell off into a kind of sleep before dawn, but she suffered so horribly in her dreams that I shook her into consciousness again. Never was dawn so long in coming. Three or four times Broughton spoke to himself. Mrs Broughton would then just tighten her hold on his arm, but she could say nothing. As for me, I can honestly say that I grew worse as the hours passed and the light strengthened. The two violent reactions had battered down my steadiness of view, and I felt that the foundations of my life had been built upon the sand. I said nothing, and after binding up my hand with a towel, I did not move. It was better so. They helped me and I helped them, and we all three knew that our reason had gone very near to ruin that night. At last, when the light came in pretty strongly, and the birds outside were chattering and singing, we felt that we must do something. Yet we never moved. You might have thought that we should particularly dislike being found as we were by the servants: yet nothing of that kind mattered a straw, and an overpowering listlessness bound us as we sat, until Chapman, Broughton's man, actually knocked and opened the door. None of us moved. Broughton, speaking hardly and stiffly, said, "Chapman, you can come back in five minutes." Chapman was a discreet man, but it would have made no difference to us if he had carried his news to the "room" at once.

'We looked at each other and I said I must go back. I meant to wait outside till Chapman returned. I simply dared not re-enter my bedroom alone. Broughton roused himself and said that he would come with me. Mrs Broughton agreed to remain in her own room for five minutes if the blinds were drawn up and all the doors left open.

'So Broughton and I, leaning stiffly one against the other, went down to my room. By the morning light that filtered past the blinds we could see our way, and I released the blinds. There was nothing wrong in the room from end to end, except smears of my own blood, on the end of the bed, on the sofa, and on the carpet where I had torn the thing to pieces.'

Colvin had finished his story. There was nothing to say. Seven bells stuttered out from the fo'c'sle, and the answering cry wailed through the darkness. I took him downstairs.

'Of course I am much better now, but it is a kindness of you to let me sleep in your cabin.'

Avalon Heights

Kay Leith

When the taxi reached level ground, Deborah Banks saw the square, white mass of Avalon Heights for the first time.

The driver swept the cab round the empty parking area, spraying pink gravel on the surrounding scrubby ground. Builders' litter at the edge of the gravel seemed to have been lying there for a long time.

Deborah left the cab eagerly and gazed upwards. The edifice seemed to sway in the immense blue sky, the windows reflecting the swiftly-scudding clouds. She walked round to the shady side, as though to make sure that her new home really did have three dimensions. The rows of balconies and blank windows were repeated.

'Looks lifeless to me,' remarked the driver as he unloaded the girl's luggage.

Deborah produced the keys and opened her purse to pay the man off, but he shook his head.

'I'll carry this lot in for you first.'

The low-ceilinged hallway was stiflingly warm. She received no reply when she knocked on the door marked 'Caretaker'.

'Lift's not working.' The young man's voice echoed sepulchrally as he opened a hatch near the marble floor, pressed something, and little arrows lit up on the indicator plate.

Deborah handed him two notes.

'Thanks, Miss. If you need a cab I'd appreciate the business.'

'I'll make a note,' she promised.

The taxi was moving off when the girl, arms waving, flung herself down the front steps. Through the rear mirror the man saw her and braked. 'What's up, then? Ghosts?'

'My food!'

Oh!' He handed out the carrier bag. 'I didn't notice ... Your husband – is he coming later?'

'Yes – tonight.'

'Oh. Well, you'll be all right, then.'

Deborah nodded swiftly and decisively. 'Of course. 'Bye now.'

But Tom couldn't arrive until the next day. The new car wouldn't be ready until Thursday, and he had to finish things off at the office. She'd lied because she'd noticed the way the man looked at her, and she didn't want to let him know that she was on her own.

She was also acutely conscious of her jewellery, smart clothes and bulging purse. She had never had the chance before to realize the burden that expensive possessions laid on one. She still didn't know whether she was on her head or on her heels. She and Tom were now rich beyond their wildest dreams.

When the purchase of the flat – arranged through an agent – was completed, she hadn't been able to wait, even for a few days, to shrug off the old life and don the trappings of wealth.

She re-locked the big glass front door. Anyone who had any right to enter would have a key.

The lift glided to a stop at the tenth floor, and Deborah deposited her things on the bright landing. She watched the lift sink out of sight. Was it automatic, or had someone pressed the button below?

A blue door on the left said 'IOA' in gold lettering. On the right was a similar door, but pale grey, marked 'IOB'.

She advanced on IOB, composing a genteel phrase or two of introduction, and rang the bell. There was no response.

Her key fitted trimly into the lock of IOA. Leaving her luggage on the landing, she wandered about the rooms which were, as yet, only sparsely furnished.

Everything in the kitchen worked perfectly and was convenient, clean, and delightfully new.

Double doors led to the balcony. The gravel road fell away and joined the main road in the distance, and beyond was the sea. To the right, at the other end of the bay, was the town.

Becoming aware of a strange, hissing sound, she went back inside. It seemed louder in the hall; even more so on the landing.

Her precious sugar was pouring itself on to the impeccable floor from a tear in the packet!

She made an indifferent job of scooping up the grains from the black tiles.

Following a light lunch of cheese and biscuits, which reminded her of the lean days, she unpacked her gay new sheets and made up the bed. Slipping off her skirt, she lay down. Ineffable silence, glorious comfort! Her novel soon fell from her hand.

Something bit her! Blinking sleep-bemused eyes, she looked around. The sun still shone yellowly; her watch showed the passage of barely fifteen minutes.

Groggily raising herself, she gaped at the red stain on the pillow. And on her blouse, too!

Rushing to the dressing-table, she saw the reason: a cut on the tip of her ear-lobe. The diamond brooch which she wore on her collar must have cut her as she moved in her sleep. But, she could have sworn she'd woken in the same position as when she'd dropped off ...

Solitude didn't trouble her, but she hadn't realized until then how isolated she was at Avalon Heights. The telephone had not yet been installed, so there was no way Tom could contact her, or she him.

The lift came obediently. The building was just as broodingly quiet as it had been earlier. A breeze had sprung up, bending the grass in the waste ground. Looking out to the sea in the misty distance, she felt as though she were the only living being on a world that had suddenly gone dead.

She might have gone for a walk, but for a peculiar reluctance either to leave the building or, once having left it, to return.

She knocked again on the caretaker's door and tried the handle. It opened, revealing a comfortably-carpeted little airlock of a hall.

'Is anyone there?' Pushing open the door opposite, she ventured inside.

A newspaper lay on the kitchen table, and there was a faint smell of pipe smoke.

A bone on the floor in a corner hinted that the man kept a dog. Perhaps he'd taken it for a walk? The tiny sitting-room was empty, and through the slightly open bedroom door she saw a neatly-made single bed.

'Have taken possession of 10A today. Mrs Banks.' She put the note on the mat outside his door – to hint that that was as far as she'd gone – and got back into the lift. Surprisingly, even the caretaker hadn't a phone.

At her flat door she paused. There was no trace of the sugar she'd spilled, not even in the groves between the tiles. Ants? Or had the caretaker swept up when she was absent?

When the sun went down Deborah stood on the balcony watching the cars which, in increasing numbers, left the town. They were like errant diamonds, escaping from a broken necklace.

None of them, however, turned on to the approach road to the flats. Deborah wished that she'd asked the taxi driver to come back. It would have been nice to have had a meal in town, or at least to have driven around for a bit.

She went inside and lit the table lamp. Some people were hard to please! She'd been in the place for barely four hours, and now she wanted to go out! Perhaps a soak in that elegant new sunken bath, with her exotic new bath oil ...

For no apparent reason the table lamp went out, plunging the flat in darkness. Panic flared. What if the caretaker had cut off the electricity supply? Why was he hiding himself? Why was everything so quiet?

Then she found the wall switch and terror receded. But, behind her, something skittered on the floor.

Quickly switching on all the lights, she searched every cupboard and recess. Then she heard the sound again, this time from above.

Cautiously she went out on to the landing. The navy blue dark looked in through the windows, a hostile witness to her fears. The service door beside the lift was locked.

Sighing with relief, she conjectured that the noise must have been made by the water tanks, and she hadn't been using water. It was imperative to find out who had.

Retrieving her handbag and keys from the lounge, she summoned the lift. All the way down to the ground floor she jammed open the lift door and rang bells, becoming increasingly perturbed. She really *was* alone! There were no other tenants!

When she reached the warm gloominess of the entrance hall she darted to the caretaker's door and rang. Her note was still on the mat.

'Oh, no!' The plaintive words slipped out and echoed in the stagnant stillness. She stared up at the lift indicator. The basement! Perhaps the infuriating man had been down there all the time!

The lift doors spilled a meagre pool of light. She reached out, clawing, and the bare bulb lit up an infinity of raw, cold concrete. The pillared vault was obviously the flats' garage.

Again, briefly, there was a scuffling sound. Mice – or rats . . . or the missing caretaker? She crept from pillar to pillar, imagining the myriads of red dots winked at her from pitch-dark corners.

There was a car – an ancient but well-cared-for saloon – parked at the side of the ramp which led up to the entrance gate. It was empty and locked. A chill breeze wafted down to her.

Perhaps, like Box and Cox, he'd been going in one door and she went out by another? Yes, that had to be it.

Making swiftly for the lift, she heard the skittering sound behind her. This time she entered the man's flat without knocking. Fear had made her bold, but he wasn't there, anyway.

Unable to stomach the idea of returning upstairs, she paced the pink and white tiles. Gradually her nerves calmed. She could picture the man: careful and middle-aged. Careful because he locked his car in a locked garage, and middle-aged because of the pipe smoke she'd smelt earlier. It all added up to a picture of wholesome ordinariness.

She longed to make contact with another human being. If she *were* the first tenant, he'd probably be glad to see her, too. But where was he?

She read the six-day-old newspaper, hardly taking in a word. Her eye fell on the bone in the corner. Fastidious men – and he certainly seemed to be one of those – were unlikely to tolerate messy dogs. Apart from the bone, there was no other indication of a dog's presence – no bowl of water or tins of dog food.

Cautiously she looked into the bedroom. Everything was neat and tidy:

underwear and shirt folded on a chair, shoes marshalled on the floor
uniform on a hanger; and, by the bedside, another bone. A few inches
away lay yet another . . .

On Thursday morning the Post Office engineers arrived at Avalon
Heights to instal telephones, and had to go back to town to get a key from
the estate agent.

The latter declared his amazement that the caretaker, or one of the
two or three tenants who had already moved in to their flats, had not
allowed the men entry.

'There's no sign of life at all,' complained the Post Office man dis-
gustedly. 'Just bones.'

'Bones?'

'Yeah – bones – like somebody's been feeding a dog in the hall.'

'Dogs are not allowed in Avalon Heights,' the agent said coldly.

'That so?' queried the telephone man. 'Well, it looks like somebody's
been breaking the rules. There's a white football lying there as well.'

'Football?' The agent blenched.

'Yes. Come to think of it, it was a funny-looking kind of football . . .'

The agent's perturbation was equal to his scorn. 'There are no children
there, either, I assure you.'

'Then it looks like you've got some checking up to do, mate.' The
telephone man paused briefly at the door. 'Oh, and another thing.
Somebody has spilled some dark red paint on the floor. It's made a proper
mess of your marble hall . . .'

The Rats in the Walls

H. P. Lovecraft

On 16 July 1923, I moved into Exham Priory after the last workman had finished his labours. The restoration had been a stupendous task, for little had remained of the deserted pile but a shell-like ruin; yet because it had been the seat of my ancestors, I let no expense deter me. The place had not been inhabited since the reign of James the First, when a tragedy of intensely hideous, though largely unexplained, nature had struck down the master, five of his children, and several servants; and driven forth under a cloud of suspicion and terror the third son, my lineal progenitor and the only survivor of the abhorred line.

With this sole heir denounced as a murderer, the estate had reverted to the crown, nor had the accused man made any attempt to exculpate himself or regain his property. Shaken by some horror greater than that of conscience or the law, and expressing only a frantic wish to exclude the ancient edifice from his sight and memory, Walter de la Poer, eleventh Baron Exham, fled to Virginia and there founded the family which by the next century had become known as Delapore.

Exham Priory had remained untenanted, though later allotted to the estates of the Norrys family and much studied because of its peculiarly composite architecture; an architecture involving Gothic towers resting on a Saxon or Romanesque substructure, whose foundation in turn was of a still earlier order or blend of orders – Roman, and even Druidic or native Cymric, if legends speak truly. This foundation was a very singular thing, being merged on one side with the solid limestone of the precipice from whose brink the priory overlooked a desolate valley three miles west of the village of Anchester.

Architects and antiquarians loved to examine this strange relic of forgotten centuries, but the country folk hated it. They had hated it hundreds of years before, when my ancestors lived there, and they hated it now, with the moss and mould of abandonment on it. I had not been a day in Anchester before I knew I came of an accursed house. And this week workmen have blown up Exham Priory, and are busy obliterating the traces of its foundations. The bare statistics of my ancestry I had always known, together with the fact that my first American forebear had come to the colonies under a strange cloud. Of details, however, I had been kept wholly ignorant through the policy of reticence always maintained by the Delapores. Unlike our planter neighbours, we seldom boasted of crusading ancestors or other mediaeval and Renaissance heroes; nor was any kind of tradition handed down except what may have been recorded in the sealed envelope left before the Civil War by every squire to his eldest son for posthumous opening. The glories we cherished were those achieved since the migration; the glories of a proud and honourable, if somewhat reserved and unsocial Virginia line.

During the war our fortunes were extinguished and our whole existence changed by the burning of Carfax, our home on the banks of the James. My grandfather, advanced in years, had perished in that incendiary outrage, and with him the envelope that had bound us all to the past. I can recall that fire today as I saw it then at the age of seven, with the Federal soldiers shouting, the women screaming, and the negroes howling and praying. My father was in the army, defending Richmond, and after many formalities my mother and I were passed through the lines to join him.

When the war ended we all moved north, whence my mother had come; and I grew to manhood, middle age, and ultimate wealth as a stolid Yankee. Neither my father nor I ever knew what our hereditary envelope had contained, and as I merged into the greyness of Massachusetts business life I lost all interest in the mysteries which evidently lurked far back in my family tree. Had I suspected their nature, how gladly I would have left Exham Priory to its moss, bats, and cobwebs!

My father died in 1904, but without any message to leave to me, or to my only child, Alfred, a motherless boy of ten. It was this boy who reversed the order of family information, for although I could give him only jesting conjectures about the past, he wrote me of some very interesting ancestral legends when the late war took him to England in 1917 as an aviation officer. Apparently the Delapores had a colourful and perhaps sinister history, for a friend of my son's, Capt. Edward Norrys of the Royal Flying Corps, dwelt near the family seat at Anchester and related some peasant superstitions which few novelists could equal for wildness and incredibility. Norrys himself, of course, did not take them so seriously; but they amused my son and made good material for his letters to me. It was this legendry which definitely turned my attention to my transatlantic heritage, and made me resolve to purchase and restore the family seat which Norrys showed to Alfred in its picturesque desertion, and offered to get for him at a surprisingly reasonable figure, since his own uncle was the present owner.

I bought Exham Priory in 1918, but was almost immediately distracted from my plans of restoration by the return of my son as a maimed invalid. During the two years that he lived I thought of nothing but his care, having even placed my business under the direction of partners.

In 1921, as I found myself bereaved and aimless, a retired manufacturer no longer young, I resolved to divert my remaining years with my new possession. Visiting Anchester in December, I was entertained by Capt. Norrys, a plump, amiable young man who had thought much of my son, and secured his assistance in gathering plans and anecdotes to guide in the coming restoration. Exham Priory itself I saw without emotion, a jumble of tottering mediaeval ruins covered with lichens and honeycombed with rooks' nests, perched perilously upon a precipice, and denuded of floors or other interior features save the stone walls of the separate towers.

As I gradually recovered the image of the edifice as it had been when my ancestors left it over three centuries before, I began to hire workmen for the reconstruction. In every case I was forced to go outside the immediate locality, for the Anchester villagers had an almost unbelievable fear and hatred of the place. This sentiment was so great that it was sometimes communicated to the outside labourers, causing numerous desertions; whilst its scope appeared to include both the priory and its ancient family.

My son had told me that he was somewhat avoided during his visits because he was a de la Poer, and I now found myself subtly ostracized for a like reason until I convinced the peasants how little I knew of my heritage. Even then they sullenly disliked me, so that I had to collect most of the village traditions through the mediation of Norrys. What the people could not forgive, perhaps, was that I had come to restore a symbol so abhorrent to them; for, rationally or not, they viewed Exham Priory as nothing less than a haunt of fiends and werewolves.

Piecing together the tales which Norrys collected for me, and supplementing them with the accounts of several savants who had studied the ruins, I deduced that Exham Priory stood on the site of a prehistoric temple; a Druidical or ante-Druidical thing which must have been contemporary with Stonehenge. That indescribable rites had been celebrated there, few doubted, and there were unpleasant tales of the transference of these rites into the Cybele-worship which the Romans had introduced.

Inscriptions still visible in the subcellar bore such unmistakable letters as 'DIV ... OPS ... MAGNA. MAT ...' sign of the Magna Mater whose dark worship was once vainly forbidden to Roman citizens. Anchester had been the camp of the third Augustan legion, as many remains attest, and it was said that the temple of Cybele was splendid and thronged with worshippers who performed nameless ceremonies at the bidding of a Phrygian priest. Tales added that the fall of the old religion did not end the orgies at the temple, but that the priests lived on in the new faith without real change. Likewise was it said that the rites did not vanish with the Roman power, and that certain among the Saxons added to what remained of the temple, and gave it the essential outline it subsequently preserved, making it the centre of a cult feared through half the heptarchy. About 1000 A.D. the place is mentioned in a chronicle as being a substantial stone priory housing a strange and powerful monastic order and surrounded by extensive gardens which needed no walls to exclude a frightened populace. It was never destroyed by the Danes, though after the Norman Conquest it must have declined tremendously; since there was no impediment when Henry the Third granted the site to my ancestor, Gilbert de la Poer, First Baron Exham, in 1261.

Of my family before this date there is no evil report, but something strange must have happened then. In one chronicle there is a reference to a de la Poer as 'cursed of God' in 1307, whilst village legendry had nothing but evil and frantic fear to tell of the castle that went up on the foundations of the old temple and priory. The fireside tales were of the most grisly description, all the ghastlier because of their frightened reticence and cloudy evasiveness. They represented my ancestors as a race of hereditary daemons beside whom Gilles de Retz and the Marquis de Sade would seem the veriest tyros, and hinted whisperingly at their responsibility for the occasional disappearances of villagers through several generations.

The worst characters, apparently, were the barons and their direct heirs; at least, most was whispered about these. If of healthier inclinations, it was said, an heir would early and mysteriously die to make way for another more typical scion. There seemed to be an inner cult in the family, presided over by the head of the house, and sometimes closed except to a few members. Temperament rather than ancestry was evidently the basis of this cult, for it was entered by several who married into the family. Lady Margaret Trevor from Cornwall, wife of Godfrey, the second son of the fifth baron, became a favourite bane of children over the countryside, and the daemon heroine of a particularly horrible old ballad not yet extinct near the Welsh border. Preserved in balladry, too, though not illustrating the same point, is the hideous tale of Lady Mary de la Poer, who shortly after her marriage to the Earl of Shrewsfield was killed by him and his mother, both of the slayers being absolved and blessed by the priest to whom they confessed what they dared not repeat to the world.

These myths and ballads, typical as they were of crude superstition, repelled me greatly. Their persistence, and their application to so long a line of my ancestors, were especially annoying; whilst the imputations of monstrous habits proved unpleasantly reminiscent of the one known scandal of my immediate forbears – the case of my cousin, young Raldolph Delapore of Carfax, who went among the negroes and became a voodoo priest after he returned from the Mexican War.

I was much less disturbed by the vaguer tales of wails and howlings in the barren, windswept valley beneath the limestone cliff; of the grave-yard stenches after the spring rains; of the floundering, squealing white thing on which Sir John Clave's horse had trod one night in a lonely field; and of the servant who had gone mad at what he saw in the priory in the full light of day. These things were hackneyed spectral lore, and I was at that time a pronounced sceptic. The accounts of vanished peasants were less to be dismissed, though not especially significant in view of mediaeval custom. Prying curiosity meant death, and more than one severed head had been publicly shown on the bastions – now effaced – around Exham Priory.

A few of the tales were exceedingly picturesque, and made me wish I had learnt more of the comparative mythology in my youth. There was, for instance, the belief that a legion of batwinged devils kept witches' sabbath each night at the priory – a legion whose sustenance might explain the disproportionate abundance of coarse vegetables harvested in the vast gardens. And, most vivid of all, there was the dramatic epic of the rats – the scampering army of obscene vermin which had burst forth from the castle three months after the tragedy that doomed it to desertion – the lean, filthy, ravenous army which had swept all before it and devoured fowl, cats, dogs, hogs, sheep, and even two hapless human beings before its fury was spent. Around that unforgettable rodent army a whole separate cycle of myths revolves, for it scattered among the village homes and brought curses and horrors in its train.

Such was the lore that assailed me as I pushed to completion, with an elderly obstinacy, the work of restoring my ancestral home. It must not be imagined for a moment that these tales formed my principal psycho-logical environment. On the other hand, I was constantly praised and encouraged by Capt. Norrys and the antiquarians who surrounded and aided me. When the task was done, over two years after its commence-ment, I viewed the great rooms, wainscotted walls, vaulted ceilings, mullioned windows, and broad staircases with a pride which fully com-pensated for the prodigious expense of the restoration.

Every attribute of the Middle Ages was cunningly reproduced, and the new parts blended perfectly with the original walls and foundations. The seat of my fathers was complete, and I looked forward to redeeming at last the local fame of the line which ended in me. I would reside here permanently, and prove that a de la Poer (for I had adopted again the original spelling of the name) need not be a fiend. My comfort was perhaps augmented by the fact, that although Exham Priory was mediaevally fitted, its interior was in truth wholly new and free from old vermin and old ghosts alike.

As I have said, I moved in on 16 July 1923. My household consisted of seven servants and nine cats, of which latter species I am particularly fond. My eldest cat, 'Nigger-Man', was seven years old and had come with me from my home in Bolton, Massachusetts; the others I had accumulated whilst living with Capt. Norrys' family during the restoration of the priory.

For five days our routine proceeded with the utmost placidity, my time being spent mostly in the codification of old family data. I had now obtained some very circumstantial accounts of the the final tragedy and flight of Walter de la Poer, which I conceived to be the probable contents of the hereditary paper lost in the fire at Carfax. It appeared that my ancestor was accused with much reason of having killed all the other members of his household, except four servant confederates, in their sleep, about two weeks after a shocking discovery which changed his whole demeanour, but which, except by implication, he disclosed to no one save perhaps the servants who assisted him and afterwards fled beyond reach.

This deliberate slaughter, which included a father, three brothers, and two sisters, was largely condoned by the villagers, and so slackly treated by the law that its perpetrator escaped honoured, unharmed, and undisguised to Virginia; the general whispered sentiment being that he had purged the land of immemorial curse. What discovery had prompted an act so terrible, I could scarcely even conjecture. Walter de la Poer must have known for years the sinister tales about his family, so that this material could have given him no fresh impulse. Had he, then, witnessed some appalling ancient rite, or stumbled upon some frightful and revealing symbol in the priory or its vicinity? He was reputed to have been a shy, gentle youth in England. In Virginia he seemed not so much hard or bitter as harassed and apprehensive. He was spoken of in the diary of another gentleman adventurer, Francis Harley of Bellview, as a man of unexampled justice, honour, and delicacy.

On 22 July occurred the first incident which, though lightly dismissed at the time, takes on a preternatural significance in relation to later events. It was so simple as to be almost negligible, and could not possibly have been noticed under the circumstances; for it must be recalled that since I was in a building practically fresh and new except for the walls, and surrounded by a well-balanced staff of servitors, apprehension would have been absurd despite the locality.

What I afterwards remembered is merely this – that my old black cat, whose moods I know so well, was undoubtedly alert and anxious to an extent wholly out of keeping with his natural character. He roved from room to room, restless and disturbed, and sniffed constantly about the walls which formed part of the Gothic structure. I realize how trite this sounds – like the inevitable dog in the ghost story, which always growls before his master sees the sheeted figure – yet I cannot consistently suppress it.

The following day a servant complained of restlessness among all the cats in the house. He came to me in my study, a loft west room on the second storey, with groined arches, black oak panelling, and a triple Gothic window overlooking the limestone cliff and desolate valley; and even as he spoke I saw the jetty form of Nigger-Man creeping along the west wall and scratching at the new panels which overlaid the ancient stone.

I told the man that there must be some singular odour or emanation from the old stonework, imperceptible to human senses, but affecting the delicate organs of cats even through the new woodwork. This I truly believed, and when the fellow suggested the presence of mice or rats, I mentioned that there had been no rats there for three hundred years, and that even the field mice of the surrounding country could hardly be found in these high walls, where they had never been known to stray. That afternoon I called on Capt. Norrys, and he assured me that it would be quite incredible for field mice to infest the priory in such a sudden and unprecedented fashion.

That night, dispensing as usual with a valet, I retired in the west tower chamber which I had chosen as my own, reached from the study by a stone staircase and short gallery – the former partly ancient, the latter entirely restored. This room was circular, very high, and without wainscotting, being hung with arras which I had myself chosen in London.

Seeing that Nigger-Man was with me, I shut the heavy Gothic door and retired by the light of the electric bulbs which so cleverly counterfeited candles, finally switching off the light and sinking on the carved and canopied four-poster, with the venerable cat in his accustomed place across my feet. I did not draw the curtains, but gazed out at the narrow north window which I faced. There was a suspicion of aurora in the sky, and the delicate traceries of the window were pleasantly silhouetted.

At some time I must have fallen quietly asleep, for I recall a distinct sense of leaving strange dreams, when the cat started violently from his placid position. I saw him in the faint auroral glow, head strained forward, forefeet on my ankles, and hind feet stretched behind. He was looking intensely at a point on the wall somewhat west of the window, a point which to my eye had nothing to mark it, but towards which all my attention was now directed.

And as I watched, I knew that Nigger-Man was not vainly excited. Whether the arras actually moved I cannot say. I think it did, very slightly. But what I can swear to is that behind it I heard a low, distinct scurrying as of rats or mice. In a moment the cat had jumped bodily on the screening tapestry, bringing the affected section to the floor with his weight, and exposing a damp, ancient wall of stone; patched here and there by the restorers, and devoid of any trace of rodent prowlers.

Nigger-Man raced up and down the floor by this part of the wall clawing the fallen arras and seemingly trying at times to insert a paw between the wall and the oaken floor. He found nothing, and after a time returned wearily to his place across my feet. I had not moved, but I did not sleep again that night.

In the morning I questioned all the servants, and found that none of them had noticed anything unusual, save that the cook remembered the actions of a cat which had rested on her windowsill. This cat had howled at some unknown hour of the night, awaking the cook in time for her to see him dart purposefully out of the open door down the stairs. I drowsed away the noontime, and in the afternoon called again on Capt. Norrys, who became exceedingly interested in what I told him. The odd incidents – so slight yet so curious – appealed to his sense of the picturesque, and elicited from him a number of reminiscences of local ghostly lore. We were genuinely perplexed at the presence of rats, and Norrys lent me some traps and Paris green, which I had the servants place in strategic localities when I returned.

I retired early, being very sleepy, but was harassed by dreams of the most horrible sort, I seemed to be looking down from an immense height upon a twilit grotto, knee-deep with filth, where a white-bearded daemon swineherd drove about with his staff a flock of fungous, flabby beasts whose appearance filled me with unutterable loathing. Then, as the swineherd paused and nodded over his task, a mighty swarm of rats rained down on the stinking abyss and fell to devouring beasts and man alike.

From this terrific vision I was abruptly awaked by the motions of Nigger-Man, who had been sleeping as usual across my feet. This time I did not have to question the source of his snarls and hisses, and of the fear which made him sink his claws into my ankle, unconscious of their effect; for on every side of the chamber the walls were alive with nauseous sound – the verminous slithering of ravenous, gigantic rats. There was no aurora to show the state of the arras – the fallen section of which had been replaced – but I was not too frightened to switch on the light.

As the bulbs leapt into radiance I saw a hideous shaking all over the tapestry, causing the somewhat peculiar designs to execute a singular dance of death. This motion disappeared almost at once, and the sound with it. Springing out of bed, I poked at the arras with the long handle of a warming-pan that rested near, and lifted one section to see what lay beneath. There was nothing but the patched stone wall, and even the cat had lost his tense realization of abnormal presences. When I examined the circular traps that had been placed in the room, I found all of the openings sprung, though no trace remained of what had been caught and had escaped.

Further sleep was out of the question, so, lighting a candle, I opened the door and went out in the gallery towards the stairs to my study, Nigger-Man following at my heels. Before we had reached the stone steps, however, the cat darted ahead of me and vanished down the ancient flight. As I descended the stairs myself, I became suddenly aware of sounds in the great room below; sounds of a nature which could not be mistaken.

The oak-panelled walls were alive with rats, scampering and milling, whilst Nigger-Man was racing about with the fury of a baffled hunter. Reaching the bottom, I switched on the light, which did not this time cause the noise to subside. The rats continued their riot, stampeding with such force and distinctness that I could finally assign to their motions a definite direction. These creatures, in numbers apparently inexhaustible, were engaged in one stupendous migration from inconceivable heights to some depth conceivably or inconceivably below.

I now heard steps in the corridor, and in another moment two servants pushed open the massive door. They were searching the house for some unknown source of disturbance which had thrown all the cats into a snarling panic and caused them to plunge precipitately down several flights of stairs and squat, yowling, before the closed door to the sub-cellar. I asked them if they had heard the rats, but they replied in the negative. And when I turned to call their attention to the sounds in the panels, I realized that the noise had ceased.

With the two men, I went down to the door of the sub-cellar, but found the cats already dispersed. Later I resolved to explore the crypt below, but for the present I merely made a round of the traps. All were sprung, yet all were tenantless. Satisfying myself that no one had heard the rats save the felines and me, I sat in my study till morning, thinking profoundly and recalling every scrap of legend I had unearthed concerning the building I inhabited.

I slept some in the forenoon, leaning back in the one comfortable library chair which my mediaeval plan of furnishing could not banish. Later I telephoned to Capt. Norrys, who came over and helped me to explore the sub-cellar.

Absolutely nothing untoward was found, although we could not repress a thrill at the knowledge that this vault was built by Roman hands. Every low arch and massive pillar was Roman – not the debased Romanesque of the bungling Saxons, but the severe and harmonious classicism of the age of the Caesars; indeed, the walls abounded with inscriptions familiar to the antiquarians who had repeatedly explored the place – things like 'P. GETAE. PROP...TEMP...DONA...' and 'L. PRAEC...VS...PONTIFI...ATYS...'

The reference to Atys made me shiver, for I had read Catullus and knew something of the hideous rites of the Eastern god, whose worship was so mixed with that of Cybele. Norrys and I, by the light of lanterns, tried to interpret the odd and nearly effaced designs on certain irregularly rectangular blocks of stone generally held to be altars, but could make nothing of them. We remembered that one pattern, a sort of rayed sun, was held by students to imply a non-Roman origin, suggesting that these altars had merely been adopted by the Roman priests from some older and perhaps aboriginal temple on the same site. On one of these blocks were some brown stains which made me wonder. The largest, in the centre of the room, had certain features on the upper surface which indicated its connection with fire – probably burnt offerings.

Such were the sights in that crypt before whose door the cats howled, and where Norrys and I now determined to pass the night. Couches were brought down by the servants, who were told not to mind any nocturnal actions of the cats, and Nigger-Man was admitted as much for help as for companionship. We decided to keep the great oak door – a modern replica with slits for ventilation – tightly closed; and, with this attended to, we retired with lanterns still burning to await whatever might occur.

The vault was very deep in the foundations of the priory, and undoubtedly far down on the face of the beetling limestone cliff overlooking the waste valley. That it had been the goal of the scuffling and unexplainable rats I could not doubt, though why, I could not tell. As we lay there expectantly, I found my vigil occasionally mixed with half-formed dreams from which the uneasy motions of the cat across my feet would rouse me.

These dreams were not wholesome, but horribly like the one I had had the night before. I saw again the twilit grotto, and the swineherd with his unmentionable fungous beasts wallowing in filth, and as I looked at these things they seemed nearer and more distinct – so distinct that I could almost observe their features. Then I did observe the flabby features of one them – and awakened with such a scream that Nigger-Man started up, whilst Capt. Norrys, who had not slept, laughed considerably. Norrys might have laughed more – or perhaps less – had he known what it was that made me scream. But I did not remember myself till later. Ultimate horror often paralyses memory in a merciful way.

Norrys waked me when the phenonema began. Out of the same frightful dream I was called by his gentle shaking and his urging to listen to the cats. Indeed, there was much to listen to, for beyond the closed door at the head of the stone steps was a veritable nightmare of feline yelling and clawing, whilst Nigger-Man, unmindful of his kindred outside, was running excitedly around the bare stone walls, in which I heard the same babel of scurrying rats that had troubled me the night before.

An acute terror now rose within me, for here were anomalies which nothing normal could well explain. These rats, if not the creatures of a madness which I shared with the cats alone, must be burrowing and sliding in Roman walls I had thought to be of solid limestone blocks

...unless perhaps the action of water through more than seventeen centuries had eaten winding tunnels which rodent bodies had worn clear and ample... But even so, the spectral horror was no less; for if these were living vermin why did not Norrys hear their disgusting commotion? Why did he urge me to watch Nigger-Man and listen to the cats outside, and why did he guess wildly and vaguely at what could have aroused them?

By the time I had managed to tell him, as rationally as I could, what I thought I was hearing, my ears gave me the last fading impression of the scurrying; which had retreated *still downward*, far underneath this deepest of sub-cellars till it seemed as if the whole cliff below were riddled with questing rats. Norrys was not as sceptical as I had anticipated, but instead seemed profoundly moved. He mentioned to me to notice that the cats at the door had ceased their clamour, as if giving up the rats for lost; whilst Nigger-Man had a burst of renewed restlessness, and was clawing frantically around the bottom of the large stone altar in the centre of the room, which was nearer Norrys' couch than mine.

My fear of the unknown was at this point very great. Something astounding had occurred, and I saw that Capt. Norrys, a younger, stouter and presumably more naturally materialistic man, was affected fully as much as myself – perhaps because of his lifelong and intimate familiarity with local legend. We could for the moment do nothing but watch the old black cat as he pawed with decreasing fervour at the base of the altar, occasionally looking up and mewing to me in that persuasive manner which he used when he wished me to perform some favour for him.

Norrys now took a lantern close to the altar and examined the place where Nigger-Man was pawing; silently kneeling and scraping away the lichens of the centuries which joined the massive pre-Roman block to the tessellated floor. He did not find anything, and was about to abandon his efforts when I noticed a trivial circumstance which made me shudder, even though it implied nothing more than I had already imagined.

I told him of it, and we both looked at its almost imperceptible manifestation with the fixedness of fascinated discovery and acknowledgement. It was only this – that the flame of the lantern set down near the altar was slightly but certainly flickering from a draught of air which it had not before received, and which came indubitably from the crevice between floor and altar where Norrys was scraping the lichens.

We spent the rest of the night in the brilliantly lighted study, nervously discussing what we should do next. The discovery that some vault deeper than the deepest known masonry of the Romans underlay this accursed pile; some vault unsuspected by the curious antiquarians of three centuries; would have been sufficient to excite us without any background of the sinister. As it was, the fascination became two-fold; and we paused in doubt whether to abandon our search and quit the priory forever in superstitious caution, or to gratify our sense of adventure and brave whatever horrors might await us in the unknown depths.

By morning we had comprised, and decided to go to London to gather a group of archaeologists and scientific men fit to cope with the mystery. It should be mentioned that before leaving the sub-cellar we had vainly tried to move the central altar which we now recognized as the gate to a new pit of nameless fear. What secret would open the gate, wiser men than we would have to find.

During many days in London Capt. Norrys and I presented our facts, conjectures, and legendary anecdotes to five eminent authorities, all men who could be trusted to respect any family disclosures which future explorations might develop. We found most of them little disposed to scoff, but, instead, intensely interested and sincerely sympathetic. It is hardly necessary to name them all, but I may say that they included Sir William Brinton, whose excavations in the Troad excited most of the world in their day. As we all took the train for Anchester I felt myself poised on the brink of frightful revelations, a sensation symbolized by the air of mourning among the many Americans at the unexpected death of the President on the other side of the world.

On the evening of 7 August we reached Exham Priory, where the servants assured me that nothing unusual had occurred. The cats, even old Nigger-Man, had been perfectly placid; and not a trap in the house had been sprung. We were to begin exploring on the following day, awaiting which I assigned well-appointed rooms to all my guests.

I myself retired in my own tower chamber, with Nigger-Man across my feet. Sleep came quickly, but hideous dreams assailed me. There was a vision of a Roman feast like that of Trimalchio, with a horror in a covered platter. Then came that damnable, recurrent thing about the swineherd and his filthy drove in the twilit grotto. Yet when I awoke it was full daylight, with normal sounds in the house below. The rats, living or spectral, had not troubled me; and Nigger-Man was still quietly asleep. On going down, I found that the same tranquillity had prevailed elsewhere; a condition which one of the assembled savants – a fellow named Thornton, devoted to the psychic – rather absurdly laid to the fact that I had now been shown the thing which certain forces had wished to show me.

All was now ready, and at 11 a.m. our entire group of seven men bearing powerful electric searchlights and implements of excavation went down to the sub-cellar and bolted the door behind us. Nigger-Man was with us, for the investigators found no occasion to despise his excitability, and were indeed anxious that he be present in case of obscure rodent manifestations. We noted the Roman inscriptions and unknown altar designs only briefly, for three of the savants had already seen them and all knew their characteristics. Prime attention was paid to th momentous central altar, and within an hour Sir William Brinton had caused it to tilt backwards, balanced by some unknown species of counterweight.

There now lay revealed such a horror as would have overwhelmed us had we not been prepared. Through a nearly square opening in the tiled floor, sprawling on a flight of stone steps so prodigously worn that it was little more than an inclined plane at the centre, was a ghastly array of human or semi-human bones. Those which retained their collocation as skeletons showed attitudes of panic, fear, and over all were the marks of rodent gnawing. The skulls denoted nothing short of utter idiocy, cretinism, or primitive semiapedom.

Above the hellishly littered steps arched a descending passage seemingly chiselled from the solid rock, and conducting a current of air. This current was not a sudden and noxious rush as from a closed vault, but a cool breeze with something of freshness in it. We did not pause long, but shiveringly began to clear a passage down the steps. It was then that Sir William, examining the hewn walls, made the odd observation that the passage, according to the direction of the strokes, must have been chiselled *from beneath*.

I must be very deliberate now, and choose my words.

After ploughing down a few steps amidst the gnawed bones we saw that there was light ahead; not any mystic phosphorescence, but a filtered daylight which could not come except from unknown fissures in the cliff that overlooked the waste valley. That such fissures had escaped notice from outside was hardly remarkable, for not only is the valley wholly uninhabited, but the cliff is so high and beetling that only an aeronaut could study its face in detail. A few steps more, and our breaths were literally snatched from us by what we saw; so literally that Thornton, the psychic investigator, actually fainted in the arms of the dazed man who stood behind him. Norrys, his plump face utterly white and flabby, simply cried out inarticulately; whilst I think that what I did was to gasp or hiss, and cover my eyes.

The man behind me – the only one of the party older than I – croaked the hackneyed 'My God!' in the most cracked voice I ever heard. Of seven cultivated men, only Sir William Brinton retained his composure, a thing the more to his credit because he led the party and must have seen the sight first.

It was a twilit grotto of enormous height, stretching away farther than any eye could see; a subterranean world of limitless mystery and horrible suggestion. There were buildings and other architectural remains – in one terrified glance I saw a weird pattern of tumuli, a savage circle of monoliths, a low-domed Roman ruin, a sprawling Saxon pile, and an early English edifice of wood – but all these were dwarfed by the ghoulish spectacle presented by the general surface of the ground. For yards about the steps extended an insane tangle of human bones, or bones at least as human as those on the steps. Like a foamy sea they stretched, some fallen apart, but others wholly or partly articulated as skeletons; these latter invariably in postures of daemoniac frenzy, either fighting off some menace or clutching other forms with cannibal intent.

When Dr Trask, the anthropologist, stopped to classify the skulls, he found a degraded mixture which utterly baffled him. They were mostly lower than the Piltdown man in the scale of evolution, but in every case definitely human. Many were of higher grade, and a very few were skulls of supremely and sensitively developed types. All the bones were gnawed, mostly by rats, but somewhat by others of the half-human drove. Mixed with them were many tiny bones of rats – fallen members of the lethal army which closed the ancient epic.

I wonder that any man among us lived and kept his sanity through that hideous day of discovery. Not Hoffman or Huysmans could conceive a scene more wildly incredible, more frenetically repellent, or more Gothically grotesque than the twilit grotto through which we seven staggered; each stumbling on revelation after revelation, and trying to keep for the nonce from thinking of the events which must have taken place there three hundred, or a thousand, or two thousand, or ten thousand years ago. It was the antechamber of hell, and poor Thornton fainted again when Trask told him that some of the skeleton things must have descended as quadrupeds through the last twenty or more generations.

Horror piled on horror as we began to interpret the architectural remains. The quadruped things – with their occasional recruits from the biped class – had been kept in stone pens, out of which they must have broken in their last delirium of hunger or rat-fear. There had been great herds of them, evidently fattened on the coarse vegetables whose remains could be found as a sort of poisonous ensilage at the bottom of huge stone bind older than Rome. I knew now why my ancestors had had such excessive gardens – would to heaven I could forget! The purpose of the herds I did not have to ask.

Sir William, standing with his searchlight in the Roman ruin, translated aloud the most shocking ritual I have ever known; and told of the diet of the antediluvian cult which the priests of Cybele found and mingled with their own. Norrys, used as he was to the trenches, could not walk straight when he came out of the English building. It was a butcher shop and kitchen – he had expected that – but it was too much to see familiar English implements in such a place, and to read familiar English *graffiti* there, some as recent as 1610. I could not go in that building – that building whose demon activities were stopped only by the dagger of my ancestor Walter de la Poer.

What I did venture to enter was the low Saxon building whose oaken door had fallen, and there I found a terrible row of ten stone cells with rusty bars. Three had tenants, all skeletons of high grade, and on the bony forefinger of one I found a seal ring with my own coat-of-arms. Sir William found a vault with far older cells below the Roman chapel, but these cells were empty. Below them was a low crypt with cases of formally arranged bones, some of them bearing parallel inscriptions carved in Latin, Greek, and the tongue of Phrygia.

Meanwhile, Dr Trask had opened one of the prehistoric tumuli, and brought to light skulls which were slightly more human than a gorilla's, and which bore indescribably ideographic carvings. Through all this horror my cat stalked unperturbed. Once I saw him monstrously perched atop a mountain of bones, and wondered at the secrets that might lie behind his yellow eyes.

Having grasped to some slight degree the frightful revelations of this twilit area — an area so hideously foreshadowed by my recurrent dream — we turned to that apparently boundless depth of midnight cavern where no ray of light from the cliff could penetrate. We shall never know what sightless Stygian worlds yawn beyond the little distance we went, for it was decided that such secrets are not good for mankind. But there was plenty to engross us close at hand, for we had not gone far before the searchlights showed that accursed infinity of pits in which the rats had feasted, and whose sudden lack of replenishment had driven the ravenous rodent army first to turn on the living herds of starving things, and then to burst from the priory in that historic orgy of devastation which the peasants will never forget.

God! those carrion black pits of sawed, picked bones and opened skulls! Those nightmare chasms choked with the pithecanthropoid, Celtic, Roman, and English bones of countless unhallowed centuries! Some of them were full, and none can say how deep they had once been. Others were still bottomless to our searchlights, and peopled by unnamable fancies. What, I thought, of the hapless rats that stumbled into such traps amidst the blackness of their quests in this grisly Tartarus?

Once my foot slipped near a horribly yawning brink, and I had a moment of ecstatic fear. I must have been musing a long time, for I could not see any of the party but the plump Capt. Norrys. Then there came a sound from that inky, boundless, farther distance that I thought I knew; and I saw my old black cat dart past me like a winged Egyptian god, straight into the illimitable gulf of the unknown. But I was not far behind, for there was no doubt after another second. It was the eldritch scurrying of those fiend-born rats, always questing for new horrors, and determined to lead me on even unto those grinning caverns of earth's centre where Nyarlathotep, the mad faceless god, howls blindly in the darkness to the piping of two amorphous idiot flute-players.

My searchlight expired, but still I ran. I heard voices, and yowls, and echoes, but above all there gently rose that impious, insidious scurrying; gently rising, rising, as a still bloated corpse gently rises above an oily river that flows under endless onyx bridges to a black, putrid sea.

Something bumped into me – something soft and plump. It must have been the rats; the viscous, gelatinous, ravenous army that feast on the dead and the living ... Why shouldn't rats eat a de la Poer as a de la Poer eats forbidden things? ... The war ate my boy, damn them all ... and the Yanks ate Carfax with flames and burned the Grandsire Delapore and the secret ... No, no, I tell you, I am *not* that demon swineherd in the twilit grotto! It was *not* Edward Norrys' fat face on that flabby fungous thing! Who says I am a de la Poer? He lived, but my boy died! ... Shall a Norrys hold the lands of a de la Poer? ... It's voodoo, I tell you ... that spotted snake ... Curse you, Thornton, I'll teach you to faint at what my family do! ... 'Sblood, thou stinkard, I'll learn ye how to gust ... wolde ye swynke me thilke wys? ... *Magna Mater! Magna Mater! ... Atys ... Dia ad aghaidh's ad aodaun ... agus bas dunach ort! Dhonas 's dholas ort, agus leatsa! ... Ungl ... ungl ... rrlh ... chchch ...*

That is what they say I said when they found me in the blackness after three hours; found me crouching in the blackness over the plump, half-eaten body of Capt. Norrys, with my own cat leaping and tearing at my throat. Now they have blown up Exham Priory, taken my Nigger-Man away from me, and shut me into this barred room at Hanwell with fearful whispers about my heredity and experience. Thornton is in the next room, but they prevent me from talking to him. They are trying, too, to suppress most of the facts concerning the priory. When I speak of poor Norrys they accuse me of a hideous thing, but they must know that I did not do it. They must know it was the rats; the slithering scurrying rats whose scampering will never let me sleep; the demon rats that race behind the padding in this room and beckon me down to greater horrors than I have ever known; the rats they can never hear; the rats, the rats in the walls.

The Haunted and the Haunters

Lord Lytton

A friend of mine, who is a man of letters and a philosopher, said to me one day, as if between jest and earnest: 'Fancy, since we last met I have discovered a haunted house in the midst of London.'

'Really haunted? – and by what? – ghosts?'

'Well, I can't answer these questions – all I know is this – six weeks ago I and my wife were in search of a furnished apartment. Passing a quiet street, we saw on the window of one of the houses a bill, "Apartments – Furnished". The situation suited us: we entered the house – liked the rooms – engaged them by the week – and left them the third day. No power on earth could have reconciled my wife to stay longer, and I don't wonder at it.'

'What did you see?'

'Excuse me – I have no desire to be ridiculed as a superstitious dreamer – nor, on the other hand, could I ask you to accept on my affirmation what you would hold to be incredible without the evidence of your own senses. Let me only say this, it was not so much what we saw or heard (in which you might fairly suppose that we were the dupes of our own excited fancy, or the victims of imposture in others) that drove us away, as it was an undefinable terror which seized both of us whenever we passed by the door of a certain unfurnished room, in which we neither saw nor heard anything. And the strangest marvel of all was, that for once in my life I agreed with my wife – silly woman though she be – and allowed, after the third night, that it was impossible to stay a fourth in that house. Accordingly, on the fourth morning, I summoned the woman who kept the house and attended on us, and told her that the rooms did not quite suit us, and we would not stay out our week. She said dryly: "I know why; you have stayed longer than any other lodger; few ever stayed a second night; none before you, a third. But I take it they have been very kind to you."

' "They – who?" I asked, affecting a smile.

' "Why, they who haunt the house, whoever they are. I don't mind them; I remember them many years ago, when I lived in this house, not as a servant; but I know they will be the death of me some day. I don't care – I'm old, and must die soon anyhow; and then I shall be with them, and in this house still.'' The woman spoke with so dreary a calmness, that really it was a sort of awe that prevented my conversing with her further. I paid for my week, and too happy were I and my wife to get off so cheaply.'

'You excite my curiosity,' said I; 'nothing I should like better than to sleep in a haunted house. Pray give me the address of the one which you left so ignominiously.'

My friend gave me the address; and when we parted, I walked straight towards the house thus indicated.

It is situated on the north side of Oxford Street, in a dull but respectable thoroughfare. I found the house shut up – no bill at the window, and no response to my knock. As I was turning away, a beer-boy, collecting pewter pots at the neighbouring areas, said to me: 'Do you want anyone in that house, sir?'

'Yes; I heard it was to let.'

'Let! – why, the woman who kept it is dead – has been dead these three weeks, and no one can be found to stay there, though Mr J—— offered ever so much. He offered Mother, who chars for him, a pound a week just to open and shut the windows, and she would not.'

'Would not! – and why?'

'The house is haunted; and the old woman who kept it was found dead in her bed, with her eyes wide open. They say the devil strangled her.'

'Pooh! – you speak of Mr J——. Is he the owner of the house?'

'Yes.'

'Where does he live?'

'In G—— Street, No.——.'

'What is he? – in any business?'

'No, sir – nothing particular; a single gentleman.'

I gave the pot-boy the gratuity earned by his liberal information, and proceeded to Mr J——, in G—— Street, which was close by the street that boasted the haunted house. I was lucky to find Mr J—— at home – an elderly man, with intelligent countenance and prepossessing manners.

I communicated my name and my business frankly. I said I heard the house was considered to be haunted – that I had a strong desire to examine a house with so equivocal a reputation – that I should be greatly obliged if he would allow me to hire it, though only for a night. I was willing to pay for that privilege whatever he might be inclined to ask. 'Sir,' said Mr J——, with great courtesy, 'the house is at your service for as short or as long a time as you please. Rent is out of the question – the obligation will be on my side should you be able to discover the cause of the strange phenomena which at present deprive it of all value. I cannot let it, for I cannot even get a servant to keep it in order or answer the door. Unluckily the house is haunted, if I may use that expression, not only by night, but by day; though at night the disturbances are of a more unpleasant and sometimes of a more alarming character.

'The poor old woman who died in it three weeks ago was a pauper whom I took out of the workhouse, for in her childhood she had been known to some of my family, and had once been in such good circumstances that she had rented that house of my uncle. She was a woman of superior education and strong mind, and was the only person I could ever induce to remain in the house. Indeed, since her death, which was sudden, and the coroner's inquest, which gave it a notoriety in the neighbourhood, I have so despaired of finding any person to take charge of it, much more a tenant, that I would willingly let it rent-free for a year to anyone who would pay its rates and taxes.'

'How long is it since the house acquired this sinister character?'

'That I can scarcely tell you, but very many years since. The old woman I spoke of said it was haunted when she rented it between thirty and forty years ago. The fact is that my life has been spent in the East Indies and in the civil service of the Company. I returned to England last year on inheriting the fortune of an uncle, amongst whose possessions was the house in question. I found it shut up and uninhabited. I was told that it was haunted, that no one would inhabit it. I smiled at what seemed to me so idle a story. I spent some money in repainting and roofing it – added to its old-fashioned furniture a few modern articles – advertised it, and obtained a lodger for a year. He was a colonel retired on half-pay. He came in with his family, a son and a daughter, and four or five servants: they all left the house the next day, and although they deposed that they had all seen something different, that something was equally terrible to all. I really could not in conscience sue, or even blame, the colonel for breach of agreement.

'Then I put in the old woman I have spoken of, and she was empowered to let the house in apartments. I never had one lodger who stayed more than three days. I do not tell you their stories – to no two lodgers have there been exactly the same phenomena repeated. It is better that you should judge for yourself, than enter the house with an imagination influenced by previous narratives; only be prepared to see and hear something or other, and take whatever precautions you yourself, please.'

'Have you never had a curiosity yourself to pass a night in that house?'

'Yes. I passed not a night, but three hours in broad daylight alone in that house. My curiosity is not satisfied, but it is quenched. I have no desire to renew the experiment. You cannot complain, you see, sir, that I am not sufficiently candid; and unless your interest be exceedingly

eager and your nerves unusually strong, I honestly advise you *not* to pass
a night in that house.'

'My interest *is* exceedingly keen,' said I, 'and though only a coward
will boast of his nerves in situations wholly unfamiliar to him, yet my
nerves have been seasoned in such variety of danger that I have the right
to rely on them – even in a haunted house.'

Mr J—— said very little more; he took the keys of the house out of
his bureau, gave them to me; and, thanking him cordially for his frank-
ness, and his urbane concession to my wish, I carried off my prize.

Impatient for the experiment, as soon as I reached home I summoned
my confidential servant, a young man of gay spirits, fearless temper, and
as free from superstitious prejudice as anyone I could think of.

'F——,' said I, 'you remember in Germany how disappointed we were
at not finding a ghost in that old castle which was said to be haunted by
a headless apparition? Well, I have heard of a house in London which,
I have reason to hope, is decidedly haunted. I mean to sleep there
tonight. From what I hear, there is no doubt that something will allow
itself to be seen or to be heard – something, perhaps, excessively horrible.
Do you think, if I take you with me, I may rely on your presence of mind,
whatever may happen?'

'Oh, sir, pray trust me,' answered F——, grinning with delight.

'Very well – then here are the keys of the house – this is the address.
Go now – select for me any bedroom you please; and since the house has
not been inhabited for weeks, make up a good fire – air the bed well –
see, of course, that there are candles as well as fuel. Take with you my
revolver and my dagger – so much for my weapons – arm yourself equally
well; and if we are not a match for a dozen ghosts, we shall be but a sorry
couple of Englishmen.'

I was engaged for the rest of the day on business so urgent that I had
not leisure to think much on the nocturnal adventure to which I had
plighted my honour. I dined alone, and very late, and while dining,
read, as is my habit. The volume I selected was one of Macaulay's
Essays. I thought to myself that I would take the book with me; there
was so much of healthfulness in the style, and practical life in the subjects,
that it would serve as an antidote against the influence of superstitious
fancy.

Accordingly, about half past nine, I put the book into my pocket, and
strolled leisurely towards the haunted house. I took with me a favourite
dog – an exceedingly sharp, bold, and vigilant bull-terrier – a dog fond
of prowling about strange ghostly corners and passages at night in search
of rats – a dog of dogs for a ghost.

It was a summer night, but chilly, the sky somewhat gloomy and
overcast. Still, there was a moon – faint and sickly, but still a moon, and
if the clouds permitted, after midnight it would be brighter.

I reached the house, knocked, and my servant opened with a cheerful smile.

'All right, sir, and very comfortable.'

'Oh!' said I, rather disappointed. 'Have you not seen nor heard anything remarkable?'

'Well, sir, I must own I have heard something queer.'

'What – what?'

'The sound of feet pattering behind me; and once or twice small noises like whispers close at my ear – nothing more.'

'You are not at all frightened?'

'I – not a bit of it, sir'; and the man's bold look reassured me on one point – viz. that, happen what might, he would not desert me.

We were in the hall, the street door closed, and my attention was now drawn to my dog. He had at first run in eagerly enough, but had sneaked back to the door, and was scratching and whining to get out. After patting him on the head, and encouraging him gently, the dog seemed to reconcile himself to the situation and followed me and F—— through the house, but keeping close at my heels instead of hurrying inquisitively in advance, which was his usual and normal habit in all strange places. We first visited the subterranean apartments, the kitchen and other offices, and especially the cellars, in which last there were two or three bottles of wine still left in a bin, covered with cobwebs, and evidently, by their appearance, undisturbed for many years. It was clear that the ghosts were not wine-bibbers.

For the rest we discovered nothing of interest. There was a gloomy little backyard, with very high walls. The stones of this yard were very damp – and what with the damp, and what with the dust and smoke-grime on the pavement, our feet left a slight impression where we passed. And now appeared the first strange phenomenon witnessed by myself in this strange abode. I saw, just before me, the print of a foot suddenly form itself, as it were. I stopped, caught hold of my servant, and pointed to it. In advance of that footprint as suddenly dropped another. We both saw it. I advanced quickly to the place; the footprint kept advancing before me, a small footprint – the foot of a child: the impression was too faint thoroughly to distinguish the shape, but it seemed to us both that it was the print of a naked foot. This phenomenon ceased when we arrived at the opposite wall, nor did it repeat itself on returning.

We remounted the stairs, and entered the rooms on the ground floor – a dining-parlour, a small back-parlour, and a still smaller third room that had been probably appropriated to a footman – as still as death. We then visited the drawing-rooms, which seemed fresh and new. In the front room I seated myself in an arm-chair. F—— placed on the table the candlestick with which he had lighted us. I told him to shut the door. As he turned to do so, a chair opposite to me moved from the wall quickly and noiselessly, and dropped itself about a yard from my own chair, immediately fronting it.

'Why, this is better than the turning-tables,' said I, with a half-laugh – and as I laughed, my dog put back his head and howled.

F——, coming back, had not observed the movement of the chair. He employed himself now in quieting the dog. I continued to gaze on the chair, and fancied I saw on it a pale-blue misty outline of a human figure, but an outline so indistinct that I could only distrust my own vision. The dog now was quiet. 'Put back that chair opposite to me,' said I to F——; 'put it back to the wall.'

F—— obeyed. 'Was that you, sir?' said he, turning abruptly.

'I – what?'

'Why, something struck me. I felt it sharply on the shoulder – just here.'

'No,' said I. 'But we have jugglers present, and though we may not discover their tricks, we shall catch *them* before they frighten *us*.'

We did not stay long in the drawing-rooms – in fact, they felt so damp and so chilly that I was glad to get to the fire upstairs. We locked the doors of the drawing-rooms – a precaution which, I should observe, we had taken with all the rooms we had searched below. The bedroom my servant had selected for me was the best on the floor – a large one, with two windows fronting the street. The four-poster bed, which took up no inconsiderable space, was opposite the fire, which burned clear and bright; a door in the wall to the left, between the bed and the window, communicated with the room which my servant appropriated to himself.

This last was a small room with a sofa-bed, and had no communication with the landing-place – no other door but that which conducted to the bedroom I was to occupy. On either side of my fireplace was a cupboard, without locks, flushed with the wall, and covered with the same dull-brown paper. We examined these cupboards – only hooks to suspend female dresses – nothing else; we sounded the walls – evidently solid – the outer walls of the building. Having finished the survey of these apartments, warmed myself a few moments, and lighted my cigar, I then, still accompanied by F——, went forth to complete my reconnoitre. In the landing-place there was another door; it was closed firmly.

'Sir,' said my servant in surprise, 'I unlocked this door with all the others when I first came; it cannot have got locked from the inside, for it is a——'

Before he had finished the sentence the door, which neither of us then was touching, opened quietly of itself. We looked at each other a single instant. The same thought seized both – some human agency might be detected here. I rushed in first, my servant followed. A small blank dreary room without furniture – a few empty boxes and hampers in a corner – a small window – the shutters closed – not even a fireplace – no other

door but that by which we had entered – no carpet on the floor, and the
floor seemed very old, uneven, worm-eaten, mended here and there, as
was shown by the whiter patches on the wood; but no living being, and
no visible place in which a living being could have hidden. As we stood
gazing around, the door by which we had entered closed as quietly as
it had before opened: we were imprisoned.

For the first time I felt a creep of undefinable horror. Not so my
servant. 'Why, they don't think to trap us, sir; I could break that
trumpery door with a kick of my boot.'

'Try first if it will open to your hand,' said I, shaking off the vague
apprehension that had seized me, 'while I open the shutters and see what
is without.'

I unbarred the shutters – the window looked on the little backyard I
have before described; there was no ledge without – nothing but sheer
descent. No man getting out of that window would have found any
footing till he had fallen on the stones below.

F——, meanwhile, was vainly attempting to open the door. He now
turned round to me, and asked my permission to use force. And I should
here state, in justice to the servant, that, far from evincing any superstitious terrors, his nerve, composure, and even gaiety amidst circumstances so extraordinary compelled my admiration, and made me
congratulate myself on having secured a companion in every way fitted
to the occasion. I willingly gave him the permission he required. But
though he was a remarkably strong man, his force was as idle as his milder
efforts; the door did not even shake to his stoutest kick. Breathless and
panting, he desisted. I then tried the door myself, equally in vain.

As I ceased from the effort, again that creep of horror came over me;
but this time it was more cold and stubborn. I felt as if some strange and
ghastly exhalation were rising up from the chinks of that rugged floor,
and filling the atmosphere with a venomous influence hostile to human
life. The door now very slowly and quietly opened as of its own accord.
We precipitated ourselves into the landing-place. We both saw a large
pale light – as large as the human figure, but shapeless and unsubstantial
– move before us, and ascend the stairs that led from the landing into the
attics. I followed the light, and my servant followed me. It entered, to
the right of the landing, a small garret, of which the door stood open. I
entered in the same instant. The light then collapsed into a small globule,
exceedingly brilliant and vivid, rested a moment on a bed in the corner,
quivered, and vanished. We approached the bed and examined it – a
half-tester, such as is commonly found in attics devoted to servants. On
the drawers that stood near it we perceived an old faded silk kerchief,
with the needle still left in a rent half repaired. The kerchief was covered
with dust; probably it had belonged to the old woman who had last died
in that house, and this might have been her sleeping-room.

I had sufficient curiosity to open the drawers; there were a few odds and ends of female dress, and two letters tied round with a narrow ribbon of faded yellow. I took the liberty to possess myself of the letters. We found nothing else in the room worth noticing – nor did the light reappear; but we distinctly heard, as we turned to go, a pattering footfall on the floor – just before us. We went through the other attics (in all, four), the footfall still preceding us. Nothing to be seen – nothing but the footfall heard. I had the letters in my hand; just as I was descending the stairs I distinctly felt my wrist seized, and a faint, soft effort made to draw the letters from my clasp. I only held them the more tightly, and the effort ceased.

We regained the bed-chamber appropriated to myself, and I then remarked that my dog had not followed us when we had left it. He was thrusting himself close to the fire, and trembling. I was impatient to examine the letters; and while I read them, my servant opened a little box in which he had deposited the weapons I had ordered him to bring, took them out, placed them on a table close at my bed-head, and then occupied himself in soothing the dog, who, however, seemed to heed him very little.

The letters were short; they were dated – the dates exactly thirty-five years ago. They were evidently from a lover to his mistress, or a husband to some young wife. Not only the terms of expression, but a distinct reference to a former voyage indicated the writer to have been a seafarer. The spelling and handwriting were those of a man imperfectly educated, but still the language itself was forcible. In the expressions of endearment there was a kind of rough wild love; but here and there were dark unintelligible hints at some secret not of love – some secret that seemed of crime. 'We ought to love each other,' was one of the sentences I remember, 'for how everyone else would execrate us if all was known.' Again: 'Don't let anyone be in the same room with you at night – you talk in your sleep.' And again: 'What's done can't be undone; and I tell you there's nothing against us unless the dead could come to life.' Here there was underlined in a better handwriting (a female's), 'They do!' At the end of the letter latest in date the same female hand had written these words: 'Lost at sea the fourth of June, the same day as——'

I put down the letters, and began to muse over their contents.

Fearing, however, that the train of thought into which I fell might unsteady my nerves, I fully determined to keep my mind in a fit state to cope with whatever of marvellous the advancing night might bring forth. I roused myself – laid the letters on the table – stirred up the fire, which was still bright and cheering – and opened my volume of Macaulay. I read quietly enough till about half past eleven. I then threw myself dressed upon the bed, and told my servant he might retire to his own room, but must keep himself awake. I bade him leave open the door between the two rooms. Thus alone, I kept two candles burning on the table by my bed-head. I placed my watch beside the weapons, and calmly resumed my Macaulay.

Opposite me the fire burned clear; and on the hearth-rug, seemingly asleep, lay the dog. In about twenty minutes I felt an exceedingly cold air pass by my cheek, like a sudden draught. I fancied the door to my right, communicating with the landing-place, must have got open; but no – it was closed. I then turned my glance to my left, and saw the flame of the candles violently swayed as by a wind. At the same moment the watch beside the revolver softly slid from the table – softly, softly – no visible hand – it was gone. I sprang up, seizing the revolver with the one hand, the dagger with the other; I was not willing that my weapons should share the fate of the watch. Thus armed, I looked round the floor – no sign of the watch. Three slow, loud, distinct knocks were now heard at the bed-head. My servant called out: 'Is that you, sir?'

'No; be on your guard.'

The dog now roused himself and sat on his haunches, his ears moving quickly backwards and forwards. He kept his eyes fixed on me with a look so strange that he concentrated all my attention on himself. Slowly he rose up, all his hair bristling, and stood perfectly rigid, and with the same wild stare. I had not time, however, to examine the dog. Presently my servant emerged from his room; and if ever I saw horror in the human face, it was then. I should not have recognized him had we met in the streets, so altered was every lineament. He passed by me quickly, saying in a whisper that seemed scarcely to come from his lips, 'Run – run, it is after me!' He gained the door to the landing, pulled it open, and rushed forth. I followed him into the landing involuntarily, calling him to stop; but, without heeding me, he bounded down the stairs, clinging to the balusters, and taking several steps at a time. I heard, where I stood, the street door open – heard it again clap to. I was left alone in the haunted house.

It was but for a moment that I remained undecided whether or not to follow my servant; pride and curiosity alike forbade so dastardly a flight. I re-entered my room, closing the door after me, and proceeded cautiously into the interior chamber. I encountered nothing to justify my servant's terror. I again carefully examined the walls, to see if there were any concealed door. I could find no trace of one – not even a seam in the dull-brown paper with which the room was hung. How, then, had the Thing, whatever it was, which had so scared him, obtained ingress except through my own chamber?

I returned to my room, shut and locked the door that opened upon the interior one, and stood on the hearth, expectant and prepared. I now perceived that the dog had slunk into an angle of the wall, and was pressing himself close against it, as if literally trying to force his way into it. I approached the animal and spoke to it; the poor brute was evidently beside itself with terror. It showed all its teeth, the slaver dropping from its jaws, and would certainly have bitten me if I had touched it. It did not seem to recognize me. Whoever has seen at the Zoological Gardens a rabbit fascinated by a serpent, cowering in a corner, may form some idea of the anguish which the dog exhibited. Finding all efforts to soothe the animal in vain, and fearing that his bite might be as venomous in that state as if in the madness of hydrophobia, I left him alone, placed my weapons on the table beside the fire, seated myself, and recommenced my Macaulay.

Perhaps in order not to appear seeking credit for a courage, or rather a coolness, which the reader may conceive I exaggerate, I may be pardoned if I pause to indulge in one or two egotistical remarks.

As I hold presence of mind, or what is called courage, to be precisely proportioned to familiarity with the circumstances that lead to it, so I should say that I had been long sufficiently familiar with all experiments that appertain to the marvellous. I had witnessed many very extra-ordinary phenomena in various parts of the world – phenomena that would be either totally disbelieved if I stated them or ascribed to super-natural agencies. Now, my theory is that the Supernatural is the Im-possible, and that what is called supernatural is only a something in the laws of nature of which we have been hitherto ignorant. Therefore, if a ghost rise before me, I have not the right to say, 'So, then, the super-natural is possible,' but rather, 'So, then, the apparition of a ghost is, contrary to received opinion, within the laws of nature – i.e. not super-natural.'

Now, in all that I had hitherto witnessed, and indeed in all the wonders which the amateurs of mystery in our age record as facts, a material living agency is always required. On the Continent you will still find magicians who assert that they can raise spirits. Assuming for the moment that what they assert is the truth, still the living material form of the magician is present; and he is the material agency by which from some constitutional peculiarities certain strange phenomena are represented to your natural senses.

Accept again, as truthful, the tales of spirit manifestation in America – musical or other sounds – writings on paper, produced by no discernible hand – articles of furniture moved about without apparent human agency – or the actual sight and touch of hands to which no bodies seem to belong – still there must be found the *medium* or living being, with constitutional peculiarities, capable of obtaining these signs. In fine, in all such marvels, supposing even that there is no imposture, there must be a human being like ourselves, by whom, or through whom, the effects presented to human beings are produced. It is so with the now familiar phenomena of mesmerism or electro-biology; the mind of the person operated on is affected through a material living agent. Nor, supposing it true that a mesmerized patient can respond to the will or passes of a mesmerizer a hundred miles distant, is the response less occasioned by a material being; it may be through a material fluid – call it Electric, call it Odic, call it what you will – which has the power of traversing space and passing obstacles, that the material effect is communicated from one to the other.

Hence all that I had hitherto witnessed, or expected to witness, in this strange house, I believed to be occasioned through some agency or medium as mortal as myself; and this idea necessarily prevented the awe with which those who regard as supernatural things that are not within the ordinary operations of nature, might have been impressed by the adventures of that memorable night.

As, then, it was my conjecture that all that was presented, or would be presented, to my senses, must originate in some human being gifted by constitution with the power so to present them, and having some motive so to do, I felt an interest in my theory which, in its way, was rather philosophical than superstitious. And I can sincerely say that I was in as tranquil a temper for observation as any practical experimentalist could be in awaiting the effects of some rare though perhaps perilous chemical combination. Of course, the more I kept my mind detached from fancy, the more the temper fitted for observation would be obtained; and I therefore riveted eye and thought on the strong daylight sense in the page of my Macaulay.

I now became aware that something interposed between the page and the light – the page was over-shadowed; I looked up, and I saw what I shall find it very difficult, perhaps impossible, to describe.

It was a Darkness shaping itself out of the air in very undefined outline. I cannot say it was of a human form, and yet it had more resemblance to a human form, or rather shadow, than anything else. As it stood, wholly apart and distinct from the air and the light around it, its dimensions seemed gigantic, the summit nearly touching the ceiling. While I gazed, a feeling of intense cold seized me. An iceberg before me could not more have chilled me; nor could the cold of an iceberg have been more purely physical. I feel convinced that it was not the cold caused by fear. As I continued to gaze, I thought – but this I cannot say with precision – that I distinguished two eyes looking down on me from the height. One moment I seemed to distinguish them clearly, the next they seemed gone; but still two rays of a pale-blue light frequently shot through the darkness, as from the height on which I half believed, half doubted that I had encountered the eyes.

I strove to speak – my voice utterly failed me; I could only think: 'Is this fear? It is *not* fear!' I strove to rise – in vain; I felt as if weighed down by an irresistible force. Indeed, my impression was that of an immense and overwhelming power opposed to my volition; that sense of utter

inadequacy to cope with a force beyond men's, which one may feel
physically in a storm at sea, in a conflagration, or when confronting some
terrible wild beast, or rather, perhaps, the shark of the ocean, I felt
morally. Opposed to my will was another will, as far superior to its strength
as storm, fire, and shark are superior in material force to the force of men.

And now, as this impression grew on me, now came, at last, horror –
horror to a degree that no words can convey. Still I retained pride, if not
courage; and in my own mind I said: 'This is horror, but it is not fear;
unless I fear, I cannot be harmed; my reason rejects this thing; it is an
illusion – I do not fear.' With a violent effort I succeeded at last in
stretching out my hand towards the weapon on the table; as I did so, on
the arm and shoulder I received a strange shock, and my arm fell to my
side powerless. And now, to add to my horror, the light began slowly to
wane from the candles – they were not, as it were, extinguished, but their
flame seemed very gradually withdrawn; it was the same with the fire –
the light was extracted from the fuel; in a few minutes the room was in
utter darkness.

The dread that came over me, to be thus in the dark with that dark
Thing, whose power was so intensely felt, brought a reaction of nerve.
In fact, terror had reached that climax, that either my senses must have
deserted me, or I must have burst through the spell. I did burst through
it. I found voice, though the voice was a shriek. I remember that I broke
forth with words like these – 'I do not fear, my soul does not fear'; and
at the same time I found the strength to rise. Still in that profound gloom
I rushed to one of the windows – tore aside the curtain – flung open the
shutters; my first thought was – LIGHT. And when I saw the moon high,
clear, and calm, I felt a joy that almost compensated for the previous
terror. There was the moon, there was also the light from the gas-lamps
in the deserted slumbrous street. I turned to look back into the room; the
moon penetrated its shadow very palely and partially – but still there was
light. The dark Thing, whatever it might be, was gone – except that I
could yet see a dim shadow which seemed the shadow of that shade,
against the opposite wall.

My eye now rested on the table, and from under the table (which was
without cloth or cover – an old mahogany round table) there rose a hand,
visible as far as the wrist. It was a hand, seemingly, as much of flesh and
blood as my own, but the hand of an aged person – lean, wrinkled, small
too – a woman's hand.

That hand very softly closed on the two letters that lay on the table:
hand and letters both vanished. There then came the same three loud
measured knocks I had heard at the bed-head before this extraordinary
drama had commenced.

As those sounds slowly ceased, I felt the whole room vibrate sensibly;
and at the far end there rose, as from the floor, sparks or globules like

bubbles of light, many-coloured – green, yellow, fire-red, azure. Up and down, to and fro, hither, thither, as tiny will-o'-the-wisps, the sparks moved, slow or swift, each at its own caprice. A chair (as in the drawing-room below) was now advanced from the wall without apparent agency, and placed at the opposite side of the table. Suddenly, as forth from the chair, there grew a shape – a woman's shape. It was distinct as a shape of life – ghastly as a shape of death. The face was that of youth, with a strange mournful beauty; the throat and shoulders were bare, the rest of the form in a loose robe of cloudy white. It began sleeking its long yellow hair, which fell over its shoulders; its eyes were not turned towards me, but to the door; it seemed listening, watching, waiting. The shadow of a shade in the background grew darker; and again I thought I beheld the eyes gleaming out from the summit of the shadow – eyes fixed upon that shape.

As if from the door, though it did not open, there grew out another shape equally distinct, equally ghastly – a man's shape – a young man's. It was in the dress of the last century, or rather in a likeness of such dress; for both the male shape and the female, though defined, were evidently unsubstantial, impalpable – simulacra – phantasms; and there was something incongruous, grotesque, yet fearful, in the contrast between the elaborate finery, the courtly precision of that old-fashioned garb, with its ruffles and lace and buckles, and the corpse-like aspect and ghost-like stillness of the flitting wearer. Just as the male shape approached the female, the dark Shadow started from the wall, all three for a moment wrapped in darkness. When the pale light returned, the two phantoms were as if in the grasp of the Shadow that towered between them; and there was a bloodstain on the breast of the female; and the phantom-male was leaning on its phantom sword, and blood seemed trickling fast from the ruffles, from the lace; and the darkness of the intermediate Shadow swallowed them up – they were gone. And again the bubbles of light shot, and sailed, and undulated, growing thicker and thicker and more wildly confused in their movements.

The closet-door to the right of the fireplace now opened, and from the aperture there came the form of a woman, aged. In her hand she held letters – the very letters over which I had seen *the* Hand close; and behind her I heard a footstep. She turned round as if to listen, then she opened the letters and seemed to read; and over her shoulder I saw a livid face, the face as of a man long drowned – bloated, bleached – seaweed tangled in its dripping hair; and at her feet lay a form of a corpse and beside the corpse there cowered a child, a miserable, squalid child, with famine in its cheeks and fear in its eyes. And as I looked in the old woman's face, the wrinkles and lines vanished, and it became a face of youth – hard-eyed, stony, but still youth; and the Shadow darted forth and darkened over these phantoms as it had darkened over the last.

Nothing now was left but the Shadow, and on that my eyes were intently fixed, till again eyes grew out of the Shadow – malignant serpent eyes. And the bubbles of light again rose and fell, and in their disordered, irregular, turbulent maze, mingled with the wan moonlight. And now from these globules themselves as from the shell of an egg, monstrous things burst out; the air grew filled with them; larvae so bloodless and so hideous that I can in no way describe them except to remind the reader of the swarming life which the solar microscope brings before his eyes in a drop of water – things transparent, supple, agile, chasing each other, devouring each other – forms like naught ever beheld by the naked eye. As the shapes were without symmetry, so their movements were without order. In their very vagrancies there was no sport; they came round me and round, thicker and faster and swifter, swarming over my head, crawling over my right arm, which was outstretched in involuntary command against all evil beings.

Sometimes I felt myself touched, but not by them; invisible hands touched me. Once I felt the clutch as of cold soft fingers at my throat. I was still equally conscious that if I gave way to fear I should be in bodily peril; and I concentrated all my faculties in the single focus of resisting, stubborn will. And I turned my sight from the Shadow – above all, from those strange serpent eyes – eyes that had now become distinctly visible. For there, though in naught else around me, I was aware that there was a *will*, and a will of intense, creative, working evil, which might crush down my own.

The pale atmosphere in the room began now to redden as if in the air of some near conflagration. The larvae grew lurid as things that live in fire. Again the room vibrated; again were heard the three measured knocks; and again all things were swallowed up in the darkness of the dark Shadow, as if out of that darkness all had come, into that darkness all returned.

As the gloom receded, the Shadow was wholly gone. Slowly as it had been withdrawn, the flame grew again into the candles on the table, again into the fuel in the grate. The whole room came once more calmly, healthfully into sight.

The two doors were still closed, the door communicating with the servants' room still locked. In the corner of the wall, into which he had so convulsively niched himself, lay the dog. I called to him – no movement; I approached – the animal was dead; his eyes protruded; his tongue out of his mouth; the froth gathered round his jaws. I took him in my arms; I brought him to the fire; I felt acute grief for the loss of my poor favourite – acute self-reproach; I accused myself of his death; I imagined he had died of fright. But what was my surprise on finding that his neck was actually broken – actually twisted out of the vertebrae. Had this been done in the dark? – must it not have been by a hand human as mine? –

must there not have been a human agency all the while in that room? Good cause to suspect it. I cannot tell. I cannot do more than state the fact fairly; the reader may draw his own inference.

Another surprising circumstance – my watch was restored to the table from which it had been so mysteriously withdrawn; but it had stopped at the very moment it was so withdrawn; nor, despite all the skill of the watchmaker, has it ever gone since – that is, it will go in a strange erratic way for a few hours, and then comes to a dead stop – it is worthless.

Nothing more chanced for the rest of the night. Nor, indeed, had I long to wait before the dawn broke. Not till it was broad daylight did I quit the haunted house. Before I did so, I revisited the little blind room in which my servant and myself had been for a time imprisoned. I had a strong impression – for which I could not account – that from that room had originated the mechanism of the phenomena – if I may use the term – which had been experienced in my chamber. And though I entered it now in the clear day, with the sun peering through the filmy window, I still felt, as I stood on its floor, the creep of the horror which I had first there experienced the night before, and which had been so aggravated by what had passed in my own chamber. I could not, indeed, bear to stay more than half a minute within those walls. I descended the stairs, and again I heard the footfall before me; and when I opened the street door, I thought I could distinguish a very low laugh. I gained my own home, expecting to find my runaway servant there. But he had not presented himself; nor did I hear more of him for three days, when I received a letter from him, dated from Liverpool, to this effect:

Honoured Sir,

I humbly entreat your pardon, though I can scarcely hope that you will think I deserve it, unless – which heaven forbid! – you saw what I did. I feel that it will be years before I can recover myself; and as to being fit for service, it is out of the question. I am therefore going to my brother-in-law at Melbourne. The ship sails tomorrow. Perhaps the long voyage will set me up. I do nothing but start and tremble, and fancy It is behind me. I humbly beg you, honoured sir, to order my clothes, and whatever wages are due to me, to be sent to my mother's, at Walworth – John knows her address.

The letter ended with additional apologies, somewhat incoherent, and explanatory details as to the effects that had been under the writer's charge.

This flight may perhaps warrant a suspicion that the man wished to go to Australia, and had been somehow or other fraudulently mixed up with the events of the night. I say nothing in refutation of that conjecture; rather, I suggest it as one that would seem to many persons the most probable solution of improbable occurrences. My own theory remained unshaken. I returned in the evening to the house, to bring away in a hack-cab the things I had left there, with my poor dog's body. In this task I was not disturbed, nor did any incident worth note befall me, except that again, on ascending and descending the stairs I heard the same footfalls in advance. On leaving the house, I went to Mr J——'s. He was at home. I returned him the keys, told him that my curiosity was sufficiently gratified, and was about to relate quickly what had passed, when he stopped me, and said, though with much politeness, that he had no longer any interest in the mystery which none had ever solved.

I determined at least to tell him of the two letters I had read, as well as of the extraordinary manner in which they had disappeared, and I then inquired if he thought they had been addressed to the woman who had died in the house, and if there were anything in her early history which could possibly confirm the dark suspicions to which the letters gave rise. Mr J—— seemed startled, and, after musing a few moments, answered: 'I know but little of the woman's earlier history, except, as I before told you, that her family were known to mine. But you revive some vague reminiscences to her prejudice. I will make inquiries, and inform you of their result. Still, even if we could admit the popular superstition that a person who had been either the perpetrator or the victim of dark crimes in life could revisit, as a restless spirit, the scene in which those crimes had been committed, I should observe that the house was infested by strange sights and sounds before the old woman died—— You smile – what would you say?'

'I would say this: that I am convinced, if we could get to the bottom of these mysteries, we should find a living human agency.'

'What, you believe it is all an imposture? For what object?'

'Not an imposture in the ordinary sense of the word. If suddenly I were to sink into a deep sleep, from which you could not awake me, but in that sleep could answer questions with an accuracy which I could not pretend to when awake – tell you what money you had in your pocket – nay, describe your very thoughts – it is not necessarily an imposture, any more than it is necessarily supernatural. I should be, unconsciously to myself, under a mesmeric influence conveyed to me from a distance by a human being who had acquired power over me by previous *rapport*.'

'Granting mesmerism, so far carried, to be a fact, you are right. And you would infer from this that a mesmerizer might produce the extra-ordinary efforts you and others have witnessed over inanimate objects – fill the air with sights and sounds?'

'Or impress our senses with the belief in them – we never having been *en rapport* with the person acting on us? No. What is commonly called mesmerism could not do this; but there may be a power akin to mes-merism, and superior to it – the power that in the old days was called

Magic. That such a power may extend to all inanimate objects of matter, I do not say; but if so, it would not be against nature, only a rare power in nature which might be given to constitutions with certain peculiarities, and cultivated by practice to an extraordinary degree. That such a power might extend over the dead – that is, over certain thoughts and memories that the dead may still retain – and compel, not that which ought properly to be called the *soul*, and which is far beyond human reach, but rather a phantom of what has been most earth-stained on earth, to make itself apparent to our senses – is a very ancient though obsolete theory, upon which I will hazard no opinion. But I do not conceive the power would be supernatural.

'Let me illustrate what I mean from an experiment which Paracelsus describes as not difficult, and which the author of the *Curiosities of Literature* cites as credible: A flower perishes; you burn it. Whatever were the elements of that flower while it lived are gone, dispersed, you know not whither; you can never discover nor re-collect them. But you can, by chemistry, out of the burnt dust of that flower, raise a spectrum of the flower, just as it seemed in life. It may be the same with the human being. The soul has so much escaped you as the essence or elements of the flower. Still you may make a spectrum of it. And this phantom, though in the popular superstition it is held to be the soul of the departed, must not be confounded with the true soul; it is but the eidolon of the dead form.

'Hence, like the best-attested stories of ghosts or spirits, the thing that most strikes us is the absence of what we hold to be soul – that is, of superior emancipated intelligence. They come for little or no object – they seldom speak, if they do come; they utter no ideas above that of an ordinary person on earth. These American spirit-seers have published volumes of communications in prose and verse, which they assert to be given in the names of the most illustrious dead – Shakespeare, Bacon – heaven knows whom. Those communications, taking the best, are certainly not a whit of higher order than would be communications from living persons of fair talent and education; they are wondrously inferior to what Bacon, Shakespeare, and Plato said and wrote when on earth.

'Nor, what is more notable, do they ever contain an idea that was not on the earth before. Wonderful, therefore, as such phenomena may be (granting them to be truthful), I see much that philosophy may question, nothing that it is incumbent on philosophy to deny – viz. nothing supernatural. They are but ideas conveyed somehow or other (we have not yet discovered the means) from one mortal brain to another. Whether, in so doing, tables walk of their own accord, or fiend-like shapes appear in a magic circle, or bodiless hands rise and remove material objects, or a Thing of Darkness, such as presented itself to me, freeze our blood – still am I persuaded that these are but agencies conveyed, as by electric wires, to my own brain from the brain of another.

'In some constitutions there is a natural chemistry, and those may produce chemic wonders – in others a natural fluid, call it electricity, and these produce electric wonders. But they differ in this from Normal Science – they are alike objectless, purposeless, puerile, frivolous. They lead on to no grand results; and therefore the world does not heed, and true sages have not cultivated them. But sure I am, that of all I saw or heard, a man, human as myself, was the remote originator; and I believe unconsciously to himself as to the exact effects produced, for this reason: no two persons, you say, have ever told you that they experienced exactly the same thing. Well, observe, no two persons ever experience exactly the same dream. If this were an ordinary imposture, the machinery would be arranged for results that would but little vary; if it were a supernatural agency permitted by the Almighty, it would surely be for some definite end.

'These phenomena belong to neither class; my persuasion is that they originate in some brain now far distant; that that brain had no distinct volition in anything that occurred; that what does occur reflects but its devious, motley, ever-shifting, half-formed thoughts; in short, that it has been but the dreams of such a brain put into action and invested with a semi-substance. That this brain is of immense power, that it can set matter into movement, that it is malignant and destructive, I believe: some material force must have killed my dog; it might, for aught I know, have sufficed to kill myself, had I been as subjugated by terror as the dog – had my intellect or my spirit given me no countervailing resistance in my will.'

'It killed your dog! That is fearful! Indeed, it is strange that no animal can be induced to stay in that house; not even a cat. Rats and mice are never found in it.'

'The instincts of the brute creation detect influences deadly to their existence. Man's reason has a sense less subtle, because it has a resisting power more supreme. But enough; do you comprehend my theory?'

'Yes, though imperfectly – and I accept any crotchet (pardon the word), however odd, rather than embrace at once the notion of ghosts and hobgoblins we imbibed in our nurseries. Still, to my unfortunate house the evil is the same. What on earth can I do with the house?'

'I will tell you what I would do. I am convinced from my own internal feelings that the small unfurnished room at right angles to the door of the bedroom which I occupied, forms a starting point or receptacle for the influences which haunt the house; and I strongly advise you to have the walls opened, the floor removed – nay, the whole room pulled down. I observe that it is detached from the body of the house, built over the small back-yard, and could be removed without injury to the rest of the building.'

'And you think if I did that——'

'You would cut off the telegraph wires. Try it. I am so persuaded that I am right, that I will pay half the expense if you will allow me to direct the operations.'

'Nay, I am well able to afford the cost; for the rest, allow me to write to you.'

About ten days afterwards I received a letter from Mr J——, telling me that he had visited the house since I had seen him; that he had found the two letters I had described, replaced in the drawer from which I had taken them; that he had read them with misgivings like my own; that he had instituted a cautious inquiry about the woman to whom I rightly conjectured they had been written. It seemed that thirty-six years ago (a year before the date of the letters), she had married, against the wish of her relatives, an American of very suspicious character; in fact, he was generally believed to have been a pirate. She herself was the daughter of very respectable tradespeople, and had served in the capacity of a nursery governess before her marriage. She had a brother, a widower, who was considered wealthy, and who had one child of about six years old. A month after the marriage, the body of this brother was found in the Thames, near London Bridge; there seemed some marks of violence about his throat, but they were not deemed sufficient to warrant the inquest in any verdict other than that of 'found drowned'.

The American and his wife took charge of the little boy, the deceased brother having by his will left his sister the guardian of his only child – and in the event of the child's death, the sister inherited. The child died about six months afterwards – it was supposed to have been neglected and ill-treated. The neighbours deposed to have heard it shriek at night. The surgeon who had examined it after death, said that it was emaciated as if from want of nourishment, and the body was covered with livid bruises. It seemed that one winter night the child had sought to escape – crept out into the back-yard – tried to scale the wall – fallen back exhausted, and been found at morning on the stones in a dying state. But though there was some evidence of cruelty, there was none of murder; and the aunt and her husband had sought to palliate cruelty by alleging the exceeding stubbornness and perversity of the child, who was declared to be half-witted. Be that as it may, at the orphan's death the aunt inherited her brother's fortune.

Before the first wedded year was out, the American quitted England abruptly, and never returned to it. He obtained a cruising vessel, which was lost in the Atlantic two years afterwards. The widow was left in affluence; but reverses of various kinds had befallen her: a bank broke – an investment failed – she went into a small business and became insolvent – then she entered into service, sinking lower and lower, from housekeeper down to maid-of-all-work – never long retaining a place, though nothing peculiar against her character was ever alleged. She was considered sober, honest, and peculiarly quiet in her ways; still nothing prospered with her. And so she had dropped into the workhouse, from which Mr J—— had taken her, to be placed in charge of the very house which she had rented as mistress in the first year of her wedded life.

Mr J—— added that he had passed an hour alone in the unfurnished room which I had urged him to destroy, and that his impressions of dread while there were so great, though he had neither heard nor seen anything, that he was eager to have the walls bared and the floors removed as I had suggested. He had engaged persons for the work, and would commence any day I would name.

The day was accordingly fixed. I repaired to the haunted house – we went into the blind dreary room, took up the skirting, and then the floors. Under the rafters, covered with rubbish, was found a trap-door, quite large enough to admit a man. It was closely nailed down, with clamps and rivets of iron. On removing these we descended into a room below, the existence of which had never been suspected. In this room there had been a window and a flue, but they had been bricked over, evidently for many years. By the help of candles we examined this place; it still retained some mouldering furniture – three chairs, an oak settee, a table – all of the fashion of about eighty years ago. There was a chest-of-drawers against the wall, in which we found, half rotted away, old-fashioned articles of a man's dress, such as might have been worn eighty or a hundred years ago by a gentleman of some rank – costly steel buckles and buttons, like those yet worn in court dresses – a handsome court sword. In a waistcoat which had once been rich with gold lace, but which was now blackened and foul with damp, we found five guineas, a few silver coins, and an ivory ticket, probably for some entertainment long since passed away. But our main discovery was in a kind of iron safe fixed to the wall, the lock of which it cost us much trouble to get picked.

In this safe were three shelves and two small drawers. Ranged on the shelves were several small bottles of crystal, hermetically stopped. They contained colourless volatile essences, of what nature I shall say no more than that they were not poisons – phosphor and ammonia entered into some of them. There were also some very curious glass tubes, and a small pointed rod of iron, with a large lump of rock-crystal, and another of amber – also a lodestone of great power.

In one of the drawers we found a miniature portrait set in gold, and retaining the freshness of its colours most remarkably, considering the length of time it had probably been there. The portrait was that of a man who might be somewhat advanced in middle life, perhaps forty-seven or forty-eight.

It was a most peculiar face – a most impressive face. If you could fancy some mighty serpent transformed into man, preserving in the human lineaments the old serpent type, you would have a better idea of that countenance than long descriptions can convey: the width and flatness of frontal – the tapering elegance of contour disguising the strength of the deadly jaw – the long, large, terrible eye, glittering and green as the emerald – and withal a certain ruthless calm, as if from the consciousness of an immense power. The strange thing was this – the instant I saw the miniature I recognized a startling likeness to one of the rarest portraits in the world – the portrait of a man of a rank only below that of royalty, who in his own day had made a considerable noise. History says little or nothing of him; but search the correspondence of his contemporaries, and you find reference to his wild daring, his bold profligacy, his restless spirit, his taste for the occult sciences. While still in the meridian of life he died and was buried, so say the chronicles, in a foreign land. He died in time to escape the grasp of the law, for he was accused of crimes which would have given him to the headsman.

After his death, the portraits of him, which had been numerous, for he had been a munificent encourager of art, were bought up and destroyed – it was supposed by his heirs, who might have been glad could they have razed his very name from their splendid line. He had enjoyed a vast wealth; a large portion of this was believed to have been embezzled by a favourite astrologer or soothsayer – at all events, it had unaccountably vanished at the time of his death. One portrait alone of him was supposed to have escaped the general destruction; I had seen it in the house of a collector some months before. It had made on me a wonderful impression, as it does on all who behold it – a face never to be forgotten; and there was that face in the miniature that lay within my hand. True, that in the miniature the man was a few years older than in the portrait I had seen, or than the original was even at the time of his death. But a few years! – why, between the date in which flourished that direful noble, and the date in which the miniature was evidently painted, there was an interval of more than two centuries. While I was thus gazing, silent and wondering, Mr J—— said:

'But is it possible? I have known this man.'

'How – where?' I cried.

'In India. He was high in the confidence of the Rajah of ——, and wellnigh drew him into a revolt which would have lost the Rajah his dominions. The man was a Frenchman – his name de V——, clever, bold, lawless. We insisted on his dismissal and banishment: it must be the same man – no two faces like his – yet this miniature seems nearly a hundred years old.'

Mechanically I turned round the miniature to examine the back of it, and on the back was engraved a pentacle; in the middle of the pentacle a ladder, and the third step of the ladder was formed by the date 1765. Examining still more minutely, I detected a spring; this, on being pressed, opened the back of the miniature as a lid. Withinside the lid was

engraved 'Mariana to thee – Be faithful in life in in death to——.' Here
follows a name that I will not mention, but it was not unfamiliar to me.
I had heard it spoken of by old men in my childhood as the name borne
by a dazzling charlatan who had made a great sensation in London for
a year or so, and had fled the country on the charge of a double murder
within his own house – that of his mistress and his rival. I said nothing
of this to Mr J——, to whom reluctantly I resigned the miniature.

We had found no difficulty in opening the first drawer within the iron
safe; we found great difficulty in opening the second: it was not locked,
but it resisted all efforts till we inserted in the chinks the edge of a chisel.
When we had thus drawn it forth, we found a very singular apparatus
in the nicest order. Upon a small thin book, or rather tablet, was placed
a saucer of crystal; this saucer was filled with a clear liquid – on that liquid
floated a kind of compass, with a needle shifting rapidly round, but
instead of the usual points of a compass were seven strange characters,
not very unlike those used by astrologers to denote the planets. A very
peculiar, but not strong nor displeasing odour came from this drawer,
which was lined with a wood that we afterwards discovered to be hazel.
Whatever the cause of this odour, it produced a material effect on the
nerves. We all felt it, even the two workmen who were in the room – a
creeping tingling sensation from the tips of the fingers to the roots of the
hair. Impatient to examine the tablet, I removed the saucer. As I did so
the needle of the compass went round and round with exceeding swiftness, and I felt a shock that ran through my whole frame, so that I
dropped the saucer on the floor. The liquid was spilt – the saucer was
broken – the compass rolled to the end of the room – and at that instant
the walls shook to and fro, as if a giant had swayed and rocked them.

The two workmen were so frightened that they ran up the ladder by
which we had descended from the trap-door; but seeing that nothing
more happened, they were easily induced to return.

Meanwhile I had opened the tablet: it was bound in a plain red
leather, with a silver clasp; it contained but one sheet of thick vellum,
and on that sheet were inscribed, within a double pentacle, words in old
monkish Latin, which are literally to be translated thus: 'On all that it
can reach within these walls – sentient or inanimate, living or dead – as
moves the needle, so work my will! Accursed be the house, and restless
be the dwellers therein.'

We found no more. Mr J—— burnt the tablet and its anathema. He
razed to the foundations the part of the building containing the secret
room with the chamber over it. He had then the courage to inhabit the
house himself for a month, and a quieter, better-conditioned house could
not be found in all London. Subsequently he let it to advantage, and his
tenant has made no complaints. But my story is not yet done. A few days
after Mr J—— had removed into the house, I paid him a visit. We were

standing by the open window and conversing. A van containing some articles of furniture which he was moving from his former house was at the door. I had just urged on him my theory that all those phenomena regarded as supermundane had emanated from a human brain; adducing the charm, or rather curse, we had found and destroyed in support of my philosophy. Mr J—— was observing in reply, 'That even if mesmerism, or whatever analogous power it might be called, could really thus work in the absence of the operator, and produce effects so extraordinary, still could those effects continue when the operator himself was dead? And if the spell had been wrought, and, indeed, the room walled up, more than seventy years ago, the probability was, that the operator had long since departed this life.' Mr J——, I say, was thus answering, when I caught hold of his arm and pointed to the street below.

A well-dressed man had crossed from the opposite side, and was accosting the carrier in charge of the van. His face, as he stood, was exactly fronting our window. It was the face of the miniature we had discovered; it was the face of the portrait of the noble three centuries ago.

'Good heavens!' cried Mr J——, 'that is the face of de V——, and scarcely a day older than when I saw it in the Rajah's court in my youth!'

Seized by the same thought, we both hastened downstairs. I was first in the street; but the man had already gone. I caught sight of him, however, not many yards in advance, and in another moment I was by his side.

I had now resolved to speak to him, but when I looked into his face I felt as if it were impossible to do so. That eye – the eye of the serpent – fixed and held me spellbound. And withal, about the man's whole person there was a dignity, an air of pride and station and superiority, that would have made anyone, habituated to the usages of the world, hesitate long before venturing upon a liberty or impertinence. And what could I say? What was it I would ask? Thus ashamed of my first impulse, I fell a few paces back, still, however, following the stranger, undecided what else to do. Meanwhile he turned the corner of the street; a plain carriage was in waiting, with a servant out of livery, dressed like a *valet-de-place*, at the carriage door. In another moment he had stepped into the carriage, and it drove off. I returned to the house. Mr J—— was still at the street-door. He had asked the carrier what the stranger had said to him.

'Merely asked whom that house now belonged to.'

The same evening I happened to go with a friend to a place in town called the Cosmopolitan Club, a place open to men of all countries, all opinions, all degrees. One orders one's coffee, smokes one's cigar. One is always sure to meet agreeable, sometimes remarkable, persons.

I had not been two minutes in the room before I beheld at a table, conversing with an acquaintance of mine, whom I will designate by the initial G——, the man – the Original of the Miniature. He was now without his hat, and the likeness was yet more startling, only I observed that while he was conversing there was less severity in the countenance; there was even a smile, though a very quiet and very cold one. The dignity of mien I had acknowledged in the street was also more striking; a dignity akin to that which invests some prince of the East – conveying the idea of supreme indifference and habitual, indisputable, indolent, but resistless power.

G—— soon after left the stranger, who then took up a scientific journal, which seemed to absorb his attention.

I drew G—— aside. 'Who and what is that gentleman?'

'That? Oh, a very remarkable man indeed. I met him last year amidst the caves of Petra – the scriptural Edom. He is the best Oriental scholar I know. We joined company, had an adventure with robbers, in which he showed a coolness that saved our lives; afterwards he invited me to spend a day with him in a house he had bought at Damascus – a house buried amongst almond blossoms and roses – the most beautiful thing! He had lived there for some years, quite as an Oriental, in grand style. I half suspect he is a renegade, immensely rich, very odd; by the by, a great mesmerizer. I have seen him with my own eyes produce an effect on inanimate things. If you take a letter from your pocket and throw it to the other end of the room, he will order it to come to his feet, and you will see the letter wriggle itself along the floor till it has obeyed his command. 'Pon my honour, 'tis true: I have seen him affect even the weather, disperse or collect clouds, by means of a glass tube or wand. But he does not like talking of these matters to strangers. He has only just arrived in England; says he has not been for a great many years. Let me introduce him to you.'

'Certainly! He is English, then? What is his name?'

'Oh! – a very homely one – Richards.'

'And what is his birth – his family?'

'How do I know? What does it signify? No doubt some *parvenu*, but rich – so infernally rich!'

G—— drew me up to the stranger, and the introduction was effected. The manners of Mr Richards were not those of an adventurous traveller. Travellers are in general constitutionally gifted with high animal spirits: they are talkative, eager, impervious. Mr Richards was calm and subdued in tone, with manners which were made distant by the loftiness of punctilious courtesy – the manners of a former age. I observed that the English he spoke was not exactly of our day. I should even have said that the accent was slightly foreign. But then Mr Richards remarked that he had been little in the habit for many years of speaking in his native tongue. The conversation fell upon the changes in the aspect of London since he had last visited our metropolis. G—— then glanced off to the moral changes – literary, social, political – the great men who were removed from the stage within the last twenty years – the new great men who were coming on. In all this Mr Richards evinced no interest. He had evidently read none of our living authors, and seemed scarcely acquainted by name with our younger statesmen. Once and only once he had laughed; it was when G—— asked him whether he had any thought of getting into Parliament. And the laugh was inward – sarcastic – sinister – a sneer raised into a laugh. After a few minutes G—— left us to talk to some other acquaintances who had just lounged into the room, and I then said quietly:

'I have seen a miniature of you, Mr Richards, in the house you once inhabited, and perhaps built, if not wholly, at least in part, in —— Street. You passed by that house this morning.'

Not till I had finished did I raise my eyes to his, and then his fixed my gaze so steadfastly that I could not withdraw it – those fascinating serpent eyes. But involuntarily, and as if the words that translated my thought were dragged from me, I added in a low whisper: 'I have been a student in the mysteries of life and nature; of those mysteries I have known the occult professors. I have the right to speak to you thus.' And I uttered a certain pass-word.

'Well,' said he, dryly, 'I concede the right – what would you ask?'

'To what extent human will in certain temperaments can extend?'

'To what extent can thought extend? Think, and before you draw breath you are in China.'

'True. But my thought has no power in China.'

'Give it expression, and it may have: you may write down a thought which, sooner or later, may alter the whole condition of China. What is a law but a thought? Therefore thought is infinite – therefore thought has power; not in proportion to its value – a bad thought may make a bad law as potent as a good thought can make a good one.'

'Yes; what you say confirms my own theory. Through invisible currents one human brain may transmit its ideas to other human brains with the same rapidity as a thought promulgated by visible means. And as thought is imperishable – as it leaves its stamp behind in the natural world even when the thinker has passed out of this world – so the thought of the living may have power to rouse up and revive the thoughts of the dead – such as those thoughts *were in life* – though the thought of the living cannot reach the thoughts which the dead *now* may entertain. Is it not so?'

'I decline to answer, if, in my judgement, thought has the limit you would fix to it; but proceed. You have a special question you wish to put.'

'Intense malignity in an intense will, engendered in a peculiar temperament, and aided by natural means within the reach of science, may produce effects like those ascribed of old to evil magic. It might thus haunt the walls of a human habitation with spectral revivals of all guilty thoughts and guilty deeds once conceived and done within those walls; all, in short, with which the evil will claims *rapport* and affinity – imperfect, incoherent, fragmentary snatches at the old dramas acted therein years ago. Thoughts thus crossing each other haphazard, as in the nightmare of a vision, growing up into phantom sights and sounds, and all serving to create horror, not because those sights and sounds are really visitations from a world without, but that they are ghastly monstrous renewals of what have been in this world itself, set into malignant play by a malignant mortal.

'And it is through the material agency of that human brain that these things would acquire even a human power – would strike as with the shock of electricity, and might kill, if the thought of the person assailed did not rise superior to the dignity of the original assailer – might kill the most powerful animal if unnerved by fear, but not injure the feeblest man, if, while his flesh crept, his mind stood out fearless. Thus, when in old stories we read of a magician rent to pieces by the fiends he had evoked – or still more, in Eastern legends, that one magician succeeds by arts in destroying another – there may be so far truth, that a material being has clothed, from its own evil propensities, certain elements and fluids, usually quiescent or harmless, with the awful shape and terrific force – just as the lightning that had lain hidden and innocent in the cloud becomes by natural law suddenly visible, takes a distinct shape to the eye, and can strike destruction on the object to which it is attracted.'

'You are not without glimpses of a very mighty secret,' said Mr Richards composedly. 'According to your view, could a mortal obtain the power you speak of, he would necessarily be a malignant and evil being.'

'If the power were exercised as I have said, most malignant and most evil – though I believe in the ancient traditions that he could not injure the good. His will could only injure those with whom it has established an affinity, or over whom it forces unresisted sway. I will now imagine an example that may be within the laws of nature, yet seem wild as the fables of a bewildered monk.

'You will remember that Albertus Magnus, after describing minutely the process by which spirits may be invoked and commanded, adds emphatically that the process will instruct and avail only to the few – that a *man must be born a magician!* – that is, born with a peculiar physical temperament, as a man is born a poet. Rarely are men in whose constitution lurks this occult power of the highest order of intellect – usually in the intellect there is some twist, perversity, or disease. But, on the other hand, they must possess, to an astonishing degree, the faculty to concentrate thought on a single object – the energetic faculty that we call *will*. Therefore, though their intellect be not sound, it is exceedingly forcible for the attainment of what it desires.

'I will imagine such a person pre-eminently gifted with this constitution and its concomitant forces. I will place him in the loftier grades of society. I will suppose his desires emphatically those of the sensualist – he has, therefore, a strong love of life. He is an absolute egotist – his will is concentrated in himself – he has fierce passions – he knows no enduring, no holy affections, but he can covet eagerly what for the moment he desires – he can hate implacably what opposes itself to his objects – he can commit fearful crimes, yet feel small remorse – he resorts rather to curses upon others than to penitence for his misdeeds. Circumstances, to which his constitution guides him, lead him to a rare knowledge of the natural secrets which may serve his egotism. He is a close observer where his passions encourage observation, he is a minute calculator, not from love of truth, but where love of self sharpens his faculties – therefore he can be a man of science.

'I suppose such a being, having by experience learned the power of his arts over others, trying what may be the power of will over his own frame, and studying all that in natural philosophy may increase that power. He loves life, he dreads death; he *wills to live on.* He cannot restore himself to youth, he cannot entirely stay the progress of death, he cannot make himself immortal in the flesh and blood; but he may arrest for a time so prolonged as to appear incredible, if I said it – that hardening of the parts which constitutes old age. A year may age him no more than an hour ages another. His intense will, scientifically trained into system, operates, in short, over the wear and tear of his own frame. He lives on. That he may not seem a portent and a miracle, he *dies* from time to time, seemingly, to certain persons. Having schemed the transfer of a wealth that suffices to his wants, he disappears from one corner of the world, and contrives that his obsequies shall be celebrated. He reappears at another corner of the world, where he resides undetected, and does not revisit the scenes of his former career till all who could remember his features are no more. He would be profoundly miserable if he had affections – he has none but for himself. No good man would accept his longevity, and to no men, good or bad, would he or could he communicate its true secret.

'Such a man might exist; such a man as I have described I see now before me! – Duke of——, in the court of ——, dividing time between lust and brawl, alchemists and wizards. Again, in the last century, charlatan and criminal, with name less noble, domiciled in the house at which you gazed today, and flying from the law you had outraged, none knew whither; traveller once more revisiting London, with the same earthly passions which filled your heart when races now no more walked through yonder streets; outlaw from the school of all the nobler and diviner mystics; execrable Image of Life in Death and Death in Life, I warn you back from the cities and homes of healthful men; back to the ruins of departed empires; back to the deserts of nature unredeemed!'

There answered me a whisper so musical, so potently musical, that it seemed to enter into my whole being, and subdue me despite myself. Thus it said:

'I have sought one like you for the last hundred years. Now I have found you, we part not till I know what I desire. The vision that sees through the Past, and cleaves through the veil of the Future, is in you at this hour; never before, never to come again. The vision of no pulling fantastic girl, of no sick-bed somnambule, but of a strong man, with a vigorous brain. Soar and look forth!'

As he spoke I felt as if I rose out of myself upon eagle wings. All the weight seemed gone from air – roofless the room, roofless the dome of space. I was not in the body – where I knew not – but aloft over time, over earth.

Again I heard the melodious whisper – 'You say right. I have mastered great secrets by the power of Will; true, by Will and by Science I can retard the process of years: but death comes not by age alone. Can I frustrate the accidents which bring death upon the young?'

'No; every accident is a providence. Before a providence snaps every human will.'

'Shall I die at last, ages and ages hence, by the slow, though inevitable, growth of time, or by the cause that I call accident?'

'By a cause you call accident.'

'Is not the end still remote?' asked the whisper with a slight tremor.

'Regarded as my life regards time, it is still remote.'

'And shall I, before then, mix with the world of men as I did ere I learned these secrets, resume eager interest in their strife and their trouble – battle with ambition, and use the power of the sage to win the power that belongs to kings?'

'You will yet play a part on the earth that will fill earth with commotion and amaze. For wondrous designs have you, a wonder yourself, been permitted to live on through the centuries. All the secrets you have stored will then have their uses – all that now makes you a stranger amidst the generations will contribute then to make you their lord. As the trees and the straws are drawn into a whirlpool – as they spin round, are sucked to the deep, and again tossed aloft by the eddies, so shall races and thrones be plucked into the charm of your vortex. Awful Destroyer – but in destroying, made, against your own will, a Constructor!'

'And that date, too, is far off?'

'Far off; when it comes, think your end in this world is at hand!'

'How and what is the end! Look east, west, south, and north.'

'In the north, where you never yet trod, towards the point whence your instincts have warned you, there a spectre will seize you. 'Tis Death! I see a ship – it is haunted – 'tis chased – it sails on. Baffled navies sail after that ship. It enters the regions of ice. It passes a sky red with meteors. Two moons stand on high, over ice-reefs. I see the ship locked between white defiles – they are ice-rocks. I see the dead strew the decks – stark and livid, green mould on their limbs. All are dead, but one man – it is you! But years, though so slowly they come, have then scathed you. There is the coming of age on your brow, and the will is relaxed in the cells of the brain. Still that will, though enfeebled, exceeds all that man knew before you; through the will you live on, gnawed with famine; and nature no longer obeys you in that death-spreading region; the sky is a sky of iron, and the air has iron clamps, and the ice-rocks wedge in the ship. Hark how it cracks and groans. Ice will imbed it as amber imbeds a straw. And a man has gone forth, living yet, from the ship and its dead; and he has clambered up the spikes of an iceberg, and the two moons gaze on his form. That man is yourself; and terror is on you – terror; and terror has swallowed your will. And I see swarming up the steep ice-rock, grey grisly things. The bears of the north have scented their quarry – they come near you and nearer, shambling and rolling their bulk. And in that day every moment shall seem to you longer than the centuries through which you have passed. And heed this – after life, moments continued make the bliss or the hell of eternity.'

'Hush,' said the whisper; 'but the day, you assure me, is far off – very far! I go back to the almond and rose of Damascus! – sleep!'

The room swam before my eyes. I became insensible. When I recovered, I found G—— holding my hand and smiling. He said: 'You who have always declared yourself proof against mesmerism have succumbed at last to my friend Richards.'

'Where is Mr Richards?'

'Gone, when you passed into a trance – saying quietly to me, "Your friend will not wake for an hour."'

I asked, as collectedly as I could, where Mr Richards lodged.

'At the Trafalgar Hotel.'

'Give me your arm,' said I to G——; 'let us call on him; I have something to say.'

When we arrived at the hotel, we were told that Mr Richards had returned twenty minutes before, paid his bill, left directions with his servant (a Greek) to pack his effects and proceed to Malta by the steamer that should leave Southampton the next day. Mr Richards had merely said of his own movements that he had visits to pay in the neighbourhood of London, and it was uncertain whether he should be able to reach Southampton in time for that steamer; if not, he should follow in the next one.

The waiter asked me my name. On my informing him, he gave me a note that Mr Richards had left for me, in case I called.

The note was as follows:

> *I wished you to utter what was in your mind. You obeyed. I have therefore established power over you. For three months from this day you can communicate to no living man what has passed between us — you cannot even show this note to the friend by your side. During three months, silence complete as to me and mine. Do you doubt my power to lay on you this command? — try to disobey me. At the end of the third month, the spell is raised. For the rest I spare you. I shall visit your grave a year and a day after it has received you.*

So ends this strange story, which I ask no one to believe. I write it down exactly three months after I received the above note. I could not write it before, nor could I show to G——, in spite of his urgent request, the note which I read under the gas-lamp by his side.

Deadline

Richard Matheson

There are at least two nights a year a doctor doesn't plan on and those are Christmas Eve and New Year's Eve. On Christmas Eve it was Bobby Dascouli's arm burns. I was salving and swathing them about the time I would have been nestled in an easy chair with Ruth eyeing the Technicolor doings of the Christmas tree.

So it came as a small surprise that ten minutes after we got to my sister Mary's house for the New Year's Eve party my answering service phoned and told me there was an emergency call downtown.

Ruth smiled at me sadly and shook her head. She kissed me on the cheek. 'Poor Bill,' she said.

'Poor Bill indeed,' I said, putting down my first drink of the evening, two-thirds full. I patted her much evident stomach.

'Don't have that baby till I get back,' I told her.

'I'll do my bestest,' she said.

I gave hurried goodbyes to everyone and left; turning up the collar of my overcoat and crunching over the snow-packed walk to the Ford; milking the choke and finally getting the engine started. Driving downtown with that look of dour reflection I've seen on many a GP's face at many a time.

It was after eleven when my tyre chains rattled on to the dark desertion of East Main Street. I drove three blocks north to the address and parked in front of what had been a refined apartment dwelling when my father was in practice. Now it was a boarding-house, ancient, smelling of decay.

In the vestibule I lined the beam of my pencil flashlight over the mail boxes but couldn't find the name. I rang the landlady's bell and stepped over to the hall door. When the buzzer sounded I pushed it open.

At the end of the hall a door opened and a heavy woman emerged. She wore a black sweater over her wrinkled green dress, striped anklets over her heavy stockings, saddle shoes over the anklets. She had no make-up on; the only colour in her face was a chapped redness in her cheeks. Wisps of steel-grey hair hung across her temples. She picked at them as she trundled down the dim hallway towards me.

'You the doctor?' she asked.

I said I was.

'I'm the one called ya,' she said. 'There's an old guy up the fourth floor says he's dyin'.'

'What room?' I asked.

'I'll show ya.'

I followed her wheezing ascent up the stairs. We stopped in front of room 47 and she rapped on the thin panelling of the door, then pushed it open.

'In here,' she said.

As I entered I saw him lying on an iron bed. His body had the flaccidity of a discarded doll. At his sides, frail hands lay motionless, topographed with knots of vein, islanded with liver spots. His skin was the brown of old page edges, his face a wasted mask. On the caseless pillow, his head lay still, its white hair straggling across the stripes like threading drifts of snow. There was a pallid stubble on his cheeks. His pale blue eyes were fixed on the ceiling.

As I slipped off my hat and coat I saw that there was no suffering evident. His expression was one of peaceful acceptance as I sat down on the bed and took his wrist. His eyes shifted and he looked at me.

'Hello,' I said, smiling.

'Hello,' I was surprised by the cognizance in his voice.

The beat of his blood was what I expected, however – a bare trickle of life, a pulsing almost lost beneath the fingers. I put down his hand and laid my palm across his forehead. There was no fever. But then he wasn't sick. He was only running down.

I patted the old man's shoulder and stood, gesturing towards the opposite side of the room. The landlady clumped there with me.

'How long has he been in bed?' I asked.

'Just since this afternoon,' she said. 'He come down to my room and said he was gonna die tonight.'

I stared at her. I'd never come in contact with such a thing. I'd read about it; everyone has. An old man or woman announces that, at a certain time, they'll die and, when the time comes, they do. Who knows what it is; will or prescience or both. All one knows is that it is a strangely awesome thing.

'Has he any relatives?' I asked.

'None I know of,' she said.

I nodded.

'Don't understand it,' she said.

'What?'

'When he first moved in about a month ago he was all right. Even this afternoon he didn't look sick.'

'You never know,' I said.

'No. You don't.' There was a haunted and uneasy flickering back deep in her eyes.

'Well, there's nothing I can do for him,' I said. 'He's not in pain. It's just a matter of time.'

The landlady nodded.

'How old is he?' I asked.

'He never said.'

'I see.' I walked back to the bed.

'I heard you,' the old man told me.

'Oh?'

'You want to know how old I am.'

'How old are you?'

He started to answer, then began coughing dryly. I saw a glass of water on the bedside table and, sitting, I propped the old man while he drank a little. Then I put him down again.

'I'm one year old,' he said.

It didn't register. I stared down at his calm face. Then, smiling nervously, I put the glass down on the table.

'You don't believe that,' he said.

'Well——' I shrugged.

'It's true enough,' he said.

I nodded and smiled again.

'I was born on December 31st, 1958,' he said, 'At midnight.'

He closed his eyes. 'What's the use?' he said, 'I've told a hundred people and none of them understood.'

'Tell me about it,' I said.

After a few moments, he drew in breath slowly.

'A week after I was born,' he said, 'I was walking and talking. I was eating by myself. My mother and father couldn't believe their eyes. They took me to a doctor. I don't know what he thought but he didn't do anything. What could he do? I wasn't sick. He sent me home with my mother and father. Precocious growth, he said.

'In another week we were back again. I remembered my mother's and father's faces when we drove there. They were afraid of me.

'The doctor didn't know what to do. He called in specialists and they didn't know what to do. I was a normal four-year-old boy. They kept me under observation. They wrote papers about me. I didn't see my father and mother any more.'

The old man stopped a moment, then went on in the same mechanical way.

'In another week I was six,' he said. 'In another week, eight. Nobody understood. They tried everything but there was no answer. And I was ten and twelve. I was fourteen and I ran away because I was sick of being stared at.'

He looked at the ceiling for almost a minute.

'You want to hear more?' he asked then.

'Yes,' I said, automatically. I was amazed at how easily he spoke.

'In the beginning I tried to fight it,' he said. 'I went to doctors and screamed at them. I told them to find out what was wrong with me. But there wasn't anything wrong with me. I was just getting two years older every week.

'Then I got the idea.'

I started a little, twitching out of the reverie of staring at him. 'Idea?' I asked.

'This is how the story got started,' the old man said.

'What story?'

'About the old year and the new year,' he said. 'The old year is an old man with a beard and a scythe. You know. And the new year is a little baby.'

The old man stopped. Down in the street I heard a tyre-screeching car turn a corner and speed past the building.

'I think there have been men like me all through time,' the old man said. 'Men who live for just a year. I don't know how it happens or why; but, once in a while, it does. That's how the story got started. After a while, people forgot how it started. They think it's a fable now. They think it's symbolic; but it isn't.'

The old man turned his worn face towards the wall.

'And I'm 1959,' he said, quietly. 'That's who I am.'

The landlady and I stood in silence looking down at him. Finally, I glanced at her. Abruptly, as if caught in guilt, she turned and hurried across the floor. The door thumped shut behind her.

I looked back at the old man. Suddenly, my breath seemed to stop. I leaned over and picked up his hand. There was no pulse. Shivering, I put down his hand and straightened up I stood looking down at him. Then, from where I don't know, a chill laced up my back. Without thought, I extended my left hand and the sleeve of my coat slid back across my watch.

To the second.

I drove back to Mary's house unable to get the old man's story out of my mind – or the weary acceptance in his eyes. I kept telling myself it was only a coincidence, but I couldn't quite convince myself.

Mary let me in. The living-room was empty.

'Don't tell me the party's broken up already?' I said.

Mary smiled. 'Not broken up,' she said. 'Just continued at the hospital.'

I stared at her, my mind swept blank. Mary took my arm.

'And you'll never guess,' she said, 'what time Ruth had the sweetest little boy.'

The House on Big Faraway

Norman Matson

'Surely the old woman told you she was *going* towards the Partelo farm, or had passed by there, something of that sort, rather than that she was staying there,' Dr Greerson said, gently correcting his host.

Bunny Brooks was positive. ' *"Staying"* was the word she used.'

Dr Greerson hesitated, seemed to decide not to argue. He was a stout man with a brown beard. He turned towards Bunny's sister. 'What did you think of her, Natalie?'

Only her grey eyes moved, meeting his. 'I did not see her.'

Young Kenneth Durham, the Doctor's nephew, laughed in his nose. He was sprawled out for six feet on the grass. The Doctor owned a farm fifteen miles away. They were, the four of them, on the newly-cut lawn of Bunny's discovery, an old farm house with a stone chimney, small window panes and clapboards black with weather. It had been unoccupied for years, standing blind and empty on its round hill. Now that all its windows looked again they saw a scene that had greatly changed. The horizon was green woods.

The only meadow left – it sloped down to the glinting pond – was covered with sumac and young birch trees, its high stone walls lost under a tangle of grape vines, elderberry and poison ivy. And there was not in all the landscape one house visible, though thirty years before all this abandoned land was farmed.

Bunny was a small, rather dapper, city man with grey hair parted neatly in the middle, a neat round face. On either side of his nose was a red mark from the grip of the glasses that usually rode there, slanted forward, gleaming. He swung the glasses now at the end of their ribbon, nervously, his forehead puckered as with some irritating thought.

'Doctor, where is this Partelo farm?'

'Half a mile that way – it's on the Big Faraway Road, too.'

'Who are they – the Partelos.'

'There aren't any Partelos.'

'Who lives there?'

'Nobody lives there.'

Young Kenneth rolled half over and looked at the reddening afternoon sky, laughed with his big mouth. He had known that was coming.

'The house is empty?'

'There isn't any house. There's nothing there but a heap of chimney stones.'

'And lilacs,' Kenneth said. 'Haw, haw.'

Bunny tucked his glasses away. He looked quite dashed.

Natalie said: 'If you're making it up Bunny, do leave off now.' She was pretty in a frail way, nostrils waxy and her ears small. Her hair was pale gold.

'No, I didn't see her, Doctor,' she said. 'I was in the back of the house. When I heard Bunny's voice I was frightened.'

'At your brother's voice?' Dr Greerson looked at her curiously.

'We've been alone here for three days. No one comes by on the road, you know, it goes nowhere but here: beyond it is quite impassable. I called out: "Bunny, are you talking to yourself?" Then I went out into the front hall and ...'

'I'll tell it,' her brother said. 'I had gone upstairs to get a coil of wire I remembered having seen in the bedroom (there's only one finished room up there; the rest is attic, you know). The door wouldn't open at first. The latch must have fallen. I had to shove hard to get in. I picked up the wire – it was rusty and quite useless I found out later – and started down again. Someone had closed the door at the bottom of the stairway.'

'I am sure I didn't,' Natalie put in quietly. She had evidently said this before as it angered her brother. He spoke loudly, turning on her: 'Very well. It was the cook we haven't got. It was a ghost. What the devil difference does it make what it was?'

'Oh, come,' Dr Greerson said reasonably, 'it was the wind.'

Kenneth winked at Natalie.

'Anyway,' Bunny went on, 'it was damned dark on that stairway. I had to grope for the catch and I came out blinking against the bright square of light from the window in the front door. When I could see clearly I was looking at *her*.'

'Who?' Kenneth asked.

'An old woman in a bonnet. Her face was close to the pane, her mouth slightly open. One tooth here at the side was gone. She was screwing up her eyes to see in, shading them with one hand. The hand had a black, fingerless mitten on it. She was looking at the air in front of me. Her eyes lifted slowly, focused into mine. They opened wide. We stared at each other through the glass. I was frightened, I'll admit, but I managed to open the door and I said: "How d'you do?"

'She said slowly in a whisper, "I don't know who you are." I didn't say anything. For a moment I wasn't sure myself who I was. She whispered: "I'm staying at the Partelo's." Then, "If you see my sister say I went to church."

'Who was her sister? Someone who had lived in this house before us? I didn't know. I realized I was rudely gaping at her, our first visitor. I said "Come in, won't you?" but she shook her black bonnet. "I'll be back," she whispered, and that was all. She went away. I watched her go along the road. She had scarlet stockings on and shiny black shoes.'

Natalie looked to Dr Greerson, wanting to know what he thought. She said: 'So I called out: "Are you talking to yourself, Bunny?" He didn't answer. I found him staring at the empty road. I ran out the back way, ran round the other side of the corn crib, my eyes all ready to see his old woman; but the air was empty. She had evaporated.'

'There's a footpath into the woods there,' Dr Greerson said. He repeated this as if he thought it was important.

'You ran after her!' Bunny exclaimed. 'That was a damned funny thing to do.'

Kenneth sat up. His eyes were bright with mischief. He picked up a blade of grass, said thoughtfully: 'Scarlet stockings!'

Bunny turned as if he had been slapped. 'Yes. I saw them. I saw her and I talked with her.'

'Man, man, we believe you,' Dr Greerson said.

'But you don't. Kenneth doesn't. Natalie doesn't. Hell, I've got feelings! Doctor, you tell me, you're supposed to know something about the mind, you tell me why I should imagine that old woman.'

'You didn't imagine her. You saw her, actually in the flesh. We all know that. But you were going to show me the old mill dam, where you plan the swimming pool. Come on, the afternoon's already gone.'

'Sorry.' Bunny got up, looked at Kenneth.

Kenneth shook his head. 'I've seen your dam.'

Bunny and the Doctor started down through the timothy grass towards the pond.

They were soon out of sight. A Bob White called, sudden as a pistol shot, and that seemed to mark the end of the day, though it was still broad daylight. A chill breath ran across the yard.

'Who was she?' Natalie reached for Kenneth and his hand met hers, held it. They were to be married, or at least so they had planned for two years. Her expression made him laugh.

'Who was she? Nobody, darling.' He tapped his forehead. 'Is Bunny often followed by funny old women? Are you?'

'No. Or,' she smiled, parting her red lips slowly, 'or generally I'm not. I do feel strange upstairs. In the bedroom – my room now – whoever was there before me and who is gone now, is still there, in a way. For years this house waited. Now we come. Still the house waits. I don't know what for. I wish I did.' He noticed goose-flesh on her arm. An actual shudder had run through her even while she smiled.

Saying how soon she would get over such notions, he put an arm around her waist, and she relaxed, pleased. All the green wood was still. It was evening.

'People walk about upstairs in these old houses, creak-creak, back and forth.' He smiled down on her, feeling superior. 'Know why? Because the wide floor-boards expand and contract with temperature changes. That's all. Bertha Bliven's no more than a thermal crack. Haw. Haw.'

'Who's Bertha Bliven?'

'She opens doors. She's in the bedroom upstairs.'

'My room!'

'Yes, and if I tell you about her you'll begin to imagine that you see her with her legs all limp, so I won't tell you.'

'Please.'

He was eager to tell, really; and he quickly made her see Bertha Bliven, a thin woman of thirty-something, of extraordinary vitality and a bitterness towards Farmer Bliven. Neither one of their two babies had lived long, and she grieved for them. Perhaps he was weary of her grief. Once he thrashed her with a bridle. Bertha's sister Matilda, who was thirteen or fourteen, would walk down the road and visit. She came one Sunday on her way to church. Bertha wouldn't go. 'I'll stay here alone,' she said.

Matilda had gone on for a mile. There she stopped. For thinking of her sister's strange expression she could not go on nor turn back. In the end she turned back, retraced her steps, passed the smithy, over the little bridge, the long bridge where the Bonacutt rushes over big stones, under the chestnuts by the white school-house. When she came to the lower barn she stopped. Here one had the first glimpse of her sister's house. It had changed. Shutters upstairs and down were tight closed, all of them.

She crept in the back door, called 'Bertha!' in the darkness. No one answered. She dared at last to call at the stair door. She went up, one step at a time, and knocked.

In the attic darkness she remembered the still clear noon-day that surrounded the house. She heard her heart.

From inside the bedroom began another pounding, rapid and irregular, growing louder. It thundered through the house. Matilda ran down and hid in the cupboard under the stairs.

When Bliven returned from church Matilda was lying on the floor, hands to her ears. To prove to her that there was nothing to be afraid of, that Bertha had merely gone back to their mother's, as she had often threatened, he forced Matilda to go back upstairs with him.

Of course, Bertha was there in the bedroom. The wire she had used had cut into her neck; blood lay long and thick down her Sunday white, and her stockinged heels had struck great holes in the plaster. In the candle-light her face seemed quite black.

'I suppose it was,' Kenneth added. 'One has to fill in here and there.'

Natalie played with her thin white hands, looking at them. She nodded slowly.

'Good story?'

'Yes, a good, dreadful story. What a dreadful thing to do to that girl. What happened to her?'

'There history is silent.'

As soon as the others returned Kenneth and Dr Greerson prepared to leave. The Doctor asked Natalie, holding her hands, 'What has he been telling you?'

'Stories.' She stood very straight like a little girl. 'Good night, Doctor. Good night, Kenneth.'

'And you, Bunny, get a lot of sunlight into that house of yours. And fires going! I'm afraid it's still damp.'

Night had fallen. They inched along in second gear to the old Providence turnpike, a mile away, fearful lest tie-rod or differential strike against a stone. On asphalt at last and rolling smoothly, Kenneth said: 'He ought to be psychoanalysed.'

Dr Greerson said: 'Bosh.'

'Well, he sees things, doesn't he? He almost had Natalie believing in that old woman. I told her there never was such a person, that she was a figment of Bunny's disordered imagination.'

'You did!'

'I certainly did!'

The Doctor found he had to think about that. He slowed down. He stopped and pulled the brake back.

'What's the matter?'

'What else did you tell her?'

The young man's voice rose. 'What else! My dear Uncle, she is my——' He broke off, with a gasp. The headlights made a clear-edged cavern in the black dark. Someone had stepped into that radiance. An old woman. A stooping old woman with a bonnet on, who grinned and showed where one tooth was gone.

In a harsh whisper, peering blindly, she asked: 'Who's that behind those glary lights?'

'Dr Greerson.'

'Good evening to you, Doctor.' She had gone back into the darkness, was walking away.

The Doctor started the car. After a minute: 'That's Matilda,' he said, 'Matilda Morris, sister to Bertha Bliven who hanged herself. Matilda's the little girl or was. She's quite all right in the mind save for that one memory. Hallo, there's a drop of rain.' He started the windshield wiper. 'She often walks this road. Walks like a man. She's strong.'

'I'd have offered her a lift but she always refuses. They say she used to go running to that house, trying to be on time you know, over and over again. The house was boarded up, of course, and the first sight of it often would straighten her out. She'd snap back to normal, but not always; she has been seen trying to open the front door, whimpering, calling out to her sister that she was coming.'

Kenneth's dry mouth finally made words. 'So you knew it was she all the time Bunny was telling us?'

'Of course.'

'And you said nothing. Explained nothing to him.'

'He's high-strung, though not as high-strung as his sister. I didn't want to feed their imaginations any more than they had already been fed.'

Here was the Greerson driveway. They left the car in an open carriage-shed and ran through pelting rain for a side door.

A gusty wind staggered against the window-panes. Greerson sat down before his fire. Kenneth paced the long room. He said:

'Which direction was she going?'

'Up the road, home – I suppose.'

'Sure?'

Dr Greerson slowly shook his head. 'Come to think of it, maybe she wasn't.'

'Maybe she was going back.'

'Back where?'

'To her sister's. To Bunny's house. For the first time she finds somebody to open the door for her. You know, I think we'd better go back there, too.'

'In this downpour? Over that road?'

'We'll say that we've actually seen the old woman, that we know who she is, that she's ... Do come, for God's sake.'

'They'll be in bed, my boy.'

'Yes. But you see, I did another wrong thing. I told Natalie about Bertha Bliven and how her little sister came calling her, too late.'

'You're a donkey,' Dr Greerson said.

Kenneth did not deny that. 'All right. But I must get there, and quickly.'

'Go ahead.'

'But you must come, we might need you.'

2

With lamps and candles darkness is always near; rooms are not filled tanks of light as with electricity. Natalie, putting dishes away in the new lean-to kitchen, walked from darkness to darkness. A whip-poor-will began loudly its witless reiteration ouside the window and bending down she looked out, saw in silhouette a large bird on the stone wall, ugly in a nameless fashion, saw how it raised its head and fluttered its wing each time it whistled, heard the slight smacking sound after. She wished it would go away.

In the big room that had been the kitchen, within the outer radiance of the fire in the huge fireplace, Bunny sat at a trestle table, as usual writing down and diagramming further plans for the farm. He did not speak as she came in from the kitchen and sat down opposite him, started to sew on pink silk. The light was on her chin and under her eyes, which were all shadow save when she looked this way and that. Then they flashed . . . It was too quiet. She wanted Bunny to say something. She did not believe in his old woman. Was he, she wondered, really a little queer despite his precise words, his neat diagrams?

Into the silence, spreading out, filling it like a quick torrent, like the rising spreading sound heard under ether, she heard one word, one straining whisper:

'Bertha!'

Natalie looked at her sewing. Bunny made another mark on his paper.

There were many other sounds, sounds in the walls. She even heard the latch of the front door click, and click again, as if it had been closed after someone entering. Her imagination was running wild. She looked across without raising her eyes, stealthily, at Bunny's hand, the one holding the pencil. Was it trembling? Was he too concealing his fears? She would have to say something.

'It's getting late.' Her voice seemed loud.

He looked up, smiled. 'Must be all of nine o'clock. How sleepy we get out here!'

'Let's go to bed.'

He yawned and agreed; went out into the front hall and locked the door. He called from there: 'Why did you lock the cupboard under the stairs?'

'I didn't lock it.'

He came back. 'Perhaps I did,' he said. 'It's no matter.'

They went upstairs, he first, said good night at the head of the stairway. 'Sleep well.'

'I'll try,' she said. His expression in the lamplight was strange; his eyes moved too quickly. Was he terrified, as she was; or was this again her imagination?

From his bed in a far corner of the great attic he called cheerfully to her. For a long time she combed her hair in the lamplight, watching herself in the mirror. Behind her on that square beam was an iron hook. Was that the one Bertha had used? Possibly. She combed very slowly. If she could only lock the door, perhaps that would make her feel better. But there was no lock, the latch was broken.

She heard, or seemed to hear, a door open downstairs in the hall. The cupboard door. One hand up with the comb she waited. It was nothing. It was the wind . . . A stair creaked, quite plainly. After a long time another creaked. She heard someone breathing out there, just outside her door.

The latch began to move.

The door opened. She, the old woman, stood in the doorway, black bonnet and shawl gleaming with rain. She was terrified, her white hands shaking as she raised them and came into the room.

Natalie moved back. The lamp went over with an outburst of brittle little sounds. For a moment it was dark, black dark. In that blindness she felt the old woman's arms tight around her.

3

Midway between highway and farm the car hit something with a clang. For a moment they sat in silence. The rain had stopped. Kenneth climbed out, flashlight in hand. Presently he said: 'Tie-rod's bent almost double. We'll have to leave her here.'

They splashed and stumbled on. At the first stone gate there was the house, and a light upstairs, reflecting on the wet leaves of an elm. They went on through the orchard. Kenneth whispered: 'Wait!' and pointed.

Under an apple tree near the house stood Matilda. She did not move. 'Good thing we came,' Kenneth whispered.

The light upstairs was brighter. Lights flickered in the downstairs windows.

Bunny's voice, high strangled, called: 'Who's that?'

'Dr Greerson and I,' Kenneth shouted. 'We came back. The car——'

'For God's sake come quickly. Natalie's gone.'

They found him crawling in the long grass. He looked up at them. 'Natalie's gone.'

He tried to tell how he had heard her screams, had found her room ablaze, had tried in vain to smother the fire.

All the windows were broadly lighted now. From the rain-soaked shingles of the great roof rose clouds of steam and smoke, and within a multitude of voices were started, crackling, whistling, whispering. The green woods stared. As flames filled the kitchen wing a dish fell. A small, deliberate crash, then another and another.

They looked over the ground for Natalie, called her name. The Doctor found her lying at Matilda's feet.

'What have you done?'

The old woman looked above his head at the glare of the fire. She was smiling. The roof-tree pitched down with a rending final cry.

'I carried her out – in time, in time,' Matilda said. Her head was filled with a weary confusion of madness and actual memories. How many times through the years she had come back here! She sighed: 'At last. At last.'

Dr Greerson on his knees listened for life. Terror, he thought. How would he tell those others. He pretended to listen.

The Three D's

Ogden Nash

Victoria was an attractive new girl at the Misses Mallisons' Female Seminary – such an attractive new girl, indeed, that it is a pity she never grew to be an old girl. Perhaps she would have, if the Misses Mallison had established their Seminary a little closer to Newburyport – or at least a little farther from Salem.

Victoria was good enough and not too good at lessons; her mouth was wide enough to console the homely girls and her eyes bright enough to include her among the pretty ones; she could weep over the death of a horse in a story and remain composed at the death of an aunt in the hospital; she would rather eat between meals than at them; she wrote to her parents once a week if in need of anything; and she truly meant to do the right thing, only so often the wrong thing was easier.

In short, Victoria was an ideal candidate for The Three D's, that night-blooming sorority which had, like the cereus, flourished after dark for many years, unscented by the precise noses of the Misses Mallison.

So felt The Three D's, so felt Victoria, and the only obstacle to her admission lay in the very title of the club itself, which members knew signified that none could gain entrance without the accomplishment of a feat Daring, Deadly, and Done-never-before. Victoria was competent at daring feats, unsurpassable at deadly feats, but where was she to discover a feat done-never-before?

Of the present membership, Amanda had leaped into a cold bath with her clothes on, Miranda had climbed the roof in her nightgown to drop a garter snake down the Misses Mallisons' chimney, Amelia had eaten cold spaghetti blindfolded thinking it was worms, and Cordelia had eaten worms blindfolded thinking they were cold spaghetti. What was left for Victoria?

It was Amanda who, at a meeting of the Steering Committee, wiped the fudge from her fingers on the inside of her dressing gown and spoke the name of Eliza Catspaugh.

'Who was she?' asked Miranda, pouring honey on a slice of coconut cake.

'A witch,' said Amanda.

'She was burned,' said Amelia.

'Hanged,' said Cordelia.

'And she couldn't get into the churchyard, so they buried her in the meadow behind the old slaughterhouse,' said Amanda.

'The gravestone is still there,' said Amelia. 'Oh, bother, the cake's all gone! Never mind, I'll eat caramels.'

'There's writing on it, too,' said Cordelia, who was not hungry, 'but you can't read it in the daytime, only by moonlight.'

'I'd forgotten how good currant jelly is on marshmallows,' said Amanda. 'The Three D's must tell Victoria about Eliza Catspaugh.'

Late next evening Victoria took her pen in hand. *Dear Father and Mother,* she wrote, *I hope you are well. I am doing well in algebra but Miss Hattie is unfair about my French ireguler verbs. I am doing well in grammar but Miss Mettie has choosen me to pick on. Dear Father, everybody elses Father sends them one dollar every week. I have lots of things to write but the bell is wringing for supper. Lots of love, your loveing daughter, Victoria.*

Victoria knew that in ten minutes Miss Hattie Mallison would open the door slightly, peer at the bed, murmur, 'Good night, Victoria, sweet dreams,' and disappear. It took Victoria seven minutes to construct a dummy out of a mop, a nightgown, and several pillows and blankets. As she lowered herself to the ground she heard the door open, heard Miss Hattie's murmur, heard the door close.

The soaring moon ran through Victoria as she marched, as she skipped, as she pranced towards the old slaughterhouse. She had for company her high moon spirits and her long shadow – the shadow which was a Victoria that no Miss Mallison could ever cage. 'No girl has ever had a taller, livelier companion than my shadow,' thought Victoria, and she breathed deeply and spread her arms, and her shadow breathed with her and spread crooked arms up the walls and across the roof of the slaughterhouse.

The moon grew brighter with each burr that Victoria struggled against on her way across the meadow that had been abandoned to burrs, the meadow where no beasts fed, the meadow where Victoria's shadow strengthened at each proud and adventurous step.

Where the burrs grew thickest, where her loyalty to The Three D's wore the thinnest, she came upon the gravestone. How hard the moon shone as Victoria leaned against the crooked slab, perhaps to catch her breath, perhaps to stand on one foot and pluck the burrs off. When the stone quivered and rocked behind her, and the gound trembled beneath her feet, she bravely remembered her purpose: that at midnight, in the moonlight, she was to prove herself a worthy companion of Amanda and Miranda, Amelia and Cordelia. Unwillingly she turned, and willfully she

read the lines which the rays of the moon lifted from the stone so obscured
by rain and moss.

Here Waits
ELIZA CATSPAUGH
Who touches this stone
on moonlight meadow
shall live no longer
than his shadow.

The job of memorizing was done, the initiation into The Three D's
handsomely undergone. 'Gracious, is that all there is to it?' thought
Victoria, and set out for the seminary.

It was natural that she should hurry, so perhaps it was natural that
she did not miss the exuberant shadow which should have escorted her
home. The moon was bright behind Victoria – who can tell how she
forgot there should have been a shadow to lead the way?

But there was no shadow – her shadow had dwindled as she ran, as
though Victoria grew shorter, or perhaps the moon grew more remote.
And if she did not miss her shadow, neither did she hear or see whatever
it may have been that rustled and scuttled past her and ahead of her.

'I hope my dear little dummy is still there,' thought Victoria as she
climbed through the window. 'I hope Miss Hattie hasn't been unfair and
shaken me.'

She tiptoed across the room in the dark to the bed, and bent to remove
the dummy. But as she reached down, the dummy, which was no longer
a dummy, reached up its dusty fingers first ...

Man-Size in Marble

E. Nesbit

Although every word of this story is as true as despair, I do not expect people to believe it. Nowadays a 'rational explanation' is required before belief is possible. Let me, then, at once offer the 'rational explanation' which finds most favour among those who have heard the tale of my life's tragedy. It is held that we were 'under a delusion,' Laura and I, on that 31st of October; and that this supposition places the whole matter on a satisfactory and believable basis. The reader can judge, when he, too, has heard my story, how far this is an 'explanation,' and in what sense it is 'rational.' There were three who took part in this: Laura and I and another man. The other man still lives, and can speak to the truth of the least credible part of my story.

I never in my life knew what it was to have as much money as I required to supply the most ordinary needs – good colours, books, and cab-fares – and when we were married we knew quite well that we should only be able to live at all by 'strict punctuality and attention to business.' I used to paint in those days, and Laura used to write, and we felt sure we could keep the pot at least simmering. Living in town was out of the question, so we went to look for a cottage in the country, which should be at once sanitary and picturesque. So rarely do these two qualities meet in one cottage that our search was for some time quite fruitless. But when we got away from friends and house-agents, on our honeymoon, our wits grew clear again, and we knew a pretty cottage when at last we saw one.

It was at Brenzett – a little village set on a hill over against the southern marshes. We had gone there, from the seaside village where we were staying, to see the church, and two fields from the church we found this cottage. It stood quite by itself, about two miles from the village. It was a long, low building, with rooms sticking out in unexpected places. There was a bit of stone-work – ivy-covered and moss-grown, just two old rooms, all that was left of a big house that had once stood there – and round this stone-work the house had grown up. Stripped of its roses and jasmine it would have been hideous. As it stood it was charming, and after a brief examination we took it. It was absurdly cheap. There was a jolly old-fashioned garden, with grass paths, and no end of hollyhocks and sunflowers, and big lilies. From the window you could see the marsh-pastures, and beyond them the blue, thin line of the sea.

We got a tall old peasant woman to do for us. Her face and figure were good, though her cooking was of the homeliest; but she understood all about gardening, and told us all the old names of the coppices and cornfields, and the stories of the smugglers and highwaymen, and, better still, of the 'things that walked,' and of the 'sights' which met one in lonely glens of a starlight night. We soon came to leave all the domestic business to Mrs Dorman, and to use her legends in little magazine stories which brought in the jingling guinea.

We had three months of married happiness, and did not have a single quarrel. One October evening I had been down to smoke a pipe with the doctor – our only neighbour – a pleasant young Irishman. Laura had stayed at home to finish a comic sketch. I left her laughing over her own jokes, and came in to find her a crumpled heap of pale muslin, weeping on the window seat.

'Good heavens, my darling, what's the matter?' I cried, taking her in my arms. 'What is the matter? Do speak.'

'It's Mrs Dorman,' she sobbed.

'What has she done?' I inquired, immensely relieved.

'She says she must go before the end of the month, and she says her niece is ill; she's gone down to see her now, but I don't believe that's the reason, because her niece is always ill. I believe someone has been setting her against us. Her manner was so queer——'

'Never mind, Pussy,' I said; 'whatever you do, don't cry, or I shall have to cry too to keep you in countenance, and then you'll never respect your man again.'

'But you see,' she went on, 'it is really serious, because these village people are so sheepy, and if one won't do a thing you may be quite sure none of the others will. And I shall have to cook the dinners and wash up the hateful greasy plates; and you'll have to carry cans of water about and clean the boots and knives – and we shall never have any time for work or earn any money or anything.'

I represented to her that even if we had to perform these duties the day would still present some margin for other toils and recreations. But she refused to see the matter in any but the greyest light.

'I'll speak to Mrs Dorman when she comes back, and see if I can't come to terms with her,' I said. 'Perhaps she wants a rise. It will be all right. Let's walk up to the church.'

The church was a large and lonely one, and we loved to go there, especially upon bright nights. The path skirted a wood, cut through it once, and ran along the crest of the hill through two meadows, and round the churchyard wall, over which the old yews loomed in black masses of shadow.

This path, which was partly paved, was called 'the bier-walk,' for it had long been the way by which the corpses had been carried to burial. The churchyard was richly treed, and was shaded by great elms which stood just outside and stretched their majestic arms in benediction over the happy dead. A large, low porch let one into the building by a Norman doorway and a heavy oak door studded with iron. Inside, the arches rose into darkness, and between them the reticulated windows, which stood out white in the moonlight. In the chancel, the windows were of rich glass, which showed in faint light their noble colouring, and made the black oak of the choir pews hardly more solid than the shadows. But on each side of the altar lay a grey marble figure of a knight in full plate armour lying upon a low slab, with hands held up in everlasting prayer, and these figures, oddly enough, were always to be seen if there was any glimmer of light in the church. Their names were lost, but the peasants told of them that they had been fierce and wicked men, marauders by land and sea, who had been the scourge of their time, and had been guilty of deeds so foul that the house they had lived in – the big house, by the way, that had stood on the site of our cottage – had been stricken by lightning and the vengeance of Heaven. But for all that, the gold of their heirs had bought them a place in the church. Looking at the bad, hard faces reproduced in the marble, this story was easily believed.

The church looked at its best and weirdest on that night, for the shadows of the yew trees fell through the windows upon the floor of the nave and touched the pillars with tattered shade. We sat down together without speaking, and watched the solemn beauty of the old church with some of that awe which inspired its early builders. We walked to the chancel and looked at the sleeping warriors. Then we rested some time on the stone seat in the porch, looking out over the stretch of quiet moonlit meadows, feeling in every fibre of our being the peace of the night and of our happy love; and came away at last with a sense that even scrubbing and black-leading were but small troubles at their worst.

Mrs Dorman had come back from the village, and I at once invited her to a *tête-à-tête*.

'Now, Mrs Dorman,' I said, when I had got her into my painting room, 'what's all this about your not staying with us?'

'I should be glad to get away, sir, before the end of the month,' she answered, with her usual placid dignity.

'Have you any fault to find, Mrs Dorman?'

'None at all, sir: you and your lady have always been most kind, I'm sure——'

'Well, what is it? Are your wages not high enough?'

'No, sir, I gets quite enough.'

'Then why not stay?'

'I'd rather not' – with some hesitation – 'my niece is ill.'

'But your niece has been ill ever since we came. Can't you stay for another month?'

'No, sir, I'm bound to go by Thursday.'

And this was Monday!

'Well, I must say, I think you might have let us know before. There's no time now to get anyone else, and your mistress is not fit to do heavy housework. Can't you stay till next week?'

'I might be able to come back next week.'

'But why must you go this week?' I persisted. 'Come out with it.'

Mrs Dorman drew the little shawl, which she always wore, tightly across her bosom, as though she were cold. Then she said, with a sort of effort:

'They say, sir, as this was a big house in Catholic times, and there was a many deeds done here.'

The nature of the 'deeds' might be vaguely inferred from the inflection of Mrs Dorman's voice – which was enough to make one's blood run cold. I was glad that Laura was not in the room. She was always nervous, as highly-strung natures are, and I felt that these tales about our house, told by this old peasant woman, with her impressive manner and contagious credulity, might have made our home less dear to my wife.

'Tell me all about it, Mrs Dorman,' I said; 'you needn't mind about telling me. I'm not like the young people who make fun of such things.'

Which was partly true.

'Well, sir' – she sank her voice – 'you may have seen in the church, beside the altar, two shapes.'

'You mean the effigies of the knights in armour,' I said cheerfully.

'I mean them two bodies, drawed out man-size in marble,' she returned, and I had to admit that her description was a thousand times more graphic than mine, to say nothing of a certain weird force and uncanniness about the phrase 'drawed out man-size in marble.'

'They do say, as on All Saints' Eve them two bodies sits up on their slabs, and gets off of them, and then walks down the aisle, *in their marble*' – (another good phrase, Mrs Dorman) – 'and as the church clock strikes eleven they walks out of the church door, and over the graves, and along the bier-walk, and if it's a wet night there's the marks of their feet in the morning.'

'And where do they go?' I asked, rather fascinated.

'They comes back here to their home, sir, and if anyone meets them——'

'Well, what then?' I asked.

But no – not another word could I get from her, save that her niece was ill and she must go.

'Whatever you do, sir, lock the door early on All Saints' Eve, and make the cross-sign over the doorstep and on the windows.'

'But has anyone ever seen these things?' I persisted. 'Who was here last year?'

'No one, sir; the lady as owned the house only stayed here in summer, and she always went to London a full month afore *the* night. And I'm sorry to inconvenience you and your lady, but my niece is ill and I must go Thursday.'

I could have shaken her for her absurd reiteration of that obvious fiction, after she had told me her real reasons.

I did not tell Laura the legend of the shapes that 'walked in their marble,' partly because a legend concerning our house might perhaps trouble my wife, and partly, I think, from some more occult reason. This was not quite the same to me as any other story, and I did not want to talk about it till the day was over. I had very soon ceased to think of the legend, however. I was painting a portrait of Laura, against the lattice window, and I could not think of much else. I had got a splendid background of yellow and grey sunset, and was working away with enthusiasm at her face. On Thursday Mrs Dorman went. She relented, at parting, so far as to say:

'Don't you put yourself about too much, ma'am, and if there's any little thing I can do next week I'm sure I shan't mind.'

Thursday passed off pretty well. Friday came. It is about what happened on that Friday that this is written.

I got up early, I remember, and lighted the kitchen fire, and had just achieved a smoky success when my little wife came running down as sunny and sweet as the clear October morning itself. We prepared breakfast together, and found it very good fun. The housework was soon done, and when brushes and brooms and pails were quiet again the house was still indeed. It is wonderful what a difference one makes in a house. We really missed Mrs Dorman, quite apart from considerations concerning pots and pans. We spent the day in dusting our books and putting them straight, and dined on cold steak and coffee. Laura was, if possible, brighter and gayer and sweeter than usual, and I began to think that a little domestic toil was really good for her. We had never been so merry since we were married, and the walk we had that afternoon was, I think, the happiest time of all my life. When we had watched the deep scarlet clouds slowly pale into leaden grey against a pale green sky and saw the white mists curl up along the hedgerows in the distant marsh we came back to the house hand in hand.

'You are sad, my darling,' I said, half-jestingly, as we sat down together in our little parlour. I expected a disclaimer, for my own silence had been the silence of complete happiness. To my surprise she said:

'Yes, I think I am sad, or, rather, I am uneasy. I don't think I'm very well. I have shivered three or four times since we came in; and it is not cold, is it?'

'No,' I said, and hoped it was not a chill caught from the treacherous mists that roll up from the marshes in the dying night. No – she said, she did not think so. Then, after a silence, she spoke suddenly:

'Do you ever have presentiments of evil?'

'No,' I said, smiling, 'and I shouldn't believe in them if I had.'

'I do,' she went on, 'the night my father died I knew it, though he was right away in the North of Scotland.' I did not answer in words.

She sat looking at the fire for some time in silence, gently stroking my hand. At last she sprang up, came behind me, and, drawing my head back, kissed me.

'There, it's over now,' she said. 'What a baby I am! Come, light the candles, and we'll have some of these new Rubinstein duets.'

And we spent a happy hour or two at the piano.

At about half past ten I began to long for the good-night pipe, but Laura looked so white that I felt it would be brutal of me to fill our sitting-room with the fumes of strong cavendish.

'I'll take my pipe outside,' I said.

'Let me come, too.'

'No, sweetheart, not tonight; you're much too tired. I shan't be long. Get to bed, or I shall have an invalid to nurse tomorrow as well as the boots to clean.'

I kissed her and was turning to go when she flung her arms round my neck and held me as if she would never let me go again. I stroked her hair.

'Come, Pussy, you're over-tired. The housework has been too much for you.'

She loosened her clasp a little and drew a deep breath.

'No. We've been very happy today, Jack, haven't we? Don't stay out too long.'

'I won't, my dearie.'

I strolled out of the front door, leaving it unlatched. What a night it was! The jagged masses of heavy dark cloud were rolling at intervals from horizon to horizon, and thin white wreaths covered the stars. Through all the rush of the cloud river the moon swam, breasting the waves and disappearing again in the darkness.

I walked up and down, drinking in the beauty of the quiet earth and the changing sky. The night was absolutely silent. Nothing seemed to be abroad. There was no scurrying of rabbits, or twitter of the half-asleep birds. And though the clouds went sailing across the sky, the wind that drove them never came low enough to rustle the dead leaves in the woodland paths. Across the meadows I could see the church tower standing out black and grey against the sky. I walked there thinking over our three months of happiness.

I heard a bell-beat from the church. Eleven already! I turned to go in, but the night held me. I could not go back into our warm rooms yet. I would go up to the church.

I looked in at the low window as I went by. Laura was half lying on her chair in front of the fire. I could not see her face, only her little head showed dark against the pale blue wall. She was quite still. Asleep, no doubt.

I walked slowly along the edge of the wood. A sound broke the stillness of the night, it was a rustling in the wood. I stopped and listened. The sound stopped too. I went on, and now distinctly heard another step than mine answer mine like an echo. It was a poacher or a wood-stealer, most likely, for these were not unknown in our Arcadian neighbourhood. But whoever it was, he was a fool not to step more lightly. I turned into the wood and now the footstep seemed to come from the path I had just left. It must be an echo, I thought. The wood looked perfect in the moonlight. The large dying ferns and the brushwood showed where through thinning foliage the pale light came down. The tree trunks stood up like Gothic columns all around me. They reminded me of the church, and I turned into the bier-walk, and passed through the corpse-gate between the graves to the low porch.

I paused for a moment on the stone seat where Laura and I had watched the fading landscape. Then I noticed that the door of the church was open, and I blamed myself for having left it unlatched the other night. We were the only people who ever cared to come to the church except on Sundays, and I was vexed to think that through our carelessness the damp autumn airs had had a chance of getting in and injuring the old fabric. I went in. It will seem strange, perhaps, that I should have gone half way up the aisle before I remembered – with a sudden chill, followed by as sudden a rush of self-contempt – that this was the very day and hour when, according to tradition, the 'shapes drawed out man-size in marble' began to walk.

Having thus remembered the legend, and remembered it with a shiver, of which I was ashamed, I could not do otherwise than walk up towards the altar, just to look at the figures – as I said to myself; really what I wanted was to assure myself, first, that I did not believe the legend, and secondly, that it was not true. I was rather glad that I had come. I thought now I could tell Mrs Dorman how vain her fancies were, and how peacefully the marble figures slept on through the ghastly hour. With my hands in my pockets I passed up the aisle. In the grey dim light the eastern end of the church looked larger than usual, and the arches above the two tombs looked larger too. The moon came out and showed me the reason. I stopped short, my heart gave a leap that nearly choked me, and then sank sickeningly.

The 'bodies drawed out man-size' *were gone*! and their marble slabs lay

wide and bare in the vague moonlight that slanted through the east
window.

Were they really gone, or was I mad? Clenching my nerves, I stooped
and passed my hand over the smooth slabs and felt their flat unbroken
surface. Had someone taken the things away? Was it some vile practical
joke? I would make sure, anyway. In an instant I had made a torch of
newspaper, which happened to be in my pocket, and, lighting it, held
it high above my head. Its yellow glare illumined the dark arches and
those slabs. The figures *were* gone. And I was alone in the church; or was
I alone?

And then a horror seized me, a horror indefinable and indescribable
– an overwhelming certainty of supreme and accomplished calamity. I
flung down the torch and tore along the aisle and out through the porch,
biting my lips as I ran to keep myself from shrieking aloud. Oh, was I
mad – or what was this that possessed me? I leaped the churchyard wall
and took the straight cut across the fields, led by the light from our
windows. Just as I got over the first stile a dark figure seemed to spring
out of the ground. Mad still with that certainty of misfortune, I made
for the thing that stood in my path, shouting, 'Get out of the way, can't
you!'

But my push met with a more vigorous resistance than I had expected.
My arms were caught just above the elbow and held as in a vice, and
the raw-boned Irish doctor actually shook me.

'Let me go, you fool,' I gasped. 'The marble figures have gone from
the church; I tell you they've gone.'

He broke into a ringing laugh. 'I'll have to give you a draught
tomorrow, I see. Ye've bin smoking too much and listening to old wives'
tales.'

'I tell you, I've seen the bare slabs.'

'Well, come back with me. I'm going up to old Palmer's – his
daughter's ill; we'll look in at the church and let me see the bare slabs.'

'You go, if you like,' I said, a little less frantic for his laughter; 'I'm
going home to my wife.'

'Rubbish, man,' said he; 'd'ye think I'll permit of that? Are ye to go
saying all yer life that ye've seen solid marble endowed with vitality, and
me to go all me life saying ye were a coward? No, sir – ye shan't do ut.'

The night air – a human voice – and I think also the physical contact
with this six feet of solid common sense, brought me back to my ordinary
self, and the word 'coward' was a mental shower-bath.

'Come on, then,' I said sullenly; 'perhaps you're right.'

He still held my arm tightly. We got over the stile and back to the
church. All was still as death. The place smelt very damp and earthly.
We walked up the aisle. I am not ashamed to confess that I shut my eyes:
I knew the figures would not be there. I heard Kelly strike a match.

'Here they are, ye see, right enough; ye've been dreaming or drinking, asking yer pardon for the imputation.'

I opened my eyes. By Kelly's expiring vesta I saw two shapes lying 'in their marble' on their slabs. I drew a deep breath.

'I'm awfully indebted to you,' I said. 'It must have been some trick of light, or I have been working rather hard, perhaps that's it. I was quite convinced they were gone.'

'I'm aware of that,' he answered rather grimly; 'ye'll have to be careful of that brain of yours, my friend, I assure ye.'

He was leaning over and looking at the right-hand figure, whose stony face was the most villainous and deadly in expression.

'By Jove,' he said, 'something has been afoot here – this hand is broken.'

And so it was. I was certain that it had been perfect the last time Laura and I had been there.

'Perhaps someone has *tried* to remove them,' said the young doctor.

'Come along,' I said, 'or my wife will be getting anxious. You'll come in and have a drop of whisky and drink confusion to ghosts and better sense to me.'

'I ought to go up to Palmer's, but it's so late now I'd best leave it till the morning,' he replied.

I think he fancied I needed him more than did Palmer's girl, so, discussing how such an illusion could have been possible, and deducing from this experience large generalities concerning ghostly apparitions, we walked up to our cottage. We saw, as we walked up the garden path, that bright light streamed out of the front door, and presently saw that the parlour door was open, too. Had she gone out?

'Come in,' I said, and Dr Kelly followed me into the parlour. It was all ablaze with candles, not only the wax ones, but at least a dozen guttering, glaring tallow dips, stuck in vases and ornaments in unlikely places. Light, I knew, was Laura's remedy for nervousness. Poor child! Why had I left her? Brute that I was.

We glanced round the room, and at first we did not see her. The window was open, and the draught set all the candles flaring one way. Her chair was empty and her handkerchief and book lay on the floor. I turned to the window. There, in the recess of the window, I saw her. Oh, my child, my love, had she gone to that window to watch for me? And what had come into the room behind her? To what had she turned with that look of frantic fear and horror? Oh, my little one, had she thought that it was I whose step she heard, and turned to meet – what?

She had fallen back across a table in the window, and her body lay half on it and half on the window-seat, and her head hung down over the table, the brown hair loosened and fallen to the carpet. Her lips were drawn back, and her eyes wide, wide open. They saw nothing now. What had they seen last?

The doctor moved towards her, but I pushed him aside and sprang to her; caught her in my arms and cried:

'It's all right, Laura! I've got you safe, wifie.'

She fell into my arms in a heap. I clasped her and kissed her, and called her by pet names, but I think I knew all the time that she was dead. Her hands were tightly clenched. In one of them she held something fast. When I was quite sure that she was dead, and that nothing mattered at all any more, I let him open her hand to see what she held.

It was a grey marble finger.

The Pit and the Pendulum

Edgar Allan Poe

Impia tortorum longas hic turba furores
Sanguinis innocui, non satiata, aluit.
Sospite nunc patria, fracto nunc funeris antro,
Mors ubi dira fuit vita salusque patent.

[*Quatrain composed for the gates of a market to be erected upon the site of the Jacobin Club House at Paris.*]

I was sick, sick unto death, with that long agony, and when they at length unbound me, and I was permitted to sit, I felt that my senses were leaving me. The sentence, the dread sentence of death, was the last of distinct accentuation which reached my ears. After that, the sound of the inquisitorial voices seemed merged in one dreamy indeterminate hum. It conveyed to my soul the idea of *revolution*, perhaps from its association in fancy with the burr of a mill-wheel. This only for a brief period, for presently I heard no more. Yet, for a while, I saw, but with how terrible an exaggeration! I saw the lips of the black-robed judges. They appeared to me white – whiter than the sheet upon which I trace these words – and thin even to grotesqueness; thin with the intensity of their expression of firmness, of immovable resolution, of stern contempt of human torture. I saw that the decrees of what to me was fate were still issuing from those lips. I saw them writhe with a deadly locution. I saw them fashion the syllables of my name, and I shuddered, because no sound succeeded. I saw, too, for a few moments of delirious horror, the soft and nearly imperceptible waving of the sable draperies which enwrapped the walls of the apartment; and then my vision fell upon the seven tall candles upon the table. At first they wore the aspect of charity, and seemed white slender angels who would save me; but then all at once there came a most deadly nausea over my spirit, and I felt every fibre in my frame thrill, as if I had touched the wire of a galvanic battery, while the angel forms became meaningless spectres, with heads of flame, and I saw that from them there would be no help. And then there stole into my fancy, like a rich musical note, the thought of what sweet rest these must be in the grave. the thought came gently and stealthily, and it seemed long before it attained full appreciation; but just as my spirit came at length properly to feel and entertain it, the figures of the judges vanished, as if magically, from before me; the tall candles sank into nothingness; their flames went out utterly; the blackness of darkness supervened; all sensations appeared swallowed up in a mad rushing descent as of the soul into Hades. Then silence, and stillness, and night were the universe.

I had swooned; but still will not say that all of consciousness was lost. What of it there remained I will not attempt to define, or even to describe; yet all was not lost. In the deepest slumber – no! In delirium – no! In a swoon – no! In death – no! Even in the grave all *is not* lost. Else there is no immortality for man. Arousing from the most profound of slumbers, we break the gossamer web of *some* dream. Yet in a second afterwards (so frail may that web have been) we remember not that we have dreamed. In the return to life from the swoon there are two stages; first, that of the sense of mental or spiritual; secondly, that of the sense of physical existence. It seems probable that if, upon reaching the second stage, we could recall the impressions of the first, we should find these impressions eloquent in memories of the gulf beyond. And that gulf is – what? How at least shall we distinguish its shadows from those of the tomb? But if the impressions of what I have termed the first stage are not at will recalled, yet, after long interval, do they not come unbidden, while we marvel whence they come? He who has never swooned is not he who finds strange palaces and wildly familiar faces in coals that glow; is not he who beholds floating in mid-air the sad visions that the many may not view; is not he who ponders over the perfume of some novel flower; is not he whose brain grows bewildered with the meaning of some musical cadence which has never before arrested his attention.

Amid frequent and thoughtful endeavours to remember, amid earnest struggles to regather some token of the state of seeming nothingness into which my soul had lapsed, there have been moments when I have dreamed of success; there have been brief, very brief periods when I have conjured up remembrances which the lucid reason of a later epoch assures me could have had reference only to that condition of seeming unconsciousness. These shadows of memory tell indistinctly of tall figures that lifted and bore me in silence down – down – still down – till a hideous dizziness oppressed me at the mere idea of the interminableness of the descent. They tell also of a vague horror at my heart on account of that heart's unnatural stillness. Then comes a sense of sudden motionlessness thoughout all things; as if those who bore me (a ghastly train!) had outrun, in their descent, the limits of the limitless, and paused from the wearisomeness of their toil. After this I call to mind flatness and dampness; and then all is *madness* – the madness of a memory which busies itself among forbidden things.

Very suddenly there came back to my soul motion and sound – the tumultuous motion of the heart, and in my ears the sound of its beating. Then a pause in which all is blank. Then again sound, and motion, and touch, a tingling sensation pervading my frame. Then the mere consciousness of existence, without thought – a condition which lasted long. Then, very suddenly, *thought*, and shuddering terror, and earnest endeavour to comprehend my true state. Then a ʼstrong desire to lapse into insensibility. Then a rushing revival of soul and a successful effort to move. And now a full memory of the trial, of the judges, of the sable draperies, of the sentence, of the sickness, of the swoon. Then entire forgetfulness of all that followed; of all that a later day and much earnestness of endeavour have enabled me vaguely to recall.

So far I had not opened my eyes. I felt that I lay upon my back unbound. I reached out my hand, and it fell heavily upon something damp and hard. There I suffered it to remain for many minutes, while I strove to imagine where and *what* I could be. I longed, yet dared not, to employ my vision. I dreaded the first glance at objects around me. It was not that I feared to look upon things horrible, but that I grew aghast lest there should be *nothing* to see. At length, with a wild desperation at heart, I quickly unclosed my eyes. My worst thoughts, then, were confirmed. The blackness of eternal night encompassed me. I struggled for breath. The intensity of the darkness seemed to oppress and stifle me. The atmosphere was intolerably close. I still lay quietly, and made effort to exercise my reason. I brought to mind the inquisitorial proceedings, and attempted from that point to deduce my real condition. The sentence had passed, and it appeared to me that a very long interval of time had since elapsed. Yet not for a moment did I suppose myself actually dead. Such a supposition, notwithstanding what we read in fiction, is altogether inconsistent with real existence; – but where and in what state was I? The condemned to death, I knew, perished usually at the *auto-da-fés*, and one of these had been held on the very night of the day of my trial. Had I been remanded to my dungeon, to await the next sacrifice, which would not take place for many months? This I at once saw could not be. Victims had been in immediate demand. Moreover my dungeon, as well as all the condemned cells at Toledo, had stone floors, and light was not altogether excluded.

A fearful idea now suddenly drove the blood in torrents upon my heart, and for a brief period I once more relapsed into insensibility. Upon recovering, I at once started to my feet, trembling convulsively in every fibre. I thrust my arms wildly above and around me in all directions. I felt nothing; yet dreaded to move a step, lest I should be impeded by the walls of a *tomb*. Perspiration burst from every pore, and stood in cold big

beads upon my forehead. The agony of suspense grew at length intolerable, and I cautiously moved forward, with my arms extended, and my
eyes straining from their sockets, in the hope of catching some faint ray
of light. I proceeded for many paces, but still all was blackness and
vacancy. I breathed more freely. It seemed evident that mine was not,
at least, the most hideous of fates.

And now, as I still continued to step cautiously onward, there came
thronging upon my recollection a thousand vague rumours of the horrors
of Toledo. Of the dungeons there had been strange things narrated –
fables I had always deemed them – but yet strange, and too ghastly to
repeat, save in a whisper. Was I left to perish of starvation in this
subterranean world of darkness; or what fate perhaps even more fearful
awaited me? That the result would be death, and a death of more than
customary bitterness, I knew too well the character of my judges to doubt.
The mode and the hour were all that occupied or distracted me.

My outstretched hands at length encountered some solid obstruction.
It was a wall, seemingly of stone masonry – very smooth, slimy, and cold.
I followed it up; stepping with all the careful distrust with which certain
antique narratives had inspired me. This process, however, afforded me
no means of ascertaining the dimensions of my dungeon; as I might make
its circuit, and return to the point whence I set out, without being aware
of the fact, so perfectly uniform seemed the wall. I therefore sought the
knife which had been in my pocket when led into the inquisitorial
chamber, but it was gone; my clothes had been exchanged for a wrapper
of coarse serge. I had thought of forcing the blade in some minute crevice
of the masonry, so as to identify my point of departure. The difficulty,
nevertheless, was but trivial, although, in the disorder of my fancy, it
seemed at first insuperable. I tore a part of the hem from the robe, and
placed the fragment at full length, and at right angles to the wall. In
groping my way around the prison, I could not fail to encounter this rag
upon completing the circuit. So, at least, I thought, but I had not counted
upon the extent of the dungeon or upon my own weakness. The ground
was moist and slippery. I staggered onward for some time, when I
stumbled and fell. My excessive fatigue induced me to remain prostrate,
and sleep soon overtook me as I lay.

Upon awaking, and stretching forth an arm, I found beside me a loaf
and a pitcher with water. I was too much exhausted to reflect upon this
circumstance, but ate and drank with avidity. Shortly afterwards I
resumed my tour around the prison, and with much toil came at last upon
the fragment of the serge. Up to the period when I fell I had counted
fifty-two paces, and upon resuming my walk I had counted forty-eight
more, when I arrived at the rag. There were in all, then, a hundred paces;
and, admitting two paces to the yard, I presumed the dungeon to be fifty
yards in circuit. I had met, however, with many angles in the wall, and

thus I could form no guess at the shape of the vault, for vault I could not help supposing it to be.

I had little object – certainly no hope – in these researches, but a vague curiosity prompted me to continue them. Quitting the wall, I resolved to cross the area of the enclosure. At first I proceeded with extreme caution, for the floor although seemingly of solid material was treacherous with slime. At length, however, I took courage and did not hesitate to step firmly – endeavouring to cross in as direct a line as possible. I had advanced some ten or twelve paces in this manner, when the remnant of the torn hem of my robe became entangled between my legs. I stepped on it, and fell violently on my face.

In the confusion attending my fall, I did not immediately apprehend a somewhat startling circumstance, which yet, in a few seconds afterwards, and while I still lay prostrate, arrested my attention. It was this: my chin rested upon the floor of the prison, but my lips, and the upper portion of my head, although seemingly at a less elevation than the chin, touched nothing. At the same time, my forehead seemed bathed in a clammy vapour, and the peculiar smell of decayed fungus arose to my nostrils. I put forward my arm, and shuddered to find that I had fallen at the very brink of a circular pit, whose extent of course I had no means of ascertaining at the moment. Groping about the masonry just below the margin, I succeeded in dislodging a small fragment, and let it fall into the abyss. For many seconds I hearkened to its reverberations as it dashed against the sides of the chasm in its descent; at length there was a sullen plunge into water, succeeded by loud echoes. At the same moment there came a sound resembling the quick opening, and as rapid closing of a door overhead, while a faint gleam of light flashed suddenly through the gloom, and as suddenly faded away.

I saw clearly the doom which had been prepared for me, and congratulated myself upon the timely accident by which I had escaped. Another step before my fall, and the world had seen me no more; and the death just avoided was of that very character which I had regarded as fabulous and frivolous in the tales respecting the Inquisition. To the victims of its tyranny, there was the choice of death with its direst physical agonies, or death with its most hideous moral horrors. I had been reserved for the latter. By long suffering my nerves had been unstrung, until I trembled at the sound of my own voice, and had become in every respect a fitting subject for the species of torture which awaited me.

Shaking in every limb, I groped my way back to the wall – resolving there to perish rather than risk the terrors of the wells, of which my imagination now pictured many in various positions about the dungeon. In other conditions of mind I might have had courage to end my misery at once by a plunge into one of these abysses; but now I was the veriest of cowards. Neither could I forget what I had read of these pits – that the *sudden* extinction of life formed no part of their most horrible plan.

Agitation of spirit kept me awake for many long hours; but at length I again slumbered. Upon arousing, I found by my side, as before, a loaf and a pitcher of water. A burning thirst consumed me, and I emptied the vessel at a draught. It must have been drugged, for scarcely had I drunk before I became irresistibly drowsy. A deep sleep fell upon me – a sleep like that of death. How long it lasted of course I know not; but when once again I unclosed my eyes the objects around me were visible. By a wild sulphurous lustre, the origin of which I could not at first determine, I was enabled to see the extent and aspect of the prison.

In its size I had been greatly mistaken. The whole circuit of its walls did not exceed twenty-five yards. For some minutes this fact occasioned me a world of vain trouble; vain indeed – for what could be of less importance, under the terrible circumstances which environed me, than the mere dimensions of my dungeon? But my soul took a wild interest in trifles, and I busied myself in endeavours to account for the error I had committed in my measurement. The truth at length flashed upon me. In my first attempt at exploration I had counted fifty-two paces up to the period when I fell; I must then have been within a pace or two of the fragment of serge; in fact I had nearly performed the circuit of the vault. I then slept, and upon awaking, I must have returned upon my steps, thus supposing the circuit nearly double what it actually was. My confusion of mind prevented me from observing that I began my tour with the wall to the left, and ended it with the wall to the right.

I had been deceived too in respect to the shape of the enclosure. In feeling my way I had found many angles, and thus deduced an idea of great irregularity, so potent is the effect of total darkness upon one arousing from lethargy or sleep! The angles were simply those of a few slight depressions or niches at odd intervals. The general shape of the prison was square. What I had taken for masonry seemed now to be iron, or some other metal, in huge plates, whose sutures or joints occasioned the depression. The entire surface of this metallic enclosure was rudely daubed in all the hideous and repulsive devices to which the charnel superstition of the monks has given rise. The figures of fiends in aspects of menace, with skeleton forms and other more really fearful images, overspread and disfigured the walls. I observed that the outlines of these monstrosities were sufficiently distinct, but that the colours seemed faded and blurred, as if from the effects of a damp atmosphere. I now noticed the floor, too, which was of stone. In the centre yawned the circular pit from whose jaws I had escaped; but it was the only one in the dungeon.

All this I saw indistinctly and by much effort, for my personal condition had been greatly changed during slumber. I now lay upon my back, and at full length, on a species of low framework of wood. To this I was securely bound by a long strap resembling a surcingle. It passed in many convolutions about my limbs and body, leaving at liberty only my head, and my left arm to such extent that I could by dint of much exertion supply myself with food from an earthen dish which lay by my side on the floor. I saw to my horror that the pitcher had been removed. I say to my horror, for I was consumed with intolerable thirst. This thirst it appeared to be the design of my persecutors to stimulate, for the food in the dish was meat pungently seasoned.

Looking upward, I surveyed the ceiling of my prison. It was some thirty or forty feet overhead, and constructed much as the side walls. In one of its panels a very singular figure riveted my whole attention. It was the painted figure of Time as he is commonly represented, save that in lieu of a scythe he held what at a casual glance I supposed to be the pictured image of a huge pendulum, such as we see on antique clocks. There was something, however, in the appearance of this machine which caused me to regard it more attentively. While I gazed directly upward at it (for its position was immediately over my own), I fancied that I saw it in motion. In an instant afterwards the fancy was confirmed. Its sweep was brief, and of course slow. I watched it for some minutes, somewhat in fear but more in wonder. Wearied at length with observing its dull movement, I turned my eyes upon the other objects in the cell.

A slight noise attracted my notice, and looking to the floor, I saw several enormous rats traversing it. They had issued from the well which lay just within view to my right. Even then while I gazed, they came up in troops, hurriedly, with ravenous eyes, allured by the scent of the meat. From this it required much effort and attention to scare them away.

It might have been half-an-hour, perhaps even an hour (for I could take but imperfect note of time) before I again cast my eyes upward. What I then saw confounded and amazed me. The sweep of the pendulum had increased in extent by nearly a yard. As a natural consequence, its velocity was also much greater. But what mainly disturbed me was the idea that it had perceptibly *descended*. I now observed, with what horror it is needless to say, that its nether extremity was formed of a crescent of glittering steel, about a foot in length from horn to horn; the horns upward, and the under edge evidently as keen as that of a razor. Like a razor also it seemed massy and heavy, tapering from the edge into a solid and broad structure above. It was appended to a weighty rod of brass, and the whole *hissed* as it swung through the air.

I could no longer doubt the doom prepared for me by monkish ingenuity in torture. My cognizance of the pit had become known to the inquisitorial agents – *the pit*, whose horrors had been destined for so bold a recusant as myself, *the pit*, typical of hell, and regarded by rumour as the Ultima Thule of all their punishments. The plunge into this pit I had avoided by the merest of accidents, and I knew that surprise or entrapment into torment formed an important portion of all the grotesquerie of these dungeon deaths. Having failed to fall, it was no part of the demon plan to hurl me into the abyss, and thus (there being no alternative) a different and a milder destruction awaited me. Milder! I half smiled in my agony as I thought of such application of such a term.

What boots it to tell of the long, long hours of horror more than mortal, during which I counted the rushing oscillations of the steel! Inch by inch – line by line – with a descent only appreciable at intervals that seemed ages – down and still down it came! Days passed – it might have been that many days passed – ere it swept so closely over me as to fan me with its acrid breath. The odour of the sharp steel forced itself into my nostrils. I prayed – I wearied heaven with my prayer for its more speedy descent. I grew frantically mad, and struggled to force myself upward against the sweep of the fearful scimitar. And then I fell suddenly calm and lay smiling at the glittering death as a child at some rare bauble.

There was another interval of utter insensibility; it was brief, for upon again lapsing into life there had been no perceptible descent in the pendulum. But it might have been long – for I knew there were demons who took note of my swoon, and who could have arrested the vibration at pleasure. Upon my recovery, too, I felt very – oh! inexpressibly – sick and weak, as if through long inanition. Even amid the agonies of that period the human nature craved food. With painful effort I outstretched my left arm as far as my bonds permitted, and took possession of the small remnant which had been spared me by the rats. As I put a portion of it within my lips there rushed to my mind a half-formed thought of joy – of hope. Yet what business had *I* with hope? It was, as I say, a half-formed thought – man has many such, which are never completed. I felt that it was of joy – of hope; but I felt also that it had perished in its formation. In vain I struggled to perfect – to regain it. Long suffering had nearly annihilated all my ordinary powers of mind. I was an imbecile – an idiot.

The vibration of the pendulum was at right angles to my length. I saw that the crescent was designed to cross the region of the heart. It would fray the serge of my robe; it would return and repeat its operations – again – and again. Notwithstanding its terrifically wide sweep (some thirty feet or more) and the hissing vigour of its descent, sufficient to sunder these very walls of iron, still the fraying of my robe would be all that, for several minutes, it would accomplish; and at this thought I paused. I dared not go farther than this reflection. I dwelt upon it with a pertinacity of attention – as if, in so dwelling, I could arrest *here* the descent of the steel. I forced myself to ponder upon the sound of the crescent as it should pass across the garment – upon the peculiar thrilling sensation which the friction of cloth produces on the nerves. I pondered upon all this frivolity until my teeth were on edge.

Down – steadily down it crept. I took a frenzied pleasure in contrasting its downward with its lateral velocity. To the right – to the left – far and wide – with the shriek of a damned spirit! to my heart with the stealthy pace of the tiger! I alternately laughed and howled, as the one or the other idea grew predominant.

Down – certainly, relentlessly down! It vibrated within three inches of my bosom! I struggled violently – furiously – to free my left arm. This was free only from the elbow to the hand. I could reach the latter, from the platter beside me to my mouth with great effort, but no farther. Could I have broken the fastenings above the elbow, I would have seized and attempted to arrest the pendulum. I might as well have attempted to arrest an avalanche!

Down – still unceasingly – still inevitably down! I gasped and struggled at each vibration. I shrunk convulsively at its every sweep. My eyes followed its outward or upward whirls with the eagerness of the most unmeaning despair; they closed themselves spasmodically at the descent, although death would have been a relief, O, how unspeakable! Still I quivered in every nerve to think how slight a sinking of the machinery would precipitate that keen glistening axe upon my bosom. It was *hope* that prompted the nerve to quiver – the frame to shrink. It was *hope* – the hope that triumphs on the rack – that whispers to the death-condemned even in the dungeons of the Inquisition.

I saw that some ten or twelve vibrations would bring the steel in actual contact with my robe, and with this observation there suddenly came over my spirit all the keen, collected calmness of despair. For the first time during many hours, or perhaps days, I *thought*. It now occurred to me that the bandage or surcingle which enveloped me was *unique*. I was tied by no separate cord. The first stroke of the razor-like crescent athwart any portion of the band would so detach it that it might be unwound from my person by means of my left hand. But how fearful, in that case, the proximity of the steel! The result of the slightest struggle, how deadly! Was it likely, moreover, that the minions of the torturer had not foreseen and provided for this possibility? Was it probable that the bandage crossed my bosom in the track of the pendulum? Dreading to find my faint, and, as it seemed, my last hope frustrated, I so far elevated my head as to obtain a distinct view of my breast. The surcingle enveloped my limbs and body close in all directions *save in the path of the destroying crescent*.

Scarcely had I dropped my head back into its original position when there flashed upon my mind what I cannot better describe than as the unformed half of that idea of deliverance to which I have previously alluded, and of which a moiety only floated indeterminately through my brain when I raised food to my burning lips. The whole thought was now present – feeble, scarcely sane, scarcely definite, but still entire. I proceeded at once, with the nervous energy of despair, to attempt its execution.

For many hours the immediate vicinity of the low framework upon which I lay had been literally swarming with rats. They were wild, bold, ravenous, their red eyes glaring upon me as if they waited but for motionlessness on my part to make me their prey. 'To what food,' I thought, 'have they been accustomed in the well?'

They had devoured, in spite of all my efforts to prevent them, all but a small remnant of the contents of the dish. I had fallen into an habitual see-saw or wave of the hand about the platter; and at length the unconscious uniformity of the movement deprived it of effect. In their voracity the vermin frequently fastened their sharp fangs in my fingers. With the particles of the oily and spicy viand which now remained, I thoroughly rubbed the bandage wherever I could reach it; then, raising my hand from the floor, I lay breathlessly still.

At first the ravenous animals were startled and terrified at the change – at the cessation of movement. They shrank alarmedly back; many sought the well. But this was only for a moment. I had not counted in vain upon their voracity. Observing that I remained without motion, one or two of the boldest leaped upon the frame-work and smelt at the surcingle. This seemed the signal for a general rush. Forth from the well they hurried in fresh troops. They clung to the wood, they overran it, and leaped in hundreds upon my person. The measured movement of the pendulum disturbed them not at all. Avoiding its strokes, they busied themselves with the anointed bandage. They pressed, they swarmed upon me in ever accumulating heaps. They writhed upon my throat; their cold lips sought my own; I was half stifled by their thronging pressure; disgust, for which the world has no name, swelled my bosom, and chilled with heavy clamminess my heart. Yet one minute and I felt that the struggle would be over. Plainly I perceived the loosening of the bandage. I knew that in more than one place it must be already severed. With a more than human resolution I lay *still*.

Nor had I erred in my calculations, nor had I endured in vain. I at length felt that I was *free*. The surcingle hung in ribands from my body. But the stroke of the pendulum already pressed upon my bosom. It had divided the serge of the robe. It had cut through the linen beneath. Twice again it swung, and a sharp sense of pain shot through every nerve. But the moment of escape had arrived. At a wave of my hand my deliverers hurried tumultuously away. With a steady movement, cautious, sidelong, shrinking, and slow, I slid from the embrace of the bandage and beyond the reach of the scimitar. For the moment, at least, *I was free*.

Free! – and in the grasp of the Inquisition! I had scarcely stepped from my wooden bed of horror upon the stone floor of the prison, when the motion of the hellish machine ceased, and I beheld it drawn up by some invisible force through the ceiling. This was a lesson which I took desperately to heart. My every motion was undoubtedly watched. Free! – I had but escaped death in one form of agony to be delivered unto worse than death in some other. With that thought I rolled my eyes nervously around on the barriers of iron that hemmed me in. Something unusual – some change which at first I could not appreciate distinctly – it was obvious had taken place in the apartment. For many minutes of a dreamy and trembling abstraction I busied myself in vain, unconnected conjecture. During this period I became aware, for the first time, of the origin of the sulphurous light which illumined the cell. It proceeded from a fissure about half-an-inch in width extending entirely around the prison at the base of the walls which thus appeared, and were completely separated from the floor. I endeavoured, but of course in vain, to look through the aperture.

As I arose from the attempt the mystery of the alteration in the chamber broke at once upon my understanding. I have observed that although the outlines of the figures upon the walls were sufficiently distinct, yet the colours seemed blurred and indefinite. These colours had now assumed, and were momentarily assuming, a startling and most intense brilliancy, that gave to the spectral and fiendish portraitures an aspect that might have thrilled even firmer nerves than my own. Demon eyes, of a wild and ghastly vivacity, glared upon me in a thousand directions where none had been visible before, and gleamed with the lurid lustre of a fire that I could not force my imagination to regard as unreal.

Unreal! – Even while I breathed there came to my nostrils the breath of the vapour of heated iron! A suffocating odour pervaded the prison! A deeper glow settled each moment in the eyes that glared at my agonies! A richer tint of crimson diffused itself over the pictured horrors of blood. I panted! I gasped for breath! There could be no doubt of the design of my tormentors – oh, most unrelenting! oh, most demoniac of men! I shrank from the glowing metal to the centre of the cell. Amid the thought of the fiery destruction that impended, the idea of the coolness of the well came over my soul like balm. I rushed to its deadly brink. I threw my straining vision below. The glare from the enkindled roof illumined its inmost recesses. Yet, for a wild moment, did my spirit refuse to comprehend the meaning of what I saw. At length it forced – it wrestled its way into my soul – it burned itself in upon my shuddering reason. O for a voice to speak! – oh, horror! – oh, any horror but this! With a shriek I rushed from the margin and buried my face in my hands – weeping bitterly.

The heat rapidly increased, and once again I looked up, shuddering as with a fit of the ague. There had been a second change in the cell – and now the change was obviously in the *form*. As before, it was in vain that I at first endeavoured to appreciate or understand what was taking place. But not long was I left in doubt. The Inquisitorial vengeance had been hurried by my two-fold escape, and there was to be no more dallying with the King of Terrors. The room had been square. I saw that two of its iron angles were now acute – two, consequently, obtuse. The fearful difference quickly increased with a low rumbling or moaning sound. In an instant the apartment had shifted its form into that of a lozenge. But the alteration stopped not here – I neither hoped nor desired it to stop. I could have clasped the red walls to my bosom as a garment of eternal peace. 'Death,' I said, 'any death but that of the pit!' Fool! might I not have known that *into the pit* it was the object of the burning iron to urge me? Could I resist its glow? or if even that, could I withstand its pressure? And now, flatter and flatter grew the lozenge, with a rapidity that left me no time for contemplation. Its centre , and of course, its greatest width, came just over the yawning gulf. I shrank back – but the closing walls pressed me resistlessly onward. At length for my seared and writhing body there was no longer an inch of foothold on the firm floor of the prison. I struggled no more, but the agony of my soul found vent in one loud, long, and final scream of despair. I felt that I tottered upon the brink – I averted my eyes——

There was a discordant hum of human voices! There was a loud blast as of many trumpets! There was a harsh grating as of a thousand thunders! The fiery walls rushed back! An outstretched arm caught my own as I fell fainting into the abyss. It was that of General Lasalle. The French army had entered Toledo. The Inquisition was in the hands of its enemies.

Headlamps

Tony Richards

There was the smell of blood that night. A breeze had sprung up from the West, coming across the Utah border into Colorado. It brought with it the scent of pine, the aroma of fresh wood, the subtlest hint of melting snow. That should have been all. It was not. The smell of blood was there, as real as your own hand. It permeated the shadows.

'Maybe I should turn in, get some sleep,' said Jethro.

'Can you?' asked Great-Uncle Luke. 'Do you think you will?'

Jethro considered that for a while. 'No, perhaps not.'

He sat up restlessly in his chair, gazed out into the darkness beyond the porch. The world had become flat, two-dimensional. Silhouettes surrounded him like headstones in a graveyard. To his left were the thirty-odd cabins which made up this tiny northern Colorado town – an isolated town with no shops or telephones or police, just a general store which doubled as a post office. To his right was Luke's lumber mill, where he was working through his college vacation. Beyond that lay the vast, impenetrable tangle of the forest. And towering over it all, purple-black and godlike, was the mountain. It suffused the corners of his view, a bulking monolith. Even as a child, it had always filled him with awe. A little fear, too, he realized. Fear of an avalanche, of being crushed beneath a thousand tons of stone. Fear of the timber wolves which dwelt in the high regions. Fear, most of all, of the treacherous, winding road which clambered along the mountainside, and of the terrible things which happened there.

The road had been built long before his time. It started at the main highway, ten miles away, forging through the dense forest to the great stone spire. There it rose, snaking up the side of the rock until it turned and disappeared high up around the mountain. From there, Jethro thought it wound back down until it joined the road to Glenwood Springs. It had been so long since anyone had used it that he was not sure.

'Something bad is going to happen tonight, isn't it?' he asked.

Great-Uncle Luke removed his home-rolled cigarette from a wrinkle that could just be called his mouth. As he leant forwards to stub it on the porch boards, his grey wispy hair fell across his forehead. He let it lie there.

'You tell me,' he said.

'I know it. I can *feel* it. Something really bad. Something ...' Jethro faltered. The statement became a question. '... to do with the road?'

Luke said nothing. He was busy rolling another cigarette. Jethro noticed, though, that the old man's nimble fingers had become unsure. That answered his quesion well enough.

Something moved high above them.

'My God, look up there! I was right!'

Out of the trees at the foot of the mountain, a pair of headlamps had appeared. Rectangular headlamps, those of a sports car. They began to traverse the mountainface like twin fireflies, moving quickly. Too quickly.

'Idiot! What's he doing up there this time of night? Don't he know *anything*?'

Luke's head came up slowly, grudgingly. The bright, distant headlamps were reflected in his narrowed eyes.

John Tarrell shifted gear from fourth right down to second, coming round the next bend. The MG protested, slowed a little. There was a thump from the trunk as the suitcases slid across. The tail nearly swung out. Tarrell brought the car swiftly under control, cursed, and dropped his speed to twenty miles per hour. Ahead of him, his headlamps were barely making an impression on the darkness. Fifteen yards of slender, rugged road was all that he could see – that and the unyielding rock wall to his right. The bends came up on him with terrifying suddenness. Worst of all, he could not make out where asphalt gave way to thin air, only guess. His imagination ran riot.

Lousy hicks, they could've at least put up a barrier.

It was some start to a holiday. He had come down from Rawlins, Wyoming, heading for Pike's Peak and his hotel. Now he realized that he should have started out earlier. Dusk had fallen soon after he crossed the state line, and night was fast on its heels. Somewhere, several miles back, he had taken the wrong fork. It was an easy enough mistake to make. Not so easy, though, was getting off the road he'd gone down. It wound tortuously through the forest for some way, getting rougher and narrower all the while, then came up on to this infernal mountain. By the time he realized his error it was too late to turn around, too far to back up, too dangerous. He had decided to go on, see where the road led. And now he was regretting it.

Cautiously, he shifted back up to third. The speedometer needle began to creep. Tarrell knew he should slow down. Better to arrive late than not at all. He found it hard, though, to fetter his impatience.

Besides, he wanted more than anything to get off the mountain. What if another car ... ?

As if his very thought had summoned them, twin headlamps appeared on the road far ahead. They were coming towards him.

'There's Old Harry,' said Luke. 'Right on time as usual.'

Jethro sprang up from his seat, began to move forwards, then stopped. He stood at the edge of the porch, his entire body trembling. To Luke, he looked like a puppet with its strings snared, all ready but incapable of motion.

'Can't we do anything?' Jethro shouted.

'Nothing except sit back and watch.'

'That's *callous*, Uncle.'

Luke seemed unperturbed. 'That's *fact*. Anyone who goes up that mountain at night can't expect help from no one but himself. Old Harry's killed fourteen motorists in the last thirty-five years he's been up there. Nothing you or I do will stop him.'

He could not seem to look directly at the mountain. His gaze kept flickering away. Above, the headlamps were closing fast. Luke's face lost some of its calmness, the lines and wrinkles deepening with sorrow.

'Course,' he went on, 'I pity that poor guy up there. All on his own. Mountain on one side and a four-hundred-foot drop on the other. And Old Harry coming at him with that big ol' dynamite truck.'

'Why does he keep doing it, though?' Jethro asked. 'Why keep on killing folks he doesn't even know?'

Luke shook his head. 'He always was like that. Mean. Unforgiving. He got hurt in a stupid, pointless way and I guess he doesn't see why he should be alone.'

'Oh, my God!' was all Tarrell could say. The words came out as little more than a gasp.

Ahead, the opposing headlamps vanished behind an outjutting rock, then reappeared, much closer. They were huge; truck lamps, he realized with a sickening shock. Huge and luminous and menacing. They grew in his vision, bearing down on him like Nemesis. The darkness might have been playing tricks on his eyes, but it seemed that they were moving even faster than he. And he was doing – he could barely shift his gaze to the speedometer – thirty!

Tarrell began to panic. Immediately, he heard an anguished squeal as his rear outside wheel left the asphalt and clung to the narrow strip of gravel by the drop. He swerved the car back in, too hard, and nearly hit the mountain.

Calm down. You're not dead. Yet.

He made sure that the car was steady, then began gently to brake, taking care not to lock the wheels. At the same time, he put his right hand firmly on the horn. It blared out in one steady, continuous note, rending the serenity which existed outside Tarrell's skull. He kept at it for what seemed like ages. His hand came free only when he realized that, surely, the truck driver could see him well enough. The other vehicle showed no sign of stopping. It was as if the driver were blind. Or crazy.

Sweat was seeping into Tarrell's eyes. His hand had become slippery on the wheel. There was a fire in him no amount of dousing would cool, and at the heart of that fire a terrible rage.

'You maniac!' he screamed at the oncoming lights. *'Stop!'*

His voice was trapped within the confines of his own car.

He was close enough to see the truck now. At first it was only a large grey shape looming out of the night. Then he could make it out in more detail. He sucked in a sharp breath. The truck was caked with mud and rust. Patches of moss grew on its sides. It was badly dented in several places, the front fender crumpled like baking foil. Just underneath the headlamps was a licence plate, local but incredibly ancient. The tyres were whirling quilts of bald rubber and patches. He had never seen anything like that on the road.

The truck was almost upon him. Tarrell looked up at the driver in the darkened cab, and screamed.

'It was the autumn of '34,' Luke was saying.

In the town, a light had come on in every house. The sports car horn had shattered the inhabitants' slumber. Pale, tired faces crowded each window. No one moved to help, though. They stayed safe inside their homes, waiting for the sports car driver to lose his nerve, plunge his vehicle right off the edge to be lost amongst the cover of the pine trees far below. As if they were spectators at some gruesome sport.

'Not a bad little year. Kind of peaceful round these parts. Nobody knew how soon the war would come, how many people would get killed. We were all getting along, minding our own business. Plenty of jobs about, too. A quarrying company had set up nearby. They were blasting on the far side of the mountain, and they hired men from this town. Pete Dane, him who owns the general store now. Jerry Driscoll, little guy, got killed in the Pacific. And Harry. They'd go up the mountain every day, on that same road. It was new then, kind of a novelty. Everybody used it in those days. It had smooth, neat asphalt and a real iron crash barrier, though that's rusted away now. Like I said, they were peaceful times. Strange that such horror could be born out of such peace.'

He grimaced round the fresh, unlit cigarette in his mouth. It was badly rolled. The paper was coming loose, the tobacco dropping out. He did not notice.

'That evening, everyone was packed up and ready to go home. All except Harry. They'd put him in charge of the explosives, and he loved it. He was a big, lumbering man like an ox, maybe a little touched. People didn't like him much. That's why they gave him that job. He didn't care – the danger never bothered him. He'd get powder all over his clothes, throw sticks of dynamite about like they were candy bars. And he was still fiddling around when it was time to go. The others left him to it.

'After a while it got dark, and Harry started back in the dynamite truck. He couldn't leave it there for fear it would get stolen. But he went slowly, carefully. What he didn't know was that back in the town some kid – he was twenty-six, actually, but he acted like a kid – had got juiced to the eyeballs on moonshine and decided to take a night time drive up that road in his car. He came roaring up at thirty-five, and Harry didn't see him till it was too late.

'God knows how they didn't both go off the edge. Harry was always a good driver, and the kid, I guess, was just drunk-lucky. The car slammed against the mountain wall, stayed there. The truck came off badly, though. And Harry even worse.'

At first Tarrell could not believe what he saw. It had to be some trick of the light. The thing he had seen driving the truck was anything but human. It was emaciated beyond belief, its face a mere skull with skin stretched across. The skin itself was burnt and black in places, scarred in others. The lips and eyelids were torn, rotten, the eyes sunken and glaring madly like hot coals in their pits. All hair was gone save for a few wild, yellowed tufts of scalp and two straggling lengths of beard. One ear was missing. But worst of all was the insane, gloating smile composed of a crescent of broken and decaying teeth. The creature leaned forward right through the windscreen, which Tarrell realized was smashed, and grinned at him. Its broken, bony fingers tightened on the wheel.

Tarrell broke away with alarm. He knew, now, that the creature intended to force him out into the abyss. And he also knew that he would not let it.

He glanced ahead, saw his chance. The road had widened very slightly and the thing driving the truck, in its eagerness to kill, had come out too far. There was a gap, not much, but maybe just enough to squeeze the MG through. At the last moment, he wrenched the car away from the drop.

The screech of metal against metal filled his ears.

'The truck skidded round,' Luke continued. 'It slammed head first into the rock. Harry, of course, went right through the windscreen. His face was caved in, cut to pieces, and some say he lost his left ear. He went half way through, then the glass caught on his belt, slashed his belly, and he slumped back moaning. Lay there for quite some time, half unconscious.

Finally he straightened up enough to realize the truck might explode. It was a blessing it hadn't already – or maybe not, thinking about it.

'By now he was on fire. Remember all that powder on his clothes? His shirt was burning right down the front as he scrabbled out of that cab. His chest got scorched, and his face, everything. That would have finished most men, but Harry was stronger than most. He ripped the shirt off and began staggering towards the other car. The kid was still there, dazed and only just sobering up, and he was going to kill him. It was then that he saw himself reflected in the kid's windscreen.'

Luke's face puckered up with the anguish of the memory.

'Poor feller. What it must have been like, seeing himself turned into something barely human. He stared a while, and then it sank through what had happened. His fingers clawed at his ruined face, like he was making sure. The last thing the kid saw, Harry was back in the truck, turning it around and heading back into the mountain. He was howling all the way like a wolf caught in a trap. He's never been down since. There's berries and nuts for him to eat up there, small animals to catch. And the truck was well supplied: tool kit, hand-crank generator, spare battery, three jerry cans of extra fuel. So Harry stays hidden up there and only comes out on those nights when someone's fool enough to use the road. Forces them off the road, and they go right down into the forest, underneath the trees where no one will ever see or find them. Come the end of October, the heavy snows come and the cars are lost for good.'

He shuddered, gestured to the forest.

'Fourteen cars somewhere out there, mouldering to dust. And in them, almost like they were in coffins, fourteen drivers who faced Harry and lost. Like I said, he never was the forgiving kind.

'The folks down here have never had the guts to hunt him down. Old Harry's got enough explosives up there to bring the entire mountain down around our heads, and folks would rather let him kill off strangers than disturb him. Oh, once in a while the County Sherriff, Henry Dobbs, comes snooping round looking for missing persons. We lie, say we've never seen them. Then Henry'll go up, have a look for himself. He finds nothing, of course. Just an empty road that no one uses any more, and that's the end of it. Folks go missing in this state all the time. It's no big deal. We could change that, I suppose, but we're all too scared.'

His gaze had fallen from the scene above. He looked up just in time to see the headlamps converge. *Number fifteen.* He covered his face with his hands.

And then Jethro shouted, 'My God, the sports car's through!'

Above the noise and the wrenching, above the fear of being crushed alive, two things in particular shocked Tarrell as he passed the truck. The first was the faded DANGER! EXPLOSIVES! painted on its side. The second was the overpowering acrid smell. He placed it in an instant. If the dynamite inside was as old as the truck, then it was sweating nitro-glycerine by the bucketful. He was amazed it had not blown up long ago. As if, it seemed, only the driver's willpower was holding the truck together.

As soon as he was through, Tarrell surveyed the damage to the MG. The left side had been scored and dented but not badly damaged. The right side, the side which had pressed against the mountainface, was wrecked. He felt glad he was carrying no passengers. All the glass of that side had been smashed, the bodywork crushed inwards. All told he had been lucky. Much too lucky.

He glanced in the rearview mirror. The truck was still there, heading down the mountain road away from him. Tarrell had hoped it might have been forced off the ledge itself, but somehow it had managed to get by. As he watched, its brake lights winked on. The truck slowed to a halt. Then it began to reverse up the gradient, fast. Tarrell moaned softly as he saw the driver lean out of the side window to stare at him.

The MG was slowing down, by now on a steep uphill slope. Tarrell put pressure on the gas. All he got in reply was a loud clanking noise from under the bonnet. Something in the engine had given. He shifted down to first and continued the tortured ascent, praying that the car would not fail him now.

The truck's rear lights were not working; either they were broken or had failed some years ago. Trying to concentrate on the road ahead, Tarrell did not see that it was upon him till it hit. A shudder ran right through the car. Tarrell was thrown against the steering wheel, then back again. His neck whiplashed. A multi-coloured skyrocket flared up from the region of his collarbone and erupted in his head. He pumped on the accelerator, but the clanking from the engine only grew worse.

It was then that he noticed the town below. So tiny was it, so engulfed by the forest, that he had not seen it in all the excitement. It was ablaze with light. *They were watching him.* And not one of them had come up to help. He sounded the horn three times in a desperate distress call.

The truck hit again. This time, the car slid forward several feet. Once more, he knew, and he would be off. He sounded the horn again.

Help me . . .

A dark chasm ahead of him caught his attention. No more than a few yards further on, the road disappeared into nothingness. It took Tarrell almost too long to realize he had come to a hairpin bend, practically driven himself off. He hauled on the wheel savagely and got the car round. A feeling of victory welled up inside him. The truck would not be able to follow him here, not backwards. He caught one glimpse of it trying to crawl round. Then it vanished.

*

'Where's it gone?' asked Jethro. 'Has it fallen?'

Luke looked puzzled for a moment, then shook his head. 'The mule trail,' he said.

'What?'

'Old Harry always was cunning. There's an old pioneer trail up there. It's a short cut, runs most of the way back up the mountain. Men built it a long time before the road, cut it out of the bare rock with no more than a few picks and shovels. It's just wide enough to let the truck through. Old Harry'll have to go slow, reversing all the way, but, even so, he'll head off the sports car further up the mountain. All he needs to do is back out into the road and he'll be facing him again.'

He had spoken a death sentence.

The two men stared at each other across the porch, Luke solemn and resigned, Jethro quivering between rage and despair. At last, rage won.

'It isn't fair!' he shouted. 'Old Harry should never have been that one to get hurt. It should have been that kid. He should have *died*.'

Luke almost wanted to laugh at his great-nephew. What was the point of raking up an injustice thirty-five years old? 'It's hard to kill a fool,' he said. 'That kid came to hardly any harm at all. Lived to a ripe old age, wiser, maybe, but not crippled. All he did was crack his head on the dashboard. Got a little scar, like T-shaped, just below the hairline.'

'I'd like to kill him,' Jethro said.

'Sure,' said Luke. 'And I'm sure sometimes he'd like to kill himself.'

The radiator was steaming by now, the car about ready to pack up. Tarrell did not care. He would buy himself a new car when he got home, now that he was able to go home. The hotel was still holding his reservation. He would drive there tomorrow, in the daylight, and have the best holiday of his life. In the bar, perhaps, celebrating. He felt in a champagne mood.

He had won, and without any help from the faint hearts in the town.

Reaching out one hand, he patted the MG's dashboard lovingly. Who would have thought that a light sports car could beat a heavy truck. He would, he thought indulgently, keep it in his garage for sentimental value.

The engine started to lose any power it had left. *Come on, baby. If you can get a truck over the side then you can finish this road.*

Then why, if the truck fell, the thought came, *didn't I hear the explosion?*

The car gave one final splutter and stopped. High above him on the road, a huge grey shape detached itself from the darkness. Tarrell's mouth went dry, his features rigid. The great round headlamps came out, dazzling him, filling his mind as they roared towards him. Tarrell was frozen in their glare.

He did not scream this time, never would again. Oblivion wrapped him in its grasp and claimed him.

The entire town came rushing out of doors as the truck exploded. They stood in the grass before the forest, mouths agape, faces alight with the pure white glow from the mountainside. It was like the Fourth of July.

The truck erupted three times, each blast louder and more violent than the last. Scorched debris was flung to the far corners of the wind. Vast gouts of flame leapt up to challenge the night sky and emblazon it with red. Some reached their zenith only to plunge down and light the tree tops far below. The small MG was invisible, enveloped in the blaze. Finally, the road itself broke up and collapsed. A number of people began to cheer.

'Listen to them,' Jethro snarled. 'A man was just killed up there.'

'The fifteenth and the last,' Luke sighed. 'A very brave man. Funny how it's always the good ones who get hurt, never the cowards and the fools.' He suddenly looked like he was going to cry. 'Well, great-nephew, it's all over now. Old Harry can rest in peace at last.'

He ran his hands through his hair. Even so briefly, his fingertips alighted on a tiny T-shaped scar just below the hairline. His eyes closed tightly shut, pressing out tears.

'Thank God I don't have to watch that any more.'

Jethro was not listening to him. He had walked right off the porch and was staring at the mountain, watching something which had moved off from the inferno.

Off to his left, a sickly hush had fallen over the crowd. For, high up on the mountain, a huge round pair of truck headlamps were moving along the road.

Except there was no longer any road.

Behind the Yellow Door

Flavia Richardson

The house was plain – stucco to the height of the first storey and brick for the remaining two. The bricks had recently been pointed; the whole building looked well kept and as if it were inhabited by well-to-do and intelligent people. Only the door was an eyesore. Yellow – not cheerful orange or even a clear lemon or saffron, but a blatant shade that could not be described by any known hue – crude chrome, perhaps, was the closest analogy.

Marcia Miles, standing on the doorstep, felt a little shiver run through her as she waited for the bell to be answered. Never given to 'feelings' or premonitions, she was at a loss to account for the cold goose-flesh sensation that attacked her ankles in spite of the warm July sun.

Then the door was opened, and she stepped into the most ordinary hall: walls papered with lincrusta for three feet from the floor and then distempered cream ... staircase turning at the half-landing with a large bowl of carnations on an oak chest in the window ... thick brown carpet, blue curtains, making a background for the pink flower-heads ... nothing could have been more sane, more conventional. And yet in her innermost heart she felt a desire to turn and run ... but why, she could not say. But companion-secretaries who have been out of work for three months, and whose qualifications are far more those of companions than of secretaries, do not run on their first day in new positions.

The maid led her upstairs to the back drawing room, which had been converted into a study. And there Mrs Merrill came to her.

Mrs Merrill was tall, slender, and good looking. Her clever, capable hands had the strength of a surgeon's. Marcia, secretly surveying her, realized why this woman had made a name as a consultant physician. She had personality ... almost hypnotic persuasion. Not a woman it would be easy to withstand.

'My correspondence is not very heavy,' she explained. 'The maid who brought you up attends to my professional appointments. She keeps the book, and you need only consult it in order to prevent my social engagements clashing.'

Marcia heaved a sigh of relief. She had been afraid, even though it had been expressly stipulated that the secretarial duties would be light. She was only too well aware of her own shortcomings from a professional point of view.

'What I really need you for,' the cool, clearly modulated tone went on, 'is as a companion for my daughter. She needs someone to be with from time to time ...'

She broke off. Marcia longed to ask the age of the daughter, but she did not like to do so. Time enough when she saw the girl. Covertly surveying Mrs Merrill, Marcia placed her as a well-preserved forty-three. Her daughter might easily be nearly grown-up – in the betwixt and between stage, probably.

The morning passed without anything of note. Marcia took down the answers to a number of letters, answered the telephone twice, and made notes of various engagements.

But all the time she was conscious of a queer undercurrent. Mrs Merrill looked at her every now and then as it were in an appraising way. Marcia fidgeted once under the scrutiny, and was aware that it was instantly withdrawn ... but she felt uncomfortable, all the same. The parlourmaid came in with a message ... and Marcia sensed that she too was looking at her more intently than was usual, even with old and valued servants. She did not like the maid. There was an opaqueness, a steeliness about the grey eyes that was almost frightening ... as though the woman's mind were always turned inwards. She looked like a woman with a mission.

Marcia tried to scold herself for her imagination. It was no business of hers. Her job was to do her work so well that Mrs Merrill would keep her as her employee for a long time to come.

Luncheon was served in a small dining room under the study, but there was no sign of the daughter. Marcia supposed she was out, but a chance remark about the tray for upstairs between Mrs Merrill and the maid made her suspect that the girl was indisposed.

More letters and odds and ends followed during the afternoon, and at last, about five o'clock, Mrs Merrill said:

'If you have finished those cards, we will go upstairs and you can meet my daughter. She will be expecting us now.'

Marcia hurried through the cards. There was a hint of something unusual in Mrs Merrill's voice that made her wonder what was to come next. Was the daughter an invalid? Had she got to amuse a fretful adolescent? She wondered anxiously how her voice would hold out if she were expected to do much reading aloud.

Mrs Merrill put aside her book, took off the tortoise-shell glasses she habitually wore for reading, and rose to her feet.

Marcia followed her docilely, but with a throb of expectation.

They went up another flight of stairs, past two doors, and then up a further flight that curled unexpectedly. Marcia realized that they were going to the attics. At the top of the stairs was a heavy door, shrouded in baize and rubber-sheathed ... and sound-proofed effectively if not in the newest manner. The sight of it seemed menacing ... Marcia hesitated involuntarily as she followed Mrs Merrill ... What lay on the other side? ... What could she not hear?

Mrs Merrill went on without a word and pushed the door open. It gave on to a small entrance lobby, dark except for the light that came in through the opened door. From it another door led. As Marcia stepped into the lobby the door behind her swung noiselessly to on its hinges. With a little gasp she realized as they stood in the dark that it had shut. Instinctively she put out a hand and pushed against it. It remained firm.

The sensation of horror deepened. In a second of time she appreciated the fact that she was shut up on the top floor of this strange house with a woman whom she did not know ... a woman who was reputed to be a brilliant pathologist, but about whom strange stories were already being whispered.

'Come in and see my daughter.' Mrs Merrill's voice was so ordinary that it almost took Marcia by surprise. She realized that she had been waiting almost rudely in the lobby, and at the same time realized that scarcely ten seconds had gone since the door had swung to at her back. Time had seemed to stand still. She pulled herself together with an effort.

'Of course,' she said, then, summoning her courage, 'Is she – is she an invalid?'

For a moment it seemed as if Mrs Merrill paused. 'Not an invalid,' she said at length, with a harsh note in her voice; 'no, not an invalid. Come in, please.'

She opened the door, and Marcia automatically followed her into the big attic. The room ran the entire length of the house, and was gay with cretonne. The floor was covered with a big straw mat, curtains hung straight in the airless July day, the canary in his cage in the window was too sleepy to sing.

For a moment Marcia glanced round ... Then it was a child, a nursery. The furniture was all on the small scale. There was a tiny chair, a table, cupboards, and wardrobe. The bed was small and beautifully carved. On it, under the lightest of summer rugs, lay a child, her face exquisitely beautiful in the Greuze style.

'Olivette,' said Mrs Merrill softly. The child stirred, flung one arm up to shield her opening eyes from the sun, and then got down from the bed.

And Marcia found herself clenching her hands till the nails began to pierce the skin of the palms in her effort to keep from crying out. For the lovely child, Olivette, beautifully made to the waist, had no semblance of beauty below. Her thighs, her legs, and ankles were barely a foot long all told. Her feet were little larger than doll's feet, and she tottered on them as she came to her mother. The beauty of the torso was made more terrible by the horror that stretched below.

'My daughter,' said Mrs Merrill, and there was a trace of defiance in her voice as she bent down to caress the child who barely reached her own waist.

Marcia held her horror in check. Leaning down to shake hands, she looked more closely at the face below, and realized that in years Olivette was no child. The features, expression, hair, the very development of the breast, betrayed the fact that she was coming to full maturity. In spite of herself, a shudder ran through her as she felt the touch of the dwarf. Noticing it, Olivette's deep-blue eyes flashed fury – her lips parted in a bitter curve.

Suddenly Marcia felt that she could stand the situation no longer. She felt faint ... she turned ... Mrs Merrill looked at her in surprise.

'Forgive me ... the heat,' gasped Marcia, as she moved to the door.

The high-pitched laughter of Olivette warned her that she was not to escape so easily. Again the foreboding swept over her like a cloud ... What would happen? Something terrible was hovering in the room ... She clutched the door handle dizzily, turned it ... It did not respond. And then she realized that she had been trapped.

Trapped for what purpose she did not know. But that she was in the hands of Mrs Merrill and the dwarf for no good purpose she was firmly convinced. She could have cried at the lack of heed she had paid earlier to the warnings of her sixth sense, yet how could she, the sane and unemotional, be expected to trouble about unknown fears and premonitions? ... For a moment she thought she would faint.

Mrs Merrill's voice brought her to herself. It was so cold, so calm, that for the moment Marcia did not take in the full purport of the words. Gradually the sense penetrated to her dulled mind.

'My daughter, Olivette ... As you see, she has never had a chance. An accident shortly before her birth ... My lovely child condemned to a life of horror and regret. I had to wait for her to come to maturity. I had to lay my plans. Now they are ready and you came in answer to my advertisement. You will do well. You are approximately the same age as Olivette. You are the size to which she ought to have grown – to which she shall grow ...'

Mrs Merrill paused. Marcia drew a deep breath. What did she mean? What was all this preamble? What were they going to do?

She gazed into the hypnotic eyes of the woman facing her and felt her strength waning. She was still conscious of her own individuality, but she was paralysed, as a rabbit before a snake.

She did not hear the door open behind her. Her whole being was concentrated on the woman who stood in front – fighting to retain awareness. So deep was her absorption that the gentle touch of silk on her wrists almost passed unnoticed. When she realized it was too late. The hard-faced parlourmaid, now in a white nurse's overall, had bound her wrists tightly behind her back.

Marcia opened her mouth to scream, but a hand was laid over her mouth and at the same time the prick of a hypodermic needle in her arm started the lapsing of her consciousness.

'She didn't give much trouble,' said the parlourmaid, as they laid the inert form on the bed. 'I didn't think she would give in so easily. And she's just what you wanted, isn't she?'

Mrs Merrill nodded. 'Just what I wanted,' she said, and her hand went out to Olivette. 'Only a little while longer, my darling, and you shall be like other girls.'

'Shall you tell her ... ?' The maid nodded at Marcia.

Mrs Merrill's eyebrows went up. 'Tell her? Of course,' she responded. 'She is to form part of a stupendous scientific experiment. Of course I shall tell her. Now help me carry her down.'

Marcia came slowly to her senses and could not for the moment realize where she was. She was lying flat on something very hard and even, not painful but definitely uncomfortable. She tried to raise her hand, but found it impossible. Then she realized that not only could she not move her head but that she could scarcely move at all. Her arms were bound tightly to her sides and her ankles were tied together. Over her chest and legs straps were passed that fastened under the table on which she was lying. Her head was held in place by a further band that passed round her neck and again under the table. If she made any effort to sit up, she felt the preliminary symptoms of strangulation.

The room was nearly dark. She must have lost consciousness for some time. The sun had sunk below the houses, and the summer twilight blurred the outlines of the furniture. Marcia tried to call out, but her voice seemed weak and distant.

The sound, however, carried further than she thought. A strong electric light was switched on at once and Mrs Merrill came into Marcia's line of vision. Marcia stared at her, first blankly, then with growing horror. She was wearing a surgeon's overall and in her hand was a case of instruments.

'What ... what ...' Marcia began feebly.

Mrs Merrill came over to the table and felt the straps. Then she nodded. 'That'll do,' she said, half to herself. Then she turned to Marcia. 'You are going to see one of the most interesting and stupendous operations that has ever been attempted in modern surgery,' she said, and there was a detached, professional note in her voice that was more alarming than any emotion. 'You and my daughter are to change lower parts of your bodies. I have been waiting for a long time to get everything ready. In a few moments I shall begin to operate. You will know nothing about it until afterwards. Then, assuming that the operation is successful, as it must be, you will find Olivette's deformed legs grafted on to your body, while Olivette will be at last able to enjoy her life as a normal human being. She has waited nearly twenty years. You have had twenty years. It is her turn.'

Marcia screamed . . . just once. Then a gag was slipped into her mouth and she found she could do nothing but gurgle helplessly. Her whole body shook with terror.

'Dorcas,' Mrs Merrill called, and the former parlourmaid came from another part of the room where she had been waiting.

'Bring Olivette in, please.'

Dorcas reappeared, and Marcia, out of the tail of her eye, could see her lay Olivette, already under an anaesthetic, on an operating table similar to the one on which she was strapped. Mrs Merrill busied herself with preparations. Then she stood up and turned to Dorcas.

'If everything is ready in the sterilizer, we'll begin,' she announced. 'Are you ready with the anaesthetic?'

Marcia struggled feebly against her bonds. Helpless, unable to cry out, fully aware that every effort was useless, she still made a frantic appeal with her eyes. But no attention was paid. She realized that she was dealing with a mad woman, a woman with so deep an obsession about her daughter that nothing else mattered – and that Dorcas had no other idea than to serve her mistress.

With a refinement of cruelty, Mrs Merrill continued her preparations within Marcia's line of vision. Try as she would, Marcia could not keep her eyes closed. She must know . . . must see how near she was coming to the fatal moment. Death or deformity? . . . She did not know if the experiment were possible . . . but, if it were a success, would not death be more kind?

And all the time she was making ready Mrs Merrill talked. 'Think what a fortunate woman you are to be the subject of such an amazing experiment,' she said, laying out one deadly instrument after another. 'And we shan't ask you to endure it without ether. I don't want you to die – dead limbs would be no good to Olivette. After all, you will be able to walk – just as she can; it is not as if we were proposing to stop with the grafting on of your limbs to her body . . . I will finish the operation properly . . .'

Involuntarily, Marcia tried to scream, but only the merest sound came from her white lips. She strained again at the straps, and fell back, choking.

'Don't be silly,' admonished Mrs Merrill. 'You will only hurt yourself, and you won't be able to stand the strain of the operation.'

'Everything is ready, madam,' said Dorcas, coming again into the line of vision.

Marcia thought wildly: 'They'll surely take the gag out before they give me the ether ... I can give one scream. This is a big street. Someone must be passing.' She lay still and tried to relax, saving her strength. Spots danced before her eyes; her lips, strained by the gag, were dry and colourless.

'Now!' Mrs Merrill approached, a surgeon's mask over her face. Only the bright eyes gleamed, brighter against the white gauze.

Suddenly the cone was dropped over Marcia's nostrils, and with the realization of despair she knew that they were not going to give her even that one poor little chance.

Hours later, Mrs Merrill lifted her face, a face so haggard that the lines and pallor could be seen even under the mask.

'Both gone?' she whispered.

Dorcas, standing between the tables, nodded. 'Both madam.'

'Failed!'

'You did your best, madam,' comforted the maid. 'Miss Olivette didn't suffer, and it was better she should die than live like – like she was. As for the other one——'

Mrs Merrill scarcely glanced at the dismembered body on the table under her hand.

'Secretaries are plentiful,' was all she said.

A Pair of Muddy Shoes

Lennox Robinson

I am going to try to write it down quite simply, just as it happened. I shall try not to exaggerate anything.

I am twenty-two years old, my parents are dead, I have no brothers or sisters; the only near relation I have is Aunt Margaret, my father's sister. She is unmarried and lives alone in a little house in the country in the west of county Cork. She is kind to me and I often spend my holidays with her, for I am poor and have few friends.

I am a school-teacher – that is to say, I teach drawing and singing. I am a visiting teacher at two or three schools in Dublin. I make a fair income, enough for a single woman to live comfortably on, but father left debts behind him, and until these are paid off I have to live very simply. I suppose I ought to eat more and eat better food. People sometimes think I am nervous and highly strung: I look rather fragile and delicate, but really I am not. I have slender hands, with pale, tapering fingers – the sort of hands people call 'artistic'.

I hoped very much that my aunt would invite me to spend Christmas with her. I happened to have very little money; I had paid off a big debt of poor father's, and that left me very short, and I felt rather weak and ill. I didn't quite know how I'd get through the holidays unless I went down to my aunt's. However, ten days before Christmas the invitation came. You may be sure I accepted it gratefully, and when my last school broke up on the 20th I packed my trunk, gathered up the old sentimental songs Aunt Margaret likes best, and set off for Rosspatrick.

It rains a great deal in West Cork in the winter: it was raining when Aunt Margaret met me at the station. 'It's been a terrible month, Peggy,' she said, as she turned the pony's head into the long road that runs for four muddy miles from the station to Rosspatrick. 'I think it's rained every day for the last six weeks. And the storms! We lost a chimney two days ago: it came through the roof, and let the rain into the ceiling of the spare bedroom. I've had to make you up a bed in the lumber-room till Jeremiah Driscoll can be got to mend the roof.'

I assured her that any place would do me; all I wanted was her society and a quiet time.

'I can guarantee you those,' she said. 'Indeed, you look tired out: you look as if you were just after a bad illness or just before one. That teaching is killing you.'

That lumber room was really very comfortable. It was a large room with two big windows; it was on the ground floor, and Aunt Margaret had never used it as a bedroom because people are often afraid of sleeping on the ground floor.

We stayed up very late talking over the fire. Aunt Margaret came with me to my bedroom; she stayed there for a long time, fussing about the room, hoping I'd be comfortable, pulling about the furniture, looking at the bedclothes.

At last I began to laugh at her. 'Why shouldn't I be comfortable? Think of my horrid little bedroom in Brunswick Street! What's wrong with this room?'

'Nothing – oh, nothing,' she said rather hurriedly, and kissed me and left me.

I slept very well. I never opened my eyes till the maid called me, and then after she had left me I dozed off again. I had a ridiculous dream. I dreamed I was interviewing a rich old lady: she offered me a thousand a year and comfortable rooms to live in. My only duty was to keep her clothes from moths; she had quantities of beautiful, costly clothes, and she seemed to have a terror of them being eaten by moths. I accepted her offer at once. I remember saying to her gaily, 'The work will be no trouble to me, I like killing moths.'

It was strange I should say that, because I really don't like killing moths – I hate killing anything. But my dream was easily explained, for when I woke a second later (as it seemed), I was holding a dead moth between my finger and thumb. It disgusted me just a little bit – that dead moth pressed between my fingers, but I dropped it quickly, jumped up, and dressed myself.

Aunt Margaret was in the dining-room, and full of profuse and anxious inquiries about the night I had spent. I soon relieved her anxieties, and we laughed together over my dream and the new position I was going to fill. It was very wet all day and I didn't stir out of the house. I sang a great many songs, I began a pencil-drawing of my aunt – a thing I had been meaning to make for years – but I didn't feel well, I felt headachy and nervous – just from being in the house all day, I suppose. I felt the greatest disinclination to go to bed. I felt afraid, I don't know of what.

Of course I didn't say a word of this to Aunt Margaret.

That night the moment I fell asleep I began to dream. I thought I was looking down at myself from a great height. I saw myself in my nightdress crouching in a corner of the bedroom. I remember wondering why I was crouching there, and I came nearer and looked at myself again, and then

I saw that it was not myself that crouched there – it was a large white cat, it was watching a mouse-hole. I was relieved and I turned away. As I did so I heard the cat spring. I started round. It had a mouse between its paws, and looked up at me, growling as a cat does. Its face was like a woman's face – was like my face. Probably that doesn't sound at all horrible to you, but it happens that I have a deadly fear of mice. The idea of holding one between my hands, of putting my mouth to one, of – oh, I can't bear even to write it.

I think I woke screaming. I know when I came to myself I had jumped out of bed and was standing on the floor. I lit the candle and searched the room. In one corner were some boxes and trunks; there might have been a mouse-hole behind them, but I hadn't the courage to pull them out and look. I kept my candle lighted and stayed awake all night.

The next day was fine and frosty. I went for a long walk in the morning and for another in the afternoon. When bedtime came I was very tired and sleepy. I went to sleep at once and slept dreamlessly all night.

It was the next day that I noticed my hands getting queer. 'Queer' perhaps isn't the right word, for, of course, cold does roughen and coarsen the skin, and the weather was frosty enough to account for that. But it wasn't only that the skin was rough, the whole hand looked larger, stronger, not like my own hand. How ridiculous this sounds, but the whole story is ridiculous.

I remember once, when I was a child at school, putting on another girl's boots by mistake one day. I had to go about till evening in them, and I was perfectly miserable. I could not stop myself from looking at my feet, and they seemed to me to be the feet of another person. That sickened me, I don't know why. I felt a little like that now when I looked at my hands. Aunt Margaret noticed how rough and swollen they were, and she gave me cold cream which I rubbed on them before I went to bed.

I lay awake for a long time. I was thinking of my hands. I didn't seem to be able not to think of them. They seemed to grow bigger and bigger in the darkness; they seemed monstrous hands, the hands of some horrible ape, they seemed to fill the whole room. Of course if I had struck a match and lit the candle I'd have calmed myself in a minute, but, frankly, I hadn't the courage. When I touched one hand with the other it seemed rough and hairy, like a man's.

At last I fell asleep. I dreamed that I got out of bed and opened the window. For several minutes I stood looking out. It was bright moonlight and bitterly cold. I felt a great desire to go for a walk. I dreamed that I dressed myself quickly, put on my slippers, and stepped out of the window. The frosty grass crunched under my feet. I walked, it seemed for miles, along a road I never remember being on before. It led uphill; I met no one as I walked.

Presently I reached the crest of the hill, and beside the road, in the middle of a bare field, stood a large house. It was a gaunt three-storeyed building, there was an air of decay about it. Maybe it had once been a gentleman's place, and was now occupied by a herd. There are many places like that in Ireland. In a window of the highest storey there was a light. I decided I would go the house and ask the way home. A gate closed the grass-grown avenue from the road; it was fastened and I could not open it, so I climbed it. It was a high gate but I climbed it easily, and I remember thinking in my dream, 'If this wasn't a dream I could never climb it so easily.'

I knocked at the door, and after I had knocked again the window of the room in which the light shone was opened, and a voice said, 'Who's there? What do you want?'

I came from a middle-aged woman with a pale face and dirty strands of grey hair hanging about her shoulders.

I said, 'Come down and speak to me; I want to know the way back to Rosspatrick.'

I had to speak two or three times to her, but at last she came down and opened the door mistrustfully. She only opened it a few inches and barred my way. I asked her the road home, and she gave me directions in a nervous, startled way.

Then I dreamed that I said, 'Let me in to warm myself.'

'It's late; you should be going home.'

But I laughed, and suddenly pushed at the door with my foot and slipped past her.

I remember she said, 'My God,' in a helpless, terrified way. It was strange that she should be frightened, and I, a young girl all alone in a strange house with a strange woman, miles from anyone I knew, should not be frightened at all. As I sat warming myself by the fire while she boiled the kettle (for I had asked for tea), and watching her timid, terrified movements, the queerness of the position struck me, and I said, laughing, 'You seem afraid of me.'

'Not at all, miss,' she replied, in a voice which almost trembled.

'You needn't be, there's not the least occasion for it,' I said, and I laid my hand on her arm.

She looked down at it as it lay there, and said again, 'Oh, my God,' and staggered back against the range.

And so for half a minute we remained. Her eyes were fixed on my hand which lay on my lap; it seemed she could never take them off it.

'What is it?' I said.

'You've the face of a girl,' she whispered, 'and – God help me – the hands of a man.'

I looked down at my hands. They were large, strong and sinewy, covered with coarse red hairs. Strange to say they no longer disgusted me:

I was proud of them – proud of their strength, the power that lay in them.

'Why should they make you afraid?' I asked. 'They are fine hands. Strong hands.'

But she only went on staring at them in a hopeless, frozen way.

'Have you ever seen such strong hands before?' I smiled at her.

'They're – they're Ned's hands,' she said at last, speaking in a whisper.

She put her own hand to her throat as if she were choking, and the fastening of her blouse gave way. It fell open. She had a long throat; it was moving as if she were finding it difficult to swallow. I wondered whether my hands would go round it.

Suddenly I knew they would, and I knew why my hands were large and sinewy, I knew why power had been given to them. I got up and caught her by the throat. She struggled so feebly; slipped down, striking her head against the range; slipped down on to the red-tiled floor and lay quite still, but her throat still moved under my hand and I never loosened my grasp.

And presently, kneeling over her, I lifted her head and bumped it gently against the flags of the floor. I did this again and again; lifting it higher, and striking it harder and harder, until it was crushed in like an egg, and she lay still. She was choked and dead.

And I left her lying there and ran from the house, and as I stepped on to the road I felt rain in my face. The thaw had come.

When I woke it was morning. Little by little my dream came back and filled me with horror. I looked at my hands. They were so tender and pale and feeble. I lifted them to my mouth and kissed them.

But when Mary called me half an hour later she broke into a long, excited story of a woman who had been murdered the night before, how the postman had found the door open and the dead body. 'And sure, miss, it was here she used to live long ago; she was near murdered once, by her husband, in this very room; he tried to choke her, she was half killed – that's why the mistress made it a lumber-room. They put him in the asylum afterwards; a month ago he died there I heard.'

My mother was Scottish, and claimed she had the gift of prevision. It was evident she had bequeathed it to me. I was enormously excited. I sat up in bed and told Mary my dream.

She was not very interested, people seldom are in other people's dreams. Besides, she wanted, I suppose, to tell her news to Aunt Margaret. She hurried away. I lay in bed and thought it all over. I almost laughed, it was so strange and fantastic.

But when I got out of bed I stumbled over something. It was a little muddy shoe. At first I hardly recognized it, then I saw it was one of a pair of evening shoes I had, the other shoe lay near it. They were a pretty little pair of dark blue satin shoes, they were a present to me from a girl I loved very much, she had given them to me only a week ago.

Last night they had been so fresh and new and smart. Now they were scratched, the satin cut, and they were covered with mud. Someone had walked miles in them.

And I remembered in my dream how I had searched for my shoes and put them on.

Sitting on the bed, feeling suddenly sick and dizzy, holding the muddy shoes in my hand, I had in a blinding instant a vision of a red-haired man who lay in this room night after night for years, hating a sleeping white-faced woman who lay beside him, longing for strength and courage to choke her. I saw him come back, years afterwards – freed by death – to this room; saw him seize on a feeble girl too weak to resist him; saw him try her, strengthen her hands, and at last – through her – accomplish his unfinished deed . . . The vision passed all in a flash as it had come. I pulled myself together. 'That is nonsense, impossible,' I told myself. 'The murderer will be found before evening.'

But in my hand I still held the muddy shoes. I seem to be holding them ever since.

The Music on the Hill

Saki

Sylvia Seltoun ate her breakfast in the morning-room at Yessney with a
pleasant sense of ultimate victory, such as a fervent Ironside might have
permitted himself on the morrow of Worcester fight. She was scarcely
pugnacious by temperament, but belonged to that more successful class
of fighters who are pugnacious by circumstance. Fate had willed that her
life should be occupied with a series of small struggles, usually with the
odds slightly against her, and usually she had just managed to come
through winning. And now she felt that she had brought her hardest and
certainly her most important struggle to a successful issue. To have
married Mortimer Seltoun, 'Dead Mortimer' as his more intimate
enemies called him, in the teeth of the cold hostility of his family, and
in spite of his unaffected indifference to women, was indeed an achievement that had needed some determination and adroitness to carry
through; yesterday she had brought her victory to its concluding stage
by wrenching her husband away from Town and its group of satellite
watering-places, and 'settling him down', in the vocabulary of her kind,
in this remote woodgirt manor farm which was his country house.

'You will never get Mortimer to go,' his mother had said carpingly,
'but if he once goes he'll stay; Yessney throws almost as much a spell over
him as Town does. One can understand what holds him to Town, but
Yessney——' and the dowager had shrugged her shoulders.

There was a sombre almost savage wildness about Yessney that was
certainly not likely to appeal to town-bred tastes, and Sylvia, notwithstanding her name, was accustomed to nothing much more sylvan
than 'leafy Kensington'. She looked on the country as something excellent and wholesome in its way, which was apt to become troublesome if
you encouraged it overmuch. Distrust of town life had been a new thing
with her, born of her marriage with Mortimer, and she had watched with
satisfaction the gradual fading of what she called 'the Jermyn-street-look'
in his eyes as the woods and heather of Yessney had closed in on them
yesternight. Her will-power and strategy had prevailed; Mortimer would
stay.

Outside the morning-room windows was a triangular slope of turf, which the indulgent might call a lawn, and beyond its low hedge of neglected fuchsia bushes a steeper slope of heather and bracken dropped down into cavernous combes overgrown with oak and yew. In its wild open savagery there seemed a stealthy linking of the joy of life with the terror of unseen things. Sylvia smiled complacently as she gazed with a School-of-Art appreciation at the landscape, and then of a sudden she almost shuddered.

'It is very wild,' she said to Mortimer, who had joined her; 'one could almost think that in such a place the worship of Pan had never quite died out.'

'The worship of Pan never has died out,' said Mortimer. 'Other newer gods have drawn aside his votaries from time to time, but he is the Nature-God to whom all must come back at last. He has been called the Father of all the Gods, but most of his children have been stillborn.'

Sylvia was religious in an honest, vaguely devotional kind of way, and did not like to hear her beliefs spoken of as mere aftergrowths, but it was at least something new and hopeful to hear Dead Mortimer speak with such energy and conviction on any subject.

'You don't really believe in Pan?' she asked incredulously.

'I've been a fool in most things,' said Mortimer quietly, 'but I'm not such a fool as not to believe in Pan when I'm down here. And if you're wise you won't disbelieve in him too boastfully while you're in his country.'

It was not until a week later, when Sylvia had exhausted the attractions of the woodland walks round Yessney, that she ventured on a tour of inspection of the farm buildings. A farmyard suggested in her mind a scene of cheerful bustle, with churns and flails and smiling dairymaids, and teams of horses drinking knee-deep in duck-crowded ponds. As she wandered among the gaunt grey buildings of Yessney manor farm her first impression was one of crushing stillness and desolation, as though she had happened on some lone deserted homestead long given over to owls and cobwebs; then came a sense of furtive watchful hostility, the same shadow of unseen things that seemed to lurk in the wooded combes and coppices. From behind heavy doors and shuttered windows came the restless stamp of hoof or rasp of chain halter, and at times a muffled bellow from some stalled beast. From a distant corner a shaggy dog watched her with intent unfriendly eyes; as she drew near it slipped quietly into its kennel, and slipped out again as noiselessly when she had passed by. A few hens, questing for food under a rick, stole away under a gate at her approach. Sylvia felt that if she had come across any human beings in this wilderness of barn and byre they would have fled wraith-like from her gaze. At last, turning a corner quickly, she came upon a living thing that did not fly from her. A-stretch in a pool of mud was an enormous sow, gigantic beyond the town-woman's wildest computation of swine-flesh, and speedily alert to resent and if necessary repel the unwonted intrusion. It was Sylvia's turn to make an unobtrusive retreat. As she threaded her way past rickyards and cowsheds and long blank walls, she started suddenly at a strange sound – the echo of a boy's laughter, golden and equivocal. Jan, the only boy employed on the farm, a tow-headed, wizen-faced yokel, was visibly at work on a potato clearing half-way up the nearest hill-side, and Mortimer, when questioned, knew of no other probable or possible begetter of the hidden mockery that had ambushed Sylvia's retreat. The memory of that untraceable echo was added to her other impressions of a furtive sinister 'something' that hung around Yessney.

Of Mortimer she saw very little; farm and woods and trout-streams seemed to swallow him up from dawn till dusk. Once, following the direction she had seen him take in the morning, she came to an open space in a nut copse, further shut in by huge yew trees, in the centre of which stood a stone pedestal surmounted by a small bronze figure of a youthful Pan. It was a beautiful piece of workmanship, but her attention was chiefly held by the fact that a newly cut bunch of grapes had been placed as an offering at its feet. Grapes were none too plentiful at the manor house, and Sylvia snatched the bunch angrily from the pedestal. Contemptuous annoyance dominated her thoughts as she strolled slowly homeward, and then gave way to a sharp feeling of something that was very near fright; across a thick tangle of undergrowth a boy's face was scowling at her, brown and beautiful, with unutterably evil eyes. It was a lonely pathway – all pathways round Yessney were lonely for the matter of that – and she sped forward without waiting to give a closer scrutiny to this sudden apparition. It was not till she had reached the house that she discovered that she had dropped the bunch of grapes in her flight.

'I saw a youth in the wood today,' she told Mortimer that evening; 'brown-faced and rather handsome, but a scoundrel to look at. A gipsy lad, I suppose.'

'A reasonable theory,' said Mortimer, 'only there aren't any gipsies in these parts at present.'

'Then who was he?' asked Sylvia, and as Mortimer appeared to have no theory of his own, she passed on to recount her finding of the votive offering.

'I suppose it was your doing,' she observed; 'it's a harmless piece of lunacy, but people would think you dreadfully silly if they knew it.'

'Did you meddle with it in any way?' asked Mortimer.

'I – I threw the grapes away. It seemed so silly,' said Sylvia, watching Mortimer's impassive face for a sign of annoyance.

'I don't think you were wise to do that,' he said reflectively. 'I've heard it said that the Wood Gods are rather horrible to those who molest them.'

'Horrible perhaps to those that believe in them, but you see I don't,' retorted Sylvia.

'All the same,' said Mortimer in his even, dispassionate tone, 'I should avoid the woods and orchards if I were you, and give a wide berth to the horned beasts on the farm.'

It was all nonsense, of course, but in that lonely woodgirt spot nonsense seemed able to rear a bastard brood of uneasiness.

'Mortimer,' said Sylvia suddenly, 'I think we will go back to Town some time soon.'

Her victory had not been so complete as she had supposed; it had carried her on to ground that she was already anxious to quit.

'I don't think you will ever go back to Town,' said Mortimer. He seemed to be paraphrasing his mother's prediction as to himself.

Sylvia noted with dissatisfaction and some self-contempt that the course of her next afternoon's ramble took her instinctively clear of the network of woods. As to the horned cattle, Mortimer's warning was scarcely needed, for she had always regarded them as of doubtful neutrality at the best: her imagination unsexed the most matronly dairy cows and turned them into bulls liable to 'see red' at any moment. The ram who fed in the narrow paddock below the orchards she had adjudged, after ample and cautious probation, to be of docile temper; today, however, she decided to leave his docility untested, for the usually tranquil beast was roaming with every sign of restlessness from corner to corner of his meadow. A low, fitful piping, as of some reedy flute, was coming from the depth of a neighbouring copse, and there seemed to be some subtle connection between the animal's restless pacing and the wild music from the wood. Sylvia turned her steps in an upward direction and climbed the heather-clad slopes that stretched in rolling shoulders high above Yessney. She had left the piping notes behind her, but across the wooded combes at her feet the wind brought her another kind of music, the straining bay of hounds in full chase. Yessney was just on the outskirts of the Devon-and-Somerset country, and the hunted deer sometimes came that way. Sylvia could presently see a dark body, breasting hill after hill, and sinking again and again out of sight as he crossed the combes, while behind him steadily swelled that relentless chorus, and she grew tense with the excited sympathy that one feels for any hunted thing in whose capture one is not directly interested. And at last he broke through the outermost line of oak scrub and fern and stood panting in the open, a fat September stag carrying a well-furnished head. His obvious course was to drop down to the brown pools of Undercombe, and thence make his way towards the red deer's favoured sanctuary, the sea. To Sylvia's surprise, however, he turned his head to the upland slope and came lumbering resolutely onward over the heather. 'It will be dreadful,' she thought, 'the hounds will pull him down under my very eyes.' But the music of the pack seemed to have died away for a moment, and in its place she heard again that wild piping, which rose now on this side, now on that, as through urging the failing stag to a final effort. Sylvia stood well aside from his path, half hidden in a thick growth of whortle bushes, and watched him swing stiffly upward, his flanks dark with sweat, the coarse hair on his neck showing light by contrast. The pipe music shrilled suddenly around her, seeming to come from the bushes at her very feet, and at the same moment the great beast slewed round and bore directly down upon her. In an instant her pity for the hunted animal was changed to wild terror at her own danger; the thick heather roots mocked her scrambling efforts at flight, and she looked frantically downward for a glimpse of oncoming hounds. The huge antler spikes were within a few yards of her, and in a flash of numbing fear she remembered Mortimer's warning, to beware of horned beasts on the farm. And then with a quick throb of joy she saw that she was not alone; a human figure stood a few paces aside, knee-deep in the whortle bushes.

'Drive it off!' she shrieked. But the figure made no answering movement.

The antlers drove straight at her breast, the acrid smell of the hunted animal was in her nostrils, but her eyes were filled with the horror of something she saw other than her oncoming death. And in her ears rang the echo of a boy's laughter, golden and equivocal.

The Villa Désirée

May Sinclair

1

He had arranged it all for her. She was to stay a week in Cannes with her aunt and then to go on to Roquebrune by herself, and he was to follow her there. She, Mildred Eve, supposed he could follow her anywhere, since they were engaged now.

There had been difficulties, but Louis Carson had got over all of them by lending her the Villa Désirée. She would be all right there, he said. The caretakers, Narcisse and Armandine, would look after her; Armandine was an excellent cook; and she wouldn't be five hundred yards from her friends, the Derings. It was so like him to think of it, to plan it all out for her. And when he came down? Oh, when he came down he would go to the Cap Martin Hotel, of course.

He understood everything without any tiresome explaining. She couldn't afford the hotels at Cap Martin and Monte Carlo; and though the Derings had asked her to stay with them, she really couldn't dump herself down on them like that, almost in the middle of their honeymoon.

Their honeymoon – she could have bitten her tongue out for saying it, for not remembering. It was awful of her to go talking to Louis Carson about honeymoons, after the appalling tragedy of *his*.

There were things she hadn't been told, that she hadn't liked to ask: Where it had happened? And how? And how long ago? She only knew it was on his wedding night, that he had gone in to the poor little girl of a bride and found her dead there, in the bed.

They said she had died in a sort of fit.

You had only to look at him to see that something terrible had happened to him sometime. You saw it when his face was doing nothing: a queer agonized look that made him strange to her while it lasted. It was more than suffering; it was almost as if he could be cruel, only he never was, he never could be. *People* were cruel, if you liked; they said his face put them off. Mildred could see what they meant. It might have put *her* off, perhaps, if she hadn't known what he had gone through. But the first time she had met him he had been pointed out to her as the man to whom just that appalling thing had happened. So, far from putting her off, that was what had drawn her to him from the beginning, made her pity him first, then love him. Their engagement had come quick, in the third week of their acquaintance.

When she asked herself, 'After all, what do I know about him?' she had her answer, 'I know *that*.' She felt that already she had entered into a mystical union with him through compassion. She *liked* the strangeness that kept other people away and left him to her altogether. He was more her own that way.

There was (Mildred Eve didn't deny it) his personal magic, the fascination of his almost abnormal beauty. His black, white, and blue. The intensely blue eyes under the straight black bars of the eyebrows, the perfect, pure, white face suddenly masked by the black moustache and small, black, pointed beard. And the rich vivid smile he had for her, the lighting up of the blue, the flash of white teeth in the black mask.

He had smiled then at her embarrassment as the awful word leaped out at him. He had taken it from her and turned the sharp edge of it.

'It would never do,' he had said, 'to spoil the *honeymoon*. You'd much better have my villa. Some day, quite soon, it'll be yours, too. You know I like anticipating things.'

That was always the excuse he made for his generosities. He had said it again when he engaged her seat in the *train de luxe* from Paris and wouldn't let her pay for it. (She had wanted to travel third class.) He was only anticipating, he said.

He was seeing her off now at the Gare de Lyons, standing on the platform with a great sheaf of blush roses in his arms. She, on the high step of the railway carriage, stood above him, swinging in the open doorway. His face was on a level with her feet; they gleamed white through the fine black stockings. Suddenly he thrust his face forwards and kissed her feet. As the train moved he ran beside it and tossed the roses into her lap.

And then she sat in the hurrying train, holding the great sheaf of blush roses in her lap, and smiling at them as she dreamed. She was in the Riviera Express; the Riviera Express. Next week she would be in Roquebrune, at the Villa Désirée. She read the three letters woven into the edges of the grey cloth cushions: PLM: Paris-Lyons-Mediterranée, Paris-Lyons-Mediterranée, over and over again. They sang themselves to the rhythm of the wheels; they wove their pattern into her dream. Every now and then, when the other passengers weren't looking, she lifted the roses to her face and kissed them.

She hardly knew how she dragged herself through the long dull week with her aunt at Cannes.

And now it was over and she was by herself at Roquebrune.

The steep narrow lane went past the Derings' house and up the face of the hill. It led up into a little olive wood, and above the wood she saw the garden terraces. The sunlight beat in and out of their golden yellow walls. Tier above tier, the blazing terraces rose, holding up their ranks of spindle-stemmed lemon and orange trees. On the topmost terrace the Villa Désirée stood white and hushed between two palms, two tall poles each topped by a head of dark-green, curving, sharp-pointed blades. A grey scrub of olive trees straggled up the hill behind it and on each side.

Rolf and Martha Dering waited for her with Narcisse and Armandine on the steps of the verandah.

'Why on earth didn't you come to us?' they said.

'I didn't want to spoil your honeymoon.'

'Honeymoon, what rot! We've got over *that* silliness. Anyhow, it's our third week of it.'

They were detached and cool in their happiness.

She went in with them, led by Narcisse and Armandine. The caretakers, subservient to Mildred Eve and visibly inimical to the Derings, left them together in the salon. It was very bright and French and fragile and worn; all faded grey and old greenish gilt; the gilt chairs and settees carved like picture frames round the gilded cane. The hot light beat in through the long windows open to the terrace, drawing up a faint powdery smell from the old floor.

Rolf Dering stared at the room, sniffing, with fine nostrils in a sort of bleak disgust.

'You'd much better have come to us,' he said.

'Oh, but – it's charming.'

'Do you *think* so?' Martha said. She was looking at her intently.

Mildred saw that they expected her to feel something, she wasn't sure what, something that they felt. They were subtle and fastidious.

'It does look a little queer and – unlived in,' she said, straining for the precise impression.

'I should say,' said Martha, 'it had been too much lived in, if you ask me.'

'Oh no. That's only dust you smell. I think, perhaps, the windows haven't been open very long.'

She resented this criticism of Louis's villa.

Armandine appeared at the doorway. Her little, slant, Chinesy eyes were screwed up and smiling. She wanted to know if Madame wouldn't like to go up and look at her room.

'We'll all go up and look at it,' said Rolf.

They followed Armandine up the steep, slender, curling staircase. A closed door faced them on the landing. Armandine opened it, and the hot golden light streamed out to them again.

The room was all golden white; it was like a great white tank filled with blond water where things shimmered, submerged in the stream; the white-painted chairs and dressing-table, the high white-painted bed, the pink-and-white striped ottoman at its foot; all vivid and still, yet quivering in the stillness, with the hot throb, throb of the light.

'Voilà, madame,' said Armandine.

They didn't answer. They stood, fixed in the room, held by the stillness, staring, all three of them, at the high white bed that rose up, enormous, with its piled mattresses and pillows, the long white counterpane hanging straight and steep, like a curtain, to the floor.

Rolf turned to Armandine.

'Why have you given Madame this room?'

Armandine shrugged her fat shoulders. Her small, Chinesy eyes blinked at him, slanting, inimical.

'Monsieur's orders, monsieur. It is the best room in the house. It was Madame's room.'

'I know. That's *why*——'

'But no, monsieur. Nobody would dislike to sleep in Madame's room. The poor little thing, she was so pretty, so sweet, so young, monsieur. Surely Madame will not dislike the room.'

'Who *was* – Madame?'

'But, Monsieur's wife, madame. Madame Carson. Poor Monsieur, it was so sad——'

'Rolf,' said Mildred, 'did he bring her here – on their honeymoon?'

'Yes.'

'Yes, madame. She died here. It was so sad. Is there anything I can do for madame?'

'No, thank you, Armandine.'

'Then I will get ready the tea.'

She turned again in the doorway, crooning in her thick, Provençal voice. '*Madame* does not dislike her room?'

'No, Armandine. No. It's a beautiful room.'

The door closed on Armandine. Martha opened it again to see whether she were listening on the landing. Then she broke out:

'Mildred – you know you loathe it. It's beastly. The whole place is beastly.'

'You can't stay in it,' said Rolf.

'Why not? Do you mean, because of Madame?'

Martha and Rolf were looking at each other, as if they were both asking what they should say. They said nothing.

'Oh, her poor little ghost won't hurt me, if that's what you mean.'

'Nonsense,' Martha said. 'Of course it isn't.'

'What is it then?'

'It's so beastly lonely, Mildred,' said Rolf.

'Not with Narcisse and Armandine.'

'Well, I wouldn't sleep a night in the place,' Martha said, 'if there wasn't any other on the Riviera. I don't like the look of it.'

Mildred went to the open lattice, turning her back on the high, rather frightening bed. Down there below the terraces she saw the grey flicker of the olive woods and, beyond them, the sea. Martha was wrong. The place was beautiful; it was adorable. She wasn't going to be afraid of poor little Madame. Louis had loved her. He loved the place. That was why he had lent it her.

She turned. Rolf had gone down again. She was alone with Martha. Martha was saying something.

'Mildred – where's Mr Carson?'

'In Paris. Why?'

'I thought he was coming here.'

'So he is, later on.'

'To the villa?'

'No. Of course not. To Cap Martin.' She laughed. 'So *that's* what you're thinking of, is it?'

She could understand her friend's fear of haunted houses, but not these previsions of impropriety.

Martha looked shy and ashamed.

'Yes,' she said. 'I suppose so.'

'How horrid of you! You might have trusted me.'

'I do trust you.' Martha held her a minute with her clear loving eyes. 'Are you sure you can trust *him*?'

'Trust him? Do *you* trust Rolf?'

'Ah – if it was like that, Mildred——'

'It *is* like that.'

'You're really not afraid?'

'What is there to be afraid of? Poor little Madame?'

'I didn't mean Madame. I meant Monsieur.'

'Oh – wait till you've seen him.'

'Is he *very* beautiful?'

'Yes. But it isn't *that*, Martha. I can't tell you what it is.'

They went downstairs, hand in hand, in the streaming light. Rolf waited for them on the verandah. They were taking Mildred back to dine with them.

'Won't you let me tell Armandine you're stopping the night?' he said.

'No, I won't. I don't want Armandine to think I'm frightened.'

She meant she didn't want Louis to think she was frightened. Besides, she was not frightened.

'Well, if you find you don't like it, you must come to us,' he said.

And they showed her the little spare-room next to theirs, with its camp-bed made up, the bedclothes turned back, all ready for her, any time of the night, in case she changed her mind. The front door was on the latch.

'You've only to open it, and creep in here and be safe,' Rolf said.

2

Armandine – subservient and no longer inimical, now that the Derings were not there – Armandine had put the candle and matches on the night-table and the bell which, she said, would summon her if Madame wanted anything in the night. And she had left her.

As the door closed softly behind Armandine, Mildred drew in her breath with a light gasp. Her face in the looking-glass, between the tall lighted candles, showed its mouth half-open, and she was aware that her heart shook slightly in its beating. She was angry with the face in the glass with its foolish mouth gaping. She said to herself. Is it possible I'm frightened? It was not possible. Rolf and Martha had made her walk too fast up the hill, that was all. Her heart always did that when she walked too fast uphill, and she supposed that her mouth always gaped when it did it.

She clenched her teeth and let her heart choke her till it stopped shaking.

She was quiet now. But the test would come when she had blown out the candles and had to cross the room in the dark to the bed.

The flame went backwards before the light puff she gave, and righted itself. She blew harder, twice, with a sense of spinning out the time. The flame writhed and went out. She extinguished the other candle at one breath. The red point of the wick pricked the darkness for a second and died, too, with a small crackling sound. At the far end of the room the high bed glimmered. She thought: Martha was right. The bed *is* awful.

She could feel her mouth set in a hard grin of defiance as she went to it, slowly, too proud to be frightened. And then suddenly, halfway, she thought about Madame.

The awful thing was, climbing into that high funeral bed that Madame had died in. Your back felt so undefended. But once she was safe between the bedclothes it would be all right. It would be all right so long as she didn't think about Madame. Very well, then, she wouldn't think about her. You could frighten yourself into anything by thinking.

Deliberately, by an intense effort of her will, she turned the sad image of Madame out of her mind and found herself thinking about Louis Carson.

This was Louis's house, the place he used to come to when he wanted to be happy. She made out that he had sent her there because he wanted to be happy in it again. She was there to drive away the unhappiness, the memory of poor little Madame. Or, perhaps, because the place was sacred to him; because they were both so sacred, she and the young dead bride who hadn't been his wife. Perhaps he didn't think about her as dead at all; he didn't want her to be driven away. The room she had died in was not awful to him. He had the faithfulness for which death doesn't exist. She wouldn't have loved him if he hadn't been faithful. You could be faithful and yet marry again.

She was convinced that whatever she was there for, it was for some beautiful reason. Anything Louis did, anything he thought or felt or wanted, would be beautiful. She thought of Louis standing on the platform in the Paris station, his beautiful face looking up at her; its sudden darting forward to kiss her feet. She drifted again into her happy hypnotizing dream, and was fast asleep before midnight.

She woke with a sense of intolerable compulsion, as if she were being dragged violently up out of her sleep. The room was grey in the twilight of the unrisen moon.

And she was not alone.

She knew that there was something there. Something that gave up the secret of the room and made it frightful and obscene. The greyness was frightful and obscene. It gathered itself; it became the containing shell of the horror.

The thing that had waked her was there with her in the room.

For she knew she was awake. Apart from her supernatural certainty, one physical sense, detached from the horror, was alert. It heard the ticking of the clock on the chimney-piece, the hard sharp shirring of the palm leaves outside, as the wind rubbed their knife-blades together. These sounds were witnesses to the fact that she was awake, and that therefore the thing that was going to happen would be real. At the first sight of the greyness she had shut her eyes again, afraid to look into the room, because she knew that what she would see there was real. But she had no more power over her eyelids than she had over her sleep. They opened under the same intolerable compulsion. And the supernatural thing forced itself now on her by sight.

It stood a little in front of her by the bedside. From the breasts downwards its body was unfinished, rudimentary, not quite born. The grey shell was still pregnant with its loathsome shapelessness. But the face – the face was perfect in absolute horror. And it was Louis Carson's face.

Between the black bars of the eyebrows and the black pointed beard she saw it, drawn back, distorted in an obscene agony, corrupt and malignant. The face and the body, flesh and not yet flesh, they were the essence made manifest of untold, unearthly abominations.

It came on to her, bending over her, peering at her, so close that the piled mattresses now hid the lower half of its body. And the frightful thing about it was that it was blind, parted from all controlling and absolving clarity, flesh and yet not flesh. It looked for her without seeing her; and she knew that, unless she could save herself that instant, it would find what it looked for. Even now, behind the barrier of the piled-up mattresses, the unfinished form defined and completed itself; she could feel it shake with the agitation of its birth.

Her heart staggered and stopped in her breast, as if her breast had been clamped down on to her backbone. She struggled against wave after wave of faintness; for the moment that she lost consciousness the appalling presence there would have its way with her. All her will rose up against it. She dragged herself upright in the bed, suddenly, and spoke to it:

'Louis! What are you doing there?'

At her cry it went, without moving; sucked back into the greyness that had borne it.

She thought: 'It'll come back. It'll come back. Even if I don't see it I shall know it's in the room.'

She knew what she would do. She would get up and go to the Derings. She longed for the open air, for Rolf and Martha, for the strong earth under her feet.

She lit the candle on the night-table and got up. She still felt that it was there, and that, standing upon the floor, she was more vulnerable, more exposed to it. Her terror was too extreme for her to stay and dress herself. She thrust her bare feet into her shoes, slipped her travelling coat over her nightgown and went downstairs and out through the house door, sliding back the bolts without a sound. She remembered that Rolf had left a lantern for her in the verandah, in case she should want it – as if they had known.

She lit the lantern and made her way down the villa garden, stumbling from terrace to terrace, through the olive wood and the steep lane to the Derings' house. Far down the hill she could see a light in the window of the spare room. The house door was on the latch. She went through and on into the lamp-lit room that waited for her.

She knew again what she would do. She would go away before Louis Carson could come to her. She would go away tomorrow, and never come back again. Rolf and Martha would bring her things down from the villa; he would take her into Italy in his car. She would get away from Louis Carson for ever. She would get away up through Italy.

3

Rolf had come back from the villa with her things and he had brought her a letter. It had been sent up that morning from Cap Martin.

It was from Louis Carson.

My Darling Mildred,

You see I couldn't wait a fortnight without seeing you. I *had* to come. I'm here at the Cap Martin Hotel.

I'll be with you some time between half past ten and eleven——

Below, at the bottom of the lane, Rolf's car waited. It was half past ten. If they went now they would meet Carson coming up the lane. They must wait till he had passed the house and gone up through the olive wood.

Martha had brought hot coffee and rolls. They sat down at the other side of the table and looked at her with kind anxious eyes as she turned sideways, watching the lane.

'Rolf,' she said suddenly, 'do you know anything about Louis Carson?' She could see them looking now at each other.

'Nothing. Only the things the people here say.'

'What sort of things?'

'Don't tell her, Rolf.'

'Yes. He *must* tell me. I've got to know.'

She had no feeling left but horror, horror that nothing could intensify.

'There's not much. Except that he was always having women with him up there. Not particularly nice women. He seems,' Rolf said, 'to have been rather an appalling beast.'

'Must have been,' said Martha, 'to have brought his poor little wife there, after——'

'Rolf, what did Mrs Carson die of?'

'Don't ask *me*,' he said.

But Martha answered: 'She died of fright. She saw something. I told you the place was beastly.'

Rolf shrugged his shoulders.

'Why, you said you felt it yourself. We both felt it.'

'Because we knew about the beastly things he did there.'

'*She* didn't know. I tell you, she saw something.'

Mildred turned her white face to them.

'I saw it too.'

'You?'

'What? What did you see?'

'Him. Louis Carson.'

'He must be dead, then, if you saw his ghost.'

'The ghosts of poor dead people don't kill you. It was what he *is*. All that beastliness in a face. A face.'

She could hear them draw in their breath short and sharp. 'Where?'

'There. In that room. Close by the bed. It was looking for me. I saw what *she* saw.'

She could see them frown now, incredulous, forcing themselves to disbelieve. She could hear them talking, their voices beating off the horror.

'Oh, but she couldn't. He wasn't there.'

'He heard her scream first.'

'Yes. He was in the other room, you know.'

'*It* wasn't. He can't keep it back.'

'Keep it back?'

'No. He was waiting to go to her.'

Her voice was dull and heavy with realization. She felt herself struggling, helpless, against their stolidity, their unbelief.

'Look at that,' she said. She pushed Carson's letter across to them.

'He was waiting to go to her,' she repeated. 'And – last night – he was waiting to come to me.'

They stared at her, stupefied.

'Oh, can't you *see*?' she cried. 'It didn't wait. It got there before him.'

The Coat

A. E. D. Smith

I am quite aware that the other fellows in the office regard me as something of an oddity – as being rather a 'queer bird', in fact. Well, of course, a man who happens to be of a studious disposition, who dislikes noise and prefers his own company to that of empty-headed companions, and who, moreover, is compelled by defective vision to wear thick glasses, is always liable to be thus misjudged by inferior minds; and ordinarily, I treat the opinion of my colleagues with the comtempt it deserves. But at this particular moment I was beginning to think that perhaps, after all, there might be something to be said for their view. For, though I might still repudiate the 'queer bird' part of the business, undoubtedly I was an ass – a first-class chump; otherwise I should have been spending my holidays in a nice comfortable way with the rest of the normal world, listening to the Pierrots or winking at the girls on the promenade of some seaside resort at home, instead of having elected to set out alone on this idiotic push-bike tour of a little-known part of France. Drenched, hungry and lost; a stranger in a strange land; dispiritedly pushing before me a heavily-laden bicycle with a gashed tyre – such was the present result of my asinine choice.

The storm had overtaken me miles from anywhere, on a wild road over a spur of the Vosges, and for nearly two hours I had trudged through the pelting rain without encountering a living soul or the least sign of human habitation.

And then, at long last, rounding a bend, I glimpsed just ahead of me the chimney-pots and gables of a fair-sized house. It was a lonely, desolate-looking place standing amid a clump of trees a little way back from the road, and somehow, even at a distance, did not convey a very inviting impression. Nevertheless, in that wilderness, it was a welcome enough sight, and in the hope of finding temporary shelter and possibly a little badly-needed refreshment, I quickened my pace towards it. Two hundred yards brought me to the entrance gates, and here I suffered a grievous disappointment; for the roofless porters' lodge, the dilapidated old gates hanging askew on their hinges, and the overgrown drive beyond, plainly indicated that the place was no longer inhabited.

I speedily comforted myself, however, with the reflection that in the circumstances even a deserted house was not to be despised as a refuge. Once under cover of some kind, I might make shift to wring out my drenched clothing and repair my damaged mount; and without further ado I pushed my bicycle up the long-neglected drive and reached the terrace in front of the house itself. It proved to be an old château, half smothered in creepers and vines that had long gone wild, and, judging by the carved stone coat-of-arms over the main entrance, had once been occupied by a person of some quality. Mounted on a pedestal on either side of the iron-studded front door stood a rusty carronade – trophies, probably, of some long-forgotten war in which the former occupier had played a part. Most of the windows had been boarded up, and it was evident that the place had stood empty for many years.

I tried the front door. To my surprise it was unfastened, and a thrust of my shoulder sent it creaking grudgingly back on its hinges. My nostrils, as I stepped into the dim, wide hall, were at once assailed by the stale, disagreeable odour of rotting woodwork and mouldy hangings and carpets. For a moment or two I stood peering uncertainly about me, with the slight feeling of eeriness that one usually experiences when entering an old, empty house. Facing me was a broad staircase, with a long, stained-glass window, almost opaque with dirt and cobwebs, at its head. I mounted the stairs, and throwing open the first door at hand, found myself looking into a spacious, handsomely furnished room that had evidently once been the chief apartment of the house, though long neglect and disuse had now reduced it to a sorry state. The ornate cornice hung here and there in strips, and in one corner the plaster of the ceiling had come down altogether. Green mould covered the eighteenth-century furniture; curtains and draperies hung in tatters; and one-half of the beautiful old Persian carpet, from a point near the door right across to the fireplace, was overspread by an evil-smelling, bright orange fungus.

The fireplace gave me an idea. Could I but find fuel I might light a fire, make myself a hot drink, and get my clothes properly dried.

A little searching in the outbuildings discovered a sufficient quantity of old sticks to serve my purpose, and with a bundle of them under my coat I re-entered the house and briskly made my way upstairs again. But on the threshold of the big room, without quite knowing why, I suddenly checked. It was as though my legs, of their own volition, had all at once become reluctant to carry me further into the apartment – as if something quite outside of me were urging me to turn about and retreat. I laid the sticks down at my feet, and for a moment or two stood there uncertainly in the doorway. I was beginning to sense some subtle suggestion of danger in the atmosphere of the place. Everything was apparently just as I had left it; yet I had an uneasy sort of feeling that during my brief absence something evil had entered the room and left it again.

I am neither a nervous nor a superstitious person; yet I found myself, a moment later, rather shamefacedly picking up my sticks and moving back towards the head of the stairs. Actually, it was not so much fear as a vague, precautionary sense of uneasiness that prompted me. It had occurred to me that perhaps I might feel more comfortable if I remained nearer to the front door, and made my fire in one of the rooms on the ground floor. If – it was an idiotic fancy, I know – but . . . well, if anything – er – queer DID happen, and I had to make a sudden bolt for it, I could get out quicker that way.

It was on this second descent of the stairs, as I faced the light from the open front door, that I suddenly noticed something that pulled me up with a decided start. Running up the centre of the staircase, and quite fresh in the thick dust, was a broad, broken sort of track, exactly as though someone had recently trailed up an empty sack or something of that nature.

From the foot of the staircase I traced this track across the hall to a spot immediately below an old, moth-eaten coat that hung from one of a row of coat-pegs on the opposite wall. And then I saw that similar tracks traversed the hall in various directions, some terminating before the doors on either side, others leading past the foot of the stairs to the rear regions of the house, but all seeming to radiate from the same point below the coat-pegs. And the queerest thing about it all was that of footprints, other than my own, there was not a sign.

Uneasiness once more assailed me. The house appeared to be uninhabited, and yet, plainly some one, or something, had recently been in the place. Who, or what, was the restless, questing creature that had made those strange tracks to and from the old coat? Was it some half-witted vagrant – a woman possibly – whose trailing draperies obliterated her own footprints?

I had a closer look at the old garment. It was a military greatcoat of ancient pattern, with one or two tarnished silver buttons still attached to it, and had evidently seen much service. Turning it round on its peg with a gingerly finger and thumb, I discovered that just below the left shoulder there was a round hole as big as a penny, surrounded by an area of scorched and stained cloth, as though a heavy pistol had been fired into it at point-blank range. If a pistol bullet had indeed made that hole, then obviously, the old coat at one period of its existence had clothed a dead man.

A sudden repugnance for the thing overcame me, and with a slight shudder I let go of it. It may have been fancy or not, but all at once it seemed to me that there was more than an odour of mould and rotting cloth emanating from the thing – that there was a taint of putrefying flesh and bone . . .

A taint of animal corruption – faint but unmistakable – I could sniff it in the air; and with it, something less definable but no less real – a sort of sixth-sense feeling that the whole atmosphere of the place was slowly becoming charged with evil emanations from a black and shameful past.

With an effort I pulled myself together. After all, what was there to be scared about? I had no need to fear human marauders, for in my hip pocket I carried a small but serviceable automatic; and as for ghosts, well, if such existed, they didn't usually 'walk' in the daytime. The place certainly felt creepy, and I shouldn't have cared to spend the night there; but it would be ridiculous to allow mere idle fancies to drive me out again into that beastly rain before I'd made myself that badly needed hot drink and mended my bicycle.

I therefore opened the door nearest to me, and entered a smallish room that apparently had once been used as a study. The fireplace was on the side opposite to the door, and the wide, ancient grate was still choked with the ashes of the last log consumed there. I picked up the poker – a cumbersome old thing with a knob as big as an orange – raked out the ashes, and laid my sticks in approved Boy Scout fashion. But the wood was damp, and after I used up half my matches, refused to do more than smoulder, whilst a back-draught from the chimney filled the room with smoke. In desperation I went down on my hands and knees and tried to rouse the embers into flame by blowing on them. And in the middle of this irksome operation I was startled by a sound of movement in the hall – a single soft 'flop', as though someone had flung down a garment.

I was on my feet in a flash, listening with every nerve a-taut. No further sound came, and, automatic in hand, I tiptoed to the door. There was nothing in the hall; nothing to be heard at all save the steady swish of the rain ouside. But from a spot on the floor directly below the old coat the dust was rising in a little eddying cloud, as though it had just been disturbed.

'Pah! A rat,' I told myself, and went back to my task.

More vigorous blowing on the embers, more raking and poking, more striking of matches – and, in the midst of it, again came that curious noise – not very loud, but plain and unmistakable.

Once more I went into the hall, and once more, except for another little cloud of dust rising from precisely the same spot as before, there was nothing to be seen. But that sixth-sense warning of imminent danger was becoming more insistent. I had the feeling now that I was no longer alone in the old, empty hall – that some unclean, invisible presence was lurking there, tainting the very air with its foulness.

'It's no use,' I said to myself. 'I may be a nervous fool, but I can't stand any more of this. I'll collect my traps and clear out whilst the going's good.'

With this, I went back into the room, and keeping a nervous eye cocked on the door, began with rather panicky haste to re-pack my haversack. And just as I was in the act of tightening the last strap there came from the hall a low, evil chuckle, followed by the sound of stealthy movement. I whipped out my weapon and stood where I was in the middle of the floor, facing the door, with my blood turning to ice. Through the chink between the door hinges I saw a shadow pass; then the door creaked a little, slowly began to open, and round it there came – the COAT.

It stood there upright in the doorway, as God is above me – swaying a little as though uncertain of its balance – collar and shoulders extended as though by an invisible wearer – the old, musty coat I had seen hanging in the hall.

For a space that seemed an eternity I stood like a man of stone, facing the Thing as it seemed to pause on the threshold. A dreadful sort of hypnotism held me rooted to the spot on which I stood – a hypnotism that completely paralysed my body, and caused the pistol to slip from my nerveless fingers, and yet left my brain clear. Mingled with my frozen terror was a feeling of deadly nausea. I knew that I was in the presence of ultimate Evil – that the very aura of the Hell-engendered Thing reared there in the doorway was contamination – that its actual touch would mean not only the instant destruction of my body, but the everlasting damnation of my soul.

And now It was coming into the room – with an indescribable bobbing sort of motion, the empty sleeves jerking grotesquely at its sides, the skirts flopping and trailing in the dust, was slowly coming towards me; and step by step, with my bulging eyes riveted in awful fascination on the Thing, I was recoiling before it. Step by step, with the rigid, unconscious movement of an automaton, I drew back until I was brought up with my back pressed into the fireplace and could retreat no further. And still, with deadly malevolent purpose, the Thing crept towards me. The empty sleeves were rising and shakily reaching out towards my throat. In another moment they would touch me, and then I knew with the most dreadful certainty that my reason would snap. A coherent thought somehow came into my burning brain – something that I had read or heard of long ago ... the power ... of the ... holy sign ... against ... the forces of evil. With a last desperate effort of will I stretched out a palsied finger and made the sign of the Cross ... And in that instant, my other hand, scrabbling frenziedly at the wall behind me, came into contact with something cold and hard and round. It was the knob of the old, heavy poker.

The touch of the cold iron seemed to give me instant re-possession of my faculties. With lightning swiftness I swung up the heavy poker and struck with all my force at the nightmare Horror before me. And lo! on the instant, the Thing collapsed, and became an old coat – nothing more – lying there in a heap at my feet. Yet, on my oath, as I cleared the hellish thing in a flying leap, and fled from the room, I saw it, out of the tail of my eye, gathering itself together and making shape, as it were to scramble after me.

Once outside that accursed house I ran as never man ran before, and I remember nothing more until I found myself, half fainting, before the door of a little inn.

'Bring wine, in the name of God!' I cried, staggering inside.

Wine was brought, and a little wondering group stood round me while I drank.

I tried to explain to them in my bad French. They continued to regard me with puzzled looks. At length a look of understanding came into the landlord's face.

'Mon Dieu!' he gasped. 'Is it possible that monsieur has been in *that place*! Quick, Juliette! Monsieur will need another bottle of wine.'

Later, I got something of the story from the landlord, though he was by no means eager to tell it. The deserted house had once been occupied by a retired officer of the first Napoleon's army – a semi-madman with a strain of African blood in him. Judging from the landlord's story, he must have been one of the worst men that God ever allowed to walk the earth. 'Most certainly, monsieur, he was a bad man – that one,' concluded my host. 'He killed his wife and tortured every living thing he could lay hands on – even, it is said, his own daughters. In the end, one of them shot him in the back. The old château has an evil name. If you offered a million francs, you would not get one of our country-folks to go near the place.'

As I said at the beginning, I know that the other fellows in the office are inclined, as it is, to regard me as being a bit queer; so I haven't told any of them this story. Nevertheless, it's perfectly true.

My brand-new bicycle and touring traps are probably still lying where I left them in the hall of that devil-ridden château. Anybody who cares to collect them may keep them.

The Seed from the Sepulchre

Clark Ashton Smith

'Yes, I found the place,' said Falmer. 'It's a queer sort of place, pretty much as the legends describe it.' He spat quickly into the fire, as if the act of speech had been physically distasteful to him, and, half averting his face from the scrutiny of Thone, stared with morose and sombre eyes into the jungle-matted Venezuelan darkness.

Thone, still weak and dizzy from the fever that had incapacitated him for continuing their journey to its end, was curiously puzzled. Falmer, he thought, had undergone an inexplicable change during the three days of his absence; a change that was too elusive in some of its phases to be fully defined or delimited.

Other phases, however, were all too obvious. Falmer, even during extreme hardship or illness, had heretofore been unquenchably loquacious and cheerful. Now he seemed sullen, uncommunicative, as if preoccupied with far-off things of disagreeable import. His bluff face had grown hollow – even pointed – and his eyes had narrowed to secretive slits. Thorne was troubled by these changes, though he tried to dismiss his impressions as mere distempered fancies due to the influence of the ebbing fever.

'But can't you tell me what the place was like?' he persisted.

'There isn't much to tell,' said Falmer, in a queer grumbling tone. 'Just a few crumbling walls and falling pillars.'

'But didn't you find the burial-pit of the Indian legend, where the gold was supposed to be?'

'I found it ... but there was no treasure,' Falmer's voice had taken on a forbidding surliness; and Thone decided to refrain from further questioning.

'I guess,' he commented lightly, 'that we had better stick to orchid-hunting. Treasure trove doesn't seem to be in our line. By the way, did you see any unusual flowers or plants during the trip?'

'Hell, no,' Falmer snapped. His face had gone suddenly ashen in the firelight, and his eyes had assumed a set glare that might have meant either fear or anger. 'Shut up, can't you? I don't want to talk. I've had a headache all day; some damned Venezuelan fever coming on, I suppose. We'd better head for the Orinoco tomorrow. I've had all I want of this trip.'

James Falmer and Roderick Thone, professional orchid hunters, with two Indian guides, had been following an obscure tributary of the upper Orinoco. The country was rich in rare flowers; and, beyond its floral wealth, they had been drawn by vague but persistent rumours among the local tribes concerning the existence of a ruined city somewhere on this tributary; a city that contained a burial pit in which vast treasures of gold, silver, and jewels had been interred together with the dead of some nameless people. The two men had thought it worthwhile to investigate these rumours. Thone had fallen sick while they were still a full day's journey from the site of the ruins, and Falmer had gone on in a canoe with one of the Indians, leaving the other to attend to Thone. He had returned at nightfall of the third day following his departure.

Thone decided after a while, as he lay staring at his companion, that the latter's taciturnity and moroseness were perhaps due to disappointment over his failure to find the treasure. It must have been that, together with some tropical infection working in the man's blood. However, he admitted doubtfully to himself, it was not like Falmer to be disappointed or downcast under such circumstances.

Falmer did not speak again, but sat glaring before him as if he saw something invisible to others beyond the labyrinth of fire-touched boughs and lianas in which the whispering, stealthy darkness crouched. Somehow, there was a shadowy fear in his aspect. Thone continued to watch him, and saw that the Indians, impassive and cryptic, were also watching him, as if with some obscure expectancy. The riddle was too much for Thone, and he gave it up after a while, lapsing into restless, fever-turbulent slumber from which he awakened at intervals, to see the set face of Falmer, dimmer and more distorted each time with the slowly dying fire and the invading shadows.

Thone felt stronger in the morning: his brain was clear, his pulse tranquil once more; and he saw with mounting concern the indisposition of Falmer, who seemed to rouse and exert himself with great difficulty, speaking hardly a word and moving with singular stiffness and sluggishness. He appeared to have forgotten his announced project of returning towards the Orinoco, and Thone took entire charge of the preparations for departure. His companion's condition puzzled him more and more: apparently there was no fever and the symptoms were wholly ambiguous. However, on general principles, he administered a stiff dose of quinine to Falmer before they started.

The paling saffron of sultry dawn sifted upon them through the jungle tops as they loaded their belongings into the dugouts and pushed off down the slow current. Thone sat near the bow of one of the boats, with Falmer in the rear, and a large bundle of orchid roots and part of their equipment filling the middle. The two Indians occupied the other boat, together with the rest of the supplies.

It was a monotonous journey. the river wound like a sluggish olive snake between dark, interminable walls of forest, from which the goblin faces of orchids leered. There were no sounds other than the splash of paddles, the furious chattering of monkeys, and petulant cries of fiery-coloured birds. The sun rose above the jungle and poured down a tide of torrid brilliance.

Thone rowed steadily looking back over his shoulder at times to address Falmer with some casual remark or friendly question. The latter, with dazed eyes and features queerly pale and pinched in the sunlight, sat dully erect and made no effort to use his paddle. He offered no reply to the queries of Thone, but shook his head at intervals with a sort of shuddering motion that was plainly involuntary. After a while he began to moan thickly, as if in pain or delirium.

They went on in this manner for hours. The heat grew more oppressive between the stifling walls of jungle. Thone became aware of a shriller cadence in the moans of his companion. Looking back, he saw that Falmer had removed his sun-helmet, seemingly oblivious of the murderous heat, and was clawing at the crown of his head with frantic fingers. Convulsions shook his entire body, the dugout began to rock dangerously as he tossed to and fro in a paroxysm of manifest agony. His voice mounted to a high un-human shrieking.

Thone made a quick decision. There was a break in the lining palisade of sombre forest, and he headed the boat for shore immediately. The Indians followed, whispering between themselves and eyeing the sick man with glances of apprehensive awe and terror that puzzled Thone tremendously. He felt that there was some devilish mystery about the whole affair; and he could not imagine what was wrong with Falmer. All the known manifestations of malignant tropical diseases rose before him like a rout of hideous fantasms; but, among them, he could not recognize the thing that had assailed his companion.

Having got Falmer ashore on a semicircle of liana-latticed beach without the aid of the Indians, who seemed unwilling to approach the sick man, Thone administered a heavy hypodermic injection of morphine from his medicine chest. This appeared to ease Falmer's suffering, and the convulsions ceased. Thone, taking advantage of their remission, proceeded to examine the crown of Falmer's head.

He was startled to find, amid the thick dishevelled hair a hard and pointed lump which resembled the tip of a beginning horn, rising under the still unbroken skin. As if endowed with erectile and resistless life, it seemed to grow beneath his fingers.

At the same time, abruptly and mysteriously, Falmer opened his eyes and appeared to regain full consciousness. For a few minutes he was more his normal self than at any time since his return from the ruins. He began to talk, as if anxious to relieve his mind of some oppressing burden. His voice was peculiarly thick and toneless, but Thone was able to follow his mutterings and piece them together.

'The pit! the pit!' said Falmer – 'the infernal thing that was in the pit, in the deep sepulchre!... I wouldn't go back there for the treasure of a dozen El Dorados... I didn't tell you much about those ruins, Thone. Somehow it was hard... impossibly hard-to-talk.

'I guess the Indian knew there was something wrong with the ruins. He led me to the place... but he wouldn't tell me anything about it: and he waited by the riverside while I searched for the treasure.

'Great grey walls there were, older than the jungle – old as death and time. They must have been quarried and reared by people from some lost planet. They loomed and leaned, at mad, unnatural angles, threatening to crush the trees about them. And there were columns too: thick, swollen columns of unholy form, whose abominable carvings the jungle had not wholly screened from view.

'There was no trouble finding that accursed burial pit. The pavement above had broken through quite recently, I think. A big tree had pried with its boa-like roots between the flagstones that were buried beneath centuries of mould. One of the flags had been tilted back on the pavement, and another had fallen through into the pit. There was a large hole, whose bottom I could see dimly in the forest-strangled light. Something glimmered palely at the bottom; but I could not be sure what it was.

'I had taken along a coil of rope, as you remember. I tied one end of it to a main root of the tree, dropped the other through the opening, and went down like a monkey. When I got to the bottom I could see little at first in the gloom, except the whitish glimmering all around me, at my feet. Something that was unspeakably brittle and friable crunched beneath me when I began to move. I turned on my flashlight, and saw that the place was fairly littered with bones. Human skeletons lay tumbled everywhere. They must have been removed long ago. I groped around amid the bones and dust, feeling pretty much like a ghoul, but couldn't find anything of value, not even a bracelet or a finger ring on any of the skeletons.

'It wasn't until I thought of climbing out that I noticed the real horror. In one of the corners – the corner nearest to the opening in the roof – I looked up and saw it in the webby shadows. Ten feet above my head it hung, and I had almost touched it, unknowing, when I descended the rope.

'It looked like a sort of white lattice work at first. Then I saw that the lattice was partly formed of human bones – a complete skeleton very tall and stalwart, like that of a warrior. A pale, withered thing grew out of the skull, like a set of fantastic antlers ending in myriads of long and stringy tendrils that had spread upward till they reached the roof. They must have lifted the skeleton, or body, along with them as they climbed.

'I examined the thing with my flashlight. It must have been a plant of some sort, and apparently it had started to grow in the cranium. Some of the branches had issued from the cloven crown, others through the eye holes, the mouth, and the nose holes, to flare upwards. And the roots of the blasphemous thing had gone downwards, trellising themselves on every bone. The very toes and fingers were ringed with them, and they drooped in writhing coils. Worst of all, the ones that had issued from the toe ends *were rooted in a second skull*, which dangled just below, with fragments of the broken-off root system. There was a litter of fallen bones on the floor in the corner.

'The sight made me feel a little weak, somehow, and more than a little nauseated – that abhorrent, inexplicable mingling of the human and the plant. I started to climb the rope, in a feverish hurry to get out, but the thing fascinated me in its abominable fashion, and I couldn't help pausing to study it a little more when I had climbed half way. I leaned towards it too fast, I guess, and the rope began to sway, bringing my face lightly against the leprous, antler-shaped boughs above the skull.

'Something broke – possibly a sort of pod on one of the branches. I found my head enveloped in a cloud of pearl-grey powder, very light, fine, and scentless. The stuff settled on my hair, it got into my nose and eyes, nearly choking and blinding me. I shook it off as well as I could. Then I climbed on and pulled myself through the opening...'

As if the effort of coherent narration had been to heavy a strain, Falmer lapsed into disconnected mumblings. The mysterious malady, whatever it was, returned upon him, and his delirious ramblings were mixed with groans of torture. But at moments he regained a flash of coherence.

'My head! my head!' he muttered. 'There must be something in my brain, something that grows and spreads; I tell you, I can feel it there. I haven't felt right at any time since I left the burial pit ... My mind has been queer ever since ... It must have been the spores of the ancient devil-plant ... The spores have taken root ... the thing is splitting my skull, going down into my brain – a plant that springs out of a human cranium – as if from a flower pot!'

The dreadful convulsions began once more, and Falmer writhed uncontrollably in his companion's arms, shrieking with agony. Thone, sick at heart, and shocked by his sufferings, abandoned all effort to restrain him and took up the hypodermic. With much difficulty, he managed to inject a triple dose, and Falmer grew quiet by degrees, and lay with open glassy eyes, breathing stertorously. Thone, for the first time, perceived an odd protrusion of his eyeballs, which seemed about to start from their sockets, making it impossible for the lids to close, and lending the drawn features an expression of mad horror. It was as if something were pushing Falmer's eyes from his head.

Thone, trembling with sudden weakness and terror, felt that he was involved in some unnatural web of nightmare. He could not, dared not, believe the story Falmer had told him, and its implications. Assuring himself that his companion had imagined it all, had been ill throughout with the incubation of some strange fever, he stooped over and found that the horn horn-shaped lump on Falmer's head had now broken through the skin.

With a sense of unreality, he stared at the object that his prying fingers had revealed amid the matted hair. It was unmistakably a plant-bud of some sort, with involuted folds of pale green and bloody pink that seemed about to expand. The thing issued above the central suture of the skull.

A nausea swept upon Thone, and he recoiled from the lolling head and its baleful outgrowth, averting his gaze. His fever was returning, there was a woeful debility in all his limbs, and he heard the muttering voice of delirium through the quinine-induced ringing in his ears. His eyes blurred with a deathly and miasmal mist.

He fought to subdue his illness and impotence. He must not give way to it wholly; he must go on with Falmer and the Indians and reach the nearest trading station, many days away on the Orinoco, where Falmer could receive aid.

As if through sheer volition, his eyes cleared, and he felt a resurgence of strength. He looked around for the guides, and saw, with a start of uncomprehending surprise, that they had vanished. Peering further, he observed that one of the boats – the dugouts used by the Indians – had also disappeared. It was plain that he and Falmer had been deserted. Perhaps the Indians had known what was wrong with the sick man, and had been afraid. At any rate, they were gone, and they had taken much of the camp equipment and most of the provisions with them.

Thone turned once more to the supine body of Falmer, conquering his repugnance, with effort. Resolutely he drew out his clasp knife, and, stooping over the stricken man, he excised the protruding bud, cutting as close to the scalp as he could with safety. The thing was unnaturally tough and rubbery; it exuded a thin, sanguinous fluid; and he shuddered when he saw its internal structure, full of nerve-like filaments, with a core that suggested cartilage. He flung it aside, quickly, on the river sand. Then, lifting Falmer in his arms, he lurched and staggered towards the remaining boat. He fell more than once, and lay half swooning across the inert body. Alternately carrying and dragging his burden, he reached the boat at last. With the remainder of his failing strength, he contrived to prop Falmer in the stern against the pile of equipment.

His fever was mounting apace. After much delay, with tedious, half-delirious exertions, he pushed off from the shore, till the fever mastered him wholly and the oar slipped from oblivious fingers...

He awoke in the yellow glare of dawn, with his brain and his senses comparatively clear. His illness had left a great languor, but his first thought was of Falmer. He twisted about, nearly falling overboard in his debility, and sat facing his companion.

Falmer still reclined, half sitting, half lying, against the pile of blankets and other impedimenta. His knees were drawn up, his hands clasping them as if in tetanic rigor. His features had grown as stark and ghastly as those of a dead man, and his whole aspect was one of mortal rigidity. It was this, however, that caused Thone to gasp with unbelieving horror.

During the interim of Thone's delirium and his lapse into slumber, the monstrous plant bud, merely stimulated, it would seem, by the act of excision, had grown again with preternatural rapidity, from Falmer's head. A loathsome pale-green stem was mounting thickly, and had started to branch like antlers after attaining a height of six or seven inches.

More dreadful than this, if possible, similar growths had issued from the eyes, and their stems, climbing vertically across the forehead, had entirely displaced the eyeballs. Already they were branching like the thing from the crown. The antlers were all tipped with pale vermilion. They appeared to quiver with repulsive animations, nodding rhythmically in the warm, windless air... From the mouth, another stem protruded, curling upwards like a long whitish tongue. It had not yet begun to bifurcate.

Thone closed his eyes to shut away the shocking vision. Beyond his lids, in a yellow dazzle of light, he still saw the cadaverous features, the climbing stems that quivered against the dawn like ghastly hydras of tomb-etiolated green. They seemed to be waving towards him, growing and lengthening as they waved. He opened his eyes again, and fancied, with a start of new terror, that the antlers were actually taller than they had been a few moments previous.

After that, he sat watching them in a sort of baleful hypnosis. The illusion of the plant's visible growth and freer movement – if it were illusion – increased upon him. Falmer, however, did not stir, and his parchment face appeared to shrivel and fall in, as if the roots of the growth were draining his blood, were devouring his very flesh in their insatiable and ghoulish hunger.

Thone wrenched his eyes away and stared at the river shore. The stream had widened and the current had grown more sluggish. He sought to recognize their location, looking vainly for some familiar landmark in the monotonous dull-green cliffs of jungle that lined the margin. He felt hopelessly lost and alienated. He seemed to be drifting on an unknown tide of madness and nightmare, accompanied by something more frightful than corruption itself.

His mind began to wander with an odd inconsequence, coming back always, in a sort of closed circle, to the thing that was devouring Falmer. With a flash of scientific curiosity, he found himself wondering to what genus it belonged. It was neither fungus nor pitcher plant, nor anything that he had ever encountered or heard of in his explorations. It must have come, as Falmer had suggested, from an alien world: it was nothing that the earth could conceivably have nourished.

He felt, with a comforting assurance, that Falmer was dead. That at least, was a mercy. But, even as he shaped the thought, he heard a low guttural moaning, and, peering at Falmer in a horrible startlement, saw that his limbs and body were twitching slightly. The twitching increased, and took on a rhythmic regularity, though at no time did it resemble the agonized and violent convulsions of the previous day. It was plainly automatic, like a sort of galvanism; and Thone saw that it was timed with the languorous and loathsome swaying of the plant. The effect on the watcher was insidiously mesmeric and somnolent; and once he caught himself beating the detestable rhythm with his foot.

He tried to pull himself together, groping desperately for something to which his sanity could cling. Ineluctably, his illness returned: fever, nausea, and revulsion worse than the loathliness of death. But, before he yielded to it utterly, he drew his loaded revolver from the holster and fired six times into Falmer's quivering body . . . He knew that he had not missed, but, after the final bullet, Falmer still moaned and twitched in unison with the evil swaying of the plant, and Thone, sliding into delirium, heard still the ceaseless, automatic moaning.

There was no time in the world of seething unreality and shoreless oblivion through which himself he drifted. When he came to himself again, he could not know if hours or weeks had elapsed. But he knew at once that the boat was no longer moving; and lifting himself dizzily, he saw that it had floated into shallow water and mud and was nosing the beach of a tiny, jungle-tufted isle in mid-river. The putrid odour of slime was about him like a stagnant pool; and he heard a strident humming of insects.

It was either late morning or early afternoon, for the sun was high in the still heavens. Lianas were drooping above him from the island trees like uncoiled serpents, and epiphytic orchids, marked with ophidian mottlings, leaned towards him grotesquely from lowering boughs. Immense butterflies went past on sumptuously spotted wings.

He sat up, feeling very giddy and lightheaded, and faced again the horror that accompanied him. The thing had grown incredibly: the three-antlered stems, mounting above Falmer's head, had become gigantic and had put out masses of ropey feelers that tossed uneasily in the air, as if searching for support – or new provender. In the topmost antlers, a prodigious blossom had opened – a sort of fleshy disc, broad as a man's face and white as leprosy.

Falmer's features had shrunken till the outlines of every bone were visible as if beneath tightened paper. He was a mere death's head in a mask of human skin; and beneath his clothing the body was little more than a skeleton. He was quite still now, except for the communicated quivering of the stems. The atrocious plant had sucked him dry, had eaten his vitals and his flesh.

Thone wanted to hurl himself forward in a mad impulse to grapple with the growth. But a strange paralysis held him back. The plant was like a living and sentient thing – a thing that watched him, that dominated him with its unclean but superior will. And the huge blossom, as he stared, took on the dim, unnatural semblance of a face. It was somehow like the face of Falmer but the lineaments were twisted all awry, and were mingled with those of something wholly devilish and non-human. Thone could not move – he could not take his eyes from the blasphemous abnormality.

By some miracle, his fever had left him; and it did not return. Instead, there came an eternity of frozen fright and madness, in which he sat facing the mesmeric plant. It towered before him from the dry, dead shell that had been Falmer, its swollen, glutted stems and branches swaying gently, its huge flower leering perpetually upon him with its impious travesty of a human face. He thought that he heard a low, singing sound, ineffably sweet, but whether it emanated from the plant or was a mere hallucination of his overwrought senses, he could not know.

The sluggish hours went by, and a gruelling sun poured down its beams like molten lead from some titanic vessel of torture. His head swam with weakness and the fetor-laden heat, but he could not relax the rigour of his posture. There was no change in the nodding monstrosity, which seemed to have attained its full growth above the head of its victim. But after a long interim Thone's eyes were drawn to the shrunken hands of Falmer, which still clasped the drawn-up knees in a spasmodic clutch. Through the ends of the fingers, tiny white rootlets had broken and were writhing slowly in the air – groping, it seemed, for a new source of nourishment. Then, from the neck and chin, other tips were breaking, and over the whole body the clothing stirred in a curious manner, as if with the crawling and lifting of hidden lizards.

At the same time the singing grew louder, sweeter, more imperious, and the swaying of the great plant assumed an indescribably seductive tempo. It was like the allurement of voluptuous sirens, the deadly languor of dancing cobras. Thone felt an irresistible compulsion: a summons was being laid upon him, and his drugged mind and body must obey it. The very fingers of Falmer, twisting viperishly, seemed beckoning to him. Suddenly he was on his hands and knees in the bottom of the boat.

Inch by inch, with terror and fascination contending his brain, he crept forward, dragging himself over the disregarded bundle of orchid-plants

– inch by inch, foot by foot, till his head was against the withered hands of Falmer, from which hung and floated the questing roots.

Some cataleptic spell had made him helpless. He felt the rootlets as they moved like delving fingers through his hair and over his face and neck, and started to strike in with agonizing, needle-sharp tips. He could not stir, he could not even close his lids. In a frozen stare, he saw the gold and carmine flash of a hovering butterfly as the roots began to pierce his pupils.

Deeper and deeper went the greedy roots, while new filaments grew out to enmesh him like a witch's net … For a while, it seemed that the dead and the living writhed together in leashed convulsions … At last Thone hung supine amid the lethal, ever-growing web; bloated and colossal, the plant lived on; and in its upper branches, through the still, stifling afternoon, a second flower began to unfold.

Satan's Circus

Lady Eleanor Smith

I once asked a circus artist whom I knew to have worked at one time with the Circus Brandt whether or not he had enjoyed travelling with this well-known show. His reply was a curious one. Swiftly distorting his features into a hideous grimace, he spat violently upon the floor. Not another word would he say. My curiosity was, however, aroused, and I went next to an old Continental clown, now retired, who had the reputation of knowing every European circus as well as he knew his own pocket.

'The Circus Brandt,' he said thoughtfully. 'Well, you know the Brandts are queer people, and have an odd reputation. They are Austrian, and their own country-people call them gipsies, by which they mean nomads, for the Brandts never pitch in their own land, but wander the whole world over as though the devil himself were at their heels. In fact, some call them "Satan's Circus."'

'I thought,' I said, 'that the Circus Brandt was supposed to be a remarkably fine show?'

'It is,' he said, and lit his pipe, 'it's expensive, ambitious, showy, well run. In their way these people are artists, and deserve more success than they have had. It's hard to say why they're so unpopular, but the fact remains that no one will stay with them more than a few months; and, what's more, wherever they go – India, Australia, Rumania, Spain, or Africa – they leave behind them a nasty, unpleasant sort of reputation as regards unpaid bills – which,' he added, blowing smoke into the air, 'is odd, for the Brandts are rich.'

'How many Brandts are there?' I inquired, for I wished to know more about Europe's most elusive circus.

'You ask too many questions,' said he, 'but this being my last reply to them, I don't mind telling you that there are two, and that they are man and wife – Carl and Lya. The lady is a bit of a mystery, but if you ask my opinion I would say that she is of Mexican blood, that she was at some time or other a charmer of snakes, and that of the two she is, on the whole, the worse, although that is saying a good deal. However, all this is pure guess-work on my part, although, having seen her, I can tell you that she's

a handsome piece, still a year or two on the right side of forty. And now,'
he said firmly, 'I will speak no more of the Circus Brandt.'

And we talked instead of Sarrasani, of Krone, of Carmo, and of
Hagebeck.

A year passed, and I forgot the Circus Brandt, which no doubt during
this period of time wandered from Tokio to San Francisco and Belgrade
up to Stockholm and back again, as though the devil himself were at its
heels.

And then I met an old friend, a famous juggler, whom I had not seen
for many months. I offered him a drink and asked him where he had been
since our last meeting. He laughed, and said that he had been in hell.
I told him I was not much of a hand at riddles. He laughed again.

'Oh – hell?' he said. 'Perhaps that's an exaggeration; but, anyhow, I've
been as near to it as ever I want to. I've been touring with Circus Brandt.'

'The Circus Brandt?'

'Exactly. The Balkan States, Spain, North Africa. Then Holland and
Belgium, and finally France. I cleared out in France. If they'd doubled
my salary I'd not have stayed with them.'

'Is the Circus Brandt, then,' I asked, 'as rough as all that?'

'Rough?' he said. 'No, it's not rough. I can stick roughness. What I
can't stand, however, is working with people who give me the creeps.
Now you're laughing, and I'm not surprised, but I can assure you that
I've lain awake at night in my wagon sweating with fear and I'm by no
means a fanciful chap.'

By this time I was keenly interested.

'Please tell me,' I asked, 'what it was that frightened you so much.'

'That I can't do,' he replied, and ordered another drink, 'for the fact
is that I, personally, was not treated badly during the tour. The Brandts
were very civil to me – too civil, in fact, for they'd ask me into their wagon
sometimes for a chat between shows, and I hated going – it gave me
gooseflesh down my back. Somehow – and you'll laugh again I know –
it was like sitting there talking to two big cats that were just waiting to
pounce after they'd finished playing with you. I swear I believed, at the
time, that Carl and Lya could see in the dark. Now, of course, that's
ridiculous, and I know it, but I still get the creeps when I think about
them. I must have been nervy – overtired, you know, at the time.'

I asked whether anyone else at the circus had been similarly affected
by the Brandts, and he wrinkled his brows, as though trying to remember,
with obvious distaste, any further details of his tour.

'There's one thing that happened so that all could see,' he remarked
after a pause, 'and that was in a wild part of Rumania, somewhere near
the Carpathian mountains. We were passing through a little village, on
our way to a town a few miles' distance, and the peasants came flocking

out to watch us pass, which was, of course, only natural, for the show is a very fine one. Then, in the village street, a van stuck, and the Brandts came out of their big living-wagon to see what had happened.'

'Well?' I asked, for he paused again.

'Well, it was funny, that's all. They scattered like rabbits – rushed into their cottages and banged the doors. The wagon was shoved out of the rut and we went on, but in the next village there was no sign of life, for everything was deserted and the doors were barred. But on every door was nailed a wreath of garlic flowers.'

'Anything else?' I asked, for he had relapsed into silence.

'Oh, one little thing I remember noticing. The menagerie. The Brandts seldom bother to inspect that part of the show. They're too busy about the ring and the ticket office. But one day she – Mme Brandt – had to go through the horse-tent and the menagerie to find some agent who was talking to the boys there. It really was a bit odd – the noise was blood-curdling. It was as though the lions and tigers were frightened; not angry, you know, or roaring for their food, but quite a different sort of row. And, when she had gone, the horses were sweating. I felt 'em myself, and it was a chilly day.'

'Really,' I said, 'it's time you came back.'

'Oh,' he replied. 'I don't expect you to believe me. Why should you? I wouldn't have talked if you hadn't asked me about the Circus Brandt. I'd just have said I was glad to be home. But as you asked me ... Oh, well, one day I'll tell you why I left them in France. It's not a pretty story. But I won't tell it tonight. I avoid the Brandts as a bedtime topic – I've been dreaming about them lately.'

It took me some time to coax the juggler's tale from him. One morning, however, as we were walking along the Unter den Linden, in pale, but radiant spring sunshine, he consented to tell it. Translated into English, this is the story:

While the Circus Brandt was touring Northern Africa, when it was, in fact, only a few days from Tangier, a man arrived asking for work. He was, he said, an Alsatian, and had been a stoker, but his ship had abandoned him at Tangier, and he had been seeking a job ever since. This man was interviewed by Carl Brandt himself, who had been accosted by him on the lot. They were a curiously contrasted pair as they stood talking together outside the steps of the Brandts' palatial living-wagon. The Alsatian was fair, a big handsome young man with thick, blond hair, a tanned skin and honest, rather stupid, blue eyes. Carl Brandt was tall, too, but emaciated, wasted, and swarthy dark; he had a smooth, darting black head like a snake's head; his long face was haggard, and yellow as old ivory; he wore a tiny dark imperial beard; his black eyes were feverishly alive in heavy purple hollows, and his teeth were sharp and broken and rotten. He was said to drug, and indeed he had very much the appearance of an addict. While the two men were talking, the door of the wagon opened and Mme Brandt appeared on the threshold, asking her husband what the stranger wanted of him. She herself was, incidentally, a remarkably handsome woman, although no longer young. She was powerfully but gracefully made, with quantities of shining blue-black hair, delicate features, oblique, heavy-lidded eyes, and one of those opaque white skins that always look like milk. She had no colour, but was all black and white. Even her lips were pale, not being painted, and her face was heart-shaped against the shadow of her dark hair. She wore white in hot countries and black in the north, but somehow one never noticed that she was not dressed in colours. She seldom looked at the person to whom she was talking, so that when she did it was rather a shock. Her voice was low, and she never showed her teeth, making one imagine that they must be bad, like her husband's.

Both Brandts stayed talking to the Alsatian for about ten minutes in the hot sunshine. It was impossible to eavesdrop, but once the Alsatian was heard reiterating rather warmly that he was a stoker by profession. Finally, however, Carl Brandt took the man off to the head keeper of the menagerie and said that he was to be given work. The Alsatian for his part said that his name was Anatole, and that he was used to rough jobs. Soon afterwards the circus went on towards Tunis.

The new hand, Anatole, was a good-natured, genial, simple fellow, who soon became popular, not only with the tent-men and grooms, but also with the more democratic of the performers, who amused themselves, during the tedium of long 'jumps', by making him sing to them, for he had a rich and beautiful voice. Generally he sang German *Lieder* or long-forgotten French music-hall songs, but sometimes he favoured them with snatches of roaring, racy, impudent ballads couched in an *argot* with which they were every one unfamiliar. On one occasion, before the evening show, when Anatole was shouting one of these coarsely cheerful songs inside the Big Top, the flap was suddenly opened to reveal Mme Brandt's pale, watchful face in the aperture.

Instantly, although some of the small audience had not seen her, a curious discomfort fell upon the gay party. Anatole, whose back was turned towards the entrance, immediately became aware of some strain or tension among his listeners, and, wheeling round, stopped abruptly in the middle of a bar. The little group scrambled awkwardly to its feet.

Mme Brandt murmured in her low voice:

'Don't let me interfere with your concert, my friends. Go on, you' – to Anatole – 'that's a lively song you were singing. Where did you pick it up?'

Anatole, standing respectfully before her, was silent. Mme Brandt did not look at him or seem to concern herself with him in any way, but sent her oblique eyes roving over the empty seats of the great tent, yet somehow, in some curious way, it became obvious to her listeners that she was stubbornly determined to drag from him an answer.

Anatole at length muttered:

'I learned the song, madame, on board a Portuguese fruit-trader many years ago.'

Mme Brandt made no sign of having heard him speak.

After this incident, however, she began to employ the odd hand on various jobs about her own living-wagon, with the result that he had less time to sing and not much time even for his work in the menagerie. Anatole, good-humoured and jovial as he was, soon conceived a violent dislike of the proprietress, and he took no pains to hide it from his friends, who were incidentally in hearty agreement with him on this point. Everyone hated the Brandts; many feared them.

The circus crossed to Spain and began to tour Andalusia. Several performers left; new acts were promptly engaged. Carl Brandt had always found it easy to rid himself of artists. Ten minutes before the show was due to open he would send for some unlucky trapezist and, pointing to the man's apparatus, complicated and heavy, slung up to one of the big poles, he would say casually:

'I want you to move that to the other side of the tent before the show.'

The artist would perhaps laugh, thinking the director was making some obscure joke.

Brandt would then continue, gently:

'You had better hurry, don't you think?'

The artist would protest indignantly.

'It's impossible, sir. How can I move my apparatus in ten minutes?'

Brandt would then watch him, sneering, for a few seconds. Then he would turn away, saying suavely:

'Discharged for insubordination,' and walk off to telegraph to his agent for a new act.

Mme Brandt took a curious perverse pleasure in teasing Anatole. She knew that he feared her, and it amused her to send for him, to keep him standing in her wagon while she polished her nails or sewed or wrote letters, utterly indifferent to his presence. After about ten minutes she would look up, glancing at some point above his head, and ask him, in her soft, languid voice, if he liked circus life, and whether he was happy with them. She would chat for some time, casually asking him searching questions about the other performers, then suddenly she would look direct at him, with a strange, brooding stare, while she said:

'Better than tramp ships, isn't it, eh? You are more comfortable here than you were as a stoker, I suppose?'

Sometimes she would add:

'Tell me something about a stoker's life, Anatole. What were your duties, and your hours?'

Always, when she dismissed him, his hair was damp with sweat.

The Circus Brandt wandered gradually northwards towards the Basque country, until the French border was almost in sight. They were to cut across France into Belgium and Holland, then back again. The Brandts could never stay long anywhere. Just before the circus entered French territory Anatole gave his notice to the head keeper. He was a hard worker and so popular with his mates that the keeper went grumbling to Carl Brandt, who agreed to an increase of salary. Anatole refused to stay on.

Mme Brandt was in the wagon when this news was told to her husband. She said to Carl: 'If you want the Alsatian to stay, I will arrange it. Leave it to me. I think I understand the trouble, and, as you say, he is a useful man.'

The next day she sent for Anatole, and after ignoring him for about five minutes she asked him listlessly what he meant by leaving them. Anatole, standing rigid near the door, stammered some awkward apology.

'Why is it?'

'I have – I have had offered me a job.'

'Better than this?' she pursued, stitching at her work.

'Yes, madame.'

'Yet,' she continued idly, 'you were happy with us in Africa, happy in Spain. Why not, then, in France?'

'Madame——'

She snapped a thread with her teeth.

'Why not in France, Anatole?'

There was no reply.

Suddenly she flung her sewing to the ground and fixed him with an unswerving glance. Something leaped into her eyes that startled him, an ugly, naked, hungry look that he had never before seen there. Her eyes burned him, like a devil's eyes. She said, speaking rapidly, scarcely moving her lips:

'I will tell you why you are afraid of France, shall I, Anatole? I have guessed your secret my friend ... You are a deserter from the Foreign Legion, and you are afraid of being recaptured. That is it, isn't it? Oh, don't trouble to lie; I have known ever since we were in Africa. It's true, isn't it, what I have said?'

He shook his head, swallowing, unable to speak.

It was a hot day and he wore only a thin shirt. In a second she sprang from her chair across the wagon and threw herself upon him, tearing at this garment with her fingers. Terrified, he struggled, but she was too swift, too violent, too relentless. The shirt ripped in two and revealed upon his white chest the seam of livid scars.

'Bullet wounds!' she laughed in his ear. 'A stoker with bullet wounds! I was right, wasn't I, Anatole?'

He was conscious, above his fear, of a strange shrinking sensation of repulsion at her proximity. 'God,' he thought, 'she's after me!' And he was sickened, as some people are sickened by the sight of a deadly snake. And then, surprisingly, he was saved. She darted away from him, sank down in her chair, snatched up her sewing.

Her quick ear had heard the footsteps of Carl Brandt. Anatole stood there dazed, clutching the great rent in his shirt. Carl Brandt entered the wagon softly, for he always wore rubber soles to his shoes. His wife addressed him in her low unflurried voice.

'You see Anatole there? He has just been telling me why he is afraid to come with us to France. He is a deserter from the Foreign Legion. Look at the wounds there, on his chest.'

Anatole gazed helplessly at the long, yellow face of Brandt, who stared at him for some moments in silence.

'A deserter?' Brandt said at length, and chuckled. 'A deserter? You needn't be afraid, my lad, to come with us to France. They've something better to do than hunt for obscure escaped legionaries there. Oh, yes, you'll be safe enough. I'll protect you.'

And he stood rubbing his hands and staring thoughtfully at Anatole with his gleaming black eyes. Anatole, to escape from them, promised to stay. He had the unpleasant sensation of having faced in the wagon that afternoon not one snake, but two. He disliked reptiles. He meant to bolt, but he had lied to Madame Brandt when he talked of a new job, and he was comfortable where he was. He was, too, an unimaginative creature, and the horrors of the Legion now seemed very remote. Soon he was in France, utterly unable to believe that he was in any danger. To his delight, his mistress ignored him after the scene in the wagon. She had obviously realized, he thought to himself, that he found her disgusting. And he would have been completely happy had he not known that he had made a dangerous enemy.

The Circus Brandt employed as lion-tamer an ex-matador, a man named 'Captain' da Silva. This individual was not best pleased with his situation. He had lost his nerve about a year before, but after working the same group of lions for ten months he had become more confident and consequently more content. Then, without any warning, Carl Brandt bought a mixed group of animals, and told da Silva to start work at once. The tamer was furious. Lions, tigers, bears, and leopards! He shrugged his shoulders and obeyed sulkily. Soon the mixed group was ready for the ring, and appeared for a week with great success.

Then one morning da Silva went to the cages and found his animals in a wild, abnormal state. Snarling, bristling, foaming at the mouth, they seemed unable even to recognize their tamer. A comrade, coming to watch, whispered in his ear:

'*She walked last night.*'

Da Silva shuddered. There was a legend in the Circus Brandt that whenever the animals were nervous or upset Lya Brandt, the 'she-devil', had walked in her sleep the night before, wandering into the menagerie and terrifying the beasts, who presumably knew her for what she was.

The tiger roared, and was answered by the lioness. Da Silva turned to his companion.

'I'm off. I wouldn't work these cats tonight for a fortune.'

In twenty minutes' time he was at the railway station.

Carl Brandt heard the news in silence. Then he raised his arm and struck his head keeper savagely on the mouth. Wrapping his black cloak about his tall, thin figure, he left the office and sought his own wagon. His wife was engaged drinking a cup of coffee. They eyed each other in silence.

Then she said calmly:

'It's da Silva, I suppose?'

'Da Silva, yes. Already he has gone. Now who will work the mixed group?'

She drained her cup and answered thoughtfully:

'I know of several tamers.'

'Probably. And how long will they take to get here?'

'Exactly,' she said, pouring out more coffee. 'That, I agree, is the great objection. Is there no one on the lot who could work the cats for a week or two?'

'What nonsense are you talking?'

She put her hand over her eyes.

'You seem to forget Anatole. An escaped Legionary in French territory. Would he disobey your orders, do you think?'

There was a pause.

'I'll send for him,' said Brandt at length.

They were silent as they waited for the Alsatian. When he came in Lya did not look at him, but began to polish her nails.

Carl Brandt turned his yellow, wrinkled face towards Anatole. His eyes were dark and smouldering hollows. He said gently:

'You know that da Silva has left?'

'Yes, sir.' Anatole was perplexed.

'There is no one now to work the animals until a new tamer is engaged.'

'No, sir.'

'It is not my custom to fail my patrons. I show always what I advertise.

The new tamer should be here in a week. It is about this week that I wish to speak.'

Another pause. Anatole's heart began to pump against his ribs.

Brandt said placidly:

'I am about to promote you, my friend. For a week you shall work the mixed group.'

Anatole turned dusky red. He was furiously angry, so angry indeed that his fear of the silent woman sitting at the table vanished entirely. No longer conscious of her presence he blurted out violently:

'What! You wish me to go in the cage with those animals? Then you must find someone else; I wouldn't do it for a fortune.'

Brandt smiled, showing his black, broken teeth. His wife, utterly indifferent, continued to paint her nails bright red. Brandt said pleasantly:

'Are you perhaps in a position to dictate, my friend? I may be wrong, of course, but I am under the impression that we are now in *French territory*. Charming words, eh?'

Anatole was silent. He thought suddenly and with horror of the Legion – blistering sun, filth, and brutality. He thought, too, of the salt-mines, that ghastly living death to which he would inevitably be condemned in the event of capture. Then he remembered the animals as he had last seen them, ferocious, maddened. He shook his head.

'That's bluff,' he said shakily. 'I'm no tamer. You can't force me into the cage.'

Carl Brandt chuckled. The delicate yellow ivory of his skin seamed itself into a thousand wrinkles. He pulled out his watch.

'Five minutes, Anatole, to come with me to the menagerie. Otherwise I telephone the police. If I may be permitted to advise you, I suggest the menagerie. Even the belly of a lion is preferable, I should imagine, to the African salt-mines. But take your choice.'

Madame Brandt, snapping an orange-stick in two, now obtruded herself quietly into the conversation.

'No, Anatole,' she said musingly, 'it will not be possible to run away in the night. The Herr Director will take trouble, great trouble, to have you traced. The Herr Director has no wish to protect criminals.'

Once again she looked directly at him, fixing him with the burning and threatening glance that was like a sword.

Brandt glanced at his watch.

'I must remind you, Anatole, that you have only two minutes left,' he said with an air of great courtesy. 'How many years did you serve in the Legion, I wonder? And is it eight years in the salt-mines for deserters, or perhaps more?'

'I'll work the animals,' said Anatole shortly. He knew that Lya Brandt had read his thoughts, and wiped the sweat from his face as he went towards the menagerie. It was not possible for the mixed group to appear

at the matinée, but it was announced to the circus in general that the
cats would work that night without fail. Anatole was to spend the afternoon rehearsing them.

His face was grey as he shut himself in the cage, armed only with a
tamer's switch. Outside the bars stood two keepers with loaded revolvers.
They, too, were nervous. The animals stood motionless to stare at the
stranger, hackles raised, restless yellow eyes fixed upon him. Around the
cage were arranged painted wooden pedestals, upon which the animals
were trained to sit at the word of command. The Alsatian now gave that
command. They took no notice. He repeated it louder, slapping the bars
with his switch, and they scattered in a sudden panic to take up their
accustomed seats. He pulled out the paper hoop through which the lions
must jump. They snarled for several minutes, striking out with their
savage paws, then, in the end, possibly deciding that obedience was less
trouble, they bounded through the loop with an ill grace. The two
keepers, and Anatole as well, were soon streaming with perspiration as
though they had been plunged into water. The Alsatian was now,
however, more confident. He turned to the bears.

Twenty minutes later Carl Brandt rejoined his wife in the living-
wagon.

'Better than I expected,' said the director coolly. Mme Brandt made
no reply, nor did she turn her head.

That evening the Alsatian was supplied with a splendid sky-blue
uniform and cherry-coloured breeches from the circus wardrobe. Out on
the lot his comrades glanced at him sympathetically. One or two, unconscious of his antecedents, warned him to defy Brandt and keep out
of the cage. Anatole merely shook his head, incapable of giving an
explanation.

It was dusk. The bandsmen, splendid in their green and gold uniforms,
played the overture inside the huge tent. A group of clowns, glittering
in brilliant spangles, stood waiting to make their comic entry. Behind the
clowns six or seven grooms were busy controlling twenty milk-white Arab
stallions with fleecy white manes and tails. These horses were magnificent
in scarlet trappings. The Chinese troupe, dark kimonos over gorgeous
brocade robes, diligently practised near the bears' cage. Anatole sat on
a bale of hay near the tigers, deaf to the advice muttered in his ear by
various comrades. The circus proceeded.

Up in the dome of the tent two muscular young men in peach-coloured
tights flung themselves from bar to bar with thrilling grace and swiftness.
Down below, the attendants rapidly constructed a vast cage, staggering
beneath sections of heavy iron bars. Soon the band crashed out a chord,
and Anatole, the Legionary, stepped into the cage, bowing modestly in
response to the applause. Then an iron door was slid aside and down the
narrow tunnel crept a file of tawny shapes.

Lions, tigers, leopards, bears. Gracefully they padded into the arena, stretching themselves, rubbing against the bars of the cage, yawning at the bright lights, showing their teeth, slinking with a cat-like agility about the ring.

Gripping his switch, Anatole uttered the first command. One minute later the animals were seated with a certain docility upon their wooden pedestals. Anatole produced his hoop. At first the people of the circus held their breath, then, gradually, as five minutes passed, they relaxed. He was doing well. They sighed with relief. The climax of the act was a tableau during the course of which the animals grouped themselves, standing erect on their hind legs about the trainer, who himself sprang upon a pedestal, arm upraised to give more effect to this subjugation of the beasts. The biggest tiger lay at his feet during the tableau, and while the other animals soon assumed their accustomed positions when ordered, the tiger was at first always unwilling to fling himself upon the sawdust.

Posing the lions and leopards, Anatole, one foot on the pedestal, spoke briskly, curtly, to the great beast, which stared at him sulkily. A second passed, seeming longer than a minute to the circus watchers. The tiger continued to stare, and Anatole, banging at the bars with his switch, pointed stubbornly at the ground at his feet.

His back was towards the ring entrance, and he did not see the grooms and attendants draw back respectfully to allow someone to pass through the red velvet curtains. His comrades did, and nudged one another, for Mme Brandt seldom came near the arena during a performance. She stood for a moment near the curtains, tall and straight in her flowing white dress, her face pale against the dense blackness of her hair.

Then, suddenly, there was tumult in the peaceful cage, as snarling furiously, the animals leaped from their pedestals to dash themselves savagely against the bars. Caught by surprise, Anatole turned, slashing with his switch, shouting, oblivious of the sullen tiger behind him. A leopard, maddened with fright, collided against him and sent him stumbling to the ground. With the fierce swiftness of a mighty hawk, the great tiger sprang. A thick choking growl that made the blood run cold, yells of terror from the crowd, and then the crack of two revolver shots. Armed with hosepipes, the menagerie men drove the animals back. The tiger was wounded in the shoulder, and clawed the ground, biting at itself in a frenzy of pain.

Anatole lay doubled up on the sawdust looking like a rag dummy, so limp and twisted was his body. On the bright blue of his uniform oozed a clotted stream of red. His face? Anatole had no longer a face; only a huge and raw and gaping wound. Opening a side door, they dragged his body from the cage and swiftly wrapped it in the gorgeous coat of a Chinese acrobat standing nearby. Screaming, weeping, cursing, the horrified audience fought, struggled and stampeded to leave the tent. In

Lady Eleanor Smith

the noise and tumult, Mme Brandt slipped through the red velvet curtains and vanished like a white shadow.

That night the body was laid temporarily in a little canvas dressing-room belonging to the clowns. It was late before the show people retired to bed, but by one o'clock in the morning all was still in the tent-town of Brandt's Circus. Only the night watchman, a stolid, unimaginative fellow, paced slowly up and down, swinging his lantern, but from time to time a lion would whimper and growl in the silence of the night.

It was the watchman, however, who afterwards related to his comrades what he saw during this lonely vigil . . . It was about an hour before dawn, and the man was lolling on a heap of hay, relieved, no doubt, to think the night would soon be over, when all at once his quick ear caught the soft sound of approaching footsteps. He turned, hiding his lantern beneath his coat. It was Mme Brandt, of course, walking slowly, like a sleepwalker, across the deserted arena towards the dressing-rooms, seeming no more tangible than a shadow, a white shadow that gleamed for a moment in the darkness, and then was gone, swallowed by the gloom of the night. Now, the watchman was a brave fellow, and inclined to be inquisitive. He slipped off his shoes and crept after her.

Madame Brandt glided straight to the little dressing-room wherein lay the mangled body of the Legionary. The watchman had not dared to bring his lantern, and it was, therefore, difficult for him to see what was happening, but at the same time he managed to observe quite enough. He glimpsed her white figure kneeling near the dark shape on the floor; as he watched, she struggled with some drapery or other, and he saw that she was trying to drag away the sheet that covered the corpse. Having apparently achieved her purpose, she remained still for a moment, staring at what she saw; this immobility, which lasted only for a second, was succeeded by a sudden revulsion of feeling more horrible than anything that had gone before; for with all the ferocity of a starving animal she flung herself upon the body, shaking it, gripping it tightly to steady its leaden weight while she thrust her face, her mouth, down upon that torn and bleeding throat . . . then in the distant menagerie the lions and tigers broke the silence of the night with sudden tumult.

'Yes,' said the juggler, after a pause, 'we liked Anatole. He was a good comrade, although, mind you, he had probably been a murderer, and most certainly a thief. But in the Circus Brandt, you know, that means nothing at all.'

'Where is the Circus Brandt now?' I asked, after another pause.

He shrugged his shoulders.

'Poland, I think, or possibly Peru. How can I tell? The Brandts are gipsies, nomads. Here today, gone tomorrow. Possibly they travel fast because there is always something to hush up. But who can say? The devil has an admirable habit of looking after his friends.'

I was silent, for I was thinking both of Lya Brandt and Anatole. Suddenly I felt rather sick.

'Look here,' I said, 'do you mind if we don't talk any more about the Circus Brandt for the moment?'

The Squaw

Bram Stoker

Nurnberg at the time was not so much exploited as it has been since then. Irving had not been playing *Faust*, and the very name of the old town was hardly known to the great bulk of the travelling public. My wife and I being in the second week of our honeymoon, naturally wanted someone else to join our party, so that when the cheery stranger, Elias P. Hutcheson, hailing from Isthmian City, Bleeding Gulch, Maple Tree County, Neb., turned up at the station at Frankfort, and casually remarked that he was going on to see the most all-fired old Methuselah of a town in Yurrup, and that he guessed that so much travelling alone was enough to send an intelligent, active citizen into the melancholy ward of a dafthouse, we took the pretty broad hint and suggested that we should join forces. We found, on comparing notes afterwards, that we had each intended to speak with some diffidence or hesitation so as not to appear too eager, such not being a good compliment to the success of our married life; but the effect was entirely marred by our both beginning to speak at the same instant – stopping simultaneously and then going on together again. Anyhow, no matter how, it was done; and Elias P. Hutcheson became one of our party. Straightway Amelia and I found the pleasant benefit; instead of quarrelling, as we had been doing, we found that the restraining influence of a third party was such that we now took every opportunity of spooning in odd corners. Amelia declares that ever since she has, as the result of that experience, advised all her friends to take a friend on the honeymoon. Well, we 'did' Nurnberg together, and much enjoyed the racy remarks of our transatlantic friend, who, from his quaint speech and his wonderful stock of adventures, might have stepped out of a novel. We kept for the last object of interest in the city to be visited the Burg, and on the day appointed for the visit strolled round the outer wall of the city by the eastern side.

The Burg is seated on a rock dominating the town, and an immensely deep fosse guards it on the northern side. Nurnberg has been happy in that it was never sacked; had it been it would certainly not be so spick-and-span perfect as it is at present. The ditch has not been used for centuries, and now its base is spread with tea gardens and orchards, of which some of the trees are of quite respectable growth. As we wandered round the wall, dawdling in the hot July sunshine, we often paused to admire the views spread before us, and in especial the great plain covered with towns and villages and bounded with a blue line of hills, like a landscape of Claude Lorraine. From this we always turned with new delight to the city itself, with its myriad of quaint old gables and acre-wide red roofs dotted with dormer windows, tier upon tier. A little to our right rose the towers of the Burg, and nearer still, standing grim, the Torture Tower, which was, and is, perhaps, the most interesting place in the city. For centuries the tradition of the Iron Virgin of Nurnberg has been handed down as an instance of the horrors of cruelty of which man is capable; we had long looked forward to seeing it; and here at last was its home.

In one of our pauses we leaned over the wall of the moat and looked down. The garden seemed quite fifty or sixty feet below us, and the sun pouring into it with an intense, moveless heat like that of an oven. Beyond rose the grey, grim wall seemingly of endless height, and losing itself right and left in the angles of bastion and counterscarp. Trees and bushes crowned the wall, and above again towered the lofty houses on whose massive beauty Time has only set the hand of approval. The sun was hot and we were lazy; time was our own, and we lingered, leaning on the wall. Just below us was a pretty sight – a great black cat lying stretched in the sun, whilst round her gambolled prettily a tiny black kitten. The mother would wave her tail for the kitten to play with, or would raise her feet and push away the little one as an encouragement to further play. They were just at the foot of the wall, and Elias P. Hutcheson, in order to help the play, stooped and took from the walk a moderate-sized pebble.

'See!' he said. 'I will drop it near the kitten, and they will both wonder where it came from.'

'Oh, be careful,' said my wife; 'you might hit the dear little thing!'

'Not me, ma'am,' said Elias P. 'Why, I'm as tender as a Maine cherry tree. Lor, bless ye, I wouldn't hurt the poor pooty little critter more'n I'd scalp a baby. An' you may bet your variegated socks on that! See, I'll drop it fur away on the outside so's not to go near her!' Thus saying, he leaned over and held his arm out at full length and dropped the stone. It may be that there is some attractive force which draws lesser matters to greater; or more probably that the wall was not plumb but sloped to its base – we not noticing the inclination from above; but the stone fell with a sickening thud that came up to us through the hot air, right on the kitten's head, and shattered out its little brains then and there. The black cat cast a swift upward glance, and we saw her eyes like green fire fixed an instant on Elias P. Hutcheson; and then her attention was given

to the kitten, which lay still with just a quiver of her tiny limbs, whilst
a thin red stream trickled from a gaping wound. With a muffled cry, such
as a human being might give, she bent over the kitten licking its wound
and moaning. Suddenly she seemed to realize that it was dead, and again
threw her eyes up at us. I shall never forget the sight, for she looked the
perfect incarnation of hate. Her green eyes blazed with lurid fire, and the
white, sharp teeth seemed to almost shine through the blood which
dabbled her mouth and whiskers. She gnashed her teeth, and her claws
stood out stark and at full length on every paw. Then she made a wild
rush up the wall as if to reach us, but when the momentum ended fell
back, and further added to her horrible appearance for she fell on the
kitten, and rose with her black fur smeared with its brains and blood.
Amelia turned quite faint, and I had to lift her back from the wall. There
was a seat close by in shade of a spreading plane tree, and here I placed
her whilst she composed herself. Then I went back to Hutcheson, who
stood without moving, looking down on the angry cat below.

As I joined him, he said:

'Wall, I guess that air the savagest beast I ever see – 'cept once when
an Apache squaw had an edge on a half breed what they nicknamed
"Splinters" 'cos of the way he fixed up her papoose which he stole on a
raid just to show that he appreciated the way they had given his mother
the fire torture. She got that kinder look so set on her face that it jest
seemed to grow there. She followed Splinters more'n three year till at last
the braves got him and handed him over to her. They did say that no
man, white or Injun, had ever been so long a-dying under the tortures
of the Apaches. The only time I ever see her smile was when I wiped her
out. I kem on the camp just in time to see Splinters pass in his checks,
and he wasn't sorry to go either. He was a hard citizen, and though I
never could shake with him after that papoose business – for it was bitter
bad, and he should have been a white man, for he looked like one – I
see he had got paid out in full. Durn me, but I took a piece of his hide
from one of his skinnin' posts an' had it made into a pocket book. It's here
now!' and he slapped the breast pocket of his coat.

Whilst he was speaking the cat was continuing her frantic efforts to get
up the wall. She would take a run back and then charge up, sometimes
reaching an incredible height. She did not seem to mind the heavy fall
which she got each time, but started with renewed vigour; and at every
tumble her appearance became more horrible. Hutcheson was a kind-
hearted man – my wife and I had both noticed little acts of kindness to
animals as well as to persons – and he seemed concerned at the state of
fury to which the cat had wrought herself.

'Wall, now!' he said, 'I du declare that that poor critter seems quite
desperate. There! there! poor thing, it was all an accident – though that
won't bring back your little one to you. Say! I wouldn't have had such

a thing happen for a thousand! Just shows what a clumsy fool of a man can do when he tries to play! Seems I'm too darned slipper-handed to even play with a cat. Say, Colonel!' – it was a pleasant way he had to bestow titles freely – 'I hope your wife don't hold no grudge against me on account of this unpleasantness? Why, I wouldn't have had it occur on no account.'

He came over to Amelia and apologized profusely, and she with her usual kindness of heart hastened to assure him that she quite understood that it was an accident. Then we all went again to the wall and looked over.

The cat missing Hutcheson's face had drawn back across the moat, and was sitting on her haunches as though ready to spring. Indeed, the very instant she saw him she did spring, and with a blind, unreasoning fury, which would have been grotesque, only that it was so frightfully real. She did not try to run up the wall, but simply launched herself at him as though hate and fury could lend her wings to pass straight through the great distance between them. Amelia, womanlike, got quite concerned, and said to Elias P. in a warning voice:

'Oh! you must be very careful. That animal would try to kill you if she were here; her eyes look like positive murder.'

He laughed out jovially. 'Excuse me, ma'am,' he said, 'but I can't help laughin'. Fancy a man that has fought grizzlies an' Injuns bein' careful of bein' murdered by a cat!'

When the cat heard him laugh, her whole demeanour seemed to change. She no longer tried to jump or run up the wall, but went quietly over and, sitting again beside the dead kitten, began to lick and fondle it as though it were alive.

'See!' said I, 'the effect of a really strong man. Even that animal in the midst of her fury recognizes the voice of a master, and bows to him!'

'Like a squaw!' was the only comment of Elias P. Hutcheson, as we moved on our way round the city fosse. Every now and then we looked over the wall and each time saw the cat following us. At first she had kept going back to the dead kitten, and then as the distance grew greater took it in her mouth and so followed. After a while, however, she abandoned this, for we saw her following all alone; she had evidently hidden the body somewhere. Amelia's alarm grew at the cat's persistence, and more than once she repeated her warning; but the American always laughed with amusement, till finally, seeing that she was beginning to be worried, he said:

'I say, ma'am, you needn't be skeered over that cat. I go heeled, I du!' Here he slapped his pistol pocket at the back of his lumbar region. 'Why, sooner'n have you worried, I'll shoot the critter, right here, an' risk the police interferin' with a citizen of the United States for carryin' arms contrairy to reg'lations!' As he spoke he looked over the wall, but the cat, on seeing him, retreated, with a growl, into a bed of tall flowers, and was hidden. He went on: 'Blest if that ar critter ain't got more sense of what's good for her than most Christians. I guess we've seen the last of her! You bet, she'll go back now to that busted kitten and have a private funeral of it, all to herself!'

Amelia did not like to say more, lest he might, in mistaken kindness to her, fulfil his threat of shooting the cat; and so we went on and crossed the little wooden bridge leading to the gateway whence ran the steep paved roadway between the Burg and the pentagonal Torture Tower. As we crossed the bridge we saw the cat again down below us. When she saw us her fury seemed to return, and she made frantic efforts to get up the steep wall. Hutcheson laughed as he looked down at her, and said:

'Goodbye, old girl. Sorry I in-jured your feelin's, but you'll get over it in time! So long!' And then we passed through the long, dim archway and came to the gate of the Burg.

When we came out again after our survey of this most beautiful old place which not even the well-intentioned efforts of the Gothic restorers of forty years ago have been able to spoil – though their restoration was then glaring white – we seemed to have quite forgotten the unpleasant episode of the morning. The old lime tree with its great trunk gnarled with the passing of nearly nine centuries, the deep well cut through the heart of the rock by those captives of old, and the lovely view from the city wall whence we heard, spread over almost a full quarter of an hour, the multitudinous chimes of the city, had all helped to wipe out from our minds the incident of the slain kitten.

We were the only visitors who had entered the Torture Tower that morning – so at least said the old custodian – and as we had the place all to ourselves were able to make a minute and more satisfactory survey than would have otherwise been possible. The custodian looking to us as the sole source of his gains for the day, was willing to meet our wishes in any way. The Torture Tower is truly a grim place, even now when many thousands of visitors have sent a stream of life, and the joy that follows life, into the place; but at the time I mention it wore its grimmest and most gruesome aspect. The dust of ages seemed to have settled on it, and the darkness and the horror of its memories seem to have become sentient in a way that would have satisfied the Pantheistic souls of Philo or Spinoza. The lower chamber where we entered was seemingly, in its normal state, filled with incarnate darkness; even the hot sunlight streaming in through the door seemed to be lost in the vast thickness of the walls, and only showed the masonry rough as when the builder's scaffolding had come down, but coated with dust and marked here and there with patches of dark stain which, if walls could speak, could have given their own dread memories of fear and pain. We were glad to pass up the dusty wooden staircase, the custodian leaving the outer door open to light us somewhat on our way; for to our eyes the one long-wick'd, evil-smelling candle stuck in a sconce on the wall gave an inadequate light. When we came up through the open trap in the corner of the chamber overhead, Amelia held on to me so tightly that I could actually feel her heart beat. I must say for my part that I was not surprised at her fear, for this room was even more gruesome than that below. Here there was certainly more light, but only just sufficient to realize the horrible surroundings of the place. The builders of the tower had evidently intended that only they who should gain the top should have any of the joys of light and prospect. There, as we had noticed from below, were ranges of windows, albeit of mediaeval smallness, but elsewhere in the tower were only a very few narrow slits such as were habitual in places of mediaeval defence. A few of these only lit the chamber, and these so high up in the wall that from no part could the sky be seen through the thickness of the walls. In racks, and leaning in disorder against the walls, were a number of headmen's swords, great double-handed weapons with broad blade and keen edge. Hard by were several blocks whereon the necks of the victims had lain, with here and there deep notches where the steel had bitten through the guard of flesh and shored into the wood. Round the chamber, placed in all sorts of irregular ways, were many implements of torture which made one's heart ache to see – chairs full of spikes which gave instant and excruciating pain; chairs and couches with dull knobs whose torture was seemingly less, but which, though slower, were equally efficacious – racks, belts, boots, gloves, collars, all made for compressing at will; steel baskets in which the head could be slowly crushed into a pulp if necessary; watchmen's hooks with long handle and knife that cut at resistance – this a specialty of the old Nurnberg police system; and many, many other devices for man's injury to man. Amelia grew quite pale with the horror of the things, but fortunately did not faint, for being a little overcome she sat down on a torture chair, but jumped up again with a shriek, all tendency to faint gone. We both pretended that it was the injury done to her dress by the dust of the chair and the rusty spikes which had upset her, and Mr Hutcheson acquiesced in accepting the explanation with a kind-hearted laugh.

But the central object in the whole of this chamber of horrors was the engine known as the Iron Virgin, which stood near the centre of the room. It was a rudely shaped figure of a woman, something of the bell order, or, to make a closer comparison, of the figure of Mrs Noah in the children's Ark, but without the slimness of waist and perfect *rondeur* of hip which marks the aesthetic type of the Noah family. One would hardly have recognized it as intended for a human figure at all had not the founder shaped on the forehead a rude semblance of a woman's face. This machine was coated with rust without and covered with dust; a rope was fastened to a ring in the front of the figure, about where the waist should have been, and was drawn through a pulley, fastened on the wooden pillar which sustained the flooring above. The custodian pulling this rope showed that a section of the front was hinged like a door at one side; we then saw that the engine was of considerable thickness, leaving just room enough inside for a man to be placed. The door was of equal thickness and of great weight, for it took the custodian all his strength, aided though he was by the contrivance of the pulley, to open it. This weight was partly due to the fact that the door was of manifest purpose hung so as to throw its weight downwards, so that it might shut of its own accord when the strain was released. The inside was honeycombed with rust – nay more, the rust alone that comes through time would hardly have eaten so deep into the iron walls; the rust of the cruel stains was deep indeed! It was only, however, when we came to look at the inside of the door that the diabolical intention was manifest to the full. Here were several long spikes, square and massive, broad at the base and sharp at the points, placed in such a position that when the door should close the upper ones would pierce the eyes of the victim, and the lower ones his heart and vitals. The sight was too much for poor Amelia, and this time she fainted dead off, and I had to carry her down the stairs and place her on a bench outside till she recovered. That she felt it to the quick was afterwards shown by the fact that my eldest son bears to this day a rude birthmark on his breast, which has, by family consent, been accepted as representing the Nurnberg Virgin.

When we got back to the chamber we found Hutcheson still opposite the Iron Virgin; he had been evidently philosophizing, and now gave us the benefits of this thought in the shape of a sort of exordium.

'Wall, I guess I've been learnin' somethin' here while madam has been gettin' over her faint. 'Pears to me that we're a long way behind the times on our side of the big drink. We uster think out on the plains that the Injun could give us points in tryin' to make a man oncomfortable; but I guess your old mediaeval law-and-order party could raise him every time. Splinters was pretty good in his bluff on the squaw, but this here young miss held a straight flush all high on him. The points of them spikes air sharp enough still, though even the edges air eaten out by what uster be on them. It'd be a good thing for our Indian section to get some specimens of this here play-toy to send round to the Reservations jest to knock the stuffin' out of the bucks, and the squaws too, by showing them as how old civilization lays over them at their best. Guess but I'll get in that box a minute jest to see how it feels!'

'Oh no! no!' said Amelia. 'It is too terrible!'

'Guess, ma'am, nothin's too terrible to the explorin' mind. I've been in some queer places in my time. Spent a night inside a dead horse while a prairie fire swept over me in Montana Territory – an' another time slept inside a dead buffler when the Comanches was on the warpath an' I didn't keer to leave my kyard on them. I've been two days in a caved-in tunnel in the Billy Broncho gold mine in New Mexico, an' was one of the four shut up for three parts of a day in the caisson what slid over on her side when we was settin' the foundations of the Buffalo Bridge. I've not funked an odd experience yet, an' I don't propose to begin now!'

We saw that he was set on the experiment, so I said: 'Well, hurry up, old man, and get through it quick.'

'All right, General,' said he, 'but I calculate we ain't quite ready yet. The gentlemen, my predecessors, what stood in that thar canister, didn't volunteer for the office – not much! And I guess there was some ornamental tyin' up before the big stroke was made. I want to go into this thing fair and square, so I must get fixed up proper first. I dare say this old galoot can rise some string and tie me up accordin' to sample?'

This was said interrogatively to the old custodian, but the latter, who understood the drift of his speech, though perhaps not appreciating to the full the niceties of dialect and imagery, shook his head. His protest was, however, only formal and made to be overcome. The American thrust a gold piece into his hand, saying, 'Take it, pard! it's your pot; and don't be skeer'd. This ain't no necktie party that you're asked to assist in!' He produced some thin frayed rope and proceeded to bind our companion with sufficient strictness for the purpose. When the upper part of his body was bound, Hutcheson said:

'Hold on a moment, Judge. Guess I'm too heavy for you to tote into the canister. You jest let me walk in, and then you can wash up regardin' my legs!'

Whilst speaking he had backed himself into the opening which was just enough to hold him. It was a close fit and no mistake. Amelia looked on with fear in her eyes, but she evidently did not like to say anything. Then the custodian completed his task by tying the American's feet together so that he was now absolutely helpless and fixed in his voluntary prison. He seemed to really enjoy it, and the incipient smile which was habitual to his face blossomed into actuality as he said:

'Guess this here Eve was made out of the rib of a dwarf! There ain't much room for a full-grown citizen of the United States to hustle. We uster make our coffins more roomier in Idaho territory. Now, Judge, you jest begin to let this door down, slow, on to me. I want to feel the same pleasure as the other jays had when those spikes began to move towards their eyes!'

'Oh no! no! no!' broke in Amelia hysterically. 'It is too terrible! I can't bear to see it! I can't! I can't!'

But the American was obdurate. 'Say, Colonel,' said he, 'why not take Madame for a little promenade? I wouldn't hurt her feelin's for the world; but now that I am here, havin' kem eight thousand miles, wouldn't it be too hard to give up the very experience I've been pinin' an' pantin' fur? A man can't get to feel like canned goods every time! Me and the Judge here'll fix up this thing in no time, an' then you'll come back, an' we'll all laugh together!'

Once more the resolution that is born of curiosity triumphed, and Amelia stayed holding tight to my arm and shivering whilst the custodian began to slacken slowly inch by inch the rope that held back the iron door. Hutcheson's face was positively radiant as his eyes followed the first movement of the spikes.

'Wall!' he said, 'I guess I've not had enjoyment like this since I left Noo York. Bar a scrap with a French sailor at Wapping – an' that warn't much of a picnic neither – I've not had a show fur real pleasure in this dod-rotted Continent, where there ain't no b'ars nor no Injuns, an' wheer nary man goes heeled. Slow there, Judge! Don't you rush this business! I want a show for my money this game – I du!'

The custodian must have had in him some of the blood of his pre-decessors in that ghastly tower, for he worked the engine with a deliberate and excruciating slowness which after five minutes, in which the outer edge of the door had not moved half as many inches, began to overcome Amelia. I saw her lips whiten and felt her hold upon my arm relax. I looked around an instant for a place whereon to lay her, and when I looked at her again found that her eye had become fixed on the side of the Virgin. Following its direction I saw the black cat crouching out of sight. Her green eyes shone like danger lamps in the gloom of the place, and their colour was heightened by the blood which still smeared her coat and reddened her mouth. I cried out:

'The cat! Look out for the cat!' for even then she sprang out before the engine. At this moment she looked like a triumphant demon. Her eyes blazed with ferocity, her hair bristled out till she seemed twice her normal size, and her tail lashed about as does a tiger's when the quarry is before it. Elias P. Hutcheson when he saw her was amused, and his eyes positively sparkled with fun as he said.

'Darned if the squaw hain't got on all her war paint! Jest give her a shove off if she comes any of her tricks on me, for I'm so fixed everlastingly by the boss, that durn my skin if I can keep my eyes from her if she wants them! Easy there, Judge! Don't you slack that ar rope or I'm euchered!'

At this moment Amelia completed her faint, and I had to clutch hold of her round the waist or she would have fallen to the floor. Whilst attending to her I saw the black cat crouching for a spring, and jumped up to turn the creature out.

But at that instant, with a sort of hellish scream, she hurled herself, not as we expected at Hutcheson, but straight at the face of the custodian. Her claws seemed to be tearing wildly as one sees in the Chinese draw-ings of the dragon rampant, and as I looked I saw one of them light on the poor man's eye, and actually tear through it and down his cheek, leaving a wide band of red where the blood seemed to spurt from every vein.

With a yell of sheer terror which came quicker than even his sense of pain, the man leaped back, dropping as he did so the rope which held back the iron door. I jumped for it, but was too late, for the cord ran like lightning through the pulley block, and the heavy mass fell forward from its own weight.

As the door closed I caught a glimpse of our poor companion's face. He seemed frozen with terror. His eyes stared with a horrible anguish, as if dazed, and no sound came from his lips.

And then the spikes did their work. Happily the end was quick, for when I wrenched open the door they had pierced so deep that they had locked in the bones of the skull through which they had crushed, and actually tore him – it – out of his own prison till, bound as he was, he fell at full length with a sickly thud upon the floor, the face turning upwards as he fell.

I rushed to my wife, lifted her up and carried her out, for I feared for her very reason if she should wake from her faint to such a scene. I laid her on the bench outside and ran back. Leaning against the wooden column was the custodian, moaning in pain while he held his reddening handkerchief to his eyes. And sitting on the head of the poor American was the cat, purring loudly as she licked the blood which trickled through the gashed socket of his eyes.

I think no one will call me cruel because I seized one of the old executioner's swords and shore her in two as she sat.

The Invaders

Terry Tapp

They came from the desert in their orderly files, a vast, rampaging army. Driven from their own land by shortage of food and an unnatural increase in population, they sought new frontiers.

The sick were left by the roadside to die; the young were carried and the elderly were murdered by their own families to conserve the food.

And as they breasted the hill the leader stopped and gazed down into the lush, green valley before him. At last the armies could stop for a while. There was food in plenty for everyone, and there would be time to rest, to eat and to make love again.

Rank on rank, the armies crowded to the top of the hill, hosts of hungry, desperate marauders. This, then, was the promised land.

Seth Kenyon rocked like the pendulum of a clock in his wickerwork chair. He hooked the jug of rough, raw spirit over his left elbow and kissed the lip of the container as if it were a woman. His tongue snaked into the jug, searching and probing; his eyes gazed down at the stained board porch as the liquid warmed and burned his throat.

When the jug was empty, all he had to do was shout for Ella to replace it, and another few hours of an interminably boring day would pass away.

Narrowing his eyes and looking southwards over the prairie, Seth could just make out the gigantic skeletons of the oil derricks striding across the horizon. He had been smart to sell the south pastures to those oil men, and, who knows, maybe there was more oil to be found on the land he had left to him.

So what was there for a man to do? The money was in the bank, and Seth had spent a small fortune diverting the mountain spring to irrigate the flat prairie land. He had paid Sam Herford for the grain and he had hired the men to plough and sow. Now it was nearly harvest time, and Seth would make a few thousand dollars more to add to his already fat bank balance.

'Ella!'

'Comin', Seth,' the voice responded wearily. 'You want another jug, honey?'

'What else would I be callin' you for?' he asked, a thin leer spreading across his unshaven face. Ella brought the jug out on to the porch, gave it to him and took the empty one in her hands. She looked at it for a moment and started to speak.

'Seth. Seth, honey ...'

'The answer is no.'

'But Seth, we got enough money to have ourselves a nice little place near town. Why can't we live near town?'

'I've told you before,' Seth growled bad-temperedly, 'I got no use for livin' near town. First thing you'll be wantin' fancy drapes and wall-coverin' like they got in the saloon. Then you'll be wantin' floor-coverin' and glossy furniture. It ain't no good goin' on that way, Ella. You see, it don't stop there. Once you get caught up in your ambitious ways, there's no tellin' what you'll want next.'

'I'd be happy with a nice little place,' Ella said. 'It don't have to be big and grand. Maybe we could have some flowers in the garden.' She grinned. 'It would be a change from acres of maize, Seth.'

'And what's so wrong with God's good corn?' Seth asked, not hesitating to use God's name when it suited him. 'Corn has been our livin', Ella. Don't you never forget it.'

'And corn liquor will be the death of you, Seth,' Ella said testily. 'Why, ever since those oil men bought the south pasture, you ain't done a day's work. You just sit out here and drink that gutrot stuff.'

'What I do is my own business,' Seth spluttered. 'I've married you, fathered a child for you and provided for you. What more do you expect of a man?'

Ella could have told him that she wanted to be loved, to be told now and then that she was pretty. She put her fingers to her face and knew that her skin was dried up and wrinkled by the heat of the sun. Dried up ...

'Where the hell's Alice got to?' Seth tried to change the subject. 'I don't favour her wanderin' out like she does.'

'She's probably near the foothills,' Ella told him absently. 'The child gets lonely, Seth.'

'Lonely, my ass!' Seth retorted.

Ella turned away. It was no good talking to Seth when he was drunk ... but then, Seth was nearly always drunk nowadays.

The sun scorched the twisted pine boards on the porch as Seth felt in his overall pocket for his pipe and puch. Away, maybe a hundred yards or so, he spied a bob-tailed rabbit. Not so long ago, he would have run into the cabin for his gun and stalked that rabbit, but Seth just let it be. There were sacks of salt meat in the cabin, and preserves, too. The larder bulged with flour and tobacco, and the cupboards were crammed with liquor. All the things Seth had been working his whole life for, and now he had them aplenty.

'If Alice don't get back, soon,' Seth called, 'you'd better get out an' look for her, Ella. Sometimes a stray cat comes down from the hills.'

He knew that the mention of mountain lions would get Ella worrying and that it wouldn't be long before she would set out to find Alice. Another swig at the jug and then a puff on the corn pipe. Yes, Seth told himself, I got everything a man could want.

He stretched his mind contentedly over the past twelve years from the time when he and Ella had first come to the prairie. It had been rough at first. The land had to be cleared, trees had to be chopped down and the cabin built. Seth grinned as he remembered the frantic race through summer to get those first few logs in place. If he didn't get the roof on the cabin and the grain sowed, they would all face starvation.

Alice was a babe in arms, and Seth had made a skin sack which he had strapped across Ella's back so that she could work, yet still be near her child. And they had worked in those days.

The cabin was soon built, and Ella made it her job to mix the mud for caulking up the framework. Every day, ten or fifteen times, she would struggle up the north hill and bring back two wooden buckets of water for making mud. Twenty, sometimes thirty or forty buckets a day. Then the dusty soil was mixed with a stick and daubed into the open cracks between the logs.

Seth had hewn the trees and sawn flat boards from them to make a floor; he had built the fireplace out of stone, and even taken time to put a mantleshelf where Ella could display the last remaining pieces of her mother's old tea set.

Side by side they had worked, out in rain and scorching heat, never caring how much their limbs screamed out in pain, so long as they were together and working to one purpose.

Purpose . . . that's what they had then.

Maybe Ella was right. Maybe they should move nearer town and take up a new challenge. Seth always felt like this during his second jug of the day. The only times that seemed to matter were when they were working together and doing things together.

'I'll go get Alice,' Ella said, coming out on to the porch and scanning the prairie with her hand over her forehead to shade her eyes from the sun. 'You reckon she's out near the foothills?'

'Either that, or up near the fork,' Seth replied.

The fork was the point where Seth had gone one day and promised Ella that she would soon have water from that spring flowing down past her front door.

'You'll never have to go up this hill again,' he had promised. 'I'm going to shift this stream for you, Ella.'

'Why, Seth!' Ella had laughed. He still remembered the laugh and the happy, admiring way she had looked at him. 'Why, Seth, you're going to kill yourself trying that.'

'Within a week,' he had promised. 'I'll have that stream paradin' past your front door within a week.'

It took him five days, and, when he finally kicked away the last few boulders to allow the stream to divert into the valley, he had felt good.

'I'll try the fork first,' Ella told him.

'No need,' Seth said. 'I see her now, runnin' like a deer.'

'Where? I can't see her ...'

'Over there,' Seth said. 'She's wavin' and shoutin'.'

'Foolishness,' Ella smiled. 'Young foolishness.'

'Yes,' Seth agreed. 'See her run, though. She's gettin' to have a figure already. I fancy she's growin' up like you used to be, Ella. She's goin' to be a fine girl.'

'Seth, there's something wrong with her ... Look!'

Alice was screaming and thrashing her arms in the air. Her hair was flying out behind her as Ella and Seth watched ...

High up on the hill, less than two miles from the cabin, the armies watched.

The legions had now all assembled and they stood like statues, waiting for the leader to give his signal. All eyes were on the tiny figure as she soundlessly screamed and ran across the prairie. The scouting party had undoubtedly seen her and would be on their way back to the main body. But the troops were hungry, and the leader knew that he couldn't hold them back for much longer.

They had been a determined and disciplined army, following the leader across the most inhospitable desert and out into the lush, green lands which lay before them. He glanced around at their emaciated bodies and tired faces.

It was time.

He raised a clawed arm above his head like a flag, held it there for a second and then brought it down sharply. The army of ravenous creatures advanced.

'Mamma! They're comin' ... comin' from the hills!' Alice screamed.

'Who, my darling? Who's coming?' Ella cried as she rushed down the porch steps to take her daughter into her open arms.

'Ant things! Thousands of them! Millions!'

Alice beat herself with her hands, brushing off the hundreds of vicious, angry creatures.

'Seth! Come over here!' Ella screamed. 'The poor child's smothered in the damn things!'

'Ants,' Seth said eaily. 'Blasted ant hills, that's what young Alice has been sittin' on.'

'They aren't ants, Seth. Bigger'n that by far,' Ella cried. 'They're bitin' her, Seth. Come over and help me.'

'And there's more of them, Dad,' Alice cried. 'Millions and millions of them. They're up on the hill there,' she said, pointing into the distance.

'Cloud shadows,' Seth reckoned, holding his hand to shield his eyes against the glare of the sun.

'Help me, Seth!' Ella screamed. 'By Christ . . . these things have bitten through to her bones.'

'What?'

'Through to her bones, I say.'

Seth walked over to examine Alice's leg. There were hundreds of the ant-like creatures gathered around an opening wound. They were raking and clawing back the skin, dipping their claws into the lake of blood and drinking. He could see it as plain as day.

'Off!' he cried. 'Get the damn things off her, Ella! By God, it's awful . . . evil!'

'Get her to the stream, Seth!' Ella screamed, frantically beating at the enraged creatures.

'Mamma! I can't stand it! Do somethin', quick!'

Seth gathered Alice in his arms and ran across the flower patch to the deepest part of the diverted stream. Without pausing, he waded into the water, brushing and slapping at Alice, scraping off the smothering mass of red creatures.

'Damned parasite things!' Seth yelled.

'You're hurting, Daddy!'

'Hold your breath, child!' Seth took Alice by the hair and dragged her under the water as Ella watched helplessly. She looked down into the creaming, crystal stream and saw her daughter and her husband. They were a million miles away. Water distorted their features, but she could plainly see Seth staring straight into Alice's face. His eyes had a look of grim determination in them – like the time when Seth was building the cabin. Then, as sure as sure, Ella knew it would be all right.

Blood from Alice's wound was gliding out of her leg, pink and filmy in the water. The terrible, bloodthirsty creatures were releasing their hold on her, letting go and floating away with the current. After what seemed to be forever, Seth emerged triumphant.

'There,' he spluttered. 'There now, child. They things won't get at you now.'

Alice looked at her father, threw her arms around his stubbly neck and cried like a new-born child.

'Come into the house,' Ella said, hardly able to keep from crying herself. 'Come into the house, my darlings.'

Arms around each other, they were walking towards the house when Seth suddenly let out a cry. 'Ella! Look over there!'

The whole hill was alive with movement as the army swept down – wave after wave of hostile, rampaging creatures. Each one was harmless enough on its own, but as an army they were invincible.

'What in hell is it?' Seth cried.

'Them ant things, Daddy,' Alice said. 'That's what I saw up there in the foothills. They're eating everything in sight.'

Like a slow motion scythe, the army cut deeply into the prairie grass, gorging, destroying and advancing all the time.

A bird shrieked in alarm, flying up high into the sky, its whole body thick with insectile life. Feathers dropped as the rapacious creatures fed, even as the bird shrieked higher and higher into the sun. Then, quite suddenly, the battle was over. With a final cry, the bird fell back to the earth, and was instantly smothered by the army of devouring creatures. And when the whole army had passed over the place where the bird had fallen ... there was nothing. There was no grass, no white bones, no feathers. The destruction was total.

'Get into the house,' Seth said slowly. 'You get into the house and put Alice up on the top bunk bed.'

Ella hurried indoors, cradling Alice in her arms.

'Water,' Seth cried. 'I'll divert the stream to the cornfields. That'll stop them.'

Grabbing a spade in his hands, he ran across to the banked-up edges of the stream and started to dig. With any luck, the stream would almost flood the corn and maybe make a crescent around the cabin. But the spade was not fast enough for him. 'Ella!' he screamed. 'You come out here and help me!'

'Seth? What is it?'

'This bank is hard as clay. If I break it with a pick-axe, you drag the lumps away. Hurry ... we don't have much time.'

'Look over there Seth ... the linny tree!'

He looked over to the edge of the cornfield where the linny tree grew. One day, he had promised, he would chop that hard tree down and make a shed out of it. One day ... when he had the time.

Together, they watched the old tree groan with anguish as it became painted red with the liquid army. It drooped its arms and fell face first into the seething lake of creatures, and within a few minutes it had entirely gone.

'Seth, we ain't going to do nothin' about them things,' Ella roared. 'We don't stand a chance. Let's run while we've got the time.'

She was right. The armies were advancing mercilessly towards the cabin. Stretched out over the hills, and back as far as the eye could see, the vast host of creatures seemed to have one target – the cabin. The sun reflected from their shiny, shell-like backs as they wrestled with grass and felled huge stems of bloated corn. Yet still they marched purposefully onward.

'Get Alice!' Seth shouted. 'You get her while I whistle up for the horse.'

Pushing his fingers into his mouth, Seth let out a piercing whistle. 'Here boy!' he yelled. 'Come over here!'

Suddenly he saw the stallion, pawing the ground near the edge of the corn. Obviously some of the scouting party of the creatures had found him already.

Seth let out a shout and ran across the grass towards the horse. 'Get off him you ... you ...' he couldn't finish. Even from this distance he could see that the stallion had given up the fight against such an army. The legs, the belly and the body filled up with them as they crawled and savaged pitilessly. Into the eyes, the nostrils and the gaping mouth. Seth actually saw the teeth shatter out of the mouth as the stallion groaned and sank to the ground, suffocating and blinded. The pain must have been too great to bear, for the great creature gave a shiver and was still. Then, after a few minutes, the dark pile of seething creatures climbed down ... dissolved away. Nothing was left.

When Seth turned his attention back to the stream, both Alice and Ella were digging away with their fingers. He ran over and knelt beside them, digging and clawing for life.

Still the army advanced, destroying every living thing – animal and vegetable. The cornfield soon became alive with them. The noise was increasing as the stems of corn fell and were devoured as if by blood-red fire.

'It's breaking!' Ella sobbed. 'The bank is breaking, Seth!'

'Faster!' Seth cried. 'Faster, darlin's. We can do it!'

With a gurgling noise, the river burst through the remaining banked-up earth and spurted out towards the cornfield. Seth, Ella and Alice were thrown on their backs by the sheer force of the water as it leaped from its prison and spread over the land.

'By Christ!' Seth cried. 'We got the bastards!'

Like a small tidal wave, the water rushed out to meet the advancing army of creatures, carrying mud, stones and even small rocks with its force. Cleaving a path through the army, the wash sent the creatures scurrying aside in panic. But most were too late. Within a few minutes, the whole cornfield was awash with floating debris and bodies.

'We done it!' Seth screamed. 'By Christ, we done it, Ella!'

Now the foothills were bare of the creatures and the cornfield was awash with the bodies of the dead. Some hundred yards away, the main army had stopped, sensing the danger ahead.

The water washed around the log cabin, almost enclosing it completely.

'I think we beat 'em,' Seth said, putting his arm around Ella. 'We beat 'em.'

'We sure did,' Ella sobbed. 'We sure beat them, Seth.' It was like the old times again, and even Alice sensed the freshness and new life as they walked into the cabin.

Meanwhile, out on the prairie, the creatures were dragging the dead bodies out of the water and piling them on top of each other in neat lines. The sun went down, and the moon provided light as the creatures worked furiously to construct a bridge of dead bodies.

And when the sun came up again, there was only a stone fireplace to mark the spot where Seth and his family had died. Just a stone fireplace, some household crockery and a couple of empty liquor jars.

The Pioneers of Pike's Peak

Basil Tozer

It was a perfect night about the end of June, the sort of night common enough in Colorado at that time of the year. At the end of the game we rose from the card-table and strolled out into the cool, refreshing air. The stars were shining with extraordinary brilliance in a sky so clear that one seemed almost to hear them winking. The moon had not yet risen above the range of mighty peaks which tower into the heavens until their crests gradually vanish into great belts of clouds, and at night seem to touch the lowermost of the celestial bodies; but a sort of halo, gradually spreading, served to show that presently the moon herself would shed a flood of light from the summit of the highest peaks down into the little village nestling at the feet of the mighty range. No sound broke the perfect stillness. The very houses seemed to sleep.

It was only when my friend and I re-entered the smoky bar saloon, where our companions, grown tired of card playing, were now quietly talking, that we noticed an odd-looking and apparently elderly stranger seated alone beside a little window at the farther end of the room. The window was open, and he was starting through it vacantly, interrupting his reverie only now and again in order to blow a long cloud of smoke into the air. My friend cast a glance of inquiry in his direction.

'He came in about five minutes ago,' one of the card-players said.

'Who is he?'

'Some crank, I suppose. He has not stirred since he sat down there.'

'What is he staring at?' someone asked presently.

'Pike's Peak, apparently,' replied Watson, the man who had called the stranger a crank.

Though the words were spoken in an undertone, the 'crank' evidently overheard them, for he turned his head and frowned. Then he resumed his former position – his vigil. Conversation drifted from one topic to another, until the subject of the Rocky Mountains in particular engrossed our attention.

'And who really was the first to reach the top of Pike's Peak?' Watson asked, looking round at us.

'Not Pike himself,' answered a man named Norton. 'They say that some man – Look out, you fellows!'

The stranger had left his seat and was approaching us with a slow, stealthy tread, his eyes oddly dilated. We all turned to face him. He was a man of immense proportions, well over six feet in height, and could not have been over fifty years of age, though he looked quite sixty. His hair was white and rather long. He had evidently been handsome in his day, but now the face, neck and hands were disfigured by numberless little sunken blotches not unlike the pits left by smallpox. He wore an old drab suit, a coon cap, thick boots, and leather leggings.

'Who did you say first reached the top of Pike's Peak?' he asked in a threatening, hollow voice. He had dropped into a chair on the opposite side of the table beside me. Norton, whom he had interrupted, came to the rescue.

'I believe that——'

'*I* was the first to reach it! You don't know the story of our ascent?'

'I know only what I have read and been told,' Norton said.

'You yourself have been up Pike's Peak?'

'I have – by the funicular.'

'You have seen the summit, then?'

'Yes.'

'And what did you see that struck you most – there, fifteen thousand feet above the sea's level?'

Norton had an inspiration.

'Do you mean the stone?' he said.

Instantly the stranger's expression changed. He looked round at us all quite intelligently.

'It *is* there then?' he inquired eagerly, bending forward across the table.

'Of course it is there,' Norton replied. 'I can give you the inscription word for word.'

'Do. What is it? Tell me, what is it?'

'The inscription says: "*This stone is erected in memory of William Dawkins, James Weston, and Walter Hellier, Pioneers of Pike's Peak, who were devoured by mountain rats while endeavouring to reach this summit.*"'

'Ah!' he ejaculated, greatly relieved. 'I am glad it is there – I am glad it is still there. Do you know the story of my friends, the story of those pioneers?'

He had grown suddenly calm. He seemed suddenly to have regained his reason. Our interest and curiosity were now thoroughly aroused. We could see that the stranger was quite sober and though his mind seemed unhinged, he had now a lucid interval.

We noticed that he poured brandy into his tumbler until it was three parts full. Just then the moon shone over the summit of the famous peak, and from where we sat the outline of the glorious mountain could be clearly discerned. Watson drew the stranger's attention to it. An odd, bitter smile flitted across his face. It was the first time we had seen him smile. He sighed once, but did not utter a word. Then his gaze became again riveted on the gigantic peak.

'Pike never would – never could have reached it. He tried several times. Finally he stood upon a hill near the stalactite caves at the base of my mountain, and, pointing with his arm at the summit, said: "No mortal man will ever tread that peak."

'But we – *we* were determined to. Our friends shook us by the hands and bade us farewell.

' "But you are fools," they said. "You will never come back. You don't know what you may meet in those mountains. You know what Pike said when he came back. You know the tale he told. And some things he would not tell."

' "Don't go, oh, don't go!" my wife cried in agony.

'I loved her, yet I forced her from me. She was but a unit. In the success of our enterprise lay the welfare of thousands. I told her that to comfort her. It was the last time I saw her alive.

'Early in the morning we started. We took with us arms, food and drink for many days, and the bare necessities of life. We carried everything ourselves. We knew where and how Pike had failed. We would succeed.

'A week later we were fairly in the midst of difficulties. The work was terribly severe, but we had determination, strength and courage. We had expected to find obstacles, and we were not disappointed. Here enormous boulders which had to be circumvented, there unlooked-for waterfalls and ravines that delayed us, besides vegetation so thick that in places we had to hack our way through it. Then the unknown dangers. There might be snakes concealed among those immense boulders; there might be death-dealing plants such as flourish in South America – indeed, we did not know what there might not be. But we did not pause to consider those things.

'Over a fortnight went by. As we mounted gradually higher and higher our spirits rose as if in sympathy. Far down in the valley we had once or twice during our progress caught glimpses of this very townlet, now called Colorado Springs, also of the village of Manitou. Tiny villages, indeed, they were in those days; and as we saw them from those great heights they looked like little chessboards upon a vast expanse of prairie. And still we fought our way upward.

'How long our expedition had been started I cannot quite remember, when our surrounding gradually changed. In place of rock and black soil we now quite remember, when our surroundings gradually changed. In place of rock and black soil we now came upon wide tracks of sandy formation. The undergrowth was still dense, however, though here and there thousands upon thousands of slim fir trees lay rotting upon the ground, evidently swept down by terrific storms, for storms in these mountains sweep down trees as a reaping machine sweeps down standing corn. Sometimes we came upon broad, open spaces, spaces swept clear apparently in early days by giant waterfalls long since dried up. Then, as we penetrated still higher, and the vegetation decreased in density, even the boulders grew smaller. They now looked as though in prehistoric times they had been flung together by a tremendous seismic disturbance.

' "Have you noticed," one of my comrades remarked one day, "what a quantity of insects there are here? And the rats are getting more plentiful. We seldom see any of those grey squirrels now."

'As he spoke he stamped his foot upon an immense brown spider that was running away. Its body burst with a crack, and glutinous liquid spurted out all round his boot. Almost instantly several spiders ran out from beneath a large stone as if to ascertain what had happened. They stopped. For a moment they seemed for all the world as if they looked at us – looked at us with a malignant, vindictive expression. Then they scuttled away.

' "I believe I felt several of those spiders scampering over my face last night," he continued. "You had better be careful; they bite like mischief. These mountains are famous for them, and – just look at that!"

'A couple of large rats were chasing an enormous spider across a long, flat boulder. A moment later spider and rats disappeared over the edge.

' "They say that mountain rats will devour any living thing." Weston said presently." They will eat us if we don't watch them!" he added in jest.

'During the early part of the afternoon we had made good progress, when suddenly we came upon a large sloping tract of bare white sand. The sun, still high in the heavens, shone down upon it, and at first sight the sand seemed to be alive with small, moving bodies.

' "Talk of spiders!" Dawkins said, laughing. "Did you ever see anything like that?'

'We had long ago, in previous expeditions, grown accustomed to surprises. Few things astonished us now. Never in our lives, however, had we seen such and assemblage. There must have been thousands upon thousands of them running about in every direction, colliding with one another and tumbling over one another apparently for no reason. The sight made me think of a gigantic ants' nest overrun with mammoth ants, and an odd sort of smell that for several days had pervaded the air struck our nostrils with renewed strength.

'Now, as we stepped forward into the open tract, a strange thing happened, for the entire space, which a moment before had been alive, became instantly motionless. The spiders were all there, right under our eyes, but of one accord they had stopped running. Oddly enough, too, every spider was now facing us. Instinctively we felt that we had become objects of intense curiosity. And as we stood there, interested and amused, we could distinctly see the spiders' great eyes sticking out and evidently watching us. The sight would have given some people "the creeps", but we rather enjoyed it.

' "Pish! you hideous things," Dawkins said, pitching a pebble into their midst. In less than a minute hardly a spider was to be seen.

' "If we describe that sight when we get back we shall be called liars," Weston said, glancing at his watch. "I've seen insects in my time, but never anything like that."

'The offensive smell was still strong in the air, and as we progressed it increased. Once or twice it became almost unbearable. We had now a long stretch of clear going before us, so we hastened to avail ourselves of it by advancing briskly. And still we saw spiders at every turn, spiders by the thousand sunning themselves on every rock and boulder, great brown spiders with fat, oval bodies, and with thick, hairy legs bent in grotesque curves. I kicked over a stunted little tree that lay rotting – ugh! Quite two or three hundred spiders must have scuttled away from under it.

' "This is getting beyond a joke," Hellier, who seldom spoke, and was generally considered to be rather surly, suddenly said. "I tell you what it is: these spiders will go for us."

' "Like Weston's rats!" Dawkins said, laughing at him, and we were still chaffing Hellier and Weston when Dawkins happened to look round.

' "Why, Harry!" he exclaimed.

'There was anxiety in his tone, and I felt his hand grip my shoulder. And no wonder. Though anything but a coward, Dawkins could not help at once realizing what we all realized a moment later – that Hellier's evil omen was more than likely to come true. A sickening feeling of fear had come over him.

'For there, barely fifty yards away, a reddish-brown mass gradually assuming the form of a crescent was steadily, swiftly gliding over the sand, steadily and swiftly overtaking us. And as it approached we could see thousands and thousands of spiders hastening towards it from every direction and quickly increasing its size. The swarm when we saw it first must have covered between twelve and fifteen square feet. Before it had glided over another twenty yards of sand the entire mass was about one-third as large again. Yet a sort of horrible fascination kept us rooted to the spot where we now stood watching the swarm approach. In order to brace up our courage we told one another that the spiders could not be pursuing us at all; that if we moved aside they would pass us by. But in our hearts we knew that we tried to think a lie. And when we moved aside in order to convince ourselves the creeping crescent immediately swayed round towards us and seemed if anything to advance more quickly.

'Suddenly the intense horror of the situation flashed across my mind and struck terror into our hearts. For what could we do to avert the terrible fate that threatened us? Savage animals we might have coped with; treacherous human beings, even, we might have bested; but now we were face to face with a peril totally unexpected, utterly loathsome and unassailable.

' "Our only chance lies in flight," Hellier said bitterly.

' "Flight! And where shall we fly to? The top of the mountain, I suppose. Look there, Hellier."

'It was Dawkins who spoke, and he spoke in tones of scorn. Looking around us, we now saw what we had not noticed before. We were surrounded. Everywhere we saw spiders – spiders approaching in brown, gliding crescents of varying sizes. And over a hundred yards away the largest and darkest mass of all could clearly be distinguished, also winding its way along the sand, also approaching, also crossing us in. And as this great crescent surged undulatingly, unswervingly across the hillocks and irregularities in the surface of the soil and sand it resembled the great wave of a sluggish, turbid stream leaving a factory sluice.

' "Fire into them!" I exclaimed, slipping a couple of shot cartridges into my gun. The two charges cut a lane in the approaching wave, but almost instantly the lane closed up and the undulating mass advanced as if nothing had happened. Together Dawkins and Weston fired four barrels. Rather a broader lane this time; but again it closed up. I had reloaded.

' "Give them a volley," Weston called out; "that may turn them."

'We did so, but by the time the smoke had cleared, the swarm had well-nigh resumed its former size and shape. Could we sweep a lane with our eight barrels and then rush through it? No, that was obviously impossible; the width of the wave was too great. And still recruits were pouring in upon every side, and as we fired volley after volley into the quickly approaching swarms in the vain hope of turning them, the distant ravines rang again and again with echoes.

' "My God, we are done for!" came despairingly from Hellier, as for the twentieth time he closed his gun with a snap.

'Our barrels had now become almost too hot to hold, and still the hideous, crawling waves, which must have contained trillions of spiders, were fast approaching with a strange swaying motion, and rapidly narrowing our little circle. In a few minutes they would be upon us, overrunning us, dragging us down. Already many stragglers were running up our legs and over our bodies. Now the first swarm was so near that we could distinctly hear it rushing up us, and – ah! the smell, how it still hangs in my nostrils . . .'

For a moment the stranger stopped. His eyes were widely distended. His limbs trembled. He clutched the table frantically, in order to support himself.

'Suddenly I saw several spiders run up Weston's face and fix upon his eyes. With a scream he dashed them away, but as he did so his eyes began to swell, for the brutes had bitten him badly.'

He stopped again. He was quivering all over with excitement. Suddenly he dashed from his seat to the farthermost corner of the room.

'Keep them from me! Keep them off!' he cried, glaring wildly all round the floor. 'Look at them now – look at them – ah! God help me! – help me! – help me! ...'

He sprang to right and left, then towards the door. Perspiration was pouring down his face. Then suddenly he snatched wildly at imaginary spiders running up his sleeves and legs, running up his body, running over his head, over his face, over his eyes, into his mouth. It was a dreadful sight.

'Stop him!' my friend cried out, jumping from his seat and rushing towards the old man; but as he approached a blindly directed blow from the stranger's fist almost stunned him, and the innkeeper and two rough-looking men entered the room.

'Hold him, boys,' the innkeeper said calmly, as the two men pounced upon the stranger and the innkeeper sauntered towards us.

'Poor fellow,' he said, 'I always have to be ready for him – look at him now, yet the doctors pronounce him sane. He often is sane, of course, but when I heard him starting on the spiders and saw him drinking brandy I knew what to expect.'

'Is there any truth in his spider story?' I asked.

'Any truth? It's all truth – at least, that's my belief. Though I was quite a lad at the time the expedition started, I can remember it well. Four of them there were, all strong and hearty when they sat out. Two months later *he* came back.'

'Did he alone escape?'

'He alone came back – came back quite done for and disfigured all over with red blotches. Afterwards they turned into pits. Some years later another expedition went up and reached the summit, but they always maintained that rats, not spiders, devoured those poor fellows, so they set a stone with an inscription on it at the top of the mountain – you have seen it, no doubt.'

'What do you yourself think they were killed by?'

'I don't think anything. As sure as you are standing there they were devoured by swarms of great spiders, as Mad Harry had told you. I have heard him tell the story often enough, and he always tells the same story. These marks are not rats' bites.'

'It's a horrible place, that mountain,' he said, looking at its rugged peak so clearly outlined in the moonlight. 'Though you can go up it now by the winding funicular, which is eight miles long, you don't know what horrors may exist in other parts of it. Many a man has gone into those mountains, but few have ever returned.'

Blind Man's Buff

H. Russell Wakefield

'Well, thank heavens that yokel seemed to know the place,' said Mr Cort to himself. ' "First to the right, second to the left, black gates." I hope the oaf in Wendover who sent me six miles out my way will freeze to death. It's not often like this in England – cold as the penny in a dead man's eye.' He'd barely reach the place before dusk. He let the car out over the rasping, frozen roads. 'First to the right' – must be this – second to the left, must be this – and there were the black gates. He got out, swung them open, and drove cautiously up a narrow, twisting drive, his headlights peering suspiciously round the bends. Those hedges wanted clipping, he thought, and this lane would have to be remetalled – full of holes. Nasty drive up on a bad night; would cost some money, though.

The car began to climb steeply and swing to the right, and presently the high hedges ended abruptly, and Mr Cort pulled up in front of Lorn Manor. He got out of the car, rubbed his hands, stamped his feet, and looked about him.

Lorn Manor was embedded half-way up a Chiltern spur and, as the agent had observed, 'commanded extensive vistas'. The place looked its age, Mr Cort decided, or rather ages, for the double Georgian brick chimneys warred with the Queen Anne left front. He could just make out the date, 1703, at the base of the nearest chimney. All that wing must have been added later. 'Big place, marvellous bargain at seven thousand; can't understand it. How those windows with their little curved eyebrows seem to frown down on one!' And then he turned and examined the 'vistas'. The trees were tinted exquisitely to an uncertain glory as the great red sinking sun flashed its rays on their crystal mantle. The Vale of Aylesbury was drowsing beneath a slowly deepening shroud of mist. Above it the hills, their crests rounded and shaded by silver and rose coppices, seemed to have set in them great smoky eyes of flame where the last rays burned in them.

'It is like some dream world,' thought Mr Cort. 'It is curious how, wherever the sun strikes it seems to make an eye, and each one fixed on

me; those hills, even those windows. But, judging from that mist, I shall
have a slow journey home; I'd better have a quick look inside, though
I have already taken a prejudice against the place – I hardly know why.
Too lonely and isolated, perhaps.' And then the eyes blinked and closed,
and it was dark. He took a key from his pocket and went up three steps
and thrust it into the key-hole of the massive oak door. The next moment
he looked forward into absolute blackness, and the door swung to and
closed behind him. This, of course, must be the 'palatial panelled hall'
which the agent described. He must strike a match and find the light-
switch. He fumbled in his pockets without success, and then he went
through them again. He thought for a moment. 'I must have left them
on the seat in the car,' he decided; 'I'll go and fetch them. The door must
be just behind me here.'

He turned and groped his way back, and then drew himself up sharply,
for it had seemed that something had slipped past him, and then he put
out his hands – to touch the back of a chair, brocaded, he judged. He
moved to the left of it and walked into a wall, changed his direction, went
back past the chair, and found the wall again. He went back to the chair,
sat down, and went through his pockets again, more thoroughly and
carefully this time. Well, there was nothing to get fussed about; he was
bound to find the door sooner or later. Now, let him think. When he came
in he had gone straight forward, three yards perhaps; but he couldn't
have gone straight back, because he'd stumbled into this chair. The door
must be a little to the left or right of it. He'd try each in turn. He turned
to the left first, and found himself going down a little narrow passage; he
could feel its sides when he stretched out his hands. Well, then, he'd try
the right. He did so, and walked into a wall. He groped his way along
it, and again it seemed as if something slipped past him. 'I wonder if
there's a bat in here?' he asked himself, and then found himself back at
the chair.

How Rachel would laugh if she could see him now. Surely he had a
stray match somewhere. He took off his overcoat and ran his hands round
the seam of every pocket, and then he did the same to the coat and
waistcoat of his suit. And then he put them on again. Will, he'd try again.
He'd follow the wall along. He did so, and found himself in a narrow
passage. Suddenly he shot out his right hand, for he had the impression
that something had brushed his face very lightly. 'I'm beginning to get
a little bored with that bat, and with this blasted room generally,' he said
to himself. 'I could imagine a more nervous person than myself getting
a little fussed and panicky; but that's the one thing not to do.' Ah, here
was that chair again. 'Now, I'll try the wall the other side.' Well, that
seemed to go on for ever, so he retraced his steps till he found the chair,
and sat down again. He whistled a little snatch resignedly. What an echo!
The little tune had been flung back at him so fiercely, almost menacingly.

Menacingly: that was just the feeble, panicky word a nervous person would use. Well, he'd go to the left again this time.

As he got up, a quick spurt of cold air fanned his face. 'Is anyone there?' he said. He had purposely not raised his voice – there was no need to shout. Of course, no one answered. Who could there have been to answer, since the caretaker was away? Now let him think it out. When he came in he must have gone straight forward and then swerved slightly on the way back; therefore – no, he was getting confused. At that moment he heard the whistle of a train, and felt reassured. The line from Wendover to Aylesbury ran half-left from the front door, so it should be about there – he pointed with his finger, got up, groped his way forward, and found himself in a little narrow passage. Well, he must turn back and go to the right this time. He did so, and something seemed to slip just past him, and then he scratched his finger slightly on the brocade of the chair. 'Talk about a maze,' he thought to himself; 'it's nothing to this.' And then he said to himself, under his breath: 'Curse this vile, Godforsaken place!' A silly, panicky thing to do he realized – almost as bad as shouting aloud. Well, it was obviously no use trying to find the door, he *couldn't* find it – *couldn't*. He'd sit in the chair till the light came. He sat down.

How very silent it was: his hands began searching in his pockets once more. Except for that sort of whispering sound over on the left somewhere – except for that, it was absolutely silent – except for that. What could it be? The caretaker was away. He turned his head slightly and listened intently. It was almost as if there were several people whispering together. One got curious sounds in old houses. How absurd it was! The chair couldn't be more than three or four yards from the door. There was no doubt about that. I must be slightly to one side or the other. He'd try the left once more. He got up, and something lightly brushed his face. 'Is anyone there?' he said, and this time he knew he had shouted. 'Who touched me? Who's whispering? Where's the door?' What a nervous fool he was to shout like that; yet someone outside might have heard him. He went groping forward again, and touched a wall. He followed along it, touching it with his finger-tips, and there was an opening.

The door, the door, it must be! And he found himself going down a little narrow passage. He turned and ran back. And then he remembered! He had put a match-booklet in his note-case! What a fool to have forgotten it, and made such an exhibition of himself. Yes, there it was; but his hands were trembling, and the booklet slipped through his fingers. He fell to his knees, and began searching about on the floor. 'It must be just here, it can't be far' – and then something icy-cold and damp was pressed against his forehead. He flung himself forward to seize it, but there was nothing there. And then he leapt to his feet, and with tears streaming down his face cried: 'Who is there? Save me! Save me!' And then he began to run round and round, his arms outstreched. At last he stumbled against something, the chair – and something touched him as it slipped past. And then he ran screaming round the room; and suddenly his screams slashed back at him, for he was in a little narrow passage.

'Now, Mr Runt,' said the coroner, 'you say you heard screaming coming from the direction of the Manor. Why didn't you go to find out what was the matter?'

'None of us chaps goes to Manor after sundown,' said Mr Runt.

'Oh, I know there's some absurd superstition about the house; but you haven't answered the question. There were screams, obviously coming from someone who wanted help. Why didn't you go to see what was the matter, instead of running away?'

'None of us chaps goes to Manor after sundown,' said Mr Runt.

'Don't fence with the question. Let me remind you that the doctor said Mr Cort must have had a seizure of some kind, but that had help been quickly forthcoming, his life might have been saved. Do you mean to tell me that, even if you had known this, you would still have acted in so cowardly a way?'

Mr Runt fixed his eyes on the ground and fingered his cap.

'None of us chaps goes to Manor after sundown,' he repeated.

Mr Loveday's Little Outing

Evelyn Waugh

I

'You will not find your father greatly changed,' remarked Lady Moping, as the car turned into the gates of the County Asylum.

'Will he be wearing a uniform?' asked Angela.

'No, dear, of course not. He is receiving the very best attention.'

It was Angela's first visit and it was being made at her own suggestion.

Ten years had passed since the showery day in late summer when Lord Moping had been taken away; a day of confused but bitter memories for her; the day of Lady Moping's annual garden party, always bitter, confused that day by the caprice of the weather which, remaining clear and brilliant with promise until the arrival of the first guests, had suddenly blackened into a squall. There had been a scuttle for cover; the marquee had capsized; a frantic carrying of cushions and chairs; a table-cloth lofted to the boughs of the monkey-puzzler, fluttering in the rain; a bright period and the cautious emergence of guests on to the soggy lawns; another squall; another twenty minutes of sunshine. It had been an abominable afternoon, culminating at about six o'clock in her father's attempted suicide.

Lord Moping habitually threatened suicide on the occasion of the garden party; that year he had been found black in the face, hanging by his braces in the orangery; some neighbours, who were sheltering there from the rain, set him on his feet again, and before dinner a van had called for him. Since then Lady Moping had paid seasonal calls at the asylum and returned in time for tea, rather reticent of her experience.

Many of her neighbours were inclined to be critical of Lord Moping's accommodation. He was not, of course, an ordinary inmate. He lived in a separate wing of the asylum, specially devoted to the segregation of wealthier lunatics. These were given every consideration which their foibles permitted. They might choose their own clothes (many indulged in the liveliest fancies), smoke the most expensive brands of cigars and, on the anniversaries of their certification, entertain any other inmates for whom they had an attachment to private dinner parties.

The fact remained, however, that it was far from being the most expensive kind of institution; the uncompromising address, 'COUNTY HOME FOR MENTAL DEFECTIVES', stamped across the notepaper, worked on the uniforms of their attendants, painted, even, upon a prominent hoarding at the main entrance, suggested the lowest associations. From time to time, with less or more tact, her friends attempted to bring to Lady Moping's notice particulars of seaside nursing homes, of 'qualified practitioners with large private grounds suitable for the charge or nervous of difficult cases', but she accepted them lightly; when her son came of age he might make any changes that he thought fit; meanwhile she felt no inclination to relax her economical régime; her husband had betrayed her basely on the one day in the year when she looked for loyal support, and was far better off than he deserved.

A few lonely figures in great-coats were shuffling and loping about the park.

'Those are the lower-class lunatics,' observed Lady Moping. 'There is a very nice little flower garden for people like your father. I sent them some cuttings last year.'

They drove past the blank, yellow brick façade to the doctor's private entrance and were received by him in the 'visitors room', set aside for interviews of this kind. The window was protected on the inside by bars and wire netting; there was no fireplace; when Angela nervously attempted to move her chair further from the radiator, she found that it was screwed to the floor.

'Lord Moping is quite ready to see you,' said the doctor.

'How is he?'

'Oh, very well, very well indeed, I'm glad to say. He had rather a nasty cold some time ago, but apart from that his condition is excellent. He spends a lot of his time in writing.'

They heard a shuffling, skipping sound approaching along the flagged passage. Outside the door a high peevish voice, which Angela recognized as her father's, said: 'I haven't the time, I tell you. Let them come back later.'

A gentler tone, with a slight rural burr, replied, 'Now come along. It is a purely formal audience. You need stay no longer than you like.'

Then the door was pushed open (it had no lock or fastening) and Lord Moping came into the room. He was attended by an elderly little man with full white hair and an expression of great kindness.

'That is Mr Loveday who acts as Lord Moping's attendant.'

'Secretary,' said Lord Moping. He moved with a jogging gait and shook hands with his wife.

'This is Angela. You remember Angela, don't you?'

'No, I can't say that I do. What does she want?'

'We just came to see you.'

'Well, you have come at an exceedingly inconvenient time. I am very busy. Have you typed out that letter to the Pope yet, Loveday?'

'No, my lord. If you remember, you asked me to look up the figures about the Newfoundland fisheries first?'

'So I did. Well, it is fortunate, as I think the whole letter will have to be redrafted. A great deal of new information has come to light since luncheon. A great deal ... You see, my dear, I am fully occupied.' He turned his restless, quizzical eyes upon Angela. 'I suppose you have come about the Danube. Well, you must come again later. Tell them it will be all right, quite all right, but I have not had time to give my full attention to it. Tell them that.'

'Very well, Papa.'

'Anyway,' said Lord Moping rather petulantly, 'it is a matter of secondary importance. There is the Elbe and the Amazon and the Tigris to be dealt with first, eh, Loveday? ... *Danube* indeed. Nasty little river. I'd only call it a stream myself. Well, can't stop, nice of you to come. I would do more for you if I could, but you see how I'm fixed. Write to me about it. That's it. *Put it in black and white.*'

And with that he left the room.

'You see,' said the doctor, 'he is in excellent condition. He is putting on weight, eating and sleeping excellently. In fact, the whole tone of his system is above reproach.'

The door opened again and Loveday returned.

'Forgive my coming back, sir, but I was afraid that the young lady might be upset at his lordship's not knowing her. You mustn't mind him, miss. Next time he'll be very pleased to see you. It's only today he's put out on account of being behind-hand with his work. You see, sir, all this week I've been helping in the library and I haven't been able to get all his lordship's reports typed out. And he's got muddled with his card index. That's all it is. He doesn't mean any harm.'

'What a nice man,' said Angela, when Loveday had gone back to his charge.

'Yes. I don't know what we should do without old Loveday. Everybody loves him, staff and patients alike.'

'I remember him well. It's a great comfort to know that you are able to get such good warders,' said Lady Moping; 'people who don't know, say such foolish things about asylums.'

'Oh, but Loveday isn't a warder,' said the doctor.

'You don't mean he's cuckoo, too?' said Angela.

The doctor corrected her.

'He is an *inmate*. It is rather an interesting case. He has been here for thirty-five years.'

'But I've never seen anyone saner,' said Angela.

'He certainly has that air,' said the doctor, 'and in the last twenty years we have treated him as such. He is the life and soul of the place. Of course he is not one of the private patients, but we allow him to mix freely with them. He plays billiards excellently, does conjuring tricks at the concert, mends their gramophones, valets them, helps them in their crossword puzzles and various – er – hobbies. We allow them to give him small tips for services rendered, and he must by now have amassed quite a little fortune. He has a way with even the most troublesome of them. An invaluable man about the place.'

'Yes, but why is he here?'

'Well, it is rather sad. When he was a very young man he killed somebody – a young woman quite unknown to him, whom he knocked off her bicycle and then throttled. He gave himself up immediately afterwards and has been here ever since.'

'But surely he is perfectly safe now. Why is he not let out?'

'Well, I suppose if it was to anyone's interest, he would be. He has no relatives except a step-sister who lives in Plymouth. She used to visit him at one time, but she hasn't been for years now. He's perfectly happy here and I can assure you *we* aren't going to take the first steps in turning him out. He's far too useful to us.'

'But it doesn't seem fair,' said Angela.

'Look at your father,' said the doctor. 'He'd be quite lost without Loveday to act as his secretary.'

'It doesn't seem fair.'

2

Angela left the asylum, oppressed by a sense of injustice. Her mother was unsympathetic.

'Think of being locked up in a looney bin all one's life.'

'He attempted to hang himself in the orangery,' replied Lady Moping, '*in front of the Chester-Martins*.'

'I don't mean Papa. I mean Mr Loveday.'

'I don't think I know him.'

'Yes, the looney they have put to look after Papa.'

'Your father's secretary. A very decent sort of man, I thought, and eminently suited to his work.'

Angela left the question for the time, but returned to it again at luncheon on the following day.

'Mums, what does one have to do to get people out of the bin?'

'The bin? Good gracious, child, I hope that you do not anticipate your father's return *here*.'

'No, no. Mr Loveday.'

'Angela, you seem to me to be totally bemused. I see it was a mistake to take you with me on out little visit yesterday.'

After luncheon Angela disappeared to the library and was soon immersed in the lunacy laws as represented in the encyclopedia.

She did not re-open the subject with her mother, but a fortnight later, when there was a question of taking some pheasants over to her father for his eleventh Certification Party she showed an unusual willingness to run over with them. Her mother was occupied with other interests and noticed nothing suspicious.

Angela drove her small car to the asylum, and after delivering the game, asked for Mr Loveday. He was busy at the time making a crown for one of his companions who expected hourly to be anointed Emperor of Brazil, but he left his work and enjoyed several minutes' conversation with her. They spoke about her father's health and spirits. After a time Angela remarked, 'Don't you ever want to get away?'

Mr Loveday looked at her with his gentle, blue-grey eyes. 'I've got very well used to the life, miss. I'm fond of the poor people here, and I think that several of them are quite fond of me. At least, I think they would miss me if I were to go.'

'But don't you ever think of being free again?'

'Oh yes, miss, I think of it – almost all the time I think of it.'

'What would you do if you got out? There must be *something* you would sooner do than stay here.'

The old man fidgeted uneasily. 'Well, miss, it sounds ungrateful, but I can't deny I should welcome a little outing, once, before I get too old to enjoy it. I expect we all have our secret ambitions, and there *is* one thing I often wish I could do. You mustn't ask me what ... It wouldn't take long. But I do feel that if I had done it, just for a day, an afternoon even, then I would die quiet. I could settle down again easier, and devote myself to the poor crazed people here with a better heart. Yes, I do feel that.'

There were tears in Angela's eyes that afternoon as she drove away. 'He *shall* have his little outing, bless him,' she said.

3

From that day onwards for many weeks Angela had a new purpose in life. She moved about the ordinary routine of her home with an abstracted air and an unfamiliar, reserved courtesy which greatly disconcerted Lady Moping.

'I believe the child's in love. I only pray that it isn't that uncouth Egbertson boy.'

She read a great deal in the library, she cross-examined any guests who had pretensions to legal or medical knowledge, she showed extreme goodwill to old Sir Roderick Lane-Foscote, their Member. The names 'alienist', 'barrister' or 'government official' now had for her the glamour that formerly surrounded film actors and professional wrestlers. She was a woman with a cause, and before the end of the hunting season she had triumphed. Mr Loveday achieved his liberty.

The doctor at the asylum showed reluctance but no real opposition. Sir Roderick wrote to the Home Office. The necessary papers were signed, and at last the day came when Mr Loveday took leave of the home where he had spent such long and useful years.

His departure was marked by some ceremony. Angela and Sir Roderick Lane-Foscote sat with the doctors on the stage of the gymnasium. Below them were assembled everyone in the institution who was thought to be stable enough to endure the excitement.

Lord Moping, with a few suitable expressions of regret, presented Mr Loveday on behalf of the wealthier lunatics with a gold cigarette case; those who supposed themselves to be emperors showered him with decorations and titles of honour. The warders gave him a silver watch and many of the non-paying inmates were in tears on the day of the presentation.

The doctor made the main speech of the afternoon. 'Remember,' he remarked, 'that you leave behind you nothing but our warmest good wishes. You are bound to us by ties that none will forget. Time will only deepen our sense of debt to you. If at any time in the future you should grow tired of your life in the world, there will always be a welcome for you here. Your post will be open.'

A dozen or so variously afflicted lunatics hopped and skipped after him down the drive until the iron gates opened and Mr Loveday stepped into his freedom. His small trunk had already gone to the station; he elected to walk. He had been reticent about his plans, but he was well provided with money, and the general impression was that he would go to London and enjoy himself a little before visiting his step-sister in Plymouth.

It was to the surprise of all that he returned within two hours of his liberation. He was smiling whimsically, a gentle, self-regarding smile of reminiscence.

'I have come back,' he informed the doctor. 'I think that now I shall be here for good.'

'But, Loveday, what a short holiday. I'm afraid that you have hardly enjoyed yourself at all.'

'Oh yes, sir, thank you, sir, I've enjoyed myself *very much*. I'd been promising myself one little treat, all these years. It was short, sir, but *most* enjoyable. Now I shall be able to settle down again to my work here without any regrets.'

Half a mile up the road from the asylum gates, they later discovered an abandoned bicycle. It was a lady's machine of some antiquity. Quite near it in the ditch lay the strangled body of a young woman, who, riding home to her tea, had chanced to overtake Mr Loveday, as he strode along, musing on his opportunities.

The Snake

Dennis Wheatley

I didn't know Carstairs at all well, mind you, but he was our nearest neighbour and a stranger to the place. He'd asked me several times to drop in for a chat, and that week-end I'd been saddled with a fellow called Jackson.

He was an engineer who had come over from South America to report on a mine my firm were interested in. We hadn't got much in common and the talk was getting a bit thin, so on the Sunday evening I thought I'd vary the entertainment by looking up Carstairs and take Jackson with me.

Carstairs was pleased enough to see us; he lived all on his own but for the servants. What he wanted with a big place like that I couldn't imagine, but that was his affair. He made us welcome and we settled down in comfortable armchairs to chat.

It was one of those still summer evenings with the scent of the flowers drifting in through the open windows, and the peace of it all makes you think for the moment that the city, on Monday morning, is nothing but a rotten, bad dream.

I think I did know in a vague way that Carstairs had made his money mining, but when, or where, I hadn't an idea. Anyhow, he and young Jackson were soon in it up to the neck, talking technicalities. That never has been my end of the business; I was content to lend them half an ear while I drank in the hush of the scented twilight; a little feller was piping away to his mate for all he was worth in the trees at the bottom of the garden.

It was the bat started it; you know how they flit in on a summer's night through the open windows, absolutely silently, before you are aware of them. How they're here one moment – and there the next, in and out of the shadows while you flap about with a newspaper like a helpless fool. They're unclean things, of course, but harmless enough, yet never in my life have I seen a big man so scared as Carstairs.

'Get it out!' he yelled. 'Get it out,' and he buried his bald head in the sofa cushions.

I think I laughed; anyhow I told him it was nothing to make a fuss about, and switched out the light.

The bat zigzagged from side to side once or twice, and then flitted out into the open as silently as it had come.

Carstairs's big red face had gone quite white when he peeped out from beneath his cushions. 'Has it gone?' he asked in a frightened whisper.

'Of course it has,' I assured him. 'Don't be silly – it might have been the Devil himself from the fuss you made!'

'Perhaps it was,' he said seriously. As he sat up I could see the whites of his rather prominent eyes surrounding the blue pupils – I should have laughed if the man hadn't been in such an obvious funk.

'Shut the windows,' he said sharply, as he moved over to the whisky and mixed himself a pretty stiff drink. It seemed a sin on a night like that, but it was his house, so Jackson drew them to.

Carstairs apologized in a hal half-hearted sort of way for making such a scene, then we settled down again.

In the circumstances it wasn't unnatural that the talk should turn to witchcraft and things like that.

Young Jackson said he'd heard some pretty queer stories in the forests of Brazil, but that didn't impress me, because he looked a good half-dago himself, for all his English name, and dagoes always believe in that sort of thing.

Carstairs was a different matter; he was as British as could be and when he asked me seriously if I believed in Black Magic – I didn't laugh, but told him just as seriously that I did not.

'You're wrong, then,' he declared firmly, 'and I'll tell you this, I shouldn't be sitting here if it wasn't for Black Magic.'

'You can't be serious,' I protested.

'I am,' he said. 'For thirteen years I roamed the Union of South Africa on my uppers, a "poor white", if you know what that means. If you don't – well, it's hell on earth. One rotten job after another with barely enough pay to keep body and soul together, and between jobs not even that, so that at times you'd even lower yourself to chum up to a black for the sake of a drink or a bit of a meal. Never a chance to get up in the world, and despised by natives and whites alike – well, I suppose I'd be at it still but that I came up against the Black Art, and that brought me big money. Once I had money I went into business. That's twenty-two years ago – I'm a rich man now, and I've come home to take my rest.'

Carstairs evidently meant every word he said, and I must confess I was impressed. There was nothing neurotic about him, he was sixteen stone of solid, prosaic Anglo-Saxon; in fact, he looked just the sort of chap you'd like to have with you in a tight corner. That's why I'd been so surprised when he got in such a blue funk about the bat.

'I'm afraid I'm rather an unbeliever,' I admitted, 'but perhaps that's because I've never come up against the real thing – won't you tell us some more about it?'

He looked at me steadily for a moment with his round, blue eyes. 'All right,' he said, 'if you like; help yourself to another peg, and your friend too.'

We refilled our glasses and he went on: 'When I as good as said just now, "that bat may be the Devil in person," I didn't mean quite that. Maybe there are people who can raise the Devil – I don't know, anyhow I've never seen it done; but there is a power of evil drifting about the world – suffused in the atmosphere, as you might say, and certain types of animals seem to be sensitive to it – they pick it up out of the ether just like a wireless receiving set.

'Take cats – they're uncanny beasts; look at the way they can see in the dark; and they can do more than that; they can see things that we can't in broad day. You must have seen them, before now, walk carefully round an object in a room that simply wasn't there.

'These animals are harmless enough in themselves, of course, but where the trouble starts is when they become used as a focus by a malignant human will. However, that's all by the way. As I was telling you, I'd hiked it up and down the Union for thirteen years, though it wasn't the Union in those days. From Durban to Damaraland, and from the Orange River to Matabel, fruit farmer, miner, salesman, wagoner, clerk – I took every job that offered, but for all the good I'd done myself I might as well have spent my time on the Breakwater instead.

'I haven't even made up my mind today which is the tougher master – the Bible-punching Dutchman, with his little piping voice, or the whisky-sodden South African Scot.

'At last I drifted into Swaziland; that's on the borders of Portuguese East, near Lourenco Marques and Delagoa Bay. As lovely a country as you could wish to see; it's all been turned into a native reserve now, but in those days there were a handful of white settlers scattered here and there.

'Anyhow, it was there in a saloon at Mbabane that I met old Benny Isaacsohn, and he offered me a job. I was down and out, so I took it, though he was one of the toughest-looking nuts that I'd ever come across. He was a bigger man than I am, with greasy black curls and a great big hook of a nose. His face was as red as a turkey cock, and his wicked black eyes were as shifty as sin. He said his storekeeper had died on him sudden, and the way he said it made me wonder just what had happened to that man.

'But it was Benny or picking up scraps from a native kraal – so I went along with him there and then.

'He took me miles up country to his famous store – two tins of sardines and a dead rat were about all he had in it, and of course I soon tumbled to it that trading honest wasn't Benny's real business. I don't doubt he'd sized me up and reckoned I wouldn't be particular. I was careful not to be too curious, because I had a sort of idea that that was what my predecessor had died of.

'After a bit he seemed to get settled in his mind about me, and didn't take much trouble to conceal his little games. He was doing a bit of gun-running for the natives from over the Portuguese border and a handsome traffic in illicit booze. Of course all our customers were blacks; there wasn't another white in a day's march except for Rebecca – Benny's old woman.

'I kept his books for him; they were all fake, of course. Brown sugar meant two dummy bullets out of five, and white, three. I remember; the dummies were cardboard painted to look like lead – cartridges come cheaper that way! Anyhow, Benny knew his ledger code all right.

'He didn't treat me badly on the whole; we had a shindy one hot night soon after I got there, and he knocked me flat with one blow from his big red fist. After that I used to go and walk it off if I felt my temper getting the best of me – and I did at times when I saw the way he used to treat those niggers. I'm not exactly squeamish myself, but the things he used to do would make you sick.

'When I got into the game, I found that gun-running and liquor weren't the end of it. Benny was a money-lender as well – that's where he over-reached himself and came up against the Black Art.

'Of the beginnings of Benny's dealings with Umtonga, the witch doctor, I know nothing. The old heathen would come to us now and again all decked out in his cowrie shells and strings of leopards' teeth, and Benny always received him in state. They'd sit drinking glass for glass of neat spirit for hours on end until Umtonga was carried away dead drunk by his men. The old villain used to sell off all the surplus virgins of his tribe to Benny, and Benny used to market them in Portuguese East, together with the wives of the poor devils who were in his clutches and couldn't pay the interest on their debts.

'The trouble started about nine months after I'd settled there; old Umtonga was a spender in his way, and there began to be a shortage of virgins in the tribe, so he started to borrow on his own account and then he couldn't pay. The interviews weren't so funny then – he began to go away sober and shaking his big black stick.

'That didn't worry Benny. He'd been threatened by people before, and he told Umtonga that if he couldn't raise enough virgins to meet his bill he'd better sell off a few of his wives himself.

'I was never present at the meetings, but I gathered a bit from what old Benny said in his more expansive moments, and I'd picked up enough Swazi to gather the gist of Umtonga's views when he aired them at parting on the stoep.

'Then one day Umtonga came with three women – it seemed that they were the equivalent of the original debt, but Benny had a special system with regard to his loans. Repayment of capital was nothing like enough – and the longer the debt was outstanding the greater the rate of interest became. By that time he wanted about thirty women, and good ones at that, to clear Umtonga off his books.

'The old witch doctor was calm and quiet; contrary to custom, he came in the evening and he did not stay more than twenty minutes. The walls were thin, so I heard most of what went on – he offered Benny the three women – or death before the morning.

'If Benny had been wise he would have taken the women, but he wasn't. He told Umtonga to go to the Devil – and Umtonga went.

'His people were waiting for him outside, about a dozen of them, and he proceeded to make a magic. They handed him a live black cock and a live white cock, and Umtonga sat down before the stoep and he killed them in a curious way.

'He examined their livers carefully, and then he began to rock backwards and forwards on his haunches, and in his old cracked voice he sang a weird, monotonous chant. The others lay down flat on the ground and wriggled round him one after the other on their bellies. They kept that up for about half an hour, and then the old wizard began to dance. I can see his belt of monkey tails swirling about him now, as he leapt and spun. You wouldn't have thought that lean old savage had the strength in him to dance like that.

'Then all of a sudden he seemed to have a fit – he went absolutely rigid and fell down flat. He dropped on his face, and when his people turned him over we could see he was frothing at the mouth. They picked him up and carried him away.

'You know how the night comes down almost at once in the tropics. Umtonga started his incantation in broad daylight, and it didn't take so very long, but by the time he'd finished it was as dark as pitch, with nothing but the Southern Cross and the Milky Way to light the hidden world.

'In those places most people still act by Nature's clock. We had the evening meal, old Rebecca, Benny, and I; he seemed a bit preoccupied, but that was no more than I would have been in the circumstances. Afterwards he went into his office room to see what he'd made on the day, as he always did, and I went off to bed.

'It was the old woman roused me about two o'clock – it seems she'd dropped off to sleep, and awoke to find that Benny ahd not come up to bed.

'We went along through the shanty, and there he was with his eyes wide and staring, gripping the arms of his office chair and all hunched up as though cowering away from something.

'He had never been a pretty sight to look at, but now there was something fiendish in the horror on his blackened face, and of course he'd been dead some hours.

'Rebecca flung her skirts over her head, and began to wail fit to bring the house down. After I'd got her out of the room, I went back to investigate – what could have killed Benny Isaacsohn? I was like you in those days – I didn't believe for a second that that toothless old fool Umtonga had the power to kill from a distance.

'I made a thorough examination of the room, but there was no trace of anybody having broken in, or even having been there. I had a good look at Benny – it seemed to me he'd died of apoplexy or some sort of fit, but what had brought it on? He'd seen something, and it must have been something pretty ghastly.

'I didn't know then that a week or two later I was to see the same thing myself.

'Well, we buried Benny the next day – there was the usual kind of primitive wake, with the women howling and the men getting free drinks – half Africa seemed to have turned up; you know how mysteriously news travels in the black man's country.

'Umtonga put in an appearance; he expressed neither regret nor pleasure, but stood looking on. I didn't know what to make of it. The only evidence against him was the mumbo-jumbo of the night before, and no sane European could count that as proof of murder. I was inclined to think that the whole thing was an amazing coincidence.

'When the burying was over he came up to me: "Why you no kill house-boys attend Big Boss before throne of Great Spirit?" he wanted to know.

'I explained that one killing in the house was quite enough at a time. Then he demanded his stick, said he had left it behind in Benny's office the night before.

'I was pretty short with him, as you can imagine, but I knew the old ruffian's stick as well as I knew my own hairbrush; so I went in to get it.

'There it was lying on the floor – a four-foot snake stick. I dare say you've seen the sort of thing I mean; they make them shorter for Europeans. They are carved out of heavy wood, the snake's head is the handle, the tail the ferrule. Between, there are from five to a dozen bands; little markings are carved all down it to represent the scales. Umtonga's was a fine one – quite thin, but as heavy as lead. It was black, and carved out of ebony, I imagine. Not an ounce of give in it, but it would have made a splendid weapon. I picked it up and gave it to him without a word.

'For about ten days I saw no more of him. Old Rebecca stopped her wailing, and got down to business. Benny must have told her about most of his deals that mattered, for I found that she knew pretty much how things stood. It was agreed that I should carry on as a sort of manager for her, and after a bit we came to the question of Umtonga. I suggested that the interest was pretty hot, and that the man might be really dangerous. Wouldn't it be better to settle with him for what we could get? But she wouldn't have it; you would have thought I was trying to draw her eye-teeth when I suggested forgoing the interest! She fairly glared at me.

' "What is it to do with you?" she screamed. "I need money, I have the future of my – er – myself to think of. Send a boy with a message that you want to see him, and when he comes – make him pay."

'Well, there was nothing to do but to agree; the old shrew was worse than Benny in some ways. I sent a boy the following morning, and the day after Umtonga turned up.

'I saw him in Benny's office while his retinue waited outside; I was sitting in Benny's chair – the chair he'd died in – and I came to the point at once.

'He sat there for a few minutes just looking at me; his wizened old face was like a dried-up fruit that had gone bad. His black boot-button eyes shone with a strange, malignant fire, then he said very slowly, "You – very brave young Baas."

' "No," I said, "just business-like, that's all."

' "You know what happen to old Baas – he died – you want to go Great Spirit yet?"

'There was something evil and powerful in his steady stare; it was horribly disconcerting, but I wouldn't give in to it, and I told him I didn't want anything except his cash that was due, or his equivalent.

' "You forget business with Umtonga?" he suggested. "You do much good business, other mens. You no forget, Umtonga make bad magic – you die."

'Well, it wasn't my business – it was the old woman's. I couldn't have let him out if I'd wanted to – so there was only one reply, the same as he'd got from Benny.

'I showed him Benny's gun, and told him that if there were any monkey tricks I'd shoot on sight. His only answer was one of the most disdainful smiles I've ever seen on a human face. With that he left me and joined his bodyguard outside.

'They then went through the same abracadabra with another black cock, and another white cock – wriggled about on their bellies, and the old man danced till he had another fit and was carried away.

'Night had fallen in the meantime, and I was none too easy in my mind. I thought of Benny's purple face and staring eyes.

'I had supper with the old hag, and then I went to Benny's room. I like my tot, but I'd been careful not to take it; I meant to remain stone cold sober and wide-awake that night.

'I had the idea that one of Umtonga's people had done something to Benny, poisoned his drink perhaps.

'I went over his room minutely, and after I'd done, there wasn't a place you could have hidden a marmoset. Then I shut the windows carefully, and tipped up a chair against each so that no one could get in without knocking it down. If I did drop off, I was bound to wake at that. I turned out the light so that they should have no target for a spear or an arrow, and then I sat down to wait.

'I never want another night like that as long as I live; you know how you can imagine things in the darkness – well, what I didn't imagine in those hours isn't worth the telling.

'The little noises of the veldt came to me as the creeping of the enemy – half a dozen times I nearly lost my nerve and put a bullet into the blacker masses of the shadows that seemed to take on curious forms, but I was pretty tough in those days and I stuck it out.

'About eleven o'clock the moon came up; you would have thought that made it better, but it didn't. It added a new sort of terror – that was all. You know how eerie moonlight can be; it is unnatural somehow, and I believe there's a lot in what they say about there being evil in the moon. Bright bars of it stood out in rows on the floor, where it streamed in silent and baleful through the slats in the jalousies. I found myself counting them over and over again. It seemed as if I were becoming mesmerised by that cold, uncanny light. I pulled myself up with a jerk.

'Then I noticed that something was different about the desk in front of me. I couldn't think what it could be – but there was something missing that had been there a moment before.

'All at once I realized what it was, and the palms of my hands became clammy with sweat. Umtonga had left his stick behind again – I had picked it up off the floor when I searched the office and leant it against the front of the desk; the top of it had been there before my eyes for the last three hours in the semi-darkness – standing up stiff and straight – and now it had disappeared.

'It couldn't have fallen, I should have heard it – my eyes must have been starting out of my head. A ghastly thought had come to me – just supposing that stick was not a stick?

'And then I saw it – the thing was lying straight and still in the moonlight, with its eight to ten wavy bands, just as I'd seen it a dozen times before; I must have dreamed I propped it against the desk – it must have been on the floor all the time, and yet, I knew deep down in me that I was fooling myself and that it had moved of its own accord.

'My eyes never left it – I watched, holding my breath to see if it moved – but I was straining so that I couldn't trust my eyesight. The bright bars of moonlight on the floor began to waver ever so slightly, and I knew that my sight was playing me tricks; I shut my eyes for a moment – it was the only thing to do – and when I opened them again the snake had raised its head.

'My vest was sticking to me, and my face was dripping wet. I knew now what had killed old Benny – I knew, too, why his face had gone black. Umtonga's stick was no stick at all, but the deadliest snake in all Africa – a thing that can move like lightning, can overtake a galloping horse, and kill its rider, so deadly that you're stiff within four minutes of its bite – I was up against a black mamba.

'I had my revolver in my hand, but it seemed a stupid, useless thing – there wasn't a chance in a hundred that I could hit it. A shot-gun's the only thing that's any good; with that I might have blown its head off, but the guns weren't kept in Benny's room, and like a fool I'd locked myself in.

'The brute moved again as I watched it; it drew up its tail with a long slithering movement. There could be no doubt now; Umtonga was a super-snake-charmer, and he'd left this foul thing behind to do his evil work.

'I sat there petrified, just as poor Benny must have done, wondering what in Heaven's name I could do to save myself, but my brain simply wouldn't work.

'It was an accident that saved me. As it rose to strike, I slipped in my attempt to get to my feet and kicked over Benny's wicker wastepaper basket; the brute went for that instead of me. The force with which they strike is tremendous – it's like the blow from a hammer or the kick of a mule. Its head went clean through the side of the basket and there it got stuck; it couldn't get its head out again.

'As luck would have it, I had been clearing out some of Benny's drawers that day, and I'd thrown away a whole lot of samples of quartz; the basket was about a third full of them and they weigh pretty heavy; a few had fallen out when it fell over, but the rest were enough to keep the mamba down.

'It thrashed about like a gigantic whiplash, but it couldn't free its head, and I didn't waste a second; I started heaving ledgers on its tail. That was the end of the business as far as the mamba was concerned – I'd got it pinned down in half the time it took you to drive out that bat. Then I took up my gun again. "Now, my beauty," I thought, "I've got you where I want you, and I'll just quietly blow your head off – I'm going to have a damn fine pair of shoes out of your skin."

'I knelt down to the job and levelled my revolver; the snake struck twice, viciously, in my direction, but it couldn't get within a foot of me and it no more than jerked the basket either time.

'I looked down the barrel of the pistol within eighteen inches of its head, and then a very strange thing happened – and this is where the Black Magic comes in.

'The moonlit room seemed to grow dark about me, so that the baleful light faded before my eyes – the snake's head disappeared from view – the walls seemed to be expanding and the queer, acrid odour of the native filled my nostrils.

'I knew that I was standing in Umtonga's hut, and where the snake had been a moment before I saw Umtonga sleeping – or in a trance, if you prefer it. He was lying with his head on the belly of one of his women, as is the custom of the country, and I stretched out a hand towards him in greeting. It seemed that, although there was nothing there, I had touched something – and then I realized with an appalling fear that my left hand was holding the wastepaper basket in which was the head of the snake.

'There was a prickling sensation on my scalp, and I felt my hair lifting – stiff with the electricity that was streaming from my body. With a tremendous effort of will-power I jerked back my hand. Umtonga shuddered in his trance – there was a thud, and I knew that the snake had struck in the place where my hand had been a moment before.

'I was half-crazy with fear, my teeth began to chatter, and it came to me suddenly that there was an icy wind blowing steadily upon me. I shivered with the deadly cold – although in reality it was a still, hot night. The wind was coming from the nostrils of the sleeping Umtonga full upon me; the bitter coldness of it was numbing me where I stood. I knew that in another moment I should fall forward on the snake.

'I concentrated every ounce of will-power in my hand that held the gun – I could not see the snake, but my eyes seemed to be focused upon Umtonga's forehead. If only my frozen finger could pull the trigger – I made a supreme effort, and then there happened a very curious thing.

'Umtonga began to talk to me in his sleep – not in words, you understand, but as spirit talks to spirit. He turned and groaned and twisted where he lay. A terrible sweat broke out on his forehead and round his skinny neck. I could see him as clearly as I can see you – he was pleading with me not to kill him, and in that deep, silent night, where space and time had ceased to exist, I knew that Umtonga and the snake were one.

'If I killed the snake, I killed Umtonga. In some strange fashion he had suborned the powers of evil, so that when at the end of the incantation he fell into a fit, his malignant spirit passed into the body of his dread familiar.

'I suppose I ought to have killed that snake and Umtonga too, but I didn't. Just as it is said that a drowning man sees his whole life pass before him at the moment of death – so I saw my own. Scene after scene out of my thirteen years of disappointment and failure flashed before me – but I saw more than that.

'I saw a clean, tidy office in Jo'burg, and I was sitting there in decent clothes. I saw this very house as you see it from the drive – although I'd never seen it in my life before – and I saw other things as well.

'At that moment I had Umtonga in my power, and he was saying as clearly as could be – "All these things will I give unto you – if only you will spare my life."

'Then the features of Umtonga faded. The darkness lightened and I saw again the moonlight streaming through the slats of old Benny's office – and the mamba's head!

'I put my revolver in my pocket, unlocked the door, and locking it again behind me, went up to bed.

'I slept as though I'd been on a ten-day forced march, I was so exhausted; I woke late, but everything that had happened in the night was clear in my memory – I knew I hadn't dreamed it. I loaded a shot-gun and went straight to Benny's office.

'There was the serpent still beside the desk – its head thrust through the wicker basket and the heavy ledgers pinning down its body. It seemed to have straightened out, though, into its usual form, and when I knocked it lightly with the barrel of the gun it remained absolutely rigid. I could hardly believe it to be anything more than a harmless piece of highly polished wood, and yet I knew that it had a hideous, hidden life, and after that I left it very carefully alone.

'Umtonga turned up a little later, as I felt sure he would; he seemed very bent and old. He didn't say very much, but he spoke again about his debt, and asked if I would not forgo some part of it – he would pay the whole if he must, but it would ruin him if he did. To sell his wives would be to lose authority with his tribe.

'I explained that it wasn't my affair, but Rebecca's; she owned every-thing now that Benny was dead.

'He seemed surprised at that; natives don't hold with women owning property. He said he'd thought that the business was mine and all that I had to do was to feed Rebecca till she died.

'Then he wanted to know if I would have helped him had that been the case. I told him that extortion wasn't my idea of business, and with that he seemed satisfied; he picked up his terrible familiar and stumped away without another word.

'The following week I had to go into Mbabane for stores. I was away a couple of nights and when I got back Rebecca was dead and buried; I heard the story from the house-boys. Umtonga had been to see her on the evening that I left. He'd made his magic again before the stoep, and they'd found her dead and black in the morning. I asked if by any chance he'd left his stick behind him, although I knew the answer before I got it – "Yes, he'd come back for it the following day."

'I started in to clear up Benny's affairs, and board by board to pull the shanty down. Benny didn't believe in banks and I knew there was a hoard hidden somewhere. It took me three weeks, but I found it. With that, and a reasonable realization of what was outstanding, I cleared up a cool ten thousand. I've turned that into a hundred thousand since, and so you see that it was through the Black Art that I come to be sitting here.'

As Carstairs came to the end of the story, something made me turn and look at Jackson; he was glaring at the older man, and his dark eyes shone with a fierce light in his sallow face.

'Your name's not Carstairs,' he cried suddenly in a harsh voice. 'It's Thompson – and mine is Isaacsohn. *I* am the child that you robbed and abandoned.'

Before I could grasp the full significance of the thing he was on his feet – I saw the knife flash as it went home in Carstairs' chest, and the young Jew shrieked, 'You fiend – you paid that devil to kill my mother.'

No Ticket

Mary Williams

The mist was quickly thickening into fog, and I wondered why I hadn't had the sense to stop at the last village and put up for the night. But before starting off on my Cornish walking trip the doctor had said, 'Whatever you do get out into the fresh air and walk. Walk yourself so tired your body will fall to sleep the moment you get to bed. It's the only way, Rogers. Breakdowns are funny things. Drugs can help at the beginning, but in the end it's only nature and commonsense will do the trick. You're a fit enough man physically. So give the brain a bit of a rest, and you'll soon find the nightmares will go.'

Naturally I'd taken his advice, and for the first week things had gone better for me than I'd expected. It was autumn, with the moors washed bronze and gold under the pale sun, and the mingled smell of fallen leaves, blackberries and distant tang of woodsmoke hovering rich in the air with the faint drift of sea-blown brine. Heady, nostalgic weather, stirring the lost emotion of youth to life again. Not difficult then to push the rat-race of London journalism behind me, forgetting even ... except in sudden rare stabs of renewed pain ... my break with Clare.

Each day I'd walked a little further, and when I came to some attractive looking old inn catering for visitors had stopped for the night, setting off again after a hearty breakfast for further exercise and adventure.

Yes, there was adventure in the experience; mostly I suppose because of the terrain ... Cornwall. Changeless in the sense of atmosphere and 'place' magic, yet at almost every corner providing a vista of alternating scene. At one moment lush and verdant between high hedges and clumps of woodland, the next opening to stretches of barren countryside dotted with the stark relics of ruined mine works and huddled granite hamlets perched above the windblown cliffs. As I trod the winding lanes and moorland roads of West Penwith this sense of agelessness and primitive challenge had deepened and drawn me on, almost as though into another dimension.

I should have stopped at The Tramping Woman of course, and ancient hostelry on the outskirts of Wikka; but ignored it and continued along the high road between coast and rocky hills, although the sun was already dying, leaving a film of pale gold beneath the greenish sky.

I'd walked almost a mile to the west when the mist started to rise; thinly at first, like a gauze veil over the fading landscape, then thickening into furry uncertainty so the boulders and windblown trees assumed gradually the menacing quality of ancient gigantic beasts and legendary creatures risen to torment and mislead. When I came at last to a crossroads with a decrepit sign-post pointing in three directions like a gibbet, I paused searching for my torch to try and locate any names given. It was impossible. The archaic lettering further distorted by the wreathing fog made no sense at all. In fact as I went close up, clinging to the post, the cloying atmosphere completely shrouded it into negation, warning me that far from improving, the light and weather were steadily getting worse.

A sickening sense of claustrophobia filled me, choking at my throat, filling my lungs with a hysterical feeling of being unable to breathe. The torch suddenly flickered and went out. I was alone, and lost, and if I hadn't forced myself to move quickly I knew I'd be there until morning, by which time, for me, it might be too late.

So I struck ahead taking what I thought ... or hoped ... was the main road.

How long I continued in this way, moving by instinct rather than any coherent sense of direction I don't know. Occasionally I lurched against a bush or humped tree ... maybe something more sinister ... that flapped me with the clammy slap of a dead hand. Once I fell against a looming slab of stone that emitted to my distorted fancy malicious elemental glee as I pulled myself away with my heart pumping furiously. I could imagine the ancient cromlechs and standing stones on the moors above leering down on my puny shape as I struggled blindly on, with my coat gripped close over my chest, head thrust forward in a futile attempt to get a clear glimpse of the ground.

Except for the dripping of the fog, the stillness was oppressive ... an entity in itself. Watchfulness encompassed me. From the furry grey walls on every side it seemed to me that eyes were peering. Secret haunted eyes of elemental evil and atavistic greed. Unconsciously I put out an arm to defend myself, knowing that I couldn't continue for much longer. My thighs already felt deadened, the breath in my body absorbed by the sucking lips and tongue of hungry fog.

And then, suddenly, I heard it; the distant thrum of an engine ... tangible evidence of reality in an unreal world. A car or bus surely? 'Thank God,' I thought, swerving to the side of the road.

A minute later headlights appeared dimly, emerging as two immense wan eyes through the curdling fitful grey. The road temporarily came into blurred focus ... snaking like some ghostly ribbon towards me until the cumbrous dark shape dimmed it again into darkness. The vehicle seemed to sway slightly and slow down as it passed; sufficiently for me to pull myself by the rail over the step inside.

I paused briefly, gasping for breath, then staggered on flinging myself into the first vacant seat. Only one dim light shone from the front, showing the dark shoulders of the driver at the wheel and above, in the vicinity of the windscreen, the glow of a printed name, ABMUT, which was a new one on me. I'd never heard of the place, and never been in such an antiquated omnibus before. It was a real 'bone-shaker', and as we jogged on, with the dripping fog flapping the windscreen, streaming in rivulets down the dreary windows, I could almost hear my own jaws and knees creaking in unison with the macabre tempo of the ancient engine.

There were about a dozen passengers inside, no more, and they were a silent crowd, sitting speechless and hunched into their grey clothes, faces pale discs of misery, eyes mere shadowed pools of emptiness in the queer half light. My presence seemed to evoke no interest whatever, the entrance of a stranger generally does on a country journey.

Thinking back now, I can't recall a single individual face except those of an aged bearded man with a kind of muffler round his head, a lantern-jawed woman wearing a grey hooded cape, and a young boy who seemed more alert than the rest, although his forehead was bandaged, and I guessed he'd been in an accident. He looked round once at me, and I saw in his eyes such supplication and pleading I hoisted myself up and went to sit beside him. No one seemed to notice. There was no comment, no flicker of surprise or movement from the crouched chill forms. Even the child himself didn't speak; but I could feel him shivering, and when my hand touched his it was icily cold. But I felt he was grateful to have me there.

How long that dreary journey to Abmut took, I've no idea. Time seemed to have died. The silence, except for the monotonous chug-chugging of the engine, was oppressive and somehow unearthly. There was only brief intervals when the landscape took form, showing a momentary glimpse of a looming hill-side or humped boulder at a corner of the lane. Still, I thought, Abmut must be our destination, and where there was a village or town, presumably there would be an inn, however primitive. I had a compulsive almost irrational desire at one point to get up and jump out. But as I made the first instinctive movement, several heads turned to look at me, and their dumb, pale, almost hostile faces filled me with such aversion I remained rooted to the spot, my hand automatically tightening on the boy's.

If there'd been a conductor I'd have forced information from him, but the vehicle was obviously a one-man affair as some still are in remote places; therefore all I could do was to hope for the best, and somehow battle against the sickening fear which was intensifying in me every moment that passed.

At last through the window I saw thankfully the first glimmer of lifting light in a fold of the moors below the road. As the bus took a sharp turn down a steep track between dripping walls of hedges, the blurred outline of a huddled hamlet took shape, dimly at first ... a mere outline of grey squat buildings that gradually clarified, assuming a quivering brilliance against that desolate landscape of grim uniformity. It was as though nature, in a quixotic moment had designed a macabre backcloth purely as a setting for this one benighted village.

And then the singing began ... from a church presumably ... although the soughing and sighing and rising and falling of the mournful yet unwelcoming chorus held, for my ears, more of the wind's moan and the sea's lonely call than the quality of human voices. At the same time I was aware of movement, a shuffling and stirring around me as one form after another moved cumbrously from each seat and waited, heads hunched forward, for the bus to stop.

It came to a halt at the top of a track about a hundred yards from the hamlet which appeared by then to emerge from a sea of vaporised grey, roof tops and church spire tipped with silver. I waited until the last of the throng, the boy, had clambered out. The driver had dismounted and was waiting to give a nod before each joined the mournful procession downwards. Then I swung myself wearily by the rail to the ground.

'Ticket?' I heard him murmur above the weird cacophony of sighs that rose and fell intermittently on a drift of rising wind. His voice was hushed yet grating, like the branch of a very ancient tree about to snap, the dark holed eyes watchful from the bearded face. Drifts of grey hair blew fitfully in the clammy air, brushing my face softly with the choking touch of a cobwebbed shroud.

Revolted, I drew away.

'I've no ticket,' I told him.

'No ticket?' He shook his head as the mist curdled and cleared again briefly, revealing a mournful dropped jaw and skeleton-like visage moving incredulously on a thin neck.

'That's right,' I said, 'I got on further back, where you slowed down? I can pay now, and the rest necessary to take me on. Or ... are you returning to Wikka?' As I spoke the wild hope stirred in me this might be so. I had a growing irrational desire to be away from Abmut as soon as possible. In spite of the gathering radiance there and the muted singing which was gradually dying into a subdued murmur, there was something odd and greedy about the place ... something sensed rather than seen that appalled me.

Then he spoke in a wheezing voice that was more of a harsh whisper, holding condemnation in it as well as a threat.

There's no return from here. No one leaves once they've come. *No one . . .* '

A crawling shuddering fear pricked my spine. I could feel my nails digging into my palms. What do you mean no one leaves? What the hell *is* this place . . . this *Abmut?*'

Before the mist clouded his face into a mere blurred disc I saw the lips stretch in an obscene grin from ear to ear. 'Not Abmut,' he muttered in the same sibilant undertone. 'Tumba. That's the name. Tumba.' And the laughter rose from his ancient throat more harsh than the sound of dried bones cracking on stone, colder and more deadly than death itself.

Forcing myself to mobility I rushed, half staggering, to the front of the bus. It was just as he said . . . TUMBA printed at the top of the front window in stygian green lettering that for a moment caught all the reflected light from the hamlet below. What I'd seen from the inside had been the wrong way round.

TUMBA.

It took some moments for the truth to register, and when at last the meaning of the word penetrated my cold brain, I rushed as though in some nightmare of doom over the rim of the slope. From there, against the quivering uncertain vista of fog mingled with luminous quivering light, the sad, limping, column of shuffling figures was visible; grey humped forms moving rhythmically and with an inevitability of purpose that I knew no human hand could allay.

Shuddering, I watched helplessly, as for a brief space of time the fog lifted, under a green sky, revealing a gaunt landscape of tumbled rock and giant standing-stones where the hamlet had formerly been. All sound except the screaming of gulls and moaning of the strengthening wind had died. There was no singing any more, no murmur of voices or whispered comment from the macabre driver, and when I turned there was no sign of him at all. Nothing but dripping negation . . . an emptiness and desolation so intense it seemed that no human foot had ever stepped there.

I looked again, towards the column of creeping shuffling beings, and as I stood watching, impelled by some dark power impossible to combat, the pale stones toppled and the earth opened with a shriek. Greedy grey arms clawed upwards through the brown earth, with skeleton fingers reaching for their own. Skulls leered and lolled among the stones, jaws bared in unholy welcome, the whole scene becoming a seething struggling vortex of death and decay . . . a lustful avaricious breeding ground for the terrifying 'earth-bound' and the damned.

Sickened I had to wait while the crowd of erstwhile passengers suddenly lunged forward and were taken to their own corruption. The ground closed over them like an immense elemental mouth devouring, with a shudder, its own.

All but the boy.

When the heaving and roaring of the earth had subsided, I saw him lying there by a shining white stone. The mist had dispersed considerably, and nothing moved over that lonely terrain but a bird's sudden flight and squawking from the undergrowth. I looked behind me; the moorland road above the slope was almost clear; pale and empty under an eerie moonlit sky. No sign of any vehicle or indication there had ever been one.

Slowly I turned and made my way to where the recumbent young form lay stretched on his back in the heather. There was no fear on his face, for the innocent have no need of it; only a tremendous loneliness and sadness for the days he should have had.

Automatically I crossed his hands over his chest and touched his cold forehead once, where the bandage had been torn away. The scar was vivid still from the impact that had taken his life. In that moment his delicate features were impressed indelibly and forever into my mind.

Just then I had neither the wish or strength to rationalise my haunting and macabre experience. It was all I could do to get to my feet, somehow making my way to the main moorland road.

Once there all initiative and sense of purpose faded into dark overwhelming negation. There was a roaring in my ears, a sound as though the universe was crumbling around me, and then I fell.

When I recovered consciousness I was aware only of greyness at first; a furry grey that slowly lifted to clean calm white. There was a face above me, a woman's face in a nurse's cap, and very gradually it dawned on me I was in hospital. My head was aching abominably, yet memory still registered with dreadful disconcerting clarity.

I think I said something about 'Tumba'. She merely smiled, took my wrist between finger and thumb, a thermometer in the other hand, and after a minute said quietly, 'You're doing fine, Mr Rogers. Rest now. The doctor will be in presently.'

'Who found me?' I asked. 'How could anyone know I was there, by that awful place?'

'The driver, of course,' she replied. 'There was an accident. You swerved in the fog ...'

'No, no,' I told her, as my heart started to pump rapidly against my ribs, 'there was no accident. I got on to a bus, a pretty nasty vehicle. And when it stopped we were at Tumba. It was ... *foul* ...'

'Shsh ...' she said, 'you mustn't excite yourself. Concussion plays strange tricks with the memory. In time everything will become normal again ...'

But it never did; not quite. Eventually I had to accept that I had been involved in some sort of a crash on that benighted moorland road. The driver of a perfectly ordinary car verified this in his statement to the police, and his word was accepted. Perhaps I might even have persuaded myself in the end there was nothing more to it, if something rather odd hadn't happened a few days later.

By then, having mostly recovered from physical cuts and shock. I was able to sit up in bed and glance at a local weekly newspaper.

At the middle page I got a start. There, facing me, was the smiling photograph of a boy. A face I well knew, of the youngster who'd ridden beside me on that ghastly bus bound for Tumba, and whose cold forehead I'd touched with my hand before making for the road again.

Beneath the heading of 'TRAFFIC ACCIDENT' I read:

Anthony Treneer, aged twelve, died yesterday when a car skidded in the fog across the moorland road above Wikka. He had been out walking with a friend and was returning to Verrys Farm, his home, when the tragedy occurred. Death was instantaneous. He was the younger son of Mr and Mrs Robert Treneer, both well known and respected members of the farming community.

I was still staring at the paragraph when my nurse entered.

'That's the boy,' I said, pointing to the photograph.

'You knew him?'

'He was on the bus with me,' I told her unthinkingly, 'the bus to Tumba.'

'Tumba?' she said half pityingly. 'You must forget all about that. It was just an illusion, a nightmare.'

Her obtuseness suddenly irritated me.

'That's what you always say I suppose when you come up against something that can't be rationally explained. The fact remains, nurse, I'm not out of my mind, and although the whole thing may appear moonshine to you, the boy was *with* me ...'

Her voice was clipped when she said, 'He can't have been. Your accident took place at least three miles from the spot where he was hit. Another thing ... there's no such place as Tumba, and there never has been. Now you really must try and put such morbid fancies behind you, Mr Rogers. Thinking that way won't help your complete recovery at all.'

Realising there was no point in further argument, I let the matter drop. Whether she realized the significance of the name 'Tumba' was doubtful. But in an ancient dictionary of mine it is alluded to as a *tomb*.

Incidentally, the evening of the boy's death was the same as that of my haunted 'bus' journey. The only difference being, I suppose, he had a ticket out of this life, whereas I had none.

Fear

P. C. Wren

I

From the first moment I disliked the bungalow intensely. Nor had this feeling anything to do with the fact that it was dirty, derelict and tumble-down; nor, again, that it was lonely, isolated and obviously long-uninhabited.

It was the atmosphere, aura, the spirit of the house that was anti-pathetic, inimical. Even outside it, one had this feeling of an emanated antagonism. Inside, the feeling deepened, and one seemed conscious almost of warning; and then of danger; and, finally, of threat.

I was reminded of that remarkable and haunting line which, once he has read it, occasionally returns to the mind of the traveller in little-visited and out-of-the-way corners of the earth:

'*The place was silent and – aware.*'

Certainly this place was silent, and undoubtedly one had an uneasy feeling of its awareness, of being watched, of being expected – and unwelcome. Not watched by human eyes, but by the place itself.

It was an old – and old-fashioned – rest-house, built on *teangs*, strong square pillars, some twelve feet in height, of *meribau* wood, that hard red wood which is proof against the attack of insects, including even the white ant.

Mounting the flight of steps that led up to the platform on which the house was built, and entering the big central room, the thought im-mediately entered my mind that 'rest-house' was a misnomer. I felt quite certain that whatever else I got here, I should get little rest.

One had frequently been in places which gave the impression that the *genius loci* was inimical. One had been conscious of the feeling, both in buildings made by hands and in places but rarely trodden by human foot; in certain swamps, cañons, dark forests, caves, and sun-blasted or wind-harried desert places.

I have had this feeling strongly when spending a dark and lonely night in Angkor Wat; and again in the brilliant sunlight of a beautiful morning on top of the hill called Doi Wieng Lek, a hill situated near Lampoun, some thirty miles from Chiengmai in the direction of Lampang, in Siam. 'Doi Wieng Lek' means 'the hill which is the place of evil spirits', a fact of which I was unaware, or at any rate, did not realize, until I had left it.

But standing on top of the hill, which I had climbed in order to admire a view of the Lampang plain and the distant hills, I was suddenly conscious of an uneasiness, which was but little removed from fear. What caused the uneasiness, and of what I should be afraid, when mental discomfort and apprehensiveness deepened into fear, I had not the slightest idea. It had nothing to do with the fact that practically every tree looked as though it had been struck by lightning, which certainly was not the case. It was not that I heard any of those sounds which, in certain places, are perturbing, if not startling; it was not because the trees seemed to have been deserted by both birds and gibbons, in spite of the fact that all the surrounding jungle was alive with the gibbons, little spidery long-armed long-legged monkeys whose bewhiskered faces are so friendly and amusing, and whose call is musical, yet so mournful . . .

But the house.

I am not psychic. I am not a nervous person nor sensitive. I am not fanciful, superstitious nor suggestible; but, like everybody else, who is not an absolute clod, I have a sense of atmosphere, whether it be social or local. And never in my life have I been so quickly or so strongly aware of an eerie and minatory atmosphere as in this abandoned rest-house. Had it been possible, I would have marched on, and left it to its loneliness and gloom. For I felt it was haunted, tragic and evil. However, I had no choice. Here I was, and here, for a period, I must remain. For, however unpleasant the place might be, to flee from it and return, the object of my journey unaccomplished, would have been more so. I should have felt ashamed of myself. Also ridiculous. For how could I possibly explain that I had found the place, according to directions given me by kindly hosts in Mualongse, had not entered into possession, but had simply fled, frightened away.

It seemed to me that my coolies disliked the place almost as much as I did, for with unwonted rapidity they unpacked the *hahps*, the big baskets made of woven bamboo, which hang at either end of a pole balanced over the shoulder, and in which one's food, clothes and other chattels are transported in that part of the world.

Nor did my jungle 'boy' appear disposed to linger, when once he had set up my camp-bed and served my dinner, a remarkably well-cooked and satisfying meal, consisting principally of a stew of tinned meat, rice, alleged mushrooms, bamboo shoots, dough-dumplings, chillies and unidentifiable odds and ends.

In view of the fact that my cook had, so far as I knew, neither materials nor apparatus for cooking, the effort was beyond praise.

Having dined, I carried my collapsible chair out on to the verandah, lit a cigarette and – told myself not to be a fool. For I felt more uncomfortable, more lonely, more apprehensive than ever before in all my life.

From where I sat, the moonlit jungle looked beautiful – but unfriendly, threatening; and the danger implicit in the threat was not from the leopard or the tiger.

Generally speaking, this was one of the best hours of the day, the march completed, dinner eaten, and a pleasant tiredness enhancing the flavour of tobacco and the enjoyment of a book. A good hour for the review of the events of the day, the making of plans for the morrow, and appreciation of one's good fortune in being far from the madding crowd and the din of an increasingly clamorous civilization.

The ocean, the desert and the jungle are the last strongholds and resorts of peace.

But here there was no peace. Silence, so far as the jungle is ever silent; utter stillness; but no peace – of mind.

Decidedly this was a bad place, or else I was going to be ill. It must be that ... Fever ... Liver ... And yet, until I came within sight of this derelict house, I had been in perfect health.

I had better go to bed.

Re-entering the big central room, on either side of which were two bedrooms, I turned up the wick of the lamp that hung from a roof-beam, and took stock of the place. What immediately caught my attention and gave me a slight shock of surprise, was the fact that, across one corner of the room, was a piano.

Now, I have had a perhaps unusually wide experience of rest-houses, *dak* bungalows, *pahngs* and such buildings, provided for the shelter of the casual traveller in India, Ceylon, Burma, Siam, Malaya, Annam, Cambodia, and certain parts of Africa and China; but never yet have I discovered one provided with a piano. I have known them to be well-fitted, well-kept houses, with one or more resident servants; and I have known them to be dirty derelict huts, with one or more resident reptiles, poisonous, domiciled and waiting – but never a piano.

And as my eye roamed round the ill-lit room, I discovered that it differed, in other respects, from the usual central hall common to the use of travellers occupying the different bedrooms – should more than one traveller be occupying the rest-house at the same time.

Such a room generally contains a dining-table and four chairs.

This room was furnished; and old, neglected, tattered, dust-covered and derelict as the furniture might be, it had once been drawing-room furniture. There was what had been a handsome screen at each door;

there were a sofa and arm-chairs; pictures had once adorned the walls, and the cracked, dirty and insect-riddled remains still hung in their places. In a teak-wood bookcase were the remains of books, now the home of the fish-insect, the ant, the cockroach and the rat. In a corner was a standard lamp, about whose glass chimney and globe still hung the tattered remnants of a silk shade. And beneath my feet was a matting of a very different quality from that of the usual plaited palm-leaf to be found in the ordinary travellers' rest-house. This was of fine Chinese reed-work and had cost money.

And incongruous, in this ghost of a long-dead drawing-room, stood a bed. Beside it, my jungle 'boy' had set up my own folding camp-bed, which looked neat, clean and positively attractive beside the much bigger one, once comparatively sumptuous, now a dubious-looking mass of discoloured, dust-covered silk and grimy linen.

Here and there a gleam of colour showed through dust which lay so thickly as to amount almost to a covering of earth or ash. Part of this, of course, would be the settling dust of years, part a precipitate of fine bamboo and other wood 'saw-dust' that had rained down upon it from the roof and rafters above, as the boring insects proceeded with their uninterrupted labours of destruction.

A truly dreadful room, suggesting to my mind an aged crone dressed in finery that she had worn for fifty years; a hag, evil and malignant, foul and filthy, yet not only alive, but retaining, beneath the dirt of ages, faint rare glimpses of a former finery.

But why sleep in this drawing-room of a nightmare, when there were apparently four bedrooms opening from this central room?

On a bedside table – who last had used that bedside table, and had it been a man or a woman? – I saw that my boy had placed my Hitchcock lamp, one of those invaluable pieces of camp-furniture which, needing neither chimney nor globe, gives an excellent if fierce light, and whose loud and insistent ticking is something that soothes or maddens the nerves of the lonely listener, according to the state of his mind, or more probably of his liver.

Picking it up, I lit it, and opened the nearest door.

In this room were two beds, a leg-rest chair, and a dressing-table with mirror. The room was in some disorder, and was evidently exactly as it had been left by its last occupants when, hurriedly, they departed.

Returning to the drawing-room and closing the door behind me, I entered the other room on the same side, and discovered similar conditions. This also was a double bedroom, or at any rate a room last occupied by two people, the almost mouldering remains of tumbled bedding, and suggestions of hurried departure, if not sudden flight.

And similarly in the case of the two other bedrooms.

Eight guests – and a ninth person, the host, who had slept in the drawing-room that fatal night, had fled in haste, leaving everything as it stood.

Having made my tour of inspection I sat down in a spacious arm-chair – and almost went through it to the floor. For one hideous moment of imprisonment I struggled in a position of great indignity and extreme discomfort, until I contrived to extricate myself from what was really a very neat trap.

'Good heavens!' thought I, as at length, breathless, I got to my feet and surveyed the now bottomless chair, 'I might have stuck their till I died,' the idiotic thought being in keeping with my frame of mind and my environment. For I should hardly have died before morning, when my boy and the coolies would have come. On the other hand, in that horrible position, with my knees firmly pressed against my chest, I might very well have died of suffocation, heart failure, or of a broken blood-vessel.

And once again, what rubbish, when my heart was as strong as that of a horse, and my arteries as soft as indiarubber. And yet, fear, horror and despair are not ridiculous; and, for a few seconds, while firmly wedged into that malevolent-seeming chair, endowed with devilish intention, I had been frightened, horrified, and despairing of ever escaping from the trap.

However, fear had its usual reaction, anger, and I felt thoroughly and savagely annoyed – a much healthier mental state.

I would undress and go to bed; and the devil and all his imps could play any game they fancied, in, around, above, and below the bungalow; and I would not so much as open an eye and cast a glance at them.

So I thought, or at any rate, so I told myself, and raising the mosquito curtain, got into bed, tucked the edge of the curtain in, turned the light down very low, closed my eyes and composed myself for sleep.

Suddenly something creaked very loudly. I opened my eyes and sat up; and sleep fled further from me than ever.

This wouldn't do. If I were going to jump up like that every time there was a creak, I should spend a restless night. But this had been no ordinary creak; and, lest it should seem strange and unreasonable that one should differentiate between one creak and another, I will mention that the sound was precisely that which I myself had made in walking across the wooden floor.

As I have said, the bungalow was supported upon *teangs*, great posts which raised it some twelve feet above the ground; and the floor was of boards, one or two of which, probably owing to shrinkage in dry weather after being swollen during the rains, creaked quite audibly when trodden on, somewhat as do the stairs in all old houses.

I was perfectly certain that someone, probably a bare-footed native, had crossed the room.

Hastily pulling out the linen border of the mosquito-curtain from under the thin mattress of the camp-bed, I turned up the lamp.

The room was empty, of course, and as I perfectly well knew.

Neither my jungle 'boy' nor any coolie would come into the room before dawn, and no dacoit would wander about in that fashion, within a minute of my getting into bed. What a dacoit would do would be to creep up the steps, glide like a ghost – damn that word ghost! – across the verandah and with a rush and a leap, drive his *kris* through my throat.

Or so I argued.

Anyway, there was nobody in the room. Nobody visible, that is to say.

And again I turned down the lamp, tucked in the mosquito curtain, turned on to my right side, firmly closed my eyes, and prayed the old English prayer:

> From bogles and bugaboos, warlocks and wurricoes,
> Ghaisties and ghoulies, long-leggity beasties,
> And things that go wump in the night,
> Good Lord, deliver us.

I closed my eyes but unfortunately I could not close my ears, and the loud creak which was obviously made by someone stepping upon one of those loose boards again sounded through the room, sudden and sharp as the crack of a pistol. That was a gross exaggeration, of course. It was more like the snapping of a twig beneath the unpractised foot in the dry jungle, the tiny resounding snap that warns the stalked prey of the approach of heavy-footed clumsy death – of murder most foul but self-defeated.

For some reason, or for no reason, I suddenly remembered my Irish batman and his favourite formula for use on all occasions.

'*Ah, to Hell wit' it then!*'

That was the proper attitude of mind and the suitable incantation.

Again the sound of stealthy footsteps ...

Bosh! That was an absolute boys'-magazine *cliché*. There was no sound of footsteps, stealthy or otherwise – only the noise of someone treading on loose boards.

But surely a ghost, a spirit, a *bhut*, *afrit*, *peh*, was imponderable, without substance, and quite incapable of depressing a warped board.

It wasn't incapable of depressing me, though, and my possibly warped mind.

A loud creak, as someone or something – or nothing – trod on another place where a board under the matting responded beneath the pressure.

'*Ah, to Hell wit' it!*'

And then, almost with a shriek, I again sprang bolt upright, for a pair of giant hands, with fingers spread from end to end of the keyboard, crashed down upon the keys of the piano, bringing forth a terrific and hideous cacophony, a horrible jangling discord, discernible through which were the sounds of breaking wires.

Good God! Angels and ministers of grace defend us!

I admit that it was with a hand decidedly inclined to tremble that I again turned up the light, and saw that there was no one at the piano, or in the room.

But really, this would not do. This was not only beyond a joke, it was beyond all reason. Clearly and definitely it was beyond reason that invisible hands should strike a crashing chord upon a piano.

I'm sure there are brave men who would have said 'Tut! tut!' Possibly have walked to the piano, played a hymn-tune – *Eternal Father, strong to save*, perhaps – and returned to bed the better for the performance.

Personally, I was much more inclined to get well down under the clothes, pull them over my head, and stay there till a cold or bony hand removed them.

What I did do was to sit and stare, wide-eyed and open-mouthed, while I burst into a cold sweat and tried to find rational explanation for this astonishing – and indeed in that place, at that hour, appalling – phenomenon.

The creaking of the loose boards I could explain away, more or less – in point of fact, very much less – satisfactorily, by remembering how furniture creaks, and indeed bangs, occasionally, in old houses, in the middle of the night. (Though why the devil it should always choose the middle of the night for that exercise is something of a mystery.)

The boards might creak and groan without having been trodden upon by human or non-human foot; it might be their playful habit and old-established custom to wait till midnight and then make precisely the noise they made when a heavy man stepped on them.

But what about the piano? I could not remember ever previously having slept in the same room as a piano, but I was prepared to wager a very large sum that though the woodwork of an aged and neglected piano might conceivably utter a creak or, through the sudden breaking of a wire, emit a doleful jangling *ping*, it could not possibly produce a hellish uproar in which a score of keys and strings were concerned.

I was prepared to admit that in the lonely stillness of the most ordinary drawing-room in the most commonplace bungalow, a piano, through the slipping of a wire, might make one unmusical sound; but it was inconceivable that it should make a hundred hideous jangling noises.

Cursing my cowardice, I turned the light right out.

Staring into the darkness, I could see nothing; and this is not so much a statement of the obvious as it sounds, for the darkness was not complete, not that darkness of a black velvet. The night without was lit by a gibbous moon and the brilliant tropic stars.

No, I could see nothing. But again someone at the piano played a rough and violent discord.

Raising my mosquito-curtain, I struck a match and lit the table-lamp. As I did so, I heard a heavy thud, followed by minor movements.

Lifting the lamp above my head with a hand undoubtedly beginning to tremble, I looked round the room. There was nothing whatsoever to be seen, save the decrepit furniture.

'Another little smoke wouldn't do us any harm,' said I aloud, to show myself how bold a fellow of yet-unshaken nerve was I.

Something rustled in reply.

'Rats!' said I. 'Rats. And this can be taken as a reference to rodents or as a derisive ejaculation.' Which statement, made solemnly and aloud, showed me that, whatever I might pretend, I was nervous. I would get up, light the hanging lamp, turn the small one up, and read until daylight.

No – damned if I would. For the rest of my life I should be ashamed to look myself in the face.

I finished my cigarette, turned out my lamp again, and, as a concession to human frailty and cowardice, took the matches into bed with me, tucked in the mosquito-curtain, and composed myself to slumber.

Never yet have I found any of the devices advocated for sleep-inducement of the slightest effect or value. Speaking for myself, the only thing is to relax, mind and body, beginning with the muscles of the toes and working up to those of the scalp, consciously relaxing and letting go all holds, one after the other, and finally making the mind a blank – or blanker than usual.

I had worked my way up to the arms, and had just made my hands and forearms utterly inert, when there was what might be called – and indeed must be called, for there is no other description – 'a ghastly cry'. And the ghastly cry was uttered within the room.

It was something between a moan, a wail, and a scream. I struck a match. It broke, fell on to the bedclothes, and went out. And in the brief half-second of light, I saw what again might be called – indeed must be called, for there is no other description – 'something white', a ghostly figure that crossed the room.

I struck another match, pulled up the mosquito-curtain with a great air of resolution and determination to look into the matter and do something, only to discover that there was no matter into which to look, and nothing to be done. There was no sound in the room, and certainly there was no 'something white'.

'And this is where another little drink wouldn't do us any harm,' said I.'

In point of fact, it had no opportunity to do any harm or any good, for I had nothing to drink save a little soda-water in the bottle left by my jungle 'boy'. There was not even the *nam tohn* of porous clay with a tin cup inverted over its neck, usually to be found in *dak* bungalows; and, had there been one, I should have hesitated to drink from it. Why, it is difficult to say. What is the difference between germ-infested water brought straight from the nearest *huey* or pond to the bungalow, and water of the native-owned soda-water shop? Of the two, perhaps the soda-water is the more dangerous, as its inhabitant microbes must be in a higher state of stimulation and activity – not to mention the mud and other filth encrusted in the neck of the soda-water bottle.

Having decided, I drank the soda-water and lay down, after noting that, according to my watch, the night was still young, the hour being but two o'clock. Well, plenty of time for plenty of doings ...

Soon I fell asleep – even as do men who await the dawn firing-party or the gaol officials who come to lead them to the scaffold. In that cheery frame of mind.

Anyhow, I must have slept, because undoubtedly I was awakened. How much of what I experienced in the act of awakening was dream, how much imagination, and how much utterly unreal reality, I don't know, but I do know that from a dream or from dreamless sleep I awoke to the knowledge that there was a party in progress in the room. I must have been in the act of opening my eyes as I saw lights, the forms of men, heard speech and laughter; and what is more, noticed that it was slurred speech and over-noisy laughter.

So certain was I of this, that, in the moment of sitting up and going to raise my mosquito-curtain once more, the feeling uppermost in my mind was one of indignation. What right had these fellows to come carousing and bingeing in my room at three or four o'clock in the morning? A most disgusting exhibition of caddish ill-manners, and I threw up the curtain, prepared to speak my mind to that effect.

Of course there were no bright lights; there was no sound of revelry by night.

But there *was* ...

They were trooping down the steps from the verandah to the garden. And as for a second I listened, now terrified rather than indignant, I knew that the merry party, insted of spreading itself over the garden with joyous whoops, drunken shouts and alcoholic song, turned in under the bungalow among the *teangs*, the great pillars of *meribau* wood that supported the house.

Distinctly I heard them. Distinctly I heard a crash, as of something heavy overturned. Distinctly I heard shouts and cries which were not merry nor amusing; and, finally, a sound such as I hope never to hear again. Those who have heard the scream of a wounded horse will have some idea of the blood-curdling horror of that dreadful cry, a clear-cut shocking shriek that seemed to freeze the marrow in my bones and cause the hair of my head to stand on end.

I had had enough.

Getting out of bed and pulling on my boots, I lit the Hitchcock lamp, turned it up until its flame was as high as it would go, and was thankful for its steady brilliance, and the fact that it needed neither globe nor chimney which might have blackened and broken and obscured the light.

And holding high my lamp, I crossed the verandah, descended the steps and boldly – yes, boldly! – plunged into the midst of whatever might be happening in the pillared gloom of the dreadful place beneath the bungalow.

For it was dreadful.

Not because of anything that was there, but because there was nothing there. No sign or sound of human being, animal, ghost or spirit briefly incarnate.

Save for the fact that it had no outer walls, the place was like a crypt, the big baulks of timber that supported the house suggesting Norman pillars of stone. Several feet above my head were the boards of the floor of the room from which I had just come. Beneath my feet was what had been hard-beaten earth, now in parts thinly covered by sickly weeds. No sign whatsoever of human visitation or occupation was there, save the collapsed timbers of what had been a big packing-case.

I was defeated: and promptly and willingly admitting defeat, fled from the place, mounted the steps and re-entered my bed-drawing-room.

Compared with the cellar-like place beneath the house, this horrible and haunted room seemed almost attractive; for inimical as was its atmosphere, it was not as fear-compelling as the other.

Here above, I felt fear. There below, I felt a horror and a terror fearful beyond fear.

A return to bed, somnolence, and an attitude of defenceless acquiescence were out of the question, and I began to dress, involuntarily glancing over my shoulder, swiftly turning about to see what was behind me, as I did so.

And on this occasion, as not infrequently before, I was glad that I was an extremely temperate person, and that for me, alcohol had no attraction. (Incidentally I really do not make this idiosyncrasy a cause for any self-approval. If I liked alcohol I should drink it.) I was glad because all that I had heard and the little I had seen, really *had* been heard and seen. There was no question of it. It was no alcohol-induced or drug-begotten fantasy. I had heard sounds when wide awake, as widely awake as I was now, doing up my buttons.

True, I had awakened suddenly to see lights and hear sounds that might have been part of a dream; but I felt absolutely convinced that they had also been part of waking experience.

Well, '*There are more things in Heaven and earth ...*'

And whether I had been imagining things, dreaming dreams and seeing visions, or not, one thing was certain: nothing on earth, absolutely nothing, would induce me to spend another night in this place; nay, nor another hour more than was necessary for my getting away from it.

2

Next night I camped in the jungle, a most unpleasant night of wind and rain and conditions that defeated even my accomplished Lao cook and jungle 'boy'. A night that should have been memorable for its acute and complicated discomfort, but which, in point of fact, is memorable for its sweet peacefulness, a sweetness unsoured by cold driving rain and devilish plucking wind, a peace unbroken by the heaviest crashes of violent thunder-storms. Sweetness and peace, because this was the jungle, and not that fear-stricken, horror-infested bungalow.

What were tigers, leopards, king cobras, scorpions, leeches – and the greatest of these is leeches – compared with one sound, one sight, in that house of dread?

The following night I slept in a *Wat*.

We reached it at sundown, and it had an air of solid comfort very reassuring to me after what I had been through. It was but a small *Wat* situated at the end of a green path which led to it from the road, a distance of about two hundred yards. Its outer court or hall of stone was clean and had a well-cared-for air about it. This outer hall had no walls and its stone roof was supported on four heavy stone pillars. Near the entrance was an ancient sacred *Boh*-tree whose branches were so heavy that each one had to be supported by a pole resting on the earth.

The *Wat* was empty save for one *poogni* in a yellow robe, who was chanting before the stone image of Buddha, and he took no notice of me, until, presently departing, he gave me the usual greeting of '*Sabai-ga?*'* to which I answered the usual '*Sabai!*'†

In front of the enormous effigy of the Buddha were arranged the heterogeneous collection of offerings which are usually to be found in these *Wats* and which never cease to astonish one, by reason of their strange variety.

There were stone jam-jars containing dead flowers, cheap alarm-clocks, such as are found in the village-shops in England, bunches of dried flowers, brightly coloured feathers, celluloid or glass balls, bits of coloured china, tin and enamel mugs. There were also numerous candles stuck in the melted wax of others long-since burnt-out. These candles are only lit at festival times, when the villagers come to make their offerings.

* 'Are you well?'   † 'Quite well.'

Here in this place was Peace, for over it brooded the spirit of the Buddha, beneficent, well-wishing; and the pious founder of the temple had been one who fain would acquire merit.

In it I slept peacefully.

On the next day my 'boy', leading our little party, suddenly turned aside and took a path even narrower and fainter than that on which we were. Some little distance down this path was a bamboo *pahng* or *sala*, built in a clearing in the jungle. It is not unusual to find these shelters in various parts of the dense forests. They are quite unfurnished and empty, and may be used by the passing traveller who happens to know where they are situated. The walls and floor are made of split bamboo. While perfectly strong and adequate, the bamboo floor is apt to be rather disconcerting when one walks on one of them for the first time, for it springs up and down with every movement, and it is difficult to keep one's balance until one becomes accustomed to the feeling of walking on springs.

This particularly *pahng* was very charmingly situated. Behind it rose a steep hillside covered with small teak-trees which were in flower. There were also many shrubs, with leaves of various shades of red and gold. In front of the *pahng* was the clearing, beyond which were the tall trees of the forest, and growing up one side of the shelter itself, was a thick bush of pale pink Honolulu creeper which someone had, at some time or other, planted there ...

Here again I slept in peace, and on the following night reached the house of an American medical missionary.

The Reverend Dr Gates proved to be a most interesting man, the soul of hospitality, as unlike the missionary of nitwit fiction as a man could be; and most definitely a doctor, an ethnologist, botanist, zoologist and general scientist long before he was a parson. When, purely for the sake of making conversation, a thing that at first has to be made when one meets a man who has not spoken his own language for months or years, I somewhat fatuously asked him if he had made many converts, he somewhat disconcertingly replied:

'Converts to what?' and later admitted modestly that he had possibly converted a few Wild Was to tameness, a few Karens and possibly one or two arboreal Mois, to elementary ideas of hygiene and handicraft.

Anyhow, shy jungle-folk came to him with their wives and other troubles, realizing that his methods of *accouchement* were better than those of their own witch-doctors, who did not invariably get the best results from their method of roasting the expectant mother before a large fire in the jungle ...

After an excellent dinner that night, we settled down to talk, and, having lived long enough to know when the most successful conversationalist is he who uses his ears far more than his mouth, I got the doctor to tell me of his life work.

And when the good doctor at length fell silent, after apologizing for having talked so much, and I had told him it was the best talk I had had for years, I introduced the subject that, even so, was uppermost in my mind.

'Do you believe in ghosts, Doctor?' I asked as he stuffed his pipe.

'Ghosts?' he laughed. 'Depends entirely on what you mean by ghosts. I haven't an unshakable belief in the chain-rattling figure of the wicked Sir Giles who crosses the moonlit hall at midnight; nor much in the Grey Lady who is discovered sitting in costume in the music room at sunset at St John's Eve. Why? Do you believe in ghosts?'

'Depends entirely on what you mean by ghosts,' I smiled, 'I didn't believe in any sort or kind of ghost until last Monday night. Now I have to do so.'

'Last Monday night. Let's see. Four marches back. Ah! That means the abandoned bungalow just over the Border, the one they tried to turn into a rest-house. Stayed a night there, did you? What happened?'

'Oh, a lot of funny things. First of all, a ghost walked up and down the room in the silence and the darkness – breaking the stillness of the night by causing the boards to creak beneath his weight.'

'The weight of a ghost!' smiled the doctor.

'Weight of something,' I said.

'Well, deal with that first. Suppose a leopard came in and padded to the end of the room and back, looking for your dog, as they do.'

'I should have smelt it.'

'Probably.'

'I should have heard its claws on the boards.'

'One doesn't, in point of fact,' said the doctor. And from the way in which he spoke, he had evidently been in the same room with a leopard and darkness by night.

'Anyway, we needn't go as far as that. The boards creaked and groaned as the temperature fell. Or, more likely still, as they imperceptibly moved back into place after your weight had rested on them.'

I nodded. 'Pass up.'

'Next thing?'

'Something – probably not a leopard – came and played the piano.'

'Recognize the tune?'

'No. There was no tune. In point of fact, it was a God Almighty (excuse me!) crash, as though some giant had suddenly struck every key in three octaves simultaneously. And so hard that some of the wires broke.'

'Yes. Very disturbing in the middle of the night, and admittedly not a leopard. I'll tell you what happened.'

'Thank you,' said I, perhaps a shade sceptically.

'An iguana fell from a horizontal roof-beam. Full length on to, and as it happened, exactly parallel to, the keyboard.'

'Yes . . .' I admitted. 'That would serve.

'Do iguanas get up in the roof?' I asked.

'Not that I know of,' admitted Dr Gates frankly. 'But there's a mighty big lizard – they call it the *goh* – up here . . .'

'What, the Siamese *toctaw*?' I asked.

'A bit bigger,' said Gates. 'Though I don't know that I've ever seen one that would cover three octaves on the piano.

'A snake could, of course,' he added.

'Yes,' I mused. 'But it would be funny if a snake fell rigid in a straight line, like that, wouldn't it?'

'Extremely funny, except for the person who was there listening to it,' admitted Gates. 'But if a big snake fell ten or fifteen feet on to a keyboard of a piano, there would be some noise.'

'Or I'll tell you what it might have been,' he continued. 'Not an iguana, but an ichneumon.'

'Civet-cat,' said I, proud of my worldly knowledge.

'Yes, same sort of thing. Now, they do inhabit roofs, and they are apt to drop most suddenly and somewhat alarmingly from the roof to the floor. It might have been an ichneumon. I had a nice little chap here, tame as a cat. Used to worry my dog frightfully, although I had taught him to accept the hitherto-wild jungle beast as a house companion. 'Tricks' was a big Airedale. Stood about a foot and a half high, and the civet-cat, Jo, used to stalk him. As Tricks walked past its hiding-place Jo would run out, climb on to Tricks's hind leg, run up and along the dog's back and perch on his head just above his nose. I'm afraid it was the bane of poor Tricks's life, but he put up with it very patiently.'

'Well, iguana, *goh, toctaw*, or ichneumon for the piano playing. Pass up. But by the way, the piano was played twice!'

'Yes, that was the iguana or *goh* scrambling off the piano, after resting, a bit winded from his fall, of course.'

'H'm. Well, the next thing was an eerie shudder-making cry in the room, and an indisputable glimpse of the "something white" of ghostly fiction. This was fact.'

'Let's see,' pondered the doctor. 'Yes, I think we can dispose of that. There's a very large white owl in these parts, whose nocturnal habits are not blameless. He's quite equal to a sudden swoop right through your bungalow, in at the back and out at the front, uttering a shriek to curdle your blood as he does so.'

'Is he intentionally offensive?'

'No – it's a – you know – '*This is the house that Jack built*' sort of sequence. Tiny insects such as mosquitoes and moths fly about; bats come in and catch the flying insects, and the huge white owl comes in to catch the bats. That was your ghost.'

I nodded. 'Pass up.'

'He's rather an interesting chap, that bird. Biggest owl in the world, and the natives always attribute its cry to a *peh*, and compare the owl to the *peh-nawk*. When they hear it, they hurry inside their huts and, if possible, shut themselves in. And curiously enough, the cicadas seem to share their fear or dislike, for they always cease their shrilling, and the jungle becomes comparatively silent for some time after the cry has been heard. Some people think the cicadas shut up because they know that the owl eats them, and they realize that their natural enemy is near at hand. Anything else?'

'Anything!' I smiled. 'These were only *hors d'oeuvres variés*. Yes, there was something else ... I fell asleep, a fact that I frankly admit, and I awoke from a dream, another fact that I frankly admit, and the dream continued for a few seconds, so to speak, as I awoke – and a rowdy party that was in my dream was continued in my room ... I am sure that, for a few seconds, or perhaps for part of one second, I was literally wide awake to the fact that this party was going on.'

'And then?' inquired Gates.

'I found that the room was in darkness, and that the party was trooping down the steps and going in under the bungalow.'

Dr Gates eyed me steadily.

'Explanations please?' I smiled.

'Ah! Now you're asking for something,' was the quiet reply. 'But haven't you ... Haven't you ... something else to tell me?'

'Well, only that I lit my lamp, got up, pulled on my boots, and went down to investigate.'

'Good for you,' said Gates. 'I know exactly how you felt, but what I meant was, haven't you something else to tell me about the – er – party?'

'No ... No ... Oh, yes. Of course! Above the laughter and voices, I distinctly heard a crash.'

'Sort of noise made by an *almirah** falling down on its face?'

'Exactly.'

'Yes ... Yes ...?'

'And then a most appalling scream. The most utterly dreadful sound I had ever heard in my life.'

'Yes,' agreed Dr Gates. And I say 'agreed' advisedly. For obviously he had been expecting me to say just what I had said.

'I might of course produce the *peh-nawk* to account for the scream, but I won't.'

'What is it? And why not?' I asked.

---

* Big cupboard or wardrobe.

'What is it? The *peh-nawk* is probably the bird I mentioned just now. It must be a bird. Nobody has seen it, but all jungle-dwellers have heard it. I rank myself as a jungle-dweller, and I have heard it. Like the natives themselves, I would pay down quite a perceptible little sum in hard cash rather than hear it again. And I'd travel a mighty long way round a place where it was likely to be heard. And the reason why I won't blame the noise you heard on to the *peh-nawk* is because it wasn't made by one.'

'By what was it made then?'

'Now, my friend, you are asking another question. I will reply with a story. A story that I think will answer that question. Also answer the first one of the series, and that was, "*Do you believe in ghosts?*" '

'Geoffrey Walsh-Kurnock built that bungalow and laid out that plantation in that particular spot because, amongst other considerations – climate, soil, water, labour and so on – it was in what he considered the Unadministered Territory. This Mission is, of course, undeniably in Unadministered Territory, and at the moment, you are neither in China nor Burma; neither in Siam nor Cambodia. You are nowhere, in fact. Not on any map, at least.

'And Geoffrey had the idea that if he made his plantation and built his bungalow where he did, he'd be free. No one would have any right to interfere with him.

'He was a curious chap and that was one of his idiosyncrasies – freedom ... As if anyone is free – anywhere.

'However, I was glad enough when he came up this way, for it made my nearest neighbour only sixty miles away. What one might call quite near. One could have a monthly chat with a fellow white man. We got along famously, with our dozen talks a year; and, though we didn't see eye to eye on many things, we had a mutual respect and the bond of total dissimilarity.

'He did me a lot of a good, broadened my outlook, and made me more tolerant; and I tried to do him a bit of good so far as that was possible without being offensive – though I must admit it ended in my insisting on his coming and seeing me here instead of my going there, for I really am an awfully poor hand at orgy-making. I don't play cards, I don't drink and – I don't like being a wet blanket. And whenever Geoffrey sent a messenger over, inviting me to his place for the first Saturday in the month, I knew what it meant. It meant, among other things, a wild party. For his monthly feasts became famous; and forest-officers and young teak men; wandering prospectors who had an idea that anybody who went off the beaten track was likely to stumble over large rubies, ingots of silver or lumps of jade; elephant hunters; and occasionally some of those wonderful people who catch large free wild beasts alive, and put them in little iron cages; were apt to be among his guests.

'Anyhow, a party, large or small, there always was, on the first Saturday in the month, at Walsh-Kurnock's place. Of course, it was famous, apart from its hospitality, by reason of its being unique, positively the only plantation in this part of the world, the only place for hundreds of miles where a white man, or any other man, tried to grow kapok, tea and rubber.

'Naturally it has all gone back to jungle now, and I doubt whether any of it would have done much good, unless, possibly, it was the kapok, though I have an idea that there was more in, and behind, Walsh-Kurnock than met the eye.'

The doctor fell silent as he eased the tobacco in his pipe and looked extremely thoughtful.

'In what way?' I asked.

'I don't know. It was no more than wild theory on my own part, but it was such an unlikely place for such an unlikely man, that there must have been more to it than met the eye. I don't know. Oil ... rubies ... jade ... silver ... a Consular official watching Chinese encroachment from the North? And then again, it might have been just agoraphobia, just his idiosyncratic love of solitude, his yearning to escape from his fellow-man. And yet there were the wild parties ... I don't know.

'Well, one Friday afternoon, the day before one of the monthly gatherings of half a score of people who came from all over half a score thousand square miles, Geoffrey Walsh-Kurnock was sitting on the verandah of that bungalow having tea, when there came along the track leading to the bungalow a party of Kamoo jungle-men, personally conducting a gigantic python. They do, you know, in the most extraordinary manner, something like a couple of agricultural labourers leading a bull, at Home. When he thinks he'll charge to the right, the man on the left pulls him back, and when he thinks he'll charge to the left, the man on the right pulls him back, and if he thinks he'll bolt straight ahead, they both pull him back.

'Same with a python. These folk tie a rattan rope round his neck, and a band of them gets at each end of it, and they lead him along. If he won't go straight ahead, they drag him. If he goes too fast, they put the brake on. If he wants to go left or right, they do exactly as the bull-leaders do.

'Perhaps you are wondering why they took the trouble to bring this great brute – over twenty-five feet long and as thick as a man's thigh – to call on Walsh-Kurnock. It was because he was assembling specimens of the fauna of this part of the world, to give, or possibly to sell, to a man who was making a collection for the New York Museum of Natural History.

'So he extended a cordial welcome to what was the very finest specimen of a snake he had ever seen.

'The next problem was how to house it worthily and safely until Brooke came for it. Suddenly he remembered a packing-case in which his piano had arrived. Incidentally, just fancy a man going to the expense and trouble of getting a piano up here.'

'How on earth did he do it?' I asked.

'Well, I should imagine every form of known transport was used between the warehouse in Bangkok and that bungalow; train, sampan, elephant, bullock-cart, and mostly human beast-of-burden. That piano must have come on men's heads through swamp and jungle, over hill-track and forest-path, like a stagbeetle carried by ants.

'Well, into the piano packing-case, without apology or ceremony, went the huge python, a big stone was placed on the lid, the Kamoo coolies then being handsomely rewarded with a five-*satang* piece – about a penny – each.

'Geoffrey returned to his tea. Nor, we may imagine, did he give the snake another thought until, at the height of the party next night, when, the champagne dinner finished – it was always champagne for the guests at Geoffrey's monthly party – and the brandy-and-soda flowing; the Devil put it into somebody's mouth to say:

'"*If you drink much more, Geoff, you'll be seeing snakes.*"

'They had been amusing themselves by trying to snuff a burning candle standing on the verandah rail, at twenty paces, with revolvers fired from the back of the room, when Walsh-Kurnock, who had been very successful, asked if anyone would let him shoot the candle off the top of his head – like William Tell and the apple.

'There was a Austrian there, a queer chap with a highly polished bald head – he was a man who was trying to grow cotton a hundred miles east of Walsh-Kurnock's place – and Geoffrey particularly wanted to drop some hot wax on his bald cranium, stick the candle in it, light it, and snuff the flame at twenty paces.

'But the Austrian, though otherwise a sensible man, objected.

'"*No, you're drunk, Geoff,*" said he. "*If you drink much more, you'll be seeing snakes in a minute.*"

'And that was what reminded him.

'"*Snakes!*" he cried. "*Adam and Eve! I'll show you a snake! I've got the very one that escaped from the Garden of Eden, downstairs. Come and have a look.*"

'And picking up the candle and telling someone else to bring the lamp, he led the way down those steps and they all trooped in under the bungalow.

'"*Here, catch hold of this,*" he said to somebody, gave him the candle, went to pull the big stone off the top of the packing-case, and overturned the whole thing.

'There was a crash, as it went over and the stone and lid fell away, releasing the enormous python. Before that lot of drunken and half-drunken and wine-excited young men knew it, that twenty-five feet of

immeasurable deadly strength was among them. The man holding the
lamp, backing away, fell over the stone, dropping the lamp as he did so.
The lamp went out. The man who held the candle fled for his life, and
as the rest turned, shouting scrambling, stumbling in the pitch darkness,
bumping into the *teangs*, they heard a scream that curdled their blood.

'It was one of them who told me all this, and I shall never forget the
phrase he used:

' *"It was a shrieking scream of agony and fear that seemed to rend the very fabric
of the night with a gigantic tearing sound that pierced one's ear-drums."*

'He wasn't an Englishman, as you may imagine.

'The first man who returned with a light held above his head saw
Geoffrey Walsh-Kurnock bound to one of the twelve-foot *teangs* by a
gigantic rope, a living rope, the python – whose open mouth and coldly
glaring eyes hovered a few inches from those of its victim, its crushed and
mangled victim, in whose body every single bone was broken a dozen
times.'

'Yes, I heard every detail of the whole affair from an eye-witness, the man
who saw him in the serpent's coils. He came straight here, just as quickly
as he could travel, and I had to nurse him for quite a while, before he
was fit to take up life again.'

We sat a while in silence.

'Before I leave this place, if I ever do,' said Dr Gates, 'I shall come to
believe that I too was an eye-witness – instead of only an ear-witness –
of what happened that night.'

'A what?'

'An ear-witness. Like yourself. The night I slept there, I heard –
exactly what you did. I don't mean the creakings of the dry floor-boards
nor the falling of the lizard on to the piano and the hooting of the owl;
but the laughter, the descent to the place beneath, the brief hubbub, and
then the cry.'

'Do we believe in ghosts, you and I, Doctor?' I asked.

'No, no, of course not. Aren't we rational, sensible men? We each
dreamed a dream, a nightmare, rather; and were wakened by the scream
of the *peh-nawk*.'

'Quite so,' I agreed. 'Obviously ... But, tell me. What was your chief
essential fundamental sensation, your real mental reaction, to that
bungalow?'

'Fear. Soul-shaking, mind-enfeebling, body-devitalizing *fear*,' he
replied.

'Mine too,' I admitted. 'There I really knew fear.'

Close Behind Him

John Wyndham

'You didn't ought to of croaked him,' Smudger said resentfully. 'What in hell did you want to do a fool thing like that for?'

Spotty turned to look at the house, a black spectre against the night sky. He shuddered.

'It was him or me,' he muttered. 'I wouldn't of done it if he hadn't come for me – and I wouldn't even then, not if he'd come ordinary ...'

'What do you mean ordinary?'

'Like anybody else. But he was queer ... He wasn't – well, I guess he was crazy – dangerous crazy ...'

'All he needed was a tap to keep him quiet,' Smudger persisted. 'There's was no call to bash his loaf in.'

'You didn't see him. I tell you, he didn't act human.' Spotty shuddered again at the recollection, and bent down to rub the calf of his right leg tenderly.

The man had come into the room while Spotty was sifting rapidly through the contents of a desk. He'd made no sound. It had been just a feeling, a natural alertness, that had brought Spotty round to see him standing there. In that very first glimpse Spotty had felt there was something queer about him. The expression on his face – his attitude – they were wrong. In his biscuit-coloured pyjamas, he should have looked just an ordinary citizen awakened from sleep, too anxious to have delayed with dressing-gown and slippers. But some way he didn't. An ordinary citizen would have shown nervousness, at least wariness; he would most likely have picked up something to use as a weapon. This man stood crouching, arms a little raised, as though he were about to spring.

Moreover, any citizen whose lips curled back as this man's did to show his tongue licking hungrily between his teeth, should have been considered sufficiently unordinary to be locked away safely. In the course of his profession Spotty had developed reliable nerves, but the look of this man rocked them. Nobody should be pleased by the discovery of a burglar at large in his house. Yet, there could be no doubt that this victim was looking at Spotty with satisfaction. An unpleasant gloating kind of satisfaction, like that which might appear on a fox's face at the sight of a plump chicken. Spotty hadn't liked the look of him at all, so he had pulled out the convenient piece of pipe that he carried for emergencies.

Far from showing alarm, the man took a step closer. He poised, sprung on his toes like a wrestler.

'You keep off me, mate,' said Spotty, holding up his nine inches of lead pipe as a warning.

Either the man did not hear – or the words held no interest for him. His long, bony face snarled. He shifted a little closer. Spotty backed up against the edge of the desk. 'I don't want no trouble. You just keep off me,' he said again.

The man crouched a little lower. Spotty watched him through narrowed eyes. An extra tensing of the man's muscles gave him a fractional warning before the attack.

The man came without feinting or rushing: he simply sprang, like an animal.

In mid-leap he encountered Spotty's boot suddenly erected like a stanchion in his way. It took him in the middle and felled him. He sprawled on the floor doubled up, with one arm hugging his belly. The other hand threatened, with fingers bent into hooks. His head turned in jerks, his jaws with their curiously sharp teeth were apart, like a dog's about to snap.

Spotty knew just as well as Smudger that what was required was a quietening tap. He had been about to deliver it with professional skill and quality when the man, by an extraordinary wriggle, had succeeded in fastening his teeth into Spotty's leg. It was unexpected, excruciating enough to ruin Spotty's aim and make the blow ineffectual. So he had hit again; harder this time. Too hard. And even then he had more or less had to pry the man's teeth out of his leg ...

But it was not so much his aching leg – nor even the fact that he had killed the man – that was the chief cause of Spotty's concern. It was the kind of man he had killed.

'Like an animal he was,' he said, and the recollection made him sweat. 'Like a bloody wild animal. And the way he looked! His eyes! Christ, they wasn't human.'

That aspect of the affair held little interest for Smudger. He'd not seen the man until he was already dead and looking like any other corpse. His present concern was that a mere matter of burglary had been abruptly transferred to the murder category – a class of work he had always kept clear of until now.

The job had looked easy enough. There shouldn't have been any trouble. A man living alone in a large house – a pretty queer customer with a pretty queer temper. On Fridays, Sundays, and sometimes on Wednesdays, there were meetings at which about twenty people came to the house and did not leave until the small hours of the following morning. All this information was according to Smudger's sister, who learned it third hand from the woman who cleaned the house. The woman was darkly speculative, but unspecific, about what went on at these gatherings. But from Smudger's point of view the important thing was that on other nights the man was alone in the house.

He seemed to be a dealer of some kind. People brought odd curios to the house to sell him. Smudger had been greatly interested to hear that they were paid for – and paid for well – in cash. That was a solid, practical consideration. Beside it, the vaguely ill reputation of the place, the queerness of its furnishings, and the rumours of strange goings-on at the gatherings, were unimportant. The only thing worthy of any attention were the facts that the man lived alone and had items of value in his possession.

Smudger had thought of it as a one-man job at first, and with a little more information he might have tackled it on his own. He discovered that there was a telephone, but no dog. He was fairly sure of the room in which the money must be kept, but unfortunately his sister's source of information had its limitations. He did not know whether there were burglar alarms or similar precautions, and he was too uncertain of the cleaning woman to attempt to get into the house by a subterfuge for a preliminary investigation. So he had taken Spotty in with him on a fifty-fifty basis.

The reluctance with which he had taken that step had now become an active regret – not only because Spotty had been foolish enough to kill the man, but because the way things had been he could easily have made a hundred per cent haul on his own – and not be fool enough to kill the man had he been detected.

The attaché case which he carried now was well-filled with bundles of notes, along with an assortment of precious-looking objects in gold and silver, probably eminently traceable, but useful if melted down. It was irritating to think that the whole load, instead of merely half of it, might have been his.

The two men stood quietly in the bushes for some minutes and listened. Satisfied, they pushed through a hole in the hedge, them moved cautiously down the length of the neighbouring field in its shadow.

Spotty's chief sensation was relief at being out of the house. He hadn't liked the place from the moment they had entered. For one thing, the furnishings weren't like those he was used to. Unpleasant idols or carved figures of some kind stood about in unexpected places, looming suddenly out of the darkness into his flashlight's beam with hideous expressions on their faces. There were pictures and pieces of tapestry that were macabre and shocking to a simple burlgar. Spotty was not particularly sensitive, but these seemed to him highly unsuitable to have about the home.

The same quality extended to more practical objects. The legs of a large oak table had been carved into mythical miscegenates of repulsive appearance. The two bowls which stood upon the table were either genuine or extremely good representations of polished human skulls. Spotty could not imagine why, in one room, anybody should want to mount a crucifix on the wall upside down and place on a shelf beneath it a row of sconces holding nine black candles – then flank the whole with two pictures of an indecency so revolting it almost took his breath away. All these things had somehow combined to rattle his usual hard-headedness.

But even though he was out of the place now, he didn't feel quite free of its influence. He decided he wouldn't feel properly himself again until they were in the car and several miles away.

After working around two fields they came to the dusty white lane off which they had parked the car. They prospected carefully. By now the sky had cleared of clouds and the moonlight showed the road empty in both directions. Spotty scrambled through the hedge, across the ditch, and stood on the road in a quietness broken only by Smudger's progress through the hedge. Then he started to walk towards the car.

He had gone about a dozen paces when Smudger's voice stopped him: 'Hey. Spotty. What've you got on your feet?'

Spotty stooped and looked down. There was nothing remarkable about his feet; his boots looked just as they had always looked.

'What?' he began.

'No! Behind you!'

Spotty looked back. From the point where he had stepped on to the road to another some five feet behind where he now stood was a series of footprints, dark in the white dust. He lifted his foot and examined the sole of his boot; the dust was clinging to it. He turned his eyes back to the footmarks once more. They looked black, and seemed to glisten.

Smudger bent down to peer more closely. When he looked up again there was a bewildered expression on his face. He gazed at Spotty's boots, and then back to the glistening marks. The prints of bare feet . . .

'There's something funny going on here,' he said inadequately.

Spotty, looking back over his shoulder, took another step forward. Five feet behind him a new mark of a bare foot appeared from nowhere.

A watery feeling swept over Spotty. He took another experimental step. As mysteriously as before, another footmark appeared. He turned widened eyes on Smudger. Smudger looked back at him. Neither said anything for a moment. Then Smudger bent down, touched one of the marks with his finger, then shone his flashlight on the finger.

'Red,' he said. 'Like blood ...'

The words broke the trance that had settled on Spotty. Panic seized him. He stared around wildly, then began to run. After him followed the footprints. Smudger ran too. He noticed that the marks were no longer the prints of a full foot but only its forepart, as if whatever made them were also running.

Spotty was frightened, but not badly enough to forget the turn where they had parked the car beneath some trees. He made for it, and clambered in. Smudger, breathing heavily, got in on the other side and dropped the attaché case in the back.

'Going to get out of this lot quick,' Spotty said, pressing the starter.

'Take it easy,' advised Smudger. 'We got to think.'

But Spotty was in no thinking mood. He got into gear, jolted out of hiding, and turned down the lane.

A mile or so farther on Smudger turned back from craning out of the window.

'Not a sign,' he said relieved. 'Reckon we've ditched it – whatever it was.' He thought for some moments, then he said: 'Look here, if those marks were behind us all the way from the house, they'll be able to follow them by daylight to where we parked the car.'

'They'd've found the car marks anyway,' Spotty replied.

'But what if they're *still* following?' Smudger suggested.

'You just said they weren't.'

'Maybe they couldn't keep up with us. But suppose they're coming along somewhere behind us, leaving a trail?'

Spotty had greatly recovered, he was almost his old practical self again. He stopped the car. 'All right. We'll see,' he said grimly. 'And if they are – what then?'

He lit a cigarette with a hand that was almost steady. Then he leaned out of the car, studying the road behind them. The moonlight was strong enough to show up any dark marks.

'What do you reckon it was?' he said, over his shoulder. 'We can't both've been seeing things.'

'They were real enough.' Smudger looked at the stain still on his finger.

On a sudden idea, Spotty pulled up his right trouser leg. The marks of the teeth were there, and there was a little blood, too, soaked into his sock, but he couldn't make that account for anything.

The minutes passed. Still there was no manifestation of footprints. Smudger got out and walked a few yards back along the road to make sure. After a moment's hesitation Spotty followed him.

'Not a sign,' Smudger said. 'I reckon – hey!' He broke off, looking beyond Spotty.

Spotty turned around. Behind him was a trail of dark, naked footprints leading *from* the car.

Spotty stared. He walked back to the car; the footprints followed. It was a chastened Spotty who sat down in the car.

'Well?'

Smudger had nothing to offer. Smudger, in fact, was considerably confused. Several aspects of the situation were competing for his attention. The footsteps were not following *him*, so he found himself less afraid of them than of their possible consequences. They were laying a noticeable trail for anyone to follow to Spotty, and the trouble was that the trail would lead to him, too, if he and Spotty kept together.

The immediate solution that occurred to him was that they split up, and Spotty take care of his own troubles. The best way would be to divide the haul right here and now. If Spotty could succeed in shaking off the footprints, good for him. After all, the killing was none of Smudger's affair.

He was about to make the suggestion when another aspect occurred to him. If Spotty were picked up with part of the stuff on him, the case would be clinched. It was also possible that Spotty, in a bad jam with nothing to lose, might spill. A far safer way would be for him to hold the stuff. Then Spotty could come for his share when, and if, he succeeded in losing the telltale prints.

It was obviously the only safe and reasonable course. The trouble was that Spotty, when it was suggested to him, did not see it that way.

They drove a few more miles, each occupied with his own thoughts. In a quiet lane they stopped once more. Again Spotty got out of the car and walked a few yards away from it. The moon was lower, but it still gave enough light to show the footprints following him. He came back looking more worried than frightened. Smudger decided to cut a possible loss and go back to his former plan.

'Look here,' he suggested, 'what say we share out the takings now, and you drop me off a bit up the road?'

Spotty looked doubtful, but Smudger pressed: 'If you can shake that trail off, well and good. If you can't – well, there's no sense in us both getting pinched, is there? Anyway, it was you who croaked him. And one has a better chance of getting away than two.'

Spotty was still not keen, but he had no alternative to offer.

Smudger pulled the attaché case out of the back and opened it between them. Spotty began to separate the bundles of notes into two piles. It had been a good haul. As Smudger watched, he felt a great sadness that half of it was going to benefit nobody when Spotty was picked up. Sheer waste, it seemed to him.

Spotty, with his head bent over his work, did not notice Smudger draw the piece of lead pipe out of his pocket. Smudger brought it down on the back of his head with such force and neatness that it is doubtful whether Spotty ever knew anything about it.

Smudger stopped the car at the next bridge and pushed Spotty's body over the low wall. He watched as the ripples widened out across the canal below. Then he drove on.

It was three days later that Smudger got home. He arrived in the kitchen soaked to the skin, and clutching his attaché case. He was looking worn, white, and ready to drop. He dragged a chair away from the table and slumped into it.

'Bill!' his wife whispered. 'What is it? Are they after you?'

'No, Liz – at least, it ain't the cops. But something is.'

He pointed to a mark close inside the door. At first she thought it was his own wet footprint.

'Get a wet cloth, Liz, and clean up the front step and the passage before anyone sees it,' he said.

She hesitated, puzzled.

'For God's sake, do it quick, Liz,' he urged her.

Still half bewildered, she went through the dark passage and opened the door. The rain was pelting down, seeming to bounce up from the road as it hit. The gutters were running like torrents. Everything streamed with wetness save the doorstep protected by the small jutting porch. And on the step was the blood-red print of a naked foot . . .

In a kind of trance she went down on her knees and swabbed it clean with the wet cloth. Closing the door, she switched on the lights and saw the prints leading towards the kitchen. When she had cleaned them up, she went back to her husband.

'You been hit, Bill?'

He looked at her, elbows on the table, his head supported between his hands.

'No,' he said. 'It ain't me what's making them marks, Liz – it's what's followin' me.'

'Following you? You mean they been following you all the way from the job?' she said incredulously. 'How did you get back?'

Smudger explained. His immediate anxiety, after pitching Spotty into the canal, had been to rid himself of the car. It had been a pinch for the job, and the number and description would have been circulated. He had parked it in a quiet spot and got out to walk, maybe pick up a lift. When he had gone a few yards he had looked back and seen the line of prints behind him. They had frightened him a good deal more than he now admitted. Until that moment he had assumed that since they had been following Spotty they would have followed him into the canal. Now, it seemed, they had transferred their attentions to himself. He tried a few more steps: they followed. With a great effort he got a grip on himself, and refrained from running. He perceived that unless he wanted to leave a clear trail he must go back to the car. He did.

Farther on he tried again, and with a sinking, hopeless feeling observed the same result. Back in the car, he lit a cigarette and considered plans with as much calmness as he could collect.

The thing to do was to find something that would not show tracks – or would not hold them. A flash of inspiration came to him, and he headed the car towards the river.

The sky was barely grey yet. He fancied that he managed to get the car down to the towpath without being seen. At any rate, no one had hailed him as he cut through the long grass to the water's edge. From there he had made his way downstream, plodding along through a few inches of water until he found a rowboat. It was a venerable and decrepit affair, but it served his purpose.

From then on his journey had been unexciting, but also uncomfortable. During the day he had become extremely hungry, but he did not dare to leave the boat until after dark, and then he moved only in the darkest streets where the marks might not be seen. Both that day and the next two he had spent hoping for rain. This morning, in a drenching downpour that looked like it might continue for hours, he had sunk the boat and made his way home, trusting that the trail would be washed away. As far as he knew, it had been.

Liz was less impressed than she ought to have been.

'I reckon it must be something on your boots,' she said practically. 'Why didn't you buy some new ones?'

He looked at her with a dull resentment. 'It ain't nothing on my boots,' he said. 'Didn't I tell you it was following me? You seen the marks. How could they come off my boots? Use your head.'

'But it don't make sense. Not the way you say it. *What's* following you?'

'How do I know,' he said bitterly. 'All I know is that it makes them marks – and they're getting closer, too.'

'How do you mean closer?'

'Just what I say. The first day they was about five feet behind me. Now they're between three and four.'

It was not the kind of thing that Liz could take in too easily.

'It don't make sense,' she repeated.

It made no sense during the days that followed, but she ceased to doubt. Smudger stayed in the house; whatever was following stayed with him. The marks of it were everywhere: on the stairs, upstairs, downstairs. Half Liz's time was spent in cleaning them up lest someone should come in and see them. They got on her nerves. But not as badly as they got on Smudger's ...

Even Liz could not deny that the feet were stepping a little more closely behind him – a little more closely each day.

'And what happens when they catch up?' Smudger demanded fearfully. 'Tell me what. What can I do? What the hell can I do?'

But Liz had no suggestions. Nor was there anyone else they dared ask about it.

Smudger began to dream nights. He'd whimper and she'd wake him up asking what was the matter. The first time he could not remember, but the dream was repeated, growing a little clearer with each recurrence. A black shape appeared to hang over him as he lay. It was vaguely manlike in form, but it hovered in the air as if suspended. Gradually it sank lower and lower until it rested upon him – but weightlessly, like a pattern of fog. It seemed to flow up towards his head, and he was in panic lest it should cover his face and smother him, but at his throat it stopped. There was a prickling at the side of his neck. He felt strangely weak, as though tiredness suddenly invaded him. At the same time, the shadow appeared to grow denser. He could feel, too, that there began to be some weight in it as it lay upon them. Then, mercifully, Liz would wake him.

So real was the sensation that he inspected his neck carefully in the mirror when he shaved. But there was no mark there.

Gradually the glistening red prints closed in behind him. A foot behind his heels, six inches, three inches . . .

Then came a morning when he awoke tired and listless. He had to force himself to get up, and when he looked in the mirror, there *was* a mark on his throat. He called Liz, in a panic. But it was only a very small mark, and she made nothing of it.

But the next morning his lassitude was greater. It needed all his willpower to drag himself up. The pallor of his face shocked Liz – and himself, too, when he saw it in the shaving mirror. The red mark on his neck stood out more vividly . . .

The next day he did not get up.

Two days later Liz became frightened enough to call in the doctor. It was a confession of desperation. Neither of them cared for the doctor, who knew or guessed uncomfortably much about the occupations of his patients. One called a doctor for remedies, not for homilies on one's way of life.

He came, he hummed, he ha'ed. He prescribed a tonic, and had a talk with Liz.

'He's seriously anaemic,' he said. 'But there's more to it than that. Something on his mind.' He looked at her. 'Have you any idea what it is?'

Liz's denial was unconvincing. He did not even pretend to believe it.

'I'm no magician,' he said. 'If you don't help me, I can't help him. Some kinds of worry can go on pressing and nagging like an abscess.'

Liz continued to deny. For a moment she had been tempted to tell about the footmarks, but caution warned her that once she began she would likely be trapped into saying more than was healthy.

'Think it over,' the doctor advised. 'And let me know tomorrow how he is.'

The next morning there was no doubt that Smudger was doing very badly. The tonic had done him no good at all. He lay in bed with his eyes, when they were open, looking unnaturally large in a drawn white face. He was so weak that she had to feed him with a spoon. He was frightened, too, that he was going to die. So was Liz. The alarm in her voice when she telephoned the doctor was unmistakably genuine.

'All right, I'll be around within an hour,' he told her. 'Have you found out what's on his mind yet?' he added.

'N-no,' Liz told him.

When he came he told her to stay downstairs while he went up to see the patient. It seemed to her that an intolerably long time passed before she heard his feet on the stairs and she went out to meet him in the hall. She looked up into his face with mute anxiety. His expression was serious, and puzzled, so that she was afraid to hear him speak.

But at last she asked: 'Is – is he going to die, Doctor?'

'He's very weak – very weak indeed,' the doctor said. After a pause, he added: 'Why didn't you tell me about those footprints he thought were following him?'

She looked up at him in alarm.

'It's all right. He's told me all about it now. I knew there was something on his mind. It's not very surprising, either.'

Liz stared at him. 'Not –?'

'In the circumstances, no,' the doctor said. 'A mind oppressed by a sense of sin can play a lot of nasty tricks. Nowadays they talk of guilt complexes and inhibitions. Names change. When I was a boy the same sort of thing was known as a bad conscience.

'When one has the main facts, these things become obvious to anyone of experience. Your husband was engaged in – well, to put it bluntly, burgling the house of a man whose interests were mystic and occult. Something that happened there gave him a shock and unbalanced his judgement.

'As a result, he has difficulty in distinguishing between the real things he sees and the imaginary ones his uneasy conscience shows him. It isn't very complicated. He feels he is being dogged. Somewhere in his subconscious lie the lines from The Ancient Mariner:

> *Because he knows, a frightful fiend*
> *Doth close behind him tread*

and the two come together. And, in addition to that, he appears to have developed a primitive, vampiric type of phobia.

'Now, once we are able to help him dispel this obsession, he ——' broke of, suddenly aware of the look on his listener's face, 'What is it?' he asked.

'But, Doctor,' Liz said. 'Those footmarks, I ——' She was cut short abruptly by a sound from above that was half groan and half scream.

The doctor was up the stairs before she could move. When she followed him, it was with a heavy certainty in her heart.

She stood in the doorway watching as he bent over the bed. In a moment he turned, grave-eyed, and gave her a slight shake of his head. He put his hand on her shoulder, then went quietly past her out of the room.

For some seconds Liz stood without moving. Then her eyes dropped from the bed to the floor. She trembled. Laughter, a high-pitched, frightening laughter shook her as she looked at the red naked footprints which led away from the bedside, across the floor and down the stairs, after the doctor ...

Acknowledgements

The Editor gratefully acknowledges permission to reprint copyright material to the following: Victor Gollancz Ltd. and the Delacorte Press for Lodgers *by Joan Aiken, from 'A Touch of Chill'. The Hutchinson Publishing Group Ltd. for* The Playfellow *by Lady Cynthia Asquith, from 'A Century of Creepy Stories'. The Estate of Enid Bagnold for* The Amorous Ghost. *Denys Val Baker for* The Face in the Mirror; © *1945 by The Briarcliff Quarterly. A. P. Watt Ltd., on behalf of the Estate of the late E. F. Benson for* Caterpillars, *from 'The Room in the Tower'. A. P. Watt Ltd., on behalf of the Estate of the late Algernon Blackwood, for* A Case of Eaves-dropping, *from 'The Empty House'. Robert Bloch and his agents, Scott Meredith Literary Agency, Inc., 845 Third Avenue, New York, N.Y. 10022, U.S.A., for* A Home Away from Home. *Jonathan Cape Ltd. and Alfred A. Knopf, Inc. for* The Cat Jumps *by Elizabeth Bowen, from 'The Cat Jumps'. A. D. Peters & Co. Ltd. for* Dearth's Farm; © *1923 by Gerald Bullett, from 'The Street of the Eye'. The Author for* Calling Card, *from 'Dark Companions'; © 1982 by Ramsey Campbell. The Author for* Undesirable Guests; © *1980 by William Charlton. The Author for* Shona and the Water-Horse; © *1972 by R. Chetwynd-Hayes. Fladgate & Co., Executors of the Estate of Sir Winston Churchill, for* Man Overboard. *The Author for* Superstitious Ignorance; © *Michael Cornish 1966. Murray Pollinger and Random House Inc. for* Georgy Porgy *by Roald Dahl, from 'Kiss Kiss', published by Michael Joseph and Penguin Books Ltd.* Woodman's Knot *is copyright © Mary Danby 1980. The Author for* The Lodger in Room 16; © *David Dixon 1982. The Author and M. B. A. Literary Agents Ltd. for* When Morning Comes; © *Elizabeth Fancett 1969. The Author and M.B.A. Literary Agents Ltd. for* The Girl from Tomango; © *Rick Ferreira 1976. The Author for* A Question of Conscience; © *Catherine Gleason 1978. Wm. Collins Sons & Co. Ltd. and Doubleday and Co. Inc. for* The Basket Chair *by Winston Graham, from 'A Japanese Girl and Other Stories'. Arkham House Publishers, Inc., Sauk City, Wisconsin, U.S.A. for* The Tsanta in the Parlour *by Stephen Grendon; © 1948 by Weird Tales; © 1953 by August Derleth. The Author for* The Frogwood Roundabout; © *Roy Harrison 1978. J. M. Dent & Sons Ltd. for* The Beast with Five Fingers *by W. F. Harvey. Edward Arnold (Publishers) Ltd. for* The Ash-Tree, *from 'Ghost Stories of M. R. James – 2nd Edition'. Laurence Pollinger Ltd. for* Jordan, *from 'Selected Short Stories by Glyn Jones'. John P. Trevaskis for* The Thing in the Cellar *by David H. Keller. Kirby McCauley Ltd. for* Suffer the Little Children *by Stephen King. Nigel Kneale and Douglas Rae (Management) Ltd. for* The Pond. *The Harold Matson Co. Inc., New York, for* The Graveyard Rats *by Henry Kuttner; © 1936, 1963 by Weird Tales, Inc. Wm. Heinemann Ltd. for* Thurnley Abbey *by Perceval Landon, from 'Raw Edges'. The Author for* Avalon Heights; © *Kay Leith 1976. The Author's Estate and their agents, Scott Meredith Literary Agency Inc., 845 Third Avenue, New York, N.Y. 10022, U.S.A., and Arkham House Publishers, Inc., Sauk City, Wisconsin, U.S.A. for* The Rats in the Walls *by H. P. Lovecraft; © 1924 by Weird Tales; copyright renewed. Harold Matson Co. Inc., New York, for* Deadline *by Richard Matheson, from 'Shock 2'; © 1959. Literistic Ltd. for* The House on Big Faraway *by Norman Matson. Curtis Brown Ltd., London, and Little, Brown & Co., on behalf of the Estate of Ogden Nash, for* The Three D's.

The Author for Headlamps; © *Tony Richards 1981. The Author and Campbell, Thomson & McLaughlin Ltd. for* Behind the Yellow Door *by Flavia Richardson. Ernest Benn Ltd. for* A Pair of Muddy Shoes *by Lennox Robinson, from the anthology 'Fear Fear Fear'. The Hutchinson Publishing Group Ltd. for* The Villa Désirée *by May Sinclair, from 'A Century of Creepy Stories'. Neville Spearman Ltd. for* The Seed from the Sepulchre *by Clark Ashton Smith. Hughes Massie Ltd., on behalf of the Estate of Lady Eleanor Smith, for* Satan's Circus, *from 'Satan's Circus'. The Author for* The Invaders; © *Terry Tapp 1979. John P. Trevaskis Jr., on behalf of the Estate of David H. Keller, for* The Thing in the Cellar. *The Estate of H. Russell Wakefield for* Blind Man's Buff, *from 'Old Man's Beard'. A. D. Peters & Co. Ltd. for* Mr. Loveday's Little Outing *by Evelyn Waugh, from 'Work Suspended and Other Stories'. The Estate of Dennis Wheatley and the Hutchinson Publishing Group Ltd. for* The Snake *William Kimber & Co. Ltd. for* No Ticket, *from 'Ghostly Carnival', published by William Kimber in 1980;* © *Mary Williams 1979. John Murray (Publishers) Ltd. for* Fear *by P. C. Wren, from 'Rough Shooting'. David Higham Associates Ltd., on behalf of the John Wyndham Estate, for* Close Behind Him, *from 'Jizzle'.*

Every effort has been made to trace the owners of the copyright material in this book. In the case of any question arising as to the use of any such material, the Editor would be pleased to receive notification of this.